CONDENSED BOOKS

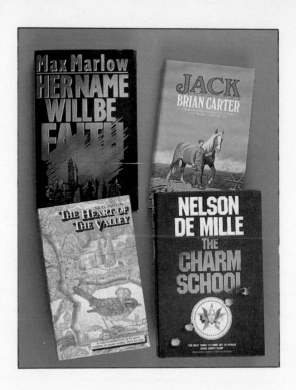

The characters and incidents in the fictional selections

THE READER'S DIGEST ASSOCIATION LIMITED
25 Berkeley Square, London W1X 6AB
THE READER'S DIGEST ASSOCIATION
SOUTH AFRICA (PTY) LTD
Reader's Digest House, 130 Strand Street, Cape Town
Printed by Petty & Sons Ltd, Leeds
Bound by Hazell, Watson & Viney Ltd, Aylesbury
Original cover design by Jeffery Matthews FSIAD

For information as to ownership
of copyright in the material in this book see last page

CONDENSED BOOKS

IN THIS VOLUME

HER NAME WILL BE FAITH
Max Marlow (page 9)

New York is in the grip of the hottest, sultriest spring for many years. More than that, water temperatures in the North Atlantic are unusually high for May. To Richard Connors, TV weatherman, that can only mean one thing: a major hurricane is being spawned.

As Hurricane Faith begins to carve a path of devastation through the Caribbean, Richard mounts a crusade to convince the authorities that it could be heading straight for Manhattan. His only ally is an attractive young journalist who is sent to interview him, and all too soon it is clear to them both that a catastrophe is inevitable.

A tense, exciting novel that gathers storm-force momentum till it reaches its furious climax.

THE HEART OF THE VALLEY
Nigel Hinton (page 155)

It is winter and the small Kent valley has been cut off by drifting snow for a week. But while the inhabitants of Little Ashden sit by a warm fire, waiting for the thaw, a deadly struggle is being waged in the hedgerows.

For the hedge sparrow, danger comes in many forms—whether from bullying magpies who steal more than their share of food, a predatory owl, a hungry fox, or simply from the paralysing cold. But if she survives the winter, then spring is sure to bring its own hazards and joys . . .

This highly-acclaimed novel opens our eyes, perhaps for the first time, to the dramas and difficulties of survival in the English countryside.

JACK
Brian Carter (page 231)

Amid the mud and squalor of the Somme valley in 1916, a young corporal searches from battery to battery for his red roan mare, Bethlehem.

The Somme is a long way from the tranquil Devon pastures where Jack McKenna had groomed and schooled Beth as a workhorse for Chancellor's Emporium. But that was in a happier age. Now, Jack has only one ambition: to release Beth from the terrors of hauling ammunition through the gas and mud and shellfire of the Front Line. And to free her from her toil he is prepared to pay any price . . .

Jack is not simply the poignant story of one man's love for a horse: it is above all a powerful testimony to the horror of war.

THE CHARM SCHOOL
Nelson DeMille (page 379)

Friday evening, Moscow. A frightened young American tourist telephones his embassy and blurts out an incredible story: American pilots are being held prisoner at a secret installation deep in the Russian woods—Mrs. Ivanova's Charm School.

Lisa Rhodes, embassy information officer, cannot believe her ears, the tale sounds just too bizarre to be true. But military attaché Sam Hollis takes the call very seriously indeed. And when the young tourist disappears, Sam's investigation takes him and Lisa to the heart of a deadly cold-war conspiracy.

What is the Charm School? And why should the KGB be so intent on keeping it hidden?

HER NAME WILL BE FAITH

A CONDENSATION OF THE BOOK BY
MAX MARLOW

ILLUSTRATED BY KEITH RITCHENS

Richard Connors is hot property. He's a talented, good-looking TV weatherman, hired by the National American Broadcasting System in New York to boost its ratings. But when he predicts that a major hurricane could strike New York that summer, nobody believes him and suddenly his career is in jeopardy.

The only person to listen is an attractive English journalist called Jo Donnelly. She is fascinated, not just because hurricanes make good news, but also because she and the rest of the Donnelly family are soon to holiday in the hurricane zone, down in the Bahamian island of Eleuthera.

As his worst fears threaten to become a reality, Richard sets out to prevent a disaster of unimaginable proportions, and to protect those he holds dear to his heart.

Wednesday 24 May

The big amphibian was alone in the sky. Four hundred miles due east of Puerto Rico. Captain Mark Hammond looked down between fleecy white clouds to the surging blue of the North Atlantic Ocean.

It was a sight with which he was familiar: since his secondment to the Florida Weather Service a year earlier, he had flown out here at least once a week, looking, watching . . . May was traditionally the quietest month of the year, weatherwise; but next Thursday would mark the official beginning of the hurricane season. If there was a tropical storm about, it was his duty to find it long before it could approach land, and let the boffins determine its potential.

Dr. Eisener came through on the intercom: "You can take her down now."

Mark gave the signal to his copilot, and the aircraft began to sink through the clouds. She was the very latest in flying laboratories, with sensors protruding from her roof, wings and belly to record every possible aspect of the atmosphere around her, and her true commander was Eisener, back in the main cabin surrounded by his staff and their various computers and radar. Satellites high above their heads might be photographing every cloud over the ocean, but it was Eisener who was going to add the fine print for the nation's weather forecasters.

There hadn't been a truly major storm, a Category Four hurricane, in the North Atlantic since before Mark had been born. Category Three storms, of which Gloria, back in 1985, remained the most famous, could do a lot of damage, but it was still the possibility of a really big one which fascinated everyone connected with Atlantic weather.

The aircraft sank lower and lower. Now Mark was skimming the surface of the sea, the huge turbos throttled back almost to stalling point as he allowed Eisener to suck sea water into his tanks. This was always the most tense part of the patrol; he breathed a sigh of relief when Eisener's voice came through: "OK, Mark, take her up."

The engines increased power, the plane rose, and a moment later it was above the clouds again.

"Home, I think," Eisener said, coming up to the flight deck.

"Anything?" Mark asked.

"Why, yes. Something."

Mark turned his head. "Today? It all looks pretty good to me."

"It all is pretty good," Eisener agreed. "Save for the water temperature. I have a reading of twenty-seven degrees centigrade."

"At the end of May? That's high."

"Interesting, isn't it?"

"Yeah, Doctor," Mark said. "Damned interesting."

THE AIRCRAFT DRONED back over Puerto Rico, gaining height to fly across the mountains of Cuba, then dipping lower over the Bahamian islands to land at Key West, Florida, soon after six. Mark went straight to the public telephone after debriefing and dialled a New York number. "Hi," he said. "Richard about?" He waited, drumming a finger on the glass wall of the booth.

"Connors," said a voice on the end of the line.

"Mark."

"Hi, old buddy. How are things back there in Florida?"

"Pretty hot. How does a water temperature of twenty-seven degrees centigrade in mid-Atlantic grab you?"

"On the twenty-fourth of May?"

"That's right. And let me give you some more." He listed numbers slowly, giving his friend time to write them down.

"Thanks a million, Mark. You coming north any time?"

"I've a furlough next month. You got an apartment yet?"

"Maybe. We're talking terms this afternoon. There'll be a bed in the lounge if you want somewhere to stay."

"So I'll see you."

"Great," Connors said. "And Mark . . . I'd be really grateful if you'd keep me up to date on those water temperatures, eh?"

"You got it," Mark said, and hung up.

Thursday 25 May

"I have Richard Connors outside, JC," Kiley said, entering the big office which looked down the length of Fifth Avenue.

J. Calthrop White grunted as he perused the financial pages of the *New*

York Times. Derek Kiley twisted his fingers together: he might be network manager for National American Broadcasting but the company president was a difficult man to work for. J.C. White was a short, thin man, whose energy belied his shock of white hair, and whose irascibility made a nonsense of his puckish features. "Who's Richard Connors?" he demanded.

"The new forecaster, JC," Kiley explained.

"From Florida," White remarked, still studying his paper. "So what decided you to bring him up here, for Chrissake?"

"Well, JC," Kiley said nervously, "down in Miami he was big. He's got it all. Looks, personality, charm, know-how . . . I reckon he'll make an impact on the ratings up here."

"Weather forecasters make impacts?"

"Everyone watches the weather, JC, it's right after the news. Give them a face they like, a guy who sounds like he knows what he's talking about, and they just start watching that particular channel."

White at last raised his head. "How much?" he asked.

Kiley hesitated. "Well, I had to go a little over the odds," he said. "But it's only a one-year contract."

"How much?" White repeated.

"Well, seventy-five."

White leaned back in his chair. "Kiley, you are paying some shavetail beachboy as much as a member of the government, just to tell me it's gonna rain tomorrow? He better be good. Show him in."

Kiley almost ran to the door.

Richard Connors entered. White looked him up and down.

The new weather forecaster was six foot three, and had an undeniably handsome face. It was easy to tell he was fit and he also exuded confidence. These were all characteristics which J. Calthrop White disliked in other men. "Kiley tells me you can forecast the weather."

"That's my job, Mr. White," Connors said, refusing to be overawed.

"So tell me what sort of a summer we're gonna have."

"It'll be hot," Connors said. "And there'll be more hurricane activity than usual."

"Now, how the hell can you tell that?"

"Because the ocean is much warmer than is usual at this time of year, Mr. White. Warm water spawns tropical storms."

"Richard is an expert on hurricanes, JC," Kiley put in eagerly.

"We don't have hurricanes in New York," White pointed out. "You're not in Florida now. Have a good day."

Connors nodded. "Thank you, Mr. White," he said, and left the office.

"Seventy-five thousand," White remarked, and pressed his buzzer. "Alice, get me Mike Donnelly senior." He released the switch to glare at Kiley. "Seventy-five thousand." He pointed. "He'd better be as good as you say, Kiley."

The phone buzzed. "I have Mr. Donnelly senior, Mr. White."

Calthrop White arranged his features into a smile. "Mike, you old son of a gun. How's it going? . . . Yeah, damned hot. How's the boy? . . . Already? I thought the yacht racing season didn't start until June? . . . Is that a fact? Mike, I want to float a stock issue." This time he had to listen somewhat longer before he could speak again. "Oh, sure, sure," he said at last. "I read the papers. But this has to be, Mike. There's a franchise coming up in England this autumn . . . I reckon a hundred and twenty-five million will do it . . . Sure, Mike, sure. I can swing my board, and my stockholders. For Chrissake, most of them are relatives anyway. Listen, why don't you come over and talk about it . . . Sure, sure, but nothing is impossible if you really get down to it. You come on over. Love to Babs and the kids." He replaced the phone, leaned back in his chair, gazed at Kiley. "Goddamned Irish jerk," he remarked. "Can't be done, he says. What the hell is a stockbroker for, Kiley? You tell me that."

Friday 26 May

The automobile lights flickered and the roll-over garage door lifted to allow Lawson Garr's sleek white Cadillac to slide into place beside his wife's Lotus. Belle and Lawson could hear the kitchen phone bleeping as her key turned in the lock. She threw her handbag on the counter and grabbed the receiver. Blonde and statuesquely beautiful—she took after her mother, Barbara Donnelly—she moved with grace, even after several cocktails. "One of your real estate clients," she said, passing the phone to her husband.

"OK, I'll be right with you." Lawson sat down on a stool, pulling an open pad towards him. "Good evening, Lawson Garr here. Can I help you?" Tall, bronzed and athletic, he was the perfect mate for Belle: the attraction between them had been instant and parent-proof—even if it had meant Belle being married to a Limey and exiled on Nassau in the Bahamas, two thousand miles from the Donnelly family in Bognor, Connecticut. That Belle shared Lawson's extravagant tastes was a more serious cause of worry to Mike and Babs Donnelly, but at least Lawson worked as hard as he played. "Why, hello, Mr. McKinley," he said. "Nice to hear from you . . ."

Liar, Belle thought, as she closed the bedroom door. Who the hell wants to hear from a client at 11.40 at night? Some people have no consideration . . . She put her dress on a hanger and threw her undies into the clothes hamper. The weather was unnaturally warm for the time of year and she was a mess of sweat, so she took a shower. Lawson was ages, and she was nearly asleep when he came in, but one look at his face brought her bolt upright in bed. "Sweetheart? What is it? You look as if you'd just fallen off the Empire State."

"I think I just did!" He sat beside her. "That was McKinley."

"I heard," Belle said. Fabian McKinley was one of the wealthiest men in the Bahamas. He owned land everywhere. "What's on his mind now?"

"He wants to sell Dolphin Point," Lawson said. Dolphin Point was the headland on Eleuthera—the most northeasterly of the Bahamian islands—where her parents had a holiday home.

"But why?" Belle asked.

"Search me. It's not my business to ask. But he wants me to handle the sale—exclusive for three months. Because I know the area, he says. The asking price is one million US dollars."

"Oh, boy," Belle said. "A million . . . you'll get twenty thousand dollars, Lawson. Oh boy." Suddenly she was anxious. "Do you think we can find a buyer? A million is a lot of loot."

"Listen, doll," Lawson said, "McKinley may want a million, and that is in line with current prices for undeveloped land. But I am damned sure that I could triple that by splitting it up into lots, laying water and electricity, having plans drawn up, maybe even starting to build."

"You mean . . ." Belle frowned at him. "Develop it yourself?"

"Why not?"

"Two reasons. One, as you've been appointed sole agent, it wouldn't be ethical. Two, we don't have a million dollars."

"Granted. But your old man does. Or could raise it."

Belle's frown deepened. "Big Mike?"

"Why not? Don't he and your brother claim to be one of the biggest stockbrokers on Wall Street? Are you going to tell me he couldn't lay hands on a million dollars if it meant a quick two million profit? One for him, one for us. Fifty-fifty. A million dollars, Belle. God, think what we could do with that! Pay off the mortgage, get those bills off our back."

Belle allowed herself to dream for a moment. Then she said, "But would it be legal? I mean, it sounds a bit like insider dealing to me. Shouldn't you be telling McKinley about this?"

Lawson leaned forward and kissed her on the nose. "McKinley isn't a good listener. And who's to know? The land goes on the market, and some rich Connecticut stockbroker snaps it up."

"Who just happens to be your father-in-law?"

"So, I told him it's worth it. There's nothing illegal in that. It's my business, for God's sake. And a million dollars, Belle. Just think of it. A million dollars!"

Belle thought of it. "Think Dad'll go for it?" she asked.

"I'll be on the phone first thing tomorrow morning," Lawson promised.

Saturday 27 May

The sky over Newport, Rhode Island, was clear blue, hazy with afternoon heat, and the water flat calm; the bridge was perfectly mirrored as the Mercedes crossed the river to the marina after the four-hour drive up from New York. Josephine Donnelly hadn't even paused to drop off the bags at her parents-in-law's house in Bognor, Connecticut: she was in a hurry to welcome Michael home from the first race of the season—and was trying not to think about the rest of the summer, when she would hardly see him.

A handsome, slender English girl in her early thirties, Jo Donnelly wore her wavy dark-brown hair cut very short. Her children sat together in the back, where they would distract her least by their constant wrangling; Owen Michael was ten and Tamsin eight. She had no sooner braked in the yacht owners' car park near *Esmeralda*'s berth than they were tumbling out to race along the pontoons.

Jo followed more slowly. She wore slacks and a loose shirt and sandals, and attracted glances from the various crews. Her grey-brown eyes searched the close-packed yachts. Michael might only have been away for a few days, but it was the first race of the season and he was a compellingly attractive man. All the Donnellys were compellingly attractive, from Big Mike and Babs, through their so-beautiful daughters, Belle and Marcia, to their so-macho sons, Michael junior and Dale. The family bubbled in a way her own had never done. Her father had been an officer in the British army and had believed it a weakness to reveal emotion of any kind. Which was probably why she had been instantly attracted to the handsome American boy doing a year at Cambridge when she was up there reading English Literature.

She sighed, as she spotted Mike's 40-foot yawl: it had all been so different, then.

Owen Michael had seen the yawl too. "There's Dad!" he shouted.

Michael Donnelly junior, tall and powerfully built, waved to them, and hurried across the intervening decks. He jumped onto the pontoon and swept the kids up into his arms . . . then turned to Jo and hugged her.

"How did it go?" she asked, pulling her head back.

"Goddamned awful," he replied. "We had a failure. A rigging screw went. Must have been faulty from the start. There was a squall the night before last, then this sudden twang and the whole boat shook, with wire flying all over the place. We damned near lost the mainmast."

"So you had to retire?"

"Yeah. What a way to start the season."

"You'll get it right. Where's your car? Can you leave now? Your folks are expecting us for dinner."

"It's at Sam's place. But there's no way I can come now. We only just got in. There's a lot of work to be done. And Sam had to go hustling off because wifey Sally had a party tonight. So I have to put the ship to bed."

"Is there so much to be done?" Jo asked. "I mean, you don't race again for a fortnight."

"Now, Angelface, you know the drill: the ship comes first." Michael

14

kissed her nose. "Listen, I will try to get down tonight, but tell Mother not to wait dinner for me."

"Oh, Daddy, we want to have you with us tonight," Tamsin begged.

"Yeah, Dad. Say, why don't you come with us now, and we'll all come and help you fix her up tomorrow?" Owen Michael offered.

"No way," Michael said. "Work first, play after." He kissed the top of Tamsin's head. "You hustle along now, and look after your mommy."

The dismal trio walked back along the pontoon in single file, and Owen Michael kicked viciously at a pebble as they neared the car, sending it skipping across another pontoon onto a boat's deck.

His mother said nothing; she could understand his resenting being rated second to a piece of plastic. Her own pleasure at seeing Michael had also quickly dissipated into resentment. Work before play, she thought bitterly. The fact was that he loved *Esmeralda* more than his family. And this was only the beginning of the season. It happened every year: what right did Michael have to abandon her and the children for twenty weekends every summer for his yacht racing? She felt like kicking a stone or two herself.

THE SQUARE, WHITE-PAINTED clapboard house stood, tall and imposing, fifty feet behind a white rail fence bordering the sidewalk in the small rural town of Bognor, Connecticut. By New England standards Pinewoods was very old, having been built in 1832, and from the moment that Big Mike and Barbara Donnelly bought it in 1971 they had taken endless pains to furnish it in authentic period style. There were stained-glass panels in the inner door of the lobby, and beautiful tiles on the hall floor. The dining room and sitting room at Pinewoods were charming and immaculate, from the gilt mirrors over the carved fire-surrounds and mantelpieces, to the wood-framed settee, armchairs, dainty round coffee tables and polished dining table with its English silver candelabra.

In the big family kitchen, however, authenticity had been partially abandoned, with tile-topped units, dishwasher, refrigerator and freezer. Even so, in one corner stood an antique but highly efficient wood-burning stove, prettily painted enamel panels set in the dull grey metal sides, and next to it were two very comfortable armchairs. Big Mike was sitting in one now, watching TV, shoulders hunched, greying black hair scattered thinly across his head, while Babs, tall and still attractive, prepared vegetables.

Dale Donnelly breezed in, wearing shorts, throwing his tennis racket onto a chair. "Hi! What's for dinner?"

"Michael and Jo and roast sirloin!" Babs tilted her face to receive her son's kiss.

"Who else?"

"The Robsons."

"Ugh!" Dale groaned. He was a languid young man who drifted from job to job, resolutely refusing to join his elder brother in the Wall Street firm. This lack of drive bothered his parents. "I suppose I'll have to entertain them."

"What's the problem?" Big Mike lit a cigarette. "Now, shut up and listen to the news." Mike concentrated on the television.

The door opened and Jo hurried in, followed by Owen Michael and Tamsin. "Hi, Babs. Hi, Dad. Dale." She kissed each in turn. "Michael sends his apologies. He's had to stay in Newport a while longer because he's got problems with the boat, but he hopes to join us later." Jo smiled brightly, but her mother-in-law was aware of Jo's disappointment—and her own.

"They nearly lost the mast," Owen Michael announced.

"Holy shit!" Big Mike remarked, ignoring his wife's frown of disapproval. "How the hell did they manage that?"

"I'm sure Michael will tell us all about it when he gets here." Babs removed her apron to join them, immediately switching off the TV set.

"Hey," Big Mike protested. "What did you do that for?"

"Neal and Meg are due here in half an hour. You haven't opened the wine yet. And those trousers are filthy. Anyway, you don't usually watch NABS."

"Yeah? Well, I wanted to see their new whiz-kid weatherman."

"Oh, Richard Connors," Jo said.

"That's the guy. You remember watching him last year when we were in Eleuthera, Babs? He was with WJQT in Miami then."

"I'm to interview him next week," Jo said.

"Is that a fact? I didn't know he was that famous."

"NABS is working on it. Seems their manager, Kiley, called my editor and suggested it."

"Well, you can watch him tomorrow," Babs said. "He can't tell us anything about the weather tonight that we can't find out for ourselves by looking out the window. Come on, Mike, be a doll." As she passed his chair he grabbed her and sat her on his knee.

"Say, will you old folks cut that out and attend to your visitors?"

"Marcia!" Babs jumped up and ran to the door to greet her younger daughter. "How are you, sweetheart?"

"To what do we owe this honour?" Big Mike held out a hand and pulled her down for a kiss. "We weren't expecting you."

"New York is hot and sticky, so we thought we'd drive up and beg dinner and a bed for the night."

"We?"

"There's someone I want you to meet. He's parking the car."

Big Mike and Babs exchanged glances: Marcia went through young men like Kleenex, but every one was *the* man, for as long as he lasted.

"That's great," Babs said. "I've set the table, but we can easily lay two more places." She opened the crockery cupboard.

"You really only need to lay one more. I doubt if Michael will be here much before ten," Jo pointed out.

At that moment Marcia heard a knock on the door, ran to open it, and pulled a dark young man proudly into the room. "This is Benny," she announced gleefully.

"THE ROBSONS ARE LATE," Jo observed, glancing at her watch as she wandered out into the kitchen.

"The Robsons are always late," Dale retorted. "They've never been on time for anything in their lives."

Babs was quite pleased about her guests' lack of punctuality: it had given the family a chance to get to know Marcia's latest young man. Benny was quiet and good-humoured, and he certainly seemed to worship Marcia. How grand it would be if Marcia could finally settle down . . . but Benny was an art student too, so it didn't look likely to happen for a while yet.

Suddenly there was a "cooee" from the front of the house. "Hope we're not late?" Margaret Robson appeared round the hall door, followed by her husband Neal.

"Not more than usual." Big Mike left his chair to kiss her.

"Oh, good." She hugged Babs. "Josephine," she said as Jo came back into the room, "my dear, how nice to see you. Is Michael still racing?"

"He's in Newport." Jo was determined not to get irritated: Margaret Robson was the only person in the world who insisted on calling her Josephine. "He had to . . ."

"Well, never mind. Where are those lovely kids of yours?"

"In bed. I've just kissed them goodnight."

"Not ill, I hope?"

"No, Meg, not ill," Babs interrupted. "Just sleepy. It's nearly nine."

"No! Is it? We *are* late. I knew it. Neal! We *are* late. I told you . . ."

"Never mind, Meg." Mike handed her a gin and Martini. "Get yourself outside that and we'll go eat."

Meg was Babs's complete opposite, nervous and excitable, and Neal adored her. Not much taller, smooth, with smiling features, he was one of those quiet, confident men who make nervous women feel safe.

Jo and Marcia helped carry the serving dishes through to the dining room where Big Mike set about carving the meat. When everyone had a heaped plate in front of them and Mike had said grace, Neal Robson rose to his feet. "Before we eat," he said, "I have something to say."

"Make it brief," Mike recommended.

Neal grinned at him. "We've done it," he said. "Bought that place in Eleuthera. The one you've been trying to talk me into for years."

"Well, son of a gun!" Mike said. "I never thought you'd go through with it."

"Oh, I am so pleased," Babs said. "We'll be down there together . . ."

"We'll be going in July, as usual," Mike said. "When are you planning on getting there?"

"Well," Neal said, "we rather thought we'd go down next month. According to the agent, that house hasn't been lived in for ten years."

"At least that," Mike agreed.

"Oh, I'm so scared," Meg admitted.

"What about?" Mike enquired.

"Well, what about things like hurricanes?"

"Hurricanes? They're no hassle."

"Oh, but when one reads the newspapers . . ."

"You don't want to believe everything you read in the newspapers," Mike announced. "We had a hurricane down there three years ago."

"Well," Babs said, "I don't think it was actually a hurricane. Didn't they call it a tropical depression, or something?"

"It was a hurricane," Mike said firmly. "Don't you remember that wind howling?"

"And the rain," Marcia said, squeezing Benny's hand. "So much got in we had to sleep in the lounge."

"It must have been awful. Weren't you terrified?" Meg asked.

The Donnellys exchanged glances.

"I'll confess I was a bit worried at first, but providing one takes the proper precautions, like boarding up the windows, why . . ." Mike spread his hands expansively. "Believe me, hurricanes aren't all they're cracked up to be."

"Anyway," Dale said, "hurricanes hardly ever hit the same place again for years and years. So Eleuthera has got to be the safest place in the Bahamas for a long time to come."

Jo remained silent as the conversation continued. She could remember that storm. It certainly hadn't been a hurricane: the winds had never risen above fifty miles an hour. Yet it had been terrifying, out on Dolphin Point, with the waves crashing onto the rocks on one side and rolling up the beach on the other, and the trees bending, and the rain teeming down, and the thunder and lightning had been continuous. They had all been scared, not least Big Mike, but in fact no real damage had been done.

"Hello there!" The front door opened and Michael stalked in. "Not too late for some food, I hope?"

"Mike!" His father leaped up and seized his hand. "Jo says you had trouble."

"Defective gear." He kissed Babs, blew one at his wife. "Kids in bed?"

"Yes," she said.

The rest of the party were already on their dessert, but Mike provided his son with a plate of roast beef, and the conversation turned to yachts and racing.

As soon as the meal ended Big Mike pushed his son into the little study. "Boy, am I glad you're back."

Michael raised his eyebrows. "Problems?"

"You have got to be kidding. Calthrop White wants to float a stock issue. By August. He's trying to buy some British TV station. Seems the franchise comes up in the fall and he reckons he can get it for a hundred and twenty-five million dollars."

Michael sat down. "What the hell does he want another network for?"

"He's ambitious, I guess. So there's work to be done. He's our best customer."

"But, Dad . . ."

"OK, OK. It shouldn't interfere with your racing. I'm letting Palmer handle most of the work on it. Now, let me give you the big one."

Michael raised his eyebrows. "Bigger than that?"

Mike winked. "For us, maybe. I had a phone call from Lawson this morning. Let me tell you what he has in mind."

Michael listened, pulling his chin. "Are you sure it's not one of his get-rich-quick schemes?"

"Sure it is. But this one could just work."

"A million bucks? Can we raise that?"

"Could be. What do you think? Are you for it?"

Michael Donnelly considered a moment longer, then stretched out his hand. "Count me in. But . . . just let's keep it amongst ourselves for the time being, eh?"

Monday 29 May

"The start of another week," Julian Summers remarked, slumping into the chair which faced that of his new senior, Richard Connors, in the NABS weather room. "Had a good weekend?"

"I hung wallpaper," Richard told him, continuing to study the various items on his desk. "Ever heard of something called *Profiles*?"

"It's a magazine. Quite up-market," Julian told him. "It's a monthly, does in-depth studies of prominent people. Why?"

"They seem to want to do me."

"You? Great balls of fire! You'll be famous. Who's interviewing you?"

Richard gave him an old-fashioned look. "Some female named Donnelly. Seems she has an appointment for Thursday."

"Don't you like females named Donnelly?"

"I don't like females named anything, right this minute," Richard told him, thinking grimly about his recent divorce. "But Kiley says I have to see her. Says it'll please JC. You seen these, Julian?"

Julian got up to lean over his shoulder. "Water temperatures? Those look kind of high for May."

"They are incredibly high for May. And look at the pattern. From mid-Atlantic right across into the Caribbean and then up into the Bahamas and the Gulf Stream. Twenty-fours and fives and sixes, and out there, twenty-seven. But see that one?"

"Twenty-two."

"Right. That was taken not thirty miles east of New York harbour."

"So it's gonna be one hot summer."

"Yeah," Richard said. "And the sea temperature needed to cause a hurricane is only around twenty-six and a half degrees centigrade, so there's probably one spawning in mid-Atlantic right this minute."

"So what's new? Thursday's the first of June: the official beginning of the hurricane season."

"Sure. But hurricanes have to have warm water, so at this time of year they fizzle when they get up here. But here we are, going into June, and there's warm water everywhere. We could have twenty-seven degrees plus up here in another month, if the weather holds. That means the whole ocean is going to be hurricane-ripe by July."

"So the guys in Florida are going to be busy. Thank God it's nothing to do with us."

"You reckon? What about hurricane Gloria in 1985? Didn't she just about knock on your door, up here?"

"She was a freak," Julian pointed out. "And she missed. Just."

"All hurricanes are freaks, Julian," Richard told him.

Julian frowned. "You really reckon a hurricane could hit New York? That would be something."

"Yeah," Richard said. "Yeah, it could happen."

Thursday 1 June

Sunlight flooded the bedroom, and Jo yawned and stretched, smiling as she touched the sleeping form beside her. She and Michael had been out to dinner the previous night, and he would probably sleep for a while yet. They had had a lot of fun.

She rolled out of bed, pulled on her dressing gown, cleaned her teeth, and began to get the world moving. Jo had worked hard to create a smart, modern home with a cosy, lived-in atmosphere. The apartment, thirty-eight floors up on Park Avenue, was light and airy, with a plate-glass picture window in the lounge giving a panoramic view over the city.

Florence had already arrived and was making coffee, while Jo got the children out of bed and dressed for school. Florence Bennett had worked for Jo since Owen Michael's appearance was imminent. A large, red-faced woman of Scottish descent, she was a total treasure.

When Florence and the children sat down to breakfast Jo returned to her bedroom, to discover Michael sitting up and scratching his head. "Um." He sighed. "Meet me at the club at eleven thirty, will you?"

"Eh?" About to step into the shower, she turned in surprise.

"I'm taking an out-of-towner to lunch, and he's got his wife with him. So I reckon it'd be good to make up a foursome: he's quite well heeled. I've booked a table at the 'Four Seasons'."

"I'm sorry." Jo shook her head. "I can't. I have an appointment at eleven fifteen."

"Cancel it."

"Now you know I can't do that, Michael. It's an interview set up by the magazine. Tell you what, though: I might be able to join you at the restaurant at about one . . ."

"Hell," he said, "what's the good of that? Do you think I want these people to know my wife works for a living?"

Jo sighed. Her going back to work had always been a bone of contention between them. "OK," she said, "then I won't come to the restaurant."

She stood beneath the shower, allowing the water to bounce off her flesh, and opened her eyes as the shower door was jerked wide.

"You are one hell of a wife," Michael declared. "Look, I am your husband, right? You are my wife, right? Now, I want you to come to the club and then out to lunch, and you are goddamned well going to do it. You're behaving like a selfish bitch who just wants to do her own thing."

He was shouting, and she prayed the children couldn't hear as she pushed him aside and reached for her towel. "Selfish!" she snapped. "You bastard. You take off in your plastic bathtub every damned weekend and you accuse me of being selfish for trying to do a job of work?"

"You . . ."

"No, *you!*" She jabbed a forefinger at his chest. "*You* are a selfish, irresponsible bastard. You never wanted a wife and children: you just wanted ornaments to show off when the occasion arose, and someone to—"

Michael swung his arm, the flat of his hand hitting the side of her face and sending her reeling across the bathroom to cannon into the wall.

The stinging blow brought moisture to her eyes, but she wasn't crying—she was too angry. She got up, wrapping herself in her dressing gown.

"The usual answer from a brainless fool." She went into the bedroom and began to dress. "Not the first time you've hit me, is it, Michael? But I promise you it will be the last." She tucked her blouse into her skirt, brushed her hair and picked up her handbag: make-up could wait until she was in the car. She left him standing there, and closed the bedroom door quietly behind her. "I'll drop the children off today, Florence," she said.

All three of them gazed at her. They had heard the raised voices, and her cheek was still red from the blow. But not a word was said, even on the drive to school. She kissed them both. "See you this afternoon," she said. "We'll do something together, shall we?"

21

MANHATTAN SHIMMERED. Even on the shady side of Fifth Avenue, heat bounced off the walls and up from the sidewalk.

Jo sighed with relief as she passed through the doors into the air-conditioned cool of the NABS building. She was shown into a small waiting room and left to herself for some fifteen minutes, which did not improve her mood. Finally Richard Connors appeared. And he didn't help matters by his opening remark: "Now, what can I do for you, Miss . . . or . . . ?"

Jo felt herself bristling, but smiled sweetly and said, "My name is Josephine Donnelly, Mr. Connors, and I would like you to talk about yourself." With which request she thought he would be happy to comply; she'd met this type before, smooth, sophisticated, too good-looking to be real.

Slowly his mouth widened into an apologetic smile. "So . . ." They sat down and he leaned back in his chair. "What do you want to know about me?"

All an act, she decided, as though he had just pressed an "on with the charm" button. Not that she wasn't used to it. Most interviewees were stiff and artificial at first—it was her job to break down that barrier and reach the real person. "You've come to NABS from WJQT in Miami, right? Have you always lived there?" A usual type of opening question.

"No. I was born in San Francisco. My father was a pharmacist there."

"What made you move to Florida?"

"I answered the advert for a weatherman, got the job. Simple as that."

"I really meant, what made you go in for forecasting? I would say you were an athlete, once upon a time."

This time his grin was more genuine. "I played football, once upon a time. But never up to professional standard. Anyway, a guy has to major in something at college, and an older cousin of mine who was keen on sailing would take me out sometimes as crew, and he was always looking at the sky and forecasting what was coming . . . so that's how I got involved myself." He paused to grin at her doubting smile. "Being a forecaster gets to be quite fun, you know."

Jo made notes on his college football career, his first job interviews, and his varied progress before moving into the world of television. But when she came to his personal life, his mood suddenly changed. "I shouldn't think that will interest anyone," he said.

"You couldn't be more wrong," she protested. "That's what it's all about."

He glanced at her ring finger. "Sorry, Mrs. Donnelly. My private life stays private."

They stared at each other, and she realised that he meant what he said. "Then talk to me about the job," she said. "Weather forecasting. And hurricanes," she added.

He frowned at her. "Hurricanes? You interested in hurricanes?"

"Sure I am. My parents-in-law have a holiday home in Eleuthera."

"Is that a fact? Say, would you really like to know how it all works?"

"Yes, I would."

"Right, I'll show you." She followed him down endless corridors, past open-plan offices where typewriters rattled, computers bleeped and coffee dispensers were in constant use.

He showed her the studio, which was like any other television centre, somewhat bare except for the various backdrops against which Richard would stand while making his forecasts, and dominated by three

23

cameras. Richard's own office was a more relaxed place, just untidy enough to look lived in. He showed her to an armchair, sat at his desk, and then smiled at her. "Now. What else would you like to know?"

"Well, tell me about your job. How exactly do you forecast weather?"

"You observe," he said. "There is really nothing much more to it than that. But the accuracy of the forecast depends on the number of observations you can get hold of, and of course on the interpretation you put on the observations; that last part can be pure experience, but it helps if you've been taught meteorology. The barometer, for instance, is one of the most important of weather forecasting instruments, because it records the atmospheric pressure around us."

"But why is pressure important?"

"From a meteorologist's point of view, the important thing is that even tiny pressure variations control the flow of wind. Wind flows from high-pressure areas to low-pressure areas, or down the pressure gradients, as we call them. Actually, winds flow *round* centres of pressure. So a glance at the millibar lines tells you the direction of the wind and just about how strong."

"What's a millibar line?"

"Very simple, it is a line drawn, as a result of reported barometric observations, through all the places on the earth's surface which have the same pressure at the same time. When all observations are received, the forecaster—or nowadays, the computer—joins all the lines of equal pressure together, making up what we call a synoptic chart."

"And that tells you what the weather is going to do?"

"Sure. Obviously, it will tell us a lot about the movements of heavy cloud and rain, say, and the millibars will tell us exactly what wind speeds to expect. When the lines are well spaced we know the wind flow will be light. When the lines appear close-packed, strong winds are indicated. In the subtropics, for example, where there is very little pressure movement at all, a drop of three millibars in one hour can very well indicate a hurricane in the vicinity."

Jo was fascinated. Not only by the subject itself, but by the total knowledge and expertise which flowed from the man. He was an expert. As well as being one of the most attractive men she had ever met. And that was dangerous thinking, in her present state of mind.

"So," he was saying, "back in the days when radio was first developed, a whole series of these weather reporting stations were set up. There were even ships at sea whose business was to maintain a certain position and do nothing but report on the weather. But of course, in the last thirty years or so, we've had the spread of satellite observation. From a satellite you can look across several hundred miles of weather at a glance."

Jo glanced up from her notes.

"May I ask you a sixty-four-thousand-dollar question?"

"Sure."

24

"Well, if all your observations and tracking systems are so accurate, how come the forecasts one hears are so often wrong?"

He held up a forefinger. "Not wrong—simply inaccurate as to timing. You see, a weather system is its own boss. Sometimes it does quite unpredictable things. For instance, we might track a system all the way from its beginning, off, say, the west coast of Africa, and for seven consecutive days it might travel due west at fifteen knots. Now, we can say with absolute certainty that there is bad weather coming. But at any moment, without warning, it may change course, increase speed, decrease speed, or stop altogether. We do know that tropical storms begin, and can only flourish, over warm water. But we can still never be absolutely certain what they are going to do next. And incidentally, a lot of people make the mistake of thinking that the faster a hurricane is travelling, the more dangerous it is. That is quite wrong. Hurricane winds are generated by heat, not by the speed of the system. Therefore, the slower a hurricane is travelling over warm water, for instance, the stronger the winds round the centre are likely to be."

"Yes," she said. "I think I have all that. Gosh . . ." She looked at her watch. "I have taken up an awful amount of your time. Really, I could sit here and talk to you for ever, but . . ."

"I haven't told you about hurricanes yet," he pointed out.

"Well, maybe . . ."

"We could talk about them over lunch," he told her.

Jo was taken by surprise. She had often lunched with interviewees, but it had never been on a day quite like this, when she should have been supporting Michael at the "Four Seasons" . . . But she only hesitated for a moment before accepting—she wanted to feel she was getting some of her own back for that slap this morning.

The restaurant was two blocks away, still on Fifth Avenue.

"I can recommend the pizzas here," Richard told her, across the red-checked tablecloth.

"I love good pizza," she said. "Pepperoni, please. And a salad."

"Make that two," he told the waiter. "And will you bring us a bottle of Frascati right away, please?"

The waiter departed, and returned to pour the pale Italian wine. Richard raised his glass. Gazing at Jo intently, he asked, "Are you English?"

"Heavens! Do I still have an accent?" She laughed and nodded. "Yes, I am."

"I can't say you have much of an accent, but it's the way you talk, and sit, and your clothes . . . they look English."

"They are."

"And happily married, I would say."

Jo shrugged. "Isn't everyone?"

"No," Richard said briefly. "Tell me about yours."

25

Between mouthfuls of pizza, Jo told him a little about herself, how she and Michael had met, her career, surprised by the number of his questions, wanting to believe his interest was genuine. "Now tell me what went wrong with yours," she asked. And he clearly knew her question was honest, more than just an attempt to gain copy for her article.

"I guess she wanted to live one way, and I another."

"I'm sorry. Are you divorced?"

He nodded.

"Is that why you left Florida?"

"I left Florida because NABS offered me twice as much as I was getting there." Then he gave a crooked grin. "Don't you believe it: I was running like hell."

They gazed at each other for several moments, then she swallowed her last mouthful. "I really should be getting back."

"But we haven't talked about hurricanes yet."

"Heavens! We haven't, have we?"

Richard signalled the waiter, ordered coffee.

"So," she said. "Can you tell me what a hurricane actually is?"

"Well, as simply as possible, it is a depression which has gotten out of hand. Depressions are caused by warm air rising, like the steam from your kettle. And when warm air rises, cold air rushes in to replace it. And, being cold air, the whole system tends to collapse fairly quickly. But over water, in the subtropics, when the water temperature is high, this new air isn't cold enough to quash the system; it merely heats up and rises itself. So we have a continual spiral of rising air which, if the other conditions are right, just gets faster and faster. You could think of a hurricane as a gigantic tornado or waterspout, only it can be hundreds of miles across. And it can generate winds of Force Twelve and up."

"Why do you say Force Twelve? What does that mean?"

He grinned at her. "I think you know that one."

"Maybe I do, but tell me anyway, so I can quote you."

"Well, it's just a reference system invented by a British admiral named Beaufort about a hundred and fifty years ago. It divides up wind speeds into readily recognisable categories. For instance, zero on the scale is flat calm. Force Three is a light breeze, say twelve knots; that's when you would get your first whitecaps at sea. When you have Force Six, which is around twenty-five knots, you have spray flying and big trees whipping to and fro. It's the sort of wind you'd have difficulty walking against. After that you get into storm territory. Force Eight is a gale, around thirty-five knots. That can be pretty serious at sea, at least to small craft. Force Ten is a storm, fifty knots. Now that really is something. You have big waves, twenty or thirty feet from trough to crest. And on land you have some trees coming down, and chimney pots and that sort of thing."

"And Force Twelve is a hurricane." Jo gazed at him over the rim of her coffee cup. "How strong is that?"

"Sixty-four knots, seventy-five miles per hour. But seventy-five miles an hour is only what we call a Category One storm. You see, although all winds of more than seventy-five miles per hour are called hurricanes, it is possible to have winds twice that speed. So the Weather Bureau divides hurricanes up into five further categories. There have only been about four Category Five hurricanes—that is, more than a hundred and fifty miles an hour—this century, at least in the western Atlantic. And when you get that, whole buildings, and I mean properly constructed buildings, can get blown down."

"But what would cause Category Five to happen?"

"Well . . ." He signalled for coffee refills. "Nobody actually knows enough about hurricanes at all. Sure, we know they won't form unless the water temperature is high enough. But that's not to say they will appear the moment the temperature reaches twenty-six and a half degrees centigrade. Just as we don't know why they sometimes fizzle and why they sometimes keep on building."

Jo regarded her notes. She had enough for a small book. "That's all just great," she said. "But tell me one thing more, Richard: how dangerous are hurricanes? I mean, compared with earthquakes or volcanoes or things like that? I know they can push up tidal waves . . ."

"We call them storm surges," he murmured. "Jo, a hurricane is the most destructive of all natural phenomena, and that includes volcanoes and earthquakes. Just as an example, even a small hurricane generates as much energy as several atomic explosions added together. It's the mightiest force known to nature."

"So it's the wind which causes the most damage?"

"Oh, no. It's the water. Figure this: a Category One storm will push up a storm surge of maybe five feet above normal water level. This surge, which may arrive several hours before the wind, might start flooding low-lying coastal areas, and then continue for as long as the wind is blowing. Also, on top of the surge there will be waves of as much as fifty feet high, breaking."

"My God! Thank heaven we don't have things like that in New York."

"You could. Don't forget Gloria."

"Back in nineteen eighty-five," she recalled. "Oh, yes. We were all panicking like mad. But she didn't turn out to be half as bad as you weather forecasters said she would be."

"That was because New York is one hell of a lucky city."

Jo smiled. "This is all great stuff, Richard. Now, let me ask you one last question: is there going to be a major storm this year?"

"That's one for the Deity, I'm afraid."

"But aren't there some signs you can use?"

"Sure. And as it happens, we have them. The ocean temperatures are higher than normal for the time of year."

"So you think there could be a big one?"

"I think there is going to be a lot more hurricane activity than usual, this year. I won't go further than that."

"Well, as I said, that was just great. But you know, what you've told me today has given me an idea. I'm sure an awful lot of people would like to know something more about hurricanes than the old wives' tales which are all they normally get. Have you thought of giving a series of talks, say at the end of a forecast? Especially now we're into the storm season."

"Have you thought of the scheduling? Kiley would throw a fit."

"I've an idea he might go for it," Jo said, remembering that it was Kiley who had set up this interview to publicise his new boy. "And what I would like to do is conduct some interviews with the man in the street, get his opinion on what you have to say. What about it? I'll have Ed Kowicz—he's my editor—give Kiley a call. And then, at the end of the season, I could interview you again."

"GOD, BUT IT'S HOT out there." Jayme, Richard Connors's secretary, delicately patted perspiration from her neck as she came into the office: she had nipped out for a sandwich between newscasts. "I bet you could fry an egg on the sidewalk. And it's only June. What do you reckon it's going to be like come August?"

"Worse than Florida," Richard commented. He was trying to concentrate on the various weather reports, but was thinking instead about Jo Donnelly. He wondered if the suggestion that he do a series on hurricanes—with its implication that they would work together—was purely professional, or if she might have had an ulterior motive. But how could she have, happily married as she was and with kids?

Jayme leaned over him. "Anything interesting on the way?"

"More of the same for us, I'm afraid. But the first storm of the season is down there in the middle of the Caribbean. They've just up-rated him into a Tropical Storm, so he has a name: Anthony."

"And is Anthony going to become a hurricane?"

"Could be. The water temperature down there is certainly high enough, but he's not going to interest us: starting where he is, he'll most certainly head off into the Gulf of Mexico."

"That's a shame," Jayme remarked. "If he'd come up here, maybe we'd get some rain to cool things off. Can't you conjure up a storm for us?"

Richard was studying the charts plotting the course of the jet stream. "I don't think I'm going to have to do that," he said. "I think one may come along of its own accord."

Sunday 4 June

The "Four Seasons" restaurant hummed with muted conversation around the vast shrubbery where prospective diners sipped apéritifs and greeted friends and guests. Michael smiled at his wife, aware how lovely she

28

looked tonight; the neck of her white dress was cut wide and low, revealing her deep tan, on which a diamond pendant gleamed, matching the sparkle of her ear-studs as she moved her head. She outshone any other woman in the room.

If only . . . if only what? If only she'd let him lead his own life? Give up her damned journalism? Stick to the role of wife and mother? But if she did, would she still be the person with whom he had fallen in love?

"Penny for your thoughts." Jo squeezed his hand.

He told her. After all, they had come here to celebrate their reconciliation—and to discuss where they went from here.

It was the opening they needed.

"Please, look at it this way." Jo gazed into his face, pleading for his understanding. "I spend an average of six hours a day, thirty hours a week, on journalism, and eight hours a day, plus all weekends, say sixty-five hours a week, on home and family. And I spend all vacations with Owen Michael and Tamsin."

Michael frowned. "Eight hours a day? How do you work that out?"

"Seven till nine in the mornings; half past twelve till two lunch time; and six till half-past ten evenings."

"Well, I do almost that."

"True. But it's the weekends and holidays which are causing the problem." She held up her hand again as he opened his mouth. "I am going to make you an offer. I'll promise to cut down my journalism by an average of one hour a day, if you'll promise to spend alternate weekends with the kids and me, and take two weeks' vacation with us every summer."

The head waiter appeared at that moment to lead them to their table, so Michael had several minutes to consider his reply. "Well, put that way, I suppose it's fair," he admitted finally. "It's just a pity the Bermuda Race this year is sailed at roughly the same time that you and the kids always go down with Dad and Mom to Eleuthera. And what with the preparations and all that . . . you do realise the Bermuda Race is the big one?"

"I know. It will be an enormous sacrifice to miss it . . ."

"Miss it? You don't mean . . . ?" He paused to study her expression. "Oh, God, yes, I see you do."

He was miserable, torn both ways. "It won't be for ever," she said gently. "In five years the thought of a holiday with us old folks will bore the kids silly. You'll be able to do what you like, then."

"But the Bermuda Race . . . we have a real chance this year of winning our section."

"Michael. You have said you have a chance of winning every year for the past seven, and you never have. Sam could replace you as skipper."

"I guess Sam could," he agreed reluctantly. "Larry could navigate . . ."

Jo noted the reluctance with a sinking feeling. Would this mean a ghastly summer holiday, with Michael sulking all the time because she had dragged him away from his sport? "You have no idea how much fun it is down there," she said. He didn't answer, but she felt his eyes on her, and looked up. Her heart lurched as she whispered, "Michael? How important to you is our marriage? Do you want to save it, honestly, or do you want us to split up?"

His eyes closed momentarily, hiding his thoughts. Then his gaze held hers as he whispered back. "My dearest Jo, our marriage, our love, is far more important than anything else in the world. It's a deal. I promise to cut back on the time I spend on *Esmeralda*. And I will hand over to Sam for the Bermuda Race."

Tears of happiness stung her eyes as she said, "And I promise to cut back on my journalism."

Monday 5 June

The phone purred beside Jo, and she picked it up. "Josephine Donnelly, good morning."

"Jo? Marcia here. How're you doing?"

"Never better, little sister. How about you? What's new?"

"Something fantastic. I've got to tell you all about it. It's so fabulous I don't know where to start."

"Try the beginning, sweetie."

"Well . . . you remember I told you that Benny's mother owned an apartment building?"

"Yes." Jo wrinkled her nose. She hadn't seen the house, but knew it was in Greenwich Village and in a rather run-down state.

"Well, the two guys who were renting the basement have moved out, so Benny's mom says we can have it."

"Oh, how super." Not quite as exciting as Jo had expected.

"But that's not all. She's not renting it to us. She's giving it. And there's more yet." Marcia paused. "Benny says that if we want to be respectable home owners, we'll have to get married and have children. So as of now we're officially engaged!"

"Marcia! How marvellous! Congratulations, babe, congratulations. Have you told your folks?"

"Not yet. I telephoned Mom and told her we'd like to come out tomorrow night. Can you and Michael come?"

"Sure we can."

"Because Belle and Lawson are flying up from Nassau, and Dale has promised to be there too. We'll surprise them."

'And I'll prepare some food," Jo said excitedly. "Bring it out so Babs won't see it."

To think that only a few days ago she had been the most miserable woman in New York.

30

Tuesday 6 June

"Run, woman, run! Move your fat ass," Big Mike shouted, then threw his racket into the air. "My God! She's missed it! Would you believe it?"

"Will you shut up, you big turkey? If you hadn't played the ball right onto Mike's racket when you had an open court . . ." Babs laughed as she went up to the net to shake Jo's hand. "Anyway, you'd have beaten us in the end. You were just too good for us today. Thanks for a lovely game."

There was applause from Owen Michael and Tamsin who were watching the game. The court had been levelled out of the gentle slope behind Pinewoods, and the sun had begun to dip towards the surrounding trees. Babs kissed her grandson, who had run over to her as soon as the tennis was finished. "Let's all go inside for a drink," she said.

Half an hour later, Marcia dashed into the house. Babs squealed with delight. "Sweetie! What a beautiful dress. And Benny! Wow! Don't you look smart. You guys going to a party?"

Jo, Michael, Owen Michael, Tamsin and Dale crowded the doorway behind Marcia and Benny, and Babs stared at them too. "You're all dressed up as well. What is this?" She looked from face to face.

Jo prodded the nervous Benny. "Er . . . well . . ." He coughed. "Well . . . Marcia-and-I-have-decided-we-want-to-get-married, and we've brought my mom too." Words spilled out in a rush, and an equally shy, plump, middle-aged woman in a smart two-piece was dragged into the room from the hallway.

Big Mike leaped up to join the whirl of excited hugs, kisses and handshakes, beaming from ear to ear. No one noticed Jo slip away to the phone, and five minutes later the excitement started all over again as Lawson and Belle walked in.

Benny was left in no doubt as to the popularity of his proposal. His natural reserve was swept away on the tide of Donnelly enthusiasm, and soon he was chatting freely, arm round his mother, explaining her generosity and all they planned to do with the apartment.

Jo was busy organising food from the car to Babs's oven, but she had time to join in every few minutes. She loved watching people—Benny's mother, swamped by the noisy and affectionate welcome; Belle, thrilled by her younger sister's happiness; and Lawson . . . but Lawson seemed to hang on the periphery of the fun, obviously preoccupied.

The meal was a great success. The table wasn't built for twelve people, but they made it, Owen Michael and Tamsin being allowed to stay up for the important occasion. After they had all held hands while Big Mike said grace, there were innumerable toasts and gradually the noise level rose.

"I have an announcement to make too," Jo said, when she could make herself heard. "You'll never guess who's vacationing with us at Dolphin Point next month."

They looked at her, and Michael drank some more wine.

31

"My husband," Jo said, smiling at him.

"Son of a gun," Big Mike said. "I never thought we'd get you down in the Bahamas again. Won't that be during the Bermuda Race?"

"Well . . ."

"I'm so glad you're coming down." Babs squeezed Michael's hand.

By 10.30 the children were virtually asleep in their chairs, and Jo took them up to bed. The others voted to clear away before taking coffee in the lounge; Benny and Dale collected glasses while the women dealt with the dishes.

Michael looked at his father, and then at Lawson. Big Mike understood the glance, as did Lawson. Big Mike nodded, motioning him to wait.

"Cigar?" he asked him.

"Love one."

"Come and take your pick. They're in my study." Followed by Michael, he led Lawson across the hall into the small room lined with loaded bookshelves. "Sit down and help yourself."

He pushed a big silver box across the table, dropped into the swivel chair behind the desk. For a moment there was a smile on his face as he watched his son. He loved all his children. He had enjoyed his business career, often at the cost of time that could have been spent with his family. Now he was easing back, letting Mike junior take over, leaving himself more time with Babs and the kids. Not that they were really kids any more. Not even Dale, the baby of the family, the leggy youngster who had just walked off his campus one day because he'd been bored, who didn't seem able to stick at any job. Dale would find his way, given time and understanding.

Just as Marcia had found hers. Marcia had never been an easy girl to understand, especially during the period when she had dyed her hair purple, with zany clothes to match. But now Marcia had her Benny and maybe even kids, someday.

He did not suppose Belle and Lawson ever would have a family. They worked and played too hard ever to consider kids. And in fact one couldn't help wondering if Michael should ever have had a family either, he spent so little time with them. The kids seemed bright and happy enough, but the thought of Jo at her job all week, and their father even more preoccupied, made him feel angry and hurt for them. Big Mike didn't approve of working mothers . . . yet he couldn't blame Jo. He remembered her saying all along that she would go back to journalism. But Michael never warned anyone, before he was married, that he would devote virtually all his leisure time to sailing.

Michael Donnelly junior. Big Mike smiled to himself, recalling how excited he'd been when the boy came home from college to say he'd like to take up the offer of a place in the firm. Michael Donnelly and Son, Stockbrokers. That had been a thrill. And so was the speed with which he had learned; nobody could have cottoned on to a business faster. Now Mike sucked vigorously on his cigar and said, "Well?"

"The ball's in your court, Big Mike," said Lawson. "Dolphin Point is officially on the market as of now. So . . . we're going to have to make a decision."

"Big local interest?"

Lawson shook his head. "A million US is a bit steep for the average Bahamian." He grinned. "No, our main interest is coming from Florida. And once the estate agents over there get in on the act . . ."

"So what d'you want from me?" Big Mike asked. "I'm thinking about raising the money, but I need another few weeks. We're up to our ears trying to float a stock issue for Calthrop White."

"Look, it'll be gone by then," Lawson said. "All it needs is a hundred thousand as a deposit. That'll tie it up, Big Mike."

"Which we lose if it doesn't work out," Michael commented.

"It has to work out," Lawson insisted. "Listen to the figures. I can lay electricity and build a cistern big enough to serve the forty-two-acre site with water for two hundred and fifty grand. Then we split the property into one hundred and sixty-eight quarter-acre lots. And you know what I reckon we'll get for them? Forty thousand dollars each. Work that one out."

Big Mike pulled his calculator towards him, jabbed the figures, and whistled. "Six million, seven hundred and twenty thousand dollars."

"That's right. Five million profit. Half for me, half for you."

Big Mike and his son exchanged glances. "We were thinking of a three-way split."

Lawson hesitated, then grinned, and shrugged. "OK, if I get my normal two per cent for every lot I sell."

"Done," Big Mike said. "I'll have that hundred thousand in your account tomorrow."

Friday 9 June

Three days later, Ed Kowicz told Jo that Kiley had agreed to give Richard an extra five minutes on Friday evenings following the early newscast, to chat about the weather, and about hurricanes in particular; he had been encouraged by Hurricane Anthony down in the Caribbean, even though it was now fading fast. "So," Ed said, "if you're serious about doing those interviews with the 'man in the street', you'd better get with it."

Jo was momentarily taken aback. She had not actually planned how she would go about it. Normally her interviews were set up by the magazine. So how did she buttonhole some perfect stranger? Then she realised that she had at least one natural starter: Washington, the giant black man who worked as porter in her apartment block.

"Washington, have you ever thought that a hurricane might hit New

York, one day?" Jo watched his face as he considered the question.

"Nope," he said at last. "Never came into my head. Hurricanes don't get this far north."

"Only because the water's too cool. But suppose one year warm water spread up here, as it must have done the year Gloria came so close?"

"Heck, I remember her," Washington said. "Jeez, that was something, eh? But she was a kind of freak, wasn't she?"

"But if she happened once, she could happen again, couldn't she?"

"I guess she could, ma'am. But you don't get freaks very often. And she didn't even hit us, Mrs. Donnelly."

"She only just missed us," Jo reminded him. "Well anyway, if a hurricane *was* heading this way, what would you do? Suppose warnings were out on TV that one was coming straight for the Battery, would you leave town?"

He nodded, slowly. "Yes, ma'am. If there was going to be a big one coming straight at us, I reckon I'd do just that. Get the wife and my daughter and her little one, and drive off to stay with my brother until it was over."

The foyer doors opened to admit several people and Washington stood up. Jo said, "Looks like you're going to be busy for a while, so I'll leave you. NABS will be doing a short feature on hurricanes after the Friday forecast at six o'clock. I'd be interested to hear what you think of it."

Monday 12 June

Florence was waiting at the elevator as Jo stepped out. "Just going to get Bert's vacation jacket from the dry-cleaners, and I'll pick up the children from school on the way back. Be about half an hour."

"Are you going to Coney Island again this year?" It amazed Jo that so many New Yorkers spent their vacations on the unattractive strip to the south of the Narrows, so close to home.

"Same as ever. Sometimes Bert and I talk about a change, but we always end up there. We like to get ourselves a good tan on the beach, once a year." Stepping into the elevator she held the door open as she added, "A gentleman called. Didn't leave a name. He said he'd call back."

"Thanks, Florence," Jo said. "Can't think who that could be." Which was a lie. As it couldn't be her boss, Ed—who would have left his name—it might well be Richard. She didn't know if she wanted that. She knew she should congratulate him on being given the extra screen time, but she hadn't as yet, because she felt guilty every time she thought of him, and remembered her mood after that silly row with Michael. How long ago that seemed . . . and it was only a couple of weeks.

When the phone buzzed an hour later she nearly jumped out of her skin. "Hi there." It was Richard. "Have you heard the good news?"

"Yes," she said. "Terrific. And I've started on my interviews with the man in the street."

"Great. I'd love to hear about them. My first chat is on Friday, and maybe I could work in some of the comments. Why don't we meet?"

Jo stared at the phone. It was a sensible idea. They were sharing a project, and pooling ideas was obvious. So why did she again feel guilty? That was absurd. "Why not?" she asked.

"What about lunch, Thursday at the pizza place? About twelve thirty?"

"OK. Thursday would be great. I'll be there."

There was a moment's silence, then he said, "See you."

"Mommy, Mommy, I have a stomachache." Owen Michael stood in the doorway, his face a mask of misery.

"Darling! I didn't hear you come in. Just a moment. Yes, Mr. Connors," she said, "Thursday at twelve thirty. Goodbye." Jo replaced the receiver and turned to put her arm round her son's shoulders. "Where is the pain, sweetheart? Tell me."

"All over. In no particular place."

Jo could see this was no minor pain: the boy's eyes swam with tears.

"Then I'll take you along to see Dr. Knapps right now. Maybe he can give you something to fix it."

INEVITABLY, BY THE TIME they reached Dr. Knapps's consulting room, Owen Michael's pain was gone.

Dr. Knapps was a charming elderly man, who smiled benevolently, trying to conceal his tolerant scepticism. Owen Michael lay on the examination couch while the doctor pressed his abdomen and asked questions. Then, when he was satisfied, Dr. Knapps said, "Hm. Let's see. Your school year finishes in a couple of weeks, I believe?"

"Yes, sir." Owen Michael nodded politely.

"So you're about to begin your exams. Hoping for good grades?"

Owen Michael grinned. "Yes, sir."

"So you've been working extra hard. Exams can be tough, can't they?" Dr. Knapps smiled again. "Not too difficult to diagnose a nervy young stomach at this time of year, is it?"

"Well . . ." Jo hesitated. "He really was in pain, Doctor."

"Of course he was, Mrs. Donnelly. Psychosomatic pain can be just as unbearable as the real thing. What we have to do is relax those stomach muscles. I'll give you a prescription . . ." He sat at his desk and scrawled on a pad. "This'll settle him down."

Wednesday 14 June

The two filing clerks Jo spoke to in the main *Profiles* office had never heard of Richard Connors, nor were they interested in hurricanes. Nor was the man on the newsstand from whom she usually bought a paper.

But when Jo asked Nancy Duval, her hairdresser, she got a tremendous response. "I was in the Bahamas once," Nancy said, "when there was a warning. God, I was scared." The girl gesticulated at Jo in the mirror. "Took Bill hours, and three vodka martinis, to calm me down. Gee, if one of those things ever hit New York . . ."

"It's highly improbable, of course," Jo said, beginning to worry about the proximity of the scissors to her ears, "but do I guess right, that if there was a hurricane warning for New York, you'd leave?"

"Leave? You can bet your life I'd leave. I'd be leading the way out of town, 'cept I reckon no one would see my heels for dust."

"Bill might not want to go," Jo suggested.

"Correct. Bill will not want to move—but he will, even if I have to drag him away by the hair."

"And your children . . ."

"Yep. I'd throw them all in the car, lock the doors, and drive like crazy. There." She stepped back. "That looks better."

Jo looked at the results in the mirror. She could have sworn the left side was shorter than the right, but she had been here long enough. "Yes, that looks great. Thanks a million."

JO LEFT THE SALON and walked down to the library. There was the usual assortment of people lounging on the steps, and she needed some more youthful reaction. Most were in groups, but there was one young man on his own, wearing a dirty sweatshirt and shorts, and a broadbrimmed western-style hat. He did not look up as she stood behind him. "You're wasting your time, sister," he said. "I don't got it."

"Got what?" Jo enquired.

"You ain't taking a survey on Aids?"

"As a matter of fact, no," she said.

At last he raised his head. He was quite a good-looking boy, early twenties, she estimated. "Well, what d'you know," he said. "What *do* you know," he repeated, as he inspected her from her ankles up the length of her summer skirt, which was almost transparent in the afternoon sun. "Well, if you're looking for sex, I guess we'll have to use your place." He grinned. "I ain't got one."

Jo opened her mouth and then closed it again. She wished she had chosen someone else. But his reaction might be interesting. "My name is Josephine Donnelly," she said. "I work for *Profiles* magazine, and I am doing research on hurricanes."

The boy leaned back and tilted his hat over his eyes. "Siddown."

Jo hesitated, then chose a relatively clean piece of step.

"You are something," he remarked. "I like your feet."

"Thank you," she said. "You ever been in a hurricane?"

"Bit of breeze," he said.

"You've seen one?"

He shrugged. "Can't say I have. You gonna let me feel your tits?"

"No," she told him. "What would you do if you were told a hurricane was coming straight for New York?"

He sat up. "You gotta be dumb."

"Imagine it," Jo recommended. "It could happen."

He gazed at her for several seconds. "I'd stand out there in the rain and say, 'Hallelujah'."

"You'd be blown away by the wind."

"That I'd have to see." He suddenly reached for her, and she had to leap to her feet.

"I'd like to see that too," Jo remarked. "You being blown away, that is." She hurried down the steps.

MICHAEL WAS STANDING at the cocktail bar with his back to the door fixing a drink, when she came in. "Hi there," he said over his shoulder.

Jo frowned. He was home at least an hour early, and suddenly she had bad vibes.

He smiled as he handed her a sherry on ice. "Let's sit down, darling. Boy, has it been hot today!" He set his bourbon and soda beside the chair, sat down, and stretched out his legs.

"Michael? What is it?"

"What's what?"

"Don't play games with me. You have something on your mind."

Michael gave a sheepish grin. "Fact is, my love . . . I won't be able to come to Eleuthera with you next month after all."

"Why not?"

"Well . . . I had to call the guys, of course, and tell them I wouldn't be available for the Bermuda Race, and they were pretty upset."

"They were, were they?"

"I did tell you that we reckon we have a good chance of a trophy this year," Michael explained. "But only if we have our best team. Sam and Larry flipped at the idea of me not skippering. And . . . ."

"No way! Absolutely no way, Michael. You made a solemn promise—"

"And on top of that, Sam would rather not skipper in so important an event. It's one thing round Long Island Sound, but on the ocean . . . ."

Jo sat back in her chair and crossed her legs. "Well, if they can't manage without you, they'll just have to scratch."

"Jo! It can't be done. I've given them my word."

"You've what?" She jumped up and stood glaring at him. "You're not serious! So tell me, Michael, who do you intend breaking your promise to, your pals, or your wife and children?"

Suddenly he was on his feet too, standing over her. "Goddamn it, you silly bitch," he hissed, "I've been trying to break it to you gently, trying to explain the predicament I'm in so you'd understand."

"Understand? Of course I understand! Did you really and truly intend

38

to drop out of the race this year? Ever? Or did you just play the yes-man to me to stop me filing for a divorce?"

He turned away, picked up the glass, drained it, and returned to the cocktail bar. "You really are the most selfish, demanding wife any poor chap ever got landed with," he remarked quietly, affecting a calm that was belied by the rattle of the decanter on the rim of his glass.

"Really?" She sat down again. "Do you base that opinion on the fact that I am asking you to keep your promise to spend some of your non-working hours with your family? And to take a vacation with them, for the first time in eight years?"

"I guess it's your training as a journalist which enables you to twist what people say to suit your purpose," he retorted. "Well, I warn you, it won't wash with me. I agreed to holiday with you this year, all things being equal. But I can't let the guys down, and I don't mean to." He drained his second drink and slammed the glass down on the counter. "If you can't even understand that, then that's it. I can't see any point in trying any more. I'm obviously just wasting my time." He opened the door. "I'll be in the study if the children want me; I've some phone calls to make."

Jo was too stunned to think for a moment. Vaguely she wondered how the situation could continue. It had been easy a fortnight ago, in a fit of fury, to threaten divorce. Now, sitting alone, she tried to visualise the possible outcome. The children having to grow up in two separate homes, learning, like so many others she knew in such circumstances, to play one parent against the other, becoming rude and aggressive in their demands. And what of the Donnellys? Babs and Big Mike, Belle, Marcia and Dale? She had come, over the past eleven years, to regard them as her family.

Her earlier anger was replaced by self-recrimination. How the hell had she been stupid enough to marry Michael in the first place? She had known of his drive for kicks from the day she met him, but she had imagined it would slacken off after marriage. Now she knew better, should she consider giving up her career to do as he asked, and devote her time to being a wife and mother? But if she did that, and the relationship continued to deteriorate, she would be left with absolutely nothing. Homeless and jobless.

Thursday 15 June

Richard Connors had the morning off. Julian was doing the ten o'clock forecast, in which there was very little to report. There was another tropical storm, just off Martinique, this one named Christopher, but Richard didn't expect it to do much. This was being the damnedest spring, the hottest in New York for some time, and yet there was only muted hurricane activity. The summer, he realised, could leave him with egg all over his face, since he had confidently predicted on the air that there would be several major storms this year.

Feeling himself trapped in the minute apartment which was all he had been able to find, he switched on his TV. The fact was, he wasn't a home-maker, at least on his own. He had moved in here a fortnight ago, and hung some wallpaper in the bedroom, but boxes of books remained stacked in a corner waiting for him to put up shelves. When Pam and he had finally agreed to split, he'd been quite keen to sample independence again, to get away from the constant emotional strain of a dead marriage. He had visualised himself as the happy bachelor, conjuring up pictures of cosy evenings with his sort of music, his kind of TV programme, hamburger in one hand and beer in the other—comfortable and contented.

Well, just about every evening since moving in he had had his music, his TV, his beer and his hamburger available—but what the hell had happened to the contentment? He'd pondered the question long enough to know the answer: he was lonely. Companionship was what he was after. A companion to eat with, walk with, go to a theatre with. He had met only one woman since coming to New York who could fill that bill. Josephine Donnelly, a married woman with children. To get her, he would have to play his image to the hilt. And he wasn't at all sure he wanted to break up a marriage. But at least they were lunching together. He could feel his way.

THEY ORDERED PIZZAS, salad and Frascati. Richard loved her in the crisp pale turquoise cotton dress she was wearing. Loved her? That was ridiculous; he hardly knew her.

". . . interviews. When school finishes for the summer . . ." He let her chat on, hardly listening, just watching her. A word sank in.

"Vacationing in Eleuthera?" he said. "That'll be fun."

"It will. All the family will be there . . . well, nearly all." A shadow passed over her face. "My husband spends most of his time yacht racing. Now, what are you going to say in your first hurricane chat?"

He felt a stab of disappointment as she backed off, and tried to get his mind back to business. "Well, I guess I'll have to begin by outlining just what a hurricane is, and hope to God I have something real to talk about next week, before JC cancels the show."

"Surely he won't cancel the show after one programme?"

"He might. He reckoned there'd be hurricane activity down south this summer which would give the chats a boost, and it isn't happening. Oh, there have been some storms, but they've all fizzled out. It's as if something out there was straining to bust loose, and hasn't been able to, yet."

"Isn't that an angle for you to use?"

He shook his head. "I'd be torn to ribbons by my fellow forecasters."

She was suddenly very aware of his black, mobile eyebrows and sleek

40

black hair, and the way he could smile with just half his mouth. She could see that he was more real and sincere than she'd first thought. She realised that he was vulnerable too.

There was a brief silence, then he asked, "Do you go racing with your husband?"

"No. Michael made it quite clear, a long time ago, that his sort of sailing is for men only."

He raised his eyebrows. "Then what are your hobbies?"

Her turn to shrug. "Being Mum, I suppose. There just isn't enough time to do anything else, if I'm going to hold down my job as well."

"But . . ." He checked what he had been going to say.

"Oh, sure, we don't need my income. That's not the point, though, is it? I have a life to live just as much as Michael, and I love journalism. But my spare time is spent being a wife and mother." She smiled. "Sometimes, after the kids are in bed—and when I can find a baby sitter—I go to a concert or a play . . . or just stay at home and listen to records. I have a super record collection."

"Really? I do too. What sort of music? Classical?" He leaned eagerly across the table. "I'd love to show you my stereo set-up; it's the only part of the apartment that's properly finished. Do you have half an hour?"

They stared at each other, both knowing the implications of his invitation. Jo's mind raced through the list of fors and againsts. She knew what she wanted to do: it was years since a man had looked at her like this—come to think of it, it was hard to recall if Michael ever had.

"Yes, I have half an hour to spare," she said, quietly but decisively.

IN THE ELEVATOR, Richard apologised for the mess she would find in the lounge. "Guess I just haven't gotten round to deciding what to do with it. I'm not too hot on interior design."

"That's because you haven't got a woman prodding you all the time," she said without thinking. But once in the apartment she immediately saw what he meant, shuddering at the mess.

He showed her his stereo system and the neat cases of compact discs. "Take your pick. Anything there you like?"

Scanning the titles, she tried to think, tried to decide what to do. Aware that he was waiting, she stammered, "I'm spoilt for choice, I love them all. How about some Chopin?"

The reproduction was exquisite. Standing beside the windows, double-glazed against the Manhattan traffic, she closed her eyes, listening, absorbing. And when she reopened them, he was beside her, filling her with an overwhelming desire to touch him, to be in his arms. And he wanted it too; she could read it in his eyes.

Silently they moved together, eyes locked. Jo felt herself drawn against him and stood trembling, wanting—yet frightened, overawed by the magnitude of her reaction to him.

41

"Jo?" His voice was scarcely above a whisper. "Darling Jo. I have dreamed of you for the past fortnight, praying, hoping and fearing it might all never happen." She felt his breath on her forehead and tilted her head to meet his mouth with hers. Suddenly a great surging joy welled up to fill her chest, her throat, her head, leaving her gasping under his soft kisses. His encircling arms moved up, and with fingers threaded in her hair he held her face in both hands and gazed at her.

His gaze turned to consternation as the doorbell rang.

"Oh, damn," he said, "just give me a moment."

She watched as he went to the door. Now was the moment to regain sanity and leave.

The door was open. "Hi, old buddy," said a young man clasping a suitcase. "Got in a shade earlier than I thought."

Jo couldn't make up her mind whether she was glad or sorry that this friend of Richard's had walked in on them. Mark Hammond was as embarrassed as they, but the ice was soon broken and they sat around chatting and drinking coffee until four o'clock. He was a navy flier, who was also, she discovered, Richard's secret source of information about the weather.

When she realised the time she hurriedly made to leave and Richard came to the door with her. "I'm real sorry about that. Can we meet again? Mark will only be here a couple of days."

"I'll call you," she promised.

Saturday 17 June

"Come on in, Mom, it's lovely," Owen Michael called from the swimming pool at Pinewoods.

"It's a bit early in the year for me," Jo replied from her lounger. But she heaved herself up and went to the edge of the pool to dip a toe in. "Hey, that's quite warm."

She dived in, slicing through the water under the children to tickle their feet and bring shrieks and squeals as they splashed to get away.

"Shame Michael isn't here," Babs murmured to Big Mike. "I thought he was only going to race every other weekend?"

"Yep. Something wrong there. You can see it in Jo's face."

Jo swam back to where they were sitting, kicked her legs and bounced up to perch on the pool edge beside them. "That's just super," she said.

"Jo, why's Michael up in Newport this weekend? Is he preparing *Esmeralda* for the Bermuda Race after all?" Big Mike was not renowned for his tact: if he had a question he usually asked it.

Babs flushed and waited.

"Yes," Jo replied, not looking at them. She did not want to discuss Michael with them—no doubt he would tell them his plans when he was good and ready.

42

"Oh, dear." Babs was well aware of the implications of Michael's absence.

Jo felt their eyes on her, knew they would have to be told something. The children were at the far end of the pool, racing from one side to the other, splashing and shouting. "Yes," she admitted. "We did have another quarrel, a big one, Wednesday night. When he told me he'd decided to race after all. I'm sorry I didn't tell you sooner—maybe I was hoping he'd change his mind again."

"Perhaps he will," Babs ventured.

Jo shrugged her wet shoulders and said nothing.

"Well . . ." Mike shook his head. "You knew he was a keen sportsman before you married, and if this is the way he wants it to be . . ." He paused, lamely.

"Quite. And he knew I was a keen journalist. Only I've kept my side of the bargain and cut back my work. So where do we go from here?" She wondered if they could help her solve her dilemma.

"Can't you discuss it together . . ." Babs started.

"We have. And it always ends in a slanging match."

They sat silently watching the children. The sky was an uninterrupted blue, but for the birds which occasionally swooped from the branches of one pine to the next. Mike rolled his feet off the lounger and stood up. "When's he coming home? I'm going to talk to him."

"I've no idea," Jo said. "We're not exactly communicating at the moment. But anyway, it's a waste of time. He'll know I've told you, and he'll accuse me of running up here whining to you." She looked at Mike and Babs, seeing the anxiety in their eyes. "I'm sorry. So sorry. He says it's all my fault, and naturally, I think it's his. I suppose we just have to accept that we're not compatible."

"Not compatible!" Mike growled. "Don't give me that. Folks are as compatible as they make up their mind to be. Look . . ." He sat on the edge of the lounger again, leaning towards her. "Don't get me wrong. I think he's behaving like a louse, breaking his promise, but dammit, it is his life, and if he wants to spend all his leisure time sailing . . ."

"He should never have got married in the first place," Jo interrupted bitterly. "I didn't marry Michael just to be his maid, valet and bear him children. I want a companion, too, to share things . . . like our children, holidays, the fun there is in life doing things that families do together." She scrambled up off the pool edge, grabbed her towel, and rushed up to the house to shower . . . and weep.

When she reappeared, made-up and smiling in a pretty sunsuit, Babs jumped up and ran to put her arms round her. "Dearest Jo, we all do love you so much. Don't give up, *please*. We'll all have a talk with Michael, and maybe . . . if you'll just be patient."

"OK." Jo hugged her back. "I love you all too, remember?" But Babs and Mike both noticed she wasn't smiling.

The phone on Jo's desk buzzed, and she picked it up, heart pounding. She still hadn't called Richard, so perhaps he had grown tired of waiting.

"Josephine Donnelly."

"Washington here, Mrs. Donnelly. There's a . . ." Washington hesitated ". . . gentleman down here to see you. Says his name is Stuart Alloan. Says you and he are old friends."

"Stuart Alloan? I've never heard of him. Oh, well, you'd better send him up." She was preoccupied with researching her next assignment, Nino Fabretti, the guitarist who was going to be in New York the following week. Stuart Alloan? She looked at her watch; it was half past three, and Florence and the children had not yet got home from school.

The doorbell rang, and she looked through the peephole, while releasing the locks. All she saw was a face which was certainly familiar, then the door was pushed in with a violence that all but knocked her over. "What on earth . . . ?" She gazed at the young man in the dirty sweatshirt and the cowboy hat from the library steps.

"Hope I didn't hurt you, ma'am," he said. "You remember me? Name's Stuart Alloan."

Jo drew a sharp breath. "Yes. I remember you, Mr. Alloan. How did you know where I lived?"

"You told me your name and the magazine you worked for, ma'am. They gave me your address."

Jo wondered who was stupid enough to do that. I must find out, she thought. But first, this lout had to be removed. "What do you want?"

He looked her up and down. Working at home, Jo wore only a housecoat, as he could certainly tell, however tightly she had retied the cord before answering the door. He closed the door behind him. "Say, some place you got here. Must be money in writing for magazines, eh?"

Jo's heart was pounding painfully. The nearest telephone was in the study—on the far side of the intruder. How on earth had she been so careless? But there was no use losing her head. "The apartment belongs to my husband," she said, "who will be home any minute."

"Is that a fact?" he asked. "You know that's what they all say?"

She licked her lips, slowly backing across the room towards the brass-edged glass table. It was used to display ornaments, one of which was a tall, slim statuette, cast in bronze. It could be a serviceable weapon.

He pointed at her. "Don't gimme any sauce, lady. I kinda like you. I just came to see if you was ready to show me those tits."

Jo reached the statue, wrapped her fingers round it and lifted it from the table. "If you don't leave right now," she said, "I am going to brain you, and then hand you over to the police."

His finger was still extended. "Now that's fighting talk, doll."

He came round the sofa, and Jo inhaled. She hadn't expected to be challenged. "I mean it," she warned. "I . . ."

Alloan moved far more quickly than she had anticipated. She swung the statue, but he easily evaded it, and then caught her arm, twisting it so that she dropped the ornament to the floor. Then his other arm went round her, clutching her against him, and his fingers were tugging at her housecoat, trying to tear it open. She gasped and twisted and used her elbows and kicked at him. She managed to get away, stumbling as she fell across the back of the sofa. Before she could recover he had seized her shoulder to hold her there, head down, legs flailing.

"No!" she screamed. "No, please . . ."

The front door opened and Florence and the children stared at the scene in front of them.

"Florence?" Jo shrieked. "Call Washington. Call the police. Call . . ." But the hand had left her shoulder as Alloan straightened, so she turned and kicked his crotch as hard as she could. Momentarily distracted by the intruders, Alloan gasped with pain.

"Nice work, Mom," Owen Michael shouted, running into the room, seizing a large Chinese vase and smashing it over the man's head.

Alloan was still bent double. Jo grabbed the statue again in both hands, swung it, and hit him on the head with all her strength.

"MAY I ASK just what the hell has been going on?" Michael Donnelly stood in the centre of his lounge and looked around him.

"Oh, it was terrible, Mr. Donnelly," Florence said.

"A man was here," Tamsin shouted.

"Assaulting Mommy," Owen Michael declared.

"But Mommy bopped him one with the statue," Tamsin informed him.

"And Owen Michael hit him with the Chinese vase," Florence added.

"Washington came, and the police, and took the man away," Tamsin said.

"The sergeant said Mommy had been awful brave," Owen Michael went on.

"And he said Owen Michael had been brave too," Tamsin added loyally.

Michael continued to glare at Jo. "I think you kids had better go do your homework," he said. "Your mother and I would like a little chat."

"Yes," Jo agreed, understanding that her ordeal was not yet over. "Run along, children. Thank you so much, Florence. You saved my life."

Michael waited until they had all left the room. Then he said, "Perhaps you'd like to explain."

"Well . . . there's not a lot to explain, Michael." She sat down. "This druggie broke in here and tried to assault me . . ."

"Is that a fact. Druggie? Broke in here? How the hell did he do that? What the hell do we pay round-the-clock porters for?"

"Well, I suppose the fault is mine. Washington called to say there was this man to see me, who said he was an old friend, and I said to send him up. I was working, and I just never thought, I guess."

Michael went to the bar and poured himself a drink. "You expect me to believe that? Entertaining hashed-up dropouts in my apartment in the middle of the afternoon . . ."

"I ought to kill you for saying that," Jo said.

He flushed. "You going to pretend you didn't know the guy? How did he know to come to this apartment?"

"Sure I knew him," Jo snapped. "He was one of the people I interviewed for my hurricane article. Nothing more than that."

"How did he know your name?"

"I told him my name," she shouted. "I always tell interviewees my name, and who I work for."

"Who you work for." His momentary embarrassment had disappeared now he had discovered another handle to twist. "That stupid job. Do you realise it could've got you raped? The kids hurt? I demand you give it up. Now."

She stared at him. She had been frightened; she could almost be tempted. If he would cooperate. "And if I do, will you come to Eleuthera next month?"

"You have got to be joking." He pointed. "You're the one out of line on this one. And I'm the poor bastard whose wife's name is going to be splashed all over the newspapers. I suppose you'll have to give evidence at the trial?"

"Of course I will. Don't worry, they tell me it won't be until after the yacht racing season."

"Bitch," he commented. "But you are giving up that job. Now."

"Go to hell," Jo told him, and went into the bedroom.

Tuesday 20 June

Richard telephoned her the following morning, at the office, just after she had finished enduring the comments and sympathy of Ed and the staff, and the apologies of one of the secretaries for having divulged her address to a total stranger.

"Jo?" Richard's voice was fraught. "I've just seen the paper. God . . ."

"Nothing happened," she assured him. "The guy was just hashed up."

"But . . . the papers say he broke in and assaulted you. That he's been charged with . . ."

"Attempted rape. He didn't get very far."

"Oh, Jo . . ."

"I'll tell you all about it when we meet."

"When?"

"I could make it today, Richard."

46

There was a moment's pause, and she could hear him riffling the pages of his diary. "You got it. Ah . . . I could arrange some time off?"

"Yes," she said. "I would like that." She realised, as she replaced the receiver, that for the second time in her life, she was falling in love.

Thursday 29 June

"There." Eisener had assumed his favourite position, on the flight deck between the two pilots, and now he pointed.

Mark Hammond followed the direction of his finger and gave a low whistle as he gazed at an apparently unbroken carpet of white cloud, lying right over the horizon even at 20,000 feet. The big bird was a very long way away from home, heading for the Cape Verdes, the group of islands that lie six hundred miles off the westernmost bulge of Africa.

The reason for the extended flight had been an unusual phenomenon: over the past week the pressure over the Cape Verde Islands had dropped much lower than usual for the time of year, and the result had been a much greater accumulation of cloud than usual. This had shown up first on satellite, and Eisener had determined to take a closer look.

"That cloud mass must stretch clear back to Africa," remarked Bob Landry, the copilot.

"Yeah, it's big," Eisener agreed. "What do you make of it, Mark?"

Mark didn't know what to reply. He had never seen anything like it. This could be what they had all been waiting for.

"There's no trace of any circulation," Landry remarked.

"No," Eisener said. "But by golly, if that mass should start to circulate . . . Let's take a closer look."

Tuesday 11 July

"That is it," J. Calthrop White declared. "Kill it, Kiley. That programme has had not the slightest effect on our ratings."

Kiley twisted his fingers together. "That's true, JC, but there could be something any day. According to Connors . . ."

"That nut? Bringing him up here is the biggest mistake you ever made, Kiley. And at seventy-five grand a year . . . my God, he's made us the laughing stock of the networks with his warnings that this could be the year of the big storm. All because it's hot?"

"Well . . . there's this big system out in the Cape Verde Islands . . ."

"The Cape Verdes? They're four thousand miles away. And it's been there for damn near a month, just sitting. That isn't going anywhere, Kiley. No, we want programmes which are going to boost our ratings. We've got to convince those Brits we can run a network. And bids for that franchise need to be in, the first of next month."

Kiley nodded. "How's the financing going, JC?"

47

"Goddamned Donnelly," JC said. "Still saying it can't be done at such short notice . . . and in the summer. What the hell has the time of year to do with it? You know something, Kiley, it's because that son of his wants to spend the summer racing. And now Mike tells me he's going to the Bahamas for at least a fortnight. Nothing to worry about, he says: my partner, Cal Palmer, is handling everything." White brooded for several seconds, then raised his head. "Now you listen to me, Kiley"—he wagged his gold pencil—"you kill those goddamned chats. And get this straight: Connors's contract will not be renewed next spring. You got that?"

"I've got it, JC," Kiley said, unhappily.

Wednesday 12 July

"Saturday," Babs said happily. "Oh, Saturday. It's just incredible that another whole year should have rolled by. But you know what, Jo, honey, every fifteenth of July I feel kind of reborn. How I love Eleuthera."

Jo watched the children playing in the pool. School had broken up a week before, to her great relief. Owen Michael's stomachache had developed into an almost nightly feature during the exams, and she had worried herself sick. But, as Dr. Knapps had prophesied, with the ending of the pressure it had just disappeared.

"When Big Mike retires . . . heck, it's in only a couple of years," Babs reflected. "I reckon we'll move down to Dolphin Point, permanently."

Jo turned her head in surprise. "You'll sell Pinewoods?"

"Well, I don't think so. I mean, Michael will take over as head of the firm. So why shouldn't you have this place? You don't want to spend the rest of your life in a New York apartment."

"Um," Jo said. She had realised that Babs, and no doubt Big Mike as well, had interpreted her happiness of the past month as meaning she and Michael had patched up their differences; fortunately Michael, absorbed with getting *Esmeralda* ready for the big race which started this weekend, had not noticed the change in her.

She still had no idea what to do. She had now been to Richard's apartment five times, had met him for lunch on nine occasions, had spoken to him on the phone at least three times a week. She was in love. But even through the euphoria she understood that she could not live the rest of her life as a lie, any more than she could give up the children. Because that was what would happen if Michael found out.

It was a rotten world, she thought. She had often dreamed of one day inheriting Pinewoods . . . but did she want it, now?

"All packed?" Babs asked, determined to keep the conversation going.

"Not really. I'll do it on Friday. There's not all that much to pack, for just the three of us," Jo pointed out. "Shorts, shirts, that's it. Anyway, I have Michael's dinner party tomorrow night."

"Oh, yes, I'd forgotten that. Will it be the usual crowd?"

"The crew and their wives, yes."

"Well, you ought to have fun." Babs hesitated, choosing her words. She and Jo hadn't really had a chance to talk about much for the past three weeks or so, but with the girl so obviously happy . . . "I can't tell you how happy it makes Mike and me to see you . . . well, to feel things are OK between Michael and you again."

"Um," Jo said.

"Sure I know it's one hell of a disappointment, him not coming down to Eleuthera with us . . . but you're not still angry about that, are you?"

"No," Jo said, with complete honesty. "Michael is welcome to spend all the time he wants in his plastic bathtub."

"Just let him do this race," Babs recommended. "And win his class. That's all he's ever wanted to do, win his class in the Bermuda. Then we'll talk him into letting go a little."

"HI." RICHARD'S VOICE drifted over the phone. "Tomorrow?"

"I can't," Jo said. "I have to prepare dinner for Michael's crew."

"Hell . . . and you're off on Saturday?"

"So I'm free Friday evening. I'll get a sitter. Michael will have left for Newport by then." They had never had the opportunity to spend even part of a night together, and she wanted that to happen.

"Oh, Jo," he said. "That'll be just marvellous. But I have to do the ten o'clock forecast that night."

"So I'll watch it, from your lounge."

"Sweetheart. Say, I have some bad news. JC has killed the chat show. Seems it hasn't had any impact on the ratings. There haven't been any storms, you see."

"But there could be one."

"Sure. As a matter of fact, you know that huge cloud mass over the Cape Verdes I've been showing on the box?"

"Yes?"

"It's started to shift to the west. Only slightly. But Jo"—now his voice was excited—"I've spoken to Mark Hammond in Florida. There are real signs of circulation."

"Oh boy. Won't that vindicate everything you've been saying?"

"Maybe. The circulation is still very weak. But if it grows, well . . . it has to come ashore somewhere."

"Where would you expect that to happen?"

"Most probably the northern West Indies. Haiti, or Puerto Rico. Not a nice thought for the people who live there. Anyway, if it does come to anything, it'll be mud in JC's eye. Something to keep me warm while you're away. Three weeks. I am going to go stark, raving mad."

"Are you?" she murmured.

"Yeah. And I've got some good news, too."

"Tell me."

"I love you."

"I love you too," she said.

Thursday 13 July

Florence was in despair: the stove wouldn't work and she couldn't get anyone to come and repair it.

Jo got on the phone and threatened the maintenance people with publicity in *Profiles* magazine, which brought a Mr. Fix-it to the apartment within twenty minutes. Owen Michael had a stomachache again. She sat him in front of the TV and told him to relax. Presumably he was getting worked up over his father's departure for Newport . . . but if he was going to have to go through life with a bellyache every time he got excited he was going to have a hard time.

Her good mood lasted all evening. Wearing a stunning little cocktail number, she welcomed Sam and Sally—Sam was Michael's best friend as well as his second-in-command on the yacht—Larry and Beth, Jon, Pete and Jerry. Actually, she liked them all, and could understand the good fellowship Michael enjoyed with them; she would have enjoyed it too, had she been allowed to share it.

Michael was at his best. He was always a superb host, and he was obviously pleased that Jo was making such an effort to play the loving wife. The party was a great success. Certainly Jo was convinced that none of the others had the slightest idea that she and Michael had not shared a bed for a month, or that their marriage might be on the verge of disintegration.

Friday 14 July

"I can't find my red sports shirt or my yacht club sweater," Michael complained, stuffing clothes into a duffle bag. "Where have you put them?"

"Haven't touched them," Jo called from the bathroom.

"Well, will you look, please? I'm in a hurry. I want to be in Newport for lunch."

"For God's sake, the race doesn't start until Sunday."

"True. But there's a lot of preparing to be done. Or hadn't you thought of that?"

"Judging by the amount of time you've spent in Newport these last six weeks one would have thought *Esmeralda* could have been refitted and ready a dozen times." She came into the bedroom, looked through his neat stack of shirts and sweaters, and carefully drew out the "missing" items. "There, under your nose," she said quietly, and strode out again.

"Are you going to keep up this farcical performance every time I go yachting?" he growled. "Now come on, for God's sake. I've got to go. Let's part friends, OK?" He was standing at the bedroom door, waiting.

Jo sighed. "OK," she said. "Let's find the kids and we'll all say goodbye together."

Tamsin and Owen Michael appeared from the family room. Jo noticed that Owen Michael was looking rather pale, and was unusually quiet.

"You'll look after Mommy and Tamsin while I'm away, won't you?" Michael held out his hand to the boy.

Owen Michael managed a smile. "Sure, Dad. And I hope you have good winds for the race."

"I'll settle for Force Six there and back, nothing more than thirty knots. But however strong the wind is, your daddy will cope."

"Are you going to come down to Eleuthera and join us when the race is over?" Tamsin asked.

Michael glanced at Jo and then away again. "No. I won't be able to do that. The fellows want to spend a week or so cruising around Bermuda before we come home. But you be sure to have lots of fun down there." He turned to Jo. "Look after yourselves." He waited.

"And you come home with that cup." She reached up and kissed his cheek. "Goodbye. Keep in touch with Sally, so that if we can't raise you on the radio we can get an update from her."

"That's my girl." Michael hugged her and the children, and headed for the elevator. He turned to wave one last time, and was gone.

JO HAD A GREAT DEAL to do. She decided to leave the packing until after lunch, but went out straightaway for some last-minute shopping. When she got back she was greeted by Dale, Michael's young brother.

"Hi!" she said in surprise, presenting her cheek for a kiss. "What brings you here?"

"I dropped in to see if I could give you a lift to Kennedy tomorrow," he said, "and found Florence worried stiff."

"Florence? Worried about what?"

"It's Owen Michael. He's in bed with bad stomach cramps."

"Oh, my God!" She rushed in to kneel beside the boy. "Darling, what's happened?"

Owen Michael was curled up on his side, flushed and shivering. An arm reached out for his mother. "Mom. It's so bad I can scarcely breathe," he sobbed.

Jo put a hand on his forehead. It was burning hot. "OK, sweetheart, we'll do something right away." She turned to Dale. "Will you carry Owen Michael down to the garage? We'll take him straight along to the clinic." She had no doubt at all that far from having a nervous tummy, her son was genuinely ill.

Dale drove the Mercedes while Jo sat beside Owen Michael in the back. When they reached the Mercy Clinic Jo ran inside to call up a

51

stretcher, and the boy was wheeled into an examination room. Dr. Matthey, a black doctor who had answered his bleeper, hurried in and with a polite nod turned to Owen Michael and gently pressed his bared abdomen. The boy screamed and Jo jumped in alarm. A nurse was sent hurrying away, and reappeared seconds later with another doctor, and the two men conferred in undertones as they examined the boy together.

"What is it?" Jo asked anxiously.

"We think he's probably got a perforated appendix. He will need immediate surgery."

Jo saw concern in the kind black face, and was frightened.

"Is he in danger?"

"His situation is critical," the doctor said carefully. "But if we get him on the table right now, we should be able to pull him through." He looked at Jo, awaiting the necessary permission. "It has to be immediately, Mrs. Donnelly."

Jo took a long breath, and nodded.

BIG MIKE DONNELLY ran along the hospital corridor, followed by Babs. "Jo!" Mike gasped, catching sight of his daughter-in-law in the waiting room. "Where is he?"

"In theatre," Jo said miserably. "They're operating now."

Babs arrived, panting. "Where's Tamsin?"

"She's stayed at the apartment with Florence."

"Michael . . . ?" Big Mike began.

Jo's shoulders heaved. "The hospital are still trying to reach him. We contacted the yacht, but he wasn't there. I . . ." She turned as a white-uniformed nurse appeared in the doorway. "Mrs. Donnelly? We have your husband on the line. You can take it in the office."

Big Mike and Babs crowded into the small room behind Jo.

"Michael?" she asked. "Michael, is that you? . . . Yes, I know the race starts at dawn tomorrow . . . yes, I know you have a lot to do, but Michael . . . oh, for God's sake, will you listen to me? Owen Michael is ill . . . yes, very ill. He has acute appendicitis . . . yes, I'm talking from the hospital. They think he's going to be all right . . ." She listened for a few moments. "For God's sake, he needs you . . . the hell with the race . . . I told you, your son needs you, Michael. We all need you . . ." Another long pause as a deep flush suffused her face. Then she slammed the phone down.

"He wouldn't come?" Babs asked, disbelievingly.

"He asked me if the doctors thought Owen Michael was going to be all right. Then he said there was no need for him to come." Jo's voice was toneless. "He couldn't let the guys down, he said."

"Oh, God!" Big Mike muttered.

Another of the phones on the desk buzzed. Jo spun round, but the

52

nurse had already picked it up. "Yes," she said. "Oh, right away." She smiled at Jo. "Dr. Matthey is waiting to see you, Mrs. Donnelly. And I think you'll find he has good news for you."

THEY FOUND A BAR just round the corner from the hospital.

Jo looked almost happy. "The appendix was perforated, as they thought," she said. "But Dr. Matthey says they cleaned him up just in time. Now, it's only a matter of recuperation."

"Jeez, what a foul-up," Big Mike muttered.

His wife knew exactly what he was thinking: they were due to leave for Eleuthera in not much over twelve hours' time. "We'll cancel our holiday, of course," she said.

"Of course you won't," Jo protested. "You can't. What about Belle and Lawson? And Dale?"

"Yes, but we can't leave you . . ."

"I'll be all right. The doc says that if all goes well, Owen Michael may be able to leave hospital next Friday. If he rests up for a few days, he should be as right as rain. We'll follow on down then."

"I guess you're right," Babs admitted. "Maybe we *should* go . . . but you can't cope on your own. You'll have to visit every day, and Florence is due for her vacation as well, isn't she? Listen, we'll take Tamsin. How about that?"

"I think that would be splendid," Jo agreed; she didn't even want Tamsin around right at this minute. She just wanted to sit and think . . . about the end of her marriage. Besides, she had another phone call to make.

"Heck, it'll work out just fine," Big Mike said. "You stay up here another ten days or so, and Michael will be back from Bermuda. You can all come down together."

BACK AT THE APARTMENT Jo telephoned Richard, who was horrified to hear about Owen Michael, and readily accepted that she would not be able to make it that night. She sent Florence home, packed a bag for Tamsin, and then the little girl was driven out to Bognor by Big Mike.

When she returned to the hospital, Owen Michael was awake. He looked ill, lying propped against his pillows, but he managed a feeble smile. She kissed him and stroked his forehead.

"Why did Dr. Knapps say it was exam nerves, Mom?" he asked.

"I guess he made a mistake, honey. Some boys and girls do get exam nerves, so maybe he thinks that's the cause of all tummyaches."

"Where's Tamsin?"

"She's going down to Dolphin Point with Granpa and Granma. Don't worry, we'll be joining them in a few days."

"When will Dad get here?" he asked, hopefully.

Jo hesitated. This was the question she had been dreading. "I don't think he will be able to make it, darling. And anyway, now that you're on the mend, you wouldn't want him to abandon the race, would you?"

"I guess not," Owen Michael agreed, not entirely convinced. "Will we really be able to go to Dolphin Point after all, Mom?"

"Of course we will. Just as soon as the doctors say so."

"I'm glad you stayed with me, Mom." Owen Michael smiled, and dozed off.

Monday 17 July

Three days later Dr. Matthey pronounced that Owen Michael was definitely on the mend. "I think you can take him home on Friday, Mrs. Donnelly," he said.

"That would be great. How about travelling, after that? We want to fly to Miami, and then across to Eleuthera."

"You have a reason for doing this?"

"Sure. The rest of the family is down there vacationing."

"Is that a fact? Well . . . I would say a couple of weeks lying in the Bahamas is just about the best way of recuperating I could think of. Go ahead and take him down. But . . ." He held up his finger. "No diving or snorkelling. Nothing which can put any kind of strain on that belly."

Jo nodded. "He'll lie quietly in the shade, Dr. Matthey, believe me. And thank you."

She was relieved: once she was back in the apartment she telephoned her travel agent and got seats on the following Monday's plane to Miami and thence on to Eleuthera by the local airline. Next she called the post office in the little Eleutheran village of Whaletown and left a message for Mr. and Mrs. Donnelly. Then she replaced the phone, and stood by the lounge window looking down at the Manhattan traffic.

The brief spurt of almost manic happiness had departed. Suddenly her whole body felt limp. She knew she was still exhausted by fear and by her bitter resentment at Michael's attitude. How could she stay married to him? She slumped into the soft white cushions of the settee and lay back, numbed. It would be bad enough going through a divorce if one didn't have children, but what the split would do to Owen Michael and Tamsin she dreaded to think. And what about Richard? They were lovers, but for her to mention the word divorce might send him running a mile, and in her present situation he was the only rock to which she could cling.

The phone buzzed insistently. It was Richard. "Sweetheart! How have you been? I've been half out of my mind with worry. How's the boy?"

Immediately her spirits lifted. She told him about Owen Michael's recovery. Deliberately she never said a word about Michael, but when she had finished he said, "Hold on a minute. Where does your husband figure in all this? Don't tell me he's gone to Newport and left you alone?"

The incredulous note in his voice made tears sting her eyes. "Of course," she said huskily. "He's racing, you see. Nothing else matters."

Richard heard the sob in her voice. "Would you like me to come over?"

To her apartment. Washington was off duty, but the other porter would record the visit. But what did it matter? She only knew she urgently needed all the love, sympathy and understanding he had to offer. "Yes. Yes, please."

"DO YOU KNOW how many times I've dreamed of just this moment?" Richard said.

"*This* moment?" Jo asked, resting her head on his shoulder. They were sitting on the settee listening to a tape after their meal.

He looked down at her. "Will you marry me, Jo?"

"Oh, God, if I can, Richard. If I can. If . . ."

"Good, that's settled." He held her close. "The how, where and when can be sorted out later, when your husband comes back from his race."

"Yes, Richard," she agreed meekly. The joy and confidence of this man swept away the last lingering clouds of uncertainty: he would solve all the problems, she had to believe that.

Then, "But what about the children? Do you really want to take on two hooligans?"

"As long as they're your hooligans, I'd like nothing better."

She smiled. "Yes. I think you would. I know you'd make a good father. Oh, Richard, how I want to . . ."

"I know." He pulled her closer. Suddenly his tenderness was replaced by tension.

"What's the matter?" She raised her head.

"It's just past midnight. There's a storm system I should get an update on."

Oh, God, she thought, not a workaholic. "I thought you were off duty."

"I am. But I told Julian, he's my assistant, that I'd keep in touch. It's that big thing just west of the Cape Verdes. You remember?"

"I remember," she said. "So you want to go off and look at a map."

"I don't particularly want to, but Julian is expecting me, and won't stop tracking until I get there. I could come back," he suggested tentatively.

"I'm expecting you'll do that," she said. "But just to make sure you do, I'll come with you and take a look at this map too."

THE LATE NIGHT NEWS programmes were finished, and the studio was quiet. Richard took Jo into the weather room, where Julian was sifting through various charts.

"You remember Josephine Donnelly, from *Profiles*?" Richard asked him casually.

55

"Hi, Jo," Julian said. "Don't tell me you want to look at that system." He laid an enlarged photograph on the desk. "Mark Hammond rang. He just got back from having a closer look. Flew right into it. He says it's tightening all the time."

"Course?" Richard asked.

"Oh, just north of west, and moving real slow, about ten knots."

Jo looked over his shoulder. She could make out the coast of Africa, and the offshore islands. A white mass was stretching from immediately west of the Cape Verdes—which were now clear of cloud—a considerable distance out into the Atlantic. "It's enormous," she whispered.

"It's the biggest I've seen," Richard agreed. "Where's the jet stream?"

Julian pulled out the latest weather chart and pointed. "Moving north all the time."

"My God!" Richard commented.

"Is that really so important?" Jo asked.

"Yes," he told her. "The jet stream is a river of air that's very big, very high, and very fast: up to two hundred miles an hour plus. Usually it has only a marginal effect on surface weather but it can be useful for dispersing hurricanes. In fact, I'm pretty sure it's been responsible for the fact that not one of the five storms we've had so far this year has developed. You see, when those storms started their upward spirals, the jet stream blew them apart, and they collapsed. But if it's now moving north, this latest system could be left to develop as much as it wants." He looked at the map again, and then at the satellite photograph. "Ten knots, you say, Julian? That means five days to Puerto Rico, on that course. Five days over some very warm water."

"So you reckon this could be the big one?" Jo said. "Your ultimate storm?"

He grinned. "Any system could become an ultimate storm, if all the conditions were right."

"And you've just said they could be right, now."

"Well . . . yes. But they've seemed to be right before."

"If it does become a storm," she asked, "what might it be called?"

"All the names are selected before the hurricane season even begins." Julian looked at the list pinned up over his desk. "As it will be number six for this year, it'll be a she, and her name will be Faith. You reckon there'll be any charity down there, Richard?"

"Nope. And even less hope, for those who can't get out of her way." He laughed and held Jo's hand as he escorted her out of the office.

Saturday 22 July

The telephone jangled. Jo had an idea who it might be. She had been expecting this call.

"Hi," Michael said.

"Hi."

"Just got in. Aren't you going to ask me how we did?"

"How did you do?"

"Well . . ." His voice was triumphant. "There are a couple of protests to be heard, but it seems certain that we've won our class." He waited for a moment. "Aren't you going to congratulate me?"

Presumably, the fact of having won the race made everything that had gone before irrelevant. "Congratulations," she said.

"It was some race," he told her. "The ship behaved like a dream. Now, tell me, how's the boy?"

"Doing well. I collected him from hospital yesterday. But he still has to rest. He's in bed."

"Well, that's great. What are your plans?"

"Owen Michael and I are flying down to Eleuthera on Monday."

"Great. He'll like that. And it's bound to do him good."

"What are *your* plans?"

"Well, like I told you before we left, the guys and I thought we'd take a week cruising around Bermuda. There's nothing for me to hurry back for, is there? Not with Owen Michael on the mend and all of you down in the Bahamas."

"Nothing at all," Jo said, and hung up. Richard had arrived just as the phone rang, and was mixing Bloody Marys for them. Now he handed her a glass. She drank, sat on the settee, brooded out of the uncurtained picture window at the skyline of New York. Richard had come here so regularly during the past week that she had ceased worrying about the porters. Now, presumably, she should be worrying about Owen Michael's reaction to him. On Dr. Matthey's recommendation she had given the boy a sedative to make sure he had no ill effects after the excitement of coming home.

"I want to talk to you," Richard said. "I don't think you should go down to Eleuthera right now."

"It'll be quite all right; Dr. Matthey says that as long as I make sure Owen Michael just lazes about, a couple of weeks in the Bahamas would be the best possible thing for him." She touched his hand. "And for me. Divorce, custody, the whole thing sounds so terrible . . . and it's difficult to make decisions when you're so close. My mind is full of you, rather than what's best for us. Can you understand that?"

"Sure I can. But I wasn't thinking about us. I was thinking about Faith. Haven't you been watching my forecasts?"

"I haven't felt like watching anything, this past week."

"Well . . . I didn't mention it before, because Tamsin's already down there and I didn't want you worrying."

Jo sat up straight. "You mean Faith's a biggie?"

"Not yet. But her winds are increasing all the time. We expect her to be upgraded to Hurricane by tonight."

"You mean she could pose a threat to the Bahamas?"

"We have no means of knowing. She could go straight across Puerto Rico into the Caribbean, she could turn up north before reaching the islands—neither would threaten Eleuthera—or she could hit Puerto Rico and then turn north, which would carry her in a straight line up the eastern Bahamas. And I'm afraid that's the most likely course."

"Oh, my God. When will this happen?"

"Well, travelling at her present speed, she could be in the Bahamas by next Wednesday."

"Good Lord!" Jo gasped. "I must get hold of them."

"Don't you think they'll have been watching the Miami forecasts?"

"Perhaps. But I really must try."

Sunday 23 July

In the morning she telephoned the Whaletown post office. It took her over an hour to get through, and then the line was bad. She asked the girl to get a message to Mr. Donnelly. Dolphin Point curved away from the mainland of North Eleuthera to form the southern arm of a huge, shallow bay; the northern arm was composed of a series of small islands of which Palm Island, on which there was a settlement, was the largest. There was a supermarket and a post office on Palm Island and, at a distance of only three miles, it was the nearest civilisation to the Point— but the Donnellys preferred as a rule to drive the ten miles into Whaletown rather than get out the small dory Big Mike kept moored to the wooden dock and brave the spray as they crossed the entrance to the sound, where the Atlantic rollers could make the passage treacherous for small boats.

Obviously, she couldn't hope to hear from Big Mike before tomorrow. And what was she going to say to him when he did call? Even if she told him she had changed her mind about coming down he was very unlikely to pack up and come home just because there was a storm in the vicinity. Nor was there any way he could send Tamsin back alone. Her anger with Michael grew. If ever a family needed two parents it was now.

"Hey, Mom." Owen Michael suddenly shouted from in front of the TV in the next room. "There's a hurricane making for Puerto Rico. It's just come through on the news. Winds of eighty miles an hour. Did you know that?"

"I heard something about it." Jo went through to him

"Say, Mom, do you think it could hit the Bahamas?"

"Of course it won't hit the Bahamas. Puerto Rico is hundreds of miles away."

"Ah, shit! I was hoping we could get down there in time."

"I wish you wouldn't use that word," Jo remarked. "And Owen Michael . . . we're not going to Dolphin Point tomorrow."

58

"Not going?" He turned away from the screen in dismay.

"Dr. Matthey has changed his mind." It wasn't exactly a lie, she had no doubt at all Dr. Matthey would agree with her. "He thinks you should stay here for at least another week."

"Aw, Mom . . ."

Jo went into the study, closed the door, and dialled Richard's number.

"Hi," he said. "Did you get through to your folks?"

"It's an out island, remember?" she told him. "I left a message for them to call me, but I don't expect to hear before tomorrow morning. Richard, do you still not know if Faith'll hit Eleuthera?"

"I can't have any idea about that until she reaches Puerto Rico, which is expected in another twelve hours. Normally she'll look for the warmest water. Trouble is, there are temperatures of over twenty-six degrees centigrade all the way up to Canada. Added to that is the way the jet stream has gone right up north . . ."

"My God!" she said. "Richard, I really am worried."

"Well, take it easy," he recommended. "There's still no indication of her getting above a Category Two Storm—say, something over one-hundred-miles-per-hour winds."

"A hundred miles per hour? Oh, my God! Richard, wouldn't I be justified in asking them to come home?"

"Sure, you would. No one sits out a hurricane who doesn't have to. As to whether they'll still get a flight . . . you'll have to make them hurry. How's Owen Michael?"

"He's fine," she said absently.

"Would you rather I didn't come round tonight?"

She hesitated. She wanted to see him badly. But she didn't want Owen Michael involved—not yet; he was still unaware of Richard's visit on Saturday. "No," she said. "I want you to come. But make it later, after Owen Michael's in bed. He's still pretty weak and easily tired; I'll have him tucked up by half past eight. Is nine OK?"

"Sure. I understand. But I may not be able to stay very long. I'll have to get back by midnight for a late update; the big white chief likes his number one weatherman on duty when the weather happens to be making news."

OWEN MICHAEL was sound asleep when Richard turned up. They drank soup and ate grilled chicken, saying little, with much on their minds.

Eventually Richard broke the silence. "Do you want to know what I think you should do when Donnelly gets back?"

"Tell me."

"You move out of here with the children, and have him served with a petition immediately. You have a pretty good case for mental cruelty and your best chance of getting custody of the kids is to leave me right out of the picture."

"Yes, I guess you're right," she agreed. "There's no point in delaying."
She noticed his eyes kept straying to the clock. "You're uptight, Richard.
Is it Faith?"

"I guess so." He sighed. "Sweetheart, I don't want to worry you when
we don't have any idea where she's heading, but the first reports have
started to come in from Puerto Rico. The hurricane winds began to hit
San Juan just before I left the studio, and the torrential rain was already
said to be causing landslips and widespread damage. The system is still
moving very slowly, and there has been a significant change in the
track, from just north of west, to northwest. That means it's still early
days. It's difficult to see how the eastern Bahamas, at any rate, can avoid
getting at least some of it. If you can get your people out of there, I most
certainly would."

Monday 24 July

The phone buzzed at eleven in the morning. Jo had deliberately stayed
in, waiting for the call. "Dad," she shouted, as she picked up the study
phone, carefully closing the door to make sure Owen Michael couldn't
overhear. "Is that you?"

"Jo? Hi, sweetheart. I got your message and came right in. Nothing
wrong, I hope? Owen Michael still OK?"

"Yes. But Dad, we're not coming down because of—"

"And Michael? Say, how did the race go?"

"He called Saturday. He's won his class, I think."

"Attaboy!" Big Mike shouted. "I knew he could do it. He must be over
the moon. Then what's all the fuss about? We thought you had an
emergency, that's why I came hustling into Whaletown to call."

"There *is* an emergency," she shouted. "Haven't you heard about
Hurricane Faith?"

"Sure," Big Mike said equably. "Seems she gave Puerto Rico quite a
clout. But the electrics have been on the blink out at the Point, and I'm
having trouble with the generator. So we didn't get last night's forecast,
except from the radio. Didn't sound too bad, though."

"Dad," Jo said, trying to speak calmly, "Faith is expected to carry
winds of more than a hundred miles an hour by tonight: that is going to
be twice as strong as we had three years ago."

"Is that a fact? Well, I guess I'll have Josh dig out those shutters again.
Actually, we could do with some rain, the cistern is kind of low."

"Dad," Jo said desperately, "we're not talking about a little bit of rain.
I think you should all get out of there while you can."

"What, run away from a bit of wind, bang in the middle of our
vacation? Heck, sweetheart, the house can take it. So can we."

"I'm thinking of Tamsin," Jo said, bluntly. "I want my daughter
brought home!"

There was a moment's silence: she had never spoken to her father-in-law like that before. At last he said, "You really are worried."

"Yes," she said. "Yes. I really am worried."

"Well, I'll tell you what I'll do. I'll hustle back out to the Point and chat it over with the others. Then I'll call you back tomorrow."

"And tell me what flight you'll be on," Jo begged.

"Ah . . . yeah, I'll call you back."

The phone went dead, and Jo rested her head on her arms.

"A HURRICANE?" MEG ROBSON screamed. "Oh, my God! Why we ever bought this place I can't imagine. I told you it was a stupid thing to do, Neal."

"Now, Meg . . ." Neal said unhappily.

"I want to go home. I want to go home, now!"

"Well, you can't, now," Lawson pointed out. "There won't be any planes out of North Eleuthera until tomorrow."

"And anyway, we have to shutter the place up," Neal told her. "Mike, I don't suppose you guys would give us a hand?"

"Sure we will," Mike said. "We have to shutter this place up too. In fact, I'll get Josh on to it now, before he goes home." The servants generally left right after lunch. "Josh!" he bawled. "Josh!" While he waited Big Mike brooded on his holiday home. Built on a low ridge lined with casuarinas, some thirty feet above the water, the setting was idyllic. The house itself was single-storeyed and U-shaped, bedrooms to the right, living rooms and kitchen to the left, linked by a wide roof which half covered the flagstoned patio. The only other house on the Point, the Robsons', was a quarter of a mile away, where the ridge dwindled to a mere ten feet above the beach.

Josh appeared from the garden. "You heard about this storm, Josh?"

"I did heah somet'ing, borse."

"Yeah? Well, I tell you what, you go on down to the generator shed and bring those storm shutters up."

"Now, borse?"

"Right now," Mike said.

Josh ambled off, somewhat disconsolately.

"Now, I tell you what we're gonna do," Mike announced. "We are going to have lunch, and then we are going to put up the shutters, and then we are going to listen to the six o'clock forecast. We'd look a right load of billygoats if we went chasing back home to get away from a storm which wasn't even gonna come near us, right? I told Jo I'd call her back tomorrow and tell her what we were doing."

Josh was back on the edge of the patio. "Borse, them shutters ain' no good. They been sittin' down in that shed t'ree year now, and they all warp up. There ain' no way them bolts goin' fit in them holes."

"Jeez." Big Mike looked at Lawson. "What the hell do we do?"

"We get some good nails and we board them up," Lawson told him. "You got a good supply of nails, Dad?"

"Of course I don't have a good supply of nails," Big Mike groused.

"OK, there's time. Josh, when you go home this afternoon, you buy some nails at the store, and bring them out tomorrow morning. Right?"

"OK, borse. I goin' do that. I goin' bring me nephew to help an' all. He is good with nails." He ambled off again.

"Lousy country," Big Mike growled, revealing his first trace of nerves. "Can't even leave some wood lying around without it warping. You'd better check yours out, Neal."

"Mine are all brand-new. Had them made the moment I got down here." Neal smiled triumphantly. "We have nothing to worry about."

"OK, FOLKS," Big Mike shouted to the world in general. "Six o'clock news time."

They straggled into the lounge, having spent an exhausting afternoon helping Neal put his shutters in place. Dale mixed up rum cocktails while they took their places in front of the TV set. Before the news was finished the Robsons had joined them.

"Now, sh," Big Mike told everyone. "This is important."

"And now for the weather, and that hurricane, folks," said a smiling young man standing in front of a huge map. "Faith is her name, and she could be heading our way . . . We have Dr. John Eisener standing by at the Coral Gables Hurricane Tracking Center to give us the latest update on that. Good evening, Dr. Eisener."

The meteorologist came up on the screen. "Good evening, Gordon."

"What's Faith doing right this minute, Doctor?"

"Well, as you know, the storm passed over Haiti last night. Then it was blowing a good ninety miles an hour around the centre, and there was some pretty heavy rainfall as well. We've reports of seventeen inches of rain in three hours."

Gordon gave an obliging whistle of amazement, as if he did not have all the figures on the desk before him.

"Winds at the centre," Eisener continued, "are now just short of a hundred miles an hour, with gales extending some hundred miles from the eye. Its position is here . . ." He turned to another huge wall map and touched it with his wand ". . . about a hundred miles southeast of Mayaguana, in the southeastern Bahamas, and it is now moving north at about fifteen knots. Mayaguana is already experiencing gale-force winds and heavy rain, and a hurricane warning has been issued by the Bahamian government to cover as far north as Cat Island. Folks in the Bahamas should prepare themselves for very high seas topped by storm surges of maybe six feet, which will mean considerable flooding in low-lying areas. Finally, Gordon, we must always bear in mind that this storm has the potential to deepen, and become a Category Three. That would

62

put her in the same class as Gloria of a few years back—and I don't have to remind you that Gloria was a very dangerous storm indeed."

Meg Robson moaned.

"Faith is moving just west of north, you said, Doctor?" Gordon asked. "Do you expect that track to be maintained?"

"Well, Gordon, as you know, one can never be certain with tropical storms. There are so many factors involved. But given what information we have, the absence of any jet stream activity in this vicinity, the water temperatures and so on, yes, I would expect her to continue on her present track for at least twenty-four hours. That would take her just east of Eleuthera and the Abacos and thence north to Bermuda."

Gordon was giving his viewers a reassuring smile. "In other words, in your opinion this storm poses no real threat to South Florida—"

Big Mike was on his feet to switch off the set. "Holy shit! No real threat to South Florida," he mimicked. "We're not *in* South Florida. Well, that's it folks. The holiday is over. Tomorrow morning first thing we are gonna put those shutters up, and then we are going to catch the first plane out of North Eleuthera." He looked round at them. "Right?"

"Right," Meg agreed.

"Right," Babs and Neal said together.

Lawson looked at Belle, who said, "If we are all going to fly out tomorrow, shouldn't someone go to the airport to book seats?"

"That won't be necessary," Big Mike assured her. "We're all going to the airport in the morning. We won't need a reservation."

"Suppose there are no seats?" Dale enquired.

"Look, the people who get out of here are going to be the ones at the airport, ready to board, not the ones sitting at home relying on a reservation. Right?"

Belle looked at Tamsin, sitting by herself, eyes big as she watched the adults. "Come on, honey," she said. "Supper for you, and bed."

She fed the little girl and then walked her across the patio.

"Aunt Belle, why can't we stay and see the hurricane?"

"Because, honey, it won't be very nice. You won't be able to see anything. The windows will be shuttered and the house all dark inside, even in the daytime. It'll be very boring."

"We could go outside and watch," Tamsin suggested.

"Honey, you'd be blown away! You can't imagine how strong the wind will be." She drew a sheet loosely over the child. "Now you get some sleep."

After the supper dishes had been washed up, Big Mike took charge again. "Come on, get with it, Dale. Help your mother pack the food: we can't leave it in the freezer, the electricity will be the first to go. Belle, you make some sandwiches for tomorrow: it'll probably be lunch time before we take off."

Everyone started doing something, halfheartedly. Mike's fear was communicating itself. This was obviously far more serious than the storm of three years before. Belle finished making the sandwiches, then went outside to put the crusts in the rubbish bin, and found her husband standing behind her. "It's such a brilliant moonlit night," she said, watching the light streaming across the water. "And there's not a breath of wind."

"That's a bad sign," said Lawson. "It means Faith is coming closer."

Tuesday 25 July

Just before dawn Belle was woken by a rain squall which blew in the mosquito screen. She reached for a light, but the power was off. Lawson was still snoring contentedly, so she got up herself to close the window. But she soon fell asleep again when she returned to bed.

When she awoke again, to broad daylight, rain was thrumming on the roof.

Josh arrived at seven with his nephew, Goodson. Josh touched his sharp-peaked cap. "I brung me nephew like I said, borse, to help wit' de shutters. We soon get um fix. Den, if it's OK wit' you, we likum get home again, quick. Got some tyin' down and t'ings to do before de storm hit.'"

Big Mike clapped him on the shoulder. "Josh! Am I glad to see you. And Goodson. Sure, we'll all work on the shutters together and then of course you must get home. Perhaps you could lift some of us to the airport on your way: we can't all fit into my car, together with the bags."

Josh frowned. "You leavin', borse? You t'ink dere goin' be planes?"

"There have to be planes," Mike insisted. "What about the two which stay overnight and fly out about ten thirty in the morning? If we hurry we can catch those, can't we?" His tone was suddenly anxious.

"Not today, borse. Dey done gorn. Flew out las' night. De wife's niece, she de agent. She tol' us dey done gorn."

"Holy. . . !" Mike bit off the word; Babs didn't like him to swear in front of the servants.

Babs, having appeared in a dressing gown, was just as alarmed. "But surely you're expecting them back?" Her eyes were wide.

"Couldn't say about dat, mam. Nassau is callin' heah. Dey tellin' us de airport is close. All de airports in de eastern region is close."

"If we had gone down to the airport yesterday afternoon we could've caught those damned planes," Mike growled.

"Beggin' you' pardon, borse," Josh put in. "But them planes was all full. People was lef' standin'. Frien' o' mine is one of de taxi drivers. He tell me las' night dere was quite a fight out dere, people pushin' and shovin'. Seems agents in de States done sold two tickets for each seat."

Blood drained from Big Mike's face. He stood, shoulders hunched, in the shelter of the porch, as wind and rain scattered bits of palm frond across the patio, fighting to control both his anger and his fear.

"What the hell is going on? They can't just maroon us."

Babs sighed. "Well, maybe we should go out to the airport anyway, just in case a plane does come in."

"Beggin' yo' pardon, mam," Melba the cook put in, "but if it was me ah wouldn't go wastin' my time out dere. Better spend de time preparin'." And seeing their horrified expressions, Melba put a comforting hand on Babs's arm. "Is all righty. Dem hurricane's no big deal. You all got good shutters. Jus' be sure you got plenny food an' water an' candles, an' oil for de hurricane lamps. Dat all yo' want. Better someone go drive down to Whaletown an' get supplied. Tin stuff, 'cause de fridge'll go wid de electrics."

"I don't believe this," Big Mike fumed. "We are just going to be abandoned on this sandbank . . ."

"But can't we keep the generator on?" Babs's mind was on the food in the freezer.

"Sure t'ing, mam, but ev'ry once in a while it got to have oil and water, and yo' tank don' hold too much fuel. Anyway, dat generator ain' too big. You got de freshwater pump for de toilets, lights, freezer . . . it goin' burn up before it take care o' dem all one time."

Lawson and Belle joined the discussion. "She's right," Lawson said. "It'd be better not to turn the thing on except for emergency lighting."

Big Mike shook his head in exasperation. "Well, that's that, folks. The decision's been made for us. Come on, you guys, let's finish getting these shutters up so these people can go home."

"What about the food supplies and the candles?" Babs asked. "Someone'll have to go down to Whaletown."

"Will it be safe going over Big Leap?" Dale peered at the rain lashing across the patio, and thought of the place where the island narrowed to such an extent that the sea came right up to the road.

"Give me a list and I'll drive down and see," Lawson volunteered. "I shouldn't think the seas are over the road yet."

"I'll come too," Belle declared. "If that's OK with you, Mom?"

"Sure. And listen, you'd better call Jo and explain the situation. Tell her there's nothing to worry about." She looked at Lawson, seeking reassurance for herself.

Lawson grinned. "We'll be snug as bugs in rugs behind these shutters. Now, have you got that list ready?"

Babs had been scribbling away. "I don't know if I've thought of everything. Candles . . . batteries. Tinned soups and beans . . ."

"And some more Log Cabin Syrup for our breakfast pancakes," Tamsin reminded her grandmother.

"Oh, lover, I nearly forgot. We'll need some more eggs, too." Babs scribbled some more, gave Belle the list. "You hurry, and take care."

"We'll hurry." Belle kissed her mother. "Who's going to go down to tell the Robsons?"

Babs sighed. "I guess it'll have to be me. I tell you what: add a really strong sedative to that list, if you can find one. We may need it for Meg when she hears we're not leaving."

THE DRIVE DOWN the coast wasn't easy. The Buick's windscreen was constantly smeared by the worn-out wipers as they were deluged by the muddy water filling the holes in the road. Big Mike had bought the auto third hand in Whaletown rather than pay to bring a car across from the mainland. They bounced and wove until a good stretch of tarmac carried them down to the neck, where they paused to see if an occasional rogue wave might swamp the road.

"The sea hasn't worked itself into a fuss yet," Belle said. "Come on, Lawson, let's go."

In fact the seas were not yet high, and with the heavy rain clouds beginning to break up to allow patches of blue and even occasional glimpses of the sun, it was a rather beautiful day. Only right down on the horizon, hardly visible, there was a ridge of cloud so dark as to be almost blue-black. They arrived at Whaletown fifteen minutes later. A very strange Whaletown, everything closed tight, windows boarded, chairs and tables stowed away, and men working with ropes to tie down suspect roofs.

The little wooden supermarket was filled with chattering women, fast emptying the shelves. Belle grabbed the last packet of candles while Lawson selected batteries, then they filled two store baskets with canned food and joined the long check-out queue. In the end, Belle left Lawson to cope and, head down against the still gusty wind, made a dash up the hill to the post office. "I want to make an international call," she said, pushing wet strands of yellow hair from her eyes.

"Dere ain' no lines," the girl said, continuing to paint her nails.

"None at all? Who's using them?"

"Nobody heah," the girl said. "Dere ain' no lines out of Nassau. Everybody speakin' at once."

"Oh, for God's sake. How soon will there be a line?"

"Ah dunno. Maybe dis afternoon. But I got a list heah of twelve people wantin' to call out. You wan' me put you down at the end?"

Belle hesitated. But there was no way she would hang about there until the afternoon. Jo would just have to wait. "No," she said, and went back to Lawson.

The rain had virtually stopped as the car headed north again. Belle and Lawson watched anxiously as they came down the steep hill to the neck, but the Atlantic was hidden from view by a high wall of rock.

"Nothing but spray seems to be coming over," Lawson commented, bending over the wheel, "so let's go."

The road was quite clear as the automobile careered down the hill and levelled off on the concrete surface of the bridge. Then Belle saw it—a massive wall of surging green water rushing straight at them. "Foot down!" she shrieked. "Go, go, go!"

As Lawson responded the giant wave crawled up the cliff face at the far end of the neck, higher and higher, then burst against the bridge. An umbrella of water opened high over the road, hung there as though waiting for the car to reach it. They were committed; it was impossible to brake in time. They could only urge the Buick on, and pray.

The water descended on the roof like a mountain of rock. They were engulfed, swept across the road and crushed against the concrete parapet. Belle was thrown into Lawson's lap, felt the car tip over, teetering on its left-hand wheels, and held her breath, waiting to crash onto the rocks beneath. But miraculously the parapet held and she was flung back against the passenger door, Lawson with her, as the car righted itself. Amazingly, the engine was still running. Now Lawson regained the wheel and accelerated, pressed the car on through the water, and then they were clear. The floor of the car was awash, and the engine spluttered as they rolled up the hill on the other side, where Lawson let it coast to a halt.

Several minutes passed before either of them spoke or moved. Then Lawson took Belle's face between his hands and kissed her.

"Oh, lover," she said, "I thought we'd had it."

He grinned at her. "We're indestructible," he said. "But I tell you what—I'm not crossing that bridge again until Faith is just a memory."

BELLE JUMPED OUT to open the garage door for Lawson to drive the Buick in, but found that the boat had been stored there, so he parked it close against the back of the house. They had passed Josh, Melba and Goodson on their way home to Whaletown just after leaving Big Leap, and had stopped to warn them of the possibility of a big sea crossing the road, but they decided not to alarm the family by telling them of their experience; they were just thankful to have survived—and Big Mike wouldn't notice the dent in the Buick's roof until after the storm.

The living room was quite a shock.

"Beds?" Belle and Lawson exclaimed together, gazing at the furniture, all pushed back against the walls to make room.

Babs laughed. "After you'd gone, Melba took charge. She said we'd not be able to get across to the bedrooms when the storm hit, so I'm afraid it's going to be dormitory style for the next couple of nights."

"Isn't it gloomy?" Dale peered at a wedge of daylight showing through a gap in the plywood boarding. "What the hell are we going to do with ourselves all day?"

"Play games and read stories," Tamsin informed her uncle gleefully.

"There's a hell of a lot of work to be done before we can play any games," Big Mike announced. "The stuff Lawson and Belle bought has to be unloaded and put away. Then the rest of us have to stow the patio furniture and get all the darned potted plants into the garage. The men will bring them up, and the women can put them away." He frowned at Belle. "You OK, sweetie? You look all shook up."

"Just wet."

"Well, change. The last thing we want is someone sneezing all over the place. Say, did you get hold of Jo?"

"No chance. There will be no lines out before this afternoon."

"Oh, heck," Babs said. "She'll be worried out of her mind."

"I'm afraid she'll just have to worry," Big Mike said, shaking his head dolefully.

JO WAITED IN all morning for the phone call from Eleuthera. When by lunch time it hadn't come, she decided to call again, and waited for even more than the usual hour while her ears were deafened by clicks and thumps. "I'm sorry," the American operator said at last, "it is quite impossible to get through to either Nassau or Eleuthera. The lines are jammed."

She felt as if she had been kicked. Perhaps they had got out already. But if they had, and had reached Miami, surely they would have phoned from there. Desperate for reassurance, she rang Richard.

"I'm afraid it doesn't look too good," he told her. "Faith has just about laid Haiti flat. She was packing winds of a hundred miles an hour, and let's face it, a lot of Haiti is shantytown: almost any strong winds knock those huts down. But first reports of the damage are horrifying. Now she's moving straight up the eastern Bahamas."

"Is she maintaining these wind strengths?" Jo asked.

There was a moment's silence. "She could be strengthening. We're talking now about a major storm. And I mean major."

Jo kept her voice level. "Tell me."

"Well, it'll be a strong enough wind to lift a car off the road, and that sort of thing. But Jo, from your father-in-law's point of view, I guess as long as he's securely shuttered and has a good roof, the house'll be in no danger."

"But what about a tidal surge?"

"Sure there'll be a tidal surge, maybe nine to twelve feet above normal. On top of the waves, of course, which could be around thirty or forty feet. But you told me your father-in-law's house is on a ridge . . ."

"Yes," she said. "Maybe twenty-five feet above normal sea level. Oh, Richard, I'm so frightened . . ."

"Take it easy, darling. Take it easy. That's the worst prognostication. On the western side of the storm the seas will be much lower. The wind strength, too. Look, I have to go now, to prepare the next forecast. There's a mass of information coming in. But I could get round later. Would you like me to do that?"

"Oh, yes, please," she said. "I want you here."

HAVING DISCONNECTED his aerial, and laid it flat beside the house, Big Mike was unable to use the television, but he invited the Robsons over that evening to listen to the news on the portable radio. There was a great deal of static, but they were able to gather that Faith was now packing winds of over 110mph, which made her by some way the biggest storm to threaten the Bahamas since the 1930s. He switched off the radio, and looked around the tense faces. Already the house was trembling to occasional gale-force gusts, and there was a good deal of distant thunder, while every so often rain squalls swept across the headland.

"OK, you guys, relax," he announced. "We're just going to sit this thing out. Now, I reckon we should break open that case of champagne. Just to put ourselves in the mood."

"Good idea," Lawson agreed. "I'll do it."

He came back from the kitchen with a tray of full champagne glasses.

"Actually," Mike announced, "I forgot to tell you, with all this going on—Michael has won his class in the Bermuda Race."

"Hey," Belle cried, "ain't that something? I'll drink to Michael. I bet he's happy he raced instead of coming down here."

"Even if Jo isn't," Dale said quietly.

"I wish Mommy was here," Tamsin said. "And Daddy," she added as an afterthought.

"I hope he gets home before this storm reaches Bermuda," Babs said. She wanted to change the subject.

"My God! What's that?" Meg Robson screamed as there was a heavier than usual squall, accompanied by a crash from outside. She was obviously full of tranquilliser and had been quite calm during the broadcast. But now her eyes were bright.

"A branch from a tree," Mike told her. "If we didn't need them for shade, I'd cut the whole damned lot down. Anyway, none of them is going to do us any damage. Now, are you folks staying to supper?"

"I think we'll get on back while we can," Neal decided. "Thanks anyway."

"But you'll remember we're here if you need us," Babs reminded him.

"Tell you what," Mike said. "Your generator running?"

"I was going to put it on when I got back," Neal said.

"You do that. Then give me a shout on your CB, so we can make sure we hear each other."

Neal nodded, and as it was not actually raining at the moment, escorted Meg outside.

Mike closed and bolted the door. "They're scared."

"So are we all," Babs pointed out. She looked at the door. "What's that roaring noise?"

"That's the sea getting up," Lawson told her. "The surf pounding on the rocks. It's going to be a wild night, folks."

Five minutes later the CB began spluttering. "Can you hear me, Mike?" Neal was asking.

Mike thumbed the handset. "Sure. Loud and clear. Keep in touch."

"WELL, HI," JO SAID, opening the door. "I didn't expect you so early."

"I came as soon as I could get away," Richard explained.

"And I'm glad to see you." Jo stepped back, and shrugged. "Owen Michael," she said, "this is a friend of . . . of your father's and mine, Richard Connors. You must have seen him on TV."

"Say, are you really the guy on TV?" Owen Michael shook hands, impressed. "Will you write in my autograph book?"

"Any time," Richard agreed.

"I'll get it." He ran to his bedroom.

Richard stared at Jo. She frowned, suddenly realising that he looked as if he'd seen a ghost. "Richard? What's the matter?"

"I came over to tell you . . ." He hesitated. "Faith's done a dirty on us. She's turned due west."

"Due west? But . . . oh, my God!"

"Yes," he said miserably. "Her new track will take her right over central Eleuthera. And Jo . . . she's increased in strength again."

"Oh, God," Jo said. Her knees gave way and she sat down. "And there's nothing any of us can do," she moaned.

He sat beside her, put his arm round her shoulders, ignoring the boy who stood in the doorway. "Not a thing. Except pray."

"WHY DO HURRICANES always come at night?" Tamsin asked.

"Well, honey . . ." Belle, engaged in tucking her in, looked at her husband for an explanation.

"They don't," Lawson said. "They just seem more scary at night."

Tamsin buried her face in her pillow. "I wish the thunder would stop."

"Thunder can't harm you, sweetheart. Now, try to get some sleep."

Big Mike stood looking out through one of the sliding glass doors; there was a board for this too, but they had left it off until they knew the storm was close, to give them some light and air. "What do you reckon it's blowing out there?" he asked when Lawson joined him.

"I reckon it's gusting about seventy miles an hour. If the forecasts are right, we shouldn't get much more than this. Say, there's a forecast on the radio in a few minutes; we'd better listen."

"Forget it. I don't want to listen to some kid in a studio telling me what I'm in the middle of."

The thunderstorm was fierce, the flashes of lightning so bright they lit up the glass in the door as if someone had switched on the outside lights; the wind whined and the rain squall slashed at the house, but it passed quickly, and it was obvious that the storm had not yet in fact arrived. Big Mike said, "I guess we should put this final shutter up."

"Not necessary, yet." Lawson shook his head. "Faith is still a long way away. Relax."

Mike glared at him, suddenly irritated by the casual confidence in his voice. "How come you know so much about it, eh?"

"I was in Martinique when David struck, oh, must have been more than ten years ago."

"Was that a big one?"

"He carried one-hundred-mile-an-hour-plus winds, just like this one is supposed to do. Come on, Dad, settle down and let's talk about what we're going to do with all that real-estate money lying just up the road."

It was the sort of chaff the family indulged in all the time, so Big Mike grinned, and said, "Well, let's see now . . ."

Just at that moment there was a particularly loud bang, which brought Tamsin upright in her bed, weeping with terror. Mike and Lawson opened the glass door and peered out. They were between rain squalls, although the air was damp with the spray thrown up by the sea on the outer side of the Point, so they ran outside. Dale followed them, and Belle and Babs stood on the patio, Tamsin between them, wind whipping their hair and clothes, to look across the garden down to the jetty. Waves crashed over the wooden platform. Built of heavy planking nailed onto stout tree trunks drilled into the seabed, normally it looked sturdy enough to withstand anything . . . but Belle wondered how long it could take a battering like this.

The men came back, looking wet and windswept, and mystified. "Can't imagine what the hell that was." Dale shrugged. "It can't have been on the property."

"Must have been," Babs said. "The noise came from right out here."

"Well, we couldn't find anything wrong."

Tamsin had to be tucked in again. Then Lawson looked at his watch. "I'll just go check the generator." They were keeping it going all night, Big Mike having decided it was essential to stay in touch with the Robsons.

Lawson opened the door and stepped outside. He was actually enjoying the weather, having experienced a similar storm before and survived without injury. He liked to feel the wind and sea spray swirling through the trees. It went with his mood, his sudden surges of euphoria; he had had to live with debt for so long it was almost unbelievable that the end was finally in sight.

AT ELEVEN THIRTY they called Neal, and were told everything was all right down there. "But say, have you had a weather update?" he asked.

"Who wants a weather update?" Mike asked. "We can give those guys one ourselves."

"I tried to get one on my portable," Neal said. "Only heard the end. Something about crossing the coast around midnight."

71

"Could be," Mike said. "I'll give you another shout later." He replaced the handset and looked at the women. "Well, there's damn all we can do now except wait. We'll board up the last door and then I suggest we go to bed."

"I'm all for that," Babs agreed.

"I'm staying in this," Belle said; she had worn a silk kaftan all evening. "Now, whose bed is which?"

That morning, with Melba's help, the television set and settee and armchairs had been pushed together to make room for the beds; first a small one for Tamsin, then a small double for Babs and Mike. Belle and Lawson shared a single, while Dale settled himself on the settee.

"Mike! You haven't put your pyjamas on," Babs protested as he made to crawl across her legs.

"You're damned right I haven't," Mike retorted. "Nobody is going to

part me from my pants tonight. God knows what I might have to get up and do in the middle of the night."

The noise was already tremendous, with constant thunder, the rain against the shutters, and waves hitting the rocks like a pride of lions growling outside the door. And there remained the awful feeling that the worst was yet to come.

Then the entire house seemed to shake with a sudden increase in wind.

"Oh, my God!" Babs said, and sat up.

"I'm going to put the kettle on," Belle announced. "It's nonsense to pretend we're going to sleep. How about some coffee?"

"Brilliant idea," Babs agreed, also getting up.

Belle made the coffee. Everyone was trying to act normally, but now the house was shaking regularly, and every so often there came a crash from outside, as if something was being torn loose.

Then the house seemed to jump into the air. At the same time, the entire room filled with brilliant light despite the shutters, and the accompanying peal of thunder was so loud it left them all dazed. Babs inhaled the scent of scorching wood. "My God!" she shouted. "We're on fire!"

Tamsin screamed.

"We've been hit by lightning, that's all," Dale told them.

Mike was switching on the lights. "Well, they're still working." He stared at the television screen, which was cracked and blackened. "Jeez! The bolt must have struck the aerial, even lying down."

"Big Mike, Big Mike," said the CB. "You guys all right?"

"Sure we are," Mike told him. "You get hit?"

"No, but it sounded awful close."

"Yeah. We had it come to call. How's Meggie taking it?"

"I've put her to bed, with a tranquilliser and whisky."

"Best thing. Keep in touch."

Babs had her arms round Tamsin. Big Mike twisted his head. "What the hell is that?" he demanded.

They all turned to look at the door, listening to a sound that was different from any they had ever heard before.

"Sounds like an express train," Dale muttered.

"My God," Lawson said. His face was pale. "That's the hurricane wind." He attempted a smile. "I guess Faith has arrived, folks."

Wednesday 26 July

Big Mike mopped his face with a towel. Since midnight the noise had been continuous, whip-like cracks of lightning striking the rocks, rain pounding on the shutters and the roof, the sea's roaring and, above all, the banshee-like howl of the wind. "How long does this last?"

"Maybe a couple of hours, until the eye passes through," Lawson said.

"Well, I think everything's working like a charm," Belle declared. "We have electricity, we don't have any water leaking in, and we've only been struck by lightning once. Who's complaining?"

"Talking about the generator, it's damn near twelve hours since it's had oil or water," Lawson remarked. "I guess we'd better do it now, then we're in the clear until well into tomorrow."

"You mean, go out in that?" Dale asked.

"Lawson's right. Look, son," Mike said. "I promised Neal we'd keep in touch, didn't I? How the hell am I to do that without power?"

"I'll come with you," Lawson volunteered.

Babs looked to Belle for support, but she just shrugged; she was used to her menfolk being macho. "Well, hurry back," Babs said.

"You bet."

The two men cautiously went outside and pressed themselves against

74

the wall. The scene was dramatic: utterly dark, yet bright as day every few seconds from the lightning flashes. In the normally calm waters of the sound there were now six-foot waves, topped with foaming whitecaps. The jetty had already disappeared, although whether it had broken up or was just under water was impossible to say. Several trees were down already. And this was the lee. Here in the patio area they were still protected by the wall that connected the two halves of the house, but they had to leave its shelter if they were to reach the generator shed.

There were two doors leading out of the patio, one at each end of the wall. They made for the south-facing exit, as the wind had swung round to the northeast. Mike slid through first, to be seized by a giant hand, it seemed, and flattened against the wall. Spread-eagled, hardly able to breathe because of the wind and rain tearing at him, Mike gazed in horror at the garden, the uprooted trees, the generator shed, still a hundred feet away, and then beyond. Another hundred feet across the unmade road the rocks began, and out there was the Atlantic. He had thought the waves in the sound big. Now he looked at immense walls of water, twenty, even thirty feet high, topped by another six foot of curling crest, smashing themselves into the rocks with a force which seemed to make the entire Point tremble, hurling spray hundreds of feet into the air. And already there was water on the road, flowing towards the drive.

Mike didn't know if they could reach the generator at all with such a wind battering at them, but even if they did, how long would the engine continue working once salt water got at it?

There was a banging sound from the wall alongside them. Grateful for the recall, they tumbled back through the door to arrive on the patio beside Belle, her hair and her kaftan blowing in the wind, and carrying a frying pan with which she had banged the wall.

"What the hell are you doing outside?" Lawson shouted at her.

"Neal is on the CB," she bawled back. "They're being flooded. And Meg's having hysterics. He wants out."

"OK," Mike growled, "tell him we're on our way."

"Crawl," Lawson told him. "Don't attempt to stand."

By staying on the bay side of the road, where the land sloped off to the west, they could obtain some shelter from the wind. But when they reached the dip down to the Robsons', they fell to their stomachs in consternation. Below them, the sea had already crossed the road. The full force of the storm was still being contained by the rocks, but the overspill of each wave, some two foot of water, was flowing across the road, round the Robsons' house, and thence down the west side of the Point to the sea. Mike realised that Dolphin Point was in danger of being cut in two right here, where the Robsons' house stood.

Lawson led the way now, crawling up to the flowing water, and then attempting to cross it. It swept him sideways, down the Robsons' drive which resembled a fast-running river, and up against the house.

There he sat up, rubbing his head and grinning ruefully. A moment later Mike had joined him. Cautiously they made their way round the house, and had almost reached the lee, when they were arrested by a huge ripping sound. Lawson recognised it, and looked up: the roof was beginning to peel back, like the lid being removed from a sardine can.

"Jeez!" Mike screamed, and reached the door to bang on it. A moment later it was opened. Inside was dark: Neal's generator had obviously failed. Mike shone his torch: the floor was covered in water, Meg lay on the settee rocking back and forth in terror, Neal was by the door, white-faced and shaking. "Let's get the hell out of here," Mike shouted. The tearing noise was growing louder.

Lawson dashed inside and pulled Meg from the settee.

"We're going to die!" she screamed. "Oh, God, we're going to die!"

"No way," Lawson told her. "But we're going to get wet."

Just then the roof finally went, with a gigantic whoosh, shattering itself in the trees. Rain and wind and salt spray descended on the wrecked house. Furniture was picked up and hurled against the walls. Glass shattered. The dresser came crashing down. The house was being systematically demolished. Even Meg's screams were lost in the noise, as the humans also were thrown about by the spiralling wind. Mike and Lawson dragged her to the door and out into the open.

It was slow going. Meg was too exhausted to fight the elements, and Neal was hardly in better shape. Slowly and painfully Mike dragged Meg up the slope, gaining some protection from the trees, yet knowing that at any moment one might come down on top of them; the noise of uprooting trunks almost competed with the howl of the wind. Then a lightning flash revealed that the Donnelly house was still intact, although water was swirling round the generator shed. Mike gave a moan of relief as the door opened to his bang, and Babs and Belle were there to help them inside.

Here too it was now utterly dark, save for an oil lamp that Belle had lit. Mike carried Meg to the nearest bed and laid her on it. "Give Meg a shot of brandy, Belle," he said. "Come to think of it, we'll all have one."

Belle poured.

"The house is gone," Neal said, sitting down with his hands dangling between his knees. "Just like that."

"Drink this," Belle said. "It'll make you feel better. Law . . ." Her voice suddenly stopped, as she peered into the gloom. "Where's Lawson?"

"Eh?" Mike jerked his head. "He was just behind us."

"Lawson!" Belle gasped.

"For God's sake, he must have fallen. He'll be just outside." Big Mike wrestled with the door, got it open, peered into the raging darkness. He felt sick. He knew that Lawson wasn't there.

"You left him behind!" Belle shrieked. "You left my husband behind!"

"REPORTS FROM THE BAHAMAS," said the NABS newsreader, "are uncertain at this time. The capital, Nassau, seems to have escaped the worst of Hurricane Faith, which passed more than fifty miles to the east of New Providence Island, although there has been considerable damage from the very heavy rainfall, and also from the storm surge. However, it is feared that the worst effects of the storm may have been felt on the island of Eleuthera, as, owing to the late alteration in Faith's course, the eye passed over the very centre of this island at about two o'clock this morning."

"Oh, my God," Jo whispered, staring at the screen. Owen Michael reached out and clutched her hand. Neither had done more than doze in their chairs all night, waiting desperately for news.

"All contact has been lost with North Eleuthera," the newsreader continued. "But I have with me here our weatherman, Richard Connors. Now, Richard, first of all, can you tell the folks what sort of weather those people on North Eleuthera might have experienced, at the height of the storm? How about the wind, for example?"

"A hundred and thirty miles an hour." Richard spoke into the camera, looking directly at Jo. "That is enough wind, Dave, to blow a man off his feet, and then some. Enough to overturn any mobile home."

"What about the buildings themselves?"

"Solidly built and well-shuttered stone structures should have been all right," Richard said. "I say shuttered, because once a wind with that kind of force gets inside any house, it can lift everything right out. Every single window and door needs to be shuttered tight."

"So you reckon that if the folks on Eleuthera knew what was coming at them, and took the proper precautions, they'd have been all right?"

Richard sighed. "I'm afraid there's no guarantee of that, Dave. You see, wind doesn't actually do the greatest damage in a hurricane, it's the storm surge. For the folks on Eleuthera, everything will have depended on their height above sea level, and their distance from the sea. With a storm which has been building for as long as Faith, one can expect a storm surge of maybe fifteen feet above normal, and you'd have to add waves of maybe thirty or forty feet to that. Now, according to my map, there are considerable areas of Eleuthera which are only a few feet above sea level."

"So you think the Nassau authorities are right to expect that there has been a major disaster up there?"

"I hope and pray not, Dave. But I think we have to brace ourselves for the worst."

Jo put her arm round Owen Michael's shoulders. Even though Richard had earlier warned her what he would have to say, each word had still thudded into her brain.

"Now, Richard, latest reports indicate that the storm has turned north again. Can you tell us where she is now?"

"Sure." Richard got up and walked to the wall map, which was already marked with an X. "She's right there at this moment, approximately two hundred and fifty miles east of Melbourne, Florida, so you see she suddenly gathered speed after striking Eleuthera, and is in fact now travelling at more than twenty knots."

"Is that good, or bad?"

"On the whole, good; it gives her less time to build any more."

"So does she pose a threat to mainland United States?"

"At the moment, no. There's a gale warning up along the entire Florida and Georgia coasts, but the folks down there are on the weaker side of the system. As long as Faith stays offshore to the east, they're not going to suffer anything more than some beach erosion. The big winds and seas are out to the northeast of the centre."

"Well, that's good news, anyway. So . . . any idea where this lady is going next?" Dave asked.

"Well, she's travelling just east of north at this minute, so I reckon the folks in Bermuda need to look out."

"And will she maintain her present force, do you think, or will she weaken as she hits the cooler waters of the North Atlantic?"

The camera suddenly zoomed in to Richard's face; the director had obviously been briefed as to what the answer would be. "There are no cooler waters up here right this minute," Richard said. "This is the hottest summer we've had in years, and the water temperatures are way above normal. Faith certainly won't weaken—and if she slows down again, she could well build. She could become one of the biggest storms we've ever seen. We have to watch what she does, very carefully, over the next four days."

"And we know that you're going to do just that, on our behalf, Richard. Thank you. That was Richard Connors, our weather expert, warning us all to keep an eye on a certain lady named Faith. Now, finally . . ."

Jo flicked the switch.

"Heck, Mom," Owen Michael said. "Do you think Tamsin is all right? And Granpa and Granma?"

"I wish I knew. We must just . . ."

The phone buzzed. Jo leaped out of her chair and ran to it.

"What's the news from Eleuthera?" Michael asked.

Her heart slowed with disappointment; she had hoped, quite unreasonably, that it might be his father. "There is none. Communications have been cut."

"That's what they're saying here too," Michael agreed. "We'll just have to assume they're all right."

"Yeah. Where are you now, Michael?"

"In the Royal Bermuda Yacht Club. We're going to leave for home at dusk. We don't want to be here when Faith arrives."

78

"Are you sure you can make it?"

"Sure I'm sure. If necessary we'll motor: we're taking on extra fuel. We'll be home in about three days."

"Listen, you should stay in Bermuda until the storm is past."

"Stay here? You have got to be crazy. This island is totally exposed. I told you, we'll be home long before that hurricane gets here; it's travelling northeast, we'll be heading northwest, and we'll have a forty-eight-hour start. What I want is the earliest possible news from Eleuthera. I'll call you tomorrow. And give my love to Owen Michael."

The phone went dead.

"That system just seems to get bigger and bigger every time we look at it," Landry remarked.

"It *does* get bigger every time we look at it," Mark Hammond agreed.

They had emerged from the clouds and climbed to twenty thousand feet, yet virtually as far as the eye could see beneath them to the north was swirling white and black.

"OK," Mark told his navigator, Mackenzie, "let's take a look at Eleuthera." He was without Eisener on this trip; the doctor was in constant demand to appear on television throughout the eastern states.

He put the aircraft into a steep turn, and they raced to the south. Below them the clouds started to break up, and as they sank into them they could see patches of white-streaked blue water. Now North Eleuthera was in sight. Mark turned to the left, to pass down the eastern, Atlantic side of the island. He heard a low whistle from Landry as they looked down on Palm Island, the roofs torn off, the collapsed buildings, the wrecked boats and overturned vehicles . . . but there were people down there too, working at clearing the damage; one or two waved at the plane. Palm Island was some forty foot above normal water level, and the town was on the lee side—it had obviously escaped the worst of the surge.

Mark waggled his wings and went on. His chart told him he was over Dolphin Point. The point had been quite heavily wooded, and now he looked at what might have been a gigantic lawn cut by an equally gigantic motor mower. "Lucky nobody lived there," Landry commented.

"Maybe somebody did," Mark said quietly. His glide down had carried him ten miles south of the Point, and now they looked down on Whaletown, or what was left of it. A wall of sea had burst through from the Atlantic side, carrying everything in its path into the calm waters of the bight enclosed by the curve of Eleuthera. The shattered remains of houses and cars could be seen in the shallows, and as the plane dipped lower yet, floating bodies could also be discerned. There were also people on the land, waving to attract their attention.

"Tell Sparky to call Nassau," Mark ordered. "Tell them there is a major emergency at Whaletown and that Palm Island will also need assistance." He waggled his wings to reassure the people that help was on its way, and then turned back to the north and west.

Now they were only a thousand feet up, following the remains of the road. The bridge connecting Dolphin Point to the mainland had collapsed. Lower and lower Mark dropped the plane, peering down into the wrecked foliage beneath him. Then they were out over the bay.

"Hey," Landry shouted. "There's someone there."

Something white was being waved, a few hundred yards north of where the water had broken through. Mark turned again, studying the bay; since the eye had passed through, the seas there had gone right down, although it was by no means calm. "Check the chart," he told Mackenzie. "What kind of depths can we expect?"

"Eight to ten feet on average. But . . . you're not thinking of putting her down? There are sandbanks all over the place."

"And you've no clearance," Landry pointed out.

"So what?" Mark said. "How long do you think one or two people stranded there are going to survive? The help is gonna go to places like Whaletown first. You guys with me?"

Landry and Mackenzie looked at each other. "You're the skipper," they said together.

"OK," Mark said. He turned the amphibian yet again, and set her down into the wind. She almost skimmed the few remaining trees on Dolphin Point, then the floats touched the water, sending huge spumes of spray away to either side, the hull bumped on the shallow waves, and she came to rest, rising and falling on the gentle swell. Mark turned her, and motored back as close to the Point as he dared, then closed the throttles. "Get that anchor down," he told Landry, "and let's prepare the boat."

The inflatable was thrust through the door, and the cord pulled. Landry passed the outboard down to Mark, who was first in. "OK, Bob," he said. "Mac and I will go see. You and Sparky stay here."

He took the tiller and they moved towards the shore. "What the hell is that?" Mackenzie asked.

"Looks like an automobile," Mark said, steering to avoid the upturned vehicle, which had been carried some thirty feet from the shore.

"You're damned right. A blue Buick."

As they neared the beach Mackenzie pointed. "There's someone!"

Mark stared at the tree line, and the young man who stood there, waving his shirt. The dinghy grounded, and Mark stepped into the shallow water with the painter to drag it clear. "You alone?"

"No," Dale said, staggering down to meet them. "No, there are others." He gestured at the trees—there had been a house there once, they could still see part of the walls—and Mark followed him, Mackenzie at their heels. They climbed a shallow slope, picking their way through tangled fallen trees and branches, and gazed at the wreckage of another house. This one had stood up to the wind and sea better than the first, but was still virtually collapsed, two walls and the roof down, furniture scattered in every direction. Further off, a large generator rested on its side.

In the shelter of the two remaining walls a group of middle-aged people huddled: two men, a woman, her eyes red with weeping, clutching a little girl to her breast, another who seemed quite unaware of his presence, tears streaming from her eyes; and also a beautiful younger woman, wearing the remnants of a torn kaftan, her face utterly closed, as if the world outside had lost all meaning.

"Can they move?" Mark asked Dale in a low voice.

"I think so."

"Well, let's get them down to the beach. We can be in Miami in half an hour. Say, I sure am glad that you all survived."

Dale's shoulders sagged. "We didn't all survive," he said.

JO'S HANDS TREMBLED as she picked up the phone: if the night had been bad, the long afternoon's wait had been worse.

"Jo?"

For a moment she didn't recognise his voice. "Dale? Oh, Dale! Where are you?"

"Miami."

"Oh, thank God for that! Tamsin . . . ?"

"She's OK. A bit shocked, I guess. I guess we all are."

Waves of relief made Jo quite dizzy; she felt sick with joy. "But you got out. Are the planes flying?"

"No. We were picked up and brought out by a navy amphibian on weather patrol."

"Oh, thank God. Dale, how are you all?"

"There's nothing left, Jo."

Jo frowned at the phone. "What do you mean, nothing left?"

"I mean, nothing. The sea just came over the point. Meg's in hospital, under sedation. I reckon Neal should be there too."

"What about Babs and Dad?"

"They're not too good, either. Listen, we're coming up tomorrow morning. Can you meet us?"

"Sure. I'll let Marcia know, too. Oh, I can hardly wait."

"Yeah. Listen, bring two cars. We'll have Belle with us."

"Oh, great. Yes, I'll have Marcia bring her car as well. Has Lawson gone straight back to Nassau?"

There was a short silence. Then Dale said, "Lawson didn't make it."

"He . . ." Jo swallowed. "You mean. . . ? But how? I mean . . ."

"He's dead!" Dale shouted. "I don't know how it happened. Nobody knows. One minute he was there, and the next he wasn't. He must have fallen and been washed away by the sea. We just don't know."

"Oh, God," Jo said. "Oh, God. Then Belle . . ."

"Yeah," Dale said. "We'll see you tomorrow."

The phone went dead, but it was several seconds before Jo replaced it.

J. CALTHROP WHITE BEAMED at his telephone. "But that is great news, Mr. Palmer. Great news! Monday, you say? That's fine. Yes, sir, just fine. Say, any word from your boss? I guess he had a little rain down there, eh? Haw, haw, haw. Anyway, you did it without him. My congratulations, Mr. Palmer." He replaced the phone, grinned at Kiley. "Palmer has financed seventy-five per cent of that issue. Now that *is* a stockbroker. I'll tell you, Kiley, that oaf Donnelly's business runs better without him and his shitty son. Now, you listen to me: I want our bid on the desk of the Licensing Authority in the UK first thing Monday morning."

"Yes, sir, JC." Kiley hesitated. "I have Connors outside."

"Well, send him in. Send him in." White leaned back expansively, grinned at Richard as he came in. "Richard!" he said. "I saw your forecast. You really socked it to them. Yes, sir. What's the latest word on this hurricane thing? Is it really as big as you said?"

"She's a big system, JC. And she could deepen further. In fact, I think she will; she's still over warm water."

"And heading at us?"

"No, sir. Thank God she's moving slowly north by east, parallel with the coast, at a distance of about two hundred miles."

"Ah." White looked disappointed that a newsworthy catastrophe could not be expected. "So you reckon there's no danger to the mainland?"

"I didn't say that, JC. We won't be out of danger until that storm is past Newfoundland. She turned west once, she can do so again."

"It could present us with a tricky situation," White mused. "This storm is causing a lot of comment, so much so I have half a mind to slot you in for another of your chats. But we have to be careful. If we start hollering wolf, and nothing happens, well . . . we lose viewers. So how do you reckon the chances?"

"I think she's a potential threat, JC. I would like to see the mayor take some precautionary steps."

"You would? What steps could he take against a hurricane?"

"Well, he could review his evacuation plan, and publicise it, so people would know when to leave and what route to take."

"What kind of evacuation area are we talking about?"

"Well, the whole coast and Jamaica Bay area. And half of Manhattan is less than fifty feet above water level; that could all be flooded."

"You mean he has a plan to evacuate Manhattan?" Kiley spoke for the first time.

"I have no idea. But he should have."

White stroked his chin, the light of battle in his eyes; he loved a political wrangle, and he was no friend of Mayor Naseby's party. "That could be interesting," he said. "And give us an angle. I tell you what you do, Richard. First thing tomorrow you round up some data. Then report back here, and we'll make one or two plans of our own."

"Yes, sir," Richard said enthusiastically.

White pointed his gold pencil at Richard. "But just bear in mind that if we take on City Hall and make this into an issue, such as pointing up the inadequacy of their plans, we have to win. That means we have to be sure of our facts. Don't let me down on this. We need that hurricane to come at least as close as Gloria did."

Or I'll be on the next plane down to Miami, looking for my old job back, Richard thought. "I won't let you down, JC," he promised. Although how the hell he was supposed to tell Faith what to do he had no idea. He frowned as he gained the elevator: did JC really want Faith actually to strike the city, in order to score a political point?

"Hi," RICHARD SAID on the phone.

"I thought you were coming over this evening," said Jo.

"I can't tonight. I have a lot on. JC is again looking on me with a smile."

"Oh," Jo said. "Because of Faith?"

"Yes. Jo . . . I spoke to Mark Hammond. I'm most terribly sorry about your brother-in-law. But at least Tamsin is safe."

"Yes. Right now, I don't know whether to laugh or weep."

"It's that kind of situation. Say, where's that husband of yours? Still in Bermuda?"

"No. I guess he's left for Newport by now."

"Can you get in touch with him?"

"I suppose so . . ." Jo snapped her fingers; she should have done so before, to let him know his folks were all right.

"Well, I would if I were you. At sea is no place to be with Faith about. So if you don't want to be a widow, I'd tell him to stay put." He blew a kiss down the line, and was gone.

Jo sat gazing at the phone for some seconds, then picked it up again to call Central Exchange for a shore-to-ship radio link.

Thursday 27 July

"Evacuation plan? What do you mean, evacuation plan?" asked Assistant Commissioner McGrath, to whom Richard had been referred by the mayor's office.

"We would like to know," Richard repeated patiently, "if the New York Police Department has a plan for the evacuation of Manhattan in the event of an emergency."

"The evacuation of Manhattan?" McGrath stared at him from under arched eyebrows. "Now I remember you, you're the guy who's been scaring people half to death with your talk about an ultimate storm. Well, how the hell do you expect us to evacuate Manhattan? Have you any idea how many people live in this city?"

"Maybe ten million," Richard ventured.

"And where do you want us to evacuate them to?"

"Look," Richard said. "All I want to know is this: does the NYPD have a plan for the evacuation of the city of Manhattan in the event of an emergency? It could be an outbreak of plague, an incipient earthquake, a major storm, or even an enemy atomic attack."

The spokesman scratched his head in bewilderment. "Say, what the hell are you talking about? Atomic bombs or weather?"

"There needn't be that much difference. Think maybe of a twenty-four-hour warning of a communist attack," Richard suggested brightly. "A Russian task force somehow spirited across the Atlantic and ready to invade."

That was a tactical error. The spokesman gave him a withering look. "You want me to tell you that, to blare over the networks? Next thing the Commies would be blowing all the bridges, and where would we be then?"

J. CALTHROP WHITE GLANCED down the page of notes. "We could have real dynamite here, Richard," he remarked. "So you're pretty sure there is no evacuation plan?"

"Pretty sure, JC. Partly because the only real emergency the authorities seem able to consider is an atomic attack, when there wouldn't be time to evacuate the population anyway."

JC glanced at Kiley. "How much time can you give him without screwing the schedule up?"

Kiley studied his timings chart. "Three minutes at the end of the early evening forecast, by cutting two news items."

"OK, Richard," White said, "you blast them this evening."

Down in the weather office, Julian showed Richard the latest chart.

Richard frowned. "She hasn't moved more than a couple of miles."

"That's right," Julian agreed. "She's stalled."

"Two hundred and twenty miles southeast of Cape Hatteras, North Carolina," Jayme added. "They're reporting seventy-mile-an-hour winds down there."

"Stalled," Richard said, and sat at his desk. Stalled, he thought. The most dangerous storms in history were always those which had stalled, because then they could go anywhere. And Faith's present position was just over five hundred miles from New York. He looked out of the window; it was raining from an overcast sky, but the wind was light. "What wind strengths?" he asked.

"Oh, they're big," Julian said. "The last navy plane into the eye recorded one hundred and fifty miles an hour. And the Hurricane Center reckons she could still build."

"So . . . you going ahead with blasting City Hall?" Jayme asked.

Richard brooded for a few seconds longer.

"Yes."

"Attaboy," Jayme shouted, and kissed him.

PASSENGERS STARTED STREAMING through the gate from the Miami flight, greeting friends and relatives, or hurrying straight for the taxis. The reporters moved closer; Jo had no idea who had told them to be here—probably Cal Palmer; she had felt obliged to call him and let him know Big Mike was all right.

"There they are!" Marcia ran forward.

Meg Robson was first out, helped by Neal. They wore clothes that had obviously been freshly bought, and had no luggage. They glanced at Marcia as if she were a stranger, ignored Jo and Owen Michael altogether, and hurried for the exit.

"Say, were you on Eleuthera?" one of the reporters called, running behind them.

"Go away," Neal snapped. "Leave us alone."

The reporter hesitated, then rejoined his rivals, who were moving forward as the Donnellys came out. Jo and Owen Michael and Marcia were in front of them as the television cameras started to whirr.

"Oh, Mom," Marcia cried, taking her mother into her arms. Like the Robsons, the Donnellys were in new clothes.

"Tamsin!" Jo swept the little girl from the floor, hugged her and kissed her, then kissed Big Mike, looked into his eyes. "Oh, Dad!" She couldn't think of anything to say.

He hugged her tightly, then turned his attention to Owen Michael. Jo looked past him at Dale, who held Belle's arm. How incredible, she thought, that Dale, the family layabout, had come through the ordeal better than anyone. "Hi, Jo." Dale kissed her.

"Belle . . ." She put her arms round her sister-in-law. She could have been hugging Babs's older sister.

"They haven't found him," Belle said. "He could still be alive, you know. People survive."

"How bad was it, Mr. Donnelly?" the reporters were asking.

"Was the island really knocked flat?"

"Do you have any idea of the loss of life?"

All the while the little group was straggling towards the exit. Now Big Mike stopped, turned, and faced the pack at their heels. "Yes," he said. "It was hell. The island was knocked flat. My property is destroyed. The waves were bigger than anything I have ever seen. And yes, there was loss of life. Now, get off my back."

They reached the automobiles. Marcia took Dale and Belle. Babs and Tamsin and Owen Michael got into the back of the Mercedes, Big Mike sat in front with Jo. "We've food at the apartment," she said. "And Cal Palmer wants you to get in touch. He says it's urgent."

"Just drive us out to Bognor," Big Mike said. "We want to go home. Cal can wait until tomorrow."

Jo hesitated, then hooted to attract Marcia's attention, and made for the Whitestone Bridge and the New England Thruway.

"Belle blames us for poor Lawson," Babs said. "She doesn't actually say it, but she does."

"But . . . it could've happened to any of you," Joe said.

"Sure," Big Mike said. "But it didn't. And then . . ." He sighed.

"She wanted the men to go back and look for him, right away," Babs explained. "But they couldn't. They'd have been killed too."

"Neal and Meggie blame us too," Mike said. "For persuading them to go down there in the first place."

"For heaven's sake," Jo protested. "They're adult human beings." Another fallout from Faith, she thought: the end of a forty-year friendship. "How bad is your house?" she asked.

"There are a couple of walls standing," Big Mike said.

"Oh, then you can rebuild it," Owen Michael suggested.

"Rebuild it? Hell! I'm never setting foot on that island again."

"What about the McKinley property?" Babs asked.

"He can keep the hundred grand," Big Mike said. "I made a mistake." Jo had no idea what they were talking about.

"Where's Michael?" Big Mike asked.

"He left Bermuda last night, for Newport."

She didn't tell them about the abuse she had received when she finally got through to the yacht and apparently dragged Michael out of his bunk to speak to her; the lack of interest he had shown even in Lawson's death, once she had told him Tamsin was safe. "He reckons he'll be home long before Faith can catch up with him. Anyway, they're travelling in different directions: he's making northwest, and the storm northeast."

"Michael will be all right," Big Mike said. "That boy knows what he's doing. No goddamned hurricane is gonna bother him."

JO REFUSED AN INVITATION for supper, and drove the children back to town. She wanted Tamsin all to herself, and she wanted the little girl to sleep in her own bed that night.

It was drizzling, although there was no wind, and it was past eight when she regained the apartment; she fed the children and put them straight to bed. Richard had left messages on her Ansaphone but she knew he would be in the studio by now, working up his ten o'clock forecast: she'd call him back after that.

She poured herself a glass of milk, fixed a plate of salad and cottage cheese, and sat herself in front of the TV. She didn't really care what she was watching, she was merely waiting for ten o'clock; and there he was, outlining Faith's position, which had moved only a little north of her midday fixing. But then, when the forecast ended, the anchorman said, "In view of the importance we attach to the matter, we are now going to repeat Richard's comments of earlier this evening." Richard promptly reappeared on screen, but wearing a different tie: this was a recording.

"There is no doubt," he was saying, "that from her present position Faith can do anything and go anywhere. There is nowhere within five hundred miles of her centre at this moment where the utmost precautions should not be being taken. And that includes this city of New York.

"Now, our experiences of past years, particularly along the Gulf Coast and in Florida, have proved beyond a shadow of a doubt that human lives can be saved by systematic evacuation of low-lying areas, if those evacuations are undertaken early enough. We all understand what an immense task it would be to evacuate Manhattan, Staten Island, Long Island or Atlantic City, but it must be understood too that any land below fifty feet above sea level could be at risk in the event of a major hurricane making a landfall in this vicinity. And there is no use waiting for the hurricane to arrive before ordering such an evacuation."

He leaned forward. "Now, I must tell you that at the time of going on the air this evening, we at NABS have been unable to discover the existence of an evacuation plan, either from the police or from the mayor's office." He paused significantly. "We now invite the city authorities to accept our offer of free air time tomorrow, either morning or evening, so that you folks sitting out there may be given the vital details of their plan for your safety, should the need arise—always supposing such a plan exists. This is Richard Connors, for the National American Broadcasting Service."

Jo switched off the set. Coming on top of everything else that had happened today, she felt numbed. Richard hadn't given her a hint that he was planning to get involved in city politics. Presumably he had been ordered to do so by J. Calthrop White.

Ten minutes later the phone buzzed, and she knew it would be him. "Hi! Who's a big bad bear, then?" she said.

"What did you think of it?"

"Richard Connors, ace reporter, straight from the shoulder. It was great, but you'd better not apply to City Hall for a building licence in the near future. Or any kind of licence, come to think of it—even a marriage one."

"Who's sounding all cheerful, then?"

"Of course I'm cheerful. I know I should be in mourning for poor Lawson, but I have my little girl back, safe and sound and tucked up in bed."

"Makes sense to me. What news of your husband?"

"Oh, he's somewhere between Hamilton and Newport."

"My God! How far out?"

"Well, he left last night, and he was going to motor if he couldn't sail. Supposing he could maintain seven knots, I suppose he'd be just about two hundred miles from Hamilton."

"Then he has time to turn back. He's about three hundred miles from the storm . . . and if he keeps on he's going to enter what sailors call the dangerous semicircle, where he'll experience the strongest winds and biggest seas of the hurricane."

"He left because he thought the boat would be in more danger in Hamilton than out at sea."

"Jo, the point is that Faith is already just about past Bermuda. They're not going to get anything but a swell. It's up to you, but . . ."

Jo looked at her watch. It was nearly eleven p.m. "I'll raise him, just as quickly as I can."

Friday 28 July

Sam Davenport climbed through the hatch of Michael's racing yawl *Esmeralda* and sniffed the air. At half past midnight it was utterly dark, with the moon and stars obliterated by the cloud cover, from which intermittent drizzle had turned everything on deck clammily wet. The wind remained light, and the sea calm, although there was a big swell out of the southwest.

"That forecast wasn't so good," Sam remarked.

Michael Donnelly sat aft, just visible in the glare of the binnacle lamp, one hand resting on the wheel. He wore orange oilskins over bathing trunks. "She's close, eh?"

"Three hundred and fifty miles."

"That figures. We must just about be crossing the top edge."

"Not according to the forecast," Sam said. "She's altered course, heading more north than we are. She's still southwest of us."

"How fast's she moving?"

"About ten knots."

"And we're making a steady seven. She won't catch us."

"Yeah. Well, I hope you're right. I got the news before the forecast. Some of what happened in Eleuthera was horrendous. They're talking of several hundred dead, and damage running into millions."

"Yeah," Michael agreed. "Including my brother-in-law and one hell of a big property deal." He shrugged. "That's the way the cookie crumbles, I guess. You ready to take over?"

"Sure." Sam swung his leg out of the companionway, then checked. "Hello, somebody's calling."

"Don't tell me," Michael groaned. "It'll be Jo again. She's a pain in the ass, sometimes."

Sam gave his skipper a curious glance, ducked back into the cabin, thumbed the handset. "You're right," he called. "It *is* Jo."

"Well, take the helm," Michael said, and went below. "*Esmeralda*," he said. "What's the trouble now? Over."

"There could be a lot of trouble," Jo said. "Have you enough fuel to get back to Hamilton? Over."

"Sure, we have. We also have enough fuel to motor into Newport. Why should we want to go back to Hamilton? Over."

"Faith is coming your way again, Michael. Didn't you get the midnight weather forecast? Over."

"Sure we did. She's over three hundred miles away from us, and only making a couple of knots more speed. OK, she's altered course. We still have time to beat her in. Over."

"Listen to me, Michael. This could be the biggest storm this century. I have spoken with a weather forecaster here and he says your only safe course is to go back to Hamilton. The storm is already past Bermuda but she's going to cross directly over your route to Newport. Over."

"I know what Faith is doing," Michael said. "And I know we can beat her in. Going back to Bermuda is out. Now, did the folks get in? Over."

"Yes," Jo said. "Yes, they got in. And Tamsin's fine. Michael, for God's sake, will you listen to me and go back to Hamilton. Over."

"Look, you go back to bed and let me run this ship, eh? We'll be in Newport Sunday night. You be there to meet us, right? *Esmeralda* over and out." He replaced the handset, looked at the anxious faces of his crew peering at him from their bunks. "So what's eating you guys?"

"Maybe she's right," Larry remarked, "and we should turn back."

Michael shot him a glance. "Say, what's gotten into you guys? You scared of a little wind? Listen, this ship is damned near hurricane proof, because I made her that way. But there's plenty for us to do to make even more sure. So all hands turn out." They grumbled, but grinned as well: they had the utmost confidence in Michael as a skipper.

"I'd like to call Sally and tell her what we're doing," Sam said. "Especially as I reckon we'll soon be out of radio range. Can you take her again for half an hour?"

"Sure, if you reckon she'll want to hear from you in the middle of the night." Michael returned on deck. "And when you've done that, carry extra lashings over the battery boxes and the radio gear—if we should get knocked down they could just come loose."

He took the helm, settled himself, thought of Jo working herself up into a fuss, and frowned. Silly bitch. There was going to have to be some very straight talking between them, when he got home.

TO HER SURPRISE, Jo slept very soundly that night, but she had set her alarm, and woke at a quarter to seven, in time to switch on the TV while her coffee percolated.

Richard smiled at her from the set, but his eyes were grave. He moved to the huge wall map. "Faith is now three hundred miles due east of Cape Hatteras, and you'll see . . ." his wand touched the last position ". . . that she is now moving northeast again, but still slowly, only about ten knots. She is just over four hundred miles southeast of New York, and in fact, if she maintains her present track, she is going to move straight out into the Atlantic and trouble no one anymore . . . except any shipping that happens to be in her way. That should all by now have moved out of her path in any event."

Jo opened her atlas, and began measuring off distances. By her reckoning the storm was within two hundred miles of where *Esmeralda* should now be. Her hand hovered over the telephone . . . but almost certainly the yacht was now out of radio range, and even if she could raise them she didn't know what they could do about it now.

"THAT WAS GOOD WORK last night, Richard," remarked J. Calthrop White. "We'll have to think about giving you some more political broadcasting to do, eh?" He glanced at Kiley, who gave an anxious smile. "Now, all we need is for Faith to act up, and give people a good enough scare to ask the same questions we have; my information is that they are already doing that. So what the hell is all this talk about she's now heading out to sea?"

Richard couldn't figure out what the old buzzard was doing in the office on a Friday morning at all; he usually went out to Long Island on Thursday night. "Well, JC . . . I'm afraid that's what she's doing."

"Hm. That's not so good. It'll give the administration a breathing space. Yes, indeed. They'll go back to the old theme of how a hurricane never will hit New York, and we'll be accused of scaremongering. So why did you say yesterday that Faith was still a possible threat to New York?"

"Because she was. She still is. She's a massive storm, she's still deepening, and she's moving very slowly . . ."

"But away from New York." JC believed in hammering the important point in any discussion. "All she's done is put down one hell of a lot of rain to spoil tomorrow's golf." He pressed a switch on his intercom. "Alice, call the garage and tell Murray I won't be staying in town this weekend after all. Tell him to have the car ready in ten minutes."

"Right away, JC," the secretary replied.

JC stood up. "I'm not blaming you, Richard. I repeat, you did a good job. And you have the face to put these things across. You look honest, and even more important, you look sincere. But there's no doubt either that we'll have lost a lot of oomph when people tune in to your next forecast and discover this storm is heading out into the Atlantic. A real pity. Have a good weekend." He left the office.

Richard and Kiley looked at each other.

"Should I start looking for another job?" Richard asked.

"Well . . . I reckon he was pretty forbearing."

"You guys have got to be crazy," Richard observed in disgust. "You *want* that storm to hit us. Do you have any idea what it would be like?"

"New York isn't some Pacific sandbank," Kiley said.

"Come over here, Mr. Kiley." Richard went to stand at the plate glass window looking down on Manhattan: it faced east. "Do we have any shutters for this window?"

"Are you crazy? We're forty floors up."

"Well, let me tell you something, Mr. Kiley: if Faith hits here that window is going to disappear, sucked out like it was paper. And if either you or JC happen to be in this office at the time, the odds are you will go with it, and most of the glass will fall into the street, in pieces as lethal as shrapnel. Now, you tell me something: how many plate-glass windows of roughly this size are there in New York?"

Kiley stared at him. "You're being hysterical," he said. "I have a luncheon date."

"Enjoy it, and pray that Faith keeps out to sea."

He took the elevator down to the weather room in a thoroughly bad temper. Jayme was out shopping; he had told her he would need her in the office over the weekend. Julian was on the phone, making notes, eyebrows bobbing at him. He replaced the receiver. "Faith has sustained winds at the centre of a hundred and sixty miles an hour, and she's still building."

"One hundred and sixty?" Richard took the pad and stared at the figures. "You ever seen wind speeds like that before, at ground level?"

"The ultimate storm, eh? But that ain't all." Julian took back the pad and flipped the page. "She's starting to wobble. There's a definite movement west of north. Look at the coordinates."

Richard reached for his phone. "Find out if Mr. White has left the building yet," he snapped at the girl on the switchboard. "If you can, stop him. Tell him I have to speak with him again, most urgently."

"I'm sorry, Mr. Connors," the switchboard said. "Mr. White has already left for Long Island."

"He has a phone in his car, hasn't he?"

"Of course, Mr. Connors, but we are under strict orders only to call him once he has left the office for the weekend in an extreme emergency."

"This *is* an extreme emergency," Richard snapped. "Get him. And get me the mayor's office as well." He replaced the phone, then picked it up again and dialled Jo.

"You really feel this is it?" Julian asked.

"This could be it. Those coordinates place the storm just three hundred and seventy miles away from us, and she could be turning this way. If something isn't done, and quick, we could be looking at the disaster of the century. Hi, Jo."

"Hi. What's happening?"

"Nothing good. Listen. I want you to pack a bag for yourself and the kids, and leave town. Go away for the weekend."

"Now? You're pulling my leg."

"I was never more serious in my life. Listen, Jo, didn't you tell me your in-laws have a house in Bognor, Connecticut?"

"Why, yes. But . . ."

"Go visit with them. Bognor should be safe enough."

"I can't just descend on them, Richard. They're still suffering from shock."

"Well, they could be going to get a lot more shock in the next couple of days. Faith is moving west."

"West? Oh, my God! But Michael . . ."

"Yeah. I know. Maybe he'll be able to outrun her. That's all I can offer. But you, Jo . . ."

"I have Mr. White on the phone, Mr. Connors," the switchboard said.

"Hell . . . I'll call you back, Jo," Richard said, and pressed the transfer button. "JC?"

"Something on your mind, Richard?" JC's tone was deceptively quiet. "Something important, I hope."

"I thought you'd like to know that Hurricane Faith has stopped moving northeast. She's starting to wobble to the west."

"Does that mean she may be coming our way after all?"

"It certainly creates that possibility."

"Splendid news, Richard. Splendid news. Keep me posted. Call me this evening at home. Well done, Richard."

"JC," Richard begged. "If she does come west, she could pose a serious threat to New York."

"Well, that's what we've been saying all along, isn't it?"

"Yes, but JC, I'd like to interrupt the schedule programming for a hurricane alert, right now."

"Richard," JC said, "listen to me, boy. I know how interested you are in this hurricane thing. But here's what you do, and this is an order. You hand over the one o'clock forecast to Julian, with strict instructions to give the coordinates and the present wind strengths and nothing more. You go home, and have a good lunch and a nap, and then you return to the studio this evening, and you call me and give me an update then."

"Mr. White, we don't have six hours to waste. This storm is carrying winds at the centre of more than one hundred and sixty miles an hour, and she is still building. She is going to be the biggest storm this century."

"Great stuff. And we predicted it. *You* predicted it, Richard. Congratulations."

"Mr. White, Faith is going to kill people. Maybe a lot of people. We have to do something, now. Get them moved out of all low-lying areas."

"Richard, you are starting to sound hysterical. How far away is this system?"

"The centre is approximately three hundred and seventy-five miles southeast of us, and moving at approximately ten knots. That is real slow, and that is additionally dangerous, because she's still building."

"But she is at least thirty-six hours away."

"Thirty-six hours isn't very long to evacuate Manhattan. And storm conditions will happen some time before the centre arrives."

"Thirty-six hours gives her one hell of a lot of time to change her course again, though." As usual, JC was concentrating on what he considered the essentials. "We'll issue our warning when we're absolutely sure she's gonna hit."

"Mr. White, that will be too late."

"We have done our bit, Richard. We forecast this storm, and we were laughed at. OK. We'd be crazy to go sticking our necks out again without proof positive. You can't have that before tonight. If Faith is still coming at us then, we'll reconsider the situation. But we do nothing further until then. Got me?" The phone went dead.

Richard looked at Julian, and Julian looked at Richard.

Richard picked up the phone and dialled City Hall. "May I speak with the mayor, please?" he asked. "This is Richard Connors, on behalf of NABS." He wondered why he was wasting his time.

"The mayor has gone to lunch."

"I thought he might have. Well, look, it is vitally important that I get a message to him, about the hurricane."

"The hurricane? Our information is that she no longer poses a threat to New York."

"Well, I have news for you." Richard kept himself from shouting with an effort. "She does pose a threat, more than ever before. She is changing direction and you can tell the mayor there is a distinct possibility that Hurricane Faith may hit this city within thirty-six hours."

"Thirty-six hours," the man said.

"And that I consider it absolutely essential that he order the evacuation of all low-lying areas of the city, immediately."

"Evacuation immediately," the man repeated; obviously he was now making notes. "Mr. Connors, the mayor isn't going to be happy to be told this. And you're not his favourite person, right this minute."

"You ask him if he's going to be happy when he has a twenty-foot wall of water rushing up Wall Street."

"Twenty foot . . . well, I'll contact him, Mr. Connors."

"And tell him NABS is ready to broadcast such an evacuation order, with details of routes to be used, and call me back here. Right?"

He replaced the phone. Julian scratched his head. "Think he'll call back? Because if JC gets to hear of this, after telling you to cool it, he's gonna have your guts for garters."

Richard got up. "I'm going to obey JC's orders, at least in part. Call me at Josephine Donnelly's apartment the moment you hear anything from the mayor."

"MY GOD, YOU'RE SOPPING WET!" Jo exclaimed as she opened the door.

"Well, it's pouring with rain out there." Richard made to kiss her, then saw the children. "Hi."

"Hi, Mr. Connors," Owen Michael said. "This is Mr. Connors, the weatherman. I have his autograph," he told Tamsin proudly.

"Maybe you'd like to stay to lunch," Jo suggested, handing him a towel to dry his hair.

"That would be very nice, Mrs. Donnelly."

"Have you any news on what's happening with Dad?" Owen Michael asked.

"Well . . . I guess he's having some rough weather out there."

"Dad doesn't worry about rough weather," Owen Michael declared.

"Well, that's great," Richard said.

"Fix yourself a drink," Jo said. "I'll have one too. And you two run along and watch TV until lunch time."

Richard watched the door close. "Jo . . ." He took her in his arms.

"Is it bad?"

"Bad, and getting worse. This is hurricane rain."

"And Michael?"

"I don't know, Jo. I simply can't imagine what it might be like out there."

She sighed, and rested her head on his shoulder. "And you want me to go up to Connecticut?"

"Don't you think you should? You have your children to think about."

They both spun round as the phone buzzed. Jo ripped it from its stand. "Jo Donnelly? Oh. It's for you."

Richard took it. "Anything good, Julian?"

"Not a damn thing."

"What about the mayor?"

"Ah . . . the guy at City Hall called back and said he'd been in touch with the mayor and had been instructed to tell us that when the mayor wishes the assistance of the National American Broadcasting Service in running New York City, he will most certainly ask for it. What do we do now?"

"What *can* we do, save wait for six o'clock? I'll be along in a couple of hours." He replaced the phone, took the glass Jo was holding for him. She watched him pace the room.

Aware of her eyes on him, he stopped and spread his arms wide in a gesture of despair. "They just don't believe it can happen."

"Surely New York has been hit by a hurricane before?" Jo said.

"Sure it has. And that's the trouble. Because the city was virtually undamaged on previous occasions, they reckon it can ride anything."

"I don't understand," she said. "If it was undamaged . . ."

"Let me give you a few facts. The centres of all those storms passed over Long Island. That means that in each of those hurricanes New York was on the left, the western side of the track, where the winds are weaker and the storm surge is minimal. New York has never been in the northeast sector, the dangerous sector. All New York has ever experienced is the navigable semicircle."

"And you think Faith is going to behave differently?"

"Ultimately, no. I think she will swing northeast after hitting land. But it's where she hits land that matters, and right now, if this turning movement continues—and don't forget that she did just this over Eleuthera on Wednesday—she could come ashore south of Manhattan, and if she does that, with the kind of winds she is generating, it's going to be like nobody can even imagine."

"Surely the mayor can see that on the weather map?"

"It's not on the weather map, as yet. All he can see is a big storm behaving exactly the same as every other big storm. Up to two hours ago he was right. The fact that she has begun to turn west won't be clearly apparent for several hours."

He drank some whisky.

"I can't prove I'm right until Faith's new track is clearly defined, and that may be too late. But you know, at the other end of the scale there are people like JC. He won't take the risk that we might be proved wrong. I'm banned from issuing any warning just in case she moves off again." He drained his glass, and Jo got up to refill it. "My darling . . ." He caught her wrist. "Will you listen to me? Believe me? Please?"

"I do believe you."

"Well, then, get out of town."

She took the glass to the bar, poured. "I can't, right now. God knows my marriage is over, Richard. But Michael is the father of my children. I have got to be where he can get in touch with me. He's out of radio range right this minute; his FM set has a maximum range of two hundred and fifty miles. But I know he'll call as soon as he nears the coast."

He sighed. "Which will be when?"

"Well . . . he should be back within range by this evening."

"By this evening, if I have my way, this entire city will be under evacuation, and there are going to be some real traffic jams. Listen, you can call him from his folks' place, surely?"

Jo hesitated. But she could see Richard was deadly serious. "OK," she said. "Listen. I'll hang on here until seven tonight, and see if I can raise him then. If Faith is still coming straight for us this evening, I promise I'll go as soon as I've spoken to the yacht."

"You don't really believe me, do you?" he said sadly.

"Well . . ." She bit her lip. "Of course I do, Richard, but I really don't want to descend on the Donnellys in their present state unless I have to. Besides . . ."

He knew what she was thinking. "Listen, Jo, I have no doubt that this is one hell of a fine building, and can stand up even to one-hundred-and-sixty-mile-an-hour winds. But what about that window? It's going to explode like a bomb. Do you really want your kids here when that happens?"

"My God," she said. "I hadn't thought of that."

"So get out while you can."

"Sure. I'll do that."

"But not until tonight?"

"We'll have time. Won't we?"

He sighed, and nodded. "OK. Tonight." He took her in his arms. "Promise?"

"Scout's honour."

"I'll be counting on that. I have an idea things are going to start to hum tonight, and I probably won't have the opportunity to call you. But if you're going to be out of town, I won't have anything to worry about."

"And what are you going to be doing? Aren't you at risk from flying glass as much as anyone?"

"Sure. But I at least know what to expect. And I have a job to do. I'll call you at Bognor, the moment I can. Now . . ." He kissed her to stop her protests. "Let's drink to Michael. I reckon he's doing it the hardest possible way, right this minute."

THE SQUALLS CONTINUED all morning, the wind speed gradually rising, and the wind gradually backing to northeast. Michael shut down the engines and even under reefed main and storm jib *Esmeralda* was making nine knots, and as the wind began to head him it was not possible to maintain a course as much north as he would have liked.

It was a peculiar day: during squalls visibility would close down to under a mile, and they seemed alone in an empty grey world. Then the rain would pass, the clouds would break and on the top of the swells they could see for ever, comfortingly aware of how busy a stretch of ocean this was. Steamers appeared and disappeared again, all heading north. Sam chatted with one huge container ship, whose radio operator remarked, "Say, you guys know what's behind you?"

"We're keeping an eye on it," Sam said.

"Well, good luck," the operator said.

The swell was now mountainous, yet *Esmeralda* coasted along very comfortably under her reduced canvas, as ready for the storm as human ingenuity could manage. Michael had sailed in the infamous Fastnet Race of 1979 when a freak storm had caused a large number of yachts to be abandoned and some fifteen men had been lost. He knew that the greatest danger any yachting crew can face in bad weather is that of a man overboard. Thus he had given instructions that no man was to leave the cabin without two safety harnesses, so that he could be clipped onto two strong points at the same time. He had also commanded that two men were to be on the helm at all times, one steering, the other ready to take over should anything happen.

At two o'clock they were hit by their first thunderstorm. Sam disconnected all his radio equipment in case of lightning; the yacht itself was perfectly safe as the mast would allow the electrical discharge to run down the steel shrouds and thence into the chainplates, from where it would plunge harmlessly over the side. But of course a strike on the aerials could blow all their electronic gear.

The first storm passed over quickly enough, but now the wind had freshened, with gusts of up to sixty knots. Even under shortened sail the yacht was racing along, soaring up the back of each swell and careering down the other side in a welter of foam.

"She's going too fast," Michael decided, as the bows nearly buried themselves in the swell. "Let's have the mainsail down."

They handed the mainsail, stuffing the wet canvas onto the boom and strapping it down with twice the normal number of sail ties. "OK," Michael said. "Jerry and I will take over now."

Larry frowned. "Peter and I have only been on two hours."

"Two-hour watches from here on. It's going to be pretty exhausting. Now, you go below and get your heads down for a couple of hours."

He connected both his harnesses, made Jerry do the same. With only her storm jib up, the yacht was travelling much more slowly.

He had been on the helm an hour, thoroughly enjoying himself, steering the boat up and down the ever-increasing swell, when Jerry looked astern. "Oh, my God!" he said.

Michael had already heard the roaring from behind him. He cast a hasty glance over his shoulder. This was a big wave, all of twenty-five feet high, and topped by another six foot of curling crest. "Close the hatch," he shouted. As it slammed shut, he concentrated. His job was to keep the yacht before the sea; if he let her yaw away to either side she might turn broadside to the waves and be rolled over and over like a car falling down a steep slope.

The roaring became louder, and he hunched his shoulders. He glanced quickly at Jerry, then he was in the middle of a foaming maelstrom of water, and the wheel was threatening to tear from his hands.

"Holy smoke!" Jerry pulled himself back to the helm. "Have you ever seen one as big as that before, skipper?"

"Yes," Michael replied, truthfully enough. He did not add that the previous occasion had been at the very height of that Force Ten storm of a few years before, and not with possibly double as much wind still to come.

Yet he was pleased with the way things were going. The ship was

handling perfectly, and the gear was standing the strain. Soon there were other waves as big as the first, but in time they became almost commonplace, as the yacht reacted to every one with perfect balance. The wind was now howling, the sea was entirely covered in flying foam, and entering the troughs was like diving down to the centre of the earth. The rain teemed down like solid grey walls, battering on their oilskins and pounding the decks. Yet it was totally exhilarating. They were fighting the elements, taking them on at their own game, and holding their own.

Just. A mammoth wave hit them and for a dreadful moment, as the stern was picked up high above the bow and Michael fought to maintain control, he thought they were going to go stern over bow.

"That's it," he bawled. "We have to get all sail off her. Get up the watch below."

Jerry banged on the hatch cover and the others came out. Larry and Peter went forward, crawling, unclipping one harness and clipping it on again before releasing the next. Then they were on the foredeck and clawing down the sail. Again the yacht was awash, and Michael held his breath as he saw them being thrown about the deck. Part of the grab rail snapped and Peter for a moment was over the side, but his harnesses held, and he scrambled back on board, and eventually the sail was handed and strapped to the deck.

"Good work," Michael said. "Get changed."

"My turn on the helm," Jon said. "Sam will keep me company."

Michael leaned over the wheel and considered the situation. Without sail the dangers of broaching were increased. To retain control he could either put out a sea anchor or trail warps astern, both to slow her down to the extent where she would be overtaken by each wave rather than carried on with it, and to keep her stern on to the seas. Neither appealed, as each would put an immense extra strain on both gear and crew. He decided to let her stand on for as long as possible.

"Just keep a lookout behind you," he suggested, and thankfully crawled through the hatch into the warmth and dryness of the cabin. Only as he stripped off his dripping oilskins and the sodden clothes beneath did he realise how much his ribs were hurting where they had been crushed against the wheel. He rolled into his bunk, listened to the immense roaring from all about him, and fell asleep. To wake as the world turned upside-down.

"HELP!" JERRY WAS SCREAMING. "We're sinking! Help!"

Michael found himself lying on the cabin roof. There seemed to be water everywhere, together with books and pots and pans and clothes and sailbags. Despite the utter darkness, he knew immediately that they had been capsized. But before he could even gather his thoughts, *Esmeralda* was coming upright again, throwing him onto the cabin floor.

He groped for the companion hatch, which had flown open, splashing through several inches of water, hearing the shouts and groans from behind him, standing on the radio, which for all its extra lashing had become dislodged.

Once on deck, Michael gave a gasp of horror as he saw the wheel spinning free. Before he could reach it, the next wave had reached them, and hurled the yacht onto her beam ends, while tons of ocean poured over her. It seemed impossible that she would not fill and go to the bottom, but the yacht came up again, bobbing like a cork, the enormous amount of air in her hull giving her buoyancy.

Michael dived aft and grabbed the helm, twisting it to bring the ship straight as she rose to the wind. He tried the engine starter, but it was dead. Yet the yacht itself did respond, if sluggishly, and just in time to ride the next wave. Once he had her under reasonable control, he could start looking for his crew. He spotted Jon, lying on the deck several feet forward of the cockpit. One of the steel harness hooks had opened straight as if made of plasticine, but the second had held, and the young man was at least still with the ship, although he appeared to be unconscious. But to Michael's horror there was no sign of Sam Davenport.

"Deck!" he screamed at the hatch. "All hands on deck!"

Larry came up the companion ladder, fell into the self-draining cockpit. Jerry followed a moment later. "We're sinking," he shouted again. "The water's up to the bunks."

"I've left Pete below—he's broken something," Larry gasped. "Maybe his shoulder. He's groaning terribly."

Michael looked aft. The men on watch each wore a life jacket, and Sam would still be floating, although as *Esmeralda* was picked up by another huge wave and rushed forward he knew there was no hope of turning back for anyone. But he saw nothing astern save for the roaring seas, and now there came a reassuring shout from the foredeck.

Both Sam's harnesses had failed, but the second one had taken the force out of the enormous power which had hurled him forward, enabling him to wrap both arms round what remained of the mainmast: it had snapped off some fifteen feet from the deck, and disappeared, taking most of its shrouds with it.

Jerry and Larry formed a human chain to drag Sam back into the cockpit. "We're sinking," Jerry gasped a third time. "She'll be gone in a moment." He reached past them in an attempt to free the canister containing the six-man life raft, strapped to the transom.

Michael released the helm with one hand long enough to slap his friend hard across the face. "Get him below," Michael snapped. "Take Jon down as well. Give me a report on him and Pete. And on damage. And start the pumps. All the pumps. Get on with it."

They hurried below, and he fought with the helm. It was still daylight, although the clouds were so low and the rain so continuous it was difficult to see more than the ship's length. It seemed an eternity, but could only have been a few minutes later, that Sam reappeared. "Pete *has* broken his shoulder," he said. "We've strapped him up and I've given him a sedative. Jon is still out. I don't like the look of him at all."

"Is he breathing?"

"Yes. But skipper . . ." His voice trembled.

"Pumps?"

"No good. The batteries have broken loose. The radio and all the instruments are out. Maybe Jerry is right and we should abandon ship."

"For the life raft? For Christ's sake, do you suppose a life raft could survive those seas? *Esmeralda* is not sinking," Michael said, his voice harsh. "Yachts don't sink unless they are holed or catch fire. You know that as well as I do. The water in the cabin came through the hatch when we were rolled over. So man the hand pump and get Larry and Jerry bailing. But first, bring me up my harnesses."

Sam blinked, noticing for the first time that his skipper was not even wearing a life jacket. He dived below for the gear, and helped Michael strap himself to the boat and the helm.

"Get to work," Michael told him. "Get bailing. All of you."

Sam disappeared, and a moment later a thin stream of water began to empty over the side. Another wave roared up with such force that Michael lost control; he sat on the transom with water round his neck. But the hatch had been bolted tight shut again, and the ship came upright. Michael laughed aloud. "You won't beat me, you bastards," he shouted at the clouds and the lightning and the rain and the waves and the wind.

As if in reply, he heard a noise. It was a noise with which he was thoroughly familiar, that of a rogue wave coming up astern. He turned his head. Behind him the entire ocean seemed to be rising in awesome fury. The white-streaked green wall went up and up and up, perhaps fifty feet, and was topped by ten foot of curling white foam. It reared above the yacht, a wall of water as high as a house, and then it was toppling over and falling.

AFTER RICHARD HAD RETURNED to the studio, Jo began making her preparations. There was a lot to do. First of all she telephoned Bognor. "Have you seen the forecasts?" she asked Big Mike.

"Yeah. Would you believe that storm seems to be following us about? Thank God we're here."

"I thank God, too. Listen, Dad, I thought the kids and I might come up for the weekend. Sounds like it's going to be a little unpleasant in town."

"Sure, do that, honey. What time were you thinking of coming?"

"Well . . ." She hesitated. She had given Richard her word to leave that evening. But it would be somewhat of an unpleasant drive in the

101

darkness and the rain; and she certainly didn't want to upset Mike and Babs all over again by suggesting there was any danger. "How about first thing in the morning, so we'll be there for breakfast?"

"Breakfast? That'll mean leaving the city before dawn."

"We're early risers," Jo assured him.

"OK. We'll expect you. Any word from Michael?"

"Not as yet. He's out of radio contact right now. I'm going to try him again this evening. Do you reckon he's all right?"

"Sure I do. Especially if the storm is turning west and he's making north. He'll run out of it." He seemed to have entirely recovered his ebullience. "Breakfast, eh? See you then."

She fed the children and put them to bed. The six o'clock forecast had revealed Faith's westward turn, but not dramatically, and Richard had been studiously relaxed about what he had had to say; she guessed he was waiting to be given his instructions by JC.

Jo began to pack for the weekend. Then she watched a mini-series on TV, and promptly fell fast asleep, to be woken with a start by a sudden flash of lightning and the almost immediate crack of thunder right overhead. The whole apartment block shuddered, a vicious reminder of what it might be like were the hurricane really to hit the city.

She got up and went into the bedrooms. Amazingly, both Owen Michael and Tamsin were still fast asleep. But that thunderclap had ended her last doubt about leaving.

Then she thought of Marcia and Benny, down in Greenwich Village. They should leave too, for the safety of Pinewoods. She reached for the phone and punched out their number, but there was no response. Her watch showed eleven o'clock, so they had to be out at a party. She'd have to try them again later. She replaced the phone, heard Julian Summers's voice on TV, and hastily turned back to the set.

"We are interrupting this programme to bring you the latest update on Hurricane Faith. Here is Richard Connors."

Richard's face was grave. "Good evening," he said. "This is Richard Connors, bringing you the latest information on Hurricane Faith. Faith is now a very big storm indeed, the biggest, in terms of wind speeds, ever recorded. She has sustained winds around the centre of approximately one hundred and seventy miles an hour, and her present position is . . . here." He stood in front of the wall map and pointed with his wand. "Two hundred and eighty miles east by north of Norfolk, Virginia, and exactly the same distance southeast of New York. You can also see from her track that it is almost certain that we are going to feel the full effects of the storm here. There is also some evidence that Faith is beginning to quicken, which means that she could be no more than twenty-four hours away from us.

"Now, this is a highly dangerous storm. Because of her size and intensity, we have little previous experience to work on, but we can

102

expect extensive damage to property. This means most roofs are going to be at risk, and all windows and doors will be extremely vulnerable. But an even greater problem will be presented by the storm surge. It could be as high as thirty foot, depending on the state of the tide when the hurricane actually touches land, but the effects will be felt some five hours before the full force of the storm is encountered. Such a storm surge would mean the flooding of vast areas of land along the coast, and indeed of a considerable portion of Manhattan itself. We at NABS feel that in these circumstances it is our duty to warn you that everyone living within five miles of the coast, in the area stretching from Atlantic City to Newport, Rhode Island, must consider themselves in grave danger. We urge everyone who can to evacuate these areas before tomorrow afternoon, and certainly all those whose dwellings are situated less than fifty foot above sea level.

"For those who cannot evacuate, instant preparations must be made. Prolonged power failures can be expected, as well as a complete failure of the telephone system. A refuge should be prepared in each apartment away from external windows and doors, and a store of drinking water ensured. The best way to do this is fill the bathtub, now, while there is uncontaminated water available."

He paused, and took a sip of water. "We have contacted the Police Department and we are looking forward to their cooperation. Now let me stress that there is absolutely no need for any kind of panic. Hurricane Faith cannot reach New York before tomorrow afternoon at the very earliest. Therefore there is ample time for every man, woman and child who wishes to do so to leave the city. This station will of course remain on the air for as long as there is power, bringing you up-dates and information as they are available. This is Richard Connors, for the National American Broadcasting Service. Thank you."

"Whew!" Julian Summers said, and wiped his brow.

"So here we go," Jayme agreed.

Richard lit a cigarette, something he very rarely did.

"I must say," Julian remarked, "I am really amazed that you finally persuaded JC to put that message out."

"Or that the police agreed to cooperate," Jayme said.

Richard stubbed out the cigarette again: he had taken only two puffs. "I didn't persuade anyone," he said. "I couldn't get hold of JC. And as for the police, I didn't waste my breath trying to get them to move. I didn't have the time. New York doesn't have the time."

They both stared at him. "Let me get this straight," Julian said at last. "You put out that warning without JC's permission, and without any reference to the NYPD? Do you have any idea what's going to be happening down there once that message percolates?"

"So, there'll be an upheaval. And the police will just have to step in and sort it out. Just as they should've been doing since this morning. But people will start to leave the city, and that's all that matters. Sorry, gang, to have landed you in it . . ."

"Oh, we're right with you," Jayme said. "But I guess we'd better barricade that door."

"And take the phones off," Julian suggested.

As he spoke, Richard's buzzed. He picked it up. "Connors."

"Oh, Mr. Connors," the switchboard said. "A Mrs. Donnelly called earlier. She wants you to call her back after your late forecast."

"Thank you, Maisie," Richard said. "She'll be out in Bognor, Connecticut. Just a moment." He checked his address book, gave her the number. "Call her there, will you?" He replaced the phone, looked at his staff. "It'll take JC a little longer than that to react, I guess."

Saturday 29 July

Jo realised that she had completely misjudged the rapidity with which the authorities would get to work. But it would still surely take an hour or so for people to react and get on the streets. She was already packed, and the Mercedes was topped up with gas.

She ran into Owen Michael's bedroom, shook him awake. "Get dressed," she said. "Quickly now."

He sat up. "Is it dawn?" he asked incredulously.

"Not quite," Jo told him. "But we're leaving early. I thought we'd surprise Granpa and Granma. Hurry." She went into Tamsin's room, got her up as well.

She returned to the lounge. The carriage clock said twenty-five minutes past twelve. She grabbed three cans of Coke and some cookies from the kitchen, jostled Owen Michael and Tamsin out of the front door, and they crammed into the elevator with their belongings.

When the elevator came to rest in the lobby Washington emerged from the office. He eyed the bags, "You folks going off somewhere, then? It sure is a poor night out there."

"Owen Michael, go on down to the garage and get yourself and Tamsin settled," Jo instructed. "Take those bags."

"I can do that, Mrs. Donnelly," Washington protested.

"You can help me with this big one," Jo said. She watched the children disappear down the stairs. "Didn't you see the latest up-date on the hurricane, Washington?" she whispered. "It's coming straight at us. So I'm taking the children out of town."

"You are? Heck." His breath came through his teeth. "No, I didn't see it. When are they expecting the storm to hit?"

"Maybe tonight, maybe tomorrow morning."

"Oh! Then there's plenty of time." He smiled.

"There isn't," Jo scolded. "Do you know how many people live in Manhattan? Maybe seven million. Can you imagine the traffic jams when

104

they all decide to leave together? Washington, I think you should wake everybody in the building, and tell them to leave. And then leave yourself."

"Oh, I couldn't do that, Mrs. Donnelly," Washington protested. "I couldn't leave anyhow until I was sure the building was evacuated, and I couldn't leave even then. Suppose somebody was to break in?"

"Washington, no one would expect you to sit here throughout a hurricane, surely?"

"I guess I could wake the old lady now and tell her to pack a bag," Washington decided. "You say that storm is coming straight for us?"

"Yes," Jo said. "Straight for us." She ran down the stairs to join the children in the Mercedes.

AT THE NEW YORK Police Department headquarters, Assistant Commissioner McGrath's phone was ringing again, and another message arrived telling of crowds and agitation in the streets.

"Hell!" McGrath took over the phone himself. "Get me the Hurricane Center. I want to speak to Eisener. Sure I know what time it is. Get him on the line." He replaced the phone. "All of you guys get back to your precincts and put extra men on the streets, we could have a major traffic snarl-up. And somebody find out who started this alarm."

"It was a television broadcast," said Captain Luther, who had just returned from checking with the duty officer. "That forecaster from NABS, Connors, went on the air just before midnight and issued a warning that Hurricane Faith is coming straight at us."

"Holy mackerel, why wasn't I told at once?" McGrath bawled. "That crazy character . . . He wanted us to plan an evacuation of the city. An evacuation!"

"Well, Connors apparently told everyone to do just that," Luther said. "He predicted all kinds of damage, suggested that the city might just about be blown flat."

"Get the commissioner," McGrath bellowed into the phone. "And the mayor. Sure, wake them up, if you have to. We could have a problem." He grabbed his other phone as it buzzed. "Oh, Dr. Eisener, John McGrath, NYPD, here. . . . Say, about this Faith thing . . . You mean that fellow Connors could be right? . . . Twenty-four hours is right? . . . maybe less? Ah . . . yeah . . . yeah, that's what's bugging us. I mean, they always have veered before . . . yeah . . . yeah, sure, we can handle it . . . yeah . . . Thanks a million, Dr. Eisener. Keep us posted." He replaced the phone. "Seems that thing *could* hit us."

"Could?" Luther enquired. "Or will?"

"Well, Eisener says it could still do anything, and he thinks Connors did the right thing. Well, hell, I sure don't agree with him."

"J. Calthrop White," Luther said. "He owns NABS. He'll have put Connors up to it. He has a running war going with City Hall anyway."

"I wouldn't mind locking that bastard up as well," McGrath growled He banged on the telephone. "Come on, come on, get me those numbers."

"Well, they're all asleep, Mr. McGrath," the girl protested.

"So wake them up. And come to think of it, wake J. Calthrop White up as well."

JO STARTED THE ENGINE, punched the red button on the wall in the underground garage, waited for the steel doors to go up—and remembered Marcia! She had completely forgotten to call her again. But she couldn't abandon her sister-in-law down in Greenwich Village, which was definitely liable to be flooded. Anyway, at this hour of the morning it would only take them ten minutes to drive down and pick up her and Benny.

Though she knew the weather had been deteriorating all evening, she was unprepared for the density of the rain that hit the automobile as she topped the ramp onto the street. And there were far more vehicles about than she had expected—it took her several minutes to edge into the stream.

"Mom, this is terrible. Can't we wait till it clears?"

"I'm freezing," Tamsin put in.

Jo flicked on both heater and demister, leaning forward to peer through the dazzle set up by the lights of the oncoming traffic.

The combination of rain, traffic and repeated red lights stretched the journey to Benny and Marcia's apartment into twenty minutes, and one glance at where they always kept their car told Jo that they weren't in.

The dashboard clock showed 1.25 a.m. They could of course still be out at their party. Equally, they could have seen Richard's telecast and already left. Jo stopped the car and got out. "I'm going to try ringing for a minute, just in case they're in after all," she told the children. She was soaked by the time she had satisfied herself that the house was empty and hurried back to the Mercedes. She was still anxious about the young couple, but she couldn't risk waiting for their return. Traffic was building up all the time.

Progress north slowed as the traffic steadily grew worse, with much shouting and swearing and honking on horns to suggest that quite a few New Yorkers had heard Richard's warning and decided to act on it. But she made steady progress uphill round the Pan-Am Building, and passed 47th Street, 48th—their own apartment block. 49th Street . . . "How long will it take to get to Bognor, Mom?" Owen Michael asked. "I've never seen the streets so busy."

"Everyone's going away for the weekend," Jo agreed. "I thought we'd be halfway there by now." The lights changed, and she braked, drawing up slowly behind a white Chevrolet which inched forward in anticipation of the change back and then leaped into gear immediately on amber. Jo followed . . . and yelled as a blue Cadillac, racing to beat the lights which had already turned against it, smashed into the Mercedes's front wing, sending it spinning into the car on their left.

Tamsin screamed as another automobile hit the Mercedes from behind, throwing it at right angles to the street. Jo shook her head, realising that she was not actually hurt, and looked at Owen Michael. If that bump had opened his stitches . . . He managed a smile. "I'm OK, Mom."

She opened her door and got out into the rain. "You stupid idiot," she bawled at the driver of the Cadillac.

He ignored her, wrenched his automobile round, tearing off some of her wing as he did so, and joined the traffic hurrying away from the lights.

"Bastard," Jo muttered, so angry she forgot to take his number, and bent to look at the damage. The right wing was pushed hard in against the wheel, and she doubted if it would turn without tearing the rubber to shreds. She needed a garage. And now the cacophony of horns and shouting drivers around her was tremendous.

"Get that wreck off the road," someone shouted.

"Yeah, lady, you're blocking the road," shouted someone else.

"How can I move the thing?" she shouted back. "I need a tow."

"Then let us help you," someone else bawled.

Before she could stop them, four men leaped from their vehicles and ran to the Mercedes. They put their shoulders to the body and began to heave, cheered on by their passengers and immediately joined by several more frustrated drivers.

"Stop that!" Jo screamed. "My children are in there!" She grabbed at their shoulders, but they shrugged her off, and she slipped and fell on the wet street, only just being missed by an automobile in the next lane, which swerved round her and slithered away down the avenue.

Jo scrambled to her feet and ran to the Mercedes, which had been pushed onto the central reservation. She pulled the door open, and Owen Michael and Tamsin tumbled out. "Are you all right?"

Tamsin threw both arms round her.

"Yeah," Owen Michael said. "Yeah. But what's got into these people?"

Jo hugged him too, and looked past him at the Mercedes. The men ran away from it, shouting and laughing. As Jo watched them drive off, she saw a police officer making his way towards her, water dripping from his cap and cape. "Did you see those men wreck my car?" she shouted.

"Yeah," he agreed. "These people sure are in a hurry."

"Well, aren't you going to do something about it?"

"Me, lady? I'd need the goddamned National Guard to stop this bunch. They're scared stiff."

"But my auto . . . You have a radio. Can't you call for a tow truck?"

He peered at the twisted metal. "It sure is a wreck. Calling a garage wouldn't do any good; they'd never get here. That vehicle ain't going anywhere tonight, lady. I reckon you have to get hold of something else if you mean to leave town."

Jo stared at him in disbelief, then at the Mercedes, then again at the traffic streaming by. At that moment she hated everyone in the world. But she knew there was Michael's Cadillac waiting in the garage only a few blocks behind her. "Thanks for your advice, officer," she said.

She wrestled the boot open, selected a suitcase—she knew she could only carry one—locked the boot again, told the boy to hold his sister's hand, and walked away through the rain.

RICHARD LOOKED DOWN at the street below. All New York was now a constant ribbon of light, and the traffic was steadily growing. It was going to be a grim dawn, with darting lightning flashes serrating the gloom, accompanied by a rumble of thunder and a succession of rain squalls. Faith was coming closer. The phone buzzed and he grabbed it.

"I have Bognor on the line, Mr. Connors."

"Hello," he said, "Mr. Donnelly?"

"Speaking," said the gruff voice. "Who the hell is that?"

"Richard Connors. I'd like to speak to Jo, please."

"To Jo? At one o'clock in the morning? Anyway, she ain't here."

Richard frowned. "But . . . aren't you expecting her?"

"Sure. Tomorrow morning. This morning, for God's sake. For breakfast! Now get off the line. You've woken up the whole goddamned house."

The phone went dead, and Richard slowly replaced it. What the devil could have happened? He picked it up again. "Call Mrs. Donnelly's Park Avenue number, please, Maisie."

"Right away, Mr. Connors." She was back in five minutes. "There's no reply, Mr. Connors. I spoke with the night porter, and he said Mrs. Donnelly and her children left the building by automobile, just after midnight."

"Thank God for that," Richard said. Just after midnight—leaving immediately after the telecast they'd have beaten the traffic build-up. She was safe, and in another hour and a half she'd be in Bognor, well away from anything more than a strong breeze: he could concentrate on the job.

The phone buzzed again. "Mr. White for you, Mr. Connors," Maisie said.

"Oh, God," he muttered, and waggled his eyebrows at Julian, who was trying to get through to the Hurricane Center. How the hell had JC got in on the act so early? "Good morning, JC," he said. "Well, it isn't such a good morning after all, is it?"

"Richard," JC said. "I have just been called by Assistant Commissione

108

McGrath, enquiring if I had authorised my station to put out an emergency warning for the evacuation of New York City. Has such a warning been issued by NABS?"

"Yes, Mr. White. I made the telecast, sir."

"On whose authority did you do that, Richard?"

"I convinced the programme controller that it was necessary to interrupt transmission. He wanted to call Mr. Kiley, but I told him I had your authority. I take full responsibility, sir."

"You do." JC did not raise his voice. "You acted on your own initiative despite an express directive from me to the contrary?"

"I felt it to be necessary, sir, in view of the direction Hurricane Faith is now taking."

"Richard, has it occurred to you that the National American Broadcasting Service may well have to face severe censure—and withdrawal of advertising revenue as a consequence—for what you have done? You have deliberately created a panic situation without any justification."

"I disagree, Mr. White. I think I have every justification. In fact, I think the service had a responsibility, in view of the facts."

"Richard, your employment is terminated as of this moment. I would like you to clear your desk and be off the studio premises by seven o'clock this morning, or you will be charged with trespass." The phone went dead.

Richard looked at it, then at Julian, then at Jayme. "I have just been fired," he said.

"Oh. Ah . . . I'll make some coffee," Jayme offered.

"Silly old bastard," Julian grunted. "So what are you going to do?"

"Stay right here until this thing is over. He says he'll charge me with trespass if I'm here after seven. So let him."

The phone buzzed.

"If that's him," Richard said, "you'd better say you're in charge."

"Yeah," Julian said, uncertainly, and picked it up. "Summers. Oh, hi. Yes, he's here." He handed it over. "The Hurricane Center."

Richard grabbed a pad and pencil and wrote, then frowned. "Hold on, Mark, old buddy, that can't be right. We got a ten o'clock update which placed her two hundred and eighty miles southeast of us. This makes her only two hundred and forty. Faith has moved forty miles in two hours?"

He listened. "But that means she'll be with us . . . my God, at two o'clock this afternoon!"

His frown deepened. "Say that again? One hundred and eighty miles an hour. God Almighty! You ever heard of that before?"

The phone went dead, and the three of them stared at each other. "Tides," Richard snapped. "Jayme—the tide tables." He snatched the booklet from her hand. "High tide eighteen minutes past one this afternoon. And it's a biggie; more than six foot."

109

"You reckon this is the biggest storm in all history?" Jayme asked.

"I don't know," Richard said. "But I reckon that we need a new category to describe it: Category Six!"

MARCIA YAWNED. "Jeez, I can hardly keep my eyes open. Where are we?" She peered through the steamed-up windscreen at the deluge outside the automobile, half blinded by the oncoming headlights. "What the hell's going on, Benny? Will you just look at all this crowd? What time is it?"

"Not two yet."

"Seems like Kitty's wasn't the only party. I'm never going to be able to get out of bed in the morning. And I'd so wanted to finish the paintwork in the lounge. It's looking pretty good, don't you think?"

"Great," Benny replied absent-mindedly. He was feeling grouchy. They had planned to leave the party early, but all the late arrivals had jammed their auto in tight and they hadn't been able to get away.

It was 2.15 when they rolled up onto the concrete parking space, and by the time they had unlocked the front door they were drenched to the skin, while thunder and lightning crashed and flashed around their heads.

"Phew, this is some storm. Must be an offshoot of the hurricane that hit your folks' place in the Bahamas, you know."

"I know," Marcia said, for a moment almost sober. Taking Belle out to Bognor had been the most traumatic experience of her life, and of course they were all still mourning poor Lawson . . . But heck, life had to go on.

Benny bolted the door on the inside, leaned against it, and yawned. "What say we take the phone off the hook and sleep in, huh?"

"OK," Marcia giggled and rubbed her wet face against his. "Come on, let's take just one look before we go up." She pulled his arm towards the lounge door. Together they stood, admiring their handiwork—the fresh wallpaper, the new white paint on door and window frames, and the alcove of shelves by the fireplace. "Whee! Isn't it exciting?" Marcia hugged Benny's arm. "It's the best looking lounge in the Village." Suddenly Marcia shivered. "Let's get out of these wet things. Either I'm catching my death of cold, or a goose just walked over my grave."

"KILEY?" ASKED J. Calthrop White. "Is that you, Kiley?"

"For God's sake . . . Oh, good morning, JC. Kind of early."

"Kiley, what the hell have you been doing?"

"I've been sleeping, JC. It's two o'clock in the morning."

"Haven't you been watching television?"

"JC, I never watch television once I get home."

"Well, let me tell you that New York is running wild. It's all the fault of that protégé of yours, Connors. I've told him to quit."

"You what? JC, I do the hiring and firing." Outrage at being awakened had given Kiley unusual courage.

110

"Well, you weren't there, were you? But that's not relevant. Listen to me, Kiley: that guy may just for once have hit the nail on the head. Seems this storm could hit New York after all. Now Kiley, did our franchise bid and the bank guarantee go off to the UK?"

"Well, no, JC. You told me specifically it was to go on Monday. Don't worry, JC, it'll be faxed out at six o'clock Monday morning. Bids close noon UK time, so it'll be there spot on."

"Kiley, what happens if there are no electrics on Monday morning? According to Connors, this storm could cause a two-day breakdown. That could mess us up. Kiley, I want you to get down to the office right away and put in that bid."

Kiley hesitated, then sighed. "OK, JC. But all bids have to be supported by bank guarantees. The bank was going to fax that on Monday as well."

"Well, they'll have to do it today."

"Saturday?"

"Get them moving. Get someone down there to do it. Come to think of it, I want *all* our funds moved out, Kiley. Personal accounts too. Get them off some place inland."

"JC, nothing can possibly happen to Wall Street."

"Yeah? It's kind of low down, right? Again, if Connors is right it could get flooded."

"JC, the computers with your accounts in them are in the vaults. Nothing can get into those vaults."

"Kiley, those vaults are underground. I want my money out of there, this morning. Now get onto it."

JO AND THE CHILDREN staggered through the glass doors into the lobby of the apartment block. It had been a dreadful walk back through the rain and the blustery wind and she was exhausted from carrying the heavy suitcase. The children were pretty weary as well, but at least they had had six hours' sleep before setting off. Now, they were all soaked to the skin, and they would have to change into dry clothes before trying again with Michael's Cadillac.

Washington's office was empty when Jo hurried Owen Michael and Tamsin to the elevator. "Say, Mom, is this Hurricane Faith?" Owen Michael asked.

"Naw," Tamsin declared, before Jo could reply. "Faith was much worse than this."

"How much worse?"

"Oh . . ." and suddenly she began to cry. She was really scared, as well as wet and miserable.

"Faith isn't going to hurt you here, darling," Jo promised her. The elevator stopped, and they ran into the apartment. "You two change while I get the car keys."

112

But the keys weren't in Michael's desk, their usual resting place. She hunted through every pocket in his closet and every drawer in the apartment.

"They must be in the pants he was wearing when he left," Owen Michael said logically, emerging from his room in dry clothes. "We'll call a cab," she said, trying to appear calm and unflustered. She flicked rapidly through the yellow pages—but either the lines were busy or just not answering. She punched over and over at the same numbers, until at last there was a reply. Hastily she gasped her request.

"Sorry, lady, but there won't be nothing available for at least two hours. If you'd like to leave your number we'll get back to you."

"Forget it," she said. Two hours! Already the wind was howling outside the plate glass window. She looked down into the street as she waited. The rain had eased temporarily, but the lightning still flashed, and the thunder was continuous, mingling with the whine of the wind. The traffic was worse than when they had come in. She was totally shattered, emotionally and physically. She did not think she had ever been so frightened in her life.

She had to get out. She had to find those keys.

Owen Michael followed his mother from room to room, watching as she emptied drawers and fished through pockets. She dialled the cab company again, but got only the engaged tone. She wanted to weep with frustration.

"Mom, we're obviously going to be here for a while," Owen Michael said. "Why don't we go back to bed for a couple of hours? We'll make a move when it's daylight."

Jo hesitated. But bed, if only for an hour, was what she wanted more than anything else in the world. If she could just put her head down for even five minutes, she'd probably be able to remember where the keys were. Just five minutes. And by then the traffic would have eased. The storm wasn't going to hit before tomorrow morning. There was still ample time to get out of town.

THE HELICOPTER DROPPED out of the dawn murk, swirling in the near gale-force gusts as it slowly settled onto the grass. Waiting staff tried to shout information to Mayor Bill Naseby as he jumped from the cabin, but he shook his head and ran towards the building: talking out there was a waste of time. He entered his office and sat behind his desk. Police Commissioner Grundy and Assistant Commissioner McGrath were already waiting. Water ran down his neck into his pullover. He was a big man, and when sufficiently roused, he could look formidable. He was certainly roused this morning. He pointed. "I've spoken with the governor, and he's turning out the National Guard. Tom . . ." He turned to Grundy. "We have to have every man on the streets. Do you know what's going on out there?"

"It's a solid traffic jam the length and breadth of the city," Grundy confessed. "Heck, Bill, there's nothing we can do without bulldozers."

"It's all the fault of that guy Connors," growled Assistant Commissioner McGrath. "When I lay hands on that idiot I am going to . . ."

"You'd better shake his hand and say, well done, boy, at least you tried to help," Naseby pointed out. "Because that's what he did. Which is more than any of us, including myself, have done so far."

McGrath scratched his head.

"Maybe he didn't go about it the right way," the mayor continued, "but at least he knew something had to be done. And Dr. Eisener from the Hurricane Center at Coral Gables confirms that it is going to be every bit as bad as Connors has claimed. He's just had a radio report from a navy plane flying into the eye, and there are gusts of over two hundred. You got that? *Two hundred* miles an hour. That storm is going to hit this city with the effect of an atomic explosion. And the eye could reach the mainland at two o'clock this afternoon. That means we are going to have hurricane force winds here in a couple of hours, and the sea is going to start to rise around nine o'clock this morning. And you know something else? The tide is going to start rising around then too."

The policemen exchanged glances; they had never seen the mayor so agitated.

"Now, you guys, listen to me," Naseby went on. "I'm trying to persuade the Governor to declare New York a disaster area and put in martial law, right now. He's worried about doing this, because it's before the event, so to speak, so he's checking with his legal department. However, he has agreed to mobilise the National Guard. So Tom, you and your men are going to move straight in and clear those streets. Otherwise we could be looking at a massacre. Use bulldozers if you have to, but get people out of town. Anyone who can't get out by noon at the outside, get them onto high ground."

"The tunnels and bridges are jammed solid," McGrath said gloomily.

"So concentrate on them first. If we get moving right away there will be time. It's the lower levels that have to be got out first. By my reckoning that includes Penn Station, Madison Square Garden, Greenwich Village, SoHo, Little Italy, and of course, Wall Street."

"You really think that'll happen, Bill?" the commissioner asked. "Surely the Narrows . . ."

"I'm told by Dr. Eisener that the Narrows won't keep this dame out," Naseby said. "In fact, they might just act as a funnel and increase the volume to a possible forty-foot tidal wave." The mayor gave a brief grin. "You guys will have noticed, I guess, that right here we'll be well below the mark. And so is the telephone exchange. So we evacuate too, right after we have got every civilian to safety."

"But the files, the records, the computers . . ."

"They go out too, right away. Not the computers, just the disks. I've

114

arranged for a helicopter fleet to lift them out. But no one leaves this building until Manhattan has been made safe."

"Where are we gonna put all these people?" Grundy said.

"Requisition every hotel that's above the fifty-foot mark. And then use Central Park."

"You're gonna send a million people to Central Park in a hurricane?"

"So you tell me when you have any better ideas," Naseby snapped. "We've been caught with our pants down. Now we just have to pull them up as best we can." He glanced at his notepad. "Now, let's get on with it. Kennedy Airport is going to be under water. Keep the planes flying as long as you can, but only out. All incoming flights are to be diverted. And by nine o'clock every last aircraft must have gone, and all personnel evacuated. Same thing for La Guardia: it'll probably be flooded as well."

Two aides hurried in. "They're reporting one-hundred-and-fifty-mile-an-hour winds in Atlantic City," one gasped. "And twenty-foot waves. The Boardwalk is just falling apart."

"There's a guy on the phone from Prospect Park Zoo asking if he should turn the animals loose," said the other.

"Holy Moses! Is he mad?" the commissioner shouted. "That's all we need, a bunch of lions and tigers running down the street."

Naseby sighed. "I'm sorry, Lou, but people have to come before animals. Anyway, Prospect Park is way above the flood line. And why is he calling me? Isn't there anyone awake down in Brooklyn? Now, shipping. All small craft should head up the rivers as far as possible."

"They're doing it," McGrath said. "The Harbour Police report there's nearly as big a crush on the water as on the street."

"The big stuff will have to sit it out," Naseby said.

"Well . . . some of them are already putting to sea. They reckon they have more chance riding it out at sea. They could be right. Those big ships are sitting ducks in harbour. A forty-foot tidal surge pushed by a two-hundred-mile-an-hour wind could just land one of them in Times Square."

"Well . . . we'll have to leave that to the judgment of individual masters." The phone buzzed. "Yes? Oh, Governor, thank God . . . yes, from all reports it's sheer hell out there . . . The President? Oh, that's great . . . OK, we're moving into action, right now." He replaced the phone. "The President has authorised the imposition of martial law; it takes effect at six o'clock. The message is being put out on all TV and radio stations. The National Guard is being assembled now, and the army is being sent in to help. We'll have to sort out the legalities afterwards. Now we have to hustle." He looked at his watch. "Four thirty. Mitch, arrange for me to make a broadcast at six, telling people what we're trying to do. Fix coverage on all networks, and on radio." He pointed at the commissioner and McGrath. "And I want things under control when I go on the air."

THE BEDROOM IN THE CONEY ISLAND hotel faced south, but the buildings opposite blocked out the sea view, even without the rain. Just their luck, Florence Bennett thought, to have weather like this for their annual Coney Island vacation.

"Looks pretty horrible out there," mumbled Bert, her husband. "What're you out of bed for, anyway?"

"The thunder woke me. Thought I'd take a look," Florence replied. "I guess this is a bit of the hurricane that hit the Donnellys' place in the Bahamas a few days ago. I wonder if it'll come up here."

They hadn't looked at television or read a newspaper since coming to Coney Island. Bert's idea of a vacation was to forget the world existed.

"Hurricanes don't come this far north, girl," he pontificated. "They kick off into the Atlantic. Come on back to bed for a cuddle."

"Now then, Bert," his wife scolded. "We can't have any of that first thing in the morning. Emmie's in the next room and the walls in this place are paper-thin."

"So what?"

Florence sighed and started to remove the curling pins from her hair—but there was a smile twitching the corners of her mouth.

"WILL YOU GET ME that Michael Donnelly number in Connecticut again, please, Maisie?" Richard said.

"Of course, Mr. Connors."

Julian had just finished putting out another update; they had a minute or two. Jayme was making coffee. It was difficult to believe that they had been on duty all night without a wink of sleep. Things were happening, officially; a camera crew had been whisked away by helicopter from the NABS roof, over the traffic jams, to enable the mayor to broadcast to his people.

"Bognor, Mr. Connors," Maisie said.

"For God's sake, not you again?" Big Mike complained. "Don't you ever sleep?"

"I wanted to make sure Mrs. Donnelly got to you OK, Mr. Donnelly."

"Look, Connors, she isn't due here until breakfast time. Right?"

"Breakfast time? She left her apartment to drive up to you just after midnight. With your grandchildren."

"The grandchildren? But that's nonsense. It doesn't take five hours to drive from New York to Bognor. Three, maximum."

"Yes," Richard said. "That's what I thought. Something's happened to her."

"Happened to her? You mean a breakdown? In this rain? Say, is it raining in New York?"

"Yes, Mr. Donnelly. It is raining in New York. Look, I'm going to have to leave this one with you. But I'd be very grateful if you'd call me back and let me know what's happened to her."

116

"Yeah," Big Mike said. "Yeah. God! What a mess!"

The phone went dead, and Richard gazed at it. It had to be a simple breakdown. And if it was outside of the city there would be no problem. And anyway there was absolutely nothing he could do about it. Even if he decided to abandon the studio, he wouldn't know where to start looking . . . The door opened and he gazed at Kiley.

A very wet and angry looking Kiley, gazing at him. "What the hell are you doing here?" he demanded. "JC fired you hours ago."

Julian chipped in. "You're kind of early, ain't you, Mr. Kiley?"

"Early!" Kiley exploded. "JC is going wild. I've spent the past three hours trying to get here. God knows if I'll ever see my automobile again. I've had to walk from the bridge. They're jammed solid, all lanes, going north. And I've got to get someone down to the bank to make some transfers. Dear God!" He wandered out, closing the door behind him.

"He doesn't know what time of day it is," Jayme commented.

"I don't think he knows what day it is," Julian said.

"Well, I think he'll soon find out." Richard picked up the phone again.

JO WOKE WITH A START to the jangling of the telephone. It was broad daylight and rain was lashing at the windows. She sat up, gasped as she saw the time on her bedside clock—six o'clock. She pushed hair from her eyes and reached for the phone.

"Jo?" The woman's voice was high.

"Oh, my God! Sally? Sally Davenport? Where are you?"

"I'm at home, Jo," Sally said. Home for Sally Davenport was ten miles outside Newport. There'd be no chaos out there . . . yet.

"Oh. Well . . . any word from the boys?"

"I was going to ask you that. I tried to raise them through the exchange here but they told me they can't handle any personal traffic right now as there's an emergency on. Have you ever heard such damned nonsense?"

"Well," Jo said, "there is a hurricane racing at us . . ."

"For Heaven's sake, Jo. You'd think in this day and age they'd be capable of coping with a hurricane," Sally complained. "Sam was supposed to call me last night; they were going to be back within radio range by then. But he hasn't. Jo, have you heard from them?"

"No. Not since midnight on Thursday. I spoke to Michael about the hurricane and suggested he turn back to Bermuda."

"And was he going to take your advice?"

"No. He said he was standing on. You know what Michael is."

"Good Lord! Aren't you worried?"

"Sally," Jo said impatiently, "of course I'm worried. But Michael was confident he could outsail the storm, and he's probably right. He usually is. Anyway, it's turned away from him. It's virtually on our doorstep down here. I have things to do. I'll call you later." She jumped out of bed,

117

and ran into the lounge, where Owen Michael was watching television.

"Hey, Mom," he called. "The mayor's on."

Jo gazed at Bill Naseby, wearing his electioneering expression—he was famous for his ability to reassure—as he filled the screen.

He seemed to be just finishing. ". . . but I will tell you this: as long as there is one life in danger in this city, I and my staff and your gallant police force will remain at our posts. And as long as there is electricity, keep your radios and televisions tuned in, to keep yourselves informed of the situation. God bless you all."

His face disappeared, and one of the anchormen replaced him. "That was the mayor of New York, William Naseby," he said. "And that telecast will be repeated every hour, on the hour, throughout the morning. And now, at this grave hour, we turn . . ."

Jo switched off the set.

"Hey, Mom, he said to leave it on," Owen Michael protested.

"I know he did. And we can put it on again later. But I have to get through to the studio."

All the studio lines were busy. She went into the bathroom to wash her face, and found only a rusty trickle coming out of the tap. The kitchen was the same. It did not seem possible for the water to have gone off while it was clouding past her windows in what seemed like solid sheets.

She tried the studio again, and heard it ring. "Mr. Connors, please," she gasped. "It really is urgent. My name is Donnelly."

To her amazement, she was through in ten seconds. "Richard!" she shrieked. "Oh, Richard! I've been trying to reach you forever."

"My darling, where are you? Did your father-in-law find you?"

"My father-in-law? I haven't seen him. I'm not in Bognor. I'm right here in the apartment."

"You're *where?*"

Swallowing, she launched into the story of their morning.

"Look, have you food and water?" he said when she had finished.

"We have food," she said. "But there's no water."

"You have nothing to drink at all?"

"Oh, there's plenty to drink. Except water." Just hearing his voice was making her feel normal again.

"OK. Listen . . . there's no way you can leave town now."

"I know that . . . what do we do? I have the children here with me."

"Keep calm, for a start. Move yourself, and everything you have to drink and a good supply of canned food, away from your windows. Into . . . how about the bathroom? Move yourself and Owen Michael and Tamsin in there and sit tight. Expect the electricity to go off sometime this morning. I'm going to try to get to you, the moment I'm of no use here."

"Richard!" she screamed. "You can't. Don't try, please. It'll be too dangerous."

118

"I won't take any chances," he promised. "Just make yourself and the kids safe and sit tight. I'll be there if it's humanly possible."

He rang off. Jo sat with drooping shoulders, staring at the phone.

Owen Michael and Tamsin, who had now woken up too, stood together, gazing at her. "What are we going to do, Mom?" Owen Michael asked.

She returned the boy's smile and squared her shoulders. If only he knew how inadequate she felt. "I guess we have to get ourselves ready to ride out the hurricane, right here. Shouldn't be too much of a problem."

"Heck, no, Mommy," Tamsin said. "I wasn't scared, down in Eleuthera, not until the roof blew off. Then it was so cold and wet and scary. But our roof won't blow off here, will it?"

"Of course it won't," Jo asserted, and stood up. Suddenly she had an almost terrifying feeling of claustrophobia, knowing that they were, so far as she was aware, alone in the huge building.

"What do we do to make ourselves ready?" Owen Michael wanted to know.

"First we decide which bathroom to use as a shelter . . ."

"Tamsin's and my bathroom," the boy interrupted. "There's no window in there to get broken."

"Good thinking." The bathroom the two children shared had only an extractor fan let into the wall of the building. "Let's all go see how we'll manage it." They stood in the bathroom doorway. "Let's fill the vanity cupboard with food, for a start," Jo said.

"How will we cook it in here?" Tamsin wanted to know.

"We won't. Cold soup. Cold ham . . . We can't make coffee because we have no water."

"Hey, Mom, we could make coffee with soda water," Tamsin cried.

Jo raised her eyebrows. "Why not?"

"There's bottles and bottles of soda water in here," Owen Michael shouted, dashing to the bar. "If we take the electric kettle into the bathroom . . ."

"It won't do us much good when the power goes off," Jo told him. "Anything we're going to boil has to be done right now."

"It's going to be pretty boring, sitting in the dark," Owen Michael declared. "I know. I'll get my torch."

"I'm hungry. I'm sure it's breakfast time," Tamsin complained.

"Of course it is," Jo agreed. "Let's make a really good, big meal," she suggested. "We can eat what's left over later, even if it's cold. I'll put some meat in the microwave to thaw."

While the meal was cooking, they hauled two single mattresses into their refuge, together with pillows and blankets. Jo found some fancy candles she used for dinner parties, and soon had the bathroom looking like the inside of a tent. By now, the howling of the wind, the roar of the thunder, the shuddering of the building in the gusts, seemed almost normal.

When they had eaten and cleared up, it was just a matter of waiting. Jo suddenly remembered that in another hour or so she was due at Pinewoods for breakfast. She picked up the phone to call them and tell them she wasn't going to make it, but it seemed all the lines in the New York telephone exchange were busy. She tried Marcia's number as well, and got no reply—though Marcia would surely be in Connecticut by now. Then she busied herself removing pictures, ornaments, everything in fact for which she could find safe storage. Plants and photo albums joined them in the bathroom, along with a precious antique tea service which had belonged to her grandmother.

"Have we got a can opener in there?" Owen Michael asked.

"Yes," she called loudly, to be heard above the storm. But she didn't know where it was, or care, for the moment. She was staring in the bathroom mirror at the fearful apparition of a woman with hair matted into dishevelled points, shoulders drooping under damp crumpled clothes, while from deep, dark shadows, terrified eyes stared back at her.

My God! Is that really me? She swallowed, and took a deep breath. What confidence could the children have, seeing her like that? She pulled out a hairbrush, rushed into the dressing room for a fresh blouse, moistened a tissue in soda water and rubbed it over her face and hands. Forcing a wide smile she said, "Let's see what's on TV."

They sat in silence, half watching some filler programme being relayed between announcements, being promised a full weather update as soon as possible, while the pictures were constantly broken up by discharges of lightning. Suddenly she was reminded of the people she had interviewed about hurricanes. What about Nancy Duval, her hairdresser? She'd have fled at the first suggestion of a storm. Washington had left early, too; she hoped he'd got all his family to safety by now.

She shuddered: Alloan. The memory of that visitation made her skin crawl. Presumably the police would have got him out of the city, along with all prisoners on remand. Ironic, in a way, that he should be saved, while possibly hundreds of decent folk would die.

IN THE MAYOR'S OFFICE Naseby rested his head on his hands for a moment, raised it again as the phone buzzed. "Naseby."

"I have Mr. Hatton from Hunt National Bank, Mr. Mayor," the girl said.

"Put him on. Good morning, Mr. Hatton. Can I help you?"

"Mr. Mayor, we are facing a serious situation."

"I know that, Mr. Hatton." Naseby gazed through his window into City Hall Park and watched the first helicopter trying to lift off, packed to the door with files and computer disks—all the million and one records that are required to operate a city. "We are doing the best we can."

120

"I'm talking about here on Wall Street. We are trying to transfer funds . . . I'm not just speaking of Hunt. I am speaking for all the banks . . ."

"You're transferring funds on a Saturday?"

"Our customers are uneasy about the situation, should this hurricane strike New York. And the wire services, the telephone system, just don't seem able to cope. Everybody must be using the phone at the same time."

"I can believe that, Mr. Hatton. Just like you and me."

"Well, really, something has got to be done about it. And now we are told that Wall Street is liable to be flooded. Perhaps you do not realise, Mr. Mayor, but it is possible that water may penetrate our vaults."

"I do realise, Mr. Hatton."

"Well, then, you will understand that as it is impossible to transfer all our accounts in time, we must move out our computer systems."

"That's a good idea. If it's possible."

"We must be assisted to do so, Mr. Mayor. A road must be cleared for us . . ."

"Forget it, Mr. Hatton. Roads are for people. Use helicopters. That's what we're doing. Charter every chopper you can . . . my God!"

The helicopter was now lifting off. But it was whipped sideways by an enormous gust of wind before it was properly airborne. It rose sharply, but it was still being pushed sideways too fast; its belly brushed a tree, and then another, and then it turned over, plummeting to the ground to burst into flames with a sickening explosion.

"Did you see that?" Mitch, his deputy, shouted, running into the office.

"I saw it," Naseby said. "That's it, Mitch. Send the rest of those guys home. We're just risking brave men."

"But . . ."

"We'll have to think of something else."

Mitch hesitated, then left the office.

"Mr. Mayor? Mr. Mayor?" Hatton asked. "What's happening? What was that noise? Do you know I can see a fire very close to City Hall?"

"I know it, Mr. Hatton," Naseby said. "It means helicopters are out. The wind is just too strong."

"But what are we to do?"

"Organise yourselves a truck convoy. We will do the same, and we'll leave together, under police escort. But Mr. Hatton, no truck leaves until I am satisfied the roads are sufficiently clear of people. They still have priority."

"COME ON, YOU GUYS, I need help with the dishes," Nancy Duval called from the kitchen. As expected, there was no reply—they were all playing deaf as usual, and they knew she expected assistance with breakfast, even on Saturdays: the hairdressing salon opened six days a week, of course. She went to the door and shouted, "I know you can hear me, you lazy bums. It's nearly eight and I'm going to be late for work again."

"Nance, shut up your bawling," Bill called from the lounge. "They've just said the mayor's gonna address the city. It's a repeat of some speech he made earlier this morning."

"What's it to do with you, Bill? You didn't vote for him last time. And I haven't got the time . . ."

"It's not an election speech," he snapped. "It's about evacuating the city. Will you shut up and listen?"

It wasn't like Bill to talk like that! Nancy hurried into the room to see what the fuss was about . . . and slowly her jaw dropped as she gaped in horror, speechless until Mayor Naseby was finished. Then, "For God's sake, let's get out of here," she gasped, untying the strings of her pinafore. "Kids, quick, get your raincoats."

"Just hold on a minute," Bill suggested. "Let's just talk about it for a moment. There's your job . . ."

"Talk? Don't be a nut. We'll talk about it when we're in Yonkers. As for my job, my job can go . . ."

The phone bleeped, and Bill reached it first. "Yeah? . . . oh, hi, Ernie. What's up? . . . Yeah, we were just watching it. What are you and Marge gonna do?" There was a long pause during which Bill's face grew longer and more serious. "OK," he said at last. "That sounds best. Let me check with Nance." He turned to his wife. "Ern says the streets are jammed and do we want to go upriver with him and Marge on the *Glory of Liberty*? It'll mean walking down across Eleventh but he's got her moored at the end of the fifty-fourth deck, so it won't be too far."

Ernest, Bill's brother, was mate on one of the pleasure boats which toured the harbour.

"But where'll we go on her?" The blonde curls were shaking with fright. "What'll we do for wheels when we get ashore? I'll bet that river's real nasty already and the storm's not due here till this afternoon. That poor old tub can't take rough weather. She'll sink." She remembered a Sunday afternoon trip on it last year, the way the bulkheads creaked and groaned as the boat nosed the current back up to her berth.

"The *Glory*'s got to be a better bet than the streets," Bill said. "Come on, if you're worried about staying . . ."

"Worried?" Her eyes filled with tears. "Of course I'm worried, Bill. I'm shit scared. We gotta get out, quick."

"Then grab your coat, sweetheart, throw some clothes in a bag, and get the kids moving. I'll lock up."

The three children soon reappeared and the young family set out, heading for the Hudson River.

"HERE'S THE EIGHT-THIRTY A.M. update from the Hurricane Center," Julian said, pulling the sheet of paper out of the teleprinter and handing it across the desk.

Richard looked at it. Faith was still nearly 120 miles away, but was now holding an absolutely steady course and speed, northwest at 20 knots. There could no longer be any question in anyone's mind that they were on the edge of a catastrophe. Even the double-glazed windows in the office were buckling. Richard would have liked to evacuate the weather room, but it was their duty to send out the news for as long as there was power, and it would be impossible to move and re-site all the computer equipment in other windowless studios.

He stood looking down into the streets, still clogged with vehicles, now mostly abandoned by their drivers. Scattered round the vehicles, or on top of them, was all manner of debris, from shattered billboards to television aerials and the branches of trees.

The lights flickered, went off, and came back on again.

"What the hell . . . ?" Julian demanded, staring in outrage at his computer screen, which had promptly returned to the "please wait" display.

"Power outages," Jayme announced, returning from down the corridor, where she had taken a copy of the weather update to their producer, Hal Waring. "Seems it's pooping out all over the place. Greenwich Village is blacked out."

"The whole lot is going to go before long," Richard warned. "There doesn't seem too much point in us all staying here. Why don't you try to get home, Julian?" Julian lived in the city, and well above the 50-foot mark. "Take Jayme with you."

"And you? Who's going to do the next update?" Julian demanded.

"I'll do it." Richard grinned. "I shouldn't think JC will be watching. And if he is, there's damn all he can do about it now." He could, and should, of course, leave the updates to Julian and get out himself, and get to Jo while he could. But this hurricane was his baby, the one he had foretold, and he wanted to be involved with it for as long as he could, which meant for as long as there was power.

Jayme and Julian looked at each other. "We'll stay, too," the girl decided. "Heck, I don't really want to go out into that; it was bad enough this morning."

"OK," Richard agreed. "Just remember that the time is going to come when you won't be able to go, even if you want to."

"So we'll set up house for the duration."

"Here's your spiel." Julian tore the sheet of paper from the print-out and placed it on Richard's desk. "Not a lot to add, really. Just—"

"God Almighty!" Jayme screamed. She had just glanced at the window. A television aerial, swept off the roof of one of the neighbouring buildings, was coming straight for them.

"Down," Richard shouted, and hurled himself across the desk at the girl, sweeping her to the floor, skidding round Julian's desk as he did so. The noise of shattering glass was enormous. The wind made the room

123

seem to swirl around them, papers, pens, computer screens, even chairs being lifted into the air. The TV monitor crashed to the floor and broke into flying splinters. Richard had to force Jayme and himself into the knee well of the desk to stop them being lifted too, but even the desk was moving, being swept across the floor, and the wind was searing through the open door and down the corridor, bringing screams of alarm from other offices.

"Get through the door," Richard yelled into Jayme's ear, and shoved her towards it. She tried to crawl, her shoes coming off, the wind inflating her trouser legs as a fresh gust sent furniture again whirling round the room. She screamed in sheer horror as the front of her white shirt inexplicably became covered in blood.

Richard and she went rolling over and over, through the doorway, helped by the wind. Men were running up the corridor, being checked by the enormous force thrusting at them, but grouping together in an attempt to push the door shut.

"Julian!" Jayme moaned. "Julian! He's still in there!"

Richard dragged her to her feet against the wall and hastily checked that the blood was not hers: she was actually unhurt except for scratches and bruises. He shouted at the men to wait, hurled himself back into the stricken office. Two others came with him and they seized Julian's arms and pulled him out through the door. Then the door was slammed shut, and he knelt beside the injured man. His heart seemed to miss a beat: Julian's throat had been cut by a jagged piece of flying glass, and he was already dead.

"WHAT?" J. CALTHROP WHITE shouted into the telephone. "What? The building damaged? How the hell? . . . A window? . . . Who the hell was the moron opened the window? . . . Blown in? . . . Whose fault was that? I want to know, by God . . . Julian Summers? Dead? Look, Kiley, what was Connors doing giving the latest update? I fired that man myself, this morning. And Kiley, has that fax gone off to London? And the transfer been made? . . . Now you look here, Kiley, I don't give a goddamn if everyone else in New York wants his money out, I want ours out, now. You tell Hatton that if he doesn't get moving he's lost my business. You tell . . ." He broke off, stared at the phone for several seconds, then raised his head to look at his wife, his English butler and his chef, who had all gathered in the hall of his Long Island mansion. "He's hung up. The bastard has hung up on me."

"James, do remember your blood pressure," his wife cautioned.

"Ahem," remarked the butler. "It is possible, sir, that the telephones have ceased to operate."

JC stared at him. "My God . . . you could be right. Where the hell is Murray?"

"Here, sir." The uniformed chauffeur, also English, had just come in.

124

"Get out the Rolls. I'm going into town. That goddamned station is falling apart."

"Now, sir?" Murray cocked his head. Even on Long Island the wind was howling and the trees in the garden were lashing back and forth.

"Now, you idiot. I need to get things under control down there."

"James," remonstrated his wife, "I think it will be a very tiresome drive, especially if the reports of traffic tailbacks are true."

"It could possibly be dangerous," the butler suggested.

"In the Rolls? For God's sake, that thing is built to last . . . I may not be back for lunch, dear. Don't wait for me; I'll grab something from the canteen." He pointed at the butler. "You're in charge should this wind get up."

The butler bowed. "Of course, Mr. White."

THE ROLLS-ROYCE slithered sideways across the road.

"What the devil is the matter with the car?" J. Calthrop White demanded.

"It's the wind, Mr. White. It really is getting strong. I wonder if we shouldn't turn back?"

"Turn back? Don't give me any bullshit, Murray. Put your foot down." Murray sighed, and rounded a corner, both hands tight on the wheel. At least there were no other vehicles around—everyone else had more sense than even to open a garage door in this weather.

The automobile slithered again. He got it straight, then lost it again when by far the strongest gust so far hit the high body. "Hell!" Murray gasped, and spun the wheel, but the Rolls still continued to move sideways.

"What the devil . . ." shouted JC. But the Rolls was already off the road, sliding down the parapet, to come to rest in a muddy ditch.

"Sorry, Mr. White, I just lost her," Murray said. The engine was still running, and he put the car in low gear and revved, but there was merely an enormous upheaval of mud and a grinding noise. "I think she's stuck."

"So do I, Murray. So I suggest you go and raise some help."

"I don't think I can walk against that wind, Mr. White."

"Do what you can, Murray!" JC's voice was quiet. "Do what you can."

Murray sighed, and opened the door.

THE TREMENDOUS BANGING on the downstairs door in the Coney Island hotel made Florence sit up. It had been so lovely, lying in bed all morning with Bert, dozing off and waking up again to listen to the howl of the wind, the distant booming of the seas on the beach.

Eventually she had got up and fetched coffee from the vending machine in the corridor, then she had gone back to bed and they had slept again, in each other's arms. At some stage her sister Emmie had banged on the bedroom door, and gone on banging for quite a while. But then they had been left alone until this much more insistent banging . . . which was now interrupted by the sound of shattering glass.

"What the hell . . ." Bert had heard it too, and jumped out of bed. "Somebody's breaking in!" He nearly lost his balance as the building shook, but he wrapped a towel round his waist and unlocked the bedroom door, to be driven back by the blast of air which came gushing into the room. "Shut that street door," he bawled down the stairwell: the little hotel, set well back from the beach front, was a walkup.

"Hey, who's there?" came back a shout. "Your name Bert Bennett?"

"Yeah. So what?"

"Your sister-in-law sent us down. She thought you'd left with everybody else, but when we got to counting heads up at Prospect . . . say, you guys deaf, or what? You didn't hear everyone else leaving?"

Florence had got out of bed as well and, wrapped in a dressing gown, stood at her husband's shoulder, gazing down the stairs at the patrolman. His cape and hat were glistening wet and the surf sounded very close, closer than she had ever heard it, almost drowning out the whine of the wind. Suddenly she was gripped by a deathly fear.

"You mean . . . everybody's gone?" Bert was asking in bewilderment. "This place was full."

"All of Coney Island was evacuated two hours ago," the patrolman told him. "Hell, you guys must've been stoned or something. Come on, we have to get the hell out of here."

"I'll just get dressed," Florence said.

"Lady," the patrolman said, "you're gonna have half the Atlantic Ocean inside that bedroom with you in half an hour. You coming now, or not? Because I sure as hell am leaving now, and I ain't coming back."

Florence looked at Bert, and they ran down the stairs together. Already several inches of water were pouring over the street, while at the intersection, even as they watched, a wave came down the alleyway, sweeping before it a collection of shattered deck chairs, plastic bottles and boxes, discarded sunhats and shoes.

"The beach . . . ?" Bert asked.

"The beach ain't there anymore," the patrolman said. He urged them on and they splashed round the corner, away from the sea, to where a patrol car was parked. Inside was another officer, using his radio. He stared at them in amazement. "What the hell . . . ?"

"That dame was right," his partner told him. "Would you believe it, Charlie? These two were in bed. In bed!" He opened the rear door and bundled them inside.

"Well, they have to be the last," Charlie said. "We're under orders to get out of here and rendezvous with the others at Prospect Park."

"Prospect?" Bert asked. "Say, we have to get home. We need clothes."

Charles gunned the motor and turned the patrol car; water was swirling round its axles. "Home being where?"

126

"We live in the Bronx," Florence told him.

"Well, you can forget that," the patrolman told her. "All the bridges and tunnels are closed. They're setting up an emergency centre at Prospect Park. They'll take care of . . . oh, for God's sake, Charlie!"

The patrol car had slowed through a larger surge of water coming down the street, and the engine coughed and died.

"Damn it!" Charlie opened his door and got out, throwing up the bonnet. He was knee-deep in water. The rain was falling so heavily there was no chance of his engine drying out in a hurry.

"We're gonna have to walk it," the patrolman said.

"In this?" Florence asked.

"Like this?" Bert put in.

The patrolman grinned. "Maybe you're better off than us, at that. Let's go." He opened the door for them, and they splashed out.

"I can't," Florence protested. "I'm freezing."

"Lady," the patrolman said, "look." He pointed. "That row of houses over there is all that's standing between us and the whole goddamned ocean. You reckon . . . oh, my God!"

Even as they looked, the houses in front of them started to collapse, windows and doors flying out before the impact of the sea.

"YEAH," SAID ASSISTANT COMMISSIONER McGrath into his radio. "Yeah. . . . Yeah . . . OK, that's it. You guys pull out." He put the handset down and looked at his waiting officers. "The tide's surging right over the Battery and starting to flood down Broadway. I've told them down there to get out while they can, and it's time we did the same. And the mayor." He picked up the radio handset again. "City Hall, City Hall, NYPD here."

"City Hall."

"The mayor about, Mitch?"

"Right here."

"Naseby speaking, McGrath, what's happening now?"

"This is it, Mr. Mayor. The Battery's gone. Water's on Broadway. That means it's only nine blocks from us. I guess we have to get out of here."

"Is the evacuation complete?"

"Well, I guess not. We're doing the best we can, but you know what these folks are like, especially the older ones. Some of them don't even answer the door, and I just don't have the men to go through every apartment building. Mr. Mayor, I want you to pull your people out."

"I promised . . ."

"Sure you did. But this city is going to need you to put it back together again when this storm is finished; you can't do that if you're dead, now can you?"

Naseby hesitated, then sighed. "OK, McGrath, I guess you're right.

127

Evacuate now. We'll do the same. Is your mobile headquarters set up?"

"Yeah, at the Plaza Hotel. We have an emergency generator up there."

"OK. Keep in touch. Let's move."

McGrath replaced the handset, crammed the last mouthful of his sandwich down his throat, swallowed, stood up. "Everybody out. Those files ready?"

Captain Luther nodded.

"OK, don't forget the cells, now. Captain Harmon mustn't let any of the bastards in custody drown. Throw them out if you have to. Let's move it now, boys, or we are going to get our feet wet. I'm going up to the chief."

Chief Grundy stood at his office window, watching the streets. "My God!" he remarked. "Look at that rain; it's coming at us horizontal."

"It's gonna be salt water in five minutes," McGrath told him. "Naseby says out. So let's go."

They put on their hats and coats, headed down the stairs; the elevator had ceased functioning when the electrics had gone. Their desks had already been cleared and everything loaded into the waiting fleet of vans.

On the headquarters ground floor, Chief Grundy stamped his feet impatiently as he watched a trickle of water come in at the door and across the lobby. "Where the hell is Harmon?" he bawled.

"Those guys down there don't want to come out," Captain Harmon called up to him from the remand cells. "They reckon they're safer down there."

"Are they nuts?" Grundy himself ran down to the lower level. The cell doors were wide open, and the remand prisoners were free to leave—indeed, they were being implored to do so, but none of them looked anxious to take advantage of the offer. "For God's sake," Grundy bellowed. "Use force, Harmon. Throw them out."

Harmon turned to the policeman with him. "You heard the chief," he said. "Get those guys out."

Stuart Alloan scrambled onto his bed, dragging Domingo Garcia with him; he reckoned staying close to the new tough friend he had made in jail was his safest course.

"You trying to drown us?" Garcia yelled. He was a little man, but he had a loud voice. "Leave us right here where it's safe, you . . ." His voice trailed away as he stared at the stairs. Grundy and Harmon turned together, to watch a four-foot-high wall of water rushing towards them.

WHEN THE PHONE went dead at around 11.15 a.m., Jo decided it was time to take shelter in the kids' bathroom. Just before, she had tried calling Marcia and Benny, only to find that all communication with Greenwich Village was cut—and then Connecticut, and finally Richard, but with no more success. At least she was able to see his face on TV

128

from time to time. Amazingly, the windows in the apartment were holding—the plate glass in the lounge faced away from the worst of the storm—but judging by the noise outside, and the heavy debris she could see flying past the apartment block, she didn't reckon they would stand up to much more. So she herded Owen Michael and Tamsin into the bathroom, bolted the door, and they sat together on the mattresses, drinking hot soup out of mugs.

"I don't think I could eat a burger as well, Mom." Tamsin eyed the meal that Jo had hastily prepared while the electricity lasted.

"Do try, sweetheart. It may be a long time before I'll be able to cook again." She could see that both the children were frightened, each determined not to reveal it to the other.

"I wonder where Dad is now?" Owen Michael said.

"Probably in sight of Newport," Jo told him. "Having the time of his life."

"I wish I was with him."

"Well, I wish you and Tamsin were with Granpa and Granma."

"And you too, Mom," Tamsin added.

Jo wasn't sure how to reply. She still wanted to be near Richard, even though the thought that he might try to reach her was terrifying.

Oh, no, my darling Richard, don't do it, she prayed silently. Nobody could get through this storm now.

But all the same, she was constantly straining to hear his voice above the din, imagining that each unidentifiable crash or bang was his knock on the door.

ALLOAN HALF RAN, half fell, dragging Garcia behind him, the two men carried along on the wind from alleyway to recessed doorway, falling against each other in the scant shelter as they tried to catch their breath. It was difficult to find protection anywhere, even in the cavern-like New York streets: apart from the driving rain and continuous thunder, the air was full of flying debris. It was a miracle the two young men had survived this long, and had not been cut by hurtling glass or crushed by the automobiles which were being picked up and thrown through the air; they had sidestepped a number of casualties, ignoring their pleas for help; they had crawled through giant tangles of fallen trees and torn power lines—if the electricity hadn't failed they'd have been fried to a crisp. Garcia was a helluva burden, pleading exhaustion and having to be hauled to his feet each time he fell. If he hadn't known that Garcia was an expert locksmith he would have abandoned him long ago; but to achieve his goal he might well need the man. He was not only driven by fear of the rising water behind him, but by anger—and an all-consuming desire.

Garcia had no idea why they were still together. In a way he wished they weren't, that he could be left in a doorway to rest his aching limbs.

But as the kid had got them out of the cells, fighting a way up the stairway through cascades of water and people screaming, gasping and being trampled underfoot to drown, subconsciously he felt obliged to force himself to keep going. He didn't know where, but the kid had some place in mind.

Alloan looked at Garcia, at the heaving chest and tinge of blue round his mouth. Might be wiser to show a bit more patience, he didn't want this character passing out on him. It was fairly sheltered just here and the storm would continue for hours yet. "OK, Domingo. We'll rest up here a while. That's it," he nodded as Garcia slid gratefully down the wall and leaned his head back, "you have yourself a rest."

THERE WAS STILL electricity at Penn Station, where they were using emergency generators. Washington Jones was told there were no more trains running north, but that he could take the cross line, under the East River, to Lorimer. He held Celestine's hand, carrying two suitcases in the other, and Patsy ran behind him, the baby in her arms. They had become part of a terrified mob of people trying to get away, driven by reports that rising flood water was within a few blocks.

Washington knew that he had left it too late—but the fault was not entirely his. It had taken him more than an hour to get home, and then he'd discovered that Celestine and Patsy had done nothing: his wife hadn't packed and his daughter hadn't called her husband. He had finally convinced them that it was urgent, and they had got to work, slowly and resentfully. He had tried calling the boy's workplace himself, over and over again, and never got through. The boy ought to have been home by nine anyway, but he hadn't come. So they had waited, and waited, because Patsy wouldn't leave without him, while the wind had grown stronger and the house had trembled and the phone and the electricity had gone dead. And at last they had realised the boy wasn't coming, for whatever reason, and Washington had been able to persuade the women to leave.

Just in time, he thought. Oh, just in time, as he tried to keep his family together in the midst of the huge crowd of people, hurrying down the corridors, jamming the stairs, filling the elevators, screaming and shouting. They had left home with three suitcases, but the one Celestine carried had caught in the elevator door and Washington made her abandon it.

They reached the platform and piled into the train, which immediately started to move off, attendants shouting at people who were trying to push their way on board and then being crammed in by those behind them. "There ain't gonna be no more trains after this one," a man said to Washington. "They say Greenwich Village is almost under water. Did you hear that, man? These electrics can't last too much longer."

Obstructing bodies prevented the train door from closing until the

130

attendants started shouting that another train would be along shortly.

"Wanna bet?" the man asked.

The train moved off very slowly, gathered speed, slowed, stopped and started again. "Holy Mother of God, we're going to be here for ever," a woman yelled. She had a little girl on her knee, wearing a straw hat with a ribbon and carrying a plastic doll with long hair.

Washington saw they were all alone and took pity on them. "Don't fret. We'll all stick together. Can't be much further now." He could feel them begin the gradual ascent on the east side of the river.

Suddenly the train stopped; at the same moment the lights went out. There was a chorus of screams and shrieks, and Washington abandoned the suitcases and put both arms round Celestine and held her close. The din was tremendous as the people shouted and pushed against each other and the doors, which remained firmly closed.

"We're going to die," Celestine gasped. "We're going to die."

Patsy wept, and the baby wailed, and the woman with the little girl kept praying, "Holy Mary, Mother of God, save us," over and over again.

They heard, faintly, an attendant out in the tunnel shouting for calm, but nobody was paying any attention to him, and the press was growing greater. Washington felt all the air being crushed out of his body, until suddenly the doors against which he was being flattened opened and he almost fell out. Celestine went with him, and Patsy and the baby. And then the crowd followed, yelling and trampling on each other. He realised that he was ankle-deep in water. But they had been first out and could move away, up along the track.

"The electric line," Celestine gasped.

"If that line was live, the train would be moving," Washington gasped back at her. "And if it comes live again we're all going to die anyway. Just hold on to my jacket with one hand and Patsy with the other. Careful now, mind your step. I'll lead the way."

He was worried by the water; it was rising. They must get out, but the other people didn't seem to be moving in any particular direction, just floundering. Thank God they had been in the front carriage. He suddenly felt compelled to do something—help these terrified folk to get out. In his youth he had been a good baritone in the church choir. Now he stood tall and called, his voice resounding down the tunnel behind him. "Just make a line, folks, and follow behind us. We'll soon be out of here. Just keep calm, and sing to the Lord." He drew a deep breath and began: "O God, our help in ages past, Our hope for years to come . . ." Celestine's soprano joined him. "Our shelter from the stormy blast . . ." and Patsy and the man who held her coat and the woman who held his hand all began to follow the strong baritone that was attempting to lead them.

Washington could feel his way along the wall of the tunnel. His fingers

131

groped and his feet stumbled and splashed. He was aware that there were a lot of people behind him not singing, just sobbing, moaning and cursing, falling and being pushed over. The hymn ended, and he started again. How long was it to the next station? And the water was rising every minute. It was past his knees, and his legs were feeling like lead. Once Celestine fell, and he had to drag her up again, soaking wet. He didn't know how much longer he could keep going, when he saw flashing lights ahead of him.

Several military policemen were peering down from a platform, waving their powerful torches. "We heard there were people in here. Listen, you gotta get out, quick. This tunnel is gonna flood any moment."

Washington helped Celestine up as one of the young men held her hand. "Son," he said, "you just show us the way."

Patsy passed the baby to another soldier and was heaved up out of the water. People began to clap and cheer, and by the dim glow of the torches several stopped to shake the big black man's hand and thank him, as he handed them up to the platform.

"Washington, come on, or we'll get separated," Celestine begged.

"She's right, mister," a military policeman said. "It's time you were with your family. You've done your bit." He offered his hand while another MP held the other to heave together: Washington Jones was a heavy man, and very tired.

More soldiers appeared with hand-held floodlights, linked to a portable generator, illuminating the stairs ahead, the crowded platform, and beyond it the swirling black water.

Washington, Celestine, and Patsy and the baby were halfway up the stairs to the street when frantic screaming exploded from the platform below them. They turned, and saw a great wall of water gush out of the tunnel they had just left, engulfing everyone on the platform, sweeping those on the outer edge away with it. Those nearest the wall clung together, clutching at rails, seats, anything that might keep them on their feet.

The water rose over them and reached even the step on which Washington was standing . . . and there, spinning at his feet for a few moments, was a little round straw hat with a ribbon. Then it was drawn away into the main stream again, and disappeared.

MARCIA COWERED BACK against the door. "Benny, I'm scared. I've never heard a noise like this. The whole house is shaking."

"Guess we're getting the edge of Faith all right," Benny agreed.

They had slept very late, and brunched on tinned soup, cheese and fruit. Occasionally they had been disturbed by the wind and the thunder. Once they thought they heard a police siren close at hand, and a loudspeaker blaring, but the noise had been confused by the pounding rain. Even later someone had knocked on the street door, several times, and then rung the bell, but they had ignored whoever it had been; in weather like this, with hangovers, bed had seemed the best place to be.

When they finally got dressed and went to the kitchen, the upper part of the house appeared to be swaying, beams and joists creaking behind the plaster, and they had to shout to be heard above the noise.

"Edge of nothing! This has to be the real thing." Marcia winced as a violent gust cracked a windowpane.

"Jeez! That whole window will go in a minute. We must nail something over it." Desperately Benny looked around. "Quick, what can we use?"

"Try the plywood back off that old bureau." Marcia tugged at the ancient piece that had served them as a dressing table.

"Yeah, that'll do. Look, I'll hold it over the window while you fetch a hammer and nails."

When the frail window was safely boarded up, they went round the other rooms, checking that everything was secured. Then the lights went out.

"Damn," Benny said. "That means we can't check the weather on TV." They groped through the gloomy daylight filtering into the hallway. "Who'd believe it was one o'clock in the afternoon?"

"Benny, do you think we're safe here?" She peered out, up the street. "Jeez, it's dead out there. Not a soul in sight."

"Sweetheart, will you just look at the bricks and tiles scattered on the road? It's dangerous outside. I reckon we're a whole lot safer inside, and obviously everybody else thinks so too. Let's get on with fixing the lounge."

"Well, I guess we could hang the curtains and put the loose covers on the settee and chairs." Anything to occupy her mind, fight off the pangs of fear which were paralysing her movements.

A sudden tremendous crash rocked the building, scattering crockery in the kitchen. It continued to boom and rattle for several minutes.

"Oh, dear God! What was that?" Marcia followed Benny to the window, then drew back in horror. The old brown house across the street, belonging to a young couple who had become good friends of theirs, was now just a heap of rubble. The roof had lifted and fallen back, breaking up as it did so, heavy tiles and supporting joists devastating the floors and walls below.

"My God, how did that happen? Could've been struck by a bomb. I must go and see if I can help them." Benny started for the door.

"No, Benny, no! They're not there. They went to Joyce's mother for the weekend. Oh, Benny . . ." Marcia flung herself into his arms. "I'm so frightened."

He held her against him, patting her shoulders. But he couldn't avoid a terrible feeling that maybe that police siren and the banging on the door

133

might have been some kind of warning. If only he had a portable radio, but he'd never bothered; he had always preferred playing his collection of tapes to the brainless chat which filled so much air time. And anyway, a hurricane . . . in Greenwich Village?

Yet to think of the place opposite. To see a house just collapse . . .

But he couldn't communicate any of his fear to Marcia; she was terrified enough as it was. He said, "Come on, and stop worrying. We've got work to do. Where are the hooks for the curtains?"

The young couple tried to concentrate, pushing the hooks into place with fumbling fingers, but they were shaken every few minutes by new bangs and crashes as lightning struck the taller buildings around them, and the wind carried chimney pots, tiles, and even sheets of plate glass slicing through the streets. Half an hour later, the curtains were all neatly in place, but it was hard to appreciate the full effect, the light was too bad.

Some of the apartment windows had old casement shutters, which Benny had securely fastened. "That last gust nearly took the house with it. We'll just have to sit in the dark unless you can find some candles. There'll have to be . . ."

He never finished the sentence. A deafening roaring, creaking, groaning, whirring, moaning sound thundered round their heads, and showers of ceiling plaster rained down on them.

Marcia screamed. Benny grabbed her and drew her towards the outer wall. It was impossible to speak, but they both knew the roof had gone. Instinctively Marcia slid down the wall to sit on the floor.

Suddenly she realised that the carpet was wet. "Ugh!" She jumped up and grabbed Benny's hand. "The rain's coming through the ceiling," she yelled in his ear.

But Benny knew it wasn't rainwater. It was already swirling round their ankles, and it smelt of sea and salt. "Upstairs," he yelled back, and started for the door, trying to drag Marcia with him.

They never reached it. With a series of massive cracks like a barrage of artillery fire, the door burst open and a cascade of water, carrying stinking flotsam, converged on them in the gloom.

"Oh, my new curtains!" Marcia cried, a split second before she was swept off her feet. She struggled, lungs bursting, seeking to surface—but she didn't know which way was up. She thought she felt Benny brush by her and made a grab for him, but it was only a chair.

"Marcia!" Benny plunged this way and that, surfaced, drew breath . . . and realised his feet were not touching; the water pouring in from the street was over his height. "Marcia!" he screamed.

There was no reply.

He dived, swam desperately, reaching out in all directions, until his lungs were exploding, then he kicked for the surface again.

But this time there was no surface—his head struck the ceiling.

As THE CENTRE of the hurricane swept in towards the land, it pushed more and more water in front of it. The seas climbed higher and higher. Fifteen miles from the Narrows, the Ambrose Lightship parted her moorings and was swept towards the beach on sixty-foot waves. In Lower New York Bay, by two o'clock the buoys and lights were scattered, Rockaway Beach, Jones Beach and Coney Island were obliterated. Some of the surging water found its way into Jamaica Bay, and the Wildlife Sanctuary was destroyed; waves broke across the runways at Kennedy and smashed through the glass doors to batter the luggage carousels to pieces. But by far the greatest volume of water was funnelled into the Narrows, where it exploded in a mountainous surging sea, bursting across an already turbulent harbour to engulf the gigantic Statue of Liberty. For some minutes the recently rebuilt structure defied the waves. Even as they struck at the finely chiselled face, the hand holding the torch continued to thrust itself above the water. Then the tremendous force of the storm proved too much for the foundations, and the great statue tottered, the noise of its fall lost in the howl of the wind.

The storm surge continued on its way, to smash into an already half-submerged Lower Manhattan. Staten Island disappeared beneath flying waves as part of the surge found its way down into Newark Bay; the main force tore up the East and Hudson Rivers.

ERNIE TURNED THE MOTORBOAT in alongside a pier in Yonkers. "This is far enough."

"You reckon?" Bill Duval asked uncertainly.

"Sure. We're fifteen miles from the harbour. All the experts say the danger is in the five miles nearest the sea, right? Besides, I'm starving. Hey, you guys," he bawled at some men who had just finished mooring their own boat, "take a line."

Nancy Duval raised her head, slowly and sadly, unable to believe that they had really come to rest at last. It had taken them more than five hours to make the journey from Lower Manhattan—just fifteen miles. She and the children had been violently sick for most of the time, the wind had been howling, the rain had been torrential, and the waves on the river had been high enough to make her feel she was in a storm at sea. The boat had leaked like a sieve through her decks, and had been leaking through her hull as well—Ernie had had to keep the bilge pump working all the time—and the roughness had been worsened by the myriad wakes carved back and forth, as it seemed everyone who owned a boat in New York was trying to take it to safety at the same time. Added to which, in the Upper Harbour, the big ships had kept their engines going as they swung and heaved at their mooring warps; many had apparently already left the harbour that morning, before the full force of the storm had actually arrived, preferring to risk themselves at sea.

Nancy wished them joy. She only wanted to get ashore, and if Ernie

136

thought that Yonkers was safe, that was good enough for her. Her sister-in-law, Marge, obviously felt the same way. "Just let Nance and the kids and me ashore," she begged. "You can do what you like, after."

"In one minute, darling," Ernie promised. "Secure that bow warp, Bill; make it good and fast."

The pier was crowded with boats already moored, and with their crews. There were a couple of restaurants across the street packed with people, either having a late lunch or drowning their sorrows. The wind was powerful up here, but not half as strong as it had been down in the harbour.

As soon as the boat was secured alongside, Marge and Nancy grabbed the children, one by each hand, and staggered up the pier and onto the land. Nancy felt like kneeling down and kissing it, even in the pouring rain. The two women got the four children across the street and into the warmth of the bar, where a huge, if somewhat hysterical, party was in progress.

Relief flooded through Nancy, as she turned round to look back at the boat, where Bill and Ernie were still securing extra warps, making sure nothing was going to damage her.

"Holy Mary, Mother of God," said an Irishman standing beside her. People crowded against them, rubbing misted breath from the glass to see better, staring at the huge wave coming up the river.

Nancy abandoned the children and ran outside. "Bill!" she screamed, her voice dissipating on the wind. "Ernie! Come ashore! Hurry!"

The men still tending their craft had seen what was coming, and were scrambling onto the pier. Ernie slipped and fell, and Bill turned back to help him. Then the tidal bore struck. It was already carrying on its fifteen-foot crest an assortment of shattered boats, driftwood and various flotsam. Now it smashed through the pier and the moored boats, sweeping them on up the river, a foaming maelstrom of destruction. The last Nancy saw of Bill and Ernie, they were clinging desperately to pieces of the destroyed pier as they were carried out of sight.

THE LIGHTS IN THE NABS building had flickered several times before finally going out. All broadcasting had naturally ceased, but by then Richard, to whom everyone left in the building had turned for leadership, had had the emergency generator started, and he had also assembled all the staff in the main studio, which had no external windows and was by far the safest place to be. They were all suffering from shock at least. In addition to Julian, several people had been badly hurt by flying glass, and had been treated and sedated as far as possible. But the building itself was a wreck: nearly all the windows had been blown in, and the resulting damage to offices was shattering. That the roof had remained intact was due not only to the strength of its construction but to the prompt closing of every possible door.

The mayor had said, justifiably enough, that the most serious danger was that of drowning, and that those in buildings situated more than fifty feet above water level would be physically safe, whatever damage their dwellings or offices might have to suffer. Julian had been in such a building, and the storm had not even reached its height when he died.

The thought of that happening to Jo was unbearable. He had tried to reach her by phone several times, but without success; now the phones were all dead. He had thought of attempting to get to her—it was only a few blocks—but he knew that no one could survive on those streets. So he waited, and now . . . others had heard it too. Heads began to raise as a huge, deathly stillness overtook the afternoon, a sudden cessation of the racket with which they had existed for so long. There were euphoric whispers; could the catastrophe be over?

"Not quite," Richard told them. "This is the eye of the storm. It's not likely to last more than half an hour at the outside. Then the wind is going to blow again, just as hard as before, only from the other direction. But we're winning. We know the storm is passing; and with the wind in the west the water level is going to get pushed back down to normal pretty rapidly. So just sit tight for another few hours, and we'll all be able to leave."

Reassured, they were chatting now. Richard went over to Jayme, who sat on the floor, staring into space. Julian had been a special friend. "Listen," he said in her ear, "I'm leaving now. If anyone wants to know where I've gone, tell them I'm trying to find out what's happening out there, and that I'll be back. But keep convincing them they're better off here than anywhere else, at least until the wind has dropped."

For a moment she just looked at him. Then her head jerked. "Going out? Where?"

"I must get to Mrs. Donnelly. She's alone in her apartment with her children . . . God knows what they must have gone through."

"Mrs. Donnelly . . ." She blinked at him, then gave a faint smile. "You and her? Well, what do you know? But you can't go outside. When the storm comes back you'll be killed."

"I reckon I have time to make it, just. I have to go, Jayme. So, see you tomorrow." Richard let himself out of one of the doors leading into a side corridor. The utter silence of the building outside the studio was uncanny. He took the stone stairs, hurrying down, panting less with exertion than apprehension.

At the bottom the street doors were closed, but he leaned on the bar and stepped out, blinking in the sudden bright daylight, looking up at blue sky above him, and then gasping at the destruction to either side. Automobiles were tumbled one on top of the other, broken glass crackled beneath his shoes, water flowed everywhere, either from flooding from the sea or from the fantastically heavy rainfall which had been unable to run off through the waterlogged sewers.

138

He hurried along the avenue towards 48th Street, picking his way through the debris, listening to sounds of returning life, windows being thrown open, people calling to each other . . . he hoped they knew that this respite was only going to be of the most temporary kind.

He was still several blocks short of 48th Street when the daylight faded, and he looked up in time for a vivid flash of lightning, accompanied simultaneously by an earsplitting clap of thunder. The blue sky had disappeared, and the black clouds were back, and with them, sudden teeming rain and the enormous roaring of the hurricane wind.

Richard knew he had to reach the nearest side street, where he could obtain a lee. But crossing the intersection wasn't going to be easy. The wind picked him up and sent him sprawling. He made no attempt to rise, clung to the sidewalk and began to inch his way to a pile of automobiles on the corner, only to be caught by another gust and sent rolling, splashing through the water running out of the gutters. He came to rest against an uprooted tree, held on to it, and worked his way once again towards the shelter of the automobiles.

Minutes later he got up and made a dash for the side street, and was thrown down again, battered and bruised, against a bent railing which had once surrounded a trash can. As he lay there, watching water bubbling out of a sewer hole only inches from his face, he thought how damned silly it would be to drown on Fifth Avenue. He pushed himself up once again and fought his way forward.

"WHAT'S IN THAT BOX, Mom?" Owen Michael asked, indicating the heap dumped in the shower stall, topped by an old cardboard box.

"Photos, waiting to be fixed in those albums."

"Can we see well enough in this light to do them?" The power had gone some while ago and they were trying to economise, using only one candle.

"Let's try." It would help occupy their minds.

Together they knelt on the bathroom floor and set the photos out in neat piles.

"That's an awful one of you skiing, Mom." Tamsin held up a shot of Jo slithering down a slope, a flurry of skis and snow in the air.

"What about this one of you and Owen Michael under water, last year?"

Owen Michael grabbed it. "Heck, I don't remember that."

Every few moments they held their breaths, listening, physically shaken even away in their shelter.

The sudden silence took them completely by surprise. "Holy shit!" Owen Michael exclaimed. "What's happening?"

"It's the eye," Tamsin said. "We had it in Eleuthera."

"You mean it's done? It's over?"

"No, it's not done," Jo told him. "Don't open the door."

"It'll start again," Tamsin said, her voice containing a sob as she remembered that terrible night. "Worse than before."

"But . . ." Owen Michael looked from her to his mother. "It must mean something good."

"Sure it does. It means we're halfway through," Jo told him. "That has to be good."

"What about Pinewoods?"

Tamsin's face was screwed up with worry. Jo put an arm round her. "That'll be all right. Bognor is twenty miles from the sea. And on a hill. No problem there."

"But they'll have a lot of wind," Owen Michael went on, pessimistically. "What if a tree falls and smashes through the roof?"

Jo gave him a warning frown over Tamsin's head; the poor child was quite upset enough. "I'm sure . . ." she began, then checked, listening.

"That was a knock on the door," he said. "I know it was."

"There it is again," Tamsin said. "Someone's outside."

Jo leaped to her feet. Richard! He'd come, during the eye. Thank God, he was safe. But she hadn't told the children he might be joining them, so she said, "I'll see who it is. Bolt the door behind me, just in case the wind gets up before I'm back."

"Mom . . ." said Owen Michael uneasily, but she had already opened the bathroom door and stepped into the corridor.

Everything was amazingly quiet. "Bolt it now," she called through the door as she closed it behind her. As soon as she heard the bolt slip into place she hurried eagerly across the lounge. It was such a relief to know Richard was here; and he was only just in time. The lounge had seemed startlingly bright compared with the enclosed bathroom, but even before she could reach the main door the room was darkening and there was a flash of lightning which made her gasp.

"Richard!" she shouted, running into the lobby to release the bolts, pull the chain free and swing open the heavy security door—to gasp in horror. It wasn't Richard. It was Stuart Alloan, and another man.

"Hi, there," Alloan said with a sneer. "My lucky day. I was afraid you might've gotten away."

The wind had returned, whistling up the stairwell and into the apartment. Jo staggered back against the lobby wall, held there momentarily by the force of the sudden gust. If only she'd had time to slam the door in their faces . . . but they had been blown into the lobby with her.

"Let's get this door closed," the second man shouted, and it took the strength of both men to swing it back onto the latch.

This gave Jo a few moments in which to recover her breath . . . and her sense. She could see that this new man was small and dark with a vicious curl to his lip. Her legs felt weak, but she had to keep her head. "What do you want?" she asked, trying to sound calm, praying that the children would remain locked in the bathroom, no matter what happened.

"That depends what you have, sister," Garcia leered.

Alloan stared at her, unsmiling. "We want you, for a start," he said. "I owe you plenty, remember. You feel like having her, too, Domingo?"

"Sure," his friend replied from the lounge. "But I feel like a drink more. Bring her in here."

Alloan advanced on Jo.

"All right," she said, trying to reject the blind panic clawing at her brain. She was about to be raped by these men. But she could stand that if it would save the children.

He caught her as she went through the door, slid his arms round her waist. She wanted to kick him but didn't dare, watched by Domingo at the bar, pouring himself neat whisky, draining the glass in two gulps. "Hell," he said, "I needed that." He turned. "You got food, sugar?"

"Yes," Jo added. Anything to keep them busy. "Let go of me." She tried to shake off Alloan. "Let me go."

His fingers scraped across her flesh, but he released her.

"It'll have to be cold," she told them. "There's no power."

"Just get it," Garcia said, sitting down. "You watch her."

Jo went into the kitchen, Alloan at her shoulder. She opened the refrigerator and he began to touch her again, playing with her belt. "Let's get these pants off," he said.

"Leave me alone," she muttered, taking out ham and tomatoes and lettuce. As she opened the kitchen drawer to find a knife, her wrists were seized. "Forget it, baby," he said. "I know you. We'll eat with our fingers. You got bread?"

"In that bin. If you'll let me go . . ."

Still holding her wrist, Alloan opened the bin and took out a loaf of bread. "Take the plates," he said.

She took both plates into the lounge, and Garcia grabbed one and started cramming food into his mouth. "Jeez!" he said. "I was hungry. And hell, we only just made it, kid. Listen to that."

The wind seemed even louder, now it was blowing directly at the building instead of coming from behind.

"Yeah." Alloan grinned, and finished eating. "But I told you we'd be snug here, Domingo. Right?"

"Right." Garcia stretched. "That feels better. Now, what d'you say we play with the dame a little?"

"Yeah," Alloan said. "Yeah."

As Jo tried to make up her mind what to do, Alloan threw his arms round her waist and stretched her across his knees on the settee. She cried out and struck at him, and he laughed and caught her wrists. "She's a fighter," he said.

"I like them best. You hold her arms." Garcia got up.

Jo strained and twisted, but Alloan merely moved from beneath her and then knelt, one hand on each wrist, pinning her to the settee. She kicked at Garcia, but he laughed and knelt beside her to unfasten her belt. "Let's see what you got in there," he said.

Suddenly the outer door burst open before the force of the wind and, because the lobby door had been left ajar, an almost solid mass of air rushed into the apartment. Jo heard a tremendous crack from behind her and knew that the picture window had at last gone.

Garcia had released her and got to his feet. "Shut that goddamned door . . ." he was shouting, when the wind picked him up and lifted him right over the back of the settee. He gave a despairing shriek as he was carried out through the huge, empty window. Alloan had released her wrists to turn and look at the door and the wind caught him too. He fell over the back of the settee with a shout of dismay. Jo, already half on the floor, lay against the heavy piece of furniture and felt it move even as she flattened against it, all the breath being crushed from her body. She heard Alloan scream again and again, the last scream being a despairing wail. But now the settee was moving with increasing speed, carrying her with it as she threw her arms around as much of it as she could hold. Then the gust slackened and the settee crashed into the wall beneath the window.

"Mom!" Owen Michael was shouting from the bathroom. "Mom!"

"Get back inside," Jo shouted. "Bolt the door."

She struggled to her feet. The wind was still strong, but she could move against it until the next big gust. She drove herself forward into the lobby. Because the outer door had only been slammed, not bolted, the Yale lock had been torn from the wood, as had the ordinary lock. But the three bolts and the chain were still intact, and the door looked solid enough. Exerting all her strength, she slowly forced it shut, shot the bolts, fixed the chain. The apartment was still a turmoil of wind, gusting in through the broken window: bottles were swept out of the bar, pictures torn from walls. From the kitchen she heard the sound of shattering glass and crockery. But she could move, and regained the inner corridor, shutting every door behind her. She banged on the bathroom door and Owen Michael let her in. She collapsed between the two children, and they gazed at her cut lip and bruised hands.

"Who was it, Mom?" Owen Michael asked.

"Nobody," Jo gasped. "He went away again."

JO COULD HARDLY BELIEVE her ears. Having actually fallen into an exhausted sleep on the bathroom floor, she awoke with a start when the shrieking, howling, crashing, faded; the noise of the wind was still tremendous, but the thunder was only a distant growl and the drumming rain had ceased.

The children were still asleep, even more exhausted than herself.

Cautiously she opened the bathroom door, stepped into the corridor and made her way through the twilight into the shambles that had been her lounge. She saw that the apartment door had been blown open again, the bolts forced out of the wood, the entire structure torn from its hinges—yet in the bathroom they had survived. She clung to the lounge door, still intact, and allowed the wind, now blowing something above gale force but seeming no more than refreshingly cool, to play over her, while she looked out through the shattered picture window, shuddering as she remembered those traumatic moments only a few hours before. Back in the bathroom she poured herself a cup of coffee from the last of the many vacuum flasks they had filled earlier and returned to the lounge, listening to slowly increasing sounds: wails and screams and cries for help, drifting up from the street. She even thought she heard several gunshots, suggesting the police were already having trouble with looters.

Then she heard a noise closer at hand. There was someone in the corridor outside the apartment, moving slowly, laboriously and cautiously towards her.

Her blood seemed to freeze—there was no way she could keep an intruder out. She ran into the kitchen to find the carving knife, any knife, but the kitchen had been gutted by the wind, and she could find nothing in the gloom. She turned, panting.

"Jo?" a man whispered. "Jo, are you alive? For God's sake, Jo!"

"Richard!" She hurled herself into his arms. "Oh, Richard!"

He hugged her close. "Sorry I took so long to get here, darling."

She stood away from him, stared at him. His jacket had been torn off and his shirt was buttonless. His hair was scattered and there were cuts and bruises on his face as well as his chest; his left arm hung awkwardly; there was blood all over him. "Oh, my God!" she cried. "You're hurt!"

"Broken glass, mainly," he said. "The street is ankle-deep in it. After I was blown down the avenue and knocked out, I crawled part of the way on my hands and knees—I think there's still quite a lot in there."

"Knocked out?" she cried. "But . . ."

"A long time," he said. "A couple of hours. I don't know for sure. I lost my watch. But then, this . . ." He touched his arm and winced.

"Oh, Richard! It looks broken."

"It sure hurts."

"Oh, darling Richard, you came through the storm . . . but what a risk you took."

He gave his crooked grin. "Well, I had to wait for the old girl to say I could. Then she changed her mind. Women are like that."

"You could have been killed." She drew him towards the bathroom. "And I had better patch you up before you bleed to death."

He had been taking in the damage to the apartment. "But you . . . and the children . . ."

"We're OK," she said, opening the bathroom door. "We're really quite

143

snug in here." She closed the bathroom door behind them and lit a candle. Suddenly she felt faint and weak—from exhaustion mostly, but also from sheer relief at Richard's presence. Despite his torn and ragged appearance, he was still a tower of strength. "Hey, kids," she said, as they woke up, "you remember Mr. Connors, the weather man from NABS. He came over to see how we've been doing. Wasn't that good of him?"

"Hi, Mr. Connors," Owen Michael said. "We're doing fine. We had no problems at all."

Richard looked at Jo.

"No problems at all," she echoed.

BY DAYBREAK, FAITH had long turned back to the northeast, and, dying, was spending the last of her energy over Cape Cod. In New York the wind was no more than fresh. The rain had stopped, the clouds had cleared, and there was blue sky to accompany the sunrise.

The flood waters had receded, and survivors began to emerge, hardly able to believe they were still alive.

Horror gripped them as they looked at the city. A jumbled mass of destroyed vehicles and dead bodies, uprooted trees, shattered buildings, some totally collapsed, even the more substantial ones badly damaged.

It was time for work.

Police Commissioner Grundy had not been seen since Police Headquarters had been flooded out, but Assistant Commissioner McGrath and a handful of patrolmen had fought their way up to the emergency police headquarters in the Plaza Hotel, along with the mayor and most of his staff, and from there McGrath assumed command of the city's law and order. Using radio, McGrath began assembling his battered and exhausted men and women to begin the job of clearing up and preventing disease.

He did not lack help: at dawn, half the available United States Army, with their medical corps, was airlifted into the disaster area to assist.

At dawn, too, James Calthrop White woke in a muddy ditch: he had slept shoulder to shoulder with his chauffeur in the back seat of the Rolls when it was obvious there was no help to be found. Amazingly, although the ditch had filled with rain, the engine started at first kick, and when an army helicopter landed nearby to see if they were all right, they managed to push the car back onto the road.

"You want to go into town, JC?" Murray asked.

"I want to go home," White said. "And have a large Scotch. Come to think of it, we'll *both* have a large Scotch."

AT EIGHT O'CLOCK the President of the United States arrived by helicopter, to be greeted by the governor and Mayor Naseby, and taken on a bird's-eye tour of the stricken city. "To think that one storm could do so much damage," the President mused. "But do you realise how lucky we were that it happened on a Saturday? And that there was adequate warning? If all the banks and business places had been open and crowded . . ." He turned to Naseby. "I have to hand it to you, Bill, that was some decision you took, to order the evacuation of the entire city, while the storm was still a good distance away. But by God, if you hadn't . . ."

Naseby looked down at the ruins beneath him. "I didn't make that decision, Mr. President. At least, not until it was forced upon me. The evacuation was ordered by a television weather man, Richard Connors, on his own initiative. Because he knew what was coming, and the rest of us wouldn't believe him."

"Then Connors is someone I'd like to meet," the President said. "Or is that confidential?"

"I think Mr. President is asking, Bill, if you are going to tell that fact to the voters," the governor put in.

Naseby grinned. "I'll have to think about that. But I sure intend to tell Mr. Connors, supposing I can find him." He looked down at the city again. "Supposing he's alive."

IN A REMARKABLE TWO DAYS life was heading back to normal. It would take months, years, to restore the city to its old, sleazy greatness, but by the time the debris was cleared away from the streets, tunnels and subways, and all the bodies that were going to be recovered had been found, services were working again on a limited scale, and the airport runways repaired and reopened. People began to pick up their lives again. With massive help pouring in, not only from the rest of the United States but from all over the world, epidemic disease was averted and the job of clearing up the demolished buildings got under way.

As soon as it was safe to leave Park Avenue, Richard took Jo and the children to his apartment, which had remained undamaged, and there they spent the next few days, while the cleanup got under way. The city was supplied with food and drinking water by the army, using great trucks and containers. Jo did not attempt to explain her emotional situation to Owen Michael and Tamsin, and they did not question it. In the aftermath of such a catastrophe questions about personal relationships seemed irrelevant.

But once power was restored Richard felt it his duty to go back to work, nothing further having been said about his dismissal. With the NABS building a shambles, news and weather reporting was primitive, but a service was provided.

Jo knew she had to regain contact with the Donnelly family, but the public telephones were still out. She and the children returned to Park Avenue, and were overwhelmed with joy to find Washington back on duty—and repairmen already at work on the building. Michael's

Cadillac was still in the garage, into which, miraculously, only a trickle of water had penetrated, and Jo now discovered that Washington had a spare set of keys for it. Sadly, he had no news of Florence, and in view of the total destruction of Coney Island the worst had to be assumed.

Nor was there any news to be had from Greenwich Village, where the destruction and loss of life had been massive; the entire area had been cordoned off by the army because bodies were still being recovered from the wreckage of houses and the risk of disease had not yet been eradicated. "Next of kin will be informed as soon as identification can be made," the major in charge told Jo. "If your sister-in-law is here, we'll find her. But . . . you'd better pray she ain't."

Jo and the children called at the *Profiles* office and found it gutted and deserted, so they drove on out to Bognor, which had been sideswiped by the storm but suffered no real damage. Once outside the storm area she stopped the car at a payphone. She lifted the receiver and heard the dialling tone. She hesitated. But she had to find out. So she dialled.

Sally Davenport said, "Jo! Yes. I'll just get Sam." Her voice sounded odd.

If Sam was back . . . Jo frowned, and waited.

"Jo? Are you OK?" His voice sounded funny too.

"Yes."

"Have you seen the folks?"

"No. I'm on my way over now."

"Heck," he said. "We've been trying to contact you for two days, but there was no way. Jo . . ."

"Who got ashore?" she asked in a low voice; the children were outside in the car.

"It was a monster wave, Jo. I swear it must've been sixty foot high. We never stood a chance. Michael never stood a chance. He was on the helm and went overboard. Jo . . . he was great. To the very end he was great. A real hero. Without him, we'd have been done far sooner."

"How many?" she asked again.

"The ship broke up. We couldn't get Pete up in time . . . he had a broken shoulder. And I think Jon had already died; he'd been flung on the deck and hit his head. Larry, Jerry and I got the life raft over, but it was torn apart by the wind, kept capsizing. We hung on, somehow, and gradually the seas started going down. We thought we were finished . . ."

"But you got ashore."

"A helicopter came and winched us up. Seems we were spotted by a plane. Larry . . . Larry didn't make it. Exposure, I guess. Jerry's OK . . ."

"And so are you, Sam. Thank God for that," Jo said.

"Listen, Michael was a hero, Jo. I told you, if it hadn't been for him we'd have gone down much sooner."

"Yes," Jo said, and thought, If it hadn't been for him you wouldn't

146

have gone down at all, you would have been snugly moored in Hamilton, Bermuda. But that was a thought she kept to herself.

She returned to the Cadillac and drove on to Pinewoods. One look at the faces of Big Mike and Babs told her that they knew . . .

Babs embraced her. "Oh, Jo," she said. "We've been hunting for you everywhere. Mike drove into town and went to the apartment, but you weren't there, and the place was wrecked . . . we were so worried."

"When was this?" Jo asked.

"Yesterday."

"Oh. We were . . . staying with a friend."

They went onto the patio; Pinewoods had suffered very little damage and the children immediately rushed off to change for the pool. Jo and Big Mike and Babs sat on the loungers silently for several moments. There were things which had to be said, questions which had to be asked, but each was afraid to start.

"Have you told the children?" Babs asked at last, watching Owen Michael and Tamsin diving into the pool.

"No. I only found out an hour ago, from Sam Davenport. I'm not quite sure how to do it."

Babs nodded. "We haven't told Belle yet. About either of them."

"Either . . ." Jo's heart sank into her stomach; the absence of Marcia had been one of the questions she had been afraid to raise. "Marcia? I tried to contact them . . . Friday night. I even went there . . . but they weren't home."

"They were home Saturday," Big Mike said. "I drove down there yesterday, when I was looking for you."

"And?" Jo prompted in a whisper.

"When I told them I was Marcia's father, they let me into the Village," Big Mike said, his voice toneless. "Two army boys came with me." His head bent, he covered his face with his hands, shoulders heaving. "They were in the kitchen. The damned building was on top of them. But they had drowned. Would you believe it? Drowned, in their own kitchen."

Jo's breath was knocked out of her body. She remembered the last time she saw them, their excitement, their pride in the transformation of their apartment.

"And then, you," Babs said. "We didn't know . . . that man Connors kept telephoning . . ."

"Oh," Jo said. "I'd told him I was leaving town. I guess he was worried."

"But you didn't leave town?" Big Mike said.

"No. We had an accident, so we went back to the apartment."

"And sat it out there," Babs said. "Was it very terrible?"

"We sat it out," Jo said, very carefully.

"Tamsin . . ."

"She's OK. I guess having Owen Michael with her helped."

"You have to tell them," Big Mike said. "They'll cry, but they have a lot to be proud of." Tears were streaming down his face. "Their daddy died a hero, and he died doing what he liked best. He defied that storm to the end. He was a hero."

"Yes," Jo said. "He was a hero. I won't let them forget that."

She went inside, and after a moment Babs followed her. "It was all over between you two, wasn't it?"

Jo's shoulders rose and fell. "That doesn't mean I don't grieve for him, Babs. I guess the shock hasn't quite got through to me, yet. He was a great guy. Just . . . not a great husband."

"I know." Babs put her arms round her daughter-in-law, and the two women wept together. "What are you going to do?" Babs asked, when she was able to control her voice.

"Oh, pick up the pieces, I guess." She attempted a smile. "There are an awful lot of pieces to be picked up."

"You're still our daughter, you know."

Jo wanted to weep afresh. She had no idea how to go about telling Babs about Richard—that would have to wait. The children had to come first, although she had an idea Owen Michael already understood the situation. He and Richard had appeared to like each other . . . but then Owen Michael had thought his father was still alive. Now . . . there were crises ahead. But she would face them, with Richard.

AFTER JO LEFT, Big Mike gazed at the pool, shoulders hunched. "Jeez," he said, "all gone. Just like that. Michael, Marcia and Benny, Lawson . . . Palmer tells me the office is wiped out . . . It'll be like starting from scratch, all over again."

"Would you like a hand, Dad?" Dale asked, quietly.

Big Mike glanced at him; the boy had hardly said a word since hearing of his brother's death.

Dale flushed. "So, I don't have a college degree. But I can learn. If you'll have me."

"Have you? God Almighty, boy, if I thought you'd settle down . . . It's going to be tough," Big Mike said. "We'll still have our clients, I guess. But sorting out the mess . . . but hell, I reckon that with all of Wall Street hit, and the Stock Exchange under several feet of water, we're all in the same boat. If you're serious . . . ."

"Try me," Dale said.

Big Mike held out his hand, and his son grasped it.

Three months later

"I want you to know, Richard," said J. Calthrop White, "that when you were publicly commended by the mayor of this city for what you did, I felt as proud as if I'd done it myself." He allowed his gaze to drift over his

148

massed employees in the main studio of the rebuilt NABS building. "But I also felt pride in my entire network, in all my employees, who remained at their posts throughout the ordeal, and who like that gallant man, Julian Summers, were prepared to die at their posts."

He paused, and there was a ripple of applause.

"But I know," JC went on, "that Julian would have wanted the station to continue on its glorious way, bringing to this great nation the best in television, regardless of the forces of nature that may be gathered against it. And that he, and all of you, will be as proud as I am myself when I tell you that NABS has been granted a franchise to operate a television company in the United Kingdom. The news came through today."

He paused to allow another ripple of applause.

"Yes, folks," he went on, "the news of the acceptance of our bid has only just been received but, and many of you will not know this, the bid was made on that fateful Saturday last July, and our success is at least partly due to the unremitting efforts of your vice-president, Derek Kiley." He beamed at Kiley. "It was Mr. Kiley who commanded the ship, if I may say so, during my absence, and it was Mr. Kiley who brought her safely through."

More applause.

"My only regret," JC continued, "is that I was unable to be here with you during those terrible hours, to share your burden. You all know how hard I tried to get to you, and how I was nearly killed, but I bitterly regret my absence. So now, Richard, it gives me great pleasure to present you with this scroll, signed by all the civic authorities and business organisations in this city, and by myself, as a small token of our appreciation of your actions during the approach of Hurricane Faith. And to offer you a new contract with NABS. I believe you have already seen the terms."

"Yes," Richard said.

"And do you accept?"

Although his decision had already been taken, and JC knew it, Richard hesitated before replying. He had been very tempted to tear the contract into pieces. But that would have been stupid—he was a weather man. If he didn't work for NABS he would have to work for some other company, and the odds were he would discover another J. Calthrop White there too. At least, here, he would be listened to in the future. "I accept, JC," he said.

JC shook hands. "Now, finally, ladies and gentlemen," he said, "it gives me great pleasure to announce Richard's engagement to Mrs. Josephine Donnelly. I guess everyone here knows that Mrs. Donnelly's husband perished heroically in the storm. So did two other members of her family. The Donnellys are my friends . . ." He paused to blow his nose. "That their family could have suffered such grievous losses and come up fighting is a fitting testimony to their characters." He shook

Richard's hand again, gave Jo a kiss on the cheek, looked uncertainly at Owen Michael and Tamsin, standing together beside their mother.

"Thank you, JC," Jo said.

"So now I guess you'll need time off for a honeymoon, Richard?"

"I would appreciate that, sir."

JC smiled as he wagged his finger. "Just be sure you're back before the hurricane season."

May

The big amphibian droned through a cloudless sky, her crew looking down on the quiet blue of an untroubled ocean.

"You reckon this has to be the most boring job ever created?" Bob Landry asked. "Day after goddamned day, just looking at sea and sky?"

"Yeah," Mark Hammond agreed. "Well, I guess that's it for today, at least." He thumbed his intercom. "You ready to turn for home, Doc? There sure ain't anything to worry about down there."

"I'd like to stand on a little further, Mark," Eisener replied. "There's a report just coming in about a large stationary cloud mass off the Cape Verdes. I think we should take a look. Don't you?"

Mark looked at Landry, who looked back. "Yeah," the two pilots said together. "We should take a look."

MAX MARLOW

Max Marlow may hold a British passport, but he has scarcely ever lived in the UK. Born of British parents, he was educated in Barbados, then lived on various West Indian islands until a recent move to Spain. His years in the Caribbean gave him more than a taste of what it's like to experience a hurricane. In fact he lived through several during his Barbadian schooldays.

With the enthusiasm of any author about to publish his first novel, Marlow described to us how he arrived at the idea for *Her Name Will Be Faith*. Long ago he knew that the Miami coast could be hit by devastating hurricanes. The last one struck in 1949, when Miami was virtually undeveloped. Now the shore is bursting with hotels, most of which are less than six foot above sea level. A storm surge would devastate the area. He sketched out a plot, but publishers said the story wouldn't sell unless the hurricane were to threaten New York, and *that* wasn't realistic. Disappointed, he put the idea on hold. "Then in 1985 Hurricane Gloria sideswiped the city and of course *Faith* began to take shape in my mind," he says.

Max Marlow now lives in a villa on the Costa Blanca in Spain. He is a keen sailor, but enjoys relaxed cruising on the Mediterranean rather than the sort of high-powered ocean racing that is Michael Donnelly's obsession in *Her Name Will Be Faith*.

More than happy to give up a successful career in banking in the West Indies in order to concentrate on writing, Marlow is now busy working on a new novel. Entitled *The Red Death*, it is the dramatic story of a virulent disease that sweeps across the world, spread in the red corpuscles of the blood. He had enormous fun researching the medical aspects of the book and he assures us, "It really could happen!"

The
Heart
of the
Valley

A CONDENSATION OF
THE BOOK BY

Nigel
Hinton

ILLUSTRATED BY
PAUL ROBINSON

On a freezing January night a little
dunnock, or hedge sparrow, crouches
shuddering on a bare branch. Many
birds and animals in the small Kentish
valley are dying because snow has
covered their food, but driven by hunger
the sparrow decides to risk all and fly off
in search of nourishment. With her mate
she finds refuge in a dry and warm hay
barn, and together they survive until the
same instinct tells them that spring is
just around the corner . . .
Without sentimentality, *The Heart of
the Valley* tells the story of a year in the
life of a hedge sparrow, and of her
unceasing fight for survival.

Chapter One

The bitter cold weather set in during the third week of January. Until then the female dunnock's first winter had been relatively easy. A long, golden autumn had lasted nearly until the end of November. Some sharp night frosts had slightly diminished the supply of insects but there had been abundant seeds to be found during the bright sunny days. An unusually mild and gently moist December had followed, bringing out some insects again, and the little hedge sparrow had fed well. She had started the new year fat and strong. Then the east wind had begun to blow and the temperature had fallen below zero.

For the first three days she spent much of the time huddled up in the thick tangle of her blackthorn bush, conserving her energy. Just before dawn on the fourth day the howling wind died away and snow began to fall. Pangs of hunger and a sudden sense of foreboding drove her out looking for food.

In the grey, early light the thick flakes soon whitened the ground and changed the shapes all around her. She set off along the outer limits of the silver birch wood, searching for seeds before they were covered. The snow filled her with terror. The constant blurring movement confused her so that she often flinched and flew to safety for no good reason. Once, though, her vision was so limited that she was still on the ground when a large form blundered past her out of the maelstrom. It was only a rabbit, but it made her even more uneasy and she spent long periods in the bushes peering out warily at the turmoil of white. She longed to return to the safety of her roost but the hunger inside her had to be satisfied.

155

She darted out again into the danger-filled open and flew in an urgent burst down the slope to a small stream. Normally the soft earth along the edge of the water yielded earthworms, and she often found seeds that had been swept down from higher in the stream's course. Today, though, the worms were locked in the jagged hardness of the frosted ground and the only sign that the stream still flowed was the flickering of air bubbles under the inch-thick ice.

She flitted from bush to bush along the stream until an explosive *tic-tic-tic* alarm call stopped her short. A robin shot from the bracken and stood puffing out his red chest. He raised his head, issued another warning skirl of notes, then hopped aggressively over the snow in her direction. She dipped her head submissively and flew back up the slope away from his territory.

As she flew she tried to make sense of the terrible change that had come over her world. Nothing was the same—the air was thick with falling shapes that, she began to understand, did not threaten her directly but that increased the menace of the outside world. Somewhere out there her enemies prowled or hovered, hidden from her view, perhaps until too late.

At the eastern end of the wood the banks of bracken on the hilltop were already solid with snow and looked like miniature hills and valleys of white. Under this upper icing, though, brown fronds could still be seen near the ground and the dunnock headed for this one familiar feature of her world. She landed just inside the cover, then hopped up onto the bent stem of a fern. The thick snow covering above had pressed the ferns and brambles down, making the tangle of undergrowth darker than ever. At least here, however, the ground was still free of snow.

She waited, motionless, peering into the gloom of the interior. Nothing large could possibly be lurking in so closely interwoven a thicket. She skipped forward into the darkness from branch to branch, stopping and checking for danger after every move. Finally, near the centre of the mass of bushes, she dared to hop down to the ground. The frosts had bitten less deeply here and she began pecking at the leaf litter. The top layer was frozen into clumps which she found hard to turn, but she persevered and managed to uncover one small patch. Here, in close-packed, decaying leaf mould she at last found food—a few seeds and moth pupae.

For the next few hours she worked her way forward, turning the leaf litter, probing for the morsels of food. As her hunger lessened, her other senses became keener. By the time her stomach was filled, every quiver of a leaf was sending her darting onto a branch for safety. The desire to leave this dark, foreign place became stronger and the security of her roost called her. When the increasing weight of the snow caused the branches suddenly to sag lower, she flew off her feeding-ground and out of the exit.

The snow was falling more thickly than ever and she flew almost blind along the edge of the wood until she came to the blackthorn bush. Her roost was right in the centre, next to the main trunk. There, long grass had bent and woven itself around the lowest branch, forming a snug tunnel just large enough for her small body. She hopped her way along the branch and into the comfort and safety of her home. Sheltered from the storm and warmed by the food inside her, she settled down and relaxed. When she fluffed out her feathers to form an insulating layer of warm air, she could feel the comforting pressure of the grass that, during the past months, had come to fit her shape.

The snow stopped at about nine in the evening. The cloud cover began to break up, and towards midnight the last ragged wisps parted to reveal a brilliant moon shining down from the cold, black depths of space. The snow crackled and hardened in the severe frost.

A barn owl, perched high in one of the birch trees, screeched. The long eerie scream woke the dunnock and she shifted closer to the trunk of the bush. The owl peered down, watching for the slightest movement. For five minutes he stayed there, motionless. Then, suddenly, as though angered by the lack of movement, he screeched again and lowered his head and swung it to and fro, snapping his bill. The loud clicks echoed through the silence like the sound of small bones snapping, and they finally unnerved a tree sparrow who was roosting in a holly bush. She fluttered her wings and hopped onto another branch. The slight scratching noise of the holly leaves caught the owl's attention. He raised his head menacingly. His eyes hooded and seemed to close, but through narrow slits he watched for another telltale sign. When none came, he tipped forward and glided down onto the top of the holly bush. He gripped a branch, raised his body, and began wildly beating his wings. The bush rocked and shook until, panic-stricken, the sparrow tumbled out into the darkness. She landed, confused, on the snow and lifted her head in time to catch a last glimpse of the moon; then the light was blocked by the swooping shape of the owl.

His sharp talons crushed the sparrow's skull, and an instant later the limp body was carried away into the night. The dunnock had heard it all, and it was a full hour before her jangling nerves calmed and she slept again.

THE NIGHT WAS LONG and terrible. Hour by hour the temperature fell, until by midnight there were sixteen degrees of frost. Down by the stream the robin who had chased the dunnock swayed on his branch, then toppled forward, dead. In the silver birch wood a tree-creeper froze to death in the ivy where she roosted. All over the area birds were dying.

The dunnock sat hunched in her roost, feathers fluffed out and wings tucked forward towards her breast. She had fed well in the past day and that gave her the strength and warmth to last the night. In all her young life she had been a solitary and independent creature—even aggressive to other birds who came too near. Now the pain and fear she was suffering roused a new desire in her, the desire for comfort from others. The dim but growing need for the shared warmth of another body.

157

AT FIRST LIGHT the dunnock hopped stiffly out of her roost and stood on the end of the branch. The air was so raw that she had to squint at the world through half-closed eyes. She flapped her wings feebly and almost overbalanced, righted herself, flapped her wings again, then took off and flew into the wood. The short flight left her dizzy, and when she landed she had to make a couple of hesitant hops across the snow to stop herself falling over. Her body was cold and she needed to move in order to ease the stiffness, but without some food she would not be able to go on moving for long.

She forced herself to fly in brief bursts through the trees, stopping every few yards to summon up the strength for the next move. At last she emerged from the darkness of the wood and perched on top of a small bullace bush.

To her left she could see the area of bracken and bramble where she had fed on the previous day. During the night a fox who was stalking a mouse had knocked down most of the snow and her feeding ground was covered with it—now the seeds would be locked and hidden beneath the frozen crust. She flew over the bracken and set down on the snow on the other side. From here the rough pastureland sloped steeply down to the valley.

At the bottom of the hill ran a hedge-bordered lane. Across that was a narrow strip of pasture, then the small river that had, over long centuries, created the valley. Beyond the line of trees on the other side of the river lay a small community of scattered houses—Brook Cottage, Little Ashden and Forge Farm. From the hedges surrounding Brook Cottage came the faint chatter of many birds. Smoke curled up from the chimney of the house, spreading out and forming a blue haze in the cold, still air along the valley.

All this area was beyond the dunnock's territory. Before this moment her life had been strictly bounded by an instinct to stay near her roost, but now two even stronger urges were pushing her: she needed food and, almost as much as food, she needed company.

For a long time fear held her back. Then a blue door at the side of Brook Cottage opened. A woman appeared and the noise of the birds stopped. A small black and white dog ran out of the door and began tearing round the garden, yapping and leaping at unseen enemies. The woman busied herself round a tall wooden object in the centre of the garden. After a few minutes she returned to the door and called. The dog stopped his wild chasing and ran inside.

The door closed. There was a short pause and then birds began flying towards the wooden object. The chattering notes began again—now shriller and more excited—and they spoke of one thing: food.

The restricting patterns of her past held the dunnock back. Then the call from below overcame her fear and gave strength to her wings. She forsook her territory and flew down into the unknown.

Chapter Two

The dunnock landed on the snow at the top of the neatly clipped hedge of Brook Cottage and looked at the hectic activity. A large bird table stood in the centre of the garden, piled high with seed, grain and breadcrumbs. Four starlings and three mistle thrushes occupied the table at that moment, feeding and squabbling with such frantic movements that they were rocking the wooden support and sending showers of food tumbling onto the snow below. On the ground, dozens of smaller birds waited for this falling harvest, flying off to various parts of the garden whenever they found a morsel too big to eat at one gulp.

The air was filled with sharp calls of alarm and threat as each bird fought for its share. The noise and rapid action scared the dunnock, but her need for food was terrible so she dropped forward from the hedge and glided down onto the trampled snow. She hopped towards a piece of crust, picked it up in her bill and flew off, to find shelter under a bent cabbage plant and begin pecking at the crust and swallowing the crumbs.

All morning the dunnock stayed near the bird table, gulping down whatever small items she could. She dived among the trampling legs and claws to snatch at crumbs and seeds, often missing them because of the need to watch out for unexpected attack. There was little aggression in her nature, so she did not spend energy chasing other birds. Instead, she hopped round gobbling each undisputed piece she could find.

Only twice was she driven away from the feeding area. The first time a short-tempered yellowhammer took a fancy to a seed which the dunnock had just taken into her bill. The yellowhammer sprang at her and chased her the length of the garden. She flew into a small gap under the wooden step up to the potting shed. He didn't bother to follow, but he called angrily at the entrance for a while and strutted importantly up and down for a final demonstration of his victory before flying back to the food. The dunnock stayed where she was, giving her already full stomach time to digest and absorb some of the food.

In mellower weather conditions she would have gone back to her roost at this point and only started to eat again later in the day. During a severe cold spell like this, though, her body needed well over one third of its own weight in food every day just to keep her blood at the right temperature. So as soon as she could cram in more food she returned to the hustling, flurrying search round the table. She kept a respectful distance from the yellowhammer, but he didn't even seem to notice her presence.

Late in the morning came the second interruption. There was a harsh calling noise and a large group of magpies flew in over the rooftop of Brook Cottage. As one, the smaller birds scattered for cover. The dunnock made for the privet hedge, pushed her way through it, and flew up the hill to the safety of the bracken.

The sun was now at its height and she perched on the bracken, absorbing its warmth and looking back to the garden. The area was now the property of the bullying magpies. A couple of them stood lurching uneasily on the table-top but most of them were hopping clumsily round the base, pecking at what remained of the food. There were frequent quarrels as one seized another's food and flew off, pursued by its shrieking rival.

For the first time since the cold had begun, the sun was shining warmly enough to melt the snow. Some branches of trees on the edge of the wood began to drip, and the dunnock flitted down to sip some drops of water from the mushy snow.

When the magpies at last flew off in a whirl of white flashing wings and long tails, the smaller birds returned to the garden. The dunnock joined them, only to find that the hour-long raid by the magpies had finished the food. The table was empty and there was nothing to be seen in the churned-up snow around it. Along with some of the others, the dunnock began patiently probing and turning the snow for seeds and crumbs that had been trampled under. As the afternoon wore on and the cold descended again, the numbers still searching for hidden pieces diminished. The snow started to crisp and freeze, and as the sun set it became impossible to move it. By this stage only a couple of starlings, a robin and the dunnock remained. Her perseverance had paid off and she was full of food. She flew up the hill, along the edge of the wood and into her roost. The hollowed grass welcomed her into its snug fit and she settled down for the night.

Once again the temperature dropped steadily and a numbing frost clamped down. The dunnock's blood, heated by the store of food she had eaten, pumped round her body, keeping out the icy clutches of the night.

NOW THAT HER HUSBAND had died and her son had gone off to college, Eve Conrad lived alone in Brook Cottage. She had just put some coke in the kitchen range and damped it down for the night, when the telephone rang. The vice-principal of her son's college broke the news gently but left her in no doubt about the seriousness of the accident. Daniel had been standing in a bus queue when a car had skidded on the icy road and mounted the pavement. He was in a London hospital. There was no immediate danger, the vice-principal said, but perhaps she would want to be with him?

Five minutes later Eve locked the house and picked up Teddy, her small black and white Yorkshire terrier. Her shoes crunched on the snow as she walked down the rough track that led to Little Ashden and Forge Farm. She was relieved to see that there was still a light on downstairs at Little Ashden.

The barn owl, perched silently in a beech tree by the river, watched her pass. He saw her go up to the door of Little Ashden and ring. He saw the door open and he heard the hurried conversation between Eve Conrad and Mary Lawrence. He saw Mary touch Eve gently on the arm, take the dog inside, then close the door. Unblinking, he followed Eve's progress back down the track into the lane, then his attention was taken by the movement of something small and black by the riverbank. The creature darted into a hole.

The owl was still peering intently at the hole when he heard a metallic whirring noise. His head spun round as he sought the source of the sound, and he focused his eyes across the river, over the narrow strip of pasture and beyond the lane. The engine of Mrs. Conrad's car whirred again, seemed to catch, coughed and stopped. Another whirr, and the engine fired and kept going. There was a roar and Eve eased the car into gear and drove steadily in the direction of the distant village and the main road.

THE DUNNOCK STAYED in her roost until late next morning, avoiding the first chilly hours of light before the sun came over the hills. This was breaking the routine of her whole lifetime, but already she had learned that the frost made it difficult to pick up food early in the day.

The hedges were already filled with birds when she got to Brook Cottage. A few were searching in the snow for fragments of the previous day's food, but were finding nothing. There was a mounting pitch of excitement in the tone of the song all round her and the dunnock joined in, giving voice to her rising anxiety as no new food appeared.

The tension increased with the passing of time, and bitter little disputes began breaking out. There were hostile notes in the song-patterns and sudden flurries and squeaks and chases. Wings were raised angrily and bills were opened in warning gapes. The dunnock felt the waves of threat and spite, and they made her uneasy. She was in foreign territory, surrounded by the noise and motion of birds who might attack her at any minute, and she was becoming weaker. She poised herself, ready to fly back to her old, familiar world. Then, high above the angry, despairing sounds of the birds round her, came the song of one of her own kind.

The song, fast and repeated over and over, came from way beyond the house, across the lane. The first few notes of its insistent pattern blared out defiance and warning, filling her with dread. Then, at the end of each round, came three notes—soft, begging and tender. When the song finally stopped, these three notes still echoed in her body.

She flew to the front hedge and paused for a moment. The lane was a divide that would separate her utterly from her known world: the hedgerow on the other side was an alien land full of possible dangers. Twice she flicked her wings in pretended flight before she shot into the air, soaring almost vertically as if up the face of an invisible wall. She peaked at about fifty feet, and just before she glided down she uttered a rapid series of calls. She landed on the opposite hedgerow at the point where it curved down the track towards Little Ashden and Forge Farm. She had crossed the divide.

~Paul Robinson~

She moved along the track, landing now on the small white gate that led into the long strip of pasture, now on the wooden handrail at the side of the bridge, now on the rusted iron posts of the low fence opposite Little Ashden. Teddy was lying mournfully on the broad windowsill, staring through the glass in the hope of seeing his beloved mistress appear. He saw the dunnock land, and sat up and yapped. His breath misted the cold glass in front of his face and his nose made a neat round mark in the mist as he yapped excitedly again. Theo Lawrence, who was reading in front of the fire, called him gently. At once Teddy forgot the dunnock, leaped to the floor, and ran to the armchair. Theo raised his paper and Teddy jumped up and settled down on his lap.

The dunnock flew on, leaving the track and crossing the field to the river. She stopped on top of a low bush near the bank and called. There was no reply, only the roar of the river as it tumbled over the five stone steps of the weir. She returned to the track and followed it up towards the two oast-houses of Forge Farm. At the base of the first oast-house she perched on the harrow that Jim Siddy had moved out of the barn earlier in the morning. The huge tyres of the tractor that Jim had used had left furrows in the snow, exposing the track beneath, and in the cinder the dunnock saw some food. She swooped down and began eating the crushed grain, following the tracks until she entered the main yard of the farm.

Intent on her feeding, the dunnock hopped nearer the entrance of one of the barns and then flinched as something moved inside it. She looked up and saw a large Sussex yearling bullock staring at her. The bullock had pushed his purple-red head through the slats in the barrier across the doorway and had got it stuck. The warm breath from his wet nostrils steamed in the cold air and his eyes rolled as he pulled and twisted his head. The violent jerks rattled the planks, and the dunnock flew off across the yard, landing on the gate that led into the farm garden.

Suddenly, the song began again—nearer and startlingly intense. The sound was coming from the roof of a long building that she had passed on her way up the track. The sun appeared to be sitting just behind the crest of this roof, and the song seemed to be flooding out from the heart of its brightness. As her eyes became accustomed to the glare, the dunnock saw a small shape on the end of the roof ridge. This silhouette trembled with the passion of its song and its wings fluttered so that the sun seemed to shine through its body.

It was a male of her kind, and his beauty struck her with joy and fear. The new feathers on his back and wings glowed and throbbed with colour, and the rich brown and black streaks made him look bigger than he was, like some powerful predator. And yet the slate-grey feathers of his neck and breast looked so soft that she wanted to lie beneath them.

Then, unexpectedly and without even a warning note, the male charged, half running and half flying. He was after her. She burst into flight, skimming over the track, through the wooden bars of the fence and over the snow-covered pasture towards the river. He darted at her from the left, and rather than dodge away from him she curved her wings and flew directly at him, forcing him to swerve away below her. This took him too low and he landed roughly on the snow while she streaked away and landed on a hazel bush by the riverbank.

Her heart beat with the excitement and exhilaration of the chase. This was not like some squabble with another bird; the fright she felt was thrilling, and the jingle of notes she started singing to him bubbled with delighted confusion. "Come. Go. Come. Go. Go. Come. Come." He responded immediately with a boasting trill that threatened *all* intruders. This was his territory, and to prove it he leaped into the air and buzzed her perch. His wing tips swept across her eyes and she nearly toppled. He landed on the branch above her and uttered a violent, shrieking rattle of notes, and at once her feelings changed. He was in earnest—his threats were real, and included her. He would chase her, fight her, even kill her, unless she left his territory.

She dashed from the bush, seized with terror. Her wings beat wildly as she followed the course of the river, her strength failing quickly as she banked and zigzagged, desperate to get away from him. At every turn she made he gained on her, threatening her now from above and now from below. She swept over the weir, flying straight through the fine mist of spray that rose in the air above it, and there ahead was the wooden bridge. She flicked her wings and glided underneath it, landing on one of the supporting struts. She crouched there, her chest heaving and the blood pounding in her head. The river swirled and bubbled below, drowning all other sounds with its hissing and gurgling. She peered fearfully back to the entrance, but there was no sign of the male.

She waited for a while, then wearily leaned forward and launched herself into the air. As she emerged into the bright light at the far side of the bridge, the male dived at her from the handrail where he'd been waiting. She summoned up all her strength and whipped her tired muscles into action, soaring up to the right, away from the river, in the direction of Little Ashden. The male followed, close on her tail, his strident cries piercing her ear.

The weariness of her shoulders knotted the muscles, and she knew she could go no further. She stopped beating her wings and held them out stiffly in a glide to the nearest perch. Exhausted, she landed where she had first seen the male, on the roof of the long outbuilding. He landed beyond her, skipped round and charged. All her instincts screamed for escape, but her body could not respond. As he swept in to attack she ducked, opened her bill wide, and let out her breath in a feeble, begging squeak. It was an act of total submission.

The male reared up. His chest puffed out and his wings spread wide until all she could see was him above her. For an instant she was torn by the desire to fight and the desire to be crushed. Then the feathers round the male's throat swelled and a tremor shook his head. He backed away, uttered three notes of pure, soft song, then flitted out of sight down the snow-laden roof.

She stayed there, neck extended and bill gaping, for a moment, then straightened up and looked around. He was gone. She turned and looked towards Brook Cottage. The male was nowhere in sight, but suddenly his voice came from somewhere below her. She glided down to the ground and jerked her head in all directions, looking for him. His voice now came from above her and she glanced up. He was perched in a small triangular hole at the edge of the glass of a narrow window near the top of the wall, his head facing into the building. He balanced on the broken edge of the glass, flicked his tail, and disappeared inside.

A moment later his voice came to her, a brief, inviting trill. She ducked her head, looking along the track, then peered back at the hole. Once more the male sang his short invitation, then he flew out and back into the hole, giving a couple of enticing flicks of his tail before he disappeared.

This time she followed, flying up to the window, trying to judge the width of the small hole. As she drew near, she drove her legs forward and her toes clamped onto the edge of the glass. At last she closed her wings and heaved herself through. The air inside the room was warm and sweet, reminding her of the rich harvest days at the end of the summer. Somewhere in the gloom of this scented warmth the male's voice called to her.

Outside, a couple of tiny snowflakes drifted past the window on the stiffening breeze. They heralded the renewal of the snow and the beginning of the worst blizzard in living memory.

Chapter Three

The large room into which the dunnock had flown contained the bales of hay that Jim Siddy had cut during the summer as winter feed for his cattle.

She landed on one of three beams that straddled the room a couple of feet below the ceiling. The male was on the floor, rooting among fallen strands of hay and evidently finding plenty to eat. Despite her hunger, the dunnock was too timid to join him. She'd never been inside a building before, and although it was warm and seemed free from danger she was overawed at being in an enclosed space. In addition, this was the male's territory—and this was his food.

At length, though, she plucked up courage and flew down to the floor a safe distance away from the male. He looked up and regarded her for a moment, then resumed his search. In front of her she saw the spiky head of a ribwort plantain, rich with seed. It was one of her favourite foods and a temptation too hard to resist. She pecked a seed, then raised her eyes to look at the male. As she did so she saw another head of plantain to her left, and another beyond that. The floor was littered with it. The sight of all this food and the male's continued indifference finally dispelled her fear and she began to eat.

When at last her hunger was satisfied, she flew up to the beam and looked through the hole in the window. Outside the snow fell heavily, driven by gale-force blasts of wind that sent it swirling back into the air before hurling it down in sudden diagonal sweeps.

A steady stream of snowflakes was being blown through the opening to melt on the floor. Part of her longed for the familiarity of her roost, but the savagery of the storm outside, the food and warmth she had found, and the presence of the male all urged her to stay. He was perched snugly on a ledge, his shoulders hunched and his head tucked down so that his bill was hidden under a wing. He raised his head drowsily and called—two soft, bubbling notes that spoke of warmth and comfort and companionship.

It was enough. She spread her wings and flew to join him.

Two hours later, standing side by side, they heard Jim Siddy's Land-Rover pass along the track. He and Jill had debated ringing some of their friends in the village to ask if they could pick up the girls, Amy and Rosa, from school and look after them overnight. In the end Jim had decided to trust the Land-Rover to get him to the village school and back. The four-mile round journey took him an hour and a half. When his headlights finally lit up the whirling snow in the yard, Jill burst out of the front door in relief to welcome her family home. The Land-Rover was the last vehicle to make the journey along the lane for more than a week.

THE SNOW FELL, whipped by the wind, for thirty-six hours. When it stopped, the valley was an almost featureless layer of white. Hedgerows and small bushes had been obliterated, and the branches of trees creaked and groaned under their shrouds of snow.

Brook Cottage, on the western side of the valley, had been hardest hit: the snow had piled up at the front almost to the level of the first-floor windows. In the back garden the bird table was so deeply buried that there was no sign of it at all.

Forge Farm, two hundred and fifty yards away on the other side of the valley, had been less affected. Jim had managed to dig a narrow trench along to the storehouse. He pushed open the door and ducked in surprise as the two dunnocks flew past his head in panic. After their long isolation this sudden intrusion of light and noise startled them, and the shock of what they found outside increased their confusion. The male instinctively headed for the fence across the track, his usual perch when he left the storeroom, only to find that it had gone.

In surprise, he set down on the snow and immediately felt his legs sink into its soft surface. The female had followed his example, and for a moment they both floundered, their wings beating and showering each other with snow, before they managed to get back into the air.

Not daring to land on the treacherous, yielding surface again, the male

166

flew in a long arc across the pasture towards the river. The female flew after him. He had shown her food and a safe roost, and now she trusted his leadership. They dodged through the maze of heavy-laden, bending branches on the riverbank, then swerved downstream.

By the time they flew back to the storehouse, Jim had taken the four bales of hay he needed and had dragged them up the deep, narrow path on the girls' sledge. Loose seeds and strands of hay were scattered outside the door and along the path. A ravenous group of birds, mostly starlings and blackbirds, had found them and were pecking and squabbling at the bottom of the sheer-sided trench in the snow. The dunnocks flew over them and through the small hole in the window.

Jill Siddy noticed the number of birds scrabbling round for scraps in the yard and resolved to put out some food for them later. She looked down towards Little Ashden. The Lawrences didn't have a phone and she wondered whether they were all right. She was reassured to see that there were lights in the house and smoke coming from the chimney.

In fact, the Lawrences were perfectly well and happy. Theo Lawrence, despite his sixty-nine years, was even feeling a childlike thrill at the adventure. He had enjoyed digging a short path from the kitchen door to the coal bunker, and now he could barely restrain a smile of pleasure from creeping across his face. Outside, the coming night would be harsh, but in here the fire glowed warmly, his wife Mary was reading in her chair, and Teddy was curled up at her feet. He closed the curtains.

In the storehouse, the dunnocks were already asleep.

EVE CONRAD HAD INTENDED to be up in London for only a couple of days but, when she rang the Siddys and heard that the valley was cut off, she was glad of the excuse to stay near Daniel. His fractured leg had been pinned and would have to remain in traction for at least a month, but there were no complications and despite the pain he managed to be relatively cheerful.

Jill rushed down to pass on the good news to the Lawrences. Jim had, at last, cleared a path to Little Ashden and although they were cut off from the rest of the world there was a frequent and friendly traffic between the two houses. Theo was more than pleased to wrap up warmly and give Jim a hand with some of the extra work on the farm. Every lunchtime both families sat down at the large kitchen table in Forge Farm and shared the meal that Jill had prepared.

A WEEK AFTER THE BLIZZARD stopped, the shared food supplies began to run out. Jim had daily expected the snowploughs to come and clear the lane, and he and Theo had widened the path along the track so that the Land-Rover would be able to leave immediately for the village. But day after day the lane had stayed closed, hidden under snow so deep that it was impossible to tell where the hedgerows were on either side. At last he rang the local council to explain the seriousness of the situation. The harassed official promised to see what he could do.

Late the next afternoon Jim and Theo were busy working in the barn when they heard the distant roar of an engine. They rushed down the track and were just in time to see the large yellow snowplough surge past, pushing an eight-foot wall of snow off the lane and into the area they had cleared. The two men gasped in disbelief at all their wasted work, and Theo laid a hand on Jim's shoulder and began to chuckle.

On his own, Jim could not have taken it so lightly but now, with a gesture of mock despair, he joined in·the laughter. They went back for their shovels and began to work at once, anxious to force a passage through, so that they could get down to the village before the shops closed. It was hard going, but Theo was pleased to be able to keep pace with Jim. He had been altogether too lazy over the last few years, since he had retired, and the past week had sharpened his appetite for physical work. He'd said as much to Jim the day before and had, half jokingly, offered his services on a casual basis after the crisis was over. Jim's immediate and enthusiastic acceptance of the offer had delighted and flattered him.

For Jim the arrangement was perfect. Running a small farm was a precarious and exhausting business and there were many times during the year when he wished he could call on some reliable assistance, but he had never been able to afford full-time help. During the past week he had been amazed at Theo's enthusiasm and energy, and they had developed an excellent relationship.

Half an hour after they started, the two men finally hacked a way through the wall of snow and took the Land-Rover down to the village to buy supplies. The isolation was over.

Chapter Four

Although the lane was now open, the journey to the village was still difficult and could only be attempted in a vehicle like the Land-Rover. The postman and the milkman tried to get to the valley, but both failed, so Jim picked up the mail and the milk when he took Amy and Rosa down to school. It was also he who went down to fetch Eve Conrad; she had driven from London but hadn't dared risk her car on the last part of the journey from the village to Brook Cottage.

Jim and Theo carved a way through the snow to her front door, then lit the fires for her. The house was icy cold, so while it warmed up she spent the rest of the day at Little Ashden, exchanging news with Mary Lawrence. Daniel was making good progress and would be out of traction in about three weeks. After that he would have to keep all weight off his leg for a couple of months and, since he had exams coming up, she and the doctors had persuaded him to come and revise for them at home.

When Eve finally went back to Brook Cottage, the house still felt chilly and unlived-in. Teddy's reaction was warm enough, though, and he followed her everywhere, his whole rear end wagging with pleasure at being home with her.

Early the next morning, Eve cleared a path through the snow and uncovered the bird table. Many times while she had been in London, she had thought about how the birds must be suffering. She felt that she had failed them at the worst possible moment.

Back at the kitchen window she watched for the first arrivals. Normally birds were waiting in the hedges for the food, but this morning it was ten minutes before a passing chaffinch landed on the roof of the potting shed and regarded the pile of seeds for a moment before flying down to the table. As he pecked with his stout bill at the first seed, he was joined by a bluetit and, shortly afterwards, by a greenfinch.

Eve smiled. Already the garden was enlivened by yellow and blue and rusty red. Already the frozen stillness was broken by bobbing tails and flicking wings. Soon the silence would be filled with the chatter and song of excited birds, and again she would be able to delight in their beauty.

THE NIGHTS WERE STILL icy cold and even in the middle of the day the temperature barely rose above freezing point, so the snow lay as deep as ever. For nearly another two weeks the countryside lay under its white shroud.

Then, suddenly, the temperature rose dramatically. A warm wind blew from the southwest and everything started to drip. So rapid was the thaw that in the low-lying pastures the ground appeared from under the snow, only to disappear under water as the river flooded.

A mist persisted for four days, hiding everything in its melancholy limpness. Then, towards the end of the fifth day, the sun could be seen glowing dimly red as it set behind the hills, and the following morning the mist lifted for good. By midday the sky was a vivid blue. The sun shone warmly and the valley throbbed with bright colour after the long weeks of monochrome.

The female dunnock flew out from the storehouse window that morning and landed on the bright red roof tiles that she had never seen before in all her time of living there. The sun warmed her back and the whole valley was bathed in its fresh light. The beauty of the scene exploded in her breast and she burst into the air, piping.

She soared high above the oast-houses, then swooped low over the grass, heading towards the river, only to wheel up above the trees in an exultant desire to use her muscles and feathers to their fullest extent.

As she swept back to the storehouse roof, the male rose to join her. Together they flew the whole width of the valley. The female felt the call of her old home-site, but the lure of the male was stronger. As she followed him in a long climb above the smoke that rose from the chimney of Brook

Cottage, she saw the valley below and her bursting heart claimed it all.

Nearly three thousand miles away there was another bird who would have bitterly disputed such a claim.

THE FEMALE CUCKOO, who was in a baobab tree trying to shelter from one of the violent afternoon thunderstorms that regularly soaked that part of Africa, had been born on the edge of the Oakdown Forest, only a couple of miles away from the valley. Her host parents had been a pair of reed warblers who, after their own offspring had been methodically ejected from the nest by the young cuckoo, had devoted all their energy to nurturing her. By the time she had been ready to leave the nest, the two reed warblers had had to stand on the huge back of their insatiable foster child in order to feed her. She had spent the rest of the summer building up her strength and perfecting her powers of flight.

Then, though she had never even known one of her own kind, she had taken to the air one day and made a journey that countless generations of her forebears had made in the past. Unerringly she had followed the same route across Europe, over the Mediterranean and down into Central Africa.

Now, in the first days of March, she was beginning to feel the pull of the valley that she thought of as her own. Soon she would be back, seeking out host nests for her eggs, indifferent to the fact that each egg she laid was like a time bomb that would wreck the nest.

THE WARM SUNNY WEATHER lasted for the whole of the first week of March. After the hardship of the winter, everything in the valley responded to the warmth and brightness. The trees that had creaked and groaned under their loads of snow now rustled and whispered in the breeze as their branches stretched and swayed and began to push out buds. Fresh green shoots were springing up among the tired, brown tussocks of grass on the hillsides, and at the end of her garden, Eve Conrad noticed, some early daffodils were beginning to unfold.

Not long after dawn each day the two dunnocks flew out from the storehouse to join in the general exultation that greeted the arrival of spring. Normally, their lives were governed solely by the deep and urgent needs of survival for themselves and their species, but for this brief period they did little but celebrate the sheer joy of being alive. They flew for no other purpose than to rejoice in the strength and mastery of flight. They shook and preened their feathers in sensuous delight in their bodies, and they sang in triumphant exhilaration at the beauty around them.

Once, exhausted after a playful chase through the sky, they landed on the roof of one of the oast-houses and looked down at the bustle in and around Forge Farm. Amy and Rosa Siddy passed, chanting about sailing away in a bonny balloon—a song that, for no good reason, they had suddenly remembered from their nursery days. They were hauling rubbish out to the edge of the field that led down to the river, where their father and Theo Lawrence were piling it onto a huge fire whose flames shimmered transparently in the sunlight.

Suddenly Will, the Siddys' black labrador, seized a large cardboard box that was waiting to be thrown onto the fire. The box was almost as large as he was, and as he gripped it in his jaws and pulled, it swung up and over his head and landed, open side down, on his back. Now a box with four glossy black legs frisked away across the field, pursued by the two men, whose laughter and high-spirited shouts were as exuberant as those of the two girls, who dropped their load and rushed to join in the game.

The same spirit of play was the starting point of the dunnocks' nest-building. The two birds were perched on the roof of the storehouse when a flock of doves, from a dovecote in the garden of one of the large houses that lay beyond the hills, wheeled overhead. As they turned abruptly and their white bodies and wings created kaleidoscopic patterns against the blue sky, a small feather fell from the breast of one of the birds. The male dunnock, intrigued by its movement, darted into the air after it. He snapped it up in his bill and carried it back to the roof. There he dropped it and watched it slide along the tiles in the puffs of wind. It had just reached the edge of the roof and was about to tumble into the gutter, when he flew after it and grabbed it again.

Then, on a sudden impulse, he continued his flight down and through the window into the storeroom. When the female followed him a few minutes later, she found him on the ledge where they slept. He had laid the feather there. She dropped to the floor, picked up a strand of hay, and flew up and laid it beside the feather. Then she pushed both of them into position up against the rafter and flew down for another strand. She, had started a nest.

Deep within both of them, the week of delight and the sense of a reborn world had stirred the need to sustain life by creating it themselves. For a while their movements and actions had been prompted by nothing more than the joy of doing them. Now, suddenly, the emphasis changed.

Before, the female had been content to follow the male and be dazzled and inspired by the glowing brightness of his feathers, the beauty of his song, and the power of his flight, but she now asserted herself at the centre of the activity. She it was who rejected and tossed aside unsuitable building material, and she it was who continually moved into the middle of the accumulating pile of hay to push and press it into the beginning of a cup shape. The male mostly stood and watched, or went hunting.

The ledge was narrow and often, as the female tried to fuss a new piece into position, her movements sent a shower of the patiently gathered material cascading off the beam onto the floor below. She hardly seemed to notice these setbacks, but patiently searched for new material.

When the light began to fade, she flew out to join the male in the hunt for food. On their return they settled down to roost on either side of the nest as

though guarding it from intruders. The next day, and half of the day after that, the female worked on the nest, and as it took shape the male spent more and more time perched on the cracked glass of the window shrilling the warning notes that told the rest of the world that this was his territory. Innocent birds who just happened to be passing were subjected to hostile displays. If they did not leave at once he flew directly at them, chittering so fiercely that they always fled rather than face his anger. Despite all this aggressive vigilance, there was one intruder that he had not bargained for.

It was nearly dusk. The main work on the nest had been completed almost two days before, but the female was still busy rearranging a piece of moss inside the cup. She prodded it into its new position, then pressed her breast against it to mould it into shape.

Earlier in the day, a large rat that lived in the sewers under Forge Farm had entered the outbuilding in search of food. He had climbed a pile of boxes and reached the ledge on which the dunnocks' nest was built. Now he stood stock-still, peering at the nest in the gathering gloom. The female's dark colouring made her almost invisible above the rim.

Satisfied, at last, with the arrangement of the moss, the female hopped out of the nest and looked critically at the result of her hard work. She bent forward and picked roughly at the external weave of the hay as if to test its ability to withstand violent jolts.

The rat watched the flicking of the female's tail and finally decided that the creature was small enough to attack. He broke into a careful run, his flank pressed against the wall and his long tail flexed over the lip of the ledge to give him extra balance. It was the slithering sound of the tail against the rough texture of the ledge that warned the female. Her head flicked up and round, and an instant later she was in the air, twittering in a shriek of alarm. The rat shot past where the dunnock had stood and jumped into the nest in the hope of finding eggs or nestlings.

The burst of flight had taken the female across the room and she landed on the central beam, her heart racing with shock and fright. Now, safe from immediate attack, she exploded into calls of indignation and rage that brought the male flying to the entrance to investigate. He perched for a second on the edge of the glass, then launched himself into a frantic defence of the nest. Chattering wildly, he flew straight at the rat, swinging in so fearlessly low that his wing tips brushed the brown fur on its back. The rat flinched at the sudden noise and blur of movement but, as the male banked away and turned for another attack, he quickly raised himself on his hind legs and bared his teeth. Again the male passed perilously close and the rat was unwisely tempted to lean out in an attempt to grab a wing. All his weight was thrown onto the front of the nest, and it tipped. His feet scrabbled frantically, but it was hopeless. He toppled forward and the nest went with him, breaking up as it fell.

The rat twisted in midair and managed to land on the floor with his legs braced for the shock. As the shower of hay and moss poured onto his back, he bounded away in panic, searching for an escape route. He dashed along one wall to the door, then bolted back towards the hay and squeezed himself into a dark gap between two bales. As he disappeared from view, the male dunnock, in useless bravado, swooped to the floor chittering threats, while the female, more concerned about the loss of the nest, flew to where it had been and looked down at the wreckage.

It was nearly dark, so it would be impossible to start rebuilding now, and anyway the rat's attack had tainted the site with an aura of fear. This room, which had kept them warm during the winter, now felt too enclosed, and heavy with menace.

Chapter Five

The morning after their nest had been destroyed, the two dunnocks set off in search of a new nesting site. From first light onwards they began crisscrossing the valley, critically examining bush after bush. They started with the shrubs along the riverbank, but the constant noise and movement of the water warned the female that it was a dangerous area. They flew past Forge Farm and investigated the stout branches of some elder bushes, and then, higher up near the sandstone rocks, the dense shrubs of broom. All the best sites already belonged to other birds and they grew accustomed to being chased away by the indignant owners.

This happened at one site that the female particularly liked. They flew along the back of the outbuildings and found a barberry bush growing up against the wall. A dog rose had woven its way through some of the lower branches, forming an intricate mesh that would be an excellent base for a nest. The male flew up to the roof of the outbuildings to check the site from there, and the female made experimental flights to determine the best route in and out of the centre of the bush. Everything seemed perfect until a hen blackbird suddenly arrived. She stood on the ground chattering angrily, claiming the territory as hers. By that time the dunnocks felt so strongly about the place that the male started to dispute with the blackbird despite her much larger size. He had only uttered a few notes, however, when the cock blackbird arrived, eyes glaring fiercely and yellow bill stabbing in an argument that brooked no reply. The dunnocks fled, pursued by the blackbirds, and took cover in the eaves of the calves' barn. They were still there a few minutes later when Theo Lawrence came out of the door below them and picked up the large wheelbarrow.

He had just finished cleaning out and refilling the calves' drinking trough and was off to the storehouse to fetch some hay. Will was lying next to his kennel and through lazy, half-closed eyes he watched Theo turn the corner. There was a pause of a couple of seconds after Theo disappeared while Will weighed up the potential interest of accompanying him, then he lumbered to his feet, shook himself, and trotted across the yard.

Theo had just parked the wheelbarrow and was reaching for the door of the storehouse when Will bounded up to him, wagging his heavy tail so enthusiastically that the whole of his hindquarters swung with it. Theo patted the dog's broad back, then gently nudged him aside so that he could open the door.

The rat had spent the night vainly looking for a way out. Now, as the door swung open, he darted towards the sudden light. Will only saw the rat at the last moment as it streaked past him and out of the door. He sprang back in astonishment, then spun round and set off in pursuit.

As the huge, panting creature grew closer, the rat tried a desperate zigzag movement, lowering his body and snaking left, then right, then left again. Out of the corner of his eye he saw the dog veer away in the wrong direction, and he headed across the track towards the field. Only at the last moment did he realise that he had been outmanoeuvred. He caught a glimpse of the large black body falling towards him, and then felt a terrible pain as he was knocked to the ground. Theo reached the doorway just in time to see the dog's final pounce. Will grabbed the rat by the back and with a quick toss of his head severed its spinal cord.

Ten minutes later, as Jim Siddy drove past the storehouse in his Land-Rover, a large crow which was on the fence eyeing the rat's body flapped into the air. The two dunnocks, perched in the scarlet branches of a dogwood bush next to the river, also saw the Land-Rover go by. They had been inspecting the bush as a possible nesting site, but the rattle and boom of the wheels on the wooden bridge startled them and they flew upstream and over the river. On the other bank they examined the potential of a bullace bush that was set back from the river, but it was too small and exposed to offer the necessary cover. So they flew on across the narrow strip of pastureland towards the lane. The female climbed high to avoid the hedge and continued climbing, over the lane, over the front garden of Brook Cottage, and up onto the roof of the house. She landed on the gutter, turned round with a quick hop, and looked for the male. She had expected him to follow her but he was nowhere in sight.

At length the call of the male began, shrill and urgent. When the female turned to trace the sound she saw him sitting safely on the hedge on the other side of the lane. His cry was so commanding now that the female sprang into the air and dived to join him. As she prepared to land, the male took off and swung down into the side of the hedge, so she adjusted her flight and followed him through the maze of branches to the interior. It was an old hedge, mostly hawthorn and hazel, that ran the whole length of the lane. At one time it had been tended and trimmed by craftsmen, but now the council sent a mechanical trimmer that ripped and savaged the sides and the top into some sort of shape each autumn. The years of skilled husbandry still showed at the heart of the hedge, where the central trunks stood thick and solid and the branches spread neatly and evenly.

It was here that the male stopped and let the female discover for herself what a fine site it was. The thin holly bush on the left provided an excellent windbreak and also secured that side against invasion by a large animal. Above, the past training of the branches had created a tightly woven network that would give shelter from the rain. Below, the thick under-growth would cut the draught, and to the right the hazel, already thick with hanging catkins, would soon form a screen of leaves. Yet despite all this cover and protection there were clear and direct flight paths in front and behind her. The closeness to the lane was a drawback, but in every other respect the site seemed perfect, and to show her consent she flew out of the hedge and returned with a twig.

For the next hour she flew in and out bringing twigs, roots and thick stems of grass. She laid them haphazardly, building up a secure base by the sheer weight and mass of the pieces.

THE FOLLOWING DAY the female dunnock was at work soon after first light. Onto the solid base she now began to place the twigs that would serve as the framework for the soft heart of the nest. Unlike the previous day when she had collected virtually any material that she could carry, this framework needed thin twigs of roughly the same length. Consequently, she ranged further afield in her search, often flying hundreds of yards and rooting around for a long time before selecting a possible item. She worked at top speed and stopped only occasionally to rest or feed, but there was no frantic haste, just the rhythm of total absorption.

MARY LAWRENCE WAS FEELING frustrated and angry. She had washed some blankets and was hanging them on the line. She had already trailed one on the ground and would have to rewash it, and now she had snagged the end of another on the rough edge of the basket. She pulled roughly at the loose thread to break it, but it only unravelled. Angrily, she jerked it again and it unravelled some more. Only when she had pulled and unravelled a whole line of thread was she forced to act calmly. Keeping her temper in check, she sought the right grip, broke the thread cleanly, rolled it into a ball and hurled it into the hedge. During the next hour the thread was blown from point to point, snagging temporarily on something, then snapping free, until it blew across the lane and into the privet hedge along the front of Brook Cottage. There it wrapped itself round a low branch.

SOON AFTER SHE HAD STARTED in the morning, the dunnock had been disturbed by the loud, throbbing roar of the tractor as it turned out of the track onto the lane, heading for the fields where Jim Siddy was planning to plant his spring barley. Eight hours later she was still hard at work putting the finishing touches to the nest, when the tractor thundered by on its way back to Forge Farm. The deafening noise shook the hedge, and the male, who had been standing guard next to the nest, blundered out into the open, followed by the female. During the day, the male had caught and eaten the occasional spider, and twice he had brought one back for the female, but they were now both very hungry and it was nearly dark. They flew high over the track just before the tractor passed, and perched on the bare branch of an old lilac bush in the garden of Little Ashden. The female flicked her bill along the rough surface of the bark in order to rub off the stickiness that had accumulated there from the twigs.

Next they flew over Little Ashden, along the outbuildings, and landed on the ground next to the manure heap. The light was fading fast so they hopped forward and began sifting round the edge of the dung looking for beetles to sustain them through the coming night.

While the dunnocks fed, Jim wearily disconnected the plough from the tractor and pulled it into the shed. His whole body ached from the hours of concentration and he too was hungry. First, though, he would have a long soak in the bath. As he crossed the yard towards the kitchen door, he stopped and looked beyond the outbuildings towards the fields that he'd ploughed. They were on the hill on the far side of the valley and the last streaks of light in the sky were gleaming on the freshly turned furrows at the top of the slope. Yesterday, those fields had been dormant but now, as a result of his work, the long parallel lines of moist soil seemed to heave with the promise of new life.

Up there in the fields he had been totally absorbed in the rhythm of each rise and each hollow as he'd concentrated on slicing his straight lines, but now he could see it whole, could see the subtle changes he had wrought on the colour and texture of the entire landscape by changing the colour and texture of part of it. That crow, too, flying lazily but steadily along the last light blue line of the horizon, was altering the valley by its shape and movement, hiding distant trees as it passed, momentarily joining the two stark silhouettes of the chimneys on Little Ashden, and now, swinging west, becoming a mere speck as the perspective shifted.

And those two dark bodies by the manure heap—dunnocks, to judge by their stooped, shuffling movements and twitching wings. How had their day led them here, to this place at this moment? What journeys had they made in the valley as they flew about their business, and how had his movements finally crossed theirs to make this particular pattern? For nearly ten minutes he stood, eyes glazed, in the stillness. Then a breeze ruffled his hair and the small birds rose in the air, tipped sideways and, as though part of the wind, blew away into the darkness. He turned and headed for the warm light streaming through the kitchen door.

Chapter Six

The male dunnock found the white thread of wool while he was rummaging along the bottom of the privet hedge in front of Brook Cottage. He pulled at the loose end and it began to unravel. He pulled again and again until the whole length untwisted except for the end that was snagged by a small knot in the fork in the twig. He tugged and tugged, and at last the knot slipped free. The short flight across the lane was achieved without problems but the real trouble began when he tried hopping through the hedge to the nest. First one bit, then another, caught on branch after branch. He managed to free it a couple of times but the end he was carrying was continually jerked out of his bill, until it became so entangled that he could not go on. At last he gave up and flew off, searching for food, but almost every time he returned he was tempted into picking up the thread and giving another vain pull at it.

The female, too, had tried a couple of times to tug the thread free when the male had first got it so near the nest, but she had quickly lost interest and had concerned herself with material that was available.

OVER THE NEXT FEW DAYS the female dunnock put the finishing touches to the nest. At times it seemed as if she might unmake the whole of the inner lining as she ruthlessly pecked at it, discarding pieces that didn't suit her. Then, suddenly, she decided it was finished. For virtually a whole day after its completion, the male sang in celebration.

The time for creating new life was growing near. Already the female's left ovary and oviduct had begun to increase in size, and the first tiny ovum had started to develop, and to form the yolk of a future egg. The female's body now needed as much nourishment as was possible.

Never far from each other, the two dunnocks moved among the tussocks of grass, their breasts low to the ground, searching for weevils and spiders. The female also started swallowing small specks of grit which her body absorbed to provide the calcium carbonate that would be needed to form shells for the eggs.

Sometimes while she was feeding she flew back to the top of the hedge to check that there was nothing threatening their territory. On these occasions she inevitably sat watching the male as he continued feeding on the ground, and she was almost mesmerised by his movements and by the colours of his feathers, which pulsed in the bright light. At these times she found herself impelled to fly down to be near him again, feeling so at one with him that her hopping, bending and pecking movements fell into absolute rhythm with his.

The male, too, was highly aware of his mate. Whenever he flew onto the hedge he was unable to resist breaking into song, partly in warning to other birds but mostly to attract the attention of the female. And when she returned for a while to sit in the nest and keep the lining in good shape by pressing it with her breast, he was always anxious to find some food which he could take to her. Whatever he found—small worm, moth larva or spider—the moment when he stood on the rim of the nest and bent to offer the food always filled them both with a trembling excitement that they could barely endure.

DURING HIS FIRST WEEK at home Daniel Conrad spent hours lying on the sofa looking out of the window. The Lawrences had helped Eve to bring his bed and desk downstairs so that he wouldn't have to tackle the steep stairs with his crutches, and they had also pushed the sofa against the window so that he could see out. The beauty of the valley helped to take his mind off the pain in his leg. Teddy loved to share these moments, curled up on his lap, luxuriating in the warm sun, and Daniel found it comforting to stroke and scratch the terrier's neck in simple communication.

Daniel had noticed the constant traffic of the dunnocks in and around the hedge opposite Brook Cottage and he guessed that they had a nest there. He found his father's old binoculars and watched them in close-up as they flew backwards and forwards. No matter how closely he peered, though, he couldn't see the nest itself, and he was looking forward to the day when he would be able to get out and about on his crutches. To get near to the hedge and see the nest would be a kind of landmark on his road to recovery.

UP ON THE HILLS, the field that Jim had ploughed had been harrowed and sown, and now over the light brown earth there was a faint haze of green where the barley was already sprouting. The days of soft winds and sunshine were daily drawing more of the shoots out of the dark into the open air.

The female dunnock was constantly aware of the birth and growth all round her. The vegetation, the breeze, the light, the sky were all alive with their own particular rhythm which filled her with a warmth and a tenderness for the world. Even other birds and animals were less threatening to her than usual.

In all this physical harmony, though, something strange happened. The male, who had recently been so close to her, began to seem mysterious and awesome. She longed to close the gap between them, but his beauty and power frightened her. He too felt the estrangement, and redoubled his efforts to entice her back. He flew close, repeatedly displaying his feathers to show off their glossiness and bright sheen. He sang to her his finest songs, and stretched his wings to the utmost in spectacular flight; but the more he tried to win her, the more intimidated she became.

The days grew longer and longer, and in response to the extended daylight the female's sexual glands reached a peak of activity. For her it simply meant an increased attraction towards the very being who, simultaneously, was growing more terrifying. A war of attraction and repulsion, a struggle between her fear of being dominated and her desire to submit, played within her.

Late one afternoon she was standing on a branch of a blackthorn bush. The white blossom was so thick round her that it made her head spin. On the ground in front of the bush the male was feeding, and she found that she could stop the spinning by fixing her gaze on him. A large bumblebee flew clumsily past and clutched feverishly at one of the blackthorn blossoms. It pushed its tongue deep into the centre of the flower and the dunnock felt the blossom begin to revolve again. At the same time the elements of fear and desire started to spiral inside her, until they became one whirling physical need. She fell forward and let her wings carry her down to the male. She landed directly in front of him, deliberately turned her back, lifted her tail and vibrated it from side to side in enticement.

For a moment the male was so surprised that he did not respond. Then, as he moved towards her, the female took to her wings. As though pulled by an invisible thread, the male followed—across the fields, along the track, past Little Ashden and onto the roof of the outbuildings where they had first met. As the female landed she went into a crouch. The male landed next to her. He stood sideways on, apparently staring off towards the fields, but suddenly he leaped round and perched lightly on her back. The extra weight unbalanced her and they both fluttered their wings to steady themselves. The male lowered his rear to meet her raised rump and their two cloacas joined, and a garbled twitter of excitement broke from

179

both their throats. Their bodies rocked, their wings flapped, and with a tremor of bursting delight his sperm passed into her.

As the convulsion faded away and they jerked free of each other, the fear that had kept them apart swept over them again. The female, in particular, had defeated all her self-protective instincts in order to take up the submissive position, and now, as those instincts reasserted themselves, she flew away as if her life depended on it.

For nearly an hour she sat trembling on the nest, drawing comfort from the warmth and protection which the enclosing cup gave her. Then, irresistibly, she felt the return of the need for union with her mate. She left the nest and flew to find him again in the twilight.

The next day they mated several times, always apprehensive beforehand and separating in a rush of nervousness afterwards. Once they mated on top of the privet hedge in front of Brook Cottage. Daniel happened to be looking out of the window and laughed at their precarious coupling.

INSIDE THE FEMALE, a ripe ovum had been fertilised. From the top of the oviduct where fertilisation had taken place, the ovum began to pass down the funnel-shaped tube towards the uterus. As she flew through the air, as she fed on the ground, as she rested in the nest, a miraculous process was at work in the dunnock's body.

The germ cell from which the embryo would grow was now resting on the top of the ovum, or yolk. In order for the embryo to develop properly, it was essential for the germ cell to remain in this position at the top, so during the journey down the oviduct a tough skin-like membrane was forming round the yolk. At either end of the membrane was a twisted piece that would be attached to the inner skin of the shell, so that the yolk would be suspended. As a result, each time the egg was moved, the yolk could rotate and the embryo would stay in the right position.

At the same time, the albumen, the white gelatinous substance, was also forming round the yolk. This would protect the yolk in two ways: first, by acting as a cushioning element if the egg was ever jarred and second, by absorbing and stopping the growth of any bacteria that managed to penetrate the shell. In addition, the albumen would eventually act as a source of protein for the growing embryo when the store of protein in the yolk was exhausted.

The contents of the egg were complete and now two layers of protective membranes were formed round the yolk and the white, so that when the egg finally entered the uterus it was like a flabby, half-inflated balloon. But this balloon was not going to be inflated with air. Through the membrane walls, the thick, sticky albumen absorbed more and more water from the uterus until its substance was thinned down and it was ninety per cent water. As this absorption took place and the inside of the egg swelled, the two outer layers of membranes were stretched tight. Now that the balloon was blown up, the calcium carbonate which the female's body had been storing began to create hard protective layers of shell over its surface, until the final glossy layer was formed.

The egg was now ready to be laid, and as it shifted in the uterus towards the cloacal opening, the female flew back to the nest in readiness. While she made her last preparations, settling herself time and again into the cup to warm it, the male stood near, on the top of the hedge, keeping guard. When she began to make a regular, soft, almost inaudible piping sound he left her alone and, in a state of high excitement, flew back and forth along the length of their territory in a ceaseless vigil.

The sounds that escaped from the female's throat were caused by the air that was gulped in and out of her lungs as she pushed downwards to expel the egg. The rhythm of her breathing regulated the contractions and expansions in the tube as the egg moved closer to the opening. When the pressure mounted to its peak, she raised her rear slightly and the egg began to bulge out of the hole. A couple more pushes, and it slid gently out of her body and nestled on the soft, warm grass lining.

At once she hopped off the nest and looked down at what she had produced. It was a perfect, tiny oval, and its colour was the exquisite light blue of the clear skies. The excited chatter that burst out of her brought the male winging in through the branches. Side by side they stood and gazed in wonder at the miracle.

THE FEVER OF CREATION was upon them now, and not long after the first egg arrived they went flying in a ritual chase, across the field and along the trees near the river, that ended in another moment of mating. In the nest, the egg began to cool, and as it shrank slightly the two outer membranes just inside the shell were pulled apart at the larger end, leaving a little pocket of air. When the chick was ready to hatch it would break the inner membrane and breathe its first lungful of air before it began the process of breaking out of the shell.

During the four days that followed, another three eggs were laid. Increasingly the female only felt at ease when she was near the nest, guarding it and making sure that the eggs stayed at the right temperature. Until the clutch was complete she wouldn't start the process of incubation but, although she did not want the temperature of the eggs to be high enough to begin the development of the embryos, she was anxious to make sure that they never fell below the heat that kept them alive. Consequently she had already spent some time sitting on them to keep them from growing too cold, and she took care to turn them frequently so that the temperature remained fairly even.

Then, with the laying of the fourth egg and the completion of her clutch, another change came over her body. As the sexual drive diminished and finally ceased, the blood which had been concentrated in those areas concerned with the growth of the eggs inside her, now pumped with greater vigour into the skin along the underside of her body. There the

181

blood capillaries flooded and swelled out, so that the maximum amount of heat was centred where her body touched the eggs.

For the next two weeks she would spend three quarters of her time giving warmth to her young. The nest was now the crucible in which the final elements of life would be forged. Patiently the female settled down to provide the fire from which the mysterious sparks would fly.

Chapter Seven

The day that the female dunnock began her period of incubation was Theo Lawrence's seventieth birthday. From early on the Saturday morning, frantic preparations were under way for a celebration lunch. Mary's arthritis limited what she could do, so Jill Siddy and Eve Conrad went over to Little Ashden to help.

It was also a special day for Daniel. At last the time was over when he had to keep his leg in a horizontal position, and so at midday, with his mother walking anxiously by his side, he hopped and swung on his crutches all the way from Brook Cottage to Little Ashden. It was tiring work after so many weeks of lying down, but it felt good to be mobile again and he was determined to make the return journey alone at the end of the party. Not until he had done that, and stopped to find that dunnocks' nest which he had so looked forward to seeing, would he consider that he was really independent again.

From twelve thirty onwards Theo's guests began arriving. The female dunnock felt edgy as she sat on her precious eggs, and she fidgeted nervously as the cars passed and the noise of slamming doors echoed across the pastureland.

Then there was a long period of calm, and she relaxed. Towards the end of the afternoon, though, her unease returned as once again doors were slammed and cars crunched and rattled down the bumpy track.

At about six the last of the guests left. Nobody would allow Theo to help clear up, so he went into the living room and stared round at the cards and presents. It had been a good party, but now he felt oddly melancholy. A long, tiring walk might help.

Reaching the end of the track, he saw Daniel hopping on his crutches along the side of the hedge, peering in through the branches. When Daniel laughed, embarrassed, and explained about his symbolic search for the nest, Theo joined in, gently pulling aside the twigs.

The female dunnock had watched with mounting fear as first one figure, then a second, started to move closer. Then a hand reached forward and lifted the screen of leaves in front of her, and two large faces loomed towards her. Already unnerved by all the noise and movement during the day, she now panicked and flew off the nest screaming in alarm, hoping to draw the attackers after her and away from the eggs.

Theo and Daniel were almost as startled by the dunnock's flapping, crashing flight as she had been by them. They both caught a quick glimpse of the blue eggs in the nest, then stepped back and let the branch swing into place, sorry to have disturbed her.

Nearly an hour later the female finally ventured back to the nest and settled down on the eggs again.

SOON AFTER DAWN on the fourth day of incubation it began to rain heavily. For a long time the branches overhead kept the rain off, but eventually the persistent pounding on the young leaves made them tilt downwards, and water started to drip through onto the nest. The female fluffed out her feathers as far as possible and spread her wings to shield the eggs and stop the edges of the nest from becoming damp.

By midmorning, when the postman and the milkman stopped in front of Brook Cottage in quick succession, the feathers on the female's back and head were streaked and darkened by the water that dripped on her with torturing regularity.

The arrival of the postman always frightened her: his van had a loose exhaust, and it rattled and banged against the underside of the chassis as he left it chugging in front of the gate. He also slammed the van door each time he got in or out, and his large boots with their metal-tipped soles scraped and clicked loudly when he walked.

On the other hand, she quite liked the soft whirring sound of the milkman's electric float. The milkman always whistled, too, even today in the pouring rain, and his arrival and departure were marked by the chiming and tinkling of the bottles, so his whole visit had a musical quality that pleased her. For the few minutes that he was around, the female was able to forget her discomfort.

Not since the worst moments in the winter had she felt as cold as she did now. The large drops of water that splattered onto her were beginning to soak through to her skin as her normally impermeable feathers became waterlogged. In addition, in spreading her wings to protect the nest, rather than tucking them round herself, she had seriously reduced her usual insulation. Her body was occasionally shaken by a fit of shivering and she was becoming terribly hungry. Not for one moment, though, did it occur to her to abandon her task—she would rather have frozen to death. So, because of her loving dedication, not one drop of water fell on the eggs and their temperature remained constant.

Inside the shells the embryos were growing fast. Most of the young birds' internal organs were taking shape – miniature heart and lungs and liver – and the limbs were beginning to form. From hour to hour new developments were taking place. In the seven hours of continuous rain that followed the departure of the milkman, amazing changes brought the embryos a few steps nearer to becoming identifiable creatures.

At the end of the seven hours, another vehicle drew up outside Brook

Cottage. Edward Sandars, an old friend of Eve Conrad's, decided to leave his car outside the gate rather than put it on the concrete forecourt of the garage, where he usually parked. No point in getting wet, and anyway, there was plenty of room for another car to squeeze past. He put his raincoat over his head, opened the door, and dashed for the warmth and shelter of the house.

THE LORRY DRIVER was achingly tired. His clothes were still clammy from the long time he'd stood in the rain unloading his delivery. All he wanted was to get home quickly and relax under a hot shower, but here he was, stuck in a long, slow-moving line of traffic on the main road. Up ahead, he knew, was a short cut across country that would save him more than five miles. The lanes were narrow and twisting and he would be breaking the width restriction, but the chances of being spotted by the police on a foul day like this were remote.

As soon as he got onto the empty lane and began to move freely, his tension and frustration drained away. This was more like driving ought to be: no traffic, and the fun of hauling the big lorry round tricky bends. He felt like a rally driver.

When he came to Brook Cottage he was forced to slow and stop. Some idiot had left a car blocking nearly half the width of the lane. He hooted, hoping that the driver might still be inside, but there was no movement behind the misted windows. Damn! Now he'd have to reverse, find a place to turn round and go back all the way he'd come. Unless, of course . . . Yes, he could probably make it if he pulled right in to the hedge.

He heaved on the wheel and swung the front of the lorry round the car, then accelerated gently.

The female dunnock had heard the lorry's roar grow louder as it approached and then seen it stop and chug menacingly. The blast on the horn had scared her and had brought the male dodging through the branches to investigate. Together they had watched in horror as the monster turned its face towards them and came nosing closer and closer, filling the air with its terrifying voice. The hedge round them had begun to shake. Then there was a violent jolt as the beast moved forward, catching the branch on which the nest stood, and pulling it with it. The female flew off the nest in terror.

The branch was bent almost to breaking point, and finally it snapped back like a catapult. The foundations of the nest disintegrated and the cup and its contents were hurled to the ground. Three of the eggs were crushed by the rear wheel of the lorry, the fourth smashed when it hit the ground.

For a while after the lorry drove away, the two dunnocks were too frightened to return to the hedge. Then, as the retreating roar finally faded from the valley, they flew back to the nest.

The pelting rain was already dissolving the thick jelly of the squashed eggs, and the presence of death overwhelmed the two birds as they stood

184

looking at the destruction. In dread they fled to the hedge, only to return almost instantly.

The female stared at the fourth egg, which had escaped the weight of the wheels. The rain was making the still-whole yolk slide to the edge of the tarmac, where water gushed along the grass verge. As it was caught by the stream and carried away, it rolled over to reveal the network of blood vessels stretching from the dark patch where the embryo had been forming. She flew a few yards ahead of it, then cocked her head to watch it swirl past her and down the rushing cataract that took the water underground to the river.

As it disappeared, a mad anguish seized her and she flew wildly into the evening gloom, crying out her horror in a frantic piping call. As the night began to close in early under the thick cloud cover, she continued to fly from perch to perch with the male in close attendance, and all the time she kept up her mourning cry.

Chapter Eight

The female cuckoo's long voyage started in the middle of the first week of April. Weeks of extra eating had built up the necessary fat for the arduous flight, and careful preening had ensured that her feathers were in perfect condition. As her body reached a peak of fitness she was gripped by an uncontrollable restlessness and anxiety. Then one afternoon she flew off the baobab tree where she roosted and climbed higher and higher into the sky until, suddenly, all her confusion and apprehension melted away.

She wheeled in a wide circle, and as she came round to face north the feeling of pleasure and rightness drew her in that direction with unhurried but steady and powerful wing beats.

For countless generations her ancestors had followed this route, forging the memory that now lay hidden deep within her.

Late on the first night she saw the glimmer of moonlight on the waters of Lake Chad. She had flown for over twelve hours but the exhilaration of being on the wing would have kept her moving on and on except for one thing. Ahead lay over a thousand miles of barren wilderness whose terrible heat and vast distances would strain her strength to the utmost. While there was even the barest shade, and the chance of water and food, she had to take advantage of it.

She spent the whole of the following day trying to avoid the direct assault of the sun in the scrubby cover of one of the thorn trees that crouched near the water. When the sun at last dipped, huge and bloody, towards the trembling line of the western horizon, the semidesert came alive again. Creatures that had hidden from the burning heat in the shade of their holes and crevices now scuttled out to hunt and, in turn, to be hunted. The cuckoo joined them, quickly replenishing her energy with the abundance of insects drawn out by the approaching dusk. When she had eaten her fill she spent a few minutes at the pool, sipping as much water as she could. It would be her last drink for more than a thousand miles.

Then, while the sky was still streaked with light, she set off. She turned northwards and settled into her regular, rhythmic flight, continually adjusting her direction so that the pattern of moon and stars produced the feeling of harmony within her that meant she was on the right course.

FOR TWO DAYS she continued her flight over the ribbed surface of a great sand-sea. The motion of her effort was so hypnotic that she barely registered the change from night to day, except for the reflex slowing of the rate of her wing beats as the heat grew. On the second day the sun's fire was fierce. It bounced back off the sand and warped the air so that the undulations of the dunes merged into a shimmering flatness. From above and below the furnace seared the cuckoo, sapping her strength.

Never before had she faced such appalling heat. Her blood had thickened and her heart was having to work harder to pump it round her body. Her muscles were starting to knot from lack of oxygen and her head pounded with pain, making her vision tremble in and out of focus.

At last the sun passed its zenith and small aubergine-coloured shadows began to spread eastwards from the curved tops of the highest dunes. As soon as she spotted one large enough, she glided down and stood panting in its shade. She spread her feathers to speed up the process of heat loss but she had to resist the temptation to close her eyes and sleep. Here on the ground, attack could come swiftly from any direction.

Indeed, danger was only three yards away, where a horned asp lay beneath the sand with only its two unblinking eyes protruding above the surface. The snake watched the cuckoo intently. The bird was obviously too big for prey, but the snake was wound up ready to strike in defence if she came too near. For some time the cuckoo stayed still, but when she took a couple of tottering steps, the snake reacted. It sprang from its coiled position, shrugging the sand off its stubby body. Its jaws opened wide and its large fangs swung to the front. The cuckoo skipped back in surprise, flapping her tired wings and overbalancing in her anxiety to take to the air. Before she had recovered, the snake had seized the opportunity to slither fast down the slope away from her and the danger had passed.

Dusk finally brought relief from the heat as a cooling breeze sent spindrifts of sand hissing down from the lip of the dune. But as the purple sky thickened into blackness, the increased threat of attack and the numbing cold of the night air forced the cuckoo to haul her tired body back into flight.

IN THE DAYS THAT FOLLOWED, the cuckoo twice passed over settlements, their lights yellow and diffuse. Gradually more and more bushes and trees showed up on the ground. Then one morning the air grew softer and more moist, and by dawn a rolling bank of mist hid all but the tops of the taller trees. When the sun rose, the mist thinned and there, ahead of her, was the glittering Mediterranean.

She stopped for a couple of hours to feed among the palm trees, then carried on, following the coastal plain. A breeze from the sea took the edge off the sun's heat and she flew easily even during the hottest hours. By the end of the day she was near Tunis.

As the sun set, the lights of the city made bewildering patterns below her and the roar that rose up from it made the air tremble. After the peace of the desert this confusion of noise and flashing lights was terrifying, and it was a great relief when it died away and she found herself once more above the empty land and sea.

There, the only sound was the soft shushing of the waves on the shore and the only light was the delicate glimmer of the dusk sky and its faint reflection on the surface of the sea. Just as the last gleam of light slipped away in the west, she landed in a gnarled olive tree. She had covered one thousand two hundred miles. The most dangerous part of the journey was over, and for the first time in five nights she could sleep.

SHE STAYED IN THE AREA for four days, recovering after crossing the desert and building up her resources again. Then, early on the fifth day, she set off and flew the hundred and twenty miles across the sea to Sardinia in just under six hours.

After the harsh glare of the rocks and sands of the Sahara, the deep, rich green of the sweet-smelling maquis and the sparkle of light on the tumbling streams was a gentle, ever-changing delight to her eyes. She found plenty of shelter and food in the wild tangle of heavily perfumed shrubs, and as soon as the sun had lost some of its intensity she flew across the narrow straits to Corsica.

She cut across the hilly southwestern quarter of the island, then flew north roughly parallel to the coastline. When the sun was dipping into the sea, she turned inland, looking for a suitable roost for the night. She had just passed over an old farmhouse and was heading for a grove of trees when something glinted red in the light of the setting sun. Some pellets had already whistled below her before she heard the sound of an explosion.

Instinctively, she dived for a moment to gain speed, then tipped rapidly upwards again and soared high above the trees and away. A young Corsican stepped out from his cover to aim his second barrel, but the cuckoo's evasive tactics had worked and he lowered his gun with a curse as she disappeared from his sight.

The suddenness of the attack put her on her guard and she flew high for another quarter of an hour before warily coming to roost in an isolated tract of woodland.

The next day, dark clouds were scudding across the sky and a strong wind from the sea shook the trees and bushes. The swaying branches and rustling leaves made her nervous, and slowed her search for food among the shrubs, so that the morning was well advanced before she set off in a northwesterly direction. The nearer she got to the French coast, the harder the wind blew, and by the time she made landfall near Sainte-Maxime she was worn out from the buffeting. She passed an uneasy night in a rocking pine tree in the hills behind the resort, then at dawn she set off across the southern foothills of the Alps. It was midafternoon before she came down into the Rhône Valley just above Avignon. There the full blast of the mistral hit her. She battled against the relentless headwind for another two hours, before heavy, driving rain made it impossible to continue.

She found a roost in a thick tangle of bramble and shrub that grew up the side of an abandoned stone hut, and spent a miserable night pressed against the base of the wall, on constant alert for attacks by ground animals. The rain finally stopped just before dawn. As soon as there was enough light she searched for food along the rows of vines in a nearby vineyard, but the rain and the recent spraying of the vines had driven off most of the insects, and it was with a nearly empty stomach that she eventually took off again into the teeth of the wind.

Her body was cold and her muscles were stiff and she flew in short bursts, resting for almost as long as she flew, looking for food whenever she stopped. It was nearly midday before she reached Montélimar. The wind's howling ferocity increased and she sought shelter in the lee of a rocky gorge that carried a small tributary down to the wide waters of the Rhône. The comparative calm between the steep cliffs overcame her reluctance to leave the northerly flight path of her ancestors, along the main valley. Instead, she followed the twisting course of the small river westwards as it bounded down from the high plateau of the Massif Central. Within four miles she had left the worst of the wind behind, and she took some rest in a tree near the top of the gorge.

HAVING FED ON SOME CATERPILLARS in the bushes at the base of the tree, the cuckoo set off again across the high open plateau with its conical hills, the rounded remnants of long-extinct volcanoes.

Although the air was comparatively still, she flew slowly, stopping frequently, partly because of fatigue but also because now that she had left her inborn route she had constantly to gauge and readjust her flight path. The sun was hidden behind dense layers of cloud, and much of the time she tried to guide herself by judging where there was the greatest luminosity in the pall of grey. This gave her a rough, general direction, but she was continually being led slightly off course by shifts in the thickness of the cloud cover. By the time she reached Mont Mezenc, the mist had nearly reached the summit of the mountain. Even while she rested briefly on a shrubby pine tree near the top, the other trees round her paled and disappeared in the swirling whiteness, making it impossible to tell what was snow and what was air.

She took off and climbed above the top of the mountain, where the air was still clear. Beneath her the blanket of mist covered the ground as far as she could see. For nearly an hour she flew on into the gathering gloom, and then suddenly, with an abrupt fall in the temperature, the ceiling of cloud came down to meet the floor of the mist. At once she beat upwards, trying to burst through the fog. She climbed for over two and a half thousand feet without escaping the muffling blanket, and then was beaten down by cold and the lack of oxygen in the thin air. Now there was only one way left: blindly down towards the ground, where every hazard – tree, hillside, telegraph wire – might be seen too late.

At near-stalling speed she glided earthwards, her wings arched to reduce her rate of descent. Every nerve was alert, straining to determine distance and height by sounds and subtle changes in the air pressure.

Something black loomed out of the mist below her and she flapped her wings quickly in order to brake, then angled them and tried to climb. Her right wing struck something and she was jerked round. Her feet scrambled wildly against the rough surface as she tried to find some purchase, then she found herself falling backwards. As she hit the ground the air was blasted out of her and she crashed into unconsciousness.

Chapter Nine

Céline had led the goats through the mist from the field at the end of the village and had just closed the stable door on them when she heard the frantic flurry of wings and the soft thump. Normally, she never went up to the church that brooded on the hill opposite her house, but now she hurried up the worn steps because she couldn't bear the thought of an animal in pain.

She found the cuckoo on the gravel to the left of the main door. Its right wing was open and the feathers were crumpled, but although it lay stunned it was alive. She knelt by its side and lifted it onto her lap. There was a small bare patch on the wing where it must have hit the church. A dark smear of blood stained the surrounding feathers, but when she felt gently along the wing there didn't seem to be any bones broken.

By the time Céline got the cuckoo home and into a cage, it had recovered sufficiently to stand on its feet. It glared through the wicker bars at her and she stared back, admiring the fierceness of its look.

During the next three days the cuckoo came to recognise Céline. The other shapes that came near the cage were mostly dark and confusing, but this one made soft noises and gave off a comforting glow. Often, too, after it had been near, there was water to drink and caterpillars and worms to eat. Apart from this one reassuring shape, though, the cuckoo found everything frightening. At times her fear turned to panic and she pushed and pecked frantically at the cage, but most of the time she crouched, still and watchful, hoping to escape attack by complete immobility.

Céline worried about the cuckoo. As far as she could tell its wing was not permanently damaged, and she was pleased to see that it had preened the feathers so that the small cut and the bare patch were no longer visible. But by the fourth day of captivity its condition was obviously beginning to deteriorate. At first it had eaten the food Céline gave it, but now the worms and caterpillars squirmed unnoticed on the bottom of the cage. The bird's eyes had lost their fierce glitter and it spent most of the time hunched despondently in the corner.

If anyone knew what to do, it would be Louis. He had a gift with animals, and her earliest and happiest memories were of the times when she'd helped him to look after them. He arrived at the house straight from work, and as he kissed Céline the cuckoo watched the new shape that glowed so brightly and made such warm, harmonious sounds. Céline had expected the bird to respond well to Louis but even she was surprised by its complete docility as he took it in his sure hands and examined it. It even hooded its eyes in sensuous pleasure as he stretched its wing and flexed it a couple of times. When he ran his finger gently from the top of its head, down its neck and along the line of its wing, it actually quivered and a soft, bubbling trill escaped from its throat. Louis' whole attention was focused on the bird, and when the trill finished he suddenly looked up at Céline and his face broke into a beautiful smile of surprise and delight that flashed straight to her heart.

Outside in the twilight they stood silently, taking a last look at the cuckoo. Then Louis kissed the top of its head and with a flowing upward swing, launched it into the air. As his hands parted and the bird was released from his grip, Céline saw it float upwards until, at the top of its trajectory, it opened its wings and continued the momentum with lazy, almost slow-motion, beats. It climbed steadily and began to merge with the dark background of the hills.

DURING THE FIRST COUPLE of minutes of freedom the cuckoo's wings had felt feeble and stiff, but by the time she reached the river that ran through the valley below Chadrinhac she was flying naturally again. It was growing dark, though, and she needed rest. She swept left up a tributary of the Loire, flying slowly. The limited depth of vision inside the house had taken the edge off her keen sight and she was in no condition to deal with the precision required for movement through a dark landscape.

The bright reflection of moonlight on a waterfall was, therefore, like a beacon to her and she flew towards it and perched in an elm tree near the base of the tumbling water. The tranquillity of the night sky, and the cool air, soothed away the fear and confusion she had felt since the accident, and the steady roar of the waterfall eased her into sleep.

She stayed in the area for six days, roosting at night in the elm and hunting by day along the river. The days were warm and sunny and there was a profusion of tasty sawfly larva to eat, so she grew steadily fatter.

A low mist was spreading out from the pool at the base of the waterfall when the cuckoo finally left the elm tree. The sun had set but there was enough light left for a group of men to still be playing *boules* in the square at Chadrinhac as the cuckoo flew over, high above the church.

Céline was just coming out of the barn but she did not look up. Nor did Louis, a quarter of an hour later when the cuckoo flew over the football field where his team was playing its crucial last match of the season. The cuckoo passed over the centre of the town, her shape clearly illuminated by the powerful lamps lighting up the cathedral and its huge statue of the Virgin Mary, and then soared away into the gathering darkness.

By first morning light she had left the Massif Central. An increasing feeling of well-being told her she was back on her inborn route. She was not back to peak fitness, though, and was forced to stop towards the end of the day and find a roost. She chose one of the tall poplars along the banks of the Loire. The following day she flew lazily upstream for a few hours to a large island, just where the river curved westwards to begin its long sweep across the central plain to the far-distant sea.

Insects and caterpillars were plentiful on the island and the cuckoo lingered there undisturbed for two days. Late in the afternoon of the second day she set off on the final stage of the journey. She reached the Channel the following morning, and without stopping crossed the narrow strip of sea and reached England just after midday. Despite all the delays, she had made the journey in a little over four weeks.

Theo Lawrence and Jim Siddy were too absorbed in mending the gate to the top pastureland to notice the cuckoo as she beat along the valley. The male dunnock saw her, though, as he searched for small worms in the soft earth near the river bank. Against the bright light of the setting sun her silhouette looked hawk-like, and he crouched low to the ground in fear until she had passed.

Chapter Ten

After the destruction of their nest, the dunnocks did not return to live in the hedge. All trace of the eggs was gone and they had no conscious memory of them, but the fragments of the nest, hanging in the branches, disturbed them. Something was missing. Something was not right.

For a couple of nights they roosted on a beam under the eaves of Little Ashden, then they passed eight nights in a small cavity behind some loose tiles on the roof of one of the oast-houses at Forge Farm.

As the weather improved and the sun drew out the insects again, they spent the days rediscovering the pleasure of living free of all responsibility. They grew stronger with the plentiful supply of food, and the hours of sunshine once more encouraged them to fly with joy. The leaves on most trees and bushes were spreading wide, and the rich green light that filtered through them was a constant blurring delight as they swept among the branches.

It was on one such carefree flight that they found their new roost.

The bullace bush leaned up against the creosoted wooden wall of the last barn at Forge Farm. Its small white flowers, shaking in front of the black background, attracted the female. She left the river, flew across the pastureland and onto its topmost branch. Almost instantly she dived down through the flowering shoots to the heart of the bush. The remains of a goldfinch's nest caught her eye. For a while she looked speculatively at the old nest, then left the bush and rejoined the male.

At dusk they flew back to the oast-house roof and squeezed through the narrow gap in the tiles. As soon as they had settled themselves, though, the female ducked outside again and stood on the edge of the gutter. She had, since that afternoon, a growing desire to build another nest. She called to the male, but when he did not appear she flew down to the bush on her own. The male had heard her call but had ignored it because he was comfortable and sleepy. When she failed to return, however, he felt uneasy. He blundered out of the hole, wriggling his shoulder-blades to lever himself through the tiles, and almost fell as he slithered out too quickly onto the steep slope of the roof.

The sky was filled with colour – the clouds aflame with reds and yellows against a background that faded from dark blue to pale green – while the light clung thickly to everything on earth, like liquid ivory.

When the male reached the other side of the roof, he looked down on the yard of Forge Farm and had almost completed the circle back to the hole when the female called to him. He found her sitting on a bullace shoot that bent and bounced under her weight. When she sprang off the shoot and dived into the heart of the bush, he followed. From that evening, it was their new home.

THE BUSH PLEASED THEM greatly as a roosting-place. The barn against which the bullace leaned was the one in which Jim kept his calves, and the sweet, warm smell of hay and dung reassured the birds whenever they woke suddenly in the darkness. At first they were disturbed by the sounds of snorts and trampling hooves and by the occasional rattling of the boards as the cattle rubbed their flanks on the walls, but gradually these noises, too, became a solid and comfortable part of their lives. Best of all was the fact that, apart from the rumble of the tractor from the other side of the barn, they were free from the noise and danger of vehicles.

Despite their contentment with the bush as a home, they did not begin building a nest at once. Only gradually did the female begin to be stimulated by all the evidence of breeding round her. After the losses during the hard winter, the urge to repopulate gripped every species of bird, and wherever she went she saw and heard the same activity. Songs of territorial defence rang from the trees and hedges. Adults, their bills crammed with items of food, flew urgent shuttles from first to last light in a hopeless attempt to satisfy the incessant chittering demands of their nestlings.

One evening at dusk, the male arrived to find the female tugging at a twig that had formed part of the foundation of the goldfinch's nest. It jerked free, and she hopped with it in her bill along the branch, then fluttered up to a higher branch. The male could hardly see her in the gloom, so he followed and found her laying the twig on top of some others that she had put across a narrow gap between two parallel branches. It was the first stage in the construction of their new nest.

Chapter Eleven

The first few days after the cuckoo's return to the valley were humid and overcast. A faint haze hung in the heavy air and distant thunder rumbled occasionally. For some time she was content simply to rest after her journey and to feed on the woolly-bear caterpillars of the garden tiger moth, which were abundant on plants and bushes in the clearings.

It was a full week after her arrival before she began to take an interest in the calls of the males that rang from the various corners of the woods. Just one long, clear, bubbling call was enough to advertise her presence and bring two of the males flying to investigate.

The first to arrive actually perched in the beech tree where she was standing, but the other, who arrived a few minutes later, stayed out of sight, tantalising her with his deep, imperious call. One look at the visible male was enough for her to dismiss him, for he was a thin, young bird, with some of the rufous feathers of immaturity still evident on his back. She uttered a harsh, laughing alarm note that startled him, then, disdainfully diving past him, she set off in pursuit of the unseen male whose mysterious behaviour was so attractive.

For over an hour they played hide-and-seek through the green cloisters of the wood. Sometimes she got so close that his mellow voice rippled all the air round her and she felt as if she were flying on the waves of his cry, certain that this time she would see him. She would glide to the nearest perch and look round expectantly, only to hear his taunting song float mockingly from the direction from which she'd just come.

At last, in a broad, sunny clearing where young chestnut trees were shooting up round the cut stumps of their parent trees, she caught a glimpse of him. She saw his chest flash white as he banked, and then caught a quick view of his white-tipped tail and sharp wings as he disappeared into the thick trees on the other side of the clearing. Increasing the rate of her wing beat, she shot after him.

Even at full speed, though, she was unable to keep pace with him, and when she reached the edge of the wood and burst out into the brightness of an open field he was nowhere to be seen. Then, as she turned back towards the wood, a single note from above caused her to look up. Somehow he had managed to soar high into the sky while her back was turned, and now he was skimming down towards her, his wings angled in a spectacular dive. He swooped past, flattened the dive into a steady glide, then slowed to stalling speed and dropped neatly onto the top of a round post next to a five-barred gate.

His flight had been proud and strong, and the female made no attempt to imitate it. Instead she performed a long, graceful circle that took her out over the field away from him and then in a teasing curve slowly back towards him. She approached at the exact height of his perch. Her outstretched wing nearly brushed him as she coasted by, tipped to the right and landed delicately on the top of the hedgerow.

He swayed slightly on his perch as though in preparation for flight, and lowered his head. The small feathers of his throat quivered, then he opened his bill and began pumping out sweet ovals of sound that rolled over and through her. She closed her eyes for a moment as the music throbbed—each double note building upon the echo of those that had already sounded, towards those that were yet to come.

When the sequence finally ended, they both stood stunned in the silence. They had now made the decision to mate together, but there were no ties. They did not roost together and in the ensuing days they spent much of the time apart.

THE CUCKOO LAID her first egg at the beginning of the fourth week of May. The unfortunate foster parents, who would see their own offspring killed by the tiny assassin which would hatch from the egg, were a pair of reed warblers who had built their nest in the reeds along the margin of a small pond. The cuckoo herself had been fostered by reed warblers and, though she was prepared to lay in a whole range of birds' nests, she certainly preferred these small brown birds whose deep-cup nests of dried grasses seemed, inevitably, so familiar to her.

She had quartered her territory searching for a suitable host family, then, having made her selection, she had patiently settled down to wait for the right moment to deposit the egg. Watching the female reed warbler lay the last of her clutch of four eggs in the morning had stimulated the cuckoo, and by early afternoon she was ready to lay. A couple of hours later the female warbler, whose head had barely been visible over the lip of the deep nest, skipped off her eggs. She sang her churring song a couple of times, then flew across the water and disappeared into the thick vegetation on the far shore.

Immediately the cuckoo swooped down. She landed on the edge of the nest, but when she tried to manoeuvre herself into a laying position, the supporting reeds trembled and swayed so much that she flew off and

194

landed on the grass bank. She lifted her tail slightly, opened her wings a little to give her balance and crouched down to lay the egg. Speed was now essential and almost before the egg had settled onto the grass she turned, picked it up in her bill, and flew back to the nest. Balancing precariously, she gently put the egg alongside the others and took one of them in exchange. In the brief time before she flew off she was satisfied to see how well her egg blended with the others. It was larger and a lighter, browner colour than the almost olive green of the reed warblers' eggs, but it closely imitated the marbling spots and streaks, which would certainly ensure that the foster parents wouldn't reject it.

She flew slowly back to the wood before cracking the egg she had stolen, and eating it, shell and all, to help provide the goodness she would need for further laying. Just forty-eight hours later she laid another egg. Again she chose a reed warblers' nest—this time on another pond that fed the first from slightly higher up in the forest.

Having exploited the available sites in the west of her territory, she now started searching for some in the south. She flew speculatively along the valley, but her real goal was Ramsell Lake, about half a mile south. This oval stretch of water, lying in a hollow with steep banks on either side, hardly deserved the title of lake, but the thick reeds all round its edge were perfect for reed warblers. She found three nests there, but only one of them, already containing four eggs, was suitable.

The cuckoo spent most of the afternoon spying on the nest from the depths of a yew tree at the top of the bank. She noted the behaviour of the reed warblers and assessed correctly that the female was waiting to lay a fifth and final egg. The cuckoo already had another egg forming inside her, but since the reed warbler would probably not leave the nest until the clutch was complete she would have to wait perhaps as long as two more days before she could lay it.

She left the yew tree and flew gently along the river on her way back to the wood. A group of about twenty house martins were swooping and soaring along the road in front of Brook Cottage, and as the cuckoo passed they all rose towards her, cheeping and whistling aggressively. For nearly half a mile they chased and harried her until they wheeled away back to their nesting ground.

THE HOUSE MARTINS were building their nests under the eaves of nearly every building around Forge Farm. In reality, the cuckoo was no threat to them but they were extra sensitive to her hawklike silhouette because they were collecting mud for their nests and felt vulnerable each time they landed on the ground. Daniel had earlier noticed the constant fly-past of martins, and now that he'd stopped revision work for the day he was sitting at the open window of Brook Cottage watching them. They came in a low arc over the hedge, turned sharply to the right, and swept down to the drying puddle in the hollow at the edge of the track leading to Forge

Farm. They landed, tipped forward with their wings half-spread on the ground for balance, scooped a pellet of mud into their bills, then blundered back into the air as though unable to bear the feel of the earth for longer than a second or two.

Although some martins always nested in the area, Daniel had never seen so many, and he spent more than an hour watching the endless circle of wheeling, darting birds. It was almost dark by the time the last martin gave up work and Daniel saw its swaying white rump fade into the night.

The following morning Daniel's physiotherapist made one of her twice-weekly visits. After pushing him through a series of gruelling exercises that made his leg throb painfully, she told him she was not satisfied with his progress and even hinted that serious measures might be necessary if he didn't soon achieve more than a forty-five degree bend. As soon as she left, Daniel was so driven by the fear of never being able to walk normally again that he decided to go outside and practise.

As he limped down the garden path to the road, he tried to reassure himself that he was obviously making progress: for a start, he no longer needed crutches. Yet he was terribly aware of how his leg dragged and how he had to swivel his hip to send it forward at each step.

When he turned the corner onto the track, he saw Mary Lawrence coming towards him, and as they saw each other's almost identical struggle to walk they both grinned wryly. They stopped to talk, while the house martins wheeled high above them. Daniel realised that he'd never paid much attention to Mrs. Lawrence's disability, but now, in response to his persistent questions, she gave him the bare details about her arthritis, which had been getting worse for the last ten years; about how she could no longer sleep in a bed but had to spend the night in an armchair; and about her hopes that she might have only a few more months to wait before her name came to the top of the list for an operation.

It was nearly an hour before they went their separate ways. As Daniel walked back towards Brook Cottage he saw the cuckoo flying slowly but deliberately across the pastureland. She landed in the yew tree above the lake and settled down, waiting for her moment to arrive.

TIME PASSED SLOWLY for the cuckoo. It was essential that the prospective parents did not see her, so she had to remain absolutely still, despite the discomfort each time her own egg shifted inside her. The egg was more than ripe for laying, though she could hold it for a few hours longer.

The female reed warbler laid her fifth egg later that morning and the cuckoo hoped that after a short spell of settling it down with the others she would go off in search of food before beginning the incubation proper. Instead, she fussed and wriggled the eggs into place, then shuffled herself down on top of them as if she wouldn't move until they hatched. The cuckoo grew increasingly uneasy—her egg had to be laid that day.

She watched every movement of the reed warbler, looking for the least

196

sign that she might be getting ready to leave the nest. Even a short flight might allow her enough time to make the substitution. Meanwhile, she was suffering cramps from having to remain so still in the yew tree, and the feeling of fullness just behind her cloaca was gradually turning to pain.

Then, early in the afternoon, the reed warbler hopped off her eggs onto the rim of the nest. The cuckoo peered down intently, waiting for further movement, but the warbler had only been disturbed by the first of a series of splashes in the centre of the lake, where a grass snake was devouring a newt. As soon as she had determined the cause of the noise, the warbler settled back on her eggs and ignored the noisy struggle that continued in the water. The cuckoo, though, was intrigued.

The newt's head had already been firmly trapped in the snake's jaws by the time they splashed to the surface, but the small amphibian refused to submit easily to its death. It twisted and twitched in an attempt to drag itself free. The snake coiled and knotted itself round the wriggling newt and inexorably crammed it deeper into her mouth.

Now, with the snake's throat muscles restricting its air and her toxic saliva already beginning to burn and gnaw at its flesh, the newt's struggle was reduced to spasmodic jerks and trembles. Yet ten minutes later, when the grass snake was at last able to head for the shore, the tip of the newt's tail still quivered from her jaws like a large tongue. The cuckoo saw the snake slide smoothly out of the water and slip away into the long grass, then she turned back to look at the nest. The reed warbler had gone.

The cuckoo inched slowly along the branch to give herself a clear view of the whole area. A pied wagtail was chasing insects along the stream at the far end of the lake but there was no sign of the reed warblers, so she hopped to the end of the branch and glided down to the nest. The supporting reeds swayed slightly as she landed, but the nest seemed secure enough for her to lay directly into it. She tipped forward to pick up one of the warblers' eggs, then decided to lay her own first; she shuffled round the rim until her rear was poised over the cup. As she lowered her tail and leaned forward, she was startled by the appearance of her reflection on the still water at the base of the reeds. She opened her bill in angry defiance at this rival for the site, and then was thrown into total confusion, for at the same time as the rival opened his beak below her, strident alarm cries burst from above and behind her.

The returning reed warblers had seen the cuckoo, and now they came shooting down in wild defence of their eggs. They flashed past the startled cuckoo and, still screaming in alarm, dived, twisted and soared in dizzying looping movements. In blind panic the cuckoo staggered off the nest, only to find the warblers already heading straight back towards her. Instinctively she flinched and dived away from them. Her large body was not, however, built for rapid manoeuvres in tight situations and she almost crashed into the lake. Her wing tips and long tail brushed the water and for a moment she felt as if she would be sucked down into it, but sheer terror gave her the strength to lift herself clear. She banked left, climbing all the time, and though the reed warblers pursued, chittering with anger, she knew she was safe.

The cuckoo had been badly scared and she beat on quickly, anxious to get well away from the lake. She crossed the river, flew high over the field where Jim was spraying the barley, and only thought of stopping when she reached the other side of the valley. There she landed in a tall oak behind Forge Farm, and crouched in the safety of the dense foliage to recover. For nearly an hour she stayed there, tense and jumpy, before a spasm of pain from the muscles inside her cloaca reminded her of the urgent need to lay her egg. If she did not find a host nest within a very short time, she would simply have to expel the egg and abandon it.

THE FEMALE DUNNOCK finished turning the last of her clutch and, fluffing up her breast feathers, settled once more on top of the four sky-blue eggs. The total satisfaction which she found in sitting on the eggs, combined with an unspecified but lingering disquiet since the loss of the first nest, had made her unwilling to leave her precious charges for more than a few moments. However, the seeming absence of any potential dangers near the nesting site had recently tempted her to give in to her growing desire to wing freely through the air for a short time and search for food.

High in her oak tree, the cuckoo saw a dunnock fly out from behind the barn and set off across the field. There was nothing of particular interest in this event, and as another spasm of pain gripped the cuckoo she was about to look away when the dunnock suddenly swerved round and headed back the way she had come. This telltale sign of anxiety and indecision caught the cuckoo's attention. It was the nervous action of a bird with something to protect—a nest, perhaps? The cuckoo's eyes, now alert to every detail, saw the dunnock disappear behind the barn, and she immediately glided to the small ash tree on the left in order to get a better view. From this angle she could see the bullace bush growing up against the barn.

A moment later the dunnock flew out again, her anxiety about whatever was hidden in the bush now obviously stilled, for she headed decisively across the field. The cuckoo watched her go; watched her as she crossed the river and landed in the strip of pasture on the far side; watched as a male hopped to greet her; and watched as they both disappeared into some dense clumps of dock. The instant they were out of sight, she leaned forward and launched herself in a sharp glide towards the bullace.

The interwoven branches and the sharp thorns made her progress difficult, but she finally wriggled her way down into the heart of the bush. From there, two easy hops took her to the side of the nest. She sensed that the life inside the four blue shells was already well advanced and would hatch before her own chick. Its chances of survival would therefore be reduced, but at least it would have a chance. She could wait no longer. Quickly plucking out one of the dunnock eggs and holding it in her bill,

198

she spread herself over the nest. She had been clutching the muscles of her cloaca so tightly that, as she relaxed them in order to lay, stabbing pains shot through her body and she was unable to ease her egg out.

She lifted her rear briefly, then settled down again. This time she pumped her muscles and tried to push the egg out, but still it would not come. When the widest part of the egg reached the opening, the pressure increased until it felt as if she would have to allow it to withdraw inside her again, but suddenly the pressure eased and she felt the egg slide down onto its pointed tip. Her muscles relaxed and the pain faded. By the time she had hopped onto the branch and had swung round to look, her egg had tumbled gently onto its side and was lying snugly next to the other three.

The bush was easier to leave than to enter, and without a second glance the cuckoo skipped and flapped her way out. She jumped to the ground with half-open wings, tossed her head and opened her bill in order to shift the egg she was carrying into a better position, then rose into the air and flew away, keeping low to the ground.

EVEN BEFORE THE FEMALE DUNNOCK reached the nest, she sensed that something had happened. A faint impression of an intruder still lingered among the branches of her home and a tremor of terror quivered through her as she hopped onto the rim of the nest. But the eggs were still there and she immediately jumped down and settled herself on top of them.

Throughout the long hours of incubating she had always managed to arrange the eggs so that they fitted snugly under her, but now no amount of shuffling and rolling them with her breast could shift them into a comfortable position. At last she jumped off, and hopped round the rim of the nest looking critically at the eggs from every angle.

The cuckoo's egg was larger than her own and its buff-green colour and distinctive marbled patterns stood out dramatically next to the sky-blue of its companions. She saw the difference and it puzzled, even frightened her, but her loyalty to the impulse of life was greater than any uncertainty she felt. She settled once more on the eggs and gladly adjusted her body to the new shape beneath her.

Chapter Twelve

The weather became changeable. An unseasonably cold wind brought solid banks of slate-grey clouds sweeping across the valley to shiver the leaves with fierce, rattling showers. When the clouds broke, and the sun sparkled and flashed in puddles, and in single drops caught on the leaves, it was the wind rather than the warmth of the sun that dried the land before the next shower.

The female dunnock did not stray far from the bush again. She still exercised her muscles by hopping and flitting through the branches, and

she occasionally flew down round the base of the barn to search for seeds, but these short breaks of a few minutes every hour or so were the only relief she got. The rest of the time she snuggled tight onto the eggs, protecting them from the cold. By the eighth day of the dunnocks' incubation period the cuckoo's egg, which had missed the first four days, was still only at the early stages of development. The tiny embryo had formed into two bulges that would become the head and the body, but there was still no recognisable feature of the bird that was to come. The three dunnock eggs, on the other hand, were well advanced.

Inside the small shells, the main limbs had formed, and there were even miniature toes at the ends of the tiny legs. All the main organs existed,

200

the beak had taken shape and the eyes looked like two black jellies.

On the eleventh day of the female's long vigil, the clouds broke up for good and the wind dropped. The sun, whose heat seemed suddenly to have intensified, rolled slowly across the sky, warming the earth and drawing all forms of life out of hiding, so that by the evening there were clouds of insects dancing in its thick golden light. Inside the cuckoo's egg, the embryo, as though sensing the disadvantage it would face by hatching late, was racing through its development, but was still three and a half days behind the dunnock embryos, which were now fully formed, and in forty-eight hours would begin to hatch.

Late on the evening of the twelfth day, the dunnock felt the first twitches of life. For some time the movements came from only one egg, but during the night her two other chicks also began to wriggle and scrape against the shells. The sudden jerks brought the unsleeping female to a fever pitch of excited anticipation, and at the first faint glimmer of dawn she burst into urgent call. The eternity of waiting was over—the new life which she had so patiently nurtured was ready to emerge. The male caught the tension of the moment and began a ceaseless ferrying of seeds to the nest. He tore impetuously at the plants, often returning with whole heads trailing from his bill and nearly as often dropping them in his haste. By chance, though, he was back at the nest to hear the first faint cheep as the most advanced of the chicks began to call through the shell. The male stood for a moment in almost terrified wonder, then dived madly out into the world, his dedication to his task redoubled by what he had heard.

The female had noted the precise source of the sound and, scrabbling this particular egg to the front of the nest, began to call encouragement. Twice she even tapped the shell with her bill to prompt the chick to begin the long, tiring task ahead. The chick—a male—felt the tapping, and sensed, rather than heard, the distant voice calling to him.

This first contact with life outside his cramped little world stimulated him, and he began hammering at the inside of the shell. These few random thrusts brought no reward, but when he swung himself round and started again his bill tore through the fabric of the inner membrane where it had separated from the outer shell as the egg had cooled. He opened his bill in surprise and gulped in the air that had been trapped there for this very moment. The delicious air filled his lungs, and he began to peck wildly at the shell in the lust for more.

Jagged lines shot out from the centre of the shell, and a moment later the first chip flew free. The effort of this hardest part of the hatching had exhausted the chick and he subsided panting to the floor of the shell.

As soon as he had recovered his strength the male chick struggled up and continued his work, chipping and tearing at the shell and levering the cracked fragments away with the blunt, horny spike at the tip of the upper half of his bill. He completed his hatching a couple of hours later. Naked and utterly helpless, he squirmed his way out of the egg and wriggled close to the warm feathers of his mother. The slow emergence had partially accustomed him to the assaulting sensations of the outside world, but he was still filled with terror and confusion by the strange loud noises, the roughness of the nest against his tender skin, and the glow that pulsed through his closed eyelids. Then, overriding everything else, came a surge of hunger. Summoning all his energy, he stretched his scrawny neck and opened his bill.

The male had scattered seeds in and around the nest but the female ignored these and flew out to search for something better. By the time she returned, the male had re-entered the bush and was standing on a branch peering down at his still-gaping offspring. The open bill and thin neck led down to a wrinkled, pink body whose skin was almost transparent, so that the internal organs showed as dark masses. It was not an attractive sight. Then his mate flew in with a small caterpillar in her bill. He watched as she stood on the edge of the nest and plunged the food directly into the back of the nestling's throat.

The chick gulped eagerly at the food, but almost before it had reached his stomach, he was gaping again—crying out, stretching, begging for food: food, the only thing that could drive away the fear and discomfort that had been torturing his delicate being since he had left the shell. This insatiable lust for the comfort of a full belly would ensure the rapid growth that he needed to make in the next week or so if he was to survive.

During the following hour the male returned twelve times with small insects to cram into that ever-eager mouth. As soon as he had placed the food at the back of the nestling's throat, he bent forward and jostled his head down into the crowded nest in search of fragments of the shattered shell. He had already carried away the two main portions and dropped them far from the bush so that they would not attract predators, but he still searched meticulously for the small chippings, because it was essential to keep the nest clean.

The second chick—a female—began to hatch late in the afternoon, and the sun had already set before the process was complete. Now two ravenous mouths gaped and squeaked in pitiful entreaty.

The few hours' head start that the male chick had over his sister was already evident on the following day. At the slightest jarring of the nest he was the first to react, and his stretched neck and importuning mouth were the obvious targets for the returning parents.

The mother invariably responded to this show of dominance and fed him, but the father often purposely waited until the female chick had struggled up and then fed her. Despite this, when night finally halted the adults' food-gathering, the male chick settled down contentedly with a swollen belly that ensured that he quickly fell into a deep sleep while the female chick, still racked with hunger, dozed only fitfully.

Worn out by the hectic activity of their day, the parent birds slept soundly, but it was a very short night. While the last stars still glimmered palely in the lightening sky, the third chick started to call from inside the shell. The mother bird snapped wide awake. She stood up to move the egg to the front of the nest and instantly woke the two chicks. While she pushed at the egg, they raised themselves, collapsed and raised themselves again in frenzies of starving excitement. The male, who had passed the night on the branch next to the nest, was woken by their piping cries and blundered mechanically out of the bush to resume his labours.

The world outside was cold and damp. The barn owl, who had five young in his nest in one of the oast-houses of Forge Farm, was returning from his last sortie across the field, a small vole hanging limply from his hooked bill. A light burned in the living room of Little Ashden where

Mary Lawrence, unable to sleep because of the pain in her hip, was reading a book. The dunnock landed in a tall clump of grass, shaking dewdrops off the stalks, and reached up to tear at the seeds.

Not long after the sun climbed above the trees on top of the rocks, the third chick hatched. Another female, she was from the start altogether stronger and more aggressive than her sister. At once, her arrival set a new level of competitiveness for food that raised the mood in the nest to one of continual squabbling and squeaking as each of the nestlings pleaded for their parents' attention.

The third-born chick managed to claim about half the amount of food her stronger brother grabbed, but it was more than enough to ensure that she would survive. Only when these two lay momentarily exhausted by their jostling rivalry did their weaker sister succeed in scrambling up to sway and call feebly for food. She ate enough to keep her alive, but while the other two grew hourly fitter and stronger she merely clung to existence, spending most of her time crouched at the bottom of the nest.

The plight of his weakest offspring often disturbed the male as he stood on the lip of the nest with a newly caught insect in his bill, but he usually succumbed to the persuasive demands of the other two and popped the food into one of their trembling throats. The mother bird showed no concern for the weakling. She was, however, concerned about the fourth egg, which still lay in the centre of the nest.

She had delayed the beginning of the incubation until the last egg arrived because her instinct had dictated that all the chicks should hatch at roughly the same time. The lateness of this one went against all the feelings of rightness that governed her life. Bit by bit the egg took on the nature of a threat, and she grew hostile to its presence. Yet on the two occasions that she determined to eject it from the nest, she sensed that there was life within it and her maternal instinct would not allow her to tip it out.

So the pattern of their lives continued. The male's days were filled with the tireless provision of food; the female's with cleaning the nest, brooding the chicks during the chillier hours, and helping her mate with the endless task of trying to satisfy the insatiable appetites of their young. Then, late one afternoon three and a half days after the male chick had hatched, a crack forked like menacing lightning across the centre of the cuckoo's egg.

Chapter Thirteen

The cuckoo hatched with frightening speed, chipping violently at the shell and pushing with such force that when the end finally broke away she fell out of the egg. Blind, her skin still wet, she lay panting next to the weakest of the dunnock nestlings. The others had paid no attention to the hatching, having been totally engrossed in begging for food.

The mother bird, however, had remained by the nest watching the arrival of the newcomer and giving small cheeps of encouragement. Now she leaned forward and took one of the broken halves of the shell in her bill. As her head brushed the neck of the cuckoo, the tiny creature turned aggressively and pecked her. The dunnock darted back in surprise and stood for a moment looking curiously at the nestling, before flying off to deposit the eggshell on the far side of the field.

By the time the last of the shell fragments had been cleared, the cuckoo was already beginning to lift her head and to open her bill in urgent demands for food. There was something about the sway of her scrawny neck and the width of her gaping bill that was more compelling than even the practised entreaties of the dunnock nestlings. Night was falling fast and the mother bird had been intending to stay on the nest to cover her offspring against the chilly air, but there was no denying this insistent command. She flew off into the dusk and began a search for insects.

The male, too, felt the power of the cuckoo when he returned with a small spider in his bill. Like his mate he had intended to stop hunting since the light had become faint, but the way the newcomer gulped the spider and immediately gaped again was irresistible. He hopped out of the dark interior of the bush and set out once more into the gloom.

The two stronger dunnocks, fierce rivals during the day, now huddled together and fell asleep. Their weaker sister, though, sensed the chance to win a good position for the next arrival of food, and she started to stumble to the side of the nest. She brushed against the cuckoo and felt the newcomer stiffen and begin to push, but she was so used to being jostled by the other nestlings that she took no notice.

The cuckoo, however, was not like the other nestlings. Still less than two hours old, she already burned with the desire for sole domination of the nest, and her killer instinct gave extraordinary power to her tiny body. When the weak female reached the side of the nest and tottered up into a standing position, the cuckoo wormed her way underneath her rump. She wriggled closer until she felt the dunnock's body touch the sensitive hollow on her back. It was only the slightest brush, but it was as if a charge of electricity had shot through the cuckoo and her whole body convulsed at the signal. Her rear end shot upwards, sweeping the dunnock off her feet so that she collapsed upside-down onto the cuckoo's back. Still as though in the grip of a fit, the cuckoo flung her legs out behind her until the tiny claws on her feet grasped the interwoven strands of the bowl of the nest. Then, using the crooks of her naked wings like elbows to push her, the cuckoo began to clamber backwards up the side of the cup.

The dunnock had been too astonished to do anything at first, but now that she felt herself being lifted she tried to escape. She turned one way then the other but was unable to roll onto her front because she was clamped between the heaving shoulder blades of the cuckoo. Her only hope lay in raising her head and trying to pull herself upright into a sitting position but her weak neck muscles were unable to take the strain. All she could do was flail helplessly as the cuckoo twitched and jerked her way nearer the edge. Once her rear had reached the lip of the nest, the cuckoo only needed to lift her elbows a little higher in order to straighten her back and the writhing burden would slide off.

She was just flexing her muscles for this heave when the dunnock's shift of weight relieved the pressure. The cuckoo jerked upwards so violently that the dunnock was flung, rather than eased, off her back.

The two small birds fell simultaneously—the cuckoo back into the soft base of the nest, and the dunnock down onto the bare soil. She hit the ground head-first, and the weight of her body broke her neck.

A few minutes later, when first the male and then the female returned, the cuckoo was too weary to raise herself to take the food they had brought her, and the dunnock nestlings, too, could not be bothered to leave the sleepy comfort they had settled into. The parents offered the food for a few moments and then, getting no response, ate it themselves. There was no question of further hunting in the dark, so the male crouched down on the branch next to the nest and hunched himself for sleep while the female settled her body gently over the cup and spread her wings slightly to protect the nestlings against the cold and the dew. After a moment she raised herself, puzzled by the feel of the shapes beneath her now that the egg had gone. Then, feeling three warm bodies stir against her breast, she lowered herself in tired contentment.

THE MALE DUNNOCK, conscious even in sleep of his precarious balance on the branch, was the first to wake as the bush swayed. A moment later the female also was alert to the presence of something below. Alarm overcame her instinct to remain quiet and hidden, and as the thing below moved again, shaking the whole bush, she chittered and squeaked in fright.

The male had been frozen in an attempt to avoid detection but now the only option was to divert attention away from the nest. He screeched his alarm call and flew out of the bush making as much noise as possible. As soon as the female heard him go, she crouched low in the nest in an effort to keep the nestlings still. The male dunnock's bravery was, in the event, unnecessary. The fox had heard the female's cry but he was in no mood to waste his time over any adventure that offered him less than a substantial meal. Climbing up through a thorny bush after a small bird did not appeal to him. He came upon the body of the dead nestling, however, and ate it in one disappointed gulp, then padded away along the barn and round the curve of the oast-house.

THE CUCKOO USED THE MORNING to concentrate on building up her reserves of food and strength, but by early afternoon her belly was sufficiently filled for her to respond to her other urge. She was aware that two competitors for the nest remained, and she had already sensed that one was weaker than the other. The more active of the two posed a greater threat in the immediate struggle for food, but she felt that she was not yet strong enough to eject him from the nest so she concentrated on the weaker female. Whenever the parent birds were away, she hounded the female nestling, stalking her relentlessly, pushing and prodding, trying to manoeuvre her into a vulnerable position.

When one of the parents returned she stopped—but only to compete for the latest titbit of food, and certainly not because she wanted to keep her murderous intention secret. Her urge to destroy her rivals was as natural to her as her urge to eat, and she knew no guilt and no need for guile. Nor was there any need for secrecy. Had she been a rat, a snake, or any of the other threats that they lived in fear of, the parent birds would have fought to the death to protect their young. What they saw in the cuckoo, however, was simply another nestling.

For nearly three hours—sometimes by chance, and sometimes through her own efforts—the dunnock nestling warded off disaster. Twice her instinct for survival brought her scrambling off the cuckoo's back at the last moment. Then, finally, almost hypnotised into submission, she was lifted to the brink and saw the dark drop below her. She moved her limbs in feeble resistance, but she had lost hope.

From the other side of the nest, the male nestling watched as his sister was hoisted higher. He caught a last glimpse of her as she slid and rolled down the cuckoo's back, before she was flung into the air and away out of sight by a quick flip of the cuckoo's rump. He felt no loss, but as the cuckoo tumbled from the edge and rolled towards him, he did feel fear.

SMALL TWIGS AND LEAVES had broken the female nestling's fall and she had rolled, rather than tumbled, her way down through the bush and into the open. As soon as the returning dunnock saw the nestling crumpled forlornly on the ground, her first instinct was to get her back under cover of the bush. She stood next to the nearest point of cover and, first with enticing calls and then with piercing commands, tried to persuade the nestling to come into shelter.

Suddenly, the dunnock saw a jay standing on the edge of the roof of the barn. There was no doubt of the big bird's intention, and the dunnock flew, screaming in alarm and trailing her tail feathers in an invitation to attack. The jay refused to be drawn into giving chase and swooped on the nestling, clamping his bill tightly on its neck. As he straightened up and flapped into the air, the nestling twitched slightly, and died. The dunnock darted in pursuit, but soon the jay was so far ahead that it was impossible for her to catch up. She watched his white rump grow smaller as he sped away and disappeared into the trees below the rocks.

DANIEL WAS SITTING on a half-sunk boulder at the base of one of the tallest rock faces. He had always loved playing in and around the rocks when he was a child, and now that he was walking so much better he came up here every day. It would be some time, of course, before he could climb up the slippery sandstone faces again, but even walking along their base or clambering up some of the easy sloping gullies to sit on top of the rocks gave him a sense of achievement.

The sun was setting now and it was growing chilly, so he ought to be getting back. As he went down the track, he met Theo Lawrence coming out of the yard of Forge Farm. Daniel forced the pace as they walked together towards Little Ashden. It jarred his leg but he hated it if he thought someone was having to slow down so that he could keep up. Even when they parted at the gate of Little Ashden he kept going fast, in case Theo could still see him from the garden.

THEO GLANCED AT HIS WATCH as he slid the key into the front door. It was late again. He really must make more of an effort to get home in time for tea, but there was so much work to do at the moment with the new calves that Jim had bought. He opened the door and called out his usual greeting to Mary. There was no reply. He called out again when he found that she was not in the front room, then once more as he started on his way to the kitchen. Silence.

Smoke was seeping out of the oven, and when he opened it a great cloud billowed out from the burnt cake inside. He switched off the oven and went to the window. As he reached up to swing it open, he saw a large wet stain on the ceiling. He ran along the hall and pounded up the stairs. Water was running out from under the bathroom door. He fumbled with the handle and pushed. Water was pouring over the rim of the bath, and Mary was lying motionless on the floor.

Chapter Fourteen

The cuckoo was developing rapidly—partly because she won nearly three quarters of the incoming food and partly because her metabolism was such that she was built to gain weight and grow twice as fast as any rivals in the nest. Already, on the third day of her life, she weighed almost as much as the remaining dunnock nestling, even though he was now six and a half days old. In every other respect, though, he was much more mature and it was this fact that kept him alive. His eyes were fully open and, beneath the fluffy down, the first stubby quills of his real feathers were beginning to protrude. He had also mastered the principle of keeping his balance and he was able to move quite rapidly round the nest on his legs.

The cuckoo, on the other hand, for all her size, was still blind and practically naked, and she was no match for the mobility and agility of the dunnock. Nevertheless, he watched her every movement because, although she was not fast, she was persistent. A couple of times on the day she had ejected the second of his sisters, he had almost suffered the same fate. In the confines of the nest he was never able to get very far away from her, and after each successful evasion he had only a brief respite before she came squirming and flopping towards him again. Even when he stood his ground and pecked savagely at her head or back as she tried to wriggle under him, he could never drive her away for long. As soon as the immediate pain had worn off, she would shuffle into the attack again.

The parent birds saw nothing of this struggle. Each time they returned to the nest with food, they saw only the natural scramble of two hungry young birds. The male felt a slight unease at the "foreignness" of the cuckoo, and occasionally resisted her bobbing, seductive pleas in order to feed his real offspring. The female, however, made no such distinction and indiscriminately fed the closest mouth, which was invariably the cuckoo's.

The adult birds' days were filled with this round of flying, hunting and feeding. When the weather was good and the food supply was abundant, they made as many as thirty trips an hour between the hunting ground and the nest. When food was more difficult to find they returned less frequently, but were, in fact, forced to work harder, flying further afield and searching more urgently. Each evening, as the days grew longer, they worked later, to take advantage of the last glimmer of light, and each morning they were out of the bush and at work before the last of the dark had left the sky. Their bodies were stretched to the limit, and during the short nights they sank into profound sleep.

BEFORE DAWN on the cuckoo's seventh day of life, the male dunnock woke and opened his eyes to a slate-blue light in which the tips of the branches of the bush were just becoming visible. Outside, a thin drizzle was coating the top leaves, and every so often they bent and twitched as drops of water swelled, ran together, and plopped onto the leaves below.

The male flinched as one of the drops hit him square on the head. His burble of surprise woke the female, whose eyes snapped open, then hooded and closed again when she saw that all was well. She would not leave the nest until the male returned with his first catch to show that food was available. Meanwhile the nestlings had to be kept warm.

The male hopped carefully onto the rim of the nest and began flicking and smoothing the damp and displaced feathers on her back. While he preened her she tipped her head upwards and closed her eyes in pleasure and appreciation. He worked up towards her shoulders, nipping the feathers into place, then ran his bill quickly up the side of her neck in a sudden memory of their lovemaking. This unexpected caress sent a shiver through her, and she hunched her neck down into her shoulders in surprise at the intense thrill of pleasure. When the nest jerked, she opened her eyes, expecting another delightful, teasing attack, but was only in time to catch a glimpse of his dark shape poised at the edge of the bush. He gave the little preflight bob that she knew so well, then darted away. His body merged with the blue richness of the early light outside and he was gone.

He flew directly to the riverbank and spent a few minutes rooting for food round the bottom of the trees, but the wind was sweeping the drizzle in under the cover of the branches so he took off again and crossed the river, looking for a drier feeding ground. He found that there was shelter from the wind and drizzle on the side of the hedge nearest the road, so he landed there and began shuffling along the bank.

After a while he hopped down onto the surface of the road and found that from there he had an eye-level view of the edge of the bank and it was much easier to peer under the foliage and spot the small insects for which he was searching. At the base of some honeysuckle he found a heaving cluster of aphids and started cramming them into his bill, excited that he had found such a rich source of food so early in the day.

SITTING AT THE WHEEL of his car, the fisherman had to keep switching his wipers on and off because, although the drizzle was heavy, it wasn't enough to wet the windscreen properly, and they kept squeaking and smearing. He always loved the drive down to the coast, loved it especially while it was still dark and his headlights carved out the path. This particular road that he was just turning onto led along an unspoilt valley with soft rounded hills on one side and an amazing outcrop of rocks on the other.

When life really got him down during the working week, he thought of this valley. Did they know how lucky they were, the people who lived in the little collection of houses he was just coming to? He would give anything to live over there in those oast-houses that he could see in the distance across the fields. Tina probably wouldn't like it—she loved the lights and the houses and the noisy streets. But the city was only an hour or so away—they could go up to it at weekends. What a turnaround that would be: being where he wanted five days of the week, and only having to face the traffic and the noise and the people at weekends. Yes, of all the places he knew, this valley would be the best possible place to live.

THE MALE DUNNOCK was just leaning forward to pluck another aphid from the stem when light flashed across his vision. He hopped out from the bank and stood on the road, staring in wonder. From out of the surrounding blue haze, lights were moving towards him. A beam of light swung directly onto him and the colours exploded into a fierce and dazzling whiteness. He cowered before the power of the light and was frozen, with his legs bent and his body poised for the spring into the air that he had started but seemed unable to finish. Then suddenly the noise reached him—a roar and a whistling and a splashing and a splattering.

The muscles of his body unfroze and he completed the spring. His wings beat wildly to lift him away from the threat, but the speeding light was nearly on him, searing his eyes and making him lose all sense of direction. He must climb! He pulled towards the cool blueness, his wings pressing down on the air and lifting him high, higher. He rose above the light, which immediately swept below him. Now he would turn. He angled his wings and began the turn when, suddenly, the wave of air caught him and he was bowled with it along the bonnet of the car. He turned one complete somersault before he was smashed against the windscreen.

The fisherman had seen a whirr of wings flash through his lights, but before his foot could touch the brake, whatever it was had slammed against the windscreen and whirled away. He had flinched and for one awful moment he'd thought he might skid right across the road. He hated running into things like that. It wasn't fair that someone who loved animals should have an accident like that. What was the matter with the crazy bird? The stupid thing had flown straight at him. It must be dead— an impact like that! He couldn't bear the thought that it might just be injured and would die in agony. But it was too late now, he'd never find it in this half-light.

The dunnock was not dead. The blows he had received had knocked him unconscious and when he came to, half an hour later, he was too weak and disabled by his injuries to move. One wing lay half folded across his back, while the other was spread out to the side. Whenever he breathed deeply, the roll of his body put too much weight onto this wing and he suffered such pain that it sank him further away from life. His head was resting on the road in such a way that one eye saw only a blurred close-up of the surface of the tarmac while the other could see the top of the hedge and the leaden sky beyond. It was this eye which, after some time, saw the crow flap down and perch on the hedge. The helplessness and fear he felt on seeing the big black bird staring down at him was too strong, and his brain refused to continue to accept the image, so it switched itself to register only the blurred picture of tarmac sent by the other eye.

The female dunnock waited for her mate's return, but eventually the restlessness of the two nestlings drove her out hunting. Insects were hard to find in this poor weather and the nestlings were in a state of raging hunger so, although she felt the absence of the male and longed to search for him, she had no alternative but to concentrate on the more immediate problem of trying to do the work of two providers. Her affinity with her mate was so strong that she certainly would have found him had she been able to spare the time to look, and she would also have stayed near him while he continued to live. As it was, he died alone.

The crow marked the precise moment when the life slipped out of the little grey bundle. She tensed, glanced round with fierce, glittering eyes to check that there were no potential rivals, then spread her wings and slid smoothly down to her waiting meal.

DANIEL SETTLED HIMSELF into the passenger seat and pulled the door to. His college friend, Mike, was still loading the suitcase into the back of the van, so he turned to look at the house and saw his mother watching from the window. She looked so lonely, with Teddy held against her and the drizzle-streaked glass making it hard to see more than a blur. Supposing she had an accident, like Mrs. Lawrence, all alone in the house?

At last Mike finished the loading and got in. Daniel waved quickly to his mother and then, as the van started off on the journey back to college, he tried to switch his thoughts off by fixing in his mind pictures of the valley. Just random details that he would be able to recall during the hectic weeks of exams that lay ahead . . . that crow, for instance, that had flown up at the last minute because it could hardly drag itself away from what it was pecking at on the road.

Chapter Fifteen

For Theo, the first few days after Mary's accident were a jumble of anxious hours of waiting, either in some grim corridor in the hospital or in the lonely silence of Little Ashden.

The fall, as she'd stepped into the bath, had badly cracked her pelvis in a couple of places, but the bones near her hip were already in such a mess from the arthritis that, despite the many X-rays, the doctors found it difficult to assess the damage. In addition to that, the skin on one side of her body was scalded from the hot water that had filled the bath and overflowed onto her. It was hardly any wonder that she was suffering from shock, and there were fears that she might develop pneumonia.

The one good thing that had come out of the accident was that Mary was likely to have her hip replaced sooner than she had anticipated. The operating list was full, but since she was already in hospital there was a good chance that she would be fitted in as soon as there was a cancellation. In the meantime, they would have to be patient.

Theo threw himself even more whole-heartedly into the work on the farm to take his mind off his worries about Mary and to fill the hours of loneliness. Rather than sit around brooding during the long evenings, he decided to dig up and replant the big vegetable patch that he had neglected for the last couple of years. This decision provided quite a number of parent birds with easily found food for their young. The female dunnock was among those who benefited. After the couple of days when she had had to fly long distances in search of food, she was relieved to find so many grubs and worms in the newly turned earth quite close to the nest.

ELSEWHERE IN THE VALLEY, the law of the survival of the fittest was already being harshly applied. One of the barn owls' nestlings, in foolhardy imitation of his parents, scrambled up from the nest and blundered out of the opening in the oast-house roof. Unlike them, however, he was unable to keep his balance on the acute angle of the tiles and, in the frightening darkness, he slid down the slope and over the edge.

212

THE SIGHT OF ONE SMALL creature's struggle for life snapped Eve Conrad out of the fit of weeping that had seized her on the morning that Daniel left. Her tears had started as she watched him go down the path to his friend's van. He still limped quite badly, and the stubborn courage with which he tried to play it down had made her eyes brim with tears.

While she boiled the water to make some coffee, she stared blankly out of the kitchen window. Then a movement on the lawn distracted her. A young mistle thrush was hopping across the grass, whirring its wings in a series of desperate attempts to fly. It had evidently fallen from its nest, and was too young and inexperienced to fly back to safety. Some of its hops were nearly transformed into flight, but its wings could not sustain the momentum. Finally it took a fearful glance round, then ducked behind the shovel that was leaning against the woodshed.

Eve quietly opened the kitchen door and peered out. There was a scrape of claws on the lino and Eve felt Teddy brush past her legs as he scrambled out into the garden. Barking, the terrier set off on his usual manic run round the garden to frighten off invisible intruders lurking threateningly just beyond the fences and hedges. She called him as sternly as she could but he was too lost in his joyous performance of his duty to hear her.

Suddenly the bird darted out from its hiding place and fluttered and skipped in fright. It stopped in the middle of the lawn, hunched tight and

low to the ground, half in terror and half in an attempt to camouflage itself. At that very moment Teddy stopped his search, bounced his way through the vegetable patch and capered out onto the lawn.

Instantly he saw the thrush and halted. He lowered his entire body a fraction and padded forward, his jaws open and his nerves coiled in anticipation of the moment when he would surge in to strike. Eve had been so intent on the drama that she was as startled as Teddy when an adult thrush came swooping across the scene, screaming an alarm call. The terrier was taken so completely unawares by the wild noise and the swiftness of the bird's pass that he rocked back on his haunches. Almost before he had time to turn his head to see what was happening, the thrush had flipped round and come screaming past in another attack.

This time, however, having succeeded in distracting the dog momentarily, the thrush's new sweep was aimed at its grounded fledgling. It came in fast and low, stalled abruptly, landed by the young bird and took off again, in a rapid demonstration of what was required and how easy it was to do. Having set the example, it landed on top of the hedge and turned, in a clear invitation to its offspring to follow. For an instant there was total stillness as Eve, the parent thrush, and Teddy all stared at the young bird. Then Teddy leaned back in preparation for a pounce, and this movement gave the young thrush the necessary impetus. If it stayed there any longer, it knew it would die. It bobbed low, summoned every nerve and muscle into action, and sprang. Its frantically flapping wings took it skimming across the lawn, its feet still brushing the grass. Then, just when it looked certain that the bird would have to drop its legs and land again, it curved into the air and winged triumphantly onto the hedgetop. The whole flight had taken only a couple of seconds, but Eve sensed the intense effort of will, daring and determination that had been crammed into the struggle, and her heart lifted at its success.

She shouted to Teddy, and hurried him back into the kitchen. She smiled in pleasure at the bird's achievement and felt strengthened and encouraged by the triumph of youth and life in the face of death.

Across the valley another struggle—between the male dunnock nestling and the cuckoo—was beginning in earnest.

THROUGHOUT THE DAY on which her mate was killed, the female worked feverishly to keep her nestlings fed.

The cuckoo, in particular, was driven frantic by raging hunger, and her jangling nerves kept her moving restlessly. Each time the adult dunnock returned to the nest, all this energy was channelled, with a rush, into a neck stretched to its very limit, a gape wider than ever, and a body that twitched and shook in greedy anticipation. Invariably she won the food and this gave momentary relief to the pent-up desperation that boiled within her.

Immediately the food had been swallowed, however, and the adult bird had departed, the cuckoo's frustration was pumped once more into hatred of the other nestling. Her eyes had recently opened, and her size and viciousness, properly directed, would have quickly eliminated the dunnock, but she still relied largely on trying to trap him on her back in order to lift him and eject him from the nest. All afternoon, with mounting irritation, she tried to manoeuvre herself into position under the dunnock, but he simply dodged away. While she continued to use this old ploy his greater mobility kept him out of danger. Then, as the lowering sky grew even gloomier, to signal an early nightfall, the cuckoo's continual failure suddenly exploded into a frenzy of violence.

Feeling the dunnock yet again slip away from her rump, she whirled round in blind anger and happened to stumble over him. The dunnock collapsed under her greater weight and size, and the cuckoo, hardly knowing what she was doing, followed up by pecking savagely at his head and back. She was surprised both by how quickly she had overwhelmed him and by what a blissful release of tension it was to peck and slash him with her bill.

She looked down at the dunnock, who was still lying dazed by the attack, and his evident helplessness excited her. She moved in and this time deliberately aimed a blow at his head. There was a satisfying squeak from her victim as her bill jarred his skull, and he cringed even lower before her vicious power. Again she pecked, and again he squeaked. She leaned back, intending to lunge really hard, but at that moment the nest shook and the mother bird was there with a pale green lacewing hanging from her bill. At once the cuckoo's entire attention was directed at the food, and she pranced and stretched so energetically that the dunnock actually had difficulty in placing the food into the usual position at the back of the cuckoo's throat. In the end she simply dropped the lacewing into the swaying mouth and flew away quickly to make at least one more trip before the light faded completely.

The cuckoo was bemused to find that the food did not slide easily and satisfyingly down her throat. Instead, the insect's large pale green body and wings stuck, jammed first out of one side of her bill and then the other. She flicked her head and gaped as widely as possible, but she was still unable to swallow it. Her struggle with the food gave the dunnock nestling time to recover. The blows had been painful, but no serious damage had been done. Now, while the cuckoo's attention was elsewhere, he stood up and moved towards her rear. If he could keep moving he would be safe.

He barely got himself into position before the cuckoo managed to gulp the lacewing. For a brief moment she sat enjoying the food, then she suddenly remembered her unfinished task. She heaved herself up and started to manoeuvre herself round so that she could once more peck at her rival. The dunnock was ready, though, and simply stayed close to her rear as she staggered round in a circle, unable to catch up with him.

Once, she stopped and backed suddenly, trying to tip him onto the hollow just above her rump, but he neatly sidestepped her and she was

forced to resume her bid to get within pecking range. It was a fruitless task, for her clumsy, heaving movements were no match for his comparative agility. On top of this, she was relatively new to the technique of keeping her eyes focused. Her brain began to swim with the strain, and she slumped to the base of the cup to rest.

The male dunnock, too, was trembling from the exertion, but he could not take the risk of settling down by the cuckoo's side, so he stood leaning against the cup to recover. It was because he was standing that he happened to get the most substantial item of food that the mother bird had found all day, the plump green larva of a skipper butterfly. The caterpillar was so big that the little male had a job to gorge it all, but he was desperately hungry and it was just what he needed. The cuckoo, meanwhile, felt the jarring of the nest as the adult bird flew away and struggled up in time to see the last of the larva disappear into her rival's bill. In fury she pecked at him and while he was still trying to swallow his meal he was forced to dart away before she knocked him down.

This time, anger and frustration drove her, and instead of simply chasing him round the nest she improvised tottering ventures across the centre of the cup to stop him getting into a safe position behind her. Only his speed and a good deal of luck kept him on his feet and able to dodge out of her way until she exhausted herself and stopped to recover her breath. She crouched, panting, and her look was filled with such malice and hostility that he could not meet her eyes. He cocked his head to the side and, still keeping a watch for the first sign of an attack, peered out into the near blackness beyond the nest.

Out there lurked unknown terrors, perhaps even worse than the stabbing bill of the cuckoo, and an overwhelming fear began to flow through his body, weakening his muscles and making him want to collapse to the floor of the nest. Had his mother not returned shortly afterwards, he would have been a submissive victim to the cuckoo's next attack.

THE TWO NESTLINGS were developing so fast that hours, let alone whole nights, brought changes in them. Although the cuckoo was already bigger than the little male dunnock, she was, when dawn broke, only entering the eighth day of a developmental period that would last at least three weeks. She still had only the lightest covering of down on her body and her muscles were not yet strong enough to allow her to make coordinated movements for any long period. She was, therefore, a long way behind the dunnock who was, on this eleventh day of his life, only forty-eight hours away from reaching full growth. Almost all of the nearly two thousand feathers that would cover his body were well advanced, so that the main hues of his markings—grey on throat and breast and brown on his back— were already apparent. His eyes had been open for days and he had learned to recognise shapes and to judge distances, albeit within the limited confines of the nest and the branches above. In addition, he was relatively steady on his feet and was quickly learning how to keep his balance by slightly raising his wings. All this relative maturity, however, was no match for the cuckoo's sheer persistence and brute force when, the following morning, the struggle for the nest began again.

The female dunnock had been so tired and had slept so deeply that she woke late. The sky had cleared just before dawn, and when she opened her eyes she saw the rays of the sun already catching the upper branches of the trees on top of the rocks. The beauty of the rich yellow beams striking the fresh green of the leaves lifted her heart.

She stretched her wings, felt the nestlings stir beneath her, and hopped onto the rim of the nest. She turned and looked as the two little balls uncurled and immediately reached up to her with wide gapes. The little male's colours had become richer and deeper overnight, and she was struck by a pang of emptiness in her life where her beautiful mate had been. Perhaps it was because of this sense of loss that she was suddenly aware of the young male in a way that she had never been before. Until this moment he had merely been another infant mouth to be fed, but now he was recognisably one of her own kind—like her, and like her absent mate

In the meantime, though, he and his fellow nestling would be dependent on her hunting skill and tireless sacrifice. But first she would need to fill her own stomach to give her strength for the long hours ahead. She flapped her wings to stretch her muscles, zipped the barbs of her wing feathers quickly through her bill to make sure they were in place, and then took off into the bright new day. The minute she was gone and there was obviously no food to beg for, the cuckoo turned on the male and pecked at his neck. He saw the blow coming, swayed too far to avoid it, staggered and fell onto his back. Before he had time to recover, the cuckoo managed to straddle his head and start to peck at his unprotected neck and chest.

The jabs and thumps hurt him but he was saved from bad injury because she was unable to get full power into her blows. Then, trying to shift herself into a better position, she accidentally trod on his head. His neck twisted as he was forced to one side and he rolled clumsily onto his half-open wing. There was a ripping pain as his muscles were pulled, and in panic he jerked upwards. The cuckoo, always unsteady, was completely unbalanced by this movement and crashed into the wall of the nest.

As soon as her weight was off him, the dunnock staggered to his feet and started scrambling up the opposite side of the nest to get as far away as possible from his enemy. He reached the rim and gripped tightly with his claws. Once or twice before he had daringly climbed up here to escape her attacks, but he hated the feeling of openness and the dizzying glimpses of the dark depths below, and he had always circled the rim quickly and found a safe place to drop back into the comforting confines of the nest. This time, however, there was no safe place. It would be better to remain up here on this unsteady perch than to risk injury in the cramped bowl.

The cuckoo, however, was not content merely to have control of the cup of the nest—she wanted him out of her sight. As soon as she recovered from her fall she charged at him again. She crashed against the wall, rocking the whole nest. He tottered, but flapped his wings to regain his balance, then skipped round the rim away from her, wings half-stretched to keep him poised on the narrow rim. Each time he tried to shift back the cuckoo's jabbing bill prodded and nudged him towards the edge again. He was confused by the whirling of the leaves and twigs as he scuffled round the rim, and the fear of the chasm at his side was sapping his will. At last, one foot trod air and he lurched so violently that his wings were unable to restore his balance. He hung for a moment, then fell.

The cuckoo hissed in triumph. At last she had what she should have had long ago—sole control of the nest. She sank to the base of the cup, contented, only to rise in astonished fury as the dunnock's head appeared again beyond the rim. He had fallen onto the branches supporting the nest. For an instant he had nearly rolled into the gap between them, but he had managed to wriggle up and find a precarious footing.

BY ALL THE GENERAL RULES of survival, the little male's ejection from the nest should have condemned him to death. Since he was still unable to fly, he could not hunt for food nor could he escape danger. In addition to this, away from the comfort and security of the nest, he was exposed to the elements. Yet in his case the expulsion was a blessing, and he thrived better out of the nest than he had done in it.

For a start, he was freed from perpetual harassment by the cuckoo. Secondly, and crucially, he now got his fair share of the food. His mother spotted him immediately when she returned with the first food of the day and, in a mixture of distress and curiosity, she ignored the beseeching squeaks of the cuckoo and hopped over to feed him. She scolded him and tried to entice him back into the nest, but when he refused to budge she flew out and returned almost at once with more food for him.

From this point onwards, the male was no longer in unequal competition with the cuckoo for food. Now the feeding pattern depended solely on whether the female went straight to the nest when she got back, or whether she flew directly to his perch on the branch. Her basic instincts drove her to remain loyal to the nest, but she was also attracted to the small creature whose familiar shape and colouring could be more clearly seen now that he was out of the nest. Drawn by his likeness to her and by his vulnerability, she fed him almost as often as she fed the cuckoo.

For the first couple of hours out of the nest, the little male shook and trembled with fear and cold. The rays of the early morning sun were not very warm, and as soon as the bush fell into the shadow of the barn the air grew quite chilly. However, as his stomach filled out as never before, the food helped to generate an internal warmth that compensated for this. By the time the afternoon sun struck the bush again, he was already so well insulated that the golden light shining warmly onto him was a welcome bonus rather than a desperately needed relief. His tremors of fear gradually subsided as the day passed and no further threat presented itself.

Only when the light thickened and the base of the bush became invisible in the gloom did he begin to be alarmed by the sifting, soughing noise of the wind and the hundreds of sounds that filled the fast-gathering night.

When his mother returned at the end of her long day and settled back onto the cuckoo, and when all was quiet, the little male climbed up the wall of the nest and crouched down, half on the rim and half on his mother's back. It was a long, cold night. The sharp air nipped and finally numbed the upper part of his body and it was only his well-stocked stomach and the warmth of his underparts where he rested on his mother's back that stopped him from dying of exposure.

When, at last, the sky began to lighten and the twelfth day of his young life dawned, he had faced his most rigorous test yet. And he had survived.

Even before his mother woke to begin hunting, he jumped off the nest, flapped his wings vigorously to ease the stiffness in his back, and hopped confidently along the branch to stand in the little pool of warmth where the sun managed to penetrate the bush. Again, the fairly regular supply of food by his mother quickly restored his temperature, and by midmorning the valley was sweltering in the early stages of a heatwave that would continue for the whole of the last part of June.

The fine weather meant that there were plenty of easily found insects, and the female managed to keep even the cuckoo's raging appetite satisfied. As for the little male, he was so well fed that he had energy to spare, and he spent much of the day jumping across the gap between two branches. An excitement inside him burst out in the need to move and explore and, as he leaped and turned and leaped again, his wings shuffled and twitched. By the end of the day he was relying less on his legs to push him over the gap and more on the muscles of his wings, which tingled with the desire to stretch themselves in serious work. His whole body was tense, and yearned for the next step in his development: the mastery of flight.

NEWS OF MARY'S OPERATION came during Theo's afternoon visit. The chief consultant suddenly appeared in the ward, almost shouting the information that an old man who had been due for the operation the next day had developed bronchitis, and that his place would be taken by Mary. All kinds of preliminary tests would have to be made immediately, so if Theo didn't mind, perhaps he would shorten his visit? He could ring at about six o'clock the following evening. The consultant left and they had hardly begun to recover from his whirlwind visit before two orderlies arrived to take Mary away. Theo's throat tightened and his eyes watered unexpectedly as he fumbled for her hand and kissed her cheek. She smiled at him, and he had to turn away before he said something to upset her.

When the train reached the village, he decided to walk home rather than phone Eve or Jim for a lift as he usually did. The air was warm, and even though he walked slowly he was soon sweating and uncomfortable. The blood beat in his ears and his legs were leaden as he trudged up the mile-long incline from the village. As he stood at the point where the road dipped towards the valley, he was suddenly swept by fear that Mary was going to die.

Arriving at the house, he sat staring blankly out of the window as the light faded and the night came. Was Mary sleeping, or was she too awake, wondering whether she would ever see him again? Tomorrow, if she died, leaving him alone in the world of the living, what would he do?

He fell asleep in Mary's chair by the window, and when he woke he watched, as she had watched so many times before him, the rising sun flood the valley with golden light.

DRIVEN BY AN EAGER VITALITY and a curiosity to explore, the little male dunnock spent that morning hopping through the bullace, rapidly learning to coordinate his eyes and muscles and preparing his body for the strain it would endure in flight.

220

The faster he hopped, the faster he panted, instinctively training his lungs for the nearly two hundred breaths a minute he would take when he was flying fast. The harder he panted, the more air he dragged into his lungs, the richer was the blood that his tiny heart, beating seven times faster than any human heart, pumped round his body.

All this activity and exploration and excitement increased his hunger and gave an added urgency to his dashes back to the nest whenever his mother returned to the bush. As he took greater risks, flapping and gliding his way across increasingly wider gaps between branches in order to get back in time for the food, he was unconsciously mastering the basic techniques of flight. Towards midday he began the final stage of preparation. He started by loosening up the pectoral muscles that lay on either side of his breastbone. These huge muscles made up one third of his whole body-weight and would be responsible for the powerful downbeats of his wings that would pull him through the air.

Slowly at first, but building to a crescendo, he flapped his wings while his claws gripped the branch to stop him from taking off. Exhaustion quickly set in, but the next time he tried it his muscles and the joints and tendons in his shoulders and wings had already become more flexible. Then suddenly there was nothing left to do but put all the separate elements together. Everything—breathing, wing beat, timing, balance, precision and power—now had to be synchronised in flight. He was on the outer half of the branch and he skipped along it until he neared the end, where it bounced and bent under his weight. Already his skill in holding onto twigs was so assured that despite the swaying he was able to focus his entire attention on his first unhindered view of the world outside the bush.

The immensity of the open sky tightened his chest and squeezed the air from his lungs. He stood awe-struck by the vastness. At last he leaned forward, hesitated for a second more, and then, as somewhere very high above him a lark started to flute her praise of the glorious freedom of the air, he used the upward spring of the branch to launch himself.

The thick, warm air caressed the underside of his body and seemed to place a soft cushion beneath his spread wings. Using only a few lazy flaps to boost his speed and determine his direction, he floated on a long, gradual descent in which the ease and pleasure of what he was doing filled him with a greater joy than any he had so far known.

So smooth and gentle was his approach angle that it would hardly have mattered how he landed; but instinctively he did everything right. Without so much as a hint of a stumble or a top-heavy forward topple, he set down in the long grass, a good twenty feet from the bullace.

The tall, lush green glowed all round him in the sun's bright light, and the throbbing warmth pulsed down onto his back. The air was filled with the hum of insects in the heat haze, and the earth trembled and swelled with growth. All these new sensations crowded together and overwhelmed him. Out here he felt tiny and defenceless—he must get back to safety.

221

Another second and he might have frozen with terror, but as it was his fear was just sufficient to give him the strong push-off he needed. As his legs straightened from the spring and he left the ground, his wings snapped open, flapped backwards and forwards to create the necessary airstream, and lifted him into a climb. Over-enthusiasm and inexperience took him shooting past the perch he had chosen, but he adjusted his aim and landed on the branch above. He teetered briefly, then settled into a secure position.

JIM KINDLY TRIED to fill Theo's day with a series of tasks that were meant to distract him, but Theo still found that the time passed agonisingly slowly. No amount of work could stop his thoughts about Mary racing in a loop from dread to hope and back again, until his head burned, and his heart lost its rhythm and seemed to jerk spasmodically in the hollow of his chest. At precisely six o'clock he rang the hospital from Forge Farm. He was told that the operation had taken place and that Mrs. Lawrence was as comfortable as could be expected.

He felt drained rather than elated. He went home, had a bath, started to prepare a meal, then realised that he wasn't hungry and that all he wanted to do was sit quietly in the living room. He was still there a couple of hours later, numbly gazing at the gathering dusk, when he heard Eve Conrad's voice calling him urgently from somewhere down the track. There was a telephone call for him. The hospital. Mary.

He ran all the way, and his blood was pounding so loudly in his ears when he picked up the phone that he could hardly hear. But it was her voice—groggy and still slightly thick from the anaesthetic. She was fine. No, no pain. It had all gone splendidly. She would have to spend five days in hospital, then go for a month's rest and re-education in a convalescent home, but at the end of that time she would be walking again. She couldn't wait to see him. Tomorrow, yes. She was tired. She was going to sleep now. She loved him.

Theo's little jig of delight as he put the phone down, and the smile which lit up his face, told Eve everything. She opened her arms and they whirled in a crazy dance of happiness, laughing and slapping each other on the back. Teddy set off in a skidding chase round the kitchen in response to the excitement that crackled in the air and filled the house with its power.

THE MALE DUNNOCK ventured out four more times on his first afternoon of flying. Each time he risked staying a little longer, but each time the intensity of the experience quickly proved too strong for him and sent him flurrying back to the security of the bush. There, comforted by the enclosing vastness of leaves and branches, he spent hours peering out at the huge open space, torn by a mixture of longing and dread.

Even when his mother came back to settle on the nest for the night, he kept to his perch at the edge of the bush. So for the first time he saw the slow sparkling spin of the night sky, and he stared so long at the wonder of the pulsing lights that when his heavy eyes closed in brief snatches of sleep the crystal beams still streaked across his vision.

Late in the night while he slept more soundly, the moon rolled up from behind the barn, and when he woke the world was visible again, but in a glowing, silvery light that softened its impact. Imperceptibly, the silver light of the moon was joined by the first faint yellow in the eastern sky, and the male dunnock's eyes took it all in as the shapes, patterns and colours of the world grew stronger. Yesterday he had stood outside it but now, as the world re-emerged in all its vigour, he felt a part of it. It had grown inside him. When, from across the field, a young thrush started her melody to the dawn, the joyous excitement inside the male swelled in his throat and he tried his first simple attempt at song. Within minutes, the valley was ringing with a complex and beautiful interplay of notes and phrases from many birds, and his high-pitched piping played its part.

He was still singing, absorbed in adding his voice to the overall harmony, when his mother whirred past him out of the bush. Without a

moment's hesitation he followed and, pursuing her, was drawn into a totally different kind of flight from his solo experiments of the day before. In a fearless ecstasy of energy and delight he raced after her, slicing through the cool morning air. She had not known that he could fly so well, and she turned and sang a phrase of surprise and pleasure.

For the rest of that day, and for the whole of the next two days, he was his mother's constant companion. In the air he was always on her tail, following her every loop and swerve so instantaneously that they seemed tied to each other. Even when they were on the ground, the male was never more than a few skips away from her and was always ready to close the gap if something suddenly frightened him, or if he saw a particularly tempting titbit in her bill. Although he was starting to find his own food, he still occasionally went into his begging posture. On those occasions she automatically gave him the food, but most of what she found was still destined for the rapacious cuckoo, back at the nest.

It was his constant attention to what she did and how she did it that was enabling the young male to race through the last stages towards complete maturity. The major part of what he was as a living being had been born within him as instinctive behaviour, but observing how his mother did things refined his instincts into expertise.

For three days he flew with her and hunted with her, unconsciously learning at every moment. With her he discovered how to prise weevils out of the tiny crevices where they hid. From her he absorbed the knowledge that insects congregated in the rich spots of evening sun along the riverbank, and that young worms could most easily be plucked from beneath leaf mould in cool places in the early morning. During the few quiet moments of the day, he stood by her side and perfected his preening technique by imitating her actions as she stroked and pulled and zipped her feathers. Then, on the fourth morning, the sharing was over.

When the female flew off the nest, the young male did not follow. She stopped short and called to him, feeling it strange not to have him shadowing her; but when he still did not come, she flew on. Her overriding duty lay in feeding her nestling.

The male lingered in the bullace. The restlessness that urged him to be gone, to strike off on his own, was balanced by the anxiety and timidity that urged him to stay. In a fever of indecision he hopped from branch to branch. He was still in the bush when, half an hour later, the female returned with the cuckoo's first meal. When she flew off again, he could no longer resist and he followed her out into the already warm sunlight.

As soon as he was flying, all his hesitation disappeared, and while his mother kept on course for the river, he banked to the right and headed towards the track. He perched briefly on the top rail of the fence opposite Little Ashden, but he felt too exposed at that height, so he dodged down onto the bottom rail where long grass reached up to give a little cover. He had hardly settled himself there, though, when a blackbird landed on the

224

garden gate just across the track. The blackbird cocked his tail and stared at him with glittering, yellow-ringed eyes, then launched himself forward and flew towards the dunnock, chittering loudly. The male threw himself off the bar in terror, flew low across the field, and sought shelter again in the familiar world of the bullace.

The fear faded quickly and the restlessness began again. Once more he flitted fretfully through the bush while the exciting sights and sounds of the outside world called to him. He became so lost in his internal struggle that it was a shock when he heard a frantic squeaking noise. When he stopped and looked down he saw that the nest was directly below him and the cuckoo nestling was swaying from side to side with her bill open wide.

He swooped down onto one of the branches that supported the nest, and the cuckoo went into a frenzy of twitching and gaping. She was now so large that she nearly filled the cup of the nest. Yet despite her size, there was, now that he looked closely at her, nothing frightening about her; indeed, there was even something appealing about her clumsy and uncoordinated attempts to attract his attention.

Wings whirred past him, and as his mother landed on the rim of the nest he automatically squatted low and lifted his bill towards her. She had intended to feed the cuckoo but she was distracted by the male's movement. She turned, uncertain which of them to feed, and in her confusion the long green caterpillar she was carrying dropped from her bill. It tumbled onto the branch and was just about to roll off when the male ducked forward and snapped it up. He flicked his head in order to twitch one end of the caterpillar into his mouth, but before he could do it the cuckoo nestling began piping pathetically and shaking the nest. Her sheer helplessness could not be ignored and, as he had seen his mother do countless times, he hopped onto the rim of the nest and offered her the caterpillar. The sharp points of her bill that had so recently stabbed at him now parted in eager acceptance. He lowered his head gently into the very jaws of his enemy and placed his gift at the back of her throat.

The female was perched on the roof of the barn when the male flew out of the bullace. She watched as he crossed the field and disappeared from sight down the track. There had been a strength and a determination and a directness about his flight that told her he was leaving for good.

Chapter Sixteen

Mary Lawrence came out of the convalescent home at the very end of July, and on the first Saturday in August there was a homecoming party at Little Ashden. The day started fine, but by midafternoon, when the guests began to arrive, dark heavy clouds filled the sky. As the air grew steadily more humid, it was obvious that it would rain before nightfall.

The female cuckoo, her work of laying her eggs long ago completed and her body once again at peak fitness, had been preparing to begin her journey back to Africa in the evening, but the threat of rain prompted her to set off early. No one saw her as she passed over Little Ashden, climbing up towards the cloud ceiling. It had been a very successful summer. She had laid twelve eggs and out of these she was leaving behind her eight nearly full-grown offspring. She had never seen a single one of them.

At the beginning of September, each would leave separately, alone and unguided, following the same route that their mother and generations of their forebears had taken. Five of them would die on the way. Of the three survivors, one would be the female who had been reared by the dunnock. After the three-thousand-mile journey she would make her roost a few miles from her mother, and next year she would be back in the valley.

THE LAWRENCES' party was an enormous success. Almost everyone had had the same thought and brought a bottle of champagne, so what had been planned as quite a quiet tea party turned into a high-spirited affair filled with laughter and chatter. Even before the champagne, the atmosphere had been charged with everyone's pleasure at seeing Mary home and in such good form. She still limped a little, but she was delighted at how mobile she was; and when somebody put some music on she had no hesitation in accepting Jim Siddy's invitation to dance.

Daniel, too, was happy to be able to dance. Everyone had commented on the fact that he was walking perfectly again, and they all seemed to have taken a liking to Stephanie, his new girlfriend. This party was a good opportunity to show her the valley and introduce her to his mother.

At the end of the party the three of them walked up to the ridge behind Brook Cottage, to look down on the valley. The young male dunnock had just settled for the night in his roost low in a rowan bush next to the brook, and he watched them go by. Although he did not know it, the blackthorn bush at the top of the slope just a few seconds' flight across the brook was the place where his mother had roosted at this time last year. All he knew was that the area filled him with contentment: there was food in plenty, and the trickling, bubbling music of the brook was a delightful background to his life. Plump and strong, and used to having to improvise and adapt, he was destined to survive the winter. Next year he would find a mate and they would build a nest, here in the rowan.

Across the valley, his mother was still roosting in the bullace bush. Life was quiet and peaceful, and the long pleasures of warm summer days and a plentiful autumn still lay ahead.

NIGEL HINTON

"I knew nothing about birds when I first moved to Kent at the age of twenty-six. It was only by walking in the countryside that I became conscious of how unobservant I was, of how much I'd taken for granted," says Nigel Hinton. An experience followed that made him even more aware of the world around him. "I was driving in my car one morning, when I hit a bird. Later that day, I couldn't get the incident out of my mind. If I had driven past five minutes earlier, or five minutes later, that bird would not have been killed. I suddenly had a powerful impression of the interconnectedness of everything. And that led me to think that our awareness of the world may be very restricted: our range of hearing and our field of vision are limited. Perhaps our very perception of the world is limited."

The Heart of the Valley was Nigel Hinton's first novel for adults. Previously he wrote for a younger market, and it was during a nine-year spell as a teacher that he produced *Collision Course*, his first novel for teenagers. He then spent a year acting in pantomime and repertory, but became disillusioned with theatre life, and decided to dedicate more of his time to writing. A major breakthrough came in 1986 when his novel *Buddy* was serialised by the BBC, starring Roger Daltry, ex-member of the rock group The Who. The series was a huge success, and Hinton still travels to schools all over the country to talk about the book, which is now included in the GCSE syllabus. He wrote a sequel, *Buddy's Song*, which is to be filmed for the cinema during 1989. As well as writing the screenplay, Hinton is currently working with Roger Daltry to produce twelve songs for the film. It's a project he is very excited about, though he confesses he's only just learned to play the electric guitar, and does so "badly"!

Away from the amplified sounds of electric guitars, and the noise of the classroom—where he still teaches on two mornings a week—Nigel Hinton lives with his French wife in a quiet and unspoilt part of the Kent countryside, close to the small valley which he made the setting for *The Heart of the Valley*.

JACK

A CONDENSATION OF THE BOOK BY
BRIAN CARTER

ILLUSTRATED BY EDWARD MORTELMANS

On the day that Bethlehem was born, young Jack McKenna made a solemn promise to the beautiful, red roan filly he had helped bring into the world—a promise which he would never break.

But that was at a time when everything seemed possible: one day Jack would save enough money to buy Beth from Old Man Chancellor, and take his own cart round the narrow Devon lanes selling provisions. And when he met pretty Kitty Widdicombe his dreams of future happiness seemed more certain than ever . . .

But that was before the Great War.

When Beth is requisitioned by the army, Jack leaves his young wife and son to follow her to the Somme valley, where it's hard to see how his promise to the beautiful young mare can ever be kept.

PROLOGUE

A shell descended and the fountain of earth rose, hung for a moment and fell apart. Fumes gusted across the road and the sergeant coughed and drew the corner of his turned-up collar over his mouth.

"Walk on," the driver said, and the two carthorses who were tandem-hitched to the ambulance strode away.

Twilight closed on the fields. Screened by trees to the west of the Front the British heavies opened up. Then a column of limbers came along the road at speed. Jack stepped aside and sat on an overturned watercart. The first team thundered past, the horses bounding through the mud. The right lead animal was familiar. Its face was white and despite the mud the marbling on its flanks and haunches was rich enough to catch the eye. Jack's scalp prickled. The horse was surging on, filling the air with spray that stank.

"Beth," he cried. "Beth!"

She swung her head and tried to dig in her feet and stop. But Milburn's whip smacked her neck and obedience won. Her stride faltered only to lengthen again.

"Beth!" Jack began to run.

"McKenna," the sergeant barked. "Stand still, man, stand still." The mud sucked at his legs and brought him to a halt.

"Beth," he groaned.

The lead driver of the next limber team was roaring at him to get out of the way. Then something hard and heavy struck his shoulder and spun him off the road.

231

"Talk about the bog Irish!" the sergeant grunted, dragging him out of the shell hole. "Where were you going, you horrible little Irishman?"

"It was my horse," Jack gasped. "My bloody horse. My Beth."

The sergeant stared at him.

"A red roan mare. Bethlehem. I helped bring her into the world. She's my horse."

"No, lad," the sergeant said. "She's the King's horse. There's nothing you can do about it. Best forget you saw her—if it was her."

Jack wiped his mouth on his sleeve and spat mud. His puttees had uncoiled and were hanging over his boots.

"We don't own anything out here, lad—least of all ourselves."

"She's mine," Jack whispered. "I made her a promise."

"I made my old lady a promise at the altar but it don't mean a lot now."

"She's mine," Jack repeated. There was a manic certainty in his voice.

PART ONE BOY AND FOAL
Chapter 1

Shortly before dawn Jack McKenna closed the front door of Number Eight Angarrick Terrace behind him and walked the deserted streets of Lansworthy out into the south Devon countryside. The air was heavy with the scents of spring, but the birdsong was quieter where the gardens of the seaside town surrendered to pasture and copse. The boy turned up the collar of his jacket against the cold, tugged down the peak of his cap and buried his hands in his trouser pockets. He liked the solitude, the slow ebb of darkness and the ring of his nailed boots on the road. It was the best part of the day, or perhaps he just loved beginnings, that warm thrill before mystery subsided into the commonplace.

He was fourteen and not long out of the Board School. "Irish" Jack they called him, partly because of his accent but mainly because he bounced between wild enthusiasm and cheerfulness—which the Devonians grudgingly admired although they pretended to disapprove. The boy was small, nimble and bright-eyed in a Celtic way that suggested alertness straying into recklessness. His eyes glistened as though he were permanently close to tears. Their blue pallor, and a broken nose which had been repaired in haste, lent his face a comical ferocity.

He stopped at Batterways Bridge and tightened a bootlace. The road smelt of rain and cattle but the wind blowing across the Channel from the Continent promised fine weather. It was shaking raindrops out of the hedges on either side as he came up the hill past the brickworks, thinking of the horses on Cider Mill Tor. They would be facing the sea, waiting for the phantom light to erupt into sunrise. The blackbird singing from the cherry tree at Clayland Cross already had sunshine in its voice.

232

Hawthorn blossom was palely visible up in the hedge that ran alongside Mary's Haven Road. The wind and last night's showers had scattered little white stars on the road, and the mist clotting the coombs had the same faint glow. Once again excitement squirmed in Jack's stomach. He was going to the horses like the first boy in the first dawn. All creation was assembling round him as spinneys, woods and high-hedged fields lifted grey and ghostly from the mist. He was glad Princess had had her foal and Melody would soon give birth. Working with horses for Chancellor's Emporium was fine, but coming to Tor Barton was an adventure. Old Mr. Sidney Chancellor, who also loved horses, understood. Pregnant mares and sick animals were sent from the Emporium's stables in Lansworthy to the farm which he owned, and Jack had been put under the head carter, Trant. The boy was steeped in horse lore. Since early childhood he had hung around the stables behind the railway station whenever he had a free moment, until he had become part of the place.

Now rooks were breaking from the elms near the cider mill and drifting down Clennon Valley. Jack turned off the road and took the cart track on to Cider Mill Tor. The weathered limestone pushed a shoulder out of the common and the boy perched on top of it and hugged his knees to his chin. The mist was thinning to reveal dawn's cool colours. Six summers ago the bonfire celebrating King Edward VII's coronation had blazed from the hilltop. They ought to light a bonfire here every summer, he thought. Bonfires cheer people up.

Over the blossoming apple trees the farmhouse could be seen standing grey under its lichened roof. Beyond the chimneys the water meadows of Clennon Valley were divided by a stream which passed under the Dartmouth Road, cut across the peat and bog and found the sea through a culvert in the Great Western Railway embankment. Northeastwards, and partly screened by Clennon Woods, was the sandstone tower of Lansworthy parish church and the rooftops of the higher part of the town. Lansworthy was the central nail in the horseshoe formed by St. Mary's Bay.

Above a harbour, facing south, the fashionable holiday resort of Abbot's Quay was parading rows of terraced villas. Across the water at the other end of the horseshoe a crab boat left the little port of Mary's Haven to sail round St. Mary's Head, under the lighthouse and the sea birds' breeding places, and into the English Channel. Gulls winged silently inland and light was spreading along the horizon.

Jack slid off the rock and ran down to the gate that opened onto a meadow. The draught horses cantered up to him, loosing their manes on the air and fluting through their nostrils. He called them by name: "Mary, Dolly, Captain, Edward, Sunny, Jan." Mares and geldings jostled around him, lowering long serious faces and wreathing him in the breath of crushed grass. Beneath the heave of life the boy sensed the power of the great animals. It vibrated in bunched muscles and arched necks and shone and rippled on the surface of their bodies. They towered over him and nudged him gently with their muzzles while the new day crept in off the sea.

He left the horses and went down the hillside to the farmhouse and knocked on the side door. The farmer's wife gave him a blank smile and told him to wait. Mrs. Maddock never invited any of the workers into her kitchen.

"Has Melody foaled, missis?" Jack said, taking the jug of tea from her.

"I don't know," came the reply, and the door closed.

Jack cupped his hands round the hot enamel and skated across the wet manure in the bullock yard to the stables. He marched along the passage with the open stalls on his right. Iona regarded him placidly as Jack put down the jug and crooned the endearments he always saved for the horses. In the next stall Princess and her filly foal, Bathsheba, waited to be let out into the paddock. The shire cross lifted her front feet and beat a tattoo of impatience.

"Hold to, hold to," the boy said and Princess's ears pricked, but she knew Jack's voice and did not flinch from his touch.

"For God's sake," the carter cried, "leave the beasts alone and get in yer with the tea."

Trant sat on an upturned pail and his thin wife leaned against Melody's manger, arms folded.

"I forgot the mugs," Jack grinned. His chilblains were jumping and he wanted to take off his boots and have a good scratch.

"That doan surprise me," the carter said. "They don't call 'ee 'Irish' Jack for nort. Bog Irish Jack, the Dublin dawbake."

"Dingle, mister. We come from Dingle."

"Bliddy Dingle dangle Dublin!—tez all the same to me, boy," Trant hissed. "Old man Chancellor may think the sun shines out your behind but I idn impressed. Has it happens I've got a cup. Just give us the jug."

Jack's grin broadened and he bent over Melody and stroked her nose. The mare turned her head as the labour pains intensified. She kicked against it but the pain grew worse. Suddenly the waters burst and the foal slid along the birth canal until its hooves and front legs protruded in a sheath of membrane from its mother's hindquarters. The watching boy had witnessed a dozen such births yet the miracle still had the power to move him.

Slowly the parcel of freshly minted life emerged from Melody and the mare lifted her head, eager to see the part of herself which would soon be a separate unique creature. One final shudder pushed the foal free. Wrapped in the glittering membrane it flopped onto the straw and Mrs. Trant slit the bag and pulled it off the newborn animal while life flowed through the umbilical cord between mother and daughter. Melody turned and manoeuvred until she was able to lick the foal.

Light slanted over the top of the stable doors and fanned out across

234

the ceiling. The windows opposite the stall held some of the sky's gleam.

"Melody," Jack whispered, dropping to his knees.

The mare drew back her upper lips and bared her teeth at him.

"She'll give you one hell of a nip if you get too close," said Trant. "Her's foal proud."

"She won't hurt me," the boy smiled. "I can talk to horses." He stooped and taking the foal's head in his hands planted a kiss on her nose.

"Good girl," Jack crooned. "Clever Melody. You've got a perfect foal, a roan. Clever girl. Clever girl."

Hidden behind films of moisture, something profoundly sad lay in the mare's eyes. Then her lids descended and rose again leaving the brown pupils empty.

"Come away, boy, and let her get on with it," the carter said. "Us've got work to do."

The foal got to her feet and the life cord broke close to her body. Like the mare she was a red roan, finely marked, with white legs and belly. The whiteness climbed her flanks, marbled her thighs and touched parts of her shoulders. Nearly every inch of her bay coat carried a dusting of white hairs. Her face right up to the eyes was white and there were white streaks in her mane and tail.

"Her's a 'ansome little sod," Trant admitted. "Her sire was a carriage horse and she won't have a lot of bulk."

For a moment she stood wobbling and swaying on legs that threatened to buckle. But Melody was upright now and nudging the foal towards her teat. Soon she was sucking. All is well, thought the boy, closing his eyes above an enormous yawn.

"What's her name, mister?" said Jack.

"Bethlehem," the carter said, blowing out the lantern. "Old man Chancellor came up with it weeks ago. If her'd been a he her would be called Joshua. The boss likes his Bible."

Then Jack was left to water and feed the mare. The sun rose and turned the cobwebs on the windows to gold. Slowly the morning flooded Bethlehem's consciousness, but uncertainty tugged her up against her mother's flanks. Melody munched the chafed straw and oats Jack had put in the manger. The steam of her breath poured from her nostrils and the corners of her mouth.

Outside the stables the farm was coming to life. The milkers and teamsters had arrived and the yard was full of cattle. Bethlehem's nostrils dilated.

The chestnut trees behind the stables were whispering and dark shapes of birds flickered across the sun dazzle on the window. Everything fascinated the foal. She returned Jack's gaze, not vacantly like a newborn human baby, but as a creature that had stepped out of another existence with its senses and intelligence already orchestrated to a fine awareness of the world.

THE WARM WEATHER PREVAILED and the mares and foals were turned out permanently into the paddock. Under the chestnut trees next to the stables was a linhay where they could shelter if it rained. But the sun shone and most nights were clear and starry. Now Bethlehem was caught between love of mother and wonder at everything around her. Running with Bathsheba through the moonlight was more than a game; and when the foals were tired they stood together on the sloping field looking across the bay. The sky leaped up from the horizon and arched over them, and the moon which was not yet full hung above the sea.

One afternoon the boy put Bethlehem in a head collar and, despite her protests, led her round the paddock. It was the first step in schooling the foal to harness. After shaking her head and prancing on hind legs for a moment she trotted away with Jack in tow, clinging to the halter.

"Her thinks her's boss," Trant said. "Later on us'll put her straight. Doan make a fuss of her, boy, or you'll have trouble when her's full-growed. A spoilt horse is worse than useless."

Jack bent to pluck bits of bramble off the foal's fetlocks and the long white hairs, or "feather" as it was known, spreading over her hooves. Bethlehem blew fluttering sighs. In her simplicity she accepted without suspicion the attention lavished on her and her kind, and the whine and hum of insects, the creak of a cart, birdsong, and all the other sounds that, lifting from the farm, entered her knowing.

She rolled in the grass and beat the air with her hooves. Amongst the stems were the pale mauve flowers of lady's-smock. A breeze trailed across the paddock and grass curled at the tips. Where the cow parsley stood in the ditch a yellowhammer sang.

THE PATTER OF CHESTNUT BLOSSOM on the linhay roof woke her. Masthead lanterns shone from the bay and the sea glittered to the horizon. One of the farm dogs began to bark and Bethlehem pressed closer to her mother. The dark green breath of the June night eddied around them.

Less than a mile away Jack lay staring up at the bedroom ceiling, only partly aware of his brothers, Michael and Sean, in the bed beside him, and his youngest sister mumbling in her sleep over by the window. The dream had made him sad. He yawned and clasped his hands together behind his head. Silver horses, he thought, struggling to reassemble the dream like a jigsaw puzzle. The tide of shining animals flashed through the darkness and was gone.

Number Eight Angarrick Terrace was not a happy house, but the trouble smouldering between husband and wife differed little from the grievances affecting most of the other working-class homes in the neighbourhood. Kevan McKenna was a pub man. His whole life revolved around the sawdust, ale, noise and comradeship of the "King William"— an inn which the devil, it seemed, had placed within easy staggering distance of the terrace.

McKenna had left the Dingle peninsula in the last years of Victoria's reign to join the Irish pick-and-shovel invasion of cities like Liverpool, Birmingham and London. He had drifted to Devon by chance and as soon as he found permanent work with the Great Western Railway had sent for his family. Some of the cheerfulness which his wife had found attractive could still break through the transparent boredom he brought home from the station. Every Friday and Saturday night especially, he whistled and sang and joked with the children while his mind waltzed ahead to the vivid hours he would soon be spending in the bar. But for the remainder of the week he was morose and dangerous. Empty pockets left him an empty man.

Mrs. McKenna hated him quietly and totally. She hated his end-of-week drunkenness and the boredom he carried in his eyes when he was broke. She hated sleeping with him and washing for him and cooking for him. The best years of her life had been squandered on Kevan McKenna, and often she looked in the mirror at the lines of drudgery and despair, wondering why she had been born. Perhaps living itself was a kind of martyrdom for poor people and the man she had married, blind to his faults, was her personal cross.

She had five children and looked nearer fifty than thirty-five. Both girls were too young to try her patience but the boys, except her oldest and favourite, Jack, were in and out of trouble. Jack was the eternal Irish paradox, the dreamer attracted to violence, someone who acted on impulse. Now she could hear him creeping along the landing and padding downstairs. She slipped out of bed.

Downstairs Jack was feeding twigs to the fire in the kitchen range. The candle burned steadily in its brass holder and the crucifix above the sideboard gleamed like gold.

"God, if you're not the tomcat," his mother smiled. "Up and about all hours of the night."

"I'm going to the farm," Jack said, tucking his shirt tail into his trousers and retrieving his boots from the regiment lined up against the fender.

"You'll turn into a horse one day."

"That would be nice," said the boy.

"Will you be home for dinner?"

He shrugged, and buttoned himself into his waistcoat. The flames leaped and the fire coughed a little smoke across the hearth. Mary McKenna glanced at the crucifix.

"Father Tynan keeps askin' why you're never at Mass, Jack. You've missed three Sundays in a row now."

"Dad doesn't go."

"Yes, well, your father's so busy going to hell he can't find time to stop anywhere along the way except the pub."

Jack laughed.

"It's not funny," she murmured, lifting a hand wearily to her brow.

237

The boy looked at her and said, "When I've got lots of money I'll buy you a pony and trap, Mum, and I'll drive you about like the old Queen."

"You and your dreams, Jack," she whispered, kissing him.

SHORTLY AFTER SUNRISE Jack opened the paddock gate and put halters on Melody and her foal. Then he rode the mare and led Bethlehem across the bullock yard and down the lane.

The broad back rolled under him as he rode away from Clennon past the orchards towards Goodrington and Cider Mill Farm. From the meadow in the bottom of the valley other horses cried out to the mare and foal, and Melody answered them. The whinnying followed them up the cart track to the road that wound white and dusty towards Dartmouth. Coming up the hill by the quarry Jack could look over flowering fields to the sea. The sight of it all tugged at his innards.

At Windy Corner the bridlepath ran down a coomb thick with bluebells to the marsh behind Broadsands beach. He brought the horses through a gap in the sea wall onto the shingle and took off their harness. Then he undressed and clambered back naked onto the mare. The tide was ebbing and the wet sand above the wavebreak was glazed with light.

Bethlehem took a couple of steps, paused and looked about her. Waves fizzed slowly over the glare. Crisp ridges of brilliance ran out to the horizon under the flash and whack of gulls' wings. Bethlehem lowered her head and sniffed the bladderwrack. Her mother was ambling into the light. The foal scuffed through drifts of shells and little sun-baked crabs. The patina of sunshine was suddenly broken by Melody's hooves. She began to trot until she was breasting the waves and Jack screwed up his eyes and gave himself to the floating sensation that had nothing to do with the sea. Holy Mary, Mother of God, he prayed, let me be like the horses. Let me understand them.

Cold water washed over his legs and he gasped. Melody turned and whinnied and was answered by the foal. Together they galloped across the shallows in a cloud of spray. At the end of the beach Jack jumped clear and watched the animals wheel to run back again, their wet coats shining and the mare's mane streaming free. The thunder of their hooves and the sight of them flying along the shore would haunt him for ever.

They came to him when he called and he took them to the marsh behind the sea wall and rolled with them in the fresh water. Bethlehem gazed curiously at the boy. He was kneeling like a small white horse beside her. Then she breathed a greeting through her nostrils and he hooked an arm round her neck. Dragonflies clicked by and the breeze swept over the scrub willow, whitening the leaves.

"WHY DID YOU DO IT? What on earth possessed you?"

Chancellor ran the tip of his tongue along the fringe of his moustache and looked sideways at Jack. The boy rammed his fists deeper into his trouser pockets, lifted his shoulders and frowned up at the white hairs crowding the old man's nostrils.

"Because the little devil's mazed," Farmer Maddock said, but Chancellor silenced him with an upraised finger.

"I watered and groomed Melody, sir," Jack said.

"After taking them bathing—you silly young sod," said Maddock, close to shouting.

"Yes, why the trip to the beach?" Chancellor pressed.

"I wanted them to have a holiday, sir. And I wanted them to be like they were before we took them over. Foxes and badgers don't have no boss. All animals were free once."

Maddock sucked in his breath but before he could comment Chancellor dismissed him.

"What will become of you, Jack?" The old man drew down his eyebrows and thought about it. "Melody might have caught a chill," he went on. "And Beth could have broken a leg galloping along that beach. You must think before you act, son. Think." He tapped Jack's head with his bunched knuckles.

"They were happy, Mr. Chancellor."

"I'm sure they were. Horses are splendid creatures. Do you know the story of how they came into the world?"

The boy shook his head.

"The Bedouins—those Arabs who live in the desert—say God looked out on creation and saw it was incomplete. So he took a handful of wind and fashioned a mare and a stallion. Now these horses were as swift as the wind, beautiful creatures, strong and brave. When Man asked for their services they gave with loyalty and love and trust. Trust, Jack—trust. It was the way of their kind and it still is."

"Yes, sir, yes," Jack said, passionately. "When we was in the sea they were like those two Arab horses and I wanted to be like them."

Chancellor smiled. "Trant thinks you'll make a good horseman."

Again the boy shook his head.

"Trant may have a sharp tongue, boy, but he cares about the animals."

Chancellor removed his hat and used it as a fan. Grey wisps of hair were glued to his forehead, but for a man on the weather side of sixty he was remarkably well preserved.

"What's your ambition, Jack? What do you hope to do with your life?"

"Look after horses, sir. Work for you, sir."

"That's all?"

"No, sir; there's something else."

"Tell me," Chancellor said, laying his forearms on top of the gate and smiling at the antics of Bethlehem and Bathsheba.

"I'd like to buy Beth off you one day, Mr. Chancellor. I'd have her pullin' my own cart."

"Selling what?"

"Fish, veg—it don't matter so long as she's mine. And she'll never go to the knacker's. Never. She'll have her own field in the summer and a warm stable in the winter. I've already promised her that."

"Where will the money come from to start your business, Jack?"

"I'm savin', sir. Where did your money come from?"

"Hard work, sweat, a bit of luck and a bank manager who knew a good thing when he saw it. Are you working at the Emporium tomorrow?"

"Yes, sir. I'm going out with the coal."

"And there'll be no more trips to the seaside for mares and foals?"

Jack shrugged and grinned. "You will sell Beth to me one day, won't you, sir?"

"Yes, Jack, I will, if you prove you can take care of her," the old man said. "These are prosperous times," he added, "and they can only get better. The Empire is growing and Chancellor's is growing with it. What are you like at sums – multiplication, subtraction and all that mumbo jumbo?".

"Hopeless," said Jack.

"But you know horses. Stick to what you know. In just a couple of months the Emporium is going to shift its premises in order to become a department store—the biggest between Exeter and Plymouth. Our vans will be delivering as far afield as Dartmouth, Totnes, Newton Abbot and Bovey Tracey. One day you could be head horseman and in a sense Beth would be yours."

"If horses are so special, Mr. Chancellor, why have you got one of those motor cars?"

"Ask my son. He bought it," the old man sighed. "Noisy, temperamental thing, always conking out. Horses aren't like that. You can rely on a mare like old Iona."

"Iona is a fine name, sir."

"It was the wife's idea. We went on this Scottish tour and sailed round the Hebrides to Fingal's Cave and Iona. Very beautiful, but it didn't measure up to Devon."

In his passion for the county he forgot his new, middle-class accent and called it "Debn". These lapses were a constant source of embarrassment to his son, Ormond.

"Can I have a rise, sir?" Jack said suddenly. "Then I'll be able to get the horse a bit quicker."

"We'll see," he said. "I dislike talking money matters on the Sabbath, McKenna. But we'll see."

Jack did not want the day to end. He had half a pasty wrapped in muslin and newspaper in his pocket, and from Cider Mill Tor the countryside swam green and seductive all the way to Dartmoor. Keeping to the high ground he walked to the River Dart at Stoke Gabriel. Children were swimming in Mill Pool but he went upriver to Hackney Creek and dawdled back through lengthening shadows along the Yalberton Road.

Chapter 2

His first chore in the morning was to take the boys' chamber pot out to the lavatory in the back yard. Michael, who was a year younger than Jack, rolled into the warm hollow left by his brother's body and spread his limbs luxuriously after a cramped night. Monday was washday and Mrs. McKenna was boiling the water and pushing clothes into the copper. The downstairs rooms were full of steam.

Jack ate breakfast by the light of a paraffin lamp. Drinking tea from a mug which bore the initials GWR in brown lettering, he thought about his father. Kevan McKenna had left for work at three o'clock. He was a shadowy figure, drifting almost casually in and out of family life. But Jack loved him.

Despite his moods and sarcastic tongue he could be funny when he chose. Full of Saturday beer he would turn a belch into the long-drawn-out squeal of a pig and dance round the living-room table on tiptoe. Only Mrs. McKenna remained aloof from these antics. Borrowing serenity from the statuette of Our Lady which stood on the sideboard, she would crouch by the range and run a gull eye over the man she had promised to love, honour and obey.

Outside in the street the sunlight took its texture from the chimney smoke. A goods engine hooted and steam billowed and vanished above the rooftops. Cockerels were crowing. Jack dug his fingers into the neck of his old grey pullover and eased up an inch of shirt collar. Small gangs of men and boys were on their way to work. Shopkeepers were sweeping the pavements outside their premises and all along the street assistants were tugging down the sunshades. The dark fragrance of ground coffee wafted from the grille above Chancellor's cellars. It had the power to draw people into the Emporium, a three-storey building crowned by the proprietor's name, which sold a bit of everything—sunblinds, silks, haberdashery, fancy goods and women's wear, grocery and provisions, toys and games, china, glass and linoleum. To Jack, who had been in and out of the place ever since he could remember, it was an Aladdin's cave cluttered with all sorts of delights.

Jack trailed down the alley beside the store and found most of the other stableboys and carters waiting in the yard. He knew them all. Ingratiating Albert Wotton, the Dunsford brothers, Will and Harold, quiet Ernie Drew, Walter Cooksley.

Nearly all the stableboys were older than Jack. One, Skilly Luscombe, had less sense than a sheep, and everyone said he was "mazed" or "looby". The simpleton's father was "all beer and smut" as Mary McKenna put it, but his heart was supposed to be in the right place. An extravagant show of affection for horses somehow redeemed Fred Luscombe's bullying in the eyes of the sentimental working-class community. Old Bob Sherwill, the senior carter, was a kind, religious man approaching retirement. Now, opening the back door, he handed out the brooms and went from floor to floor supervising the sweeping and making sure everything was ready for the counter staff. His approval was communicated in slow nods—hence his nickname, Old Bob.

Jack enjoyed the ritualistic start to the day, because he would be shut off from the horses and the sun for only a little while. The Emporium was a magnificent dead place full of dead things. Outside in the open air birds flashed and called, and in the sky light was strengthening.

Behind Dartmouth Road, Station Lane ran parallel to the railway goods depot. It was a shambles of Victorian warehouses, sheds and yards divided by sandstone walls. Here the Co-op, the Great Western Railway, Lansworthy Mill and Chancellor's stabled their horses. Most mornings over a hundred animals left the lane between the shafts of carts or wagons. The wooden stalls of Chancellor's stables were intersected by a gangway of scrubbed bricks and the horses faced each other over the half-doors.

The other lads remained in the yard to clean the wagons and vans, but Jack had horse chores. Soon he was part of the noise and bustle. The carters came staggering along the gangway, water slopping from their pails, and Jack went from stall to stall checking the salt licks while the horses drank and the carters sieved oats into the cribs.

Chancellor's kept a small stud of trotters and walkers to pull carts, vans and wagons loaded with a variety of goods. Mares and geldings lived under the same roof and when the fleet was ready to take to the streets the chestnuts, bays, greys and roans made a fine show. Outstanding among them were the shires with their shining black manes and great, steel-faced shoes. They were immensely strong, but for all their beauty and gentleness Jack preferred the half-bred Clydesdales. Lighter-boned and cow-hocked, they had the dispositions of angels.

The horsemaster had slung the harnesses on posts between the stalls. He walked the gangway checking the progress of men and animals. His name was Tom Palfrey and he had fought in the Second Boer War. A tall loose-limbed peasant from the Dartmoor in-county he was still the sunny side of forty. Before speaking he removed his pipe and weighed his words. It was his habit to amble along but when he was harnessing a horse or backing it into the shafts he moved nimbly and quickly.

Once the animals had been watered, fed and groomed they were put in their gear and the bedding-out began. The stableboys struggled to wheel barrow-loads of soiled straw out into the yard, giggling and cursing as they slipped on the wet bricks. When the job was done they collected the nosebags and took them to the wagons. It was like a military operation.

"Us've got a new lad startin'," Fred Luscombe said to Jack. "Ern Lacey's boy; and he's as handy with his fists as you are with your mouth, Jack. Step on Arthur Lacey's toes and he'll make you sing."

Jack grinned.

"Jack," the horsemaster called from the stable door. "Ride with Harold today. Down the coal yard."

The working day had begun.

ARTHUR LACEY WAS TOO HANDSOME. His near perfect features, long-lashed brown eyes and brown hair found their greatest admirer in himself. He was a tall, slim sixteen-year-old whose reputation as a fist-fighter had received plenty of advance publicity from Fred Luscombe. The Laceys had moved from Abbot's Quay to Lansworthy's St. Michael's Road, to take over a small fish-and-chip shop left them by an aunt. Suddenly they were business people and Arthur boasted of his father's independence, claiming he provided a service, like the vet and the dentist. The absurdity did not escape comment.

"Visit Dr. Lacey, the potato surgeon," Jack declared solemnly. "Let him remove the eyes from your spuds."

For the first time since he had started work at Chancellor's stables, Arthur Lacey felt he was treading close to disaster.

"Watch your lip, Irish," he rasped.

"Or what?"

"Or I'll button it for you."

Old Bob intervened, but from then on the two boys walked carefully round each other.

When the new department store opened all it meant to Jack was more floor space to sweep and new blood in the stables. But one morning before the fleet took to the road a girl appeared at the yard with a message for the horsemaster. She was a junior from the store and was very self-conscious in the Chancellor "uniform" of dark, ankle-length grey dress and white apron.

Jack guessed she was fifteen at the most, probably younger. He led one of the geldings out to the van and made a show of squaring the horse up and backing him into the shafts. It was a smooth, professional perform-ance which the girl watched admiringly. Beside the horse Jack's smallness was exaggerated but the way he danced around the animal was impressive and attractive. He was very much the master of the situation. Sticking his thumbs in his waistcoat pocket he swaggered over to her, grinning so broadly she had to smile. Her hair was the colour of hay and a pair of large green eyes brought a startling, catlike vitality to a face that was pretty rather than beautiful.

She rubbed the side of her nose with a fingertip and said, "The old horse knows you'm boss."

Jack shook his head. "No," he said, "Solomon and me are friends. All the horses are my friends."

"You're Irish, aren't you?"

"Irish Jack," he said, colouring.

"Jack's a nice name. Mine's Kitty. I work up in the store."

"And you like it?"

"Better than my last job. I was in service." Her voice dropped. "And that was awful."

"Here," Fred Luscombe bawled across the yard. "Look at our bantam cock. Cock-a-doodle-doo, Jack. You watch him, maid—they Irish bantams be lil buggers. Don't go behind the stables with 'e."

Skilly Luscombe's brays of laughter set the other boys going and Lacey was quick to score at Jack's expense. Sweeping off his cap in a deep bow he said, "Is Irish botherin' you, ma'am? You can't trust these foreigners. If he's said anything out of place I'll take a stick to un."

The horsemaster emerged from one of the sheds behind the vans and ambled up to them.

"Lacey," he said, pointing the stem of his pipe at the boy. "Give your tongue a rest and get forking out."

"What about Irish, Mr. Palfrey?"

"McKenna don't need tellin'. He gets on with the job."

The girl handed Palfrey a folded piece of notepaper.

"From the head cashier," she said. "There idn no reply, sir."

Palfrey nodded, stuck the pipe back in his smile and walked away.

"Bye, Jack," she said.

"Bye-bye, Jack," Skilly cried and the rest of the lads joined in: "Bye, Jack—goodbye, sweet Jackie boy, bye-bye. Bye-bye."

"Bloody fools," Jack laughed.

"Irish is soft on Kitty Widdicombe," a thin boy from Windy Corner said derisively.

"But her wudn look twice at him with his crooked conk," crowed Lacey.

"I've seen better faces than yours under dogs' tails," Jack said, wondering how the hatred had grown between them.

Fortunately Old Bob, the senior carter, bustled out of the harness room barking orders, and the men boarded their vehicles. One by one the vans and wagons rolled out of the yard.

Sitting beside Albert Wotton, Jack looked up at the high-flying gulls. He was thinking of Kitty's eyes and neat little hands. A train left the station, loosing puffs of steam. Then the old woman from the cottage by the railway crossing walked along the lane shovelling horse manure into a pail. Palfrey's dog, Mullah, raked its ribs with a stiff hind leg and gazed after Jack's cart. Silence closed round the stables.

KITTY WIDDICOMBE brought a marvellous charm to Chancellor's Emporium. If Jack was close enough to Victoria Street during his lunch hour he paced up and down the pavement opposite the ornate cream and sepia façade, praying she would appear. He was slow to realise staff used the delivery entrance at the back. Then one day Ernie Drew spent his noon break in the "Crown and Anchor" with the cart tucked away behind the pub. The barmaid kept him engrossed and he drank too much.

"Come back near half one, boy," he said. "And don't gab about this. Us've got a cushy round. All I want is a bit of time to get acquainted with the lady. I'll keep an eye on Solomon so you can run off and get yourself an ice cream or somethin'."

Jack climbed the wall facing the back doors and hid among the lilac leaves, but after twenty minutes Kitty had not appeared so he sauntered down to Station Square. Miraculously she was perched on the edge of the water trough under the lamp at the carriage stand, wearing a white blouse and a straw boater with a black band. And aren't all the angels jealous of her? Jack thought. Warmth rose from his stomach and took his breath away.

"Hello," he said huskily.

Her eyes lifted, full of recognition, and she smiled. "Where are your friends the horses?"

"Out and about. I'm going as far as the seafront." Then in a gush of boldness, "Have you got time for a bit of a stroll?"

"My friends are supposed to be meeting me here. They'm over the station talking to some of the boys."

"My dad works there," Jack faltered. They stared silently at each other for a moment. "You won't be coming down the front, then?" he said at last.

"Yes—I'd like to. Tidn no fun waitin' for they silly maids."

"You're not walking out with anyone?"

"Mind your own business," she giggled.

They moved off slowly together.

"How come I've never seen you before?" he grinned.

"Us live at Churston and I went to school at Mary's Haven."

Like all locals she pronounced the name "Marris-havven".

"How d'you get home a night?"

"Bus, train. But when it's fine I walk."

"Can I walk with you, Kitty? On the way I'd show you Melody's foal."

"More horses," she laughed. "Up the store they say you'm horse mazed."

"One day I'm going to have my own cart and I'll take Bethlehem off old man Chancellor."

"Who's Bethlehem? As if I didn know!"

He told her the story of the foal's birth and found himself speaking his most private thoughts, dwelling on the dream of the silver horses and the ride in the waves at Broadsands. Kitty was entirely fascinated and would stop and wait while he fumbled for the right words to colour his feelings.

They drifted along the broad, tree-fringed pavement of Lansworthy Road. On either hand were shops under dusty awnings. Old ladies gossiped over tea outside Deller's Café and younger ladies passed with a swish of gowns. How cool and elegant they are, Jack thought, letting a vision of his mother eclipse the moment.

One day, she would have a white dress and a new parasol and he'd take her and Kitty out in a carriage, like royalty. When Michael got a job she would have three wages coming in. Guiltily he recalled the money he was saving to buy Bethlehem. But it would bring her a new life as well as help him out of the dead end.

"What you done to your nose?" Kitty asked.

"Broke it—twice. Once fallin' off a horse, the other time fighting. Old Dr. Burgess, who died last year, was drunk when he set it. That's why it's a bit skewwhiff."

"It suits you," she laughed and her voice softened. "Your hair is so black it've got a blue shine to it, like a jackdaw's wing."

"My mother's got black hair."

They crossed the Esplanade onto the green by Lansworthy House, and sat on the sea wall looking across the sand to the bathing machines and tents on the tideline.

"I can't wait to see Beth. Her sounds a little beauty." Kitty slid her hand into his and their fingers dovetailed.

"Would you mind if I kissed you, Kitty?" he said.

"I would," she laughed. A gentle tug released her hand. "I've only knowed 'ee five minutes. Do you go round kissin' all the maids?"

He shook his head and his eyes twinkled. "The horses don't object when I kiss them."

"I idn no horse," she giggled, reaching out and squeezing his arm.

"But you'll come to Tor Barton with me this evening?"

When she nodded, a honey-coloured curl escaped from her boater and fell over her brow.

"You know the Big Tree at the bottom of Fisher Street where it joins Dartmouth Road?" Jack said. "Whoever finishes work first sits there and waits for the other. Does that suit you?"

Once more the curl bobbed on her forehead.

THE EVENING WAS SWEATY and the smell of the yard hung on the threat of thunder. Jack watered and fed the gelding and wisped him down with handfuls of straw to dry his coat. Ernie Drew had brought the van back late, so drunk he could hardly walk, and certainly in no condition to stable an animal. Kitty won't wait, Jack thought. He clenched his teeth on the misery. Cockchafers tapped against the windows and the screams of the swifts flying at rooftop level filled the yard. Solomon turned and looked at him like a great trusting child.

"Hold still, my beauty," Jack whispered. "Hold still."

Beginning behind the horse's ear he kept his forearm rigid and eased the currycomb through the animal's coat. Every so often he tapped the comb on the rear wall to shake out the dirt. He groomed meticulously according to the drill the horsemaster had developed out of his army service and own experience.

"Where's Drew?" said Palfrey's voice.

"Colic," Jack grunted.

"And you can cope, boy?"

"Yes, Mr. Palfrey. Me and Solomon are good friends."

The horsemaster drew on his pipe and the spittle sizzled in the hot bowl. "Colic, hey?"

"Colic, mister."

Palfrey sniffed and yawned. "Don't forget to clean round his eyes and nostrils."

"I won't, Mr. Palfrey."

Oh God, he thought, she'll be walking through Waterside by now, hating me, thinking I've forgotten. God, don't let it be like this. Let her be there.

An hour before sunset he washed the grime off his face and dashed out of the yard. But halfway up Station Lane he screwed his face into an expression of despair and stuffed his fists in his pockets. He had to go to the Big Tree, knowing the bench would be empty. And it was.

Chapter 3

Old Bob made sure their boots were really clean before letting them in the new store. Compared to the Emporium it was palatial and the boys and carters spoke in whispers as though they were attending a church service rather than sweeping out.

That morning the sweeping-out finished later than usual because one of the boys was caught stealing from the silver and electroplate department. The police sergeant was called but when Mr. Ormond Chancellor drove in from Roundham he insisted on all the boys being searched. His condescending tone might have been borrowed from an African explorer addressing the natives.

Old Bob registered his disapproval in blunt terms but one by one the boys were questioned and stripped. Sidney Chancellor hurried to the stables as soon as he was informed and tried to repair the damage done by his son, who had never been popular. He was too pompous and high-handed, and his mousy moustache bequeathed a sulkiness to a face it was easy to dislike.

"Bloody cheek," Old Bob said, slamming the door behind him. "Sorry about that, lads. That bloody young fool Wesmacott will get what he deserves but Mr. Ormond had no right to treat 'ee like criminals."

Yet the delay worked wonderfully on Jack's behalf. Kitty was among the juniors in the delivery yard waiting to go to her department and polish the brass. Old Bob saw Jack's face brighten. "Check they barrels over there, McKenna." He winked at Jack. "See if there's ort for the stables. We'll meet you back at the yard."

Jack coloured and glanced at Kitty. She was kneeling now to do up a bootlace. Then they were alone.

"I waited ages," she said. "Ages. I had to go or our mum would've played up. So I caught the bus." Her voice broke and she whispered, "Did you come?"

He nodded. "Drew got drunk and we got back late—too late. I dreamed about you last night."

Large drops of rain splattered down, drilling holes in the dust. A cloud drifted across the blue.

"I finish at quarter past eight tonight," she said.

"Whatever happens, Kitty, I'll be at the Big Tree."

"Promise?"

"God's honour."

Her thin little body was suddenly graceful and as full of life and beauty as a spring flower.

The day dragged but Ernie Drew had a conscience and made sure the van was back in the yard before the rest of the fleet. Solomon was too tired to be groomed so he was watered, given a light meal and left to himself.

The evening possessed the quality of hallucination. Thunder continued to threaten and the sultry weather persisted. An hour before sunset the heat still shimmered on the road and their boots kicked up the dust. Light streamed through the brim of her straw hat bringing a faint buttercup glow to her face. She was curious about his home and family and spoke of her own life in the farm labourer's cottage at Churston. Her cheerfulness matched his own and her enthusiasm was irresistible.

They left the road beyond the big house next to the railway line and walked into Clennon Valley, following the cattle-creep across the water meadows. A corncrake was rasping its thin croaks from the reeds.

"That old rape-scrape," Kitty laughed. "He's more frog than bird."

Jack parted the willowherb, foxgloves and nettles for her to climb the bank into the lane. She gathered her skirts and looked very grown-up and feminine. A blackbird fluted its alarm through a hush full of the scent of haystacks. Where the fields met the sky partridges whirred away and Bethlehem's ears pricked forward.

The foal had heard the boy's laughter and stood alert on her long white legs at the paddock gate. Melody and Princess were also curious but Bathsheba lay under the hedge dozing in the last of the day's warmth. The rickyard was deserted and bats were squeaking round the outbuildings, picking off winged insects.

"Her's a little gem of a sorrel," Kitty whispered.

"She's grown," said Jack. "I've had her on the bit lately."

"Doan her play up?"

"No, she's used to it now. You just gentle her along."

248

The foal laid her chin on the gate and crinkled her nostrils. Dark eyes stared from the flat white face.

"Lil dear," Kitty murmured, trailing her knuckles across Beth's upper lip, but the foal pulled away and waggled her head.

"Come here, Beth," Jack said softly and he held out his hands. The voice and smell belonged to a creature whose gentleness was known and sought after by the foal. She took two steps to the right and slid her face deliberately into his palms.

"I idn good enough for her," Kitty laughed, taking off her hat and shaking free her curls. "Will her let me stroke her now?"

"Try. Talk quietly to her."

The other horses walked up to them and jostled for attention. They had been grazing and the regular, rolling, sideways shift of their lower jaws produced a chomp of the teeth that made the boy and girl grin.

"Look, Kitty," Jack said suddenly, "I'd like to meet you every night and walk you home."

"You'd soon tire of it," she laughed. "If you really think I'm worth it we could see each other Wednesdays, Saturdays and Sundays. The other days I'm nearly always dead on my feet." Her eyes met his own and the fair lashes descended.

"I finish early Saturday," he said.

"Saturday's late turn," she sighed.

"But we could have some chips and I could go home with you on the train."

"You idn just sayin' that, Jack?"

"No," he said solemnly.

"Mum and Dad go down the pub Saturday nights," she continued.

"And Sunday?"

"Don't you go to church or Sunday School?"

He shook his head. "Lately I've been givin' it a miss."

"You won't go to hebn," she laughed.

"The Blue Hungarian Band is playing in the main shelter on Lansworthy Green Saturday night."

"I've never heard them," said Kitty. "I can see you after dinner on Sunday. I'll come into town on the two o'clock bus." She narrowed her eyes and inhaled slowly through her nostrils. "I'm glad we met."

"So am I," he said.

"You can kiss me if you want to," she said, taking off her hat and holding up her face, eyes and mouth firmly closed. Jack wrapped his arms round her, planted the kiss and held her close. She responded briefly before placing her hands on his chest and gently pushing him away.

A blackbird was singing but the lowing of cattle on Sugar Loaf Hill died to a hush. The wind dropped and the sea turned to glass. Then the last bus came and departed with her on the top deck, waving until the bend hid her from view.

THE CHILDREN CIRCLED the hurdy-gurdy at the top of the terrace, laughing and chatting as music filled the dusk. Jack fastened the top button of his Norfolk jacket and straightened his tie.

"You're late out this evening, Jack," said Mary McKenna. "And I can't remember the last time I saw you with your hair brushed."

"He's sweet on Kitty Widdicombe," Michael blurted.

"Who's she when she's at home?" frowned the boys' mother, watching young Blanche and Lily playing in the street.

"A little scrap of a thing from Churston," Michael said. "She works at the store."

"And you're sneaking off to meet her now," Mary McKenna went on, half mockingly.

Jack laughed. "I'm not sneaking. I'm walking."

"You're too young to be courtin' the girls," she said in a voice suggesting the contrary. "Those Chancellor hussies are on the road to ruin, showin' their ankles like them scarlet women who hang around the 'King'."

"Eatin' chips with a nice girl at Dimeo's won't have me sproutin' horns. But if it's a sin I can always go to confession and ask God's forgiveness. Sorry, Lord—I have sinned. I ate chips with Kitty Widdicombe."

"With or without scribbles?" Michael said gravely, referring to the little crisp pieces of fried batter the children prized as much as the chips.

"Well, you are growing up, Jack," his mother sighed, and her fingers swiftly raked his hair. "That's better. I can't bear you looking so damned neat and tidy."

SO CHIPS, PEAS AND SCRIBBLES became a regular feature of their Saturday nights, although if it was too warm they settled for ice cream from the hokey-pokey cart. But those first Saturdays in the steamy little café up Winner Street past Lansworthy Mill's shop, the smell of boiled pigs' knuckles wafting round them, were particularly cosy and intimate. They drank ginger beer and chattered like long-established lovers, sharing secrets and hopes, joys and sorrows with a candour maturity prohibits.

Over the road the pub doors and windows were open and men were singing. The warm, malty fragrance of beer drifted on the night air.

"It'll rain when the fair comes," Kitty said. "It always does on Regatta."

"Not this year."

Keeping a little apart they strolled along Palace Avenue into Victoria Street. Kitty looked up at Chancellor's and said, "I wish Monday would never come."

"Are you unhappy there?"

"No, of course not. It's a bit boring but a thousand times better than being in service. That was terrible. Awful. They treated me worse'n a donkey. All that cleaning, polishing, mending and lugging till I was asleep on my feet, dog-tired and too miserable to cry. At least the ladies who shop in our store usually give me a smile. Tidn all that bad I suppose."

"What would you really like to do?"

"Something worthwhile. I wish I knew more about things. They didn teach us much at school, but I wanted to learn."

Then she smiled into his face. "I'd like to be married to you, Jack. Us would do lots of exciting things together."

There was a dance at Deller's Café and the strains of a waltz crept up Lansworthy Road. Behind the gold glowing curtains the silhouettes sailed by like the ghosts of some impossibly distant adult world. Other children sat on the wall outside, watching and listening.

"We'll go there one day," said Jack.

MOST SUNDAY MORNINGS the Salvation Army band marched down Fisher Street and stopped at the entrance to the terrace as if that particular neighbourhood needed redemption more than sleep. The thump of the bass drum drove Mrs. Endacott wild and she would send her gormless thirty-year-old son, Moony, out to disrupt proceedings. But Moony liked the music and would caper round the players singing snatches of hymns, his heavy, blue-jowled face one vast beam of pleasure.

The small Catholic community rejoiced in its geographical ascendancy over the Anglicans. Mrs. McKenna and Jack's brothers and sisters went to sing Mass in the chapel of the seminary for young priests at the top of St. Mary's Hill. The chapel sat amongst fields with the white statue of the Virgin gleaming on its rooftop as close as possible to God.

From Cider Mill Tor the statue was visible against the haze of Abbot's Quay. Standing on the tor Jack could hear the parish church bells ring out to answer the bells of Collaton, Stoke Gabriel, Churston and Mary's Haven.

Immediately below the rock the grass was full of poppies and when he called, the horses cantered through the red flowers. The mares and foals had been put in with the farm horses. They milled around the tor until he jumped down to pet them. Bethlehem bowed her head so that he could pass his comb through her mane and speak softly to her. Then Melody intruded and her nose had to be scratched. All the animals wanted attention but Bethlehem pursued him, speaking with her eyes. And when she rolled in the grass the geldings joined her, their thrashing hooves severing the poppies and scattering them like drops of blood.

He carried the image home.

"Father Tynan is worryin' me to death," said Mrs. McKenna. She sighed. "I want you at Mass next Sunday and I swear I'll get your dad to kick you up the road if you object. It's bad enough having one godless brute for a lodger."

"Will it really make you happy, Mum?" he smiled.

"Yes," she replied and unpinned her hat and laid it carefully on the table. "The parable of the prodigal, Jack. Home to God. I can't keep makin' excuses every time you mooch off. You can't be lookin' after horses every Sunday."

"But I never left God. He made the horses and I was with them just now. He's everywhere and everything."

"Then you won't mind meeting Him up the hill once in a while."

Michael grinned. The other children were quarrelling in the scullery. The smell of the roast cooking in the oven always made Sunday a warm, lazy day.

"It will make me happy, Jack," she added with the hardness gone from her voice. "I can't look the Father in the face."

THAT AFTERNOON he met Kitty's bus and after tea he walked her home as far as Windy Corner and kissed her good night. The breeze died to a hush broken by his footfalls. Turning once he found her waving and for a moment the evening was cheerless. He thrust his hands in his pockets and thought of Beth while his depression faded and he returned to the moment.

The lane carried him between fields of wheat and cabbages. High up where the blue deepened swifts were shrilling, and coming over the brow of the hill to begin the descent into Waterside, Jack saw the lights of Lansworthy and Abbot's Quay. The air was soft and warm, and clouds of gnats hung between the hedges. His pace quickened. Across the coomb lanterns shone from Tor Barton Farm and he could hear men's voices.

Maddock, his son Arthur, Trant and a labourer were rounding up some bullocks which had stampeded between the outbuildings and were blocking the lane leading to the paddock. Jack ran up the hill towards the cider mill and headed off a couple of strays. By the time he had driven them back to the yard everything seemed to be under control.

"Did 'ee see Beth?" Maddock growled.

Jack shook his head, looking from man to man.

"Her's away up yonder somewhere—thanks to that bliddy ornament." The farmer swung his stick at Arthur. "Drove the bullocks like one of they bliddy cowboys—whoopin' his head off. And early on he went and left the paddock gate open. Beth and Sheba was in the lane. Us got Sheba but Beth must be halfway to Stoke Gabriel by now."

"I'll find her," Jack said, crouching to take off his boots.

"Take a head halter, boy," said Maddock. "Soon as I've saddled one of the mares I'll follow 'ee. Her woan go far."

BETH RAN TO THE CROSSROADS the other side of the mill and stopped. Panic no longer gripped her and already she was missing her mother. The lane behind her led back to all that was familiar and secure, but as she was about to turn towards home a mongrel came hurtling out of a nearby cottage garden to snarl and snap round her legs.

Beth galloped along the Mary's Haven Road and, meeting some

252

labourers who had been drinking cider, bolted down to Yalberton. Pacing nervously in the direction of Stoke Gabriel she had a confrontation with the motor bus and went racing off into a side lane that led to the hamlet of Aish. By now she was totally disorientated and frightened. The tops of the hedges arched to entwine and create a tunnel of foliage. Then it opened suddenly onto a narrow road and she was trotting uphill under pine trees. Three children hurried from a wayside house and tried to trap her against the garden wall, but Beth swerved and swung onto a cart track. She was lathered and miserable. The starry sky showed in blinks between branches and leaves. Cattle lowed, ghost moths fluttered about her head. The night was hostile.

Jack received directions first from the drunks, then from a woman who had left the Stoke Gabriel bus at Yalberton. The children at Aish giggled when he came padding up the lane in his bare feet, clutching the halter, but he got the information he wanted and set off down the track which led to the duck marsh and the River Dart. Near Aish Farm the track was blocked by a timber wagon. To the left a footpath followed the edge of the marsh and soon he was lengthening his stride in the dew-drenched grass where the smudges of fresh hoofprints could be seen.

Long before Jack reached Aish, Beth was trotting along the path beside the marsh, starting whenever a duck flopped down into the reeds among the shallows. Before her the hills were silhouetted black against the sky. On each side the valley climbed wooded slopes to the glow of twilight. Where the path met the river and swung abruptly downstream it was blocked by cattle. To Beth's right was a sluice, steeply banked with mud and fed by a narrow stream that flowed into the river. Beyond it was Aish Quay and the hulk of an old sand barge. Beth slithered down the bank and the mud oozed round her hocks. Desperately she splashed through the stream, to find herself in deeper mud, and struggling to free herself she keeled over on her side. A final effort left her with hind legs submerged and her body at an awkward angle, neck and head held rigidly clear of the morass. A whinny faded to a snuffle of despair. Then she lay motionless, breathing deeply, before the next jolt of panic had her thrashing about.

The moon was rising above the hills on the far side of the Dart as Jack reached the sluice. Cattle walked up to him inquisitively, but he had seen Beth and squelched down the bank to join her. She looked at him, the mud caking round her lips and nostrils.

"What have you been up to, my little darling?" he whispered.

The mud was cold and thigh-deep. He crouched and floundered through it. Beth's neck arched and she ran her tongue over her muzzle. For a gut-constricting moment he thought they were in quicksand but he managed to reach her and wrap his arms round her neck, swallowing his fear.

"Lie still," he murmured, putting the halter on her head and knowing with a sinking of the heart that he would not be able to drag her clear. All he could do was stand there holding up her head until help arrived. It was a chilling prospect.

Ten minutes later he realised his strength would give out and he began to yell for help, but no one came and presently he fell silent. Trying to pull Beth up the bank was an idea he quickly rejected. Then on a sudden surge of horror he noticed that the stream seemed to have stopped flowing and had become a little wider. The tide was coming in.

"Mother of God preserve us," he breathed. He would have to leave her and go for assistance while she was still able to keep her head out of the mud. But no sooner had he released the halter and turned to go than Beth was snuffling in alarm. A slow-motion crawl brought him to the stream.

"And would I leave you?" he grunted, looking over his shoulder. "I never will. Never."

The mud on the stream bed was ankle-deep and his feet were slipping on slimy pebbles. Relief brought a savage half-snarl, half-smile to his face. He splashed upstream until the channel shelved to deeper water. The bank beyond was gentle and grassy.

Returning to Beth he stood over her and said, "Get up, girl, come on, now. Come on. Up, up."

The foal's front legs beat at the mud and her body twisted and heaved.

"Up, Beth. Come on, girl—you can do it. Come on, my darling."

He tugged the halter rope but she sank back again, unable to free her hind legs. Once more his command drilled through her distress, and she rolled onto her back, right over until she was standing. Before she lost her balance as the mud sucked at her limbs he jerked her head round and she managed a couple of awkward steps and flopped onto her side. His voice inspired an immediate response and the next staggering bound brought her almost to the water's edge. Now the mud was shallower and a high-stepping action of the legs sent Beth crashing into the stream. Jack took her head in his hands. She was quivering and the moonlight touching her muddy coat gave it a metallic sheen.

"Good girl," the boy smiled.

Beth regarded him from a gaze that was no longer perplexed. Although she was cold, wet and dirty she had lost her fear, and her trust in Jack was absolute.

He led her into the floodwater, which was brackish, and together they swam to the bank and clambered out. Then he ran before her holding the rope and making her trot to get warm until they reached a linhay below Aish Farm. Here he ripped up some old meal sacks for cloths to dry her off, and some straw twisted into wisps. His own discomfort was ignored in his anxiety to prevent her catching cold. When the grooming was over he stripped and tied a meal bag round his waist like a kilt.

Beth shivered in spasms so he made her lie down in the straw and covered her body with sacks. Then he curled up beside her, close enough to take her breath on his face. Her eyes were open and they held some of the

254

moonlight which crept through the doorway. Her breathing was easy, regular, and she had stopped shivering. Outside an owl called. Jack closed his eyes, thinking of the Celtic warriors who lay down in the ferns with their horses in that far-off time when men were more animal than human.

THE FOLLOWING WEDNESDAY the Venners of Number Fifteen lost their young daughter Florence. She died of tuberculosis and the curtains were drawn in all the terraced houses until she was buried. There was no laughter on the cobbles after dark for many evenings. Moony Endacott, who had worshipped the thin, mousy-haired girl, was inconsolable. The women and children followed the hearse to the cemetery and Moony's wailing sent tears rolling down faces which hard living had set firm and seemingly impervious to sorrow.

Shortly after the funeral Wotton and Jack took the smart blue van to Morning House, Sidney Chancellor's villa on Roundham Head overlooking the harbour. Chancellor's eldest granddaughter was soon to be married and the van was loaded with a variety of fancy goods.

The black-gabled house, with its mullioned windows, tall chimneys and pointed tower, faced east. A hedge of macrocarpa and beech protected the lawns and flower gardens from the winter winds. In the centre of the largest lawn was a flagpole round which the Chancellors, their guests, an assortment of children and dogs, and a pony were gathered. Bees thrummed on the scent of honeysuckle.

This was the scene that greeted Jack after the housemaid had told him the master wished to see him. The boy wiped his hands on his apron and stuffed his cap in his trouser pocket so he would not have to lift it to fools like Ormond Chancellor.

"Come over here, Jack," Mr. Sidney said warmly.

Years later when Jack pieced together the incident it seemed that everything had been orchestrated to embellish the girl's beauty. A faint mother-of-pearl luminosity flowed over her pink dress. Her straw hat was trimmed with flowers and tied at the chin with a pink ribbon. Masses of glossy brown hair tumbled over her shoulders as she extended an arm and patted the pony's nose. The well-dressed boy clutching the reins smiled indulgently. Jack recognised him as Ormond Chancellor's young son, Rupert. Boys and girls of similar age looked on while their parents stood a little apart. The Daubenys from the villa next door were visiting their neighbours.

Sidney Chancellor beckoned to Jack and added, "Have a look at the pony—a good look. Miss Daubeny's father is considering buying the mare. It's the young lady's birthday tomorrow."

Jack nodded and stole another glance at the girl.

"Would you buy the pony?" Chancellor persisted.

"I would not, sir."

"Why?" the girl demanded.

"She's a bit cock-throttled and goes back at the knee."

"What?" The girl wrinkled her nose.

Mr. Daubeny turned enquiringly to Chancellor.

"The brute's got a neck like a fowl," said the old man. "It's not pronounced but Irish Jack would spot it instantly."

"And she does go back at the knee," Daubeny murmured, frowning at the slightly concave joints.

"Well, I still think she's gorgeous," the girl said peevishly.

"Isn't that the best reason for having her?" Jack asked.

An embarrassed silence greeted the remark.

"Run along then, Jack," said Sidney Chancellor.

The boy coloured and looked down at his boots for a moment before departing.

"I do wish you'd stop showing off McKenna, Father," Ormond said. "You parade him like a clever ape."

"Because I like him. He's got tremendous spirit and he lives for the horses. What does Helen think of him?"

He smiled, but the girl in the pink dress could not conceal her displeasure. "His fingernails were dirty," she said. "Is he a gypsy?"

"Irish," laughed her brother Edward.

"The Irish certainly have a way with animals," Mr. Daubeny admitted.

"Does this mean you'll not buy the pony, Father?" Helen said. "That horrid boy's so ugly and my pony is beautiful."

"And cock-throttled," smiled Edward.

"Cock-throttled or not I love her," his sister exclaimed passionately.

"Then she's yours, Helen," Mr. Daubeny said and the girl flung herself into his arms.

Chapter 4

Chancellor's staff outing began well enough. Three wagons were planked out and the shires had their tails plaited and were paraded in the show brasses. They moved out of Lansworthy, pulling their cargoes of high-spirited employees to follow the long country road to Becky Falls. At the Dartmoor beauty spot sandwiches, scones and cream were eaten and washed down with cider. Jack could not get Kitty alone but the company was merry and he was content to sit drinking medium sweet from the jar. Lacey became objectionable as the cider loosened his tongue. His remarks made some of the older women blush but the men encouraged him and he staggered about laughing and joking, usually at Skilly's expense.

Fred Luscombe had an eye on the sixteen-year-old Cundy girl who had the face of a Pre-Raphaelite princess and the body of a mature woman. The day was warm and sunny and several holiday romances bloomed. Then Jack noticed that Kitty and Lacey were missing, but before he could get to his feet they emerged from the bushes to a chorus of hoots. Lacey came and leered down at Jack. "I tell 'ee what, Irish—her doan know how to kiss. There's more warmth in a dead duck's arse."

"Cut that out," Old Bob said. "Us won't have that filthy talk with ladies present."

Lacey giggled and some of the stablelads laughed. But the carters had seen the frown on Old Bob's face and kept quiet.

"No more scrumpy for that ornament," said Ernie Drew.

Jack glanced at Kitty but she sat crosslegged, her hands in her lap and her head bowed.

Lacey rocked quietly on his heels and tapped his fists together. "Bog Irish idn much cop when it comes to romancin'," he laughed. "But Bog Irish idn a lot of cop anyway."

"Lacey," Old Bob growled.

"Let 'em get on with it, Bob," Ernie Drew interjected. "It'll clear the air."

Jack was quivering and the tin mug rattled against his teeth when he drank the remains of his cider. He put down the mug and got to his feet.

Lacey's grin twisted into a sneer. "You'm all a-tremble, boy," he breathed. "Say sorry and your Uncle Arthur won't do ort."

"Leave him alone, Lacey," cried one of the women. "You bully—you're bigger than him."

Balling his fists, Lacey took a step back. "Are you apologising, Irish?" Jack grinned.

"Hit the bugger," Luscombe grated. "Drop un, Arthur."

"Yes, hit me, Arthur," Jack whispered, and on a lurch of fear and panic Lacey realised the grin was not a real grin at all; it was a disguised snarl concealing something intrinsically animal. The pale blue eyes steadily returning his gaze were devoid of fear.

"Just—just watch it, Irish," he began, and Jack caught him with a right and a left delivered at remarkable speed which made him grunt and spit blood.

"I bit my tongue," he mumbled. "You—you—"

"Don't say it," Jack said, wagging a finger in Lacey's face.

Lacey pressed a handkerchief to his lips and began to sob, but his opponent was walking away towards the waterfall.

"It idn finished," Lacey shouted.

"You and your mouth," said Ernie Drew, baffled by the boy's stupidity.

They took the end doors off the wagons and Jack sat with his legs dangling. Shortly before the homeward journey began Kitty joined him, and he smiled at her.

"Do 'ee want to know what happened?" she whispered.

He nodded and took her hand.

"I had to go behind the bushes or—or I would've wet myself. Then he was there on the path waitin' for me. I couldn get past and when I tried to dodge he caught me hold and gave me a kiss. It wadn nice, Jack. It wadn like it is when us do it."

He wrapped an arm round her shoulders. The wagon wheels rumbled over the stony road, and the music of the harness jingled along with them. Up ahead they were singing and someone in their wagon took up the tune:

" 'Midst pleasures and palaces, wherever you may roam,
Be it ever so humble there's no place like home..."

The road fell away behind them and was lost in dust haze.

LACEY RETAINED MOST of his cronies despite his poor performance at Becky Falls.

On August Bank Holiday Monday he and Skilly and a couple of the more daring stableboys were passing the jug again in the park. The fair jerked Angarrick Terrace out of its summer torpor. Laughing gangs of teenagers went to the green arm in arm while their mothers trailed behind with the toddlers, gossiping all the way down to the swings, booths, stalls and merry-go-rounds which had sprung up beneath the big wheel. The men would gravitate more slowly from the "King Bill" to the beer tent and then pub-crawl home in the evening.

The genteel visitors pretended to be absorbed in the regatta although Edward Daubeny impressed the youths gathered at the coconut shy.

"He spends an awful lot of time in the school nets," Rupert Chancellor explained ruefully as his friend collected his third coconut.

On an impulse the tall, good-looking Daubeny boy presented the prize to the nearest girl. It was graciously accepted and he found himself staring into a startling pair of eyes. Their owner also possessed a mass of blonde hair and a broad, pretty face.

"Who was that?" he asked as they strolled back to the promenade and the Chancellor party.

"One of the Widdicombe girls," said Rupert. "Dora. Her sister works at the store. I don't know what she does—something rural I suppose. They live at Churston. She's rather stunning, isn't she?"

"Rather," Edward grinned. Greenish-gold eyes, he thought, and such dark lashes.

Out on the bay the sailing dinghies slowly tacked together, scrounging wind from a breeze that was hardly strong enough to unhook the dandelion seeds. A swimmer launched herself from a bathing machine and kicked up white splashes, while out of the sunshine Kitty and Jack were walking under the pier.

"Tis so dark and cold," Kitty shuddered. "They say bats live up beneath they floorboards."

Footsteps ringing on the pier above them sounded eerie, and the convoluted wrought iron where pillars met woodwork in the half-darkness was like the vaulting of some awful dungeon.

She caught his hand and dragged him out into the sunlight that smelt of wet dogs and ladies' perfume.

"Have you ever been roller-skatin', Jack?"

"No," he laughed. "I'd need wheels on my backside."

"You can do it on the pier," she said. "I've only ever been on the pier once."

He pushed his fingers into his pocket and teased the warm, heavy coins. They would bring him a week closer to owning Beth. But Kitty was lovely, with her breath of apples and eyes greener than spring leaves.

"Come on," he said. "Let's go up there."

"But I've only got a tanner!"

He jingled his loose change and winked. Then she screwed up her eyes and laughed and kissed him.

The thunder of the fairground steam-organs coloured the moment. Jack and Kitty joined the crowd pouring up the steps into the brilliantly lit pavilion. The wealthy, who lived most of their lives in public, moved about sedately, wearing smiles and an air of spiritual fatigue. But on the roller-skating rink the young of all classes mingled unselfconsciously.

Helen Daubeny surfaced for a moment from a field of flower-trimmed hats. She was laughing helplessly. Then the crowd closed around her once more and she was gone.

Kitty Widdicombe sat sidesaddle on a gold and scarlet horse. The steam organ started up and the merry-go-round went round with all the other gold and scarlet horses rising and falling under the canopy. Kitty's eyes closed tight on her laughter. Then she was waving and vanishing, and the horses undulated by until she was back again.

Big frightened eyes stared from the painted heads of the roundabout animals. They fixed on Jack, until the broad wavy bands of gold and scarlet blurred and deposited him at the brink of dizziness. Bursting from a fog of colour Melody and her foal abandoned the roundabout and cantered off along the shore. Behind them the rainbows dissolved and silence spread over the water. The sun going down was colder and duller than the moon.

Jack shivered and folded his hands at the base of his head.

"Are you all right?" said Kitty's voice.

The fairground reassembled round him and he smiled at her. Gold light swung across her face. Over her shoulder the roundabout horses continued to seesaw as they cut their circle of brilliance like creatures escaped from mythology. Mist had softened the sunlight.

"Jack?"

Reaching out he took her hand.

THEN THE GHOST MOTHS DANCED around the lamps and the "Three Towns" slowly vanished under dusk. The fairground was a cauldron of noise and lights filtering through Kevan McKenna's alcoholic trance.

A final stout in the beer tent had lifted him to a plateau of dazed well-being which his cronies shared. They strolled along the familiar holiday trail stopping at their favourite pubs: the "Crown and Anchor", the "Globe", the "Oldenburgh", before finishing up in the "King Bill". By this time nausea was gaining ground but this did not prevent McKenna bringing an equally drunk companion home for supper. Both men were rocking on their heels ready to drop, and Mary McKenna had no difficulty persuading the unwelcome guest to leave.

"Get some shuteye, Kev," he slurred, ricocheting off the wall into the darkness. "Get your head down, pal."

Farewells were exchanged until Mary McKenna dragged her husband inside and shut the door.

"Look at the state of you," she said. "You ought to be sleepin' with the pig."

He threw off his cap and jacket. "I will be in a minute. Gi'us a kiss, Mary—my rose of Tralee."

"You've more chance of becoming the next Pope than getting a kiss off me."

Jack and Michael glanced at each other and tried to hide their laughter.

"Bloody funny, isn't it?" McKenna roared. "You've all ganged up on me—all of you. Wife, sons, daughters. Where's the bottle, Mary?"

"You'll not have another drink, Kevan."

"And who'll stop me?"

"You'll never get to work in the morning."

"Don't be so bloody daft. I'll have a little nightcap while you go and warm my side of the bed."

"Over my dead body!"

"Bloody right. That's just about it. God! but you make love like the priest's watchin' you."

She buried her face in her hands. "You can say that in front of the boys? Have you so little regard for my feelings? Go to bed, please."

"There's a bottle of light ale in my jacket pocket," the man persisted. "Have one yourself, woman."

"If you open that bottle I'll swing for you, Kevan. By Our Lady I will."

McKenna staggered to his feet. With a low, animal grunt of rage he punched her and broke the skin under her eye. He was about to deliver another blow when Jack tripped him and brought him crashing down. His attempts to rise reminded Jack of a boxer he had seen felled in the fairground booth. The drink which had inflamed him was becoming an anaesthetic.

"Where the hell am I going, Mary?" he sobbed. "What's it all about? Why are we here? Why?" Then, on a burst of defiance, "I'll fix you, you bitch. God, I will." And he went to sleep, flat on his back, an arm crooked behind his head.

"Leave him there," said Mary McKenna. "He can sort himself out in the morning." She fingered the lump that was starting to close her eye.

"It was the drink," Jack said, lamely.

"It always is. Knowing why you've got cancer doesn't make the pain go away. Go to bed, Jack. It'll be all right now."

THE NEXT MORNING Kevan McKenna washed in the scullery and changed reluctantly into his working clothes. His head swam but he got out of the house and walked unsteadily through the darkness to the railway station. The drizzle swirled round the lanterns in the goods yard. Rails and trucks gleamed and the damp smell of steam drifted across his hangover. He was sweating. The shunter's pole was greasy in his fist but the trucks were on the move as the Saddle Tank engine warmed to the work. McKenna groaned. Somehow he controlled his nausea and swung the pole with the hook on the end to lift the chain and connect the two wagons. Then his name was called.

Giddiness nudged him into a new dimension of misery.

"McKenna. For God's sake—McKenna."

The alcohol broke from his pores and trickled through his chest hair. He ducked under the chains and was confronted by another line of trucks. They were trundling gently along the rails and he waited for a gap wide enough to dodge between them. Then the ground heaved, but he was already stumbling and fighting to keep his footing. He cleared the near rail and skidded on the sleeper. Something darker than the darkness loomed above him. McKenna screamed and clawed at the wagon. His arms clamped onto metal and he was lifted and carried gently up against the buffer he knew was waiting behind him. The moment of searing agony and disbelief ended almost instantly in nothingness as he was sandwiched between the metal discs. Heels clipping the sleeper he was dragged along until the wagons separated, leaving his crushed and mangled body on the tracks.

So the black carriage returned to Angarrick Terrace. It was one of those grey, misty days created for funerals. Mary McKenna stood at the graveside, white-faced, dry-eyed, while Jack's sisters, Lily and Blanche, wept tears of genuine grief. Earth pattered onto the coffin and Kevan McKenna was no more than an emptiness round his children's hearts. After a week his boots vanished from the fender.

The kitchen clock clipped away at Jack's distress. His mother was beyond tears, yet sadness prevailed. The evenings were drawing in and they sat round the fire with the brasswork twinkling and gold light on the move. Sean and the girls were chatting at the table, and Michael was out. Jack watched his mother darning socks. When their glances met they smiled. The fire lent her face a glowing youthfulness which would not survive the night. The black eye rendered it even more pathetic.

The girls were put in her bedroom and Jack had his own bed by the window. When the moon rose above the terrace a small rectangle of light projected the pattern of the lace curtains onto the ceiling. Lying there he let grief churn up the memories. Then the hooting of the trains had a new significance.

"FOLK DON'T SEEM real to me," he said. "People are sort of dream things—even Mam."

"And me?" Kitty said.

"Yes. Something from a nice dream."

"Like the horses?"

"No. They're always real. I suppose it's because I touch them and stroke them. I know their shape, the way they're made. People don't touch each other enough."

"You put your arm round me and catch hold my hand," she said. "And you kiss me."

"Like we're part of a dream," he said. "It's not a bad thing, Kitty. I can't help how I feel."

Leaves shook against the sky, branches swung, twigs bent and swayed. He tugged a handful of berries off the hawthorn tree. All outside, he thought. Everything's outside of me—the whole world. And what's Dad now? Nothing daft like the white marble angels up the cemetery. Misery knotted in his stomach and he brought his teeth together.

"Don't be unhappy," Kitty pleaded.

Clouds were piling up along the base of the evening sky which the sun and moon shared. Smoke from the stubble fires wreathed the valley as thousands of starlings settled screaming in the ash trees above Cider Mill Tor. When the birds had fallen silent the horses could be heard calling in the dusk.

"You get so dirty on the farm," Mary McKenna said, with nothing but affection in her voice. "You were the proper little man when you were down Chancellor's yard. He could have sent any of the boys to Tor Barton."

"Beth's nearly weaned," said Jack as if it were sufficient explanation for his move to the farm.

"Beth, Beth, Beth," laughed the woman, as she slit a rabbit open and scooped out the entrails. "You can bring that girl home, you know. Pretty Kitty. I won't eat her."

"Can I have a dog, Mam—and a cat?"

"A little kitty?" she mocked, and he grinned.

"They got collie pups out the farm—and kittens."

"I had a dog once," she said. "Dando. He was old when I met your father. I couldn't bring him to England. Poor Dando."

She shivered and muttered a swift little prayer. "Put some coal on the fire, Jack. I don't know what we'll do when that lot's gone. Your dad used to bring home a coupla hundredweight of Newcastle Bright every month. He was good at things like that."

The door flew open and Jack's little sisters, Blanche and Lily, waltzed in, their shadows leaping as the candles guttered. Maybe he was there, a shadow among shadows. Kevan McKenna, mute now but wanting to say I love you, Jack. I always loved you and your mother. Maybe the long owl-cry of the goods train was himself calling from the grave.

Jack bent over the fire and tried to blot out the horror. Crushed between two trucks! Mother of God! Mother of God! Bang your thumb with a hammer and it hurts like hell. To die like that! But his mother no longer sobbed herself to sleep and the owls crying from the darkness did not really sound like the trains.

"I DOAN NEED NO EXTRA HELP," Trant sniffed. "Maddock's eldest boy is always handy if us wants ort. The way old Chancellor fusses over you he must have Irish blood."

"The old man told me there idn no one knows as much about horses as you, mister," Jack said. "I want to learn everything about them."

"Do 'ee now?" Trant said, melting before the boy's enthusiasm.

"Then I can buy Beth one day."

"Her's a sweet-tempered little animal," said the carter. "So's Bathsheba. Didn they learn 'ee down Station Lane? I thought Palfrey was the cat's whiskers."

"He is," Jack said. "But all the horses are full-grown and I only know a bit about breaking and training."

"Tidn no game."

"It's all I want to do, Mr. Trant. Old man Chancellor says I have to watch you and do what you tell me."

"And report back," the carter sneered, allowing his inner ugliness to cast a shadow on the moment.

"I don't carry tales," Jack said quietly.

"Anyway," Trant continued, "I'm sorry about your dad. Have 'ee asked the old man for a rise?"

Jack nodded and smiled. "He saw to that without me pesterin' him."

"I ought to chuck in farm work and get down the yard," said Trant. "There's no money up yer."

The September sun warmed Jack's shoulders but the shadows creeping across the yard were pale as one of the carters led down Melody and Princess and began to put them into harness.

"Check the foals and then take Melody up the orchard," said Trant. "There's bagged apples to haul. When us've got a load us'll take 'em up over to the mill."

Starlings enveloped the hill and the foals, who were desperate for their mothers, reacted nervously. They galloped around, showing their teeth and whinnying.

"Whoa, girl," Jack called. "Whoa, Beth."

The flat white face was lowered and he tugged at her ears, one at a time, until her breathing became quiet and regular. Bathsheba pushed her muzzle against his shoulder and he spoke to the foals while his hands calmed them. Bethlehem's forelock fell over her eyes. His smell and unhurried movements pleased her. Love flowed through his fingers into her body.

Now he was standing close to her, his shoulder pressed against her, and he was lifting her foot and scraping the bottom of the hoof. The hoof-pick cleared away the clotted dung and winkled out small stones.

Trant voiced his approval. "Pamper her but doan spoil her. Talk to her all the time you'm groomin', boy."

"What's going to happen to Iona, mister? I mean when she's really old."

"Her is really old, boy. Give her a few more summers and her'll beg us to cart her off to the knacker's."

"Why does it always end like that? After all they give us."

"Listen," Trant said gruffly, tensing his features. "At the end of their lives old horses suffer. When us puts 'em down us do 'em a kindness. They can't sit round like old folk smokin' and jawin' and being looked after. They'd suffer. So we give 'em death like we give 'em mash on Sundays. Tis part of the service, part of our duty. We've got to help them along—just like the Old Man helped you along."

"Helped me along where?" Jack frowned.

"Away from the goods yard," said Trant. "He told Maddock Beth would help 'ee get over what happened to your dad."

Gradually Jack's misery faded and towards the end of the month he came to work whistling. As usual Bethlehem was standing at the gate above the orchard, and for Jack she was the first foal in the first dawn of creation.

Beside her, Bathsheba swung from side to side, rubbing her chin on the top bar of the gate. Restlessly the geldings waited as the carters sauntered up the track to the tor. Melody and Princess went unwillingly from their daughters and the foals cried after them.

The men kept mostly to themselves. There was a good deal of backbiting but their quiet lunch breaks suited Jack. Most of the labourers were content to work silently. The animals provided enough companionship, he thought, sitting sideways on Melody and riding her down the track. The mares were tied together at their bits but only until the yard was reached. Behind the cow house Trant was ready to put Princess in the shafts of the tip-cart and haul logs. The boy was told to cart manure.

"Don't push Melody," Trant said. "Her's with foal again and Beth's giving her a hard time. Walk her easy, boy."

The sun flashed on the prongs of the dung fork and the sounds of the yard hedged in his thoughts. The moments blurred behind the jingle and creak of the cart.

Shortly after midday Maddock brought the team back to the stables. They wore the lather of hard work and welcomed the opportunity to cool down. Jack fed and watered them, smiling when they snorted the dust off the chafed oats he had tipped into the mangers. Then he brushed them, gave them another small meal and permitted them to slake their thirst at the trough.

The equinoctial gales washed over Clennon Valley. Leaves and birds filled the sky and the wood was roaring. Dark, rain-lashed evenings made the stables seem especially warm and cosy. Then the smoking flame of the lantern had phantoms leaping along the walls and the horses tossed their heads and stamped their nervousness. For Jack it was the finest hour. The animals stood at their hayracks and golden gleams danced on the partitions between the stalls. Beneath polished hides the tremor and quake of muscle magicked the light alive. Standing before the geldings Jack could picture heavy horses striding across the fields of Genesis. Perhaps his father had reached that place. Perhaps dying was a flight back towards the first sunrise. Perhaps the autumn cancelled out personal sadness with its vast decay.

EVENING DEEPENED the blackness of the Big Tree's foliage and they sat beneath it waiting for Kitty's bus.

"It's a shame Beth has to be taken from her mother," she said. "You ought to hear the cows bawlin' for their calves when they'm parted."

"She'll have Iona and Bathsheba for company. Everything has to grow up, Kitty."

His arm encircled her waist and he tried to kiss her neck but was pushed away. "I don't like that, Jack. It's what the sailors do to them awful women on the fish quay at Mary's Haven. If you want to be rude you'd better take Hazel Cundy home."

"Rude?" he laughed. "You let me kiss your eyes, and ears. So what's rude about kissin' your neck?"

She stroked the creases out of her skirt and stared miserably down at her hands. Her fifteenth birthday had left her feeling closer to womanhood than childhood. Yet looking in the mirror she wondered sometimes what he saw in her.

"You don't hate me, do you?" he said.

"Course not. I couldn stop lovin' you no more than you could stop lovin' that foal."

Dusk smelled sharply of bonfires. The bus rumbled up the smoking street, its sidelamps blazing. Kitty jumped aboard and turned to wave to him. He lifted an arm and let it drop again, the loneliness hollowing his stomach.

THE SMELL OF FRYING BACON made Jack hungry as he crossed the bullock yard. Men's voices were sifted through the cowshed wall and passing the half-doors Jack heard the hiss, spurt and purr of milk filling the pails.

266

"Time us got Beth away from her mother, boy," Trant said. "Both foals can stand on their own feet now. I've spoken to Palfrey and he's arranged for the mares to do some light work on the streets. Best the separation be complete. The youngsters won't like it much to start with, but they'll get used to it."

Melody sensed what was happening. She and Princess jerked at their halters and cried repeatedly to their young. The foals ran up and down the lower hedge, shrilling their misery while the mares' anguished whinnying faded into the distance.

"I woan need 'ee for a while," Trant told the boy. "Go up the paddock and see if everything's all right."

The foal studied his approach, trying to puzzle out her predicament from his looks and actions. But Bathsheba reared on her hind legs and beat the air with flailing hooves. The animals were snuffling and snorting as he opened the gate. Then they set off in a frantic gallop round the paddock until panic abated and he was permitted to go up to them.

Beth's grave face was lowered to his fingers, the nostrils rounded to take in his smell. She stood motionless, breathing quietly now. Her ears twitched forward whenever a chestnut fell onto the linhay roof leaving its spiky shell gaping on the tiles. He took out his handkerchief and wiped round her eyes and nostrils. Beth gently nuzzled his shoulder. Moving round her he drew his hands one after the other down her coat, stroking her while he crooned endearments.

PART TWO CHANCELLOR'S MARE
Chapter 5

At dusk the mist rolled in and the foals stood side by side as the sky settled on them, dusting their coats with points of brilliance no bigger than money spiders. Those were occasions when recollection of their mothers sharpened to pain and Bethlehem paced down to the gate expecting to see Melody coming out of the bullock yard, weary from the day's work.

The year was turning, and a southwestern shift of air brought more fog and rain. Then the labourers worked with sacks slung round their shoulders and waists, hating the land and what it was doing to them.

Throughout winter the weather altered the face of the landscape. Sleet fell from a bitter wind and the puddles hardened. Under the grass the soil was like iron and the young horses trod gingerly over it, sniffing at the whiteness which their breath melted. Standing on the tor Bethlehem and Bathsheba saw the gleam of breakers sweeping across the bay. The pounding of surf blurred to a continuous thunder and the sun would rise from this, offering no warmth. Bethlehem slept standing up, unaware that she had become a yearling in January.

Congregating in the yard at Station Lane the boys blew on their fingernails, dreading the rounds which would chill them to the marrow, but there was no respite for the sheep huddled against the hedge at the top of the orchard. Sleet turned to rain. The downpour streamed off the Roman noses of the shires. Trant ran a hand over his charges, checking their condition but knowing at a glance they were trim enough for anything. Most of the horses had been harnessed for field work but the mare Magdalene, who had been brought to the farm for a rest, was cart-harnessed.

The rain eased. Blue showed between clouds and the cold intensified. A shower fell, this time of snow. Cider Mill Tor was white. Smoke climbed from the farmhouse chimney and was swept away.

"Beth's in her stall," Trant said to Arthur Maddock. "Bring her out and us'll get on with it."

The tethering did not appear to upset her. She stood daydreaming, but Jack's entry brought a swift change.

"Beth," he said. "Beth, my beauty."

And she raised her head high and fixed her gaze on some far-off place that was not part of his world.

"Beth."

Her ears pointed forward and she listened. Bathsheba, pulling at her own tether, was apprehensive and executed a little sideways shuffle. Beth's movements were alert and eager now. In the corner of the stall a tabby she-cat was uncoiling from sleep.

Jack laid his head on the yearling's neck and murmured the words she loved and expected to hear. She had known he would come. It was the order of things. She allowed herself to be led into the yard.

Trant said, "Let her bide there a bit for her must learn to stand. Once her's in the shafts her'll spend a long time just moochin' about. Tether her for a while. Soon as farmer goes up Stuggy Lane with the steers us'll fit a bit to her bridle. Her's a patient little soul and the discipline will come easy. Remember to keep praisin' her. Don't rush anything and don't be tempted to spoil her. Without discipline her will be useless. Arthur can do the same for Sheba."

The yearling had grown but was still leggy. Despite the weather her white mane, tail and feather had the lustre of well-being due to Jack's constant use of the currycomb.

"When you walk her round in her bridle," Trant said, "see you don't tug on the bit. Us doan want her to get a hard mouth. Treat an animal firm but kind, Irish, and it'll give 'ee its best. Don't scold her if you lose your temper. Always gentle the animal along. Most boys expect too much too soon. Horses get round to obeying you in their own time—some sooner than others." He allowed himself the luxury of a smile and added, "There's no doubt her's going to be a handsome mare. Red roans always look good. Do 'ee still mean to buy her?"

268

Jack nodded.

"You'd give everything in the world to own her, wouldn 'ee, Irish?"

Again the lively nod and the pale blue eyes lighting up. Trant grinned and drew his sleeve across his nose. It was difficult to dislike the boy.

"WHAT PULLS THE SWALLOWS back to the sun in those foreign lands? I don't know enough about things—the world, animals, birds and stuff. I know what three and three is, and the date of the Battle of Hastings, but I don't understand how those birds cross the sky to the warm countries."

Kitty was solemn. "Dad says they only teach you enough to get you by. If us got a proper education we'd start questioning everything."

"Like what?"

"The way things are—them havin' lots; us havin' nothing. If you lock up a dog in a coal shed all his life all he knows is darkness. According to Dad the Empire idn built on our ships patrolling the Seven Seas or our soldiers fightin' the savages. It's built on our ignorance. We're like dogs in the coal shed. My sister Dora goes white with rage when her gets on her soapbox. 'Workers of the world unite' and all that crazy rubbish."

Jack smiled. "If your dad keeps blabbin' in public he'll get the push. Old Lord Warborough will have his guts for garters."

"Don't 'ee ever think of anything except Beth?"

"No. I know what I want. Maybe your dad wants so much he'll end up with nothing."

"But you've got to fight for what you believe in, Jack."

"I only want you and Beth. The world can look after itself."

She shook her head, smiling unhappily.

"Am I stupid for not wantin' much, Kitty?"

"You idn like the rest and that's for certain," she said.

Later, sitting up behind Melody on Wotton's cart he recalled the conversation. A fresh snowfall had whitened the streets, which were crisscrossed with wheel tracks. Lansworthy sparkled under sunlight.

"Tez all right on the Christmas cards," Wotton sniffed.

"LANSWORTHY IS NOT like London, there's no real poverty here." Ormond Chancellor broached a subject rarely touched on in the drawing room. "The old age pension has removed the threat of the workhouse but I don't think business will gain from it. It's the sort of liberal softness the lower classes will latch onto and milk for all it's worth. A lead-swinger can gloat over his employer, knowing he'll have enough cash coming in when he's old to keep the wolf from the door. Letting the donkey have the carrot before it has reached its destination seems to me the height of folly."

Daubeny ran a fingertip lightly over the tiny skin cancers on his cheeks. Too much foreign sun had left his complexion sallow. Unlike the local businessmen present he did not voice agreement. Seated at a table beside the pianola Edward Daubeny and Rupert Chancellor were flattered to be included in adult male society. Even though Edward thought Ormond's remarks mindless he continued to smile and nod, wondering why his father tolerated the odious snob. And a pianola! The boy sighed. He rose and went to the windows. The wind drove across the lawns, bringing sleet showers to the hills enclosing Lansworthy Bay. A coppery tinge on the horizon foretold of a worsening of the weather. Poor Rupert! thought Edward. Having a father who couldn't stop wallowing in self-esteem.

"Fear of hunger and the workhouse just about kept the labour force ticking over," Ormond relentlessly ploughed on. "But basically they are a scrounging, workshy, shiftless lot."

"What about men like Palfrey, whom your father admires and constantly refers to as a pillar of society?" Daubeny enquired, rather mischievously his son thought.

"I don't suppose he's saved five guineas in the ten or eleven years he's been with us," Chancellor snorted. "Thousands of destitute old people flock to the workhouse because they've never saved a penny, never planned for tomorrow. All their money went on beer and tobacco. If the lower classes were thrifty the workhouse would be empty."

"And you seriously believe the old age pension will dynamite the system?" Daubeny said.

"Yes," Chancellor blustered. "Give the masses something for nothing and you have a very dangerous situation."

"But haven't they earned their pensions? And surely the five or six shillings the old can expect is less than a pathetic gesture?"

Chancellor was intelligent enough to recognise opposition.

"I'm not a hard man, Daubeny," he said. "But if we're to maintain decent standards and keep property sacrosanct they have to toe the line. Socialism is an insult to the thinking man."

Thinking man, Edward reflected. For some curious reason the tall willowy girl from Churston came to mind, and Irish Jack. Both of them had intelligent eyes. Really the situation was far too complex for drawing-room drivel. He smiled at Rupert, feeling older than his sixteen years. The pianola rolled out something bland. No, not bland, he decided, as sleet pattered again on the window, vacuous—music created especially for the mediocre.

WHEN COLDS KEPT WOTTON and Cooksley at home the horse-master reluctantly promoted Lacey to carter. Jack, who was in line for the job, was still too young, but if it had been left to Palfrey the boy would have taken Melody onto the streets. Luscombe was eager to share Lacey's triumph. The pair stood together in the yard watching the boys muck out on one of those cold, damp February mornings which get into the soul.

"Buck up, Irish," Lacey jeered. "Empty that horseshit and let the men get on with the job."

270

The warmth in Jack's grin had not reached his eyes and his face had hardened round the cheekbones. He pushed the wheelbarrow to the spoil heap and tipped it.

Harold Dunsford frowned at Lacey. "You'll never learn, never. One day that little Irish boy will break every bone in your body. But you'll never learn."

"I was drunk the last time he hit me," Lacey said, pressing his fists into a greatcoat so large it made him appear puny and shrivelled.

"Here, Lacey," Old Bob bawled. "Don't stand around like you'm foreman. Get mucking out with the rest of the boys."

"But I'm taking the reins today, Mr. Sherwill."

"You may be a carter by name but you'm a muck shifter by nature," Old Bob grinned. "Get shovellin'."

"Why do they all think the sun shines out your arse, McKenna?" said Luscombe as Melody backed into the shafts.

Jack shrugged, shook his head and coughed.

The horses were beautiful in the snow. They steamed and danced sideways, swinging their vehicles this way and that until the carters stilled them. Palfrey marched up and down before them, sucking at his pipe but saying nothing. Jack watched him from the muzzy depression that presages illness. His right lung hurt and he was sweating. The phlegm was on his chest and no amount of coughing would throw it up.

It was obvious he was too ill to work. By the time he had walked home he was sticky with sweat and too tired to take off his boots. Wrapped in a towel he sat with his feet in a mustard bath while Mary McKenna put a couple of hot-water bottles in his bed. The girls and Sean were told to keep quiet and she went off to get him something from the chemist. Snuggling under the blankets watching the snowflakes flatten and melt on the window was a luxury he had almost forgotten. It was so quiet the mice could be heard running about the roof.

At lunchtime Kitty called but Mrs. McKenna did not leave them alone. Woman and girl sat stiffly on hard-backed chairs exchanging the odd smile and glance between chat. Her first visit, Jack thought, and in my bedroom! The strangeness of it all brought the grin back to his face although the pain in his chest was like a hot knife.

"When the phlegm breaks you'll feel better, love," said his mother. Kitty had gone and the afternoon was losing its light.

"Don't go sending for the doctor," he said.

"I will if I think it's necessary."

"Then you'll take the money from the Horse Fund."

"I will not!"

"We won't need no doctor. I'll shake this off."

"Your dad used to sweat it out with hot-water bottles and whisky."

"I'll try the whisky before I go to sleep. If that don't work there's Chancellor's new service."

"New service?"

"Undertaking," he laughed, then coughed and felt the phlegm shift. "The hearse is bigger and blacker and shinier than the Co-op's. Fit for royalty, I heard Mr. Ormond say."

"Those sorts of joke aren't funny," his mother sighed. She shook her head and tucked in the bedclothes. "Have a nap before supper and I'll get you a candle, unless you want to lie up here in the dark."

"A candle would be nice."

SPRING WAS THERE beneath the countryside waiting to flood the world. Off Roundham Head the dark figures of crabbers stood in their open boats hauling the pots. Atlantic swells climbed the harbour wall to fall again leaving the stonework glistening.

"You need a shave," Kitty said, laughing through her surprise. He clamped her in his arms and rubbed his chin against her cheek.

"Don't," she giggled.

Arm in arm they walked over the meadows to Goodrington Sands.

"You're so small," he said.

"I idn. You'm getting taller."

"I won't get much taller," he said. "My dad was five nine and Mum's no more than a dwarf."

"I know. We met, remember, when you had bronch? Sittin' there with her watchin' us was terribly embarrassing. I think I'd die if you came home to our house. Dad's so serious. He expects everyone to share his views. He gets so worked up about politics Mum can hardly stop herself laughing."

"Lefty" Widdicombe they called him down the yard, but Jack did not tell Kitty. According to the Dunsford brothers he was still breathing fire and revolution in the pubs every Saturday. "I'm surprised old Warborough puts up with it, him being such a blue-blooded Tory," Harold Dunsford said.

His lordship's tolerance was short-lived. The estate bailiff dismissed Widdicombe soon after the March sowing. The misery which had left Kitty's face drawn and haggard registered in her voice when she broke the news at their Saturday evening rendezvous.

"Us'll be out on the street," she faltered. "God knows who'll put us up. Dad's brothers are in Canada and Mum's family doan want nothing to do with a Socialist. They'm all in tied cottages as it is. Yes I know, you warned me old Warborough would have his guts for garters."

He shook his head mutely and wrapped his arms round her, but Kitty wriggled free.

"We'm penniless, Jack, and Dad can't keep his mouth shut. Mum's ill with worry. Surely the truth idn that important? Why won't he hold his tongue?"

She pushed the plate away, poured some salt onto the table and using a fingertip drew a face. The mouth, Jack noted, turned down at the corners.

272

"You will come and live with us," Jack said. "Mum likes you."

"All of us? Mother, Dad, me, Dora and the others?" Her sad smile fell across his heart. "I can't abandon them, Jack. They all love me. Don't order any tea, please—I don't want anything."

When she wept the other customers pretended everything was normal although there was sympathy in the odd, furtive glance. No one will do anything, Jack thought. None of them cares enough unless misfortune touches them directly. The inertia of his class angered and puzzled him. How easy it would be for them to come together and act together, like a big fist. That was the way to deal with bullies. Why hadn't it happened at school? The bullies and the rich could get away with murder.

But Charlie Widdicombe did get a job, on a farm near Slapton owned by Quakers.

"We'm lucky I suppose, they'm good bosses," Kitty said.

"But Slapton's miles away."

"Miles away from the workhouse."

"Yes. I'm sorry, I'm sorry. When do you go?"

"Thursday—on the Kingsbridge bus. Dog, cats, us, our bits and pieces."

"Oh Kitty!"

"Don't worry," she said. "I'll be out of the way and you'll soon forget me. You've got the horse."

Then the words would not rise out of his unhappiness. The rain dripped off the peak of his cap.

"Will you write?" she said in a barely audible whisper. Her fingertips brushed his eyelashes.

"Don't you ever cry, Jack?"

"No."

They met under the Big Tree when the rooks were putting the finishing touches to their nests.

"Spring is a bad time for things to end," he said.

"Darling," she wrote a week or so later, "us have got a dismal little place about two miles from nowhere. It is very damp and the chimney smokes. But Mum and Dad are happy. Dora isn't. I have got a job, too, in service. Let us hope it will be better than the last time. I miss Chancellor's and I miss you. Eternal love, Kitty."

Chapter 6

An important stage in the breaking of the yearlings was getting them accustomed to the weight of the harness. At first it was never the complete gear, but enough leather for the young animals to feel they were carrying something other than sunlight. Throughout spring and early summer Jack and Arthur Maddock led them round the paddock or left them standing like advertisements for patience which the horsemen never took for granted.

Jack's love for Kitty was honed to desperation not only by her absence but through knowing she was unhappy in her job. By the light of the lantern in the stables he wrote, "Dearest, gentle Kitty. Every day I climb the tree behind the linhay and think of how my heart holds you and your heart holds me. Iona has been ill but she is better now. Beth and Sheba are growing fast. Working on the farm I don't get much time off but when I go down the yard again I will come and see you. Everyone at the store misses you. Keep your chin up. Things will get better. If the moon is out on my way home at night I can see the White Lady of Lansworthy and I ask her to keep an eye on you. Things aren't right without you. All my love, Jack."

THE CORN WAGONS had brought the harvest to the rickyard and small creatures had taken possession of the stacks. Jack looked at the red soil turning to dust in his hands. Summer was never hard-edged like winter. The ageless farmland sailed through the season under the hum of insects.The wonder left him breathless with an excitement that communicated itself to the yearlings and to Iona. There was still fire in the old horse. She was loved and admired and her services were appreciated. Carting half a load of potatoes did not tax her strength. Iona was working again and she knew it was only a matter of time before *he* came back to attend to her needs, the one who had taken her onto the streets summer after summer, who could smile across the lantern light and whisper the words meant only for her ears.

"Her was young Sid Anning's mare," Trant said. "They did the local deliveries back along when Chancellor's wadn so posh."

The horses puffed into their nosebags as the white-domed cumulus of midday sent the shadows flowing up the far hillsides. Jack waited for the carter to continue.

"Sid died of appendix but her hasn forgot him. Horses like Iona don't forget."

So that's what she's waiting for, Jack thought as he tugged the tiny ears of grain off a stem of wild rye.

AUTUMN'S RAIN lacked real sting Jack reflected, taking Solomon onto the streets alone one wet morning and sitting on the tip-cart in his oilskins and sou'wester. At the back of Jack's mind while he flicked the reins and set the horse trotting along the Esplanade was the certainty of Sunday's freedom. And Kitty had the afternoon off. I'll see her, he sang inside himself as the rain smacked against the oilskin.

"You can't go wishing your life away," Mrs. McKenna had said when she heard Jack say for the third time one evening a week or two before how he couldn't wait for autumn.

"I know," she had added, stopping him short as he hastened to explain.

"By then you'll be back at the yard and free to gallivant off to see that girl."

"She isn't 'that' girl, she's Kitty, like you are Mother and not 'that' woman."

"I'm sorry," she had smiled. "Just don't keep living for tomorrow or you'll have nothing to look back on."

Now the clop of hooves and the wheels grating and grinding over the cobbles carried him buoyantly through work. He was delivering parcels to guesthouses and villas all the way to Abbot's Quay and back through Compton and Marldon. Other vehicles rumbled by: vans and drays, wagons loaded with farm provender, cabs, buses, a coal cart. Clasping the reins was different from taking the lines of horses yoked to farm implements. The horses trotted obediently and Jack dozed and let Kitty occupy his thoughts. Yet whenever they approached the gangs working on the tramlines which would link Abbot's Quay and Lansworthy he was on the alert. Palfrey's creed governed all his dealings with the horses. "Treat them as green animals who know little about the carrier trade and you and they will always be safe."

Death is so strange, Jack thought. He and his horses were alive and breathing, living parts of everything around them. But his father was gone. A door had been slammed in the wind and a flame snuffed out. Where did it all go, the life your heart measured in little, regular thuds? Where did it come from? He recalled Bethlehem's birth and the things he had read in her eyes.

THE CHURCH LIFTED ITS TOWER like a grey, rigid finger proclaiming "Thou shalt not" to all believers. Behind it light was filling the sky.

He cycled through a hamlet of half a dozen cottages thrown untidily round another church. The bicycle wheels hissed moistly through the mud, tossing up a fine, red spray. On either hand were hedges, fields and dark, still woods. Then he crossed a bridge, walked his machine up the hill and found himself in that curious limbo where the familiar ends and speculation begins.

At Cotterbury Forge he stood the bicycle against a gate and picked an ivy leaf from the hedge. Then he put it under his cap and went on to the village of Strete. A wagon loaded with logs was crawling up the hill behind a pair of shires. The animals were in bad condition but the man at the business end of the lines looked happy enough. He waved to Jack who let gravity and the gradient take over. Ahead was a breathtaking view of Start Bay, Slapton Sands and Start Point. The mist was still thinning and the sky ascended to great heights in the east.

He raced along the track that was littered with shingle and pebbles. The freshwater ley was to his right and the sea on the other side. The track ran straight to the hamlet of Torcross, and Kitty was sitting on the wall where the bus stopped. He waved and she stood up.

"You must be worn out," Kitty said, taking his kiss on her lips.

He cupped her face in his hands. "Kitty, Kitty."

"I idn going to fly away," she whispered but tears were at the back of her smile, and as he wrapped her in his arms she began to cry bitterly and quietly. His face was wet with her heartbreak when he stood back and produced the ivy leaf.

"Fidelity," she said. "An ivy leaf for fidelity and marriage."

They sat on the wall and the ducks called from the water behind them.

"Did you have to walk far?" he said.

"A mile or so. It was heaven after doing for them at the Big House."

"There's a job for you at Chancellor's. I'd find you good lodgings and you could send money home."

"I couldn. Mum would die. Her idn very well as it is. My little sister Maude's got croup and Mum is up all hours of the night. If only I had a different job, but there's nort round here except domestic service. When the wind's blowin' and the rain shuts that awful house off from everywhere else I want to die."

He shook his head, mutely. Feeling as he did and finding it impossible to put his emotions into words was almost as painful as absorbing some of her misery.

"To make things worse," she suddenly announced, "I've got toothache—in one of me back ones."

"You really are in the wars, love."

They left the bicycle leaning against the wall and walked the sands which they had to themselves. Crab boats were lying keels upwards, above the high-water mark. Start Bay was the colour of steel under an ash-grey sky. The beach curved gently into the distance.

The love had to be proclaimed and the kisses were sweeter than he had imagined. Kitty was still small but her body had lost some of its angularity.

"Are you walkin' out with any other maids?" she asked, half serious despite the cajoling tone.

"Only about five or six and Hazel Cundy."

"Don't joke, please. That terrible Hazel Cundy!"

"Lacey's sweetheart."

"Anybody's sweetheart. How's your real lady-friend? You did look in on her this morning before you set off to see me?"

"I did. I brushed her mane and put a sheen on her feather and gave her a kiss."

She giggled. "You and that 'orse!"

"Our horse. One day we'll put our belongings in the cart and Beth will take us away somewhere where you won't have to black ranges and polish fish knives for flinty-hearted toffs. We'll have a fine hoolie and take to the road."

"A fine what?" she laughed.

"Hoolie, shindig, celebration. I'll show you how to dance with a horse."

Abruptly the beach shelved to deep water. Waves stood up and collapsed with a roar. Again Jack seemed to drift on forces beyond his control: the ebb and flow of light and noise, the shift of pain as her words opened new areas of unhappiness. But it was necessary for her to talk about her work like a sick person reciting the minutiae of an ailment. He could not conceive anything more horrific than being imprisoned in a house doing chores from dawn to dark.

"Fourteen pounds a year," she concluded. "And this is what scares me: some women do it all their lives."

"Not you," he said, tossing a pebble far out into the water. "Sir Jack will come riding up on his charger to carry you off to the castle."

"In Angarrick Terrace?" she sighed.

"Forget the terrace, Kitty. I want a home with some land to stable the horse and grow some veg."

"My dad don't believe in private ownership."

"He has his ideas, I got mine. Is he still up on that soapbox?"

"Not at work. Mum stopped that. Her woan have un sacrificing us to his principles ever again. Her doan want to be married to another Tolpuddle martyr."

"Tallpiddle what?"

"You'm so dumb, Jack," she laughed.

"Bog Irish."

"Lovely Irish. All you need is a horse and a dream and you'm happy. My dad's bleeding inside for the whole working class and most of them doan care if he lives or dies. It's breaking his heart."

The beach and the road remained deserted, and Jack and Kitty felt loneliness creep off the sea.

"The future scares me," she continued. "So many honest people have a bad ending. At night sometimes I lie in bed thinking of all those poor, sick old people who die without a candle to light their darkness or a hand to catch hold of."

"Gloom and doom," he groaned, breaking away from her and stalking to the wavebreak, a hand raised theatrically to his brow. "All is gloom and doom. Cruel sea, take me to thy bosom. I can face this life no more. Doomed, doomed I tell you."

And he fell backwards onto the shingle, clutching his heart.

"You idiot," she laughed but there was tenderness in her voice and her kiss was warm.

They sat on the pebble bank and watched the waves break and fall apart. Kitty took the leaf from her purse and held it to the sky.

"What are you going to do with it?" he asked. The breeze spread strands of dull blonde hair across her face.

"Press it in our Bible. Keep it always."

"On Psalm twenty-three," he said.

"'The Lord is my shepherd; I shall not want,'" she said, and waited for him to complete it.

"'He maketh me to lie down in green pastures: he leadeth me beside the still waters. He restoreth my soul...'. Beth and me will have our green pastures one day, Kitty. You'll be happy when you see us there and know we're waiting for you to join us after the workday."

Then the wind coming off the sea had a foretaste of winter in its chill, and her fingers closing round his hands were like ice.

"WELL," SAID MADDOCK, one morning, "the old King's daid."

He folded the newspaper carefully and had one last glance at the headlines. "He went at midnight. Bloody bad chest like the illness that saw off my father."

"It'll be some funeral," said Trant. "They'll all be there, all your kings and queens. England won't be the same without un."

The horses worked unaware that anything momentous had disturbed the human world. Spring's succulence oozed between their teeth as they tugged mouthfuls of new grass. Calm, moth-haunted nights added a new dimension to the outdoor living, but the fillies were two years old, approaching the time when they would be initiated fully into the worklife.

To begin with there was the shoeing. It would happen the morning after Empire Day at the St. Michael's Road forge. Bethlehem and Bathsheba were carted along the Mary's Haven Road to Tweenaway and on to the smithy. The shire gelding pulling them was to have his back teeth filed and stood placidly in line with the other horses while the fillies stamped and shifted apprehensively. The ring of metal on metal was an exciting if disturbing sound.

"Hush now," Jack said, tightening his grip on the halters.

Trant turned and frowned at the youngsters and said, "They've got a whiff of the scorched horn."

"A funny old smell," said Jack.

"Tidn painful, though. Archie Diamond knows his job."

Jack chatted with the grooms and farmboys who were holding a variety of animals from hacks and hunters to work heavies. The clanging of the hammer and anvil, and the acrid stink of horn burning to the kiss of hot new shoes gave the smithy an atmosphere of its own. Sparks streamed through the half-dark where the fire glowed and the bellows sucked and roared.

"I'll take the roan first," said Diamond. He was a dark, well-built man carrying no spare flesh.

"She's no trouble, mister," Jack said.

"Good," said the smith, lifting one of Bethlehem's hind feet to clean the hoof. Then he trimmed and pared the horn and the filly blew quietly through her nose.

"You'll get used to it, maid," Diamond said, plucking the shoe out of the forge. He used the shoe-tongs to work it on the anvil, beating it into shape with a turning hammer. Before placing the metal to the hoof he tapped it on the anvil to knock off the cinders and scale. Smoke lofted in a smelly puff.

The scorch marks served as a pattern for the fitting, and the shoe was thrust into the fire again and hammered into something that pleased the blacksmith's eye. He applied the metal expertly, nailed it home and rasped down the clenches. The small boys standing in a tight half-circle round the anvil watched the performance with admiration. Diamond worked from foot to foot, cleaning, trimming and banging home the shoes, making the anvil sing.

"Us'll have a drink before you walk 'em back to the farm," said Trant when the job was done. "I want 'em to get the feel of the road."

Most of Chancellor's draught horses were shod twice a week, but farm work was kinder on the feet and the Tor Barton animals made fewer visits to the smithy. Afterwards it was customary for Palfrey, Trant and Old Bob to meet for a noonday pint at the "King William" in Fisher Street. Jack hung on their every word for there was over a century of horsecraft between them. He loved the argot, the exclusiveness of it all. He saw himself in years to come, filling Palfrey's pewter mug, swapping news on equal terms. And Beth would be tethered outside as she was now, the cold spring rain fading round her and blue sky showing in the puddles at her feet.

"Him down Cider Mill as got a couple of real jibbers," Trant chuckled. "What old Higgs knows about horses could be writ on a sparrow's eyelid with a fencepost."

"You woan make a jibber out of Beth, will 'ee, boy?" said Old Bob, slyly probing at Jack's knowledge.

"No, mister. I'll not start her off in a cart that's too heavy. I'm not stupid."

The men laughed. Behind the rain they knew warm weather was creeping in from the sea.

Things were going smoothly, but Kitty's letter brought the chill back to Jack's heart.

"Dad," she wrote, "has the chance of a job at Lansworthy Mill. One of the men is leaving after Christmas. It's owned by Quakers and his boss will put in a good word for him. I hope he gets it because I'll be able to see you again. I do miss you, Jack. I hate it here and I couldn't face another winter under this roof working for these dreadful people. I'm afraid you'll stop loving me if I'm away too long. Sometimes I wish I was dead. Anyway, fingers crossed. Hope us will all be back soon. Lots of love, Kitty."

He read the letter for the tenth time and was sticking it back in his pocket when Helen and Edward Daubeny rode into the bullock yard with Rupert Chancellor. Jack recalled it was Saturday and his visitors were probably home from school on some sort of weekend holiday.

"Good Lord!" Rupert exclaimed, eyeing Bethlehem. "Hasn't young atsername grown?"

"Beth," said Jack, and he tied the halter line to the ring in the wall.

"If only she were a pony I'd have her," Helen said. "Those eyes and that ane! She makes poor Pru look quite dowdy."

Pru was not only cock-throttled, Jack noted; she was also a "star azer". Every so often she pulled and pointed her nose straight at the sky. he young lady was not good with horses, he decided. By the looks of it he pony had a hard mouth as well as a mournful gaze.

Young Rupert Chancellor helped Helen dismount and the three of them tood admiring the roan filly. Jack sat on the farmhouse steps and watched hem.

"What's so special about Clydesdales, McKenna?" Rupert asked. Grandfather has a soft spot for shires."

"Beth's a sort of Clydesdale cross," he said. "Shires are heavy-legged nd as big as churches. But for my money these crosses are regular work aachines. Beth's mother has enough weight and stamina. Her behaviour a her gear is all you could ask for. Her legs are strong and she's got tough eet. Beth will have all them things come autumn when we start breakin' er proper. Also, she has the sweetest temper. The only thing lacking is the ure Clydesdale's bulk. If it wasn't for the feather you could saddle her nd ride her to hounds."

"I wonder if Father would buy her for me?" Helen said, turning from ack. "She's too beautiful for farm work and carting and awful things like hat."

"Mr. Sidney won't sell her to you," Jack said softly. "I'm having her. t's promised. You'd spoil her to death."

"Watch your tongue, McKenna," Rupert said.

"And will you make me?"

"Leave it, Rupert," said Edward, and he smiled at Jack. "Don't upset ourself; Helen's only teasing. She's too fond of it."

"But that doesn't excuse your insolence, McKenna," Rupert said. Apologise to Miss Daubeny."

"For what?"

"Grandfather shall hear of this. You won't be able to buy the damned orse if you haven't a job."

"You won't say a word if you're my friend," Edward said. "Helen asked or it. Come on, Rupert, be a good fellow and promise you'll keep mum."

"Very well. But next time . . ."

"She's a fine animal," Edward said to Jack. The other two were lattering down the lane and calling back to him. "Will Mr. Chancellor art with her?"

Jack shrugged. "He says I can buy her come Christmas nineteen fifteen. 'll have the money then—but she's already mine in her heart. No one can ake her from me."

"Filthy little gyppo," Helen declared viciously when her brother caugh her up. "How can you bear to talk to him, Edward, as if he's an equal?"

"Because I like him. He has spirit."

"Father will knock that out of him," said Rupert.

"Why on earth should he want to? By all accounts McKenna i conscientious, totally trustworthy and highly skilled. Why does you father want to break him?"

"Because he has ideas above his station," Rupert said, colouring.

"He isn't servile," Edward admitted. "But I don't find that offensive The roan is probably the only thing he wants in life—his one rea ambition. We have no right to take that from him."

"But these people aren't like us," Rupert said. "They are dumb, sulle brutes."

"I don't agree," Edward smiled.

"Why do the Irish bring ducks, chickens and donkeys into the livin room at night?" Rupert chuckled, glad to be off the hook.

Edward shook his head.

"It improves the conversation."

"You ass!" and Edward laughed despite his rancour.

Chapter 7

"Farmer's dog got caught in a badger gin last night," Mrs. Trant said addressing the stable door and her husband, but directing the news a Jack. "Pike found un when he called the cows."

Trant blew his nose. "Daid?"

"A broke leg. It was one of his hind legs, broke in two. Pike shot un." Her jaws snapped shut, like a trap.

"Dad reckons a fox made old Sam break his rope and take off," Arthur said.

"He never had much of a life," said Jack, shouldering the harness. He recalled the desperate collie with its one dead, blue-glazed eye, leaping at the end of the rope.

"Dogs' lives idn supposed to be fun."

"My dog's life will be."

"You habn got a dog, Jack."

"I will have, one day."

Arthur smiled. "And a horse."

The hens strutted round them and wasps cruised through the pale sunlight between the cider orchards. In a gin trap all night after spending its last years tied up! There was something awful about the business, something that left Jack feeling cold and dirty inside. Then he wondered if he was in the right frame of mind to begin the breaking.

Trant walked a little behind them up to the paddock. He watched the boys put the bridles on Bethlehem and Bathsheba, and checked to make sure the bits sat firm against the corners of their mouths.

"Don't jerk they lines," he said. "Do what I learned 'ee, nice and smooth. Have Beth walk about a bit, boy, and don't be afraid to call her by name. Arthur will stay quiet. Her's got to know that he at the end of the line is boss. The rope in your hand is to hold her. The lines and Jack do all the talking, for her must get used to being driven like her's in the shafts."

Jack flicked the lines and said, "Walk on, Beth," and the filly strode across the paddock with the boy keeping pace at the rear.

"Don't jerk." Trant's expressive gesture emphasised the point. "Now, turn her to the right. Good. And the left. Slack right line, tight left. Stop her now."

Jack leaned back and pulled gently on both lines, crying, "Whoa, Beth. Whoa, girl."

Bethlehem champed on the bit and turned her head to quiz him.

"Good girl. Beautiful girl."

Maddock's elderly assistant, Pike, had patiently undertaken much of the schooling. He showed the boys how to shorten the lines using half hitches, for the breaking of the fillies was also an exercise in controlling them safely.

Letting them get the feel of things was important. The boys took turns holding and driving, and the horses, who wished to please them, played the game for an hour or so each day. The weight of the leather was now part of a daily ritual that ended in good food and grooming. At sunset they stood under the linhay roof and the human voices crooned their praise. Currycombs and brushes brought them to the edge of drowsiness. Then Bathsheba's chestnut coat gleamed in the moonlight which was sometimes wild with scattered leaves.

JACK WAS AT TOR BARTON for a week each month and spent the rest of the time down the yard. Here he found Lacey concentrating on a new victim, Moony Endacott, possibly because Moony had less sense than Skilly and no father to curtail the baiting. The horsemaster had thought the two simpletons would take to each other but they rarely spoke or made any sort of contact, as if they were aware that the one conspicuously mirrored the other's oddness. In the uncompromising environment they competed for kindness but the dice was loaded in Skilly's favour. Even Fred Luscombe seemed relieved to discover a creature dafter than his son.

So Moony was sent on impossible errands and became the butt of the cruel mindless humour flying about the yard. But he was happy earning enough money to put meat on the table and a smile on his mother's face.

One foggy morning Jack asked Lacey why he took such delight in "bullying cuckoos". The carters were breakfasting under the awning outside the grain stores and Moony had been trotting about trying to borrow a magic hammer for knocking nails into glass.

"You know your trouble, Irish—apart from being Irish?" Lacey said. "You haven't got a sense of humour."

"Come on, Arthur," Jack grinned. "You make me laugh. Me and Moony fell about when you pitched off the cart the other day and landed on your ass—bruising your brains."

"Don't you two ever give up?" Ernie Cooksley asked.

Suddenly Luscombe appeared and boomed from the fog, "McKenna, have you heard the latest? Iona's copped it. She'll be catmeat by tomorrow. Catmeat and glue."

Old Bob was waiting at the stable door. Jack ran over to him.

"Is it true, mister?"

"About the horse? Yes, boy. Her was put down last night. Palfrey was goin' to tell 'ee but Mr. Chancellor wanted him up the store."

"Down the bloody knacker's just like that," Jack said. "A lifetime of service—and chop! All over, finished, all bloody forgotten."

"The knacker's is part of the business of caring for horses, boy. Most animals end up there. But Iona didn get the poleaxe. She slipped in the lane coming down to the stables and the vet shot her. The fall broke her back."

Jack nodded and closed his eyes. Some of the day's greyness had crept into his face.

"Iona is going to be buried like a real Christian," Bob continued. "Chancellor will make sure of that. Maddock don't like it but . . ." The old man lifted his shoulders and let them fall with a sigh. "The boss had a soft spot for the mare, or at least his late wife did."

Before long a headstone appeared on the mound marking Iona's grave on Cider Mill Tor. The inscription read: "Iona, a true friend of man".

As winter set in and the breaking followed its course Jack was often comforted by the thought of the old mare lying in the hill she had once walked over. At least she hadn't known the stink of the knacker's yard. Pike had buried the collie, Sam, so why shouldn't Chancellor bury his favourite horse? Putting Bethlehem in her gear the boy considered how he loved her and valued her life more than that of humans like Fred Luscombe. On the one hand was the innocence of the horse; on the other a mess of inner ugliness. Moony possessed some of that spiritual purity which time could never touch, it was there, too, in Kitty's eyes—something fine, left over from childhood. Soon, Bethlehem had to be put through her paces. Jack put her in and out of the stream and trotted her through the deep puddles.

"Us can't have her afraid of water," Trant said. "You can always tell a horse broken by a fool. The beast will pull up hard at a ford and have to be dragged across. You try it, boy. On a winter's day it idn no joke."

The winter sun was paler than a sparrowhawk's eye and frost rimed the valley. Some mornings Bethlehem and Bathsheba wore the farm gear and on others they were fitted for the streets. The collar brought only a mild protest from Bathsheba but when Trant decided the horses were ready to xperience the hauling, they disapproved. The heavy log attached to the wingletree behind Bethlehem surprised her when she tried to walk orward. Suddenly something very heavy was pressing against her houlders and she staggered and tried to bolt sideways. But again she was hecked.

"Steady, girl," Jack said. "Walk forward." But she was attempting to etreat and escape.

"Beth," Jack said, gritting his teeth. "Walk forward."

And she knew, despite the spurt of panic, that if he wanted her to walk, verything would be all right. She stamped her forefeet and the pressure egistered. For a moment the weight restrained her then yielded and she aced on.

By the time the blossom was on the blackthorn both fillies knew what it vas like to be yoked to farm implements. Apart from the hauling they vere also held back after the loads were removed to sample the strange ew lightness. Melody provided steadiness when the two fillies graduated o teamwork.

Pulling the harrow across the five-acre field with her mother presented ifficulties which Bethlehem soon overcame. She was far brighter than her tablemate in learning inside and outside speed. The lines relayed Jack's vishes and she lengthened or shortened her stride according to her osition at the turn—inside, short; outside, long.

One day, Kitty was there, watching the team's progress over the hillside. The metal teeth of the harrow rattled through the stony soil, raking up the ust. Out of the wind the sun was warm. It was a good day to come home, ven if the Widdicombes' new house in Winner Street was more cramped han the cottage they had vacated at dawn.

Standing hunched under the wayside elms, Kitty drew her chin down nto her scarf and felt the wind tug at her hat.

"Jack," she called as the team jingled by, and he came running through he dust cloud in his shirtsleeves and braces, a huge smile on his face. Silently she opened her arms. Her lips quivered. The horses stood and egarded the boy and girl.

Holding her at arm's length he said, "Why didn't you let me know? God, I was thinking about you, wondering what you were doing."

She was a little figure in grey and black, with a cold, funny nose.

"I wanted to surprise you," she gasped. "Careful, you'll break me."

The kiss left her breathless. She blew her nose and sniffed.

"Kitten," he whispered, hugging her again. "My little blonde kitten."

"I'm going to cry, my heart's that big," she said. The tears were gathering under her lashes.

"I'd rather you laughed," he said and his fingers dug into her ribs.

"Beth is watchin' us, Jack McKenna," she squealed.

"Sure, she's old enough. I'll have her walkin' the streets for me in the pring." His eyes sparkled.

285

"Jack!"

He was serious now. "Are you home for good, Kitty? No more partings or pining?"

She nodded and cupped his face in her hands.

"No more partings, Jack. I love you. I love you."

The tension had left her face and her cheeks were hot and red.

LARKS SANG AND CATKINS DANCED in the wind along the edge of the water meadows. Daffodils had sprung up in the orchard above the paddock and Bethlehem could smell sunlight on the air.

The fillies had reached the final stages of the breaking. Two long fence-posts had been cocked up on the gate, one end of each resting on the third bar, the other on the cobbles, like the shafts of a cart. Then the fillies were backed in and led out again, repeatedly, until they could be relied on to negotiate real shafts without breaking them.

The bullock yard was ideal for tip-cart work. The wheels rattled and sang over the cobbles and Bethlehem was forced to execute some tight turns while Jack reduced or increased the load.

Jack and Bethlehem were happy. The filly gazed at him as he wiped her eyes and nostrils. Gently she snuffled, soliciting attention.

"Yes, yes," he murmured. "You are still the lovely lady."

She was trotted and walked from the yard to Cider Mill Farm and back. En route Arthur Maddock supplied the sort of noises and situations she could expect to meet on the streets. He would stand in the hedge and whirl his crow clapper or swing a dead rook past her eyes on a piece of cord. All the Maddock children were brought into the drama. They ran about in front of the horses, shouting and banging tins while the dogs pranced and barked. Then Beth and Solomon were hitched to a variety of vehicles until Trant finally had them between the shafts of the heavy wagon. The filly's performance convinced the horseman she was ready for the road.

BETH'S BEAUTY attracted comment the first time she took to the streets drawing one of Chancellor's blue vans. Her hooves were oiled, her tail plaited and her harness gleamed. Easing her through the light Lansworthy traffic Jack felt she was his in every sense save the most important. And he had begun to doubt Chancellor's promise. She and Melody were the best-behaved animals in the stud and good brood mares were the lifeblood of the trade.

"You have his word," said Mary McKenna. "And if he's the Christian you think he is there's no need for all this worry." The gauntness had gone from her face and she appeared to have shed the extra years which poverty and worry had bequeathed. Sean had started work on a crabber so there was meat on her table three times a week now.

"People sometimes have a change of heart," Jack said.

His mother looked at him. "You're not growing a moustache, are you?"

286

"I was considering it."

"Well, don't. A moustache won't make a man of you."

He grinned and coloured, and Mary's tone mellowed. "A moustache on a boy is a comical thing—like a caterpillar on a beach."

"I suppose you agree with her," Jack said as he led Kitty up the hill to the tor where the primroses were thickest.

"Monkeys have hairy faces," she said mysteriously, stooping to pick the little yellow flowers as Lansworthy church bells flooded the Sabbath morning with their harmonies.

"The bells make me sad," Kitty added. "Funny old Sunday. When us used to go primrosing at Churston the bells were always ringing away."

"I like them," he said, unable to think clearly about anything except her face holding the primrose light whenever she bent over the flowers. The straw hat with the black ribbon was faded and the catkin dust on her new brown jersey was darker than the weak sun which clothed the hillside.

They sat on the tor, their arms round each other, and Kitty took off her hat. The breeze rising from the sea smoothed back her hair to reveal her ears.

"Like little pink shells," he murmured, kissing one then searching for her mouth. From a husky whisper she called his name and drew his head down and pressed half a dozen butterfly kisses to his face. When their lips met again he was sucked into the hot quicksand but her fingers closed over his own as he fumbled the buttons on her jersey.

"No, Jack. I idn Hazel Cundy."

"And I'm no priest," he grinned, pressing his face into the primroses they had bunched and tied with blue wool. "Surely to God it's natural."

"Yes, and that's what marriage is for—to make it right."

"But you've got to have a bit of practice, Kitty."

She pushed her fingers through her curls and blushed. "If you really love me, you'll wait."

"Of course I will, but it's not easy and it's no fun."

"You'd best go primrosin' with Hazel Cundy, then."

"I'd have to join the queue."

"You idiot," she laughed, but now his face was serious.

"Listen," he said, taking her by the shoulders. "Always remember this. There's no one but you and there never will be. No matter what happens you'll always have my love. All we have to do is think of each other."

Then the tenderness made words unnecessary. They sat together on the rock above Iona's grave and the farm horses broke the hush as they came over the brow of the hill, stepping, so it seemed, from the sky.

THROUGHOUT THE EARLY HOURS Beth was wakened by hooting. A sea mist blanketed the bay and the colliers coming to anchor off Abbot's Quay were sounding their horns.

In the next stall Bathsheba was climbing awkwardly to her feet. She had

287

come late off the streets, too tired to be groomed. Then the stable door creaked and Palfrey's dog, Mullah, ran in, wagging his tail and slavering. The aroma of the horsemaster's pipe tobacco heralded the start of a new workday, and Beth waited for the boy's footsteps.

The carters were breakfasting when Old Bob met Jack leaving the harness room. "Have you seen Ormond's contraption?" he said. "Go and have a look, boy. It's parked over by the grain sheds."

Jack found Ormond Chancellor and his father ambling round a royal-blue motor van while the store manager stood smiling his approval. Large gilt capitals on the sides proclaimed "Chancellor's for Quality".

"Solid tyres," Ormond was saying. "And the latest acetylene headlamps."

"And you know how to keep it going?" said Mr. Sidney.

"Piece of cake. They're easier and cheaper to run than horses."

"But so ugly and noisy and dangerous."

"Like steam engines," Ormond said. "Without steam the Empire would be in a mess. In a few years we'll have a fleet of motor vehicles, Father. Move with the times—change, adapt and progress."

"What about my animals?"

Ormond shrugged. "The motor van will do the town deliveries and we'll use the horses for the out-of-the-way jobs."

"What do you think, McKenna?" Mr. Sidney said, catching sight of the boy.

"I want to be a horseman, mister, and to me that thing's just a heap of rubbish."

Ormond was nettled. "Your future may depend on how quickly you learn to handle that expensive heap of rubbish, McKenna—always assuming you have a future with Chancellor's."

"Mr. Sidney asked me a question, mister."

"Yes, well, get back to work and concentrate on the things you are paid to do."

"Looking after the horses," Jack grinned.

"Off you go," Sidney Chancellor said, reading his son's mood and disliking it.

So the motor van became part of yard life despite the carters' resentment. Cooksley was taught to drive it and gloom prevailed when the men learned that Ormond had ordered two more.

But the van's first trip into town was disastrous. It broke down, with all the horses busy elsewhere. Palfrey had it towed back to the yard by a shire at dusk to the cheers of the departing carters. The following day produced three more breakdowns and Ormond was heard bellowing into the telephone. The order for the other vans was cancelled and Sidney Chancellor's smile was something the Cheshire cat would have envied.

The following Saturday Jack put the shires in their show brasses and hitched them to one of the heavy wagons. The vehicle was planked over

288

and three hampers loaded in the rear. Then he took it to Morning House to collect young Chancellor's party for a hayride. It was Rupert's idea. The party was to picnic on Churston Point, close to the sea.

"I'll ride with the driver," Edward Daubeny said, getting up beside Jack. He had a smooth face, untouched by care, large brown eyes and a neat head of chestnut hair.

The horses walked under the jingle of their harness into the haze that was firming into an unsteady wall of heat. Edward was afraid one of the noisy youngsters behind would snare him into small talk.

"How's Beth?" he asked Jack.

"Out on the streets, earning her keep."

Daubeny wondered if it was a gibe. People like McKenna led such odd lives. He could not imagine a childhood without books or nice things; but perhaps the McKennas of the world didn't have childhoods.

"What you goin' to be when your schooling's finished?" Jack asked, and the boldness of the question surprised Edward. No "sir" or "Master Edward". But I have created this situation, he thought, and now it has become man to man I'm retreating into class and convention. One either remains aloof or becomes involved. Lord! It is so difficult.

"I'm keen on geography," he said. "I suppose I'll come down from Cambridge and traipse off to some corner of the world exploring and mapping."

"That sounds fine."

"And you?"

"Me and Beth will traipse off to some corner of Devon, doing anything to earn a bob or two. It'll be nothing to make the Empire stop and stare." He laughed and flicked the reins.

"But that's what you want?"

"Of course. Fame and fortune is for the likes of you. We had one famous man in our family on my mother's side, but we don't talk about him."

"Really? What did he do?"

"He was a bosun on a tea clipper. And once, after the ship lost her masts and half the crew in a storm, him and the other survivors ate the cabin boy."

"That's awful," Edward said, aghast but laughing.

"But it's true."

"And did he regret it?"

"Yes. The boy wasn't very well cooked and they all got indigestion." They fell silent for a time, then Edward broke the silence.

"The Widdicombes lived near here, didn't they?" he asked, a little too casually to be convincing.

Jack answered the real question. "Dora and her family have a house in Winner Street now."

"She probably has dozens of admirers."

"Loads," Jack laughed and gave his companion a long, sideways look.

THREE MILES AWAY Beth was hauling the light canvas-covered van up the hill out of Lansworthy when a nail penetrated the frog of her left forefoot. Instantly she reared, but the belly band kept the shafts down and sent her tottering to the side.

Lacey tugged savagely on the reins so that the bit cut into the corners of Beth's mouth. "Hold still. Whoa. Whoa."

She never behaved like this for the Irishman. He stood up to use the whip with maximum effect. Four blows stung Beth's neck and she whinnied, pulling hard to the right. The tram rattling down the hill added to her confusion. Her hooves scrabbled on the tramlines and she slipped and fell on her side, snapping a shaft. As the van tipped and the tram braked Lacey jumped clear, glimpsing the broken shaft raking Beth's flanks. Then he was on his knees and the van smashed down, narrowly missing him. Beth struggled to rise but the weight of the vehicle held her down. Blood puddled under her and she was throwing her head about in bewilderment.

"Get up, you crazy bastard," Lacey hissed. He snatched the reins and jerked them viciously. "Crazy"—jerk—"bastard"—jerk.

Shock left Beth numb. She lay on her side, flanks heaving, feeling the pain but expecting the boy to stop it and free her.

"Up," Lacey roared.

"How can she, with all that holding her down?" said the tram driver. The passengers crowded round him.

"Unhitch her," he went on. "Unhitch her, empty the van and we'll right it. Get in touch with Chancellor's and they'll send for the vet."

"What about me?" said Lacey. He held up his grazed fingers. "It wadn my fault."

"You'll live," the tram driver sneered. "Let's have the animal on her feet."

"Stupid brute," grunted Lacey.

"She's bleeding badly," said a gentleman bending over Beth.

"I don't know what got into her, sir, she's seen trams before."

"Maybe it was the whipping you gave her," a woman remarked.

The tears sprang to his eyes. "It idn my fault," he wavered.

The same expression was on his tongue again back at the yard but this time Palfrey gave him the benefit of the doubt. The electric trams had been responsible for several accidents and Beth's large S-shaped gash was not deep. Josephs soon stitched it up and she was standing placidly when Jack visited her that evening.

"Lacey's fed and groomed her," said Old Bob. "But her's still poorly. Nothing's broke but her took a hell of tumble."

Jack ran his hands over her and found two horizontal cuts a little below her right ear. "Those were made by a whip," he said. "And the corners of her mouth are sore."

"Us can't be certain," said Old Bob.

"A whip," Jack said emphatically, murderously.

"If Beth was playing up and got onto the tramlines Lacey was right to use the whip."

"Beth doesn't play up unless she's scared."

He lifted her feet one at a time and saw the swollen frog.

"A bloody rusty nail, mister. I'll need the iodine."

"He said he looked at her. Can't that ornament do nothing right?"

"He can lie," said Jack.

"BUT WHY DOES LACEY HATE YOU?" Kitty asked Jack. She stood on tiptoe to peer at the red admiral butterfly that had settled on the buddleia near the yard gates.

"Because Jack is everything he wants to be and can't be," interrupted her sister, Dora.

The butterfly zigzagged to another flower and spread its wings.

"Jack idn special," Kitty smiled. "Only to me."

"And the horse," said Dora. Her hands flew up to tug at the brim of her hat and straighten it. Jack's arm encircled her waist, playfully.

"Are you coming back to our place for tea, Dora?" he said. "Mum wouldn't mind. There's plenty of room at the table and plenty of grub."

"I'm going for a walk."

"Oh yes?" Kitty said, and her eyebrows arched.

"Why must every walk a young woman takes end in a rendezvous with a man? I'm simply strolling down to the harbour and back. When I'm alone I think clearer."

"Think about what?" said Jack.

"How to help me dad and his friends change the world."

Dora was tall and her features lacked the coarseness typical of even the most beautiful working-class woman. If it hadn't been for her soft Devon accent, Jack reflected, she could have fitted quite easily into the Chancellors' hayride party.

"You ought to meet Dad," she went on.

"Kitty won't take me home. She's too shy."

The colour rose in Kitty's cheeks. "You doan know my sisters. And Mum would make fun of me."

"Dad wouldn."

"But he'd jaw about the Labour Party and bore Jack to death. Dad's always preachin'."

"Preaching the truth. You should be proud of him."

"I am," Kitty cried. "But there's things just as important as politics and votes for women."

"When you've got the other things, what then?"

"I doan know. Tomorrow can look after itself." Her voice dropped to a whisper. "I idn askin' for much, Dora."

"Don't worry," Dora said, kissing her sister. "You'll get what you want. I suppose the secret is not aiming too high. A husband, babies, and a horse should come fairly easily."

"I want to be happy."

"You will be. Meanwhile I'll try to help Dad sort out society so tomorrow will come as a pleasant surprise."

"GET A MOVE ON, you old devil," Lacey barked.

Again the whip cracked and Gabriel, the old shire, winced. Rain and leaves gusted round the cart. The lash chewing into Gabriel's side got rid of some of Lacey's spite but he felt like whipping the world and continued to vent his spleen on the old horse all the way up the road. Cart and animal were now travelling at such a speed it was impossible to take the bend at the junction. Lacey clawed the brake but his wet hand failed to find purchase. Instinctively Gabriel swung to the left as the pavement and garden wall raced to meet them.

It was happening again like the tramway mishap. Gabriel mounted the pavement and made a desperate attempt to avoid the wall. But he struck it with his right knee and keeled over. The weight of the cart thrown by the kerb pushed him over a low stone balustrade into the rockery, breaking his hind legs. The cart came to rest at a drunken angle, its wheels spinning and goods crashing down on the stricken animal.

Lacey had landed unhurt in the road but when Gabriel began to whinny the horror of the situation filtered through to him. He looked round for help and saw people emerging from nearby houses.

"Send for the vet," he bawled, but Gabriel's high snuffling was louder and shriller. He covered his ears with his hands and tottered away; and Gabriel continued to thrash about until the vet came and put a bullet in the animal's brain.

"What happened?" Old Bob said as Lacey crept into the yard. The other vehicles were on the streets and the stables were deserted. "Where's your cart?"

"Crashed—back there, up Midvale Road."

"And Gabriel? He's hurt and you left un?"

"There wadn nothing I could do. He went over the wall. It wadn my fault."

"God! Where exactly? Come on, you snivelling bloody coward. Show me. Two accidents in as many months and all you can think of is yourself."

"I can't show you. Up the end of the road. You'll find it. They've sent for the vet. I idn goin' back."

"What about Gabriel?" the old man shouted and he gripped the front of Lacey's oilskin.

"The blighter bolted. Twadn my fault."

"It never is." Old Bob was shaking him. "Never your fault. By God I'll beat the hell out of you if that horse has to be destroyed."

The blood hammered at the base of Lacey's skull. He looked down at the white, blue-veined fists clenched on the oilskin. "You and the soddin' horses and whole soddin' yard can go to hell," he roared. "You've had it in for me ever since I came here. You"—Lacey's fist crunched into Bob's face—"and Palfrey"—punctuated by another blow—"and that Irish bastard."

Something hard thudded against the side of his head and sent him reeling.

Jack spat on his fists. "It's the Irish bastard, Arthur. Aren't you the bucko when it comes to knockin' old men about?"

Old Bob was sitting in a puddle of rain and horses' urine.

"Leave un be, Jack," he gasped. "He's finished here. Go and see what's happened to Gabriel, there's a good lad."

Jack stooped to take the old man under the arms.

"There's a good lad," Lacey snarled.

Standing against a heap of barrels was a long-handled shovel. He snatched it and swung it as Jack turned. Metal rang on bone and the force of the blow numbed Lacey's arm to the elbow. Jack fell like a tree and lay motionless.

"Now you've done it," Bob whispered.

"Twadn my fault," Lacey cried. "For God's sake—it wadn my fault. He would've had me. He's been waitin' for the chance. Oh yes, you'm all against me."

He walked from the yard with the steps of a man for whom the future has ceased to exist. It was raining heavily and yellow sycamore leaves were glued to the surface of the lane. Lacey lurched to a halt, placed his hands on his knees and vomited.

Two days later the lump on Jack's brow had swelled to close his eye. Beth gazed at him and laid back her ears.

"You're like one of they Halloween masks," chuckled Old Bob. "Her doan recognise 'ee."

Chapter 8

Beth enjoyed leaving the yard in the grey first light, her hooves scuffing drifts of fallen leaves and her senses taking all the morning had to offer. The collar sat comfortably on her shoulders and the shaft was perfectly hitched to her harness. Neither she nor Bathsheba showed any nervousness even amongst the growing number of motor vehicles. When old Chancellor commented on this Palfrey told him rather smugly that both fillies had been correctly schooled. And the horsemaster forecast unparalleled success at next summer's Cart Horse Parade which Chancellor's had chosen to ignore in the past.

"Why did Lacey get the push?" Moony asked Jack as they were riding Beth and Bathsheba to the smithy.

"He got a horse killed," said Jack.

"I didn like un, no sir. I didn. I didn."

He scratched the stubble on his chin and drew down the corners of his mouth. Chancellor's peak caps had been issued and Moony's was too large. It sat on his ears, throwing them out. Like jug handles, Jack thought, grinning to himself and wondering if his own cap looked daft.

Their turn at the anvil came. Sweat beaded the farrier's brow and dripped off his nose and chin. His face had the leathery sheen of his apron. The stink of scorched horn spread. The shoe was nailed and clenched home.

A carter from the Great Western Railway gave Jack a "good morning".

"Seen your mate Arthur gettin' on the early train," he said. "He had a suitcase with un. Goin' to London, to some fancy job he reckoned."

"Not with horses, I hope," said Jack.

The carter lit a Woodbine. "That was a bad do, boy. Anyone who ill-treats a horse idn fit to live." He squinted at the young Irishman and liked what he saw. Jack was of medium height, well muscled and slightly bow-legged. His greatcoat was slung across his arm and his cap tipped back. The shock of black hair and the crooked nose were things he could have borrowed from any street urchin.

THE WESTERING SUN was touching the hills so that the frost sparkled as red as the berries on the holly the children brought home from the fields. The front room and kitchen at Angarrick Terrace were decorated and the Christmas spirit was caught in the laughter of the children playing their street games while they said silent prayers for snow. Then Father Tynan went away to London, to die, Mary McKenna said. The old man had some terrible disease, which had probably accounted for his increasing aloofness over the past year, Jack thought. But he took an instant liking to the new priest.

Father O'Driscoll had been trained in Dublin. He smoked cigarettes and was older than Tynan, with a limp and a watery eye. The Irish brogue and cheerful smile made Mass less of a penance. Although he sensed Jack's doubts he bided his time and waited for the young man to come in search of Christ. Some you drove, he mused, some you coaxed, others were best left to tread through their confusion at their own pace.

On Christmas Eve he settled comfortably in the kitchen of Number Eight and allowed Mary to pour him a large Scotch. Kitty, who was helping the girls at the table, was bubbling over and the priest noted the looks that sparked between her and Jack. Eating cake alone with Mary McKenna in the front room he said, "And are they to wed?"

The woman blushed. "She's a lovely girl, but she's not a Catholic."

"I thought I hadn't seen her at Mass," he smiled.

"It's hard work getting Jack to walk up the hill," Mary McKenna said apologetically. "If you'll forgive me, Father, he couldn't take to Father Tynan. It was the English accent."

"And the horses," said the priest. "From what I hear the horses kept him from Mass. He has a way with them, so they say."

"Like St. Francis. There's no wickedness in Jack, Father. He thinks too much, that's his trouble."

O'Driscoll nodded. "He and the girl seem very close."

"They've been walking out together for over three years."

"She intends coming into the Church?"

"I honestly don't know, Father. But she has promised to bring up the children as good Catholics."

Again the priest nodded and smiled, and lifted his glass for a refill.

Mary McKenna regretted there were no grandparents to grace the family Christmas. Old age could be a barren place. Sons and daughters went off into the world to make their own lives and the stillness of a home without a husband or children would be too much like a tomb. But now the little terraced house was the heart of Christmas. Mary and the girls darted about the kitchen in a cloud of spicy steam. The low-ceilinged, lamplit room was full of jars, basins, pots, pans, bowls and plates; pickled cabbage, pickled onions, hams, herbs, sausages, loaves and tarts had been assembled like treasure trove. Mincemeat nestled in cradles of dough; pies lay ready for the oven; potatoes were being peeled and baptised in the great saucepan while Blanche skilfully operated on a white cabbage. The cake had to be iced and the hams boiled and the goose plucked.

Sean and the girls reached a point around which excitement whirl-pooled. They went to bed late, tipsy on the ruby wine, and fought sleep until it took them by surprise. Then, suddenly, their room was glorious with the light of Christmas morning and they were tearing open their parcels as the bells began to ring from the parish church.

The occasion reached its zenith at lunchtime. The family sat at the best table in the living room, under the huge, gloomy print of the play scene from *Hamlet*. The fire smoked and light sparkled on the glassware. Mary McKenna said grace and set the carving knife to the bird. A plume of steam saluted the first cut, followed by a gasp of delight from the children.

Jack and Michael toasted their mother with the best port—the stuff that made them cough as it hit the back of their throats.

"Go and fetch the pudding, you pair of idiots," she said, the tears twinkling in her eyes.

So they went to the kitchen and blacked their faces with a burnt cork. Michael, who was working on the railway station now, had drunk a lot of port and was loose-kneed. He could not take three steps without colliding with the furniture.

"Ready?" said Jack, and Michael nodded. From his neck, on a piece of string, hung an empty biscuit tin which he banged with a couple of wooden spoons. Jack lifted the pudding on its holly-trimmed plate and they marched noisily back to the living room that smelled of cigar smoke. Mrs. McKenna and the youngsters cheered and clapped as the pudding was set down in its place of honour. The ruins of the feast dismayed everyone but the wine kept them cheerful. Christmas was slipping away as it did every year.

Boxing Day was a drowsy anticlimax. Moony and his mother called and after they had gone Kitty came to supper. Jack wanted the gluttony and goodwill to last for ever. He had something special to celebrate and at the appropriate moment called for silence. Kitty and Mrs. McKenna were seated facing each other across the fire with the rest of the McKennas squatting on the hearth. The fire shifted and gold danced on the walls and ceiling.

"Kitty and me are engaged," he said stiffly. "She got the ring as a Christmas present. Her mother and father are happy for us. I hope you lot are."

Kitty raised the hand she had kept tucked in her lap and the firelight flashed on the tiny stone set in the band of gold. The face she swung from Jack to his mother was radiant.

"Oh my dear girl," Mrs. McKenna whispered, opening her arms. "Let me kiss you—quick, before I start bawlin' like a baby."

A CAT LOPED across the pavement before them and clawed at someone's front door. Fog had already sealed off half the sky, and one by one the stars were going out. As if they're being turned off, Jack thought. His grip tightened on Kitty's hand.

"Does being engaged make you feel different?" he said in the deep pleasant voice he had inherited from his mother.

"Grown-up," she murmured, pressing her cheek against his shoulder. "I can't wait to show the girls at Chancellor's. They'll be so jealous when they see the ring on me finger."

"And the one in my nose," he laughed.

"But you really do love me, don't you, Jack?" she said and the anxiety in her voice surprised him.

"God, yes," he said, lowering his face and negotiating the brim of her hat to kiss her. "And love's the only thing, kitten. It's bigger and brighter than them stars. If it's true, it's in your heart till you die, like a light nothing can put out."

THE SUNSET WAS TOO MAGNIFICENT to ignore. They had collected half a cartload of barley from Aish and rattled and rumbled back through the lanes with the sidelamps lit.

After the faded colour of the winter countryside Lansworthy had life flowing along its thoroughfares. The lamps glowed in a warm, inviting way and urchins ran beside the van or hung on the tailboards. At the corner of Winner Street and Palace Avenue was a brazier of hot coals and workmen labouring in a pit. Around the fire were the silhouettes of children and tramps. A pauper family in drab, patched clothes trailed past the park in the middle of the avenue. Their heads were bowed but a girl with a little pinched face glanced up and looked at Jack. Her misery reached to him and he wanted to speak but let Beth pace on because words were never enough. How do you fight the suffering, he thought, when you can only put your hand in your pocket and come up with a bit of loose change? Maybe Dora Widdicombe had the answers.

Sitting beside Jack was Charlie Wotton, the new stableboy. He was Albert Wotton's nephew.

"You got a dog, Jack?" he said.

"No. I keep meaning to get one but . . ." He shrugged.

"Us've got Laddie and two cats. They'm handsome. Mum lets 'em sleep on my bed. Animals make good pals, doan 'em, Jack? Dad says you'm magic with 'orses and you'll learn me everything about 'em."

"You really want to be a horseman?"

"Crikey, yes! Beth's bliddy lovely." ·

Charlie's eyes blazed and Jack smiled.

"How old are you, Charlie?"

"Just fifteen." He coloured. "I idn very big for me age."

"You'll grow, don't worry," said Jack.

The other carters were gone when they reached the yard, but Palfrey and Old Bob were busy in the harness room when Jack came in with Beth's gear.

"Plant your behind on that stool and have a drop of rum, boy," said the horsemaster. "Will 'ee be takin' the young mares up the forge tomorrow?"

"I thought I'd let Charlie and Moony have a go at it by themselves."

"Charlie's all right then?" said Old Bob.

"The horses like him and he likes them. He's a good lad."

There was a moment's silence as the men drank.

"Mr. Sidney wants you to go out with the vet in the mornin'." Palfrey frowned at his pipe and got out the matches. "He'll be up round Tor Barton and all over, tendin' horses. The old man reckons you'll pick up a thing or two, things I can't learn 'ee."

The rum and the prospect of doing something different brought the colour to Jack's face. Palfrey smiled and went across to the peg on the wall where his coat was hanging.

"Go home and read this," he said, pushing a small book into Jack's hands. "The old man wants 'ee to be top dog. What you've done with Beth has pleased un no end."

"Most of it was Mr. Trant's doing."

Palfrey blew smoke and plucked the pipe from his mouth. "Trant's a farm horseman. I keep a town stud. But you could be the best all-rounder I've ever knowed. Listen to Josephs the vet and study that book."

Jack read the title, *Animal Management*, and the smaller print on the cover, "Prepared by the War Office". He flicked through the pages. There were a lot of long words and puzzling phrases: "Animal structure and function", "The points of the horse, colours, markings and age", "Stable construction and fittings", "Stable Management".

"I'll need a dictionary to get through this," he grinned.

"Then buy a dictionary," said Palfrey. "That's a complete manual of horsemanship for soldiers, but most of the principles can be applied to a town stud. Take it all in, Jack. Old Bob's retirin' soon and I suggested to Chancellor that you take his place. More responsibility and more money."

"I'm sorry Bob's goin'," Jack said, and the old man was touched by his sincerity.

"Pensioned off, boy," he sniffed. "I idn up to this caper no more but I'll be happy if I know you'm filling the gap."

"I can't break my promise to Beth," the boy grinned. "One day I'll have her and my own round."

"Maybe you'll change your mind," said Palfrey.

"I won't, mister."

"We'll see. Anyway, the job's yours. I'll tell Mr. Sidney you'll take it."

"Whain I'm gone, of course," Old Bob chuckled.

THE DAY SPENT with Josephs the vet was rewarding. Until then Jack had not realised how many horses in poor condition were scattered around Lansworthy. Their ailments varied from injuries to the ridge of the spine to girth galls and cracked heels, as well as colic and staggers. The practical experience added a new dimension to the evening's study, and Kitty was impressed by his new knowledge.

"Head carter at your age!" she exclaimed. "Us've got a fine start in life, Jack. Dad wants 'ee to come to tea on Sunday. He've been badgerin' me for months but now I think you'm ready to sit down with the family."

"I hadn't realised what a dreadful snob you are, Kitty Widdicombe."

"I only want 'em to like 'ee," and she blushed. "They do leg-pull something awful. It would have been so humiliating if they didn take us serious. Tez all Dora in our house. You'd think her was a saint."

Later that week Jack carted palings to the Daubeny residence. Helen was exercising a couple of retriever pups on the back lawn but he did not expect her to acknowledge him. Her coat was trimmed with silver-flecked fur and she looked like a Russian princess.

Returning for the last armful of palings his eyes were on her, and he failed to notice Ormond Chancellor approaching with Rupert.

"Look where you're going," Ormond barked when a collision seemed inevitable. "Keep your eyes on the path and your mind on the job. Have you finished here?" he added, and received a nod.

"Don't nod your head at me, McKenna," the man roared.

"I'm sorry, mister," Jack said, "my mind was elsewhere."

"I know where your mind was. Get back to your cart before I sack you."

"For what, mister?"

" *'What for, sir!'* "

"What for, sir?" Jack repeated woodenly.

"I don't need a reason. We pay you to work, not daydream. Now, get out of my way."

The sequel to this skirmish did little for Ormond Chancellor's vanity. The motor van broke down at Tweenaway and no one could restart it.

"Damned shoddy workmanship," Ormond bleated.

Jack was crowing when he was sent out with Beth and the van to off-load the chinaware destined for the vicarage at Berry Pomeroy.

"You can't trust them motor things, mister," he said. "Put a horse in front of that and it'll go all day, no trouble."

Ormond glared at him. He cleared his throat. "McKenna."

"Yes, mister?"

" 'Yes, *sir.*' " He spat out the monosyllable.

"Yes, sir."

"Come down, I want a word with you."

"Yes, sir?"

"You are under the illusion that you have some claim on the horse. No—don't interrupt. Just listen. She is part of the Chancellor stud and I will make sure she remains in it until she is ready for the knacker's. Beth will never be yours. You will never own that horse."

Looking him straight in the eye Jack said, "And your father's promise, mister?"

"Have you got it in writing, McKenna?"

"He gave his word." The cold got into Jack and he shivered.

Ormond smiled. "Off you go and make sure none of the crockery gets broken or you'll pay for it. The roan can manage without you, but can you manage without the roan?"

Beth swung her head to look at Jack. The snow which was lying on her coat had begun to melt and steam.

Oh Beth, Beth. He repeated her name constantly to himself. Then he said, "Walk on, girl." Anger hardened to an ache in his chest.

SKILLY'S ACCIDENT harvested the usual crop of "ifs". If Wotton had not left the wagon to go and urinate things would have turned out differently. If the the cat had not chosen to crouch under Solomon as he stood with Boxer in the shafts Mullah, Palfrey's dog, would not have gone crazy. The cat was a stray tom whom Mullah hated. The bull terrier hit him like a thunderbolt and Solomon bolted, taking Boxer with him. At that moment Skilly was mounting the wagon wheel and the jolt dislodged his feet from the spokes. The first revolution of the wheel trapped his legs and shattered them. For a horrifying moment he was dragged thrashing across the yard until Old Bob caught Solomon's bridle and calmed the horse.

When they pulled Skilly clear he was unconscious and Palfrey, who had seen similar injuries in the Transvaal, said it was lucky he had passed out. The blood and splinters of bone were too much for some of the boys and they took their greenish-white faces behind the shed to throw up.

"They had to chop his left leg off at the knee," said Mrs. McKenna. "And he may lose the other one. The poor devil. Perhaps that father of his will stop knockin' him about now."

Jack and Kitty walked to the beach.

"It makes you wonder what God's up to," Jack said.

Easter sunlight was tinting Kitty's hair as the breeze curled it across her face. They sat on the sea wall by the pavilion.

"As if having an idiot son in the first place isn't a big enough cross without crippling him when his parents are getting old."

Skilly had been transferred from Lansworthy cottage hospital to the asylum infirmary. His father did not appear too upset although cider made him lachrymose and sentimental.

"Mrs. Luscombe walks round like death warmed up," said Mary McKenna. "There are many ways of committing suicide. God! I hope you lot won't see me buried by the parish."

"You'll outlive us all, Mum," said Michael.

Her face blanched. "Don't say that. Never say that again. What sort of life would it be—outliving my children?"

The clock behind the crucifix chimed. Lily yawned and coughed. The curtains lifted on a breeze loaded with the warmth of early summer and the scents of Grosvenor Road's gardens.

ONE OF LAZEWELL'S even-tempered stallions was brought to the farm to cover Beth and Bathsheba. Palfrey approved the match because Mr. Sidney was running the stables on similar lines to a thoroughbred stud and the animals from Lazewell's farm rarely failed to sire good foals.

The dark, terrible strength of the stallion passed to Beth and became part of her in a coupling that awed Jack. Afterwards when the stallion was led away and the mares stood together Jack sat on the outcrop looking across the trees at the figure of the White Lady on the chapel roof. Mother of God, Mother Earth, so why God the Father? It was difficult to puzzle out. How could someone like Father Tynan or Father O'Driscoll guide young people who were in love? What did they know about lust and passion and tenderness? If the feeling was so good why was it wrong? And there was O'Driscoll worrying away at them to get Kitty converted and the unborn children promised to the Faith.

He drew the grass stem through his fingers and nibbled it. The Church was like the workhouse. You had to conform and obey as if the rules were everything. He let his confusion settle. I love Kitty, he thought. I love nature, and the horses who live in nature. The horse's life is like a prayer because it never breaks faith with creation.

He heard the drumming of the mare's hooves below the tor, and the cries of the geldings. Children and animals, he reflected, had a naked awareness of the wonder which existed beyond the walls of dogma. To enjoy truth and beauty all you needed was freedom. Leaders, prophets and priests were unnecessary. The bond with the living world was a birthright.

Beth gazed up at him and Jack sighed. He could push his mind no further across the problem. The things he intuitively felt supplied no facts, but the sunlight was a symbol of something more potent than the Bible stories. It was inseparable from spring and the birth of animals and the re-emergence of life from the soil.

Chapter 9

He ran a critical eye over Charlie's performance and said, "Make sure none of her mane's stuck under the collar."

The boy worked confidently and quickly until he came to the belly band.

"That's too loose," said Jack. "Buckle it snug or she'll lift a hoof one day to scat off a blowfly, get hooked up and you'll have a three-legged banshee dancing in the shafts."

Although the normal yard work continued, the stable staff had been preparing for weeks for the Lansworthy Carthorse Show and Parade. Ormond had persuaded his father to enter the In-hand, Harness and Wagon classes which the GWR stud had previously dominated. The prizes were to be presented by the High Sheriff of Devonshire's wife and the show promised to attract a large section of county society.

Saturday broke fine and warm from the haze over the bay and by breakfast time the council labourers had erected the tents and marquees on the green in front of the Palace Hotel. Then the show secretary arrived to organise all the celebrity wagons and to push back the surrounding side-shows, swings and roundabouts.

In the Station Lane yards the carters were putting their best horses in the specials. The narrow leathers were decorated with star-shaped brass studs and the brasses clipped to the broader harness.

"Show-off stuff," Old Bob called it as he fastened a brass-mounted buckle. But Palfrey would not entertain false martingales or face-pieces hanging from brown bands. It was, he insisted, a question of taste and balance, just enough brass and shining leather to set off the beauty of the animals.

"Some of 'em get tarted up like bliddy gypsy caravans," he said. "Especially the Co-op horses. They got capes like garden gates."

Capes were stiff pieces of upright leather festooned with brass and tassels, set behind the harness.

Excitement filtered through the morning chores. Jack took Beth into the yard which the boys had scrubbed clean, and worked on her coat, brushing out the scurf and the detritus deposited among the hairs by her sweat glands. The vigorous action of the bristles stimulated the oil glands and turned her shagginess to dull gloss. He washed her legs, and shaped, rinsed and dusted her feather before oiling her hooves which had been freshly shod the evening before. Jack watched Palfrey plait Beth's mane with green ribbon, starting behind the ears and working down the arch of her neck. Her tail was plaited at the top leaving the bulk hanging like a great, silken tassel. She was put in a white halter and Charlie held her while Jack changed into the clothes Mr. Sidney had bought for the occasion.

"What a toff!" Harold Dunsford whistled as Jack emerged self-consciously into the brightness.

"Show a bit of respect," Jack said, straightening his bowler and screwing a penny into his eye like a monocle.

His gaiters and boots, breeches and Prussian blue jacket, his white shirt, black tie and tan waistcoat were regarded with more admiration than envy by the other carters. If anyone could bring a championship rosette back to the yard it was Jack, with Beth. The mare was well fleshed and lustrous. The white of her legs had turned to ivory and she possessed the alertness and controlled urgency of a thoroughbred.

Melody was also competing in the In-hand class, Bathsheba in the Harness and four shire geldings had been hitched to a decorated wagon for the heavy horse turnouts. Led by Beth they clattered along Station Lane to the jeers of the other studs and processed down Lansworthy Road which was already crowded with people heading for the show.

Palfrey assembled his contingent in front of the pier and supervised last-minute preparations. The dust was brushed off the horses' hooves and oil applied again. Then the carters lightly buffed the shires' coats with paraffin-dampened cloths to fetch their shine into brilliance.

"Let's have those animals in the collecting ring," the steward said. He was a puffy-faced little man who kept consulting his fob watch.

The crowd parted and let Beth and Melody through. It was a boisterous, tightly packed crowd, a mixture of blazers, best suits and summer dresses. People had gathered from all over the "Three Towns"— farmers and their families, clerks, fisherfolk, a scattering of the well-off from the villas of Abbot's Quay. Rows of carriages and motor cars blocked the promenade, along with carriers' carts and hawkers' hand-carts. Life was spilling from the stands and tradesmen's stalls to the ringside, where women with baskets on their hips offered soused mackerel or pasties, cakes and fruit, while their daughters sold cut flowers.

"Where do 'em come from?" Kitty said, linking arms with Dora. She was serious and watchful despite her excitement. Some of the season's colour was in her hair and eyes. Her straw hat, too, displaying a new, ice-blue band and large cloth moon-daisy, belonged to the summer. Dora gazed at her, smiling. It was like taking a child to the zoo.

The girls strolled between the tradesmen's stands where the saddlemakers, wheelwrights, farriers and ropemakers were displaying their wares and expertise. The heat thickened. Then they bumped into Moony. His billycock hat emphasised the oddness of his head which was long-skulled.

"Mornin' Miss Dora, Miss Kitty," he beamed. "Look—I gotta dog."

The tan mongrel swiftly encircled him, wrapping the string attached to its collar round its master's knees.

"I found un half starved over Clennon. Mum doan mind—long as I feeds un." He tripped and sat down, and the girls left him to untangle himself from his new pet.

"Jack's mum is here with the rest of the family," Kitty said.

"Do you want to try and find her?" Dora said, detecting the contrary in her sister's tone.

"I suppose we'd better. She gets a bit funny sometimes."

"She's afraid Protestantism or socialism is contagious."

They pushed through the throng at the ringside, knowing Mrs. McKenna would be near the front. The Chancellors, Daubenys and other important visitors were already seated on the planked-out hay wagons. The pastel shades of their clothes added to the illusion of coolness, of persons detached from the masses and heat. Helen Daubeny was shielding her face with a white-gloved hand and laughing. She rocked forward and back and Rupert Chancellor leaned over to whisper in her ear.

Dora's auburn-tinted blondeness suddenly caught the sun and flashed as she tugged off her hat. Both Helen and her brother looked across at her and were held by the wonderful eyes. Edward continued to stare secretly from under his lashes until Rupert recaptured him with a question. Dora smiled.

"Mrs. McKenna is right over the other side," said Kitty, and she waved.

"Then we've an excuse for not joining her," Dora said. Her straw hat, when she replaced it, Edward noted, was encircled with a band of artificial dog roses.

"I wish they'd start," Kitty sighed. "The horses have been waiting ages in this terrible heat."

But the animals continued to stand patiently in the collecting ring. Every so often they twitched their skins or lifted a leg and slammed it down to dislodge the flies. A shire gelding was first off the mark.

"Walk in and around," said the steward.

Beth made a beautifully paced entrance when her turn came. Light gleamed on the faces crowding Beth but she never faltered in her progress round the ring. Her ears pricked forward whenever a child squealed but neither the noise nor the movement alarmed her. The breeze freshened. Flags flapped, dropped and flapped again. Jack was asked to make her trot and on his command she complied. Then she was halted and stood foursquare, and an old gentleman in a bowler ran his hands over her legs, gazed intently at her head and body.

"Does she bite?" he asked.

"No, sir," Jack said.

The plaited mane made it impossible to ignore the arch of Bethlehem's neck. Her alertness communicated itself to the crowd. Here, said the ripple of muscles and the brightness of her eye, is a fine animal. Everything about her proclaimed health and strength. The judge continued patting and stroking her. Then he examined her ears, teeth and eyes and noted the shape of her head.

"Look at that stance," Old Bob said, and Palfrey smiled.

"Like her's waiting to carry St. George against the dragon."

The beauty of her limbs ending in the splendid white feather brought a favourable grunt from a rival horsemaster, who was not a generous competitor.

Obediently Beth lifted her feet while Jack flicked the flies off her face.

The judge murmured appreciatively at the shoes. Then with his eyes elsewhere, he asked, "How did she get the big S-shaped scar on her side?"

Jack explained and let the bitterness wing out of his heart. The bloody scar! Bloody Lacey's signature! All that beauty marred by a few moments of neglect. Now she wouldn't get the winner's rosette.

The judge went behind Beth and told Jack to step back.

"Now trot her round once more."

In the collecting ring Jack was downcast.

"The scar don't matter, boy," Palfrey consoled him. "Us get branded animals being showed. Brigadier Dearson knows what it's all about. Beth's got plenty of flesh on her and her moved sweetly when her was trotting. Us had a champion before her left the yard."

The High Sheriff's wife clipped the rosette to Beth's bridle and turned, smiling, to shake Jack's hand. "Such a divine creature," she said.

Melody took the runner's-up ribbon and Bathsheba won the In-harness class. But Moony gave Beth a great wet kiss on the nose before the parade set off along the Esplanade behind the Totnes Town Brass Band.

"A magnificent spectacle," old Chancellor said. He and the brigadier stood a little apart from the rest of the company. "It easily rivals the purebred shows—despite the animals being all shapes and sizes."

"We won't see many more," sighed the brigadier. "The world's changing, Chancellor—and not for the better. Germany's sabre rattling, motor carriages are running the horse off the road, traditional values are being scorned by all sections of society."

"I'm determined to keep my fleet on the streets for as long as I live."

The brigadier nodded. "Does your son share your enthusiasm?"

"No," Chancellor said ruefully. "More's the pity, because I have someone special in McKenna—the Irish boy walking Bethlehem." He smiled, pinched the end of his nose and sniffed. "The ruffian wants to buy the roan and start his own business but I hope to persuade him to abandon the idea. His real future is down in the yard."

"Real future," the brigadier mused. "There is definitely a rapport between that boy and the roan. Can't remember seeing a finer mare. She would be better saddled than between the shafts."

"A labour of love," said Chancellor. "McKenna's dealings with her are legendary. The natives believe he can talk to horses."

LANSWORTHY CARNIVAL QUEEN and her attendants sat in a heavy wagon at the front of the parade, drawn by four dark shires in their show gear. Then came the In-hand class, the Harness animals and the winning dray followed by the heavy horse turnouts and the Shand Mason steam fire engine. Various horse-drawn omnibuses, council and other commercial vehicles brought up the rear.

"Did you see our Jack?" Mrs. McKenna said with a flush of pride. Instinctively she reached for Kitty's hand, excluding Dora. They found a space at the far end of the green and sat down. Other families were picnicking on the grass which was littered with nannies, prams and lovers. Dora regarded Mrs. McKenna and Kitty sardonically. They were transfigured by happiness. All around them the dilapidated faces of the poor seemed to have picked up the glow. The horses had awoken something in them, something fine that transcended drudgery and the monotony of existence. Looking about her Dora knew what united and uplifted them. It was the need for change and escape, not singly but as an entire community. None of them desired a lone journey. The most unacceptable thing in their lives was uncertainty. Maybe Jack's love for horses stemmed from this knowledge.

Then the sky darkened and rain fell. Big drops beat into the crowd, and people fled back to the tents.

"Dora," Kitty cried, running with the McKennas. But her sister remained on the green. The smell of drenched grass nudged other summer afternoons into clarity. Pieces of childhood floated back; episodes like lantern slides with nothing in between.

"Come on, Dora."

Hunching her shoulders against the rain she walked back to the show.

THEN THE YEAR HAD to take a downward swing. Beth walked and trotted through the summer while the buddleia behind the GWR sidings bloomed and died and the cider apples ripened on Tor Barton's trees. Her pregnancy confirmed, she continued to draw on Jack's devotion. Mornings became mistier and the days shorter. And Mr. Sidney would sometimes stand at the top of Station Lane to watch the fleets leaving the yards. Scores of carts and wagons took to the streets within minutes of each other, testifying to the pride of the rival horsemasters. Raising their whips the carters saluted the old man who had come to admire not pry. Usually he would make Jack draw rein so he could make a fuss of Beth.

"No titbits, hey Jack?" he smiled. "We mustn't spoil her."

306

"No, sir," said Jack, thinking of the sovereigns in the tin in his bedroom and the day Beth would be his.

Jack often came early to the stables and went from stall to stall speaking the animal's names as he had done during his boyhood. He valued their trust and regard, for he had divined in them a magnanimity of spirit. They accepted whatever life offered. They never destroyed anything, never questioned their state or carped about their lot. Confronted daily by the gentle horses he promised himself that Beth would have all he could give her.

One morning he came early to the stables. The day was cold. It made his eyes water and the tip of his nose ache. In the nearest stalls the geldings were showing an eagerness to take to the streets. Their huge hooves skidded and grated across the flags as they trampled the bedding.

"You're up bright and early, Jack," said Mr. Sidney.

Jack had not heard the old gentleman's approach. All around them the animals were stirring.

"One of the mares had a bellyful of red worm, sir. Mr. Palfrey asked me to come in and see to her."

"And how is Beth?"

"Fine. She'll give us a good foal, sir. So will Sheba."

Chancellor smiled. There were bird droppings on his bowler. He stood tall and upright, looking down, Jack thought, from the dignity of his social position.

"Having a horse's loyalty is a great privilege. I didn't bury Iona simply because I'm a rich, sentimental old fool. My wife and I knew that animal from the very beginning and we loved her. The thought of her ending up as glue and pet food and what have you was too much. So I put her in the hill, close at hand, part of what's going on. Do you understand, Jack?"

"Yes, sir. If they aren't suffering, all workhorses should be turned out to pasture. Beth will be—I've promised her that."

"Will you stay with the firm, Jack?"

"I may, sir, I'm happy here."

"I hope you do," Chancellor said warmly. "You know why I've come to see you, don't you?"

"I can guess, sir."

"Bob Sherwill left us yesterday and I wanted to confirm that you are now head carter."

"Assistant horsemaster, sir," Jack grinned.

"Ah yes! I forgot how touchy the fraternity is when it comes to correct titles and things. What will you do with the extra money?"

"Get married, sir. Me and Kitty Widdicombe are engaged."

"Good show! Marry, settle down; stay with Chancellor's."

"Yes, sir, I'll think about it."

"Stay with us and I'll guarantee Beth has her green pastures when her working life is over."

He followed Jack along the gangway to Beth's stall. Beth watched the men from under her lashes.

"What do you like most about horses, McKenna?"

"Their peacefulness, sir." And their beauty and innocence, he thought as the old man extended an arm and smoothed Beth's nose.

"Skilly's home, sir," Jack said suddenly. "Can he come back to work?"

"With a wooden leg!"

"The horses don't know he's got a wooden leg."

"You think he's up to it?"

"It's all he knows. He loves it here. They shouldn't have sent him to the loony bin. He's just a toddler inside his head. Something just stopped him growing up, that's all. He's not crazy."

"Lucky perhaps—despite his mishaps. Tell Palfrey to start him back tomorrow."

"You're a good man, mister," Jack said.

"Think about your own future too, McKenna," Chancellor said gruffly. But he was touched by Jack's sincerity. In business and society one opted for the conventional deceits. Honesty was refreshing. Walking to the store he was aware of having shed important things on the way to prosperity.

MRS. ENDACOTT COULD NOT COPE with Moony's rowdy pup, which was part lurcher and part collie. One suppertime Moony appeared at the McKennas' front door in tears, saying his mother was prepared to leave home if the mongrel stayed. So Jack acquired a dog and the simpleton went away happy because the creature would always be close at hand.

"Our lives are ruled by animals," Mary McKenna pretended to complain. The dog leaped onto her lap and washed her face with its kisses.

"Get the silly mutt off me," she laughed but Jack could see she was flattered by the attention she had received.

"What'll we call it?" said Sean.

"Rover," said Blanche.

"Pal," said Lily. "Or—or—Georgie."

"Why Georgie?" Mary laughed.

"Any old name won't do," said Jack. "And the animal isn't an it; he's a he. The table is an it."

"Let Mum name him," Sean said.

Mrs. McKenna thought a moment and said, "We'll call him Dando."

"After your old dog," Lily said, and she knelt to cuddle the dog who squirmed away and went from person to person in an orgy of affection.

"Dando," Mary McKenna said softly. Then everyone was repeating the dog's name, and it sat on the hearth-rug thumping out the rhythm of ecstasy with its tail.

"Another mouth to feed," Mary McKenna sighed. "Sure, but he's a fine little chap."

"Little!" Jack grinned.

"Well, little enough."

"All we need now is a cat and everything will be just right," said Blanche.

"Dando would eat it," Michael observed.

"Poor pussy," said Lily and she began to cry.

"It's a joke, silly," said her mother, glaring at Michael.

The Widdicombes had a couple of cats and both were sleek, private creatures that gave their affections sparingly. Mr. Widdicombe would sit with the orange-and-black female on his lap, smoothing her as he spoke. The little house in Winner Street was full of books and pamphlets. Like the McKenna household it had an indefinable, lived-in atmosphere and was never really silent. But Jack and Kitty craved solitude and the long dark evenings after Christmas provided few opportunities for them to be alone unless it was in a shivering embrace somewhere cold and uncomfortable. They could eat fish and chips together at Dimeo's and dance at Deller's Café but passion was difficult to foster on a draughty doorstep with Mrs. Widdicombe calling her daughter from inside.

"Is it hard for 'ee, Jack?" Kitty whispered. "I know how you feel."

"You feel it?"

"Yes. Tidn easy to fight—but we must."

"Why?"

"I want to go to church in white and I doan want it to be a lie."

"Bloody church," Jack grated.

"Don't make me feel bad. I've made up my mind; I'm going to become a Catholic."

God, he wanted to roar, as if that's important. Having Father O'Driscoll beaming and hauling in the net full of souls. Yet he saw the felicity in her eyes and her devotion humbled him. Then tenderness eclipsed desire and left them clinging together like children. To love was to be part of the goodness embracing all life. It was their birthright, and no dogmas or taboos could impair its beauty or dictate its course.

THE MORNING WAS FROSTY but the sun was creeping over the mist. Jack was waiting to collect a load of sewing machines at the station when the Paddington train steamed in. The usual bunch of old men and layabouts were hanging round the platform waiting for the pubs to open. Doors slammed and then Lacey stepped down from the third-class compartment and set his bowler at a jaunty angle. Jack had forgotten how tall he was. The dark grey suit and patent-leather shoes proclaimed an elegance that was London commercial. His tie was silk and on his suitcases were several stickers, the mementos, it seemed, of foreign travel: Cairo, Venice, Baden-Baden. The cane and well-groomed moustache contributed to the image of man-about-town, the rakish young entrepreneur the Empire fostered and admired.

Michael McKenna, on duty as a porter, regarded him with disbelief.

"The bags," Lacey said. A little cockney had intruded into the Devon accent but no one was fooled. "Carry them bags to a cab for me. You're paid to do it."

"Go to hell," Michael grated. "The only thin' I'll carry for you, Lacey, is your coffin—so long as you're in it."

"I'll carry 'em, sir," one of the layabouts said, touching his cap.

"Carefully," Lacey said. His eyes settled briefly on Jack and he sneered. "Still playing Ben Hur with Chancellor's bonebags, Irish?"

"Don't bite, Jack," Michael cried, but he was too late.

Lacey used his cane like a sword only to find Jack coming in a rush under the first wild swing. They grappled and slammed against the side of the carriage. Blind with rage Jack clawed at Lacey's throat but his brother and some of the other men overpowered him and dragged him off.

Lacey straightened his tie and pointed a trembling finger. "Next time," he panted, "I'll go to the police. Stay away from me, you mad Irish bastard."

"If you watched your mouth you wouldn't be in trouble every time you opened it," said Michael. "I'd get in your cab if I was you, before Jack ruins your suit." He held on to his brother's arm and wondered how long he could restrain the hard, muscular body.

"I looked at him," Jack said as the brothers walked together to the van, "and all I saw was Gabriel lying broken and dead in someone's bloody front garden."

"Let it drop, now, or you'll end up in jug."

"I don't care."

"What about Kitty? If they put you away what will happen to her and Beth? Let Lacey alone."

"I don't think I'll be able to keep my hands off him, Mike."

"When you get punchy try me for size," Michael grinned.

"You're just a child," said Jack. Their boxing had all the elements of love and comradeship.

Lacey's new occupation soon became known. He was a commercial traveller for a famous brand of whisky. Over the next few weeks Jack sometimes met him on his rounds but he rapidly became a background figure, no more disturbing than Ormond Chancellor. The men used different pubs and even when their paths crossed at Deller's Café dances Jack found it easy to maintain a stony indifference.

"He looks every inch the gent till he opens his mouth," said Dora. "And the romance loses its gloss when you learn he's livin' above the chip shop in St. Michael's Road. Tidn all that dashing. Keep ignoring him, Jack. Kickin' his behind won't bring Gabriel back to life."

"But it makes me feel good."

"That should impress the magistrate!"

Greenness came back to the countryside. Showers fell and rainbows arched over the valley to dim again and appear elsewhere. A little cuckoo now lay as it always did among the daffodils and primroses, but the curlews were crying in courtship flight. Then the swifts returned to Station Lane and the bluebells under Clennon's oaks took on their deep radiance. The days lengthened and when the blossom had firmed in the cider orchards of Tor Barton, Beth had her foal.

The event took everyone by surprise. Since they had been let out of the shafts the mares had done the normal light farm work. As the time approached Trant studied them with increasing interest. Bathsheba's walk became heavier, her teats swelled and the telltale wax formed on them. But Beth's body offered none of these clues. Jack, who had often felt the unborn creature stirring inside her when he was grooming her, was deceived and told old Mr. Chancellor he thought she would probably foal in a week or so.

The weather was mild but Bathsheba had a cold and was confined to the linhay while Beth was given the run of the paddock. At Jack's suggestion the top ditch had been fenced off that winter so the roan could safely be left to herself as her companion's time approached.

Then Bathsheba went into long, disastrous labour and Josephs extracted a dead foal from her body. Throughout the small hours of the new day he and Jack worked to save the mare's life. Bathsheba, who was too ill to sniff the lifeless package the men had removed, was none the wiser. Something strange had happened to her, but they would make her well. The voices were kind and the pain gradually subsided. Laying her head back on the straw she was unaware of the birdsong and light creeping over the hill.

Trant took the dead foal outside and placed it on the grass. Jack and the vet watched him silently. Dew and the first flush of sunlight added to the pathos. Eleven months inside Sheba only to come dead into the world. Jack grimaced. It was one of those nasty ironies spring could produce from its plenitude.

He gazed across the paddock. Beth was standing against the far hedge and a small creature was wobbling round her hindquarters.

"God!" Jack cried. "She's done it!"

He began to run, but nearing the roan he brought his excitement under control and called her name. She glanced up at him and her ears twitched forward.

"You crafty old girl," he grinned. Trant and Josephs joined him.

The chestnut foal thrust hard against Beth's teats and guzzled. It was a sturdy little colt with a large head and long legs. The birth wetness still clung to its coat.

"He's steady enough on his pins," said Josephs. "Beth must have waited till we were all shut up in the linhay last night and dropped him under the hedge, privately."

"Win some, lose some," Trant smiled.

Jack approached dam and foal, crooning the familiar endearments as he came. At first she lowered her head and nudged him away with a whicker of irritation. Then his smell and voice penetrated emotions clouded by motherhood, and he was permitted to touch the creature the night had magicked out of her body.

PART THREE   ALL THE KING'S HORSES
Chapter 10

Gazing down the valley from the shade of the hawthorns on Cider Mill Tor, Beth shared the calm of the foal sleeping beside her. The fullness of the summer season echoed her contentment. She touched the foal with her muzzle and the little animal stiffened its legs in a luxurious stretch of well-being. The fox trotting down off the tor paused, and their glances met for a moment before he loped away. Pigeons shattered the hush as they left the farmhouse roof and exercised their wings. Then stillness poured back, leaving the afternoon to the rooks and the lark. Beth lay on her side and slept.

LESS THAN A WEEK LATER, on Derby Day 1913, Emily Wilding Davison, a young suffragette, threw herself in front of the King's horse, killing herself and the animal.

"Poor horse," said Mary McKenna. "What on earth was that idiot thinking of? They ought to bang them women in gaol and throw away the key."

Jack glanced up from his Friday mackerel. Her face was hard and pale. Michael drew the side of his hand across his nose, hiding the grin he had brought home from the pub.

"Just imagine that happening to your precious Beth," Mary McKenna continued, sawing viciously through the loaf.

"Jack loves her," said Blanche.

"Worships her," said the mother scornfully.

The lamplight could not soften her expression. Jack ate the fish and new potatoes and pushed the plate to one side.

"They've nearly finished the Picture House down by the level crossing," Sean said, disliking the quiet that filled the house after dark.

"You'll never get me in that place," said Mary McKenna. She folded her hands on her knitting and frowned at Dando. The dog yawned and laid its chin on its front paws. The lamplight's gold climbed the walls and flushed the samplers which bore hand-stitched legends: "God made the Country, Man made the Town"; "The King's carriage must stop for the sheep". Jack grinned. Then he thought of the horses on Cider Mill Tor. Beth and her son, Mischief, standing in the starshine.

A little before the foal was weaned Jack cycled along the Old Mary's

Haven Road at cockcrow. The October moon still shone over the South Hams although sunrise was catching the peaks of the waves from Hope's Nose to St. Mary's Head. Leaves scattered in the wind that set the beech trees roaring and Jack whooped with the excitement of it all—the wind punching his body, the Sunday morning full of flying leaves and the smell of damp farmland.

Then he came down the cart track past Cider Mill Tor, and the horses pursued him. The shires slithering across the pastures were massive under their aura of gentleness. So by the time he reached the paddock and caught sight of the roan she seemed quite small and elegant. Mischief galloped around her, kicking his hind legs. His shrill whinny of joy had the mares calling from the hill but Beth remained silent. Her watchfulness was reassuring. The trees thrashing in the sky, the birds darting in and out of shadows, the constant shift of light, were regarded from brown, un-troubled eyes. She stood under the coomb, suckling her foal while the dizzy fall of leaves continued as the sun climbed off the horizon.

"I hate winter," Kitty said one Friday night with a shiver. "Everything's so grey and dark."

The wind gusted along the pavement and they stepped into a shop doorway to finish their chips. The puddles vibrated and became flat and still once more until a station rank cab rattled by.

"I finish early on Wednesday," said Jack. "Do you want to go to the cinema?"

"The Picture House?" she exclaimed, delighted. "Dora went last Saturday and her said tis much posher than the Burlington. What are they showing?"

"I don't know," he smiled, amused by her enthusiasm. "Michael took Mum a couple of days after the place opened. He told her there was a religious motion picture on and the place was full of Catholics. For all her squawkin' she allowed herself to be hauled into the building. Now wild horses wouldn't keep her away. She's like that—against everything till she's tried it."

"Mrs. Butt from Palace Avenue plays the piano down there," said Kitty. "Our mum went to school with her."

She chattered all the way home, clinging to his arm and throwing back her head to laugh at his jokes. The night was no longer gloomy. Everything takes it colour from the way we feel, Jack thought.

IT WAS MISCHIEF'S DESTINY to be sold to a farm at Yalberton, but the colt occupied a corner of Beth's being which the passing of time could not touch.

Three of the farm geldings were being rested, so she and Bathsheba plodded between Tor Barton and the yard. The hushed countryside was a direct contrast to the noise and excitement of Station Lane and the work was harder. On icy mornings the bit was so cold it burnt the corners of her lips, and if one of the carters neglected to warm her collar it made her tense up and tread irritably into the day.

For the labourers, the winter work was the usual penance. Frozen fingers stammered over broken chains and knotted lines. Curses came out in white puffs. The hush of snow on the fields had the texture of nightmare and men and animals responded silently, miserably.

Standing at the front door one evening Mary McKenna noted for the first time that the spring had gone out of Jack's step, and the realisation chilled her. She saw Kevan and her father and the young men of her past. The cold hours spent perched on cart and wagon were taking their toll. He stooped a little and groaned as he bent to unlace his boots.

It was the way of things, she thought. The sadness of loss made it difficult to hold back the tears. The boy had gone and the man raised so many sorrows, sitting there toasting the winter out of his bones. She took the teapot off the hob and filled his mug.

"Frank Emmet in Number Three passed away this morning," she said. "He had that terrible chest for months and was coughing blood. God rest his soul. Elsie will be going back to her relatives in Abbot's Quay as soon as possible. She never liked it here since her boy Charlie went off to be a gamekeeper in North Devon. If you want the place she'll put in a good word for you with the landlord. Old Vickery isn't a bad fella."

Jack whistled as he buttoned his shirt. The material was crisp and warm from the iron.

"Well?" Mary McKenna persisted.

"Me and Kitty wanted somewhere in the country."

"The terrace isn't good enough for you, I suppose—you being the assistant horsemaster?"

Her sarcasm brought a smile to his lips. He ran the comb through his hair and said, "We'd like a bit of garden and a place to stable the horse— somewhere Beth would feel free to run about."

"Sure, and won't that come later? There's good grazing up behind St. Michael's Road and old man Pottinger has a couple of sheds in his field."

"I'll think about it, Mum. I'll ask Kitty."

"You could do it up nice, the pair of you."

"And you could help."

"Oh yes—I'd like that, Jack. My son, my life."

Kitty's reaction surprised him for he had expected disappointment, recalling her scornful remarks about "Sir Jack" and the "castle" in Angarrick Terrace. But she was enthusiastic and hung round his neck kissing his lips as he spoke. Then he realised how much marriage meant to her. She would have settled for a hovel providing they could be united in the eyes of God. Dreams get humbler as we get older, he thought.

"We can get married in April," he said. "I'll start paying the rent as soon as Mrs. Emmet moves out. That'll stop old Vickery goin' an' lettin' it to someone else."

314

"Mum can start makin' me wedding gown." Kitty whispered, her eyes bright and moist.

"And Beth can be a bridesmaid," said Jack.

"Lily and Blanche and my little sisters Maude and Vicky."

"You've got it all planned."

"Well, us've only got a few weeks to arrange things," she said, pushing him away. "Oh God! Maybe us should wait till June."

"I may go off you by then."

"Tidn no joke. Is April too early?"

"Not the end of April."

"Idn it romantic?" she exclaimed, laughing with her eyes closed, like a child at the Christmas tree.

THE COLD STRENGTHENED, and east winds brought snow from the Continent. Beth and Bathsheba were back at Station Lane, where work had come to a halt. The carters had been laid off and the horses left in the care of Jack and Palfrey. Whenever there was a lull in the blizzard the animals were led out and walked round the yard. At first they lifted their legs high but soon discovered they could push through the drifts.

Beth liked the snow beneath her hooves and the flakes whispering down. Pieces of it settled on her nostrils and vanished. She arched her neck and whinnied, to be answered by Bathsheba and Melody. The whiteness had no scent but the shire geldings could not resist rolling on it, snuffling with joy and kicking out their legs. Soon the yard was full of animals churning up the snow under the mist of their body heat.

Jack's heart went out to them in their rapture, dark and glistening under the grey light and the snow driving hard again off the sea.

It was not long before the snow had gone even from the hilltops, but the rain was cold and the sun cheerless. Maddock and Ormond Chancellor shot wildfowl on the salt marsh. Curlew, snipe and mallard lay side by side in the canvas bags and the evening flights continued despite the noise of the guns. Then Jack would go home and join Kitty, Dora and his mother in the empty house, whitewashing the kitchen and wallpapering the bedrooms.

"Best paper in the front room," said Mrs. McKenna.

"For the Co-op insurance man to see," Jack grinned. "Why do front rooms have to be stupid showpieces for visitors? Sure, it would be better if ours was used as a bedroom instead of us all crowdin' together upstairs."

"Wouldn be proper," said Kitty. "If anyone called where would us put 'em—in the kitchen?"

"Why not? For heaven's sake! Why not?"

"Because it's a game, Jack," said Dora. "Ape your betters."

"Betters!" he snorted. "Ormond Chancellor better than me!"

"Society thinks so," she laughed.

Mary McKenna was running an approving eye over the wallpaper. "Now that looks splendid, Kitty."

"Of course it does," said Jack. "You chose it, Mother."

"Chancellor's. Ten per cent discount," Kitty smiled.

He returned to the kitchen and the whitewashing.

"Is this what it's all about, Jack?" said Dora. She folded her arms and leaned against the door. "Wallpaper and furniture and lino and a bit in the bank?"

"I honestly don't know."

"Don't let it take over completely." By candlelight her beauty was ethereal. She was so calm and relaxed. "Dreams are no good unless you do something about them, Jack."

Mrs. McKenna called Dora and interrupted the conversation.

Next morning he walked to work under the stars and joined some of the carters on their way up Fisher Street. Dora's words cut into his thoughts. He was nineteen years old and already in a rut. Nothing could be more futile than grafting for wages until old age shouldered you onto the scrapheap. He glanced at his companions. Albert Wotton had spent his entire life in Lansworthy working for Chancellor's. He went from house to yard to pub to house day after day, and most of Sunday was spent in bed. By the time Jack had joined Palfrey he was on the edge of desperation.

Beth was to be harnessed for the town van and the Lansworthy round. I've enough to buy her now, Jack thought. Surely the old man would take the gold and let the horse go? Excitement welled and left his mouth dry. He would ride her bareback out of town and over the hills to Dartmoor and on through Wales to catch the Irish ferry. There were places facing the sunset where horses were still regarded as fabulous creatures. He would take her along the stormy beaches on the journey that had no ending...

But then as he walked home with Moony his mood changed, and his entire being cried out for the fireside and hot food. The smack of skipping-ropes, the chanted rhymes and the laughter filled the dusk with friendliness. The sight of the small figures circling the lamp usually produced an inner glow and Jack came to the hearth pursued by his sisters.

A week passed, darker and colder than anything else the New Year had managed. Yet the days were imperceptibly lengthening, and bringing Beth and Melody up King's Ash Hill, Jack was relieved to see blossom on the blackthorn. He stopped the wagon beneath the branches for a closer look. The tiny white florets stirred against a sky the colour of pewter. The horses turned their heads and stared at him. "Spring, my lovelies," he murmured. "For me it always begins here, on these trees."

But Jack knew spring had really come one morning when his mother opened the bedroom window to shake her duster and let the scent of rain-soaked flowers flood the house. And the King's Ash blackthorns were in tiny leaf when he and Kitty were married.

316

THE MORNING WAS SHOWERY. Blossom from the ornamental cherry trees floated on the puddles all down the path to the chapel. Guests caught in the rain ran under their umbrellas with the women gathering up their skirts and squealing. Throughout the ceremony sunlight illumined the stained glass windows and faded and swelled as clouds passed; but nothing could take the glow from Kitty's face.

They walked down the hill together to the reception in the Co-op hall. It was a small affair. Michael and Sean acted the fool, Mary McKenna cried, his new in-laws and their relatives danced to the music of a hired gramophone, and when Kitty turned to kiss him she had pastry crumbs round her mouth. He laughed and brushed them away with a fingertip.

"Tidn much of a do is it?" She blushed.

"Sausage rolls, light ale and your dad crankin' the gramophone? It's everything I imagined and more. Legless Mike and witless Sean doin' the jig; Mother weepin' buckets; Father O'Driscoll half blotto; and you and me sittin' here jawing when we should be in bed."

"Oh Jack."

"I'm only joking."

"The presents are nice, aren't they? Especially old Mr. Chancellor's. Fancy him thinking of you!"

"He was thinking of the horses."

But when evening blued to dusk, company was no longer desired. They drew the curtains and Kitty sat on his lap in the armchair, aching to drag him upstairs but unwilling to advertise her appetite for what went on between the sheets.

"Your mum might walk in," she whispered, and he laughed and led her up the short flight of stairs to the bedroom. The honeysuckle in the back yard shook its fragrance through the open window.

Bed then, and no embarrassment or hesitation except in the undressing.

"Put the candle out," she whispered, wriggling free of the flannel nightshirt and settling beside him.

Chapter 11

Maybe the news from Sarajevo cast its shadow over Dora's mind. In another summer in another place she was to recall laying down the *Daily Mail* after reading about the assassination of the Archduke Franz Ferdinand and going to the front door. The first shoppers came clumping down Winner Street and then Jack passed, upright on the cart with Beth in the shafts. He turned, waved and smiled, ignoring the motor cars and vans crawling along behind him, eager to overtake.

It occurred to Dora in a flash that the man and horse had one thing in common: no future. The motor car would see to that, the motor car and progress. It registered more as a shudder than a thought. The early editions of the *Illustrated London News* were full of scenes from Sarajevo

"There will be war," said Mr. Widdicombe, and he sighed. "Everyone's talking about it down the mill. The mazed muggers want it to happen. The working class are their own worst enemy."

Yet summer took its normal course. The wagon sailed down lanes of red dust, bumping and juddering behind Beth and Melody, the load threatening to tip at every jolt. They reached a hilltop and at their feet the whole of south Devon melted into something more mysterious than haze. Everything was perfectly still and the light around them was soft and vibrant. The far-off places held humans and animals spellbound.

Kitty was singing when Jack crept in through the front door late one evening. The clamour of swifts flying high above the terrace brought summer right into the house. He took off his boots quietly and came to the kitchen on tiptoe.

"You are an angel, Mrs. McKenna," he breathed, folding his arms round Kitty from behind.

"My clean apron!" she squealed, wriggling free. "And don't come up on me like that again. I nearly passed out. Stop it! Don't you want your supper? Wash your hands and I'll bring it in."

He was sitting at the table when she called, "Have you seen today's paper?"

Jack plucked the *Mail* off the arm of the easy chair.

"'Austria declares war on Serbia'," he read. "'Powder keg of Balkans ready to go up'." The small print elaborated on Europe's gloomy prospects.

Kitty set down the steak and kidney pie and poured the tea.

"Dad reckons it's really serious now. The Germans are dying to get at our throats."

"Not before supper, I hope. If they've got any decency they'll invade us in the boss's time."

"Jack," she laughed.

"Brooding about what might happen won't help."

She was a pretty, wide-eyed child, fearing her happiness was under attack. "Life scares me, Jack," she said, and her voice shook.

He lit the lamp against the darkness, but outside the swifts continued to scream.

ALL EUROPE WAS ARMING while the corn ripened and the skies remained blue above parched landscapes. Beth, Melody and Bathsheba were loaned to Tor Barton again, to replace some animals which had fallen sick after eating horsetail ferns down in the valley. For the yard mares those nights loose upon the tor were precious interludes. They swished through the long grass, glad of the comradeship and content to be there. Standing on the rock with the moon behind them their silhouettes were silver-edged.

Then Germany declared war on Russia as a consequence of an

318

inevitable chain reaction of alliances and counteralliances. The next day the Kaiser's armies invaded Belgium en route to France, and Lansworthy, like the rest of Britain, was gripped by war fever.

"I don't believe it," Widdicombe said. "Down the 'Crown and Anchor' last night they were baying for German blood. Your mate Lacey led the chorus. The Kaiser would quake in his boots if he knew what the lads had in store for un. Lacey talks one hell of a war."

"But it'll be all right, Dad—won't it?" said Kitty.

She was black-leading the kitchen range.

"No. It will get worse. The whole world has a sudden appetite for slaughter."

"I haven't," Jack said.

Widdicombe grinned. "You'll do what you'm told, boy."

"Will I?" Jack grinned.

The Regatta Fair drew the crowds to Lansworthy seafront and few people were aware of the khaki figures boarding the noon train.

NEXT MORNING TIME DRAGGED. The "Three Towns" smouldered until evening once more released the masses and they flocked to Lansworthy Green. The government had given the Germans an ultimatum to withdraw from Belgium, and it was due to expire at midnight—eleven o'clock British time. As the hour approached a crowd gathered outside the town hall singing "Land of Hope and Glory". The minutes ticked away and the night seemed to hold its breath, but the multitude broke into the national anthem and then fell silent. The parish church clock struck eleven times and after a long pause the town clerk raised his voice and said, "The German government has not replied. We are at war."

"War," the crowd echoed. Fists and hats were held aloft and shaken. A roar of joy and defiance rang across the bay and was answered by the cheers of the ratings on the dreadnoughts and cruisers off Abbot's Quay.

"War," Lacey cried, and Rupert Chancellor flung the word back into the cauldron of noise.

War was on the lips of the young men dashing down the streets to crowd the bars. Like the Klondike, Dora thought, and everyone had struck gold. They were singing the national anthem again as she turned and walked along Totnes Road into Victoria Street. Chancellor's windows were lit up and a huge Union Jack hung over the entrance.

"Why aren't you cheering?" said a voice in her ear.

"Cheering what?" she said.

Edward Daubeny was unsmiling. His arm encircled her waist and met no resistance. Dora did not offer the usual platitudes of coy defence. She closed her eyes, parted her lips and returned his kiss. Then she went with him towards the seafront, knowing it was right and glad she was true to herself. Now the crowd assembled at the pier sang "Dolly Gray", but Edward and Dora did not join in. They walked on the beach and the firework display, which had been put back an hour, banged and crackled into life.

Starlight quivered on the bay but the sudden arc of rockets was brighter. The hills ran black to horizons where the light was full of noise. Beth picked her way cautiously off the tor, her eyes alert. One by one the other horses came and stood baffled by what was going on below.

THE POLICE WERE GOING from door to door delivering wires to the reservists. War meant adventure, but even so Jack was surprised at the number of boys and carters who failed to show for the morning work. The Dunsford brothers made a brief apologetic appearance.

"We'm joining up," Harold said, his eyes blazing. "Lord Kitchener wants a hundred thousand men, and me and Will want to show the Hun we mean business."

Palfrey took his pipe from his lips and tapped it on the stable door. Then he looked at Jack.

"Who else has enlisted?"

"Practically everyone—Moony, little Charlie Wotton, Rupert Chancellor, bliddy Lacey, Arthur Maddock, the Daubeny boy, hundreds of 'em. They've opened a recruiting office below the billiards emporium in Station Square. Your brother Mike was there, Jack."

Jack nodded but said nothing.

"There's this Royal Artillery sergeant in his dress uniform," said Will. "He could charm the birds off the trees! Lacey's going to an infantry regiment, but all the lads from the yard and Tor Barton have joined the Gunners. So've Rupert Chancellor and his pal, Edward. The sergeant said they were looking for real horsemen. We hope we'll all be together. Can you manage without us, Mr. Palfrey?"

"I'll try," smiled the horsemaster and they shook hands.

"Idn you coming, Jack?" Harold said.

"No," said Jack.

"Someone's got to look after the horses," Albert Wotton interjected.

"You'll find enough old fellas to help 'ee," Harold mumbled.

"And they reckon it'll be over by Christmas."

Jack went into the stables.

"What's up with Irish?" Harold asked. "I never thought I'd see un turn his back on a fight?"

"Perhaps he don't feel it's his fight," said Palfrey.

"Damn it, Mr. Palfrey," Harold cried. "Tez everyone's fight. The bliddy Hun's in Belgium givin' folk a roasting. If us doan help out he'll be over here. Anyway, what's it like?"

"What's what like?"

"Action. Fighting."

Palfrey had served in the Boer War. He thought for a moment. "Tidn all it's cracked up to be. Let's hope Kaiser Bill will back off now we're

320

showing the flag. Maybe it'll end with the politicians chinwagging round the table."

"Spoilsport," Harold laughed.

MARY MCKENNA COULD NOT disguise her pride over Michael's enlistment. Half a dozen other young men from the terrace had taken the King's shilling and for a while Jack's refusal to run with the herd was hardly noticed. But Jack's growing isolation became apparent when he brought the carrier's van to the store one morning. He was loading up at the front, where a knot of figures in blue serge tunics were receiving free cigarettes from Ormond Chancellor. Among them was Lacey.

"Where's your shilling, Irish?" he crowed.

"Bloody laggard," came a shout.

"Bloody Irish."

"Us won't let Fritz hurt 'ee, boy. You stay home by the fire with the maids."

Jack's Irishness was proposed as a reason for him shirking his duty. Michael was "a different animal altogether", to quote Ormond. "We have the fighting Irish and creatures like McKenna." His father was astonished, but Helen Daubeny merely thought Jack was reverting to type.

"The backstreet bully boy would always show his scut in a crisis."

Jack returned to the terrace via the "King Bill". The half-mumbled remarks intended to be heard, and the glances of the elderly, left him unruffled. Kitty had stepped from the bath in front of the fire when he came home. She towelled herself with a bashfulness she never displayed upstairs, as though nudity and sex were improper in the living room. Her body gleamed pink and gold, and water beaded and fell from her breasts. The firelight threw her shadow on the far wall but his mind was elsewhere.

"What's wrong?" she whispered.

"I remembered something that struck me the night war was declared. In the big children's room at school they had this picture of the Charge of the Light Brigade. Grey horses were galloping into the cannon fire and dying horribly. It was a corner of horse hell, and when the fireworks were banging to celebrate the start of this all I could see was those animals flying into death. And I knew it would happen again."

"To Beth?"

"Perhaps. She's a horse."

"Old Chancellor wouldn't sell her, never. He loves her almost as much as you do."

"What if he hasn't any choice? Palfrey says the army is short of horses."

"It won't happen, Jack." She wriggled into her nightshirt and began drying her hair. "They've got motor cars and lorries and things these days. Beth's a draught animal. No self-respecting gent would want to chuck a saddle on her."

"She's built like a carriage horse. They'd find a use for her. A use!" He

321

shut his eyes and grimaced. "All that comradeship and trust and loyalty betrayed. They never get considered."

He rested a foot on the fender, trying to fight the misery.

"All them horses in all the wars, killed or maimed in battle. Heroes ridin' the real heroes—no, not heroes, innocents. Like they were riding dumb children to their deaths."

"Stop it, Jack. Please."

"That's the trouble. I can't tell anyone. I can't make Mum understand, or you understand. I'm walking down a road in the rain by myself. It's always been that way. Always."

"You idn alone, dear. I love you and I'm here with you. I'm glad you didn't join up. I'd die if you went."

"The horses never know what we've got in store for them. They never suspect us or doubt us, and they can't question us. They just go on giving all the time, right to the end. And we've used them."

"The army have got their own horses."

"Yes." He grinned mirthlessly. "Ready to trot into the jaws of death again. A touch of the spurs, gee-up and off you go."

"But not Beth."

"Beth's kind. And the lads from the yard who went off waving bloody flags and singing 'Rule Britannia' are part of the damned awful deceit."

His eyes glistened and she touched them with her fingertips, astonished. "Jack, you'm crying!"

"Must be the booze."

"Let's go to bed, sweetheart."

"Yes."

Then there was the sharp blaze of passion and her bare white arms held up to the ceiling.

Chapter 12

The war was in possession of the national consciousness, and the minds fluttering over the newspaper headlines measured the passing weeks in battles: 23 August, the Battle of Mons and the retreat; 6 September, the opening of the Battle of the Marne and the German retreat to the Aisne where the Battle of the Aisne commenced on 13 September. But swift victory was no nearer as the chestnut leaves yellowed and the plough teams opened the earth.

"Why did they take Moony?" said Kitty. "He's more trouble than he's worth."

"But he's also big and strong," her mother-in-law smiled. "And he does what he's told. Michael, on the other hand, will have them officers hoppin'."

It's still a game, Dora thought, laying down her book. Toy soldiers charging around and banging drums and marching up and down hills. Mrs. McKenna actually believed the story of the Angels of Mons who the newspapers claimed had helped the British troops. The boys had all gone off to play, only this time when they were shot there would be no counting to twenty and swift smiling resurrection.

Dora sighed. Jack had become more of an enigma. The reluctance of the Lansworthy Mill Quakers to kill fellow Christians was understandable but who would have credited him with strong principles? The three women sat before the fire drinking tea from Kitty's best china.

"Anyone home?" called Jack's voice.

Mrs. McKenna and her daughter-in-law grinned at each other like children sharing a secret.

"Are you going to tell him, Kitty?" said the older woman.

"Shouldn't I wait till he's had his supper?"

"Lord, no! Tell him this instant."

So when Jack padded to the fireside in his socks he learned he was to be a father.

Watching husband and wife embrace, Dora felt a pang of jealousy.

DEAD LEAVES DRIFTED across their euphoria, and the dark, persistent rains of November brought with them rumours of another Allied offensive. "Wipers" Mr. Widdicombe called it. He took off his cap and the sweat gleamed on his bald head.

"I looked it up in the atlas. It's a town in Flanders. Apparently we're doing fine. Doing fine! That's a joke. Kitchener's pals pretended we didn't exist a few months ago. Now the lads are khaki heroes. Our betters have let us out of the slums and ghettos to fight their war. That's nice of them. But when it's over they'll make sure everything's back to normal."

"It's our country, too, Dad," said Kitty.

"Don't be bloody daft. We rent a few rooms and keep out of the way. It's their country."

"You and Dora never let up," she said.

"Dora's applied for a job down Chancellor's yard."

"Doing what?"

"Carting. They're short of men."

"Tidn proper," Kitty said, the colour rising in her face. "All them boys gawpin' at her."

"She'll cope."

"She'll enjoy it!"

Lansworthy lay in the silence of an autumn morning. Mist hid the bay and the wind slept. Another small fleet of Belgian fishing boats carrying Belgian refugees crept to the quayside at Mary's Haven, but the battle on foreign soil remained impossibly remote and romantic. The "bestial Hun" who "bayoneted babies" and "raped nuns" was tasting "British cold steel". Charlie Widdicombe crumpled the newspaper in his fists. Kitty was

323

hooking the bath up in the yard. No matter what happened, Widdicombe thought, trivia had the final say because terrible things always happened elsewhere to other people.

November proved a cruel month. Arthur Maddock and Moony were killed when their gun exploded on the firing range, and Rupert Chancellor and Charlie Wotton fell at Ypres.

"Died instantly," said Albert Wotton through his tears. "Didn feel a thing. Well, I suppose us should be grateful—poor lil tacker."

Sidney Chancellor visited the yard to console the carter and share the grief.

"They died doing their duty."

Jack ran the currycomb through Beth's mane, waiting for a chance to speak, but the old man turned abruptly and walked away.

"Mr. Chancellor," Jack called, but the tall figure squared its shoulders and was gone.

"He's seen through your brown-nosing," Luscombe said, and Jack grabbed him by the lapels of his greatcoat.

"Not another word, you tub of lard. Not a word—now or ever again. Understand?"

Luscombe choked and nodded.

"Fine. So you keep your mouth shut and get out on the streets or one of Dora Widdicombe's mates can have your job."

The "Three Towns" rang their bells for the dead soldiers. As if they care, Jack thought, ramming his fists into the trouser pockets of his best suit. A thrush sang from one of Grosvenor Road's plane trees. The melody washed over his recollection of Mrs. Endacott's wan face of ill health and grief. Moony was lying alone in the French soil, alone for ever. "For ever." He closed his eyes and clenched his teeth, but the bird continued its song.

MORE THAN EVER Jack was conscious of the dignity of horses. He would loose Beth from her gear and attend to her needs, reluctant to speak to anyone. At the end of the grooming after a hard round he found Palfrey waiting for him in the gangway.

"Ormond's keen to sell some of the animals to the army," said the horsemaster. "We've a surplus of horses and the army is crying out for them."

"And Beth will have to go?"

"Not necessarily. You know how the old man feels about her. We'll probably lose half the animals."

"That bastard Ormond."

"He's given a lot to the war effort—including a son. It's about time you started to think of something other than horseflesh."

"It's our war, not theirs. No one's asked the horses if they want to take the King's shilling."

"Do you think that when you work them? No one asks them if they enjoy hauling carts in the rain from dawn to dusk. Don't be bloody daft, boy. It's never that simple."

Jack brushed him aside, speechless with rage.

"You can't alter the way things are," Palfrey called after him.

With Christmas approaching the band was out again in Station Square; so were the flags, and girls from Helen Daubeny's set dispensing patriotism and cigarettes. The widows stayed at home as late that afternoon the train steamed into Lansworthy station full of soldiers who had once been merely brothers, husbands or sons. Among them were a handful of what the press called "our glorious wounded". The cheering was hushed when the badly injured were carried to the ambulances, but the noise swelled as the walking wounded emerged. The crowd sang "Tipperary" and saw off the setting sun with "Land of Hope and Glory".

"Edward Daubeny has a bandaged head," said Dora, standing on tiptoe.

"Officers get the best wounds," Mary McKenna smiled.

"He picked up a bit of shrapnel at the Front," said Old Bob.

"And Mike picked up a bit of shrapnel in his backside," Jack grinned. "Look, Mum," he added, "the lad will want to have a drink before he comes home for the hero treatment. Give him a kiss and go on back with Kitty. I'll try to keep him sober."

Michael's shuffling gait he put down to his buttock wound.

"How did you manage to cop one in the bum if you were pointing in the right direction?" Jack said, shouldering his brother's kitbag.

"Arse first. Old Gunner drill," he said with a look of smiling despair.

They shook hands. Michael's greatcoat smelled of stale cigarette smoke and trench mud. His cap was perched on the back of his head but he was a pasty-faced, hollow-cheeked stranger whose unsteady movements belonged to old age. "Why do they keep singin' and shoutin'?"

"They're glad to see you."

"Well, I'm not glad to see those dozy buggers," he said, in an impassioned outburst. Then he giggled. "Good old Jack, you always know what's best. You guessed from the very beginning it was just a dirty bloody trick didn't you?" He groaned and wiped his forehead. "Why don't the noisy idiots shut up! I shout at the guns but they never stop."

"It'll be quiet up the 'Globe'."

"Nothing happens in Flanders, except blokes get killed."

"You haven't," said Jack.

"Not yet. Give Jerry a chance and he'll soon put that straight."

"Mum would give you hell if you got killed."

The noise faded behind them and they had Palace Avenue to themselves. Michael laid a hand on his brother's arm. "All she cares about is you. So stay home—keep her happy."

He laughed and coughed and staggered like an uncertain child play-acting. On the corner of the avenue and Winner Street five or six young ladies had formed a half-circle to sing patriotic songs. Another of their group was waiting to hand a rose to anyone in uniform who passed. Christmas shoppers stood close by, applauding and cheering whenever she made a successful pounce. Jack glanced at his brother. The manic, fixed grin had turned his face into a Halloween mask, but he took the rose, and the crowd, which was growing by the minute, voiced its approval. The young ladies sang on, and reached the "God who made ye mighty" part of "Land of Hope and Glory".

"Sing up, tommy," laughed the girl with the flowers. "Sing up, sing up—it's your song."

"Bloody sing? Sing that rubbish?" Michael shouted. Savagely he plucked the red petals off the rose and scattered them at his feet. Most of the choir fell silent, sensing something unpleasant developing.

"You stupid cow. There's no glory. There's nothing." His chin jutted and his eyes were tightly shut. "There's just cold bloody awful nothing."

He dredged up a great sob and the rest of the choir faltered into silence.

"Give the rose a medal. Save this—this rubbish for the poor stupid bastards about to go out there."

His shoulders shook and the tears came in a gush. Then the young lady dropped her roses and recoiled, lifting her hands to her face.

"Bloody go," he sobbed, "you and your bloody lies. Go."

Jack wrapped an arm round Michael's shoulders and led him up Winner Street. Dusk was creeping over the far building, and the lights were on. Shop windows laid rectangles of light on the pavements.

"God! I wanted to come home. When I copped a Blighty wound I could hardly stop myself dancin' with joy. Now I'm here I wish I was back with the lads."

He shuddered and the church bells began to peal again. "Merry Christmas, Jack," he smiled, unlatching the pub door.

They took their drinks to a corner table, glad the bar was nearly empty. A whippet sprawled before the fire.

"As long as there's no 'Rule Britannia'," Michael said as he took off his cap.

The curls Jack remembered had been cropped to sweat-greased stubble which exaggerated the size and darkness of his eyes. He lifted the pint pot to his lips and gulped.

"Nectar of the gods after that foreign beer—God! What a bloody hole it is over there. D'you know what the war is, Jack? It's cold, wet, noisy fear. You crouch in your hole by the gun and they shell you. Then you give it back. Holes and sweat and cold and noise. But you can't run because you're too scared, paralysed."

"The papers speak of a stalemate," Jack said.

Michael paused, blinked. "Don't let them trick you into khaki. Stay home. The war will never end. The generals don't want it to because

326

they're mad. Now get us a double rum, there's a good chap. The stuff the battery gets is no more than coloured water. The CO is a teetotal bastard."

His left eyelid closed and twitched, and he giggled. Jack turned away, afraid to speak.

WINTER PROVIDED the stage props for pessimism—the carcass of a sheep hollowed out by foxes, withered leaves in the hedge bottom, water lying dead under ice. Yet the horses galloping over the fields were as alive as the stream gliding down the valley. Beth did not like the cold but a spell at Tor Barton with a minor eye infection meant the chance to kick her heels and run free of the shafts.

On the way home one evening Jack called at the "King Bill" for a pint. He found the Friday-night bar crowded. The lamps were lit and the curtains drawn but there was room at the fireside and he stood resting an elbow on the mantelpiece. Flames swarmed up the chimney and again Michael came to mind. The boy had loved fires. Their father would have been proud of his replica, the easy-going, beer-swilling soldier. Jack smiled and tilted his glass.

"Enjoy your ale," said a sharp female voice behind him. "While you are pouring it down your gullet my brother and thousands like him are doing their duty."

Jack set down his glass and turned to face her. Helen Daubeny's look of contempt was more theatrical than the expressions worn by her companions. The young ladies were wrapped up against the cold, for their mission meant a lot of walking and Lansworthy had a lot of pubs.

"Workers and fighters defending the shirkers," Helen continued. "Aren't you ashamed—or is the word unknown to cowards?"

Jack blushed, but he was trapped and the woman knew it.

"Why are you here," she said, "when you should be over there?"

The hand she withdrew from her muff held a white feather. Deftly she planted it in his buttonhole and some of the older men grunted their approval. Jack nodded, unable to react beyond a pretence of coolness.

When the women had departed he drank his beer without haste while the blood hammered at the base of his skull. His humiliation was indelibly printed on the evening. Men would talk about it for years.

The feather, he noticed, had come from a dove.

KITTY AND MARY MCKENNA were knitting for the men at the Front— mittens, waistcoats, scarves. The clicking needles brought them closer to Michael and his comrades. The crusade had frozen to a halt in the mud and squalor of trench warfare, but the newspapers continued to drum up enthusiasm at home. Letters from serving soldiers were printed in the *Lansworthy Observer*. Reading them Jack kept seeing Michael and his bitterness. He lay in the candlelight and kissed the blue-shadowed curve of his wife's belly, knowing a child was there.

328

As always the first intimations of spring and an inauspicious St. Patrick's Day. Then with March less than two weeks old, Michael was killed at Neuve Chapelle. The official letter coincided with the official first day of spring, an irony which Jack was alone in noticing.

Madam,
It is my painful duty to inform you that a report has this day been received from the War Office notifying the death of [Michael's serial number, rank, name, regiment and the date of his demise], and I am to express to you the sympathy and regret of the Army Council at your loss. The cause of death was [and a firm hand had written in the appropriate space] killed in action.

Mary McKenna's face said everything. She sat in the fireside chair, the rest of the world excluded by her grief. Kitty's company was enough. The women held hands, the one pregnant and close to having her child, the other barren and full of loss. Wisps of grey hair lay across her brow and she looked old and ill and defeated.

"Mother of God," she groaned. "Mother of God, help me."

Her grip on Kitty's hand tightened. Then she swallowed half a dozen times, like a scared dog.

"Help me. Help me. Help me." Tears gushed on a prolonged wail of grief. She was shivering although the room was uncomfortably warm. Clearly then Jack saw Michael coming through the door from work, the fog grey on his railway uniform.

"Oh Mike," Jack whispered. "Poor old lad." Never coming home. Never. Shrugging off his thoughts he smiled across the room at Kitty.

Dreamily she traced the curve of her pregnancy with a double set of fingertips and he was puzzled why the action should annoy him.

Day after day she continued the slow, downward sweep until the labour pains began and the baby was delivered.

Mary McKenna placed Jack's supper on the table.

"A boy," she said. "And I know what you'll call him."

"I'm going up to see Kit," said Jack.

"She's all right, son—strong as a horse. Eat your supper."

"No. Put it back in the oven. I want to see Kitty."

She nodded and smiled, on the brink of sarcasm.

"Don't say anything bad," Jack said.

His mother thought a moment behind closed eyes.

"Sean wants to join up," she murmured. "When you're a mother there's no winning this war."

"Please," Jack said, fixing her with his pale gaze.

Spring sunlight dappled the bedroom walls and ceiling, and the blackbird sang from the garden wall.

"It doesn't matter."

"What doesn't?" Kitty murmured.

"Nothing—except you and the baby."

"And we'll call him Michael?"

"You don't mind?"

She smiled from the pillow and shook her head. In her arms was something very small.

The next day Sean joined the Devons and left another space at the McKenna fireside. The new Michael did not fill the gap left by the other. A birth could not cancel out a grief or lend meaning to a death.

Sunday's curious enervation touched the "Three Towns". Jack watered and fed Beth and threw a rug over her back. Riding her through the deserted streets was like going backwards in time. They came off Roundham to Goodrington and galloped through the shallows. Her mane flowed loose and her hooves smashed into the small waves. She was alive in all her senses.

Returning along the shore she saw the sun blood-red on the horizon and the bay running at her. The gleam beneath her hooves was delightful and his weight on her back reassuring. Horse and rider were transformed to light by the light of the new day whose scent was sharp as a knife. Her nostrils flared. Waves no higher than spring grass broke and melted back into the bay. Jack was rubbing Beth down later, when old Mr. Chancellor entered the stall. Rupert's death had deepened the lines in his face.

"I thought you'd be here, McKenna. Some things never change."

"How are you keeping, sir?"

"Well enough. And you?"

"A bit under the weather. My brother Mike got killed in Flanders."

"Yes, I know. I'm sorry. So many brave boys have—have . . ."

Their eyes met across the silence of the unfinished remark. Beth tugged hay through the bars of her crib and champed a mouthful.

"Pity we're not like her," Chancellor said. "The world would be a splendid place if we were."

He leaned forward on his cane and watched the mare feed.

"I have given Old Bob his job back, hoping you will decide to enlist. What on earth's kept you out of uniform, McKenna? You're not like the Quakers up the road or the rest of the pacifists."

"I've got my reasons, sir."

"And you don't mind people thinking you're a shirker?"

Jack picked up some fresh straw and continued the wisping of Beth's flanks. "Folk can think what they like."

"It's everyone's fight, lad, and you owe it to your pals not to stand back and watch. We're talking about the highest form of duty."

"The highest form of duty, sir?"

"Defending your country and the Empire."

"My brother said it was a bloody great trick and a mess."

"It's a mess that someone has to clear up," Chancellor said, squaring his shoulders.

330

"Maybe they ought to put it to the soldiers on both sides. Ask them what they think."

"That wouldn't do at all, McKenna. There are areas of life best left in the hands of those who know the ropes—our betters."

"Then maybe they ought to fight it out among themselves, sir—general against general."

"An Irish solution," Chancellor said with the faintest of smiles, but his disapproval was obvious. Working away at Beth's legs Jack knew an episode of his life had come to an end.

"What about Beth, sir? Can I still buy her? I've got the cash."

Chancellor's brow furrowed. "We'll have to see. The war has altered things, McKenna. We must all pull together for King and country."

"She hasn't got a king or an empire."

"But I have and so have you," said Chancellor, his tone sharpening.

"Is that all that counts, sir—someone almost as invisible and distant as God, and the red bits on the map?"

"Get on with the grooming. Stick to what you understand and do as you're told, McKenna. In the end life is all about pulling your weight."

THE FILMS AT THE PICTURE HOUSE continued to fan the emotions of those stranded on the Home Front. *England's Call* produced spontaneous applause as the national heroes—Raleigh, Nelson and Wellington—stepped from their portraits to demand more recruits. *Britain Prepared* revealed Kitchener's army in training. But that autumn the British came to the River Somme and faced the German line from Hébuterne to Thiepval on the Ancre, and from Thiepval to the banks of the Somme.

At home the lovely quiet days left their mark on the Devon countryside. In the yard, Jack worked with the bristle brush, putting his weight behind each downward stroke and removing the dirt of the day's round from Beth's coat. The mud caked on her legs crumbled away under the currycomb. Then he picked out her hooves and washed and dried her feather, and combed her mane. Finally, after a brisk hand-massage, she was wiped down.

Every so often the roan swung her head to look at him in the lantern light ringed with shadows. She had drunk fresh water, and eaten oats and hay. Her bedding was clean. Everything was as it should be and he was the source of her contentment. He brought nothing but joy and kindness into her life. She was never put into a cold collar or carelessly hitched to a shaft. Whenever he came up the gangway at dawn her heart quickened and she snuffled a greeting and laid her muzzle eagerly in his hands.

"YOU'RE STILL WITH US, then, McKenna?" said old Mr. Chancellor.

Jack lowered the tea chest to the pavement and grinned. "But my young brother Sean is in France, mister."

331

"Good show. When are you joining him?"

"I'm not."

The old man turned crimson. His cane rattled on the cartwheel before it was pointed at Jack.

"I credited you with bags of pluck, McKenna, and thought you'd be good for the firm. Now I can see I was wrong."

"I give you a fair day's work, but I don't belong to Chancellor's. My life's my own."

"Lucky the lads at the Front don't think that way. Lucky for England there are enough Charlie Wottons and Ruperts to cover up for the laggards. Lucky we have ladies like Nurse Cavell who are prepared to die for their country."

Chancellor's outburst came to a breathless halt.

"What about your promise, mister?" Jack said. "I'm to get Beth before Christmas this year. You gave your word."

"My word?" Chancellor said harshly. "My one and only obligation is to my country. I am offering as much as I can give to the war effort. Even my son is joining up. So do not speak to me about that animal, or what went on between us in peacetime. Damn it all, man! Your own brother is pointing the finger at you."

The ice water shifted in Jack's guts but he would not be silenced.

"Then the army will get the horses?"

"Not all of them. Obviously with the petrol shortage we'll have to keep some."

"Will you keep Beth, sir?"

"I'm leaving it to Mr. Ormond. He's organising things for the Remount Commission. It really is a question of duty, McKenna. And if my horses can help bring a swift end to the war then the army shall have them, and Rupert won't have died in vain."

Listening to the old man Jack knew he would have to take Beth off somewhere to hide her. There were plenty of coombs on Dartmoor where they could live rough. They would travel the back lanes in the dark and he would get her to Ireland. Maybe her green pastures lay over the water in the land his mother had created from fireside stories.

The following day he was told his services would no longer be required from the end of the week. It was a cold, misty morning with rumours of the requisitioning flying round the yard.

"They'm taking folks' pets as well as draught animals, hacks and hunters," said Albert Wotton. "Any horse above fifteen and a half hands is on the list. Stan Mugford up the GWR stud reckons something's happening today at Newton Abbot. Exeter's already copped it."

"You know I've got the sack, Albert."

"Yes, boy, and I'm sorry."

Old Bob was also unhappy when he came into Beth's stall.

"Leave her, Jack," he said, lowering his glance. "Perce Hancock habn

332

showed up for work, so Tom wants 'ee to hitch Rosie and Zion to the heavy wagon and take some stuff to the big house in Harbertonford—a new kitchen range, a pianola and a couple of mangles; it's all on your sheet."

"Beth has to go to the farrier," said Jack.

"One of the boys can take care of her. You'd best get on your way. Tis a long trip, and Jack"—he cleared his throat with his eyes still on the ground—"you know how us feels about you having to leave. Move sharpish, son. Ormond will be buzzin' round the yard after breakfast and I doan suppose he's your favourite human being."

The Clydesdale and the shire-cross gelding were a good pair. They paced amiably out of the mist into the sunshine. Well, Jack thought, this is it. Soon he would be excluded from Beth's life, with the Remount Commission breathing down her neck, unless he acted quickly. On Saturday when he finished he would steal one of Palfrey's stable keys and come back for her around midnight. Then they would move across country to the moors. He had the Horse Fund, and once he was clear of the county he would be just another farm labourer travelling the road to market. He might even get work in Wales and send for Kitty before going to Ireland.

At Berry Pomeroy he met an old man and boy mounted on carthorses, and leading another four. Jack was stopped and asked for a light but could not oblige. The old man had a nervous shift of the eyes.

"Where you off to?" Jack said.

"Newton Abbot and the muster."

"What muster?"

"The Remount. They'm paying good prices for draught animals." Jack's heart sank as he watched the horses walk up the hill. More heavies passed, heading for the same destination. Most of them had the confident, rolling gait of creatures about to start a day's work.

The country road ran over high ground until it looped down to the South Hams village of Harbertonford. Jack braked and as the wagon began its long descent he suddenly realised why Old Bob had given him that particular job.

Chancellor's would be sending horses to the muster. Beth, Bathsheba and Solomon would be there now with the other registered animals on the first stage of their journey to France.

"God," he cried, throwing back his head. "God!"

The old horses started at the sound of his voice. He sifted through panic and anger, letting in all sorts of absurd hopes. Maybe Chancellor had relented. Maybe the war was over. Maybe Beth was out on a safe country round.

"Don't let it happen, God."

The road ran into nightmare now and cold, fluttering sickness curdled to despair.

THE BREAKUP OF THE STABLES began shortly after the morning parade. Instead of being hitched to cars or wagons, half the stud were led to the goods yard where the cattle trucks waited. Yet even the darkness and unsteady journey left them placid. Emerging at Newton Abbot, Beth walked between Solomon and Bathsheba to the muster in the market-place. Here several hundred horses had already been assembled—hunters, hacks and cobs as well as draught animals. They stood in a nervous mass while the soldiers strode among them checking their condition. Those which were accepted after the veterinary inspection were given the broad arrow brand on the quarter and had their tails docked and manes hogged.

Playfully Beth leaned forward to snip a button off the subaltern's tunic.

"The sorrel has spirit, anyway," he said.

"Gun team material," said his companion. "There's some Clydesdale in her but we can't be too fussy. She carries herself like a good un."

The young subaltern nodded sadly. "Too good for the mess out there."

"Chin up, old lad," said the captain. "The war will probably be over by the time these animals are ready for the Front."

"Do you believe that, Frank?"

"No, but if I keep saying it it may come true."

The remounts were herded down the street to the station and Beth and her companions were once again driven into a cattle truck. The door slammed and the animals stood anxiously wondering what was happening. Each of them expected to hear the special human voice that controlled their workday. Their senses were alert to catch familiar smells and sounds, but they were not dismayed by the darkness and the company of strangers.

The train moved off. Trucks clanked and jerked forward, throwing some of the horses off balance. The younger, more excitable animals whinnied until the peace of their elders silenced them. Sunlight fanned through the slats. Beth, Solomon and Bathsheba stood together, breathing each other's smell and drawing strength from their fellowship. It was just another night, however strange and unexpected; but it would end, then Jack would come whistling to open the door and splash water into Beth's trough.

THE STABLES WERE HALF EMPTY and the staff had gone home but Palfrey sat reading his newspaper in the tack room. Beth's stall was dark and silent, and Jack could think of nothing else as he loosed the horses from their gear and watered them. They were too tired to be groomed. Then he brought the lantern to Beth's stall and stood there making no effort to fight the misery. Palfrey's boots rang on the gangway.

"Old Bob did you a kindness, boy. Ormond came round just after you got on the road. If he had had his way you would have been told to walk Beth to the station yourself. Bob couldn hold back the tears when the animals were led into the trucks and the train pulled out."

"Where has she gone?" Jack said quietly.

Palfrey took the pipe from his mouth and tapped the stem on the side of his nose.

"The Artillery, more'n likely. She's not too bulky and is light enough for the eighteen pounders. They'll trim the feather off her fetlocks and stick her in a gun team. Failing that it'll be a watercart or general service wagon. In a few months' time she'll be over there."

"Beth, Bathsheba, Solomon, Janner, Tacker, Rook and Goosie," Jack whispered.

"And Major and Prince," Palfrey said. "They've half-stripped the railway's stud and the Co-op. Folk will just have to come and get most of the stuff themselves."

"It's like takin' children and setting them up for lunatics to shoot at."

Palfrey nodded and placed the pipe back between his teeth.

Jack sighed. "I love that horse and I swear she'll have her green pastures. I swear it."

"What green pastures, Jack?"

"Just something I promised her when she was a foal." His face darkened. He turned and set off along the gangway, but before he reached the stable doors he stopped and said, "They've sent my horse to the knacker's."

"Go home, Jack," Tom Palfrey urged gently, hating the emptiness of the stalls; hating, too, his own helplessness.

DRUGGED WITH MISERY and lack of sleep Kitty said, "I suppose you'll abandon us now." She blew into her cocoa.

"Abandon you?" he frowned, kicking off his boots and holding his feet to the blaze.

"You'll go after that horse—go and get killed. It's always been Beth, Beth, bloody Beth, above everything else."

The baby began to cry.

"You will go, won't you, Jack? Won't you? Damn you."

"Kitty."

"Don't go, darling. Please. Please. What would us do if anything happened to 'ee?"

She came across the hearth-rug on her knees and raised her face to him. Reaching out he stroked her hair.

"Promise me, Jack."

He shook his head and cupped her face in his hands. They've betrayed us like they've betrayed the horses, he thought. Don't you understand?

She went to bed and he raked the embers to keep the fire alive for morning, recalling his Irish West Coast ancestry.

> I preserve the fire as Christ preserves all.
> Brigid at each end of the house,
> Jesus in the centre.

The three angels
And the three apostles
Who are highest in the Kingdom of Grace,
Protect this house
And all in it, until dawn.

Chapter 13

"Sit in Michael's chair," said Mary McKenna, moving Dando. "I had a letter from Sean this morning. He's doing well."

Like it's a Boy Scout spree, Jack thought. But Michael's death had occurred in a far-off elsewhere so it lacked reality. He wondered then if his mother thought of the boy as just being away for good—an absentee time would never touch. Licking his lips and trying to swallow the misery, he imagined Beth in a strange place waiting for him to come and put things right. Dando thrust his muzzle into his hands and whined.

"Why aren't you at work?" Mary asked suddenly.

"I got the sack. Anyway, it's dead there now."

"And how do you intend to live and keep your family?"

"Chancellor's isn't the only stud round here."

"I'm surprised you didn't put two and two together about the muster."

"I thought Ormond would wait for the Commission to come to Lansworthy. Then he could make a big thing of parting with the horses. Palfrey didn't let on. He's got a heart. So has Old Bob."

"Kitty's right. You'll go now, just like your brothers. You won't rest till you're lying next to Michael."

"Don't cry," he said gently.

Her head rocked from side to side as the tears flowed. "Do you suppose Michael has flowers on his grave?"

"Of course," said Jack. "France is a Christian country."

He had to escape from the terrace, nagged by the memory of Beth galloping off Cider Mill Tor to greet him at the gate. The pain corkscrewed as he pushed the bicycle from the front door and pulled his cap down tight on his head.

"You idn goin' far, Jack?" Kitty cried.

"Just down the road. I've got something to do but I'll be home for supper."

"Wrap up warm, love; tez goin' to snow."

It would be Christmas in a couple of weeks but there was nothing festive about the year's end. The ache for Beth returned again. The dark browns, blacks and greys of the season had come together to create a landscape which was an extension of his grief. He pedalled aimlessly into it and from the high ground above Totnes saw the hills of Dartmoor dusted with the first snows of winter.

The road brought him to Hay Tor and he left his bicycle and crunched up through the snow to the rock. All about him he could feel winter preparing to launch itself on the lowlands. Greyness spread on all sides and he felt he had reached the centre of something. She is waiting for me, he thought. Despair gave way to elation. He knew he would go and find her and keep the promise he had made during the first summer of her life. He wanted Kitty and the baby and all the things the future might hold, but nothing could break the covenant.

THE HORSES WERE UNHAPPY in transit, and none more than the sensitive Clydesdales and Clydesdale crosses. Throughout the long, slow journey Bathsheba fretted, and most of the animals in the cattle trucks who came from happy homes were distressed; but they waited patiently for release.

It was late afternoon when the train arrived at the marshalling yard and the horses were driven out of the city to the Remount Depot. Beth, Bathsheba and Solomon, and a few of the other light draught animals that were trim enough to be ridden, were allotted to the Royal Field Artillery. Their good fortune persisted and they were kept together.

The Norman cathedral dominated what had once been the capital of Saxon England. The smell and feel of the place perplexed Beth and some of the horses round her, but she knew Jack would be there at the end to feed and groom her. No matter how strange the day it would close in comfort and friendship.

Rain fell and turned to sleet as the blackness became inky. The horses were brought into stables with a single line of open stalls. Here they were tethered to the bars which served as gates and allowed to cool down. Then they were watered, fed and groomed.

Again Beth's heart lifted. Men in khaki jodhpurs and puttees came whistling along the gangway, but he was not among them and her head drooped. The building was too clean. There were none of the pleasant, layered smells she had encountered in the yard or up at the farm. Left alone for the night the horses stood waiting for their surroundings to take the shape of home. Outside, the darkness was shaken by the wind and squalls of sleet. No trucks clanked, no owls cried and there was no Mullah to run barking after stray cats.

THE REST PERIOD PASSED, homesickness faded and the animals began to come to terms with their new life. They had good food and exercise and were well treated. The vet and farrier paid regular visits, and Beth lost her feather. Like the other horses she gave her best, all things made tolerable by the certainty of his coming. She galloped in the company of fine, intelligent hacks and a carriage mare called Grace.

Work was not hard. The light draught horses had to be broken to the saddle in preparation for pulling guns and ammunition limbers. They did not object to the weight of men on their backs and were in and out of the riding school in a fortnight. Beth and Bathsheba became the lead pair of a six-horse gun team, followed by Solomon and Grace and a couple of hacks called Chance and Liza. Each pair had its own driver who held two sets of crossed reins in his left hand and a short-handled whip in the other. Most of the men were as new to the business as the four-legged recruits, and there were some comical mishaps.

But training in snow or freezing rain left little time for cheerfulness. The open countryside with its clumps of Scots pines had a doleful air and while the wind blew across the plain the batteries wheeled and swung through their exercises. The teams galloped the eighteen pounders into position, learning to think and act as one.

The weeks passed, and each drill was practised and mastered. Then Beth's battery was moved closer to Winchester where, despite her allegiance to Jack, she began to respond to the kindness of her driver.

Stan Milburn was a middle-aged Geordie who had come to horses late in life, first as a Co-op coalman and now as an Artillery driver. Tall, ungainly and shortsighted he would stare at the red roan through his glasses and keep his voice low, recalling how he used to speak to his dog back in Durham. The smell of his pipe tobacco put Beth in mind of Palfrey and how things were before the world changed.

WHEN MORNING BROKE there was stormlight in the sky and the hills were white. The drivers led their pairs out for their exercise with the wind flattening to a whisper and sparrows massing at the grain-shed doors.

"Come on, my girls," Stan grunted.

The pole bar was supported on neck, hip and withers and the team pulled the gun back and forth over the meadow. Soon the horses were steaming but the drill continued. The ammunition in the light wagon called a limber was attached to the gun trail and hauled at speed to the emplacements on the range. Here the eighteen pounder was unhitched and brought into position while Beth and her companions were returned to the picket lines.

The barking of the quick-fire guns disturbed the horses but the majority had been broken to town work and did not kick up a fuss. Those that became unmanageable were discharged.

The lucky ones, Stan thought, feeding shells into the baskets which were stacked horizontally on the limbers. A whiff of cordite carried to the lines and the teams shifted nervously. Then the battery commander galloped up, shouting orders. Number Seven Battery was sent across the plain with all its guns, general service wagons and limbers, and the men dug fresh pits. The grey sky had separated into small, sun-flushed clouds. Loneliness rose from the landscape and Beth wondered why he did not come.

Being herd animals the horses felt secure in their own company although memories of past life would tug at them, especially after dark.

The drivers were moved by their trust and willingness to serve; indeed, the number of tough Artillery men who doted on the animals surprised many subalterns.

As the weeks passed a rapport developed between driver and pair and each member of the team. The gun drill had all the elements of ritual. Sometimes they worked to a lather and Bathsheba's body-smell mingled with Beth's in the steam of effort. Grace was unused to hauling for long periods but the exercise rapidly built up her stamina and if she flagged, the other horses slowed to accommodate her. So between the five mares and the gelding a bond was born; yet Jack remained behind Beth's thoughts.

One day a clear sharp morning dawned unlike any other. The men went about their stable chores chattering and laughing. There was an air of excitement which gripped the entire battery. Then they left the camp—teams, guns, general service wagons and carts, officers mounted on their own horses. Soon the road to Southampton rang to the crunch and grate of wheels and the jingle of harness. Gradually the noise died as the column vanished beneath the valley mist.

EDWARD DAUBENY CAME HOME on leave and to his parents' chagrin took Dora out to the theatre in Abbot's Quay and to local restaurants. Charlie Widdicombe also disapproved.

"Edward would like to meet you again, Jack," Dora said, holding Dando off her best coat. "On Sunday morning at Goodrington beach if you can manage it."

"What on earth have he and Jack in common?" Mary KcKenna asked derisively.

Dora shrugged. "Integrity, compassion."

"But the Daubeny boy is in uniform and an officer."

"They got on, Mrs. KcKenna," said Dora.

"Is he a Socialist?"

"Unfortunately no—just a nice human being."

Kitty giggled. "Dora's sweet on him."

"No, Kit—I'm in love with him. When he's away I can hardly breathe with the worrying."

They stared at her, too moved and surprised to speak.

"Old level-headed, votes-for-women Dora in love with an officer and a gentleman." She sighed and gazed up at the ceiling.

"Are you goin' to marry un?" Kitty said.

"Of course not. Apart from anything else he doesn't want me to join the ranks of widows."

"You sound as if you expect him to get killed."

"He expects to get killed. All his friends are dead."

"Oh this bloody awful war," Mary McKenna whispered. "So many good boys turned to corpses."

"But his sister gave Jack a white feather," said Kitty.

"She's an empty-headed little so-and-so." Dora smiled.

Rain fell, light and warm and good for the crops. On Sunday, Jack walked the beach which the ebbing tide had wrinkled. Melody and her foal ran before him, only to melt into greyness. His heart lurched.

"Jack? Jack McKenna?"

The collar of Daubeny's waterproof was turned up against the rain that beaded the peak of his service cap. He looked older than his twenty-one years and some of the day's greyness was in his face.

"Like a gasper? No? I smoke all the time now."

The cigarette was lit between cupped hands and Daubeny chuckled.

"God! It's good to be here by the sea knowing the bloody shells can't reach Lansworthy Bay."

They strolled together along the wavebreak.

"Listen, Jack, I hope you aren't contemplating taking the King's shilling." Daubeny flicked his cigarette into the water. He was tall, slow-moving and rather graceful, although he had the habit of hunching his shoulders. "It would be another victory for the asses at the top who are responsible for this mess. Stay home and the men in the trenches will love you for it. It's a rotten do over there. I suppose when the last poor sod cops the last Blighty wound they'll have to blow the whistle on the whole business. Every fresh volunteer prolongs it. God knows what conscription will do."

He lit another cigarette and inhaled—or disguised, perhaps, an indrawn sigh of despair.

"Me and Rupert thought it would be one great cavalry charge into glory. Most of the chaps had that notion. They were decent enough and bloody brave—officers and men. Then they were pitchforked into hell, all of them, and no one at home seems to know the score."

"Michael told me."

They had reached the low line of rocks which divided North Sands from South Sands. The rain stopped but the sky remained overcast and oystercatchers were prising open shells.

"I'm sorry about Bethlehem."

"Where will they have put her, Edward?"

"Probably the Field Artillery at Winchester. There are thousands of horses at the Front. God, man, you'd have a job finding her."

"But I will," Jack said softly.

"Is she so important?"

"She is."

"More important than your wife and child?"

"No. It's a different kind of caring. I can't let her down. If you saw a child drowning in the surf, you'd try to save it, wouldn't you?"

"I suppose so," Daubeny conceded, "although I can't raise any enthusiasm for heroics."

"If she's at Winchester I'll have her out and away with no heroics."

"Ah! I see," Daubeny chuckled. "Well, that's a perfectly sane scheme, McKenna. Where will you take her?"

"Ireland, I suppose. My mother says horses are understood in Kerry. Horse is a second language over there."

Daubeny began to laugh. He wrapped an arm round Jack's shoulders and the two of them staggered about howling helplessly, knowing the idea was doomed and idiotic but loving it all the same. Daubeny's hat came off and he groped for it on his knees, still laughing.

THE HOUR BEFORE DAWN was a threshold Jack had been unable to resist since childhood. He slid out of bed praying the baby would remain silent. Kitty was dead to the world, her face pressed in the pillow. He kissed her head and took in the fragrance of her hair. The darkness breathed. It was warm and comforting and hard to leave.

But the atmosphere at Number Eight had become tomblike. Too many women under one roof perhaps, Jack thought. Everything had revolved around the baby until Sean came back for good after being gassed. Mrs. McKenna tried to winkle him out of his shell but he would sit by the fire nodding mutely, unwilling or unable to speak about his experiences. When he drew breath he sounded like a sick sheep.

Jack lit a candle and opened the Horse Fund box. One banknote would be sufficient for his needs; the remainder would see the family all right for months. He placed the money on top of his letter on the kitchen table, and closed the front door gently behind him.

THE CARRIAGE WINDOW had steamed up. He rubbed a sleeve over the condensation and peered out. The countryside was still dark but dawn had broken and there was a high bank of cloud, grey, the colour of a herring gull's back. The conscripts opposite him slept, mouths gaping and heads resting on the nearest shoulder.

The train puffed through wetlands dotted here and there with pollard willow. Its progress was stealthy. Everything has come to an end, Jack thought. Tom Palfrey, Josephs, Ormond Chancellor, the boys, the carters, the horses—they were all gone now, and he had sneaked off into the night. France was the only place to go. Everyone he knew, living or dead, was on the other side of the Channel.

As he walked through Winchester, he stared out of his unhappiness at the cathedral. Pigeons burst silently from the tower and scattered behind the trees and rooftops. He hesitated at the barrack gates, and the guards and military policemen looked him up and down.

"Have you got any horses in there, mister?"

"A few," said the sergeant.

"Can I have a look at them?"

"Why? Ain't you seen one before?"

"I like horses."

The sergeant nodded and his companions smiled.

"When you're in uniform you'll get all the horses you want. Follow me, lad. The King can use experts like you. You are an expert, aren't you?" The irony amused his companions.

"I was assistant horsemaster at the stud back home."

"Comfortin' news," the sergeant observed, shepherding Jack through the gates into the camp. "Now you go in that 'ut and the nice officer will sort you out. Soon you'll have all the horses you want."

Jack felt curiously detached, like an onlooker at a mysterious event. He entered a room where half a dozen men in their thirties or early forties sat with a crowd of boys who were probably eighteen but could have passed for fifteen-year-olds.

After the interviews the medical proved something of a formality and everyone seemed elated when they took the King's shilling and the oath. They collected their kit and were marched to the billets to join the other new recruits. Jack had a bed between a west countryman who was surly and obsessively neat, and an amiable Scot. The hut was cold. He was wearing khaki trousers, puttees and a shirt that was too big. His hair was cropped and he was miserably homesick; and as he sat writing to Kitty he knew his last bridge was burning.

THE FERRY HAD BEEN CONVERTED to carry horses and mules which, because the journey was short, were stabled on deck. Beth led the team onto the ship and took her place in one of the pens that held four animals. The world tilted under her hooves but like her companions she stood relaxed, facing inwards and tethered to the breast rail. Immediately before embarkation all of them had been shod. Now they stood placidly, aware of the comings and goings of the men, and the gulls overhead.

The French coast appeared, the noise died and the deck no longer tilted. One by one the animals were walked off onto the quay. Without haste the column assembled and while men and horses waited to move to the train the clamour of church bells crept out of the distance.

The faintest suggestion of spring was on the air but it failed to lift the hearts of the Devon horses. Their confusion mounted to anxiety as the train staggered across the French countryside, stopping for long periods, and starting again, jerkily, with blasts of steam.

Then the railhead was reached and they were coaxed from the trucks into the remains of a fine afternoon. To the east guns could be heard loud enough to prick Bathsheba's ears. Beth and her companions were watered, fed and walked off along grey, cobbled streets. Half the army seemed to be pouring in and out of Albert, choking the thoroughfares which found their way to the marketplace. The last sunlight illumined the basilica of the church that had been hit by enemy artillery fire. A shell had toppled the gilded statue of the Virgin and Child from the tower, and it hung face downwards directly above the market, secured by wires as if the church were afraid the Madonna would take flight.

The column moved up the valley behind the front line to the rest camp behind the Brigade's wagon lines.

Resting drowsily in the twilight, Beth heard the curlews pass on their way to the marshy breeding sites beside the Somme.

Chapter 14

He was one step behind her although he never knew it. The conscripts had swelled the training camp to twice its normal size and acres of canvas covered the fields under the downs. Whenever he had the chance Jack searched the stables and horse lines, but the handful of roans he discovered lacked her refinement and the distinctive S-shaped scar. Once or twice his heart leaped only to sink again.

The west countryman, Sercombe, came from St. Austell and had the most difficult temperament Jack had encountered. Relaxed in a bar he was easy-going but under pressure he could be abrasive. Tall, lean Wattie Maxwell was a Galloway man, soft-spoken and perceptive, and just the wrong side of forty. "The most ineligible bachelor north of Hadrian's Wall," he grinned. "Maybe I'm lucky, though," he added, noticing the shadow on Jack's face. "There's only my mother to grieve for me."

Sitting by himself in the canteen Jack reread Kitty's letter.

My own dearest Jack, I cannot tell you how I cried after you went. You must know how I feel but they say conscription would have taken you anyway in the spring. So it's no use going on. God, I do miss you.

Me and Baby are so lonely and I worry all the time. But everyone here is thinking of you and Mr. Chancellor called to say "well done". He's a good old man, really. Everyone in the terrace sends their regards. Darling, *please* look after yourself and come back to me and Mike, but whatever happens may God protect you and bring you home safe and sound.

All my love and lots of sweet kisses, Kitty.

"Letters are a luxury," Maxwell said shortly before lights out.

"Don't you get any, Max?" said Jack.

A shake of the head, fingers raking back the gingerish hair and a smile appearing on the dark, moustached face.

"Mither canna read nor write—but God! she can yap."

Jack grinned. His eyelids descended and he thought of Beth sleeping in the straw under the same stars. Then he saw Kitty nursing the baby, and heard the church bells of the "Three Towns" lapping over his sisters' laughter. He dozed and let the ache for Kitty have its way.

ONE OF THE PROBLEMS was the conscripts' innocence. Very few had worked with horses and before long everyone in the battery recognised Jack's expertise. Some NCOs resented this but the majority drew on his knowledge and even the sergeant major knew where to go if a difficult horse failed to respond to training.

After the evening meal Jack would walk through the stables and say good night to the animals. One evening he was joined unexpectedly by the battery's second-in-command, a couple of subalterns and the sergeant major. They had come to inspect the conditions.

"McKenna," said Captain Berry. "I understand from the sergeant major that you've worked with draught horses all your life."

"Since I was a nipper, sir," Jack grinned.

"Stand up straight and take that wet grin off your face, lad," the sergeant major roared. "Don't grin unless you're told to."

"Sure, and isn't it daft? Grinning's not something you do to order."

"Stand still, you Irish clown, and answer the officer's questions."

Captain Berry coughed into his fist and his eyes twinkled. He was a pleasant young man, passionate about horses and the regiment. His Charlie Chaplin moustache and large, aquiline nose were like a novelty set a child could buy at a joke shop.

"Why did you join the Artillery and not the Cavalry, McKenna?" he said. "Can you only handle carthorses?"

"No, sir. We had carriage horses and crosses of all kinds. Some of our stud were good enough for any gun team. A lot of the light draught crossbreds are built like carriage animals and their temperaments are better."

"Did you think that by becoming a driver you'd have a cushy number?"

"It never entered my head, sir. They took my horse and I just came after her."

"Your horse?"

So Jack was compelled to explain.

"But surely a Clydesdale crossbred roan would end up pulling siege guns?" said Berry.

"She's hardly a carthorse, sir. She's small and elegant with a big S-shaped scar on her right flank. Hauling heavy stuff would break her."

"Does it ring a bell, Sergeant Major?" Berry asked.

"Roans aren't common, sir, but we're desperate enough to take anything these days. Can't say I've seen her, though. A horse is a horse and thousands have passed through this camp."

"Thousands," Jack whispered, shaking his head.

Once during the gun-team drills on the downs Jack's battery passed within a hundred yards of the Seventh. It was the only time that winter when he and Beth came close to each other.

Dull days passed. Snow powdered down but did not lie for long and the teams rattled through the flawed sunlight to the emplacements. Unwillingly Jack was warming to the power play of horse and man. The gallop to the gun pits left drivers and teams exhilarated, for what lay over the horizon had no substance. The wagon lines, horse lines, guns, shells, the limbers and the ammunition runs were parts of an exclusively male game that had been played since the beginning of history. The equipment changed but the rules rarely altered.

By the time spring arrived Jack McKenna was very good at it.

ALONG THE WHITE ROADS came the men of the Thirty-first Division, either up to the Front or back to the rest camps. They came singing through the sunshine and the peasants on the dung carts waved and shouted greetings. Always the infantry continued their march towards the high ground held by the Germans, although the front line was impossibly remote to the gunners and drivers who worked stripped to the waist. The fine weather held. Teeth flashed white in sunburnt faces and between the trenches wild flowers choked those strips of open ground called no-man's-land.

On an afternoon in late spring Corporal Jack McKenna stood under the basilica of Notre Dame des Brebières and gazed up at the leaning figure of the Virgin.

"When she falls," said Sergeant Turnbull, "the war will end."

"And who will win?" asked Maxwell.

"Us, of course. The padre says God's on our side." His broad Somerset accent rendered practically everything he uttered comical.

Jack and Maxwell grinned. Last night's French beer leaked from their pores and beaded their brows. They were glad the journey was nearly over, glad to stand in the shadows on the edge of all the noise and bustle. A rapt expression lit Maxwell's face. The boots of marching men crunched out their regular beat until the clatter of hooves filled the square. The friends turned and saw dozens of Percheron draught horses walking in pairs over the cobbles. Troops paused to watch the animals go by. The traffic came to a halt and no one spoke or moved until they were gone.

"Them good old boys," Sergeant Turnbull muttered.

The battery joined the constant stream of convoys travelling down the road to Hédauville.

THE FARM WAS A PLEASANT shambles at the end of a track a little to the south of the hamlet. It had been vacated by another battery whose field guns had been taken to emplacements less than a mile behind the Front. A shell had removed the chimney and one of the middens was in ruins but its position in a shallow coomb had saved it from total destruction.

Like everyone else at the Front, Jack knew the offensive was a matter of weeks away. The lorries grating their gears at night on the Hédauville road were reminders of the build-up that never ceased. But men and animals went about their business optimistically. The Big Push would end the war.

The throb and rumble of artillery opening up as night fell was like the voice of authority laying about German ears.

"I never saw so many guns," said Sergeant Turnbull. "Hundreds of them, and the whole countryside back there is thick with horses. When we give Fritz his iron rations he'll bugger off back to Germany with his tail between his legs."

"Aye, what's left of him," Maxwell grinned.

In the outlying orchards men were cleaning the guns and the thin reek of paraffin was on the air. A kestrel hovered above the vegetable gardens but did not fall.

"I didn't know there was hawks in France," said Maxwell. "I always thought the French had different birds to ours."

"Is Galloway like this, Max?" Jack said, heaving the harness over a fallen apple tree and checking it for wear.

"Lord no, man. Galloway's got muscle."

"Like Devon," Jack grinnned.

They worked for half an hour to the chirr and zither of insects. Then Maxwell asked him if he had looked over the horses in the battery up the road.

"Not a roan among them," came the reply.

"When were you there?" Maxwell said. The burnished leather caught the sunlight.

"The other morning after exercise."

"For Christ's sake! You'll get shot."

Jack smiled. "I just put a saddle on Lady and rode up the coomb like I was on army business. No one challenged me."

A boy called Maunder from the Devon village of Chagford had a harmonica. He sat crosslegged by the fire waiting for the tea to brew and gave them "Roses of Picardy".

Jack lay down in the grass thinking of Chancellor's yard, but when he dozed off he dreamed of Beth pulling the open carriage with his mother in white smiling from beneath her white parasol.

The next day the battery was moved forward a mile to the north of Beth's brigade, and the field guns were hauled to the battle zone close to the eighteen pounders of the Seventh. A period of frantic activity followed, with the limber teams racing along the military road to stockpile ammunition at the pits.

THE KESTREL QUARTERED the surface of the wheatfield that was green and shining. A German plane droned high above the British lines and waggled its wings. Instantly the antiaircraft guns opened up with horizontal jets of smoke. Small white cloudlets of exploding shells surrounded the Taube and it made a lazy turn to drone back towards Beaumont Hamel. Water dripped from Beth's muzzle and she raised her head from the trough to gaze at the sky. The other horses were also watchful.

346

For the past month the battery had occupied pits behind a knoll where the flash of discharge was invisible to enemy observers. The new wagon and horse lines were a few miles behind the emplacements on the edge of a wood. Every day the teams took up ammunition, provisions and mail for the gunners. Only occasionally were the limbers caught in one of the random strafes as the enemy guns probed the British positions. But the battery's good fortune held and there were no casualties.

After they had come under fire for the first time, Milburn patted Beth's neck and knew in that awful moment that both he and the mare had strayed to the frontiers of something dark and immensely evil. The minister of his Baptist chapel back home would have called it "the inferno".

Yet the sunlight was benign. It glinted on the convoys which continued hurrying war materials up to the Front. Rain had fallen and the roads were grey and wet, but the poppies in the cornfields glistened.

Beth rounded her nostrils to read the scents lifting off the farmland, listening for his voice among the babble of other noises. Packing down tobacco in his pipe Milburn wondered why the sorrel was forever staring out of a daydream.

"She's an odd creature," he remarked to his sergeant. "I swear she's waiting for someone."

"No horse is the same," the sergeant said. "Some like work, others don't. Some are bright, others dopey."

"That mare is a gem," Milburn said. "I wish to God she was somewhere else. All this is, well—shameful, bad. The horses get really scared, Sarge."

"It ain't my fault, mate. None of this is my fault or yours or anyone's except Kaiser Bill. He's sent more than one of my mates west."

"The Big Push will do it. End all this."

"Yes, Jerry won't know what's hit him. It can't fail this time. We've enough guns to blow Germany off the map."

The limber runs kept Milburn from brooding during the third week of June 1916. Riding Beth through the warm nights left him breathless with excitement. Beth and Bathsheba were an accomplished lead pair that could have made the trip blindfolded. Leaving the wood, the road ran east towards the battle zone, crossing an exposed countryside of fields and isolated farms. Eventually the emplacements, which had been dug in the slopes, were reached and the shells unloaded.

Providing the enemy guns were quiet Beth enjoyed the canter back to the picket lines. Then they were unharnessed and left to cool off before the grooming. Behind them the wood rustled, the ghost moths danced and once in the hush after gunfire a nightingale sang from the depths of the wood.

JACK SAT OUTSIDE the dugout watching the moon's halo dilate and thin. He was tired. Drugged with summer scents he let Beth into his thoughts. He and Kitty were on her back, riding her down a lane buried under hawthorn blossom. The baby was laughing in Kitty's arms, birds were singing and the bells gave the "Three Towns" their Sabbath charm.

They rode towards the sea but never reached the shore. The lane went on for ever under the chorus of songbirds, winding through sun-speckled shadows into a calmness nothing could shatter.

Chapter 15

South of Redan Ridge the British front line was being shelled. The horses shook their heads while the drivers held them and the ammunition was unloaded. Highly strung Grace cast about in her traces, deaf to the words breathed by the man clutching her bridle. When the work was done the team came back down the road at the gallop, sniffing something more than tension on the night wind, and voicing their alarm as other horses passed hauling full limbers. Then the bombardment began.

Every gun the British and French had brought to the Somme opened up, and Beth and her companions froze. They were caught beneath an immense dome of noise that set Bathsheba and Grace bucking. Up they jerked on their hind legs with Milburn and the other drivers fighting to hold them. Instinctively the men ducked as hundreds of high-explosive shells poured overhead in a torrent to rip into the German defences.

The shriek of the shells filled the night like the sound of express trains travelling at unimaginable speeds. Westward the sky was torn by the white flash of siege guns. The night boomed, cracked and seemed to gallop after the horses who were running wildly now. A chain of thuds shook the ground close at hand. Limber horses that were out of control passed in an eye-rolling mass, but Beth pounded on.

The enemy was retaliating. Five-nines came over with the deep awful drone men and animals dreaded. Towers of fire rose in the fields, scattering shell splinters. Earth lifted and pattered down as the team slithered through the liquid excrement left by other horses.

The horizon behind them was ablaze and cobbled with noise. Flinging a glance over her shoulder Beth's fear became almost ungovernable. The feeling had gone out of her knees and her legs did not belong to her. She moved automatically, half aware of animals calling above the crash of exploding shells. A team had been hit. Horses lay kicking and writhing. Milburn shut his eyes on the horror. Shells opened the road before him and he slowed his team to negotiate the wreckage of limbers, men and animals. The air was rank with the intensity of animal suffering.

"Keep them moving," the subaltern cried.

Earth splattered Beth's face. Bathsheba flung herself to the side but was held. The air smelled of scorched horsehair and metal. Beth forced herself on, and the limber immediately ahead became a red blur, disintegrating in a hiatus of blinding white light. Human and animal debris rose, fanned out and scattered on a roar, and Milburn's team was pulling hard to avoid the crater. As they gained the shelter of the woods the barrage lifted and the sky was left to the rush and drone of British shells. A gentle breeze ghosted across the landscape from Serre, driving the smoke and fumes towards the picket lines.

Other horses were being hitched to the limbers. The sergeant yelled instructions, ignoring the returning teams. Beth was in a lather and Bathsheba on the point of collapse. Legs buckling she stood and slobbered, her whole body racked by spasms of terror. Milburn slid to the ground.

"There, girl, there," he gasped. "Bide still, don't fret."

His words struck him as absurd. Don't fret! For God's sake, why shouldn't she fret?

"Load up," the sergeant said. "Come on, Milburn, you're slower than the second coming of Christ."

Milburn groaned.

"Get them bonebags to the ammo dump sharpish, lad."

Sweat trickled into Milburn's eyes. The din crescendoed and pressed down on him. Grace and Solomon were out of control, dancing broadside and threatening to overturn the limber.

And so it continued, the loading, the runs to the gun pits and the return journey beneath the invisible arcs of shells. The bombardment showed no sign of abating but before dawn the guns of the Seventh Battery were taken to fresh emplacements with a view of the enemy trenches. Right down the Ancre valley the telltale orange spurts betrayed field-gun positions. Beth gazed across at the great firework display of howitzer shells exploding. Her ears drooped and her head was bowed. Why hadn't he come to ride her out of the agony? Glimmers of the new day were behind the explosions. Milburn's team made their return to the lines and collected another load. Before the gun pits were reached the sun was rising from mist into the promise of a fine morning.

LEADING HIS TEAM BACK to the pickets Jack deliberately let his mind go slack. The memories could not be held at bay. The poplars wavered in the heat haze and ignoring the gunfire, swallows hawked the air. A chill gripped his heart. Where was Beth? How could he find her? Maybe he would just get up one night and go from battery to battery, pretending he was a runner. But in the dark there was no chance. Back home, a dawn of sleeping rooftops would be printed on the mist, and cattle would be ambling out of Clennon Valley to the milking sheds of Tor Barton.

During the brew-up he had a chance to read Kitty's last letter again:

My own dearest Jack, I enclose a photograph of little Mike. God bless him. He's the spitting image of you, and your mum thinks the world of him. I hope you are in the pink as we all are except Lily who is chesty again. All the neighbours send their regards, and the tradesmen up Winner Street. Sad to say Mrs. Endacott passed away last week and the Prowses in Number Two lost their eldest boy over where you are. Have you found Beth? Your mum says tis only a matter of time. Listen, idn you due any leave? Come home, Jack, please, as soon as you can. All my love and kisses, Kitty.

The baby stared solemnly out of the sepia-tinted photograph, and Jack grinned. He eased himself off the empty limber and something small lying in the grass caught his eye. He knelt and cupped his hands round a lark. It had been killed by the concussion of an exploding shell, but was still warm.

Maxwell appeared at his side. "A wee lark," he whispered, reading his friend's thoughts. "That's sad."

But it was all sad, Jack reflected—the exhausted and terrified horses, the men light-headed and hallucinating from lack of sleep, and what they were doing to the foe. The Germans occupied a great Babylon of entrenchments and fortress villages just "over the way". Tons of shells had rained on them throughout the night. Listening to the field guns barking he considered the plight of the men dug into the ridge; and still the high-explosive and shrapnel shells descended.

Up by the gun pits he saw the barrage striking home. Black smoke from the heavies was mixing with the whitish-grey puffs of detonating shrapnel shells. Here and there the cloud had a yellowish tinge. Giant flames lofted, dimmed and vanished. An aeroplane caught the sunlight on its fuselage. Maxwell began unloading and stacking the shells. The stink of cordite enveloped the teams but Jack held the horses and spoke to them.

ON THE THIRD DAY the weather broke and became showery and cool. But the bombardment lost none of its ferocity and the limber teams were constantly employed. Heavy rain on June 27 and 28 covered the road in mud and half flooded the craters. Soon hooves and wheels had created difficult tracks each side of it where teams could become bogged down.

The Friday night before the offensive saw the roads leading to the Front congested as the battalions left the rest billets and moved up. Throughout the half-dozen hours of darkness the guns punched away at the German positions, and the German trenches disappeared under a pall of smoke. The ground shook and the horses were trembling and fighting their ropes.

One explosion dwarfed all others. The huge mine planted under Hawthorn Redoubt in front of Beaumont Hamel, on the breast of the hill overlooking the British trenches, was detonated at twenty past seven. The column of earth, smoke and shattered bodies was massive. Ten minutes later, at Zero, the bombardment lifted and in the lull before the guns extended their range, Beth and her companions could hear the wood whispering, and birdsong gusting off the fields. What they did not hear were the whistles shrilling all along the British forward trenches where men were swarming up ladders to pace across no-man's-land. Nor did the horses cropping in the grass hear the chatter of German machine guns and the cries of the British soldiers being slaughtered on the slopes of Redan Ridge.

Before noon the grass between the wire entanglements was choked with the dead and dying, and the Thirty-first Division had been cut to ribbons. Serre had been taken and lost again, and things were much as they had been except for the British casualties.

Rain fell and the mud on the road to the gun pits and beside it was churned to a morass. The horses squelched unsteadily through the darkness; darkness without end. The whine of shells became the screams of men and animals but Beth could not voice her despair. She slithered and kicked and fought the mud over the last two or three hundred yards to the gun pits.

Orange flames leaped and fell in a line across the night where the eighteen pounders were directing their fire over the rising ground at the German trenches. No-man's-land was lit by star shells that trembled around the flash and glow of exploding sixty-pound bombs. From dilated pupils the horses regarded the spectacle. Then the limbers were empty and the teams running again.

WHEN HIS BATTERY was mauled by the enemy Jack's stamina and skill were stretched to the limit. He and three other NCOs were mending wheels and harnesses or helping the veterinary section recover injured animals from the road. They saw horses they knew and loved having wounds dressed before the ambulance journey back to the field stations.

"Jerry abandons his," the veterinary sergeant said as they eased a bay gelding into the cart. "He don't shoot 'em or try to heal them. He just gives them the elbow." He grimaced and hung the green label on the horse's halter. "Green for surgical," he explained. "White for medical, red for contagious diseases."

"Then back to this," said Jack.

The sergeant shrugged. "It stops another animal being sent out from Blighty."

Misery shifted in the bay's eyes.

"They know," Jack whispered. "They bloody know and they can't tell us."

"Would it make it any better if they could?" said the sergeant.

"It would make it harder to use them."

Recollection of the Chancellor shires rolling in the snow tore at his heart. Great, glossy children kicking up the snow, calling to each other and arching their necks under the smoke of their body heat. Great, happy children. A shell descended and the fountain of earth rose, hung for a moment and fell apart. Fumes gusted across the road and the sergeant coughed and drew the corner of his turned-up collar over his mouth.

351

"Walk on," the driver said, and the two carthorses who were tandem-hitched to the ambulance strode away.

Twilight closed on the fields. Screened by trees to the west of the Front the British heavies opened up. Then a column of limbers came along the road at speed. Jack stepped aside and sat on an overturned watercart. The first team thundered past, the horses bounding through the mud. The right lead animal was familiar. Its face was white and despite the mud the marbling on its flanks and haunches was rich enough to catch the eye. Jack's skin prickled. The horse was surging on, filling the air with spray that stank.

"Beth," he cried. "Beth!"

She swung her head and tried to dig in her feet and stop. But Milburn's whip smacked her neck and obedience won. Her stride faltered only to lengthen again.

"Beth!" Jack began to run.

"McKenna," the sergeant barked. "Stand still, man, stand still."

The mud sucked at his legs and brought him to a halt.

"Beth," he groaned.

The lead driver of the next limber team was roaring at him to get out of the way. Then something hard and heavy struck Jack's shoulder and spun him off the road.

"Talk about the bog Irish!" the sergeant grunted, dragging him out of the shell hole. "Where were you going, you horrible little Irishman?"

"It was my horse," Jack gasped. "My bloody horse. My Beth."

The sergeant stared at him.

"A red roan mare. Bethlehem. I helped bring her into the world. She's my horse."

"No lad," the sergeant said. "She's the King's horse. There's nothing you can do about it. Best forget her—if it was her."

Jack wiped his mouth on his sleeve and spat mud. His puttees had uncoiled and were hanging over his boots.

"We don't own anything out here, lad—least of all ourselves."

"She's mine," Jack whispered. "I made her a promise."

"I made my old lady a promise at the altar but it don't mean a lot now."

"She's mine," Jack repeated. There was a manic certainty in his voice.

BEHIND THE WAGON LINES were the mass graves where they had buried the men who had died at the field hospital.

The wheels spun in the mud as the lorry slewed sideways round a shell hole and struggled to regain the road. It was one of many carrying the battery out of action to refit and rest behind the wagon lines. The horses were also brought to safe fields.

The great adventure, Maxwell decided, had turned sour. In the back of the lorry he and Jack swapped glances. Each side of the road were men of the pioneer battalions up to their ankles in mud waiting to continue with the repairs. Like creatures released on parole from the abattoir, Jack thought. And I'm no different than the worst of them. I'm trapped in the mess and Beth's back there with nowhere to hide and nothing to cling to. If I had any guts I'd go and find her. But he was drained and could hardly lift a cigarette to his lips. At that moment all he wanted to do was sleep; sleep and go home.

Everything swept away like a childhood summer—Melody, Beth, Iona, the long grass curling on Cider Mill Tor, laughter as evening closed round the yard. Why had it gone? What had happened to all the warmth and happiness and hope? Each of the lives in the back of the lorry was a small, anonymous stream that had run to this place.

He let the smoke drift from his nostrils as he pulled on the cigarette. They were entering a village. The lorry stopped and the sergeant major began bellowing into a megaphone.

"Don't you lot even dream of mixing with the infantry. Behave yourselves and report to me at 0-seven hundred hours tomorrow for fatigues. *Comprée?*"

The village was one long broad street with houses on each side and no pavements. Sitting in the sun, Jack thought of other Augusts and harvests brought home from fields above the bay. But time was meaningless. He heard Maxwell laugh and saw the group of drivers round the farrier's fire. Sercombe raised his voice and gesticulated. The horses were being watered before the shoeing. Captain Berry and another officer strolled along the line chatting with the men.

The high-explosive shells which the soldiers called coal boxes rushed out of the afternoon's calm, followed by three enormous explosions. Mud and scraps of flesh showered down on a tide of fumes. The ringing in Jack's ears gradually faded and the screaming and snorting and moans spread with the smoke. Upwards of fifty animals and nearly that number of men were dead. A subaltern walked among the maimed and mortally wounded pointing his Webley at a head which might have been horse or human.

It was all so horribly casual, an incident scribbled on the fabric of the summer day like obscene graffiti. Jack got up and walked away trying to fight nausea. Maxwell and Sercombe were gone. Nothing remained as proof of their previous existence. They were the emptiness at the centre of a smoking hole.

The boy from Chagford came out of what had once been a walled garden, followed by half a dozen drivers in shirtsleeves and braces.

"Don't go over there," Jack said. "Don't. That's an order."

"Who bought it, Corp?"

"The bloody lot—Max, Sercombe, Berry, all of them."

He lit a cigarette, astonished at the steadiness of his hands. Down the road laboured the returning teams, and muffled thunder rolled across the Front. Beyond the wagon lines peasants were cutting the corn.

353

MORE RAIN AND COOL WEATHER hastened the end of summer. Now the hoof prints at the lines were silvered with the webs of money spiders and dew persisted, often till noon. Bathsheba's cough had worsened but she gave of her best on the limber runs, requiring no more than the company of Beth and Solomon.

They were picketed badly in a marshy hollow and sleep did not come easily despite hours of gut-wrenching toil fuelled by nervous energy. Their rugs were wet and heavy and fear was never absent. Another offensive had begun and the field guns were rarely silent. The British front line had been pushed forward although the situation north of Beaumont Hamel had altered little since the beginning of July.

During the first week of September the battery's gun emplacements were again changed and the teams sweated on the runs over open ground. While the guns were being unhitched and rolled into position they came under fire from howitzers and four-twos. The barrage lasted nearly a minute and was intense. Three guns caught between the emplacements were destroyed with great loss of life. Then the pits were strafed and two more guns put out of action by explosions which left a tangle of dying men and animals.

Beth's team took shelter in the furthest pit where the drivers held the horses' heads and tried to soothe them. Gouts of chalk spurted out of the shell smoke, and behind the crash of each detonation there was the keening of animals so badly wounded that the men going to their aid wept.

The pole bar off a limber whirled over the pits, followed by shell splinters. The driver next to Milburn was struck in the neck. "God," he grunted as he died, and it was a cry of disgust, not a plea. Milburn loosened the hands clenched on the reins but Solomon and Grace would have panicked if the sergeant major had not leaped into the pit. Then the surviving eighteen pounder opened up a counterstrafe and the heavies came to its assistance.

"Think you can get these poor devils back to the lines, Milburn? We need ammo and the wounded need help."

Beth fixed her eyes on Bathsheba and saw a reflection of her own terror. The mares were lathered all over in sweat, unable to move. Milburn walked them slowly, for the fear had not left them. Twice they made way for horse-drawn ambulances. Bathsheba's body sagged and her wheezing breath distressed her companions and worried Milburn.

The fields glistened and the horses seemed to draw strength from the calm that rose off the landscape. Southward the land rolled into the Ancre valley and the intense melancholy of dusk held the horses spellbound.

Once more rain filled the gaps between bombardments, giving the landscape a bloom of cold beauty. The horses waited to be fed. Walking the lines their drivers tried to comfort them. As moonlight fanned across the fields Beth continued to search the distances for Jack, unwilling to part with the dream of what had been.

354

WHAT WAS GOING ON at the Front did not concern Jack. He would lift a grubby face, sniff the wind and listen to the horses puffing into their nosebags. He cared about Maxwell's death but his eyes stayed dry.

During mid-September the fighting was hampered by bad weather and the limber teams struggled slowly along the flooded roads to the pits. Returning from one such trip Milburn learned his battery was to be amalgamated with another whose losses had been similar. Around noon limbers, wagons and animals came briskly out of the rainy gloom. The horses were tethered and all the men save one sought the shelter of the dugouts.

Milburn was at the lines making sure his team did not trample their hay, and he regarded the approaching stranger curiously. The man looked at each horse in turn until he reached Beth. The recognition was instant. The roan's head jerked up, her eyes widened and she loosed a whinny of joy.

"Oh Beth," Jack whispered, the tears streaming down his face. Her soul stared out at him and he placed his hands on her head. "Bethlehem, my beauty."

The heavy lashes descended and she took a step forward to lay her muzzle on his shoulder. His arms encircled her neck and they stood together. For a long while she gathered his smell and the love that came from his touch and the sound of his voice.

Bathsheba and Solomon whickered their eagerness to share the reunion but Jack and Beth were lost to the world. He had come to her in the place that was not home. Now everything would be fine. Now he would ride her out of the darkness and misery back to the warm stall and the hilltop above the sea.

"What have they done to you, girl?" He pulled off the sodden rug. Her mane was no more than a crest of muddy tufts. Jack's heart swelled. Between him and the animal, elements of the past they had shared swelled to clarity. She was breaking free of the sluice at Aish again—a small leggy creature quivering as they took to the floodwater. The wet coldness flowed over his body but she was safe there in the summer the war could not reach.

Suddenly the sorrow was too painful to endure and he began to dredge up great sobs, tapping his forehead gently against Beth's muzzle. In her warmth and gentle breathing was a force he had imagined was inextinguishable. He clenched his teeth, swallowed, and the sobbing stopped. It was a moment of agony mingled with relief.

He wanted her to be safe and away from it all. The war had left him famished for things he had taken for granted. To walk through Clennon Valley in the spring would be a kind of resurrection. The good times were waiting for them on the hill above the sea, facing the sunrise. Mother of God, he prayed, let me take her home.

Beth watched him carefully. She was happy and her movements had

355

a new alertness. Beyond his voice and touch she could see the familiar places. But the mare's beauty had gone, leaving her thin and dirty. Only her eyes retained some of the splendour that she had brought with her from her birth.

Chapter 16

Autumn sunlight twinkled on beaks and berries, and small birds rocked the hogweed in a noisy flock before flitting over the women to vanish behind the copse. The sunlight smelled of woodsmoke. Blanche and Lily ran ahead, stopping to pick the best button mushrooms. Kitty walked a little apart from the group, hands behind her back and Dando at her side.

The mushroom was cold in Mary McKenna's fist. On a gush of emotion she recalled other autumn expeditions to the fields and Jack's laughter, and the way he brought her things as if God had just made them: ripe blackberries; a handful of hazelnuts; a chaffinch's tail feather.

"Them bloody conchies," Kitty said suddenly. "They ought to shoot the lot, or force 'em to walk in front of our boys when they go at the Germans. Tidn fair."

"Jack's all right, darling," said her mother-in-law. "Jack always comes home. I bet him and the other lads are kickin' up hell with the old Hun."

Kitty nodded. The wind lifting off the bay swept her hair across her face, and struggling to push it back under her hat she remembered how he would part the tresses to kiss her. Life had become a strange routine of walks, conversations by the fire, and sick anticipation of the knock and the telegram. It was easy to believe the whole of Lansworthy had a son or brother or father at the Front. Newspaper victories were celebrated in bold headlines: "Great Day on the Somme" and "British Advances Shatter the Hun". The khaki heroes were surging forward to scourge the enemy with bare steel. Haig's crusaders were winning, so all the heroism and sacrifice was reaping its reward.

Yet the hospital trains and ambulances bringing home the wounded shocked even staunch patriots like Sidney Chancellor and the Daubenys. The front page of the *Lansworthy Observer* was one great casualty list, decorated with photographs of the dead. All over town were bereaved mothers, and young wives aged by the loss of a man who had seen fewer summers than there are hours in a day. The grey of the sky and the grey sea subdued the "Three Towns". Greyness seemed to have risen like a fog as if the war required it. But up on Cider Mill Tor the owls still called and the hares waited with the horses for the stars to appear.

DUCK PASSED HIGH and silent across the sunset behind the battle zone. All along the picket lines the drivers were rubbing down their animals and grumbling about the rain which had fallen for days. The clear evening amplified the thunder of gunfire, and the telltale glow quaked on the horizon.

Beth's ears pricked but she was content under Jack's hands. All the warmth of the past enfolded her and she stood placidly while he wiped down her flanks. Milburn shook his head and wiped the mist off his glasses. Jack's story had rekindled his belief. He was happy to take over Grace and Solomon and leave the mare to the young Irishman.

The village was occupied by artillery and infantry personnel, but there was no shelter for the horses. They stood at the lines, which were spread on ground that held water, and this disturbed Jack. He recalled the quagmire on Lansworthy Green if it rained during the Regatta Fair. So he approached the subaltern in charge of his section and suggested they set up two more lines which the horses could use alternately. This would alleviate the discomfort of standing in deep mud night after night.

Bathsheba had a cold and was isolated at the end of the line, but Jack and Milburn kept it to themselves for fear she would be slaughtered or sold to the local peasants. The RSPCA hospital was full, the rumours claimed, although their ambulances were still busy.

Bathsheba's case was not unique. All the animals at the picket lines were in bad shape. The cool nights, shortage of fodder, and the continual drain on their nervous systems made them lose weight and the will to do anything other than brood. Jack knew it was important to keep up their body temperature and produce the energy a workday demanded. They needed hay to replace the salt they had sweated out, but hay was difficult to acquire. When a third of what was asked for arrived it was yellow and limp and had neither sweetness nor fragrance. Black English oats, split beans, a little linseed cake, sliced carrot and some wheat straw as chafe reached the pickets in small quantities. When bran was available Jack made a mash to build up Beth, and he fed oatmeal gruel to Bathsheba. His presence at the lines impressed his superiors and cheered up his men.

Coming out of action for a rest and refit gave the drivers a chance to scrounge extra fodder for the animals, but there was little to be had. Yet more draught and carriage horses poured in from the Remount Centre. They passed through the village, heads erect and coats all rain-glossed. The infantry coming up from base were also well-groomed.

The general service wagons, omnibuses and carts left deep ruts in the muddy streets which quickly filled with water. Then the rain passed leaving the day showery.

The oil lamp and open iron stove smoked into the *estaminet*. Madame beamed through the fug and collected the money for a refill. She returned to the table holding a jug of thin unpalatable beer in both hands, but Jack waved her on. He sat in the corner trying to rough out a letter to Kitty, when the door opened and an officer entered with his trench coat slung over an arm.

"Don't stand," he said. "Is that beer? God! I've got a thirst on."

357

The voice was enough. Before his eyes lifted from the letter Jack knew it was Edward Daubeny crossing to the stove, the three pips glinting on his shoulder. A lump came to Jack's throat. He got to his feet and, stepping back to let Madame through with her jug, Daubeny caught sight of him.

His handshake was firm. For Daubeny the war, like life, was a question of reaffirming priorities, so it was easy to ignore the subalterns' glances.

"Captain Daubeny," Jack grinned.

"*Acting* Captain, Corporal McKenna, if you please," he said with a sardonic smile.

"Will you join me in a drink, sir?"

"Are you buying?"

"Why not? Doo beers, Madame, sil voo play."

"That's pretty good French."

"All the lads can speak a bit of the Froggy lingo."

Daubeny accepted one of Jack's cigarettes and said, "*Et deux cognacs aussi, Madame.*"

It transpired that his presence was no coincidence. Dora had given him Jack's serial number, battery and brigade. To get a transfer was simple, considering the "wastage" of officers in the regiment. "Wastage" was Daubeny's expression. It was the official term to denote numbers of animals killed in action.

"But why my battery?" Jack said.

"You are minus a second-in-command I believe."

Daubeny tried to blow a smoke ring and failed. His moustache was quite bushy and lent a solemn note to his countenance.

"Also, Dora wants me to make sure you don't do anything daft. Remember our conversation on Goodrington Beach? I was more than a bit dingo then, coming home like that straight out of action. Well, don't try anything dodgy out here or they'll shoot you as a deserter. Have you found Beth?"

"Yes."

"And you plan to walk off with her? Just walk on and on to, say, Brittany and get a boat to Ireland?"

"Something like that."

"Forget it. It's too fantastic for words. They'd catch you and shoot you for certain. Then they'd send her back to the Front—with no one to care whether she lives or dies."

"They can try."

"Listen, Corporal, the woods round here are full of deserters who aren't going anywhere. You might crouch in a covert till the war's over but what about Beth? Stay put—there's a good chap. Keep an eye on her. After all, you know the ropes. You're her one real chance."

They threw back the cognacs and sipped the beer.

"God!" Daubeny said, wrinkling his nose and shuddering, "I'd forgotten how bad this is. You'll pull in your horns, then?" he pressed again.

Jack nodded.

"Good show! Now, where is this blessed roan?"

"Under cover for the first time in months. Up the road at the farm. Beth, Bathsheba and Solomon."

"God Almighty! You're a magician, Corporal."

"Will you have another cognac, sir? Those subalterns are giving us some funny looks."

"Do you know them?"

"Yes—they're A 1."

"Subalterns generally are. Shall I call them over?"

"Why don't you go and join them? Tell them I was your groom or something back in Blighty."

"Not my pal?"

Jack grinned again. "We're all pals out here, sir, but you don't have to talk about it. That would spoil everything."

MEN AND HORSES DIED in a landscape that grew darker and more alien as autumn progressed. Cold drizzle passed over the grey fields. Across this desolation the horses journeyed. Stark perception of their plight kept them miserable, although Beth had a little vitality now and shared it with her companions.

The fighting of mid-September had run through a series of attacks and counterattacks to a great artillery battle near the end of the month, but the heavy rains of October failed to wash away the confusion at the gun pits and wagon lines. During the afternoon meal five-nines had fallen close to the road and all the horses were apprehensive, but Bathsheba's distress was heightened by illness. She gasped throughout the loading of the limber, while Jack held her muzzle and spoke to her. That excitable temperament could not come to terms with the nightmare.

Rain swooped, and the light faded to pitch-black darkness, lit now and then by the flash of the field guns. Weighed down by wet topcoats the men emptied the limbers, crouching whenever a shell landed. The road back was a gleaming catwalk of mud and flooded shell holes. Whenever the moon shone the landscape swelled and the sea of mud vibrated under a fresh barrage. One of the limbers took a direct hit and exploded, leaving a heap of bodies and some smoke. Beth threw back her head and snorted. The men were dead and the sole surviving horse was quivering into stillness. More five-nines descended close at hand. Then Solomon flopped onto his side, dragging Grace with him. The moon chose that moment to sail free of the clouds. Jack, Milburn and the wheel driver gathered round the old horse.

"God," Jack spat through clenched teeth. "Oh God, God!"

The shell cap had smashed Solomon's left foreleg below the knee, splintering the bone and almost severing the limb. He managed to sit back on his hindquarters but an attempt to stand brought him over on his side again. The rest of the team went berserk and Milburn and the other driver struggled to calm them.

Solomon breathed a high-pitched neigh of agony and raised his head, unable to comprehend, and expecting help from the man crouching over him. Jack wiped the filth from the horse's nostrils. Blood oozed black into the black slime partly covering the wound. Solomon groaned. Sick with horror Jack turned to the subaltern but the young man was appalled.

"Do it, sir."

Solomon's great brown eyes were full of question and pain. What have you done to me? they pleaded. Why am I here like this?

"Sir."

The eyes rolled but they held a glimmer of hope after the bullet had stilled Solomon's brain. Jack tipped back his helmet and shook his head. Beth was struggling to turn, perpetually shrilling her anguish. She and Bathsheba lamented the passing of their stablemate. They swung their heads from side to side, and stamped their feet as Jack released the gelding from his gear for the last time.

The rain returned, washing the mud off Solomon's face. The drivers remounted and took the team forward. Half the sky was starry and moonlit, the remainder black. The shelling stopped. Through the hush came the gasp and snort of animals, and Milburn blaspheming.

JACK AND DAUBENY had very little contact as autumn wore on. Daubeny did not regret coming to the Brigade. One corner of the slaughterhouse was very much like another. But apart from the horse and the memory of a few seaside summers he felt he had nothing in common with the Irishman. Sharing a love of truth was hardly the basis for a friendship rendered almost impossible by class barriers. Yet Daubeny's respect for Jack endured. He continued to admire the horsemaster and the way he handled the picket-line animals.

Once near the rest camp a thin woman offered her body for money. Jack grinned and dug into his pockets and gave her a handful of loose change before leading her to the door.

Outside he said, "Go home, and God go with you."

Oh Kitty. Let me lay my lips on your flower-scented hair, he thought. Reconstructing their lovemaking behind his eyes was never easy. The bath-water beaded on her breasts, her lashes quivered, light streamed down her curves. He was consumed by the phantom of her beauty—the movement of an arm, the arching back, eyes full of his reflected image.

"Go home," he choked.

Rain swept the tableland and the horses bowed their heads. Bathsheba gazed at the horse occupying Solomon's place. The loss of the gelding nagged away at her and she would not be consoled. Lifting her nose she whickered and waited for him to answer.

Rain continued to fall, heavy and silent. Now Bathsheba was refusing her food. Putting her in her gear Milburn was conscious of the piercing look she gave him. Right down the line horses were restless and ill. The brigade veterinary officer despaired but did what he could, weeding out the worst cases for hospitalisation.

To this small corner of the Western Front came the staff officers. The drivers were loafing about unshaven in their jerkins and muddy puttees, for the limber runs through the previous night had been particularly arduous.

"Good lord," drawled the red-tab colonel. "What is this, Daubeny—a tramps' convention? Get the riff-raff in line."

"They've been up and down to the guns all night, sir."

"That's no excuse for slovenliness: Put those men on a charge. Have I made myself clear?"

The colonel had cut himself shaving but otherwise he was perfectly groomed. The mud oozing over his polished riding-boots delighted Daubeny and the subalterns.

"This really is a shambles. Can't you find any fatigues for these men? The brigadier hates idleness."

"My drivers have come under enemy fire for three days in succession," Daubeny said. "They are exhausted, hungry and close to breaking."

"Rot! If every C.O. along the Front thought like that morale would be nonexistent and the Boche would be in our trenches now. Don't let these men go back to base for another dose of idleness. This sort of thing stems from slack command."

Daubeny nodded and Sergeant Turnbull could see the jaw muscles twitching as the captain fought for self-control. The party moved across to the picket lines.

"It simply won't do, Daubeny," the colonel said. "These animals need grooming, and look at the state of their rugs!"

The horses stood in liquid mud. They were lifting their feet one at a time in an effort to ease their discomfort. Tissues and joints were inflamed, and the pus ran from head wounds.

"They aren't clipped," the colonel said triumphantly. He pointed his riding whip at Bathsheba. "Regulations insist all animals are clipped in November. November began three days ago. See that they are trace-clipped, Captain. I'll be back in a day or so, and God help you and your slackers if things haven't improved."

"You clip them horses, sir," Jack blurted, "and they might as well lie down and die right now. Standin' out in all weathers with half their coat gone will finish them off."

"Put that man under arrest, Sergeant Turnbull," Daubeny barked. "Bring him to my dugout as soon as the colonel's gone."

Walking back to the staff officers' transport with the colonel, he said, "I think, sir, what the corporal meant was the animals have pretty thick coats, waterproofed to a certain extent by their own oils. Clipping them will make them vulnerable to debility. The wastage here is phenomenal as it is."

"Corporals are not running this show, Captain," came the haughty reply. "Clip them. The brigadier does things by the book."

"With the greatest respect, sir, the brigadier does not have to stand out in all weathers, day and night."

Colour suffused the colonel's face. "I shall be having strong words with your C.O. Captain. Slackness cannot be tolerated."

The horses remained unclipped. Major Dellow, the battery commander, was no fool. In a memo to Brigade he regretted the loss of clipping irons and noted tersely that there were more important jobs to be done than primping animals.

Enemy shelling accounted for only a small percentage of limber-horse deaths. Standing in the rain, deterioration was rapid, and the shortage of food left them desperate with hunger. Some tried to eat their own harness and their neighbours' rugs. Those at the end of the lines gnawed the picket posts. During the dark hours, when even the guns were still, the "chug-chug" of hooves being withdrawn from the mud and set down again was a most harrowing sound.

Among the victims was Bathsheba. Weakened by exposure and grief she no longer wished to live. Eventually her heart broke and she keeled over and died without a sound. As gently as possible Jack removed her halter and scraped the mud off her face. Beth's head dropped and she pawed the ground.

Chapter 17

Beth had been resting behind the wagon lines and looked fitter than she had for weeks. Somehow Daubeny had obtained a load of hay and oats. The subalterns said it was his connections at Brigade but no one cared. It was pleasant to hear the animals chomping their fodder in the sunlight, and the larks singing again.

"Hark at the little beauties," Milburn smiled, pulling on his pipe. "What've they got to sing about?"

"It must be a relief not to know anything," someone said.

"This can't go on for ever. Jerry must be as cheesed off as us," said Milburn. "Poor old Jerry."

"Why shouldn't it go on for ever?" Sergeant Turnbull said. "Hell's for ever, ain't it?"

"We'll run out of animals," Jack said.

"Then the staff officers will get us"—as he said "us" Turnbull stuck a finger in his chest—"to haul the limbers and guns. Further down the line I hear they're eating horseflesh regular."

Jack buried his hands in his pockets and walked off. Towards the top of the picket line Milburn caught up with him.

"Turnbull was only having you on, son."

"I know. He don't bother me. He's not a bad bloke."

"What's up then?"

"I've got to get Beth off the limber runs before she joins Sheba and Solomon."

"You can't steal a horse and just ride it away. They'd have thee as a deserter."

"Then I'll have to do what I should have done before the bastards took her. Dora was right."

"Dora?"

"My sister-in-law. She told me to cripple her but I couldn't. To me Beth's perfect. It's not just the way she looks, it's what she is. To interfere with all that purity would be evil."

"But if you cripple her she'll get the bullet."

"I won't give her a bad injury—just something to get her sold off to a French farmer. Daubeny says that happens sometimes. The farmers need workhorses and they don't eat everything on four legs. Anyway, at least she'll have a chance, Stan. Here she's doomed. I'll have to see to it on the run back tonight."

BETH OPENED HER EYES. Jack drew the currycomb over her body, feeling the bones where the flesh had once been firm and round. Sensing his heartache she lowered her head to his hands.

"Get her in harness, Jack lad," Milburn said gently.

"I'm doing it tonight, Stan, on the homeward run. I mean it." He produced the jagged shell splinter and returned it again to his greatcoat pocket.

Chance had been promoted to the lead position and she was in remarkable shape considering the way things were. Beside her Beth looked old, ready for the knacker's, Jack thought. Oh no you don't, God. Not her.

It was the last run of the night and dawn was close. They moved onto the road, starlight gleaming on helmets and harness and the prairie of mud. Jack steered the team among the flooded shell holes and dead mules, following the subaltern who rode ahead tracing the route.

Fear took his breath away. Dried mud made his topcoat stiff as well as heavy, and the sweat was cooling under his balaclava. Outside his discomfort the nightmare was busy. The limber behind them went off the road into a crater and between shellbursts men and animals could be heard screaming as they sank.

"Keep going," the subaltern cried. "Keep going," he half sobbed, half snarled.

Dark figures were struggling to drag a mule out of the wayside slime.

363

Hands fought to free the ammunition panniers which gave the mule a value above that of his life or carcass. The air was full of fumes and the stench of mud and decaying things. The cannonade crescendoed as the British eighteen pounders struck back.

Treading cautiously on the brushwood and duckboards which had been put down to make the approach to the emplacements possible, Jack's team toiled up to the guns. All the animals were lathered and steaming. By the orange light of gunfire Jack and Milburn stared at each other. The horses stood resigned to the violence breaking around them.

What sort of wound? Jack thought, climbing onto Beth's back and urging the team to the road again. He considered the horse's anatomy. A lame animal would be of no use to a farmer, so any injury to the legs was out. Withers, croup, shoulders, stifle? Not her face.

Dawn broke grey, misty and dry, and the Allied bombardment began with the mighty roar of siege guns. It produced swift German retaliation, forcing the battalions waiting to reinforce the impending advance to cower in the reserve trenches.

Here, they had a clear view of the limber teams crawling through the mud in the grim first light. The foremost wagon vanished on the edge of an explosion. More shells crashed down and the little column was hidden by smoke.

When it cleared, some horses could be seen staggering about by a roadside littered with mutilated creatures and wreckage. Four black holes were filling with mud and water. More horses climbed to their feet and joined their companions but nothing living stirred on the road ahead or behind them. They were stranded in a sea of mud.

Jack heard the descending whine and saw the flash that had lifted him off Beth. Then he was aware of nothing until he opened his eyes and heard the wild, low screaming. Something warm lay under his head. It was Chance's dead body. He raised himself on his elbows. Milburn lay a few yards away on his back in the mud making inhuman noises. His spectacles had been driven deep into his face.

"Stan." Jack tried to get up but nausea and giddiness pinned him down.

For a long time Milburn screamed and all of a sudden stopped. Daylight swelled behind the smoke.

"Are you all right, Corporal?" the subaltern said, bending over him.

"Shall be in a minute, sir. A bit dizzy."

"When you're fit we'll round up the horses—those that are left. All the men are dead, except a couple of lucky so-an'-sos back there. They can't walk. It's Blighty for them."

"My horse," Jack whispered.

"Your team copped it badly, I'm afraid. Only one on its feet. A few of the others are in a bad state." He took out his revolver.

"Beth," Jack breathed, struggling again to drag himself up.

"Lie still for a bit," the subaltern said. "You caught one on the head."

The noise of dying horses was beyond belief, and the officer left him and went to do something about it. Eventually the subaltern stooped over Jack again.

"How are you feeling, old chap?"

"Could you help me up, sir? If I can get on a horse I'll be as right as rain."

"Good show." The young, smooth face smiled. "Hang on, I'll put this away."

He straightened and was returning the Webley to its holster when the shrapnel ripped through his spine, killing him instantly. He crumpled rather than fell, and lay curled up like a sleeping child. Jack turned away, the corpse stench of mud in his nostrils. A shell splinter had opened his forehead to the bone. His helmet had gone and blood dribbled into his eyes. He pawed at them, letting the dizziness do as it pleased. The chill of muddy water crept over his flesh and he began to shiver. There was no need to get up, nothing to get up for. He blinked his eyes on the redness clogging his lashes.

A FEW HOURS BEFORE Jack's team made its run, Arthur Lacey's war took a new twist. His descent into nightmare since the heady summer of 1914 had been rapid, and two years of bluff and terror had pushed him close to breakdown. Yet he survived even the first days of the Somme offensive, where luck carried him across no-man's-land and back again. A Blighty wound which turned septic kept him out of action until November when France reclaimed him.

His regiment was in the front line and Lacey did his best to avoid action. He reported sick three times claiming to be suffering from dysentery, then a chest infection and finally dizziness and blackouts. The medical officer marked him down as a slacker and one starry night he found himself on the fire step of the forward trench, his body pressed against the sand-bagged revetment, waiting for "a little remedial treatment".

He and another private named Chard were going on a scouting expedition into no-man's-land with Lieutenant Nicholson. The sergeant major had insisted he volunteer.

They went over the sandbags on their bellies, using knees and elbows to get them past the forward sap. The path through the wire was not a dead end and the subaltern breathed a sigh of relief as he led his men into the shell hole and two feet of water that stank like a gangrenous limb.

Lacey had never felt more vulnerable. They were in the middle of no-man's-land, close enough to the German trenches to catch snatches of laughter and conversation. Lacey knew what the subaltern intended. The mad fool was going to have a go at wiping out the machine gun nest with grenades. That would make them a target for every trigger-happy Hun in their line. Get out of this one, Arthur, said the voice in his head.

Nicholson and Chard were about to wriggle forward again. The wind sang in the barbed wire; Lacey's face was a mask of sweat and his knees were lifeless. A rat ran over his hand and he choked back his cry of horror. A shell exploded, filling the air with shrapnel but his head was already down. Chard had been on his hands and knees peering over the rim of the crater at the moment of detonation. The small black holes in his face and throat were clues to how he had died. One of our shells, Lacey reflected without emotion. He was safe and comfortable. Bringing his knees up to his chin he assumed the foetal position.

"Get out of there—you damned coward," Nicholson slurred.

The subaltern knelt on the edge of the crater and when the next Very light fell Lacey saw blood glistening on the face snarling down at him. Nicholson held the wreckage of his left arm across his chest.

"Lacey." He waved his revolver as numbness spread. Then the side of the crater collapsed and he slid gently face downwards into the morass. Raising himself on his good arm he tried to shake the mud from his eyes.

"I'll see you court-martialled, you damned coward."

"Tidn my fault," Lacey wailed.

Nicholson's strength gave out and he vanished, to emerge once more spitting mud. Lacey leaned over and pressed down on the helmeted head with all his weight. For a moment an arm flailed then Nicholson lay still, but Lacey continued holding the corpse under until his muscles ached.

Afterwards he rested and considered his next move. On a flash of inspiration it came to him. Slithering and grunting he hauled Nicholson's body clear of the crater, slung it across his shoulders, and came staggering to the barbed wire in front of his own lines. A star shell descended but the gap in the entanglement was close now. Then a bullet crunched into the corpse shielding his back. The sniper was hampered by the smoke and Lacey was clear of the wire before the machine gun crew spotted him. The Maxim opened up as he struggled over the last few yards. Suddenly there was a searing pain in his right leg but his impetus carried him and the body over the parapet into the trench.

"Bloody well done, lad," the sergeant major grunted, rolling up the greatcoat and placing it under his head.

"Lieutenant Nicholson?" Lacey gasped.

"The officer is dead, but it was one hell of a brave effort."

Lacey nodded and groaned. The pain pulsed from the black cavity that had once housed his right kneecap.

"Chard bought it, too," he managed, refusing a cigarette.

"That leg is your ticket out of the war—for good. So cheer up, lad. There are worse ways of gettin' home. You're one of them khaki heroes newspapers write about," the sergeant major said.

And Lacey went down the heroes' trail, stage by stage, with the nightmare ebbing the further he travelled from the Front. Stretcher-bearers brought him to the Aid Post for iodine and bandages; then he was carted to the Advanced Dressing Station and on to the Casualty Clearing

Station for surgery. Here he lost a limb and gained the Military Medal. During his convalescence he was to dwell often on his stroke of good fortune. Almost everyone he knew had two legs, but the medal and the crutches set him apart.

SOMETHING WARM AND MOIST fluttered over Jack's face. He tried to open his eyes but the lashes were gummed up with blood. Beneath his head Chance's body was no longer warm. He sighed, waiting for Sean to kick out in sleep or his mother to cry from the adjoining bedroom. But he wasn't at home. The miserable truth seeped through with the stink of mud. He was cold and wet and his head ached. Maybe if he lay there long enough he would become part of the dream. At the top of the terrace the band was playing and the skipping-ropes beat out their rhythm. He could smell the Sunday breakfast, hear the bacon crisping.

The warm moistness on his face made him conscious of his wound. Working his eyelids free he saw Beth's muzzle a few inches from his nose. Gently she nudged him. The nausea passed and he could stand without feeling giddy. He tugged off his balaclava. Beth stared at him while the thunder of the guns rippled across their thoughts. Her eyes were placid, and the sunlight reflected in them was also turning the mud on her body to silver.

Horses dragging their traces gathered round her and stood waiting. Some were wounded, all were shocked. Elsewhere the more seriously injured animals cried out for release. Taking the dead officer's revolver Jack went among them and ended their suffering. Then he hauled himself onto Beth's back and rounded up the rest of the strays until over a dozen were ready to be led to safety.

Their progress was watched by the infantry herded into the reserve trenches. As the little group picked a path among the debris and shell holes every man watching them willed their escape.

Beth splashed along the road, holding her head erect. Her stride lengthened and she went in and out of the mud like a filly. The roundabout horse, Jack thought, and there was Kitty on the merry-go-round, rising and falling until she disappeared. The earth lifted and roared and he was down in the mud again, unable to hear anything save the thrum of life at the base of his skull. The feeling had gone from his back and his chest was cold. Each breath was a jolt of agony. Not yet, he said to himself. Please, not yet. Beth was on her knees beside him and a groan rose from the trenches as the smoke cleared. Two animals lay motionless, another was on its back, legs threshing, and the driver had gone. Then Jack was up, coaxing Beth to her feet, deaf to the cheering soldiers.

She had lost an eye and the left side of her face was a sticky mask of blood.

"They've made such a mess of you," Jack choked. "Come on, my lovely—let's get you out of here."

At birth we are given the whole world as a gift. Yes, he grinned, yes. Nothing had changed. But oh God, never to see another spring or Kitty's face or the bay full of stars! He tried to lift a hand to his forehead but the movement fanned the pain in his chest and he coughed blood. His mother smiled in her white gown from under the white parasol. Then the carriage glided by.

"Mother." The blood frothed between his clenched teeth and dribbled down his chin. Shells exploded nearby but beyond the wood the ground was firmer and the road was jammed with ambulances and limber teams bound for the pits. Everything came to a halt. Men drew rein and stared in horror at the apparition galloping towards them. The rider and his horse were grey but their faces were blood-smeared red. At their heels stampeded six or seven loose animals, madness staring from their eyes.

Daubeny knew it was Jack and Beth. They passed in a flurry of mud and spray, and he spurred his horse after them. They were beyond commands or threats or words of any sort. The horses went unchallenged through the wagon lines and met the road a little south of Hédauville. Here a military police patrol tried to stop them, only to be brushed aside.

"Animals for the veterinary hospital," Daubeny shouted. Now they were running west, pounding through the sunlight into the start of the British bombardment. The siege guns roared and the sky was racked by the rush and drone of shells. Lather covered Beth from head to tail but she had no desire to rest. Over the low hedge she flew and ran on towards the village that was there behind the apple trees.

"Jack," Daubeny cried, overtaking him and grabbing Beth's bridle; but Jack's chin was down on his chest. Beth turned and whinnied before she

369

was pulled up under the apple boughs. A handful of curled, yellow leaves idled down the windless air and Jack followed them into the grass. He could hear the voice but not the words. Kneeling beside him Daubeny saw the darkness on his face, and his eyes round and full of agony. The world went up and down and Jack was riding it like a horse out of torment.

"Jack."

Blood from the wound in his back flooded both lungs, cancelling breath and pain, blotting out the sun. Daubeny closed the eyelids and still on his knees lit a cigarette. Jack's features had relaxed and his hands were clenched on the grass.

When Daubeny got to his feet he saw the old people and children among the horses.

"*Il est mort?*" demanded a little girl. She had a pale, serious face and long brown hair.

Daubeny nodded.

"*Mon frère est mort aussi.*"

Again Daubeny nodded. "Please fetch the priest—*le curé, s'il vous plaît. Mon ami est Catholique.*"

He looked about him. Whatever spirit presided over the Western Front it was not a familiar deity. He closed his eyes, hollowed his cheeks and inhaled. The gunfire brutalising the morning angered him. "Our Father which art in heaven." He looked up at the sky. There were no birds.

The children fed handfuls of grass to the horses, withdrawing their fingers quickly for fear of a nip. But Beth stood absolutely still over Jack, her head lowered and her breath ruffling his hair. She uttered no sound, yet Daubeny could feel the intensity of her grief. Her entire world had gone. Slowly then she walked round the body, nudging it in a silent plea for him to come back to her.

Later, when they had carried Jack away, she resumed her vigil while the leaves fell and the thunder of the bombardment pealed between the Ancre and the Somme.

A ONE-EYED HORSE could pull a plough or a muck cart or turn the wheel of a cider press. Daubeny had the vet brand her as unfit for action, and made sure she went to a good home in the village where Jack had died.

"If I survive I'll come back for her," Daubeny said. "Do not part with her, *m'sieur*. Have I your word of honour?"

The old farmer smiled. "*Ma parole, m'sieur*," and they shook hands.

"Take this money and look after her, please. I will help feed her for as long as I am able. Meanwhile she is in your care."

The bombardment was over. Little, it seemed, had been gained by the fresh offensive. Daubeny stood in the rain beside Jack's grave. The children had laid bunches of flowers at the foot of the wooden cross. But the soil was grey, not red like the Devon plough, and the robin's song in the failing light was poignant.

Chapter 18

Life at Number Eight Angarrick Terrace continued although the blinds were down in the front room window. The children still played round the lamppost after dark, Dando was taken for walks and the Salvation Army band struck up every Sunday morning. It was this uninterrupted flow of the ordinary that distressed Mary McKenna. She sat by the fire, gazing at the things his eyes had rested on: the wallpaper, the range, the teapot, dishes, jars, cruets, the knocked-about furniture. Mary needed no persuasion from Father O'Driscoll to believe Jack was with Michael at Jesus's right hand. But every so often the sickness and grief swelled and swamped everything. She would rock back and forth, eyes closed, reliving the moment when the official notification had arrived: a sharp rap at the door, Blanche's bare feet padding on the lino, voices, a cry. The horror caught her again and the colour vanished from her face. The words swam before her, but he was alive despite the piece of paper she had crumpled and tossed aside. He was a child again and safe from it all, there with his head tucked into the folds of her skirt. Not gone for ever. For ever. She rocked and moaned and the girls stared at her, unable to do anything.

Kitty's stoicism surprised everyone, but most of all Dora. She bore the loss well for in her heart she had known Jack would never return once the war got its hooks into him. Old Chancellor had visited the house full of guilt to speak of the dead heroes and tell her she would be getting a small pension from the store.

Edward Daubeny's news that Beth was alive on a French farm left Kitty unmoved. Again it seemed inevitable—Jack dead, the horse alive, she and the baby alone. Father O'Driscoll could not explain any of it, and "God moving in a mysterious way" was no consolation. But Mary McKenna knew that if the horse lived then so did part of her son. She knew it from an instinct whose roots ran deeper than her faith, right back to the folk history of Ireland. Man and horse, woman and hawk, all one in the spirit life that creatures shared. So she smiled and patted Dando's head.

THE SEASONS PASSED, and the war continued, measured by other battles, but nothing that was to come could match the prolonged slaughter of the Somme.

Three springs after Jack's death there were many crosses in the paddock beyond the apple trees. Fallen blossom lay on the graves and a blackbird sang in the orchard. Beth's ears twitched as she caught the melody on her return to evening grass. Her workmate was an old Percheron cross named Marie who was for ever seeking to comfort her. Yet Beth's habit of standing perfectly still every dawn and dusk, like a creature expecting to find something in the bottom of the sky, baffled her companion, and the farmer. She had a vague recollection of Jack lying in the field with his eyes

371

closed. Where had he gone? When would he return? This time there was no certainty of reunion, and she was low.

The farmer treated her well despite the shortage of hay and oats, and Daubeny's visits made her perk up until she discovered the voice calling her name was not the voice she craved. But her mane and feather had grown again and she had lost some of her thinness. When the work day was over she would permit the farmer's granddaughter to groom her. Then the scent of apple blossom would resurrect the vision of the other orchard at the top of the Devon valley. The curlews passing between the Ancre and the Somme called their sweet double notes and opened the heartache. Larks were aloft and singing, and the chalk dust drifted over the countryside, hazing distance. Munching her way across the paddock she did not know that Jack was there under one of the crosses. She thought of him as alive and was desperate to join him in the good place, where he would come up from the orchards calling her name to put her in harness and take her to the yard.

DORA AND EDWARD strolled together along Station Lane and went through the gates into Chancellor's stables. Old Bob sat in the tack room by himself. He greeted them warmly and they spoke of the war and how things were before 1914. The old man was struggling to come to terms with the enormity of the holocaust.

"Most of them have gone. Tom Palfrey was gassed at Passchendaele and he's an invalid; the Dunsfords, Drew, little Charlie Wotton, Moony, some of the other stableboys and Jack, all daid and buried. I doan know what to make of it. All they harmless men and boys and horses. Bliddy war. Bliddy waste. Still, it made a few unlikely heroes. Who would've thought that ornament Lacey would go and get chopped up tryin' to save an officer? I never thought he had it in him. Do'ee know they've made un landlord of the 'King Bill'? Tidn the 'King Bill' now, of course, because the brewery have renamed it the 'Lord Kitchener'."

Dora turned away in disgust. "After that prize idiot!"

Edward walked her down to Lansworthy beach, through the drizzle of early May.

"Jack didn get a medal," she said in a small, unhappy voice. "I can't bear to think of that boy and all the others under the soil out there."

"A medal is the last thing Jack would have wanted."

"Did he suffer, Edward?"

"Lord, no! He went out like a light, peaceful as a lamb."

She looked at him and he averted his eyes.

"Tell Kitty, please. It's the best sort of lie."

"Will you marry me, Dora?"

"No—and in your heart you don't want me to."

She smiled and kissed him. The wet, gritty sand crunched under their boots. Gulls swooped round the pier where a child was flying a kite.

"I shall go to London and push the cause. We can see each other often. Please," she added firmly, "don't go on about it, Edward. That kind of marriage could never work. Love isn't enough. I'm not ready for domesticity and I certainly couldn't put up with the sort of social daftness your sister and her set pursue. Come on, you'll get over it. You've got your chums and cricket and your books and things."

"But I haven't got you."

"I can't see myself as something for the trophy cabinet."

She laughed and he cupped her lovely, expressive face in his hands.

"Honestly, Edward, I'd make an awful wife—ask Kitty. All I want to do is lug my soapbox round street corners preaching to all them deprived slum dwellers."

"Sounds beastly depressing."

"But a little more fulfilling than working out menus for dinner parties or scolding nanny for slackness in the nursery."

Under the pier they were out of the rain. Part of the luminosity the sky borrowed from the sea flushed the shadows.

"There was a letter addressed to me in Jack's things," Edward said, taking it from his wallet and handing it to her.

"'Dear Edward'," Dora read. "'If I cop a bad one I'd like you to try and bring Beth home. I hope I can get her out of this mess but she won't have those green pastures until she is back in Clennon Valley. If I can't see this through I hope you won't let her down. I made her a promise. Best of luck, Jack McKenna.'"

Her eyes lifted to his face. "What will you do?"

"Go to France and bring Beth home. I would have done it even if he hadn't asked. Chancellor wanted to pay my expenses but that's out of the question. I need to do this for my own sake. Apart from anything else I've been wondering what it would be like to make that journey free of terror."

She slipped her arms round his neck and kissed him, feeling the tears pricking the back of her eyes.

ON THE FERRY old memories and fears crowded in, and all suffering came to a head during the journey from seaport to front-line destination. Like a mirage the village grew on the horizon. First there were the fields and lines of peasants hoeing crops, then the paddock which had become a cemetery for British soldiers, and finally the orchards, farms and houses.

"*Elle est une mignonne, m'sieur*," the farmer said. "*Très belle et gentille, et un peu étrange.*"

"*Etrange?*" said Edward with a lift of the eyebrows.

The priest accompanying them tried to explain. "After the work is finished she rests absolutely still and goes inside herself." He tapped a fingertip against his temple. "*Où le rêve commence.* She is a strange animal."

Edward nodded, and that was how she was when he came to the

373

cemetery. She stood in the grass, unmoving, waiting on the threshold of a dream. She was haggard, half blind and one of her knees was swollen. The tears streamed down Edward's face as he drew the flat of his hand down her neck.

"Bethlehem."

At the sound of her name she swung her head to look at him, but it was not Jack and her interest died. She stared into the dust haze, shutting out the rest of the world. Daubeny lingered for a while beside Jack's grave and said as much of Psalm 23 as he could remember.

Maybe, he reflected, the war had achieved something, if only to sweep away well-worn deceits from so many smug corners. To be alive was a privilege. To be alive and warm and free from terror.

BROUGHT BACK to Tor Barton she hobbled awkwardly into the sunlight on Cider Mill Tor, and the farm horses gathered to sniff her. She was recognised by some of the older animals. But where was he in this place which breathed peacefulness and was alive with his love?

Kitty and her son came to make a fuss of her.

"She's yours now, my dear," Chancellor said. "This is her home and when the little boy is big enough he can ride her. Jack did. Jack was a bundle of mischief."

"A bliddy nuisance, sir," Trant said with a bleak smile.

"She's still his horse," Kitty said, stroking Beth's face.

Walking home over the water meadows she wept for all that would never be again: his body laid on her own, his smile and voice, and the brightness of his eyes in those summers they had shared. The curlew calls followed her down Tanners Lane but she did not hear them.

And Bathsheba, Solomon and those the mud and noise and cold had taken away, they were there with Beth in the grass and sunlight. Was the wind a dream—the warmth and greenness merely shadows of what had risen from his love? She turned and lifted her head when he called; and they came, the mares and geldings, arching their necks and loosing their manes. They lived in her and were the grass and the summer rain and the sun that never ages.

She lowered her muzzle to the meadow and Solomon was not sitting in the greyness waiting to be led out of pain. The wind sent the shadows swimming around her.

"Beth. My Beth. Walk on, girl. Walk on."

Muffled hoofbeats announced the arrival of the farm horses. Solomon, Bathsheba, Melody, Iona. She started forward, her whole body vibrant with recognition. He was on the tor against the sun, part of the brilliance. The horses thundered up to brush her flanks with their bodies. Beth's lashes descended and her chest heaved. All about her the grass whispered her name, and the fields ran with the life of summer down to the sea.

374

BRIAN CARTER

"As a boy, I used to love to feed and water the horses on a farm in Clennon Valley, South Devon," Brian Carter remembers. "Yes, there's quite a lot of my own childhood distilled into Jack McKenna's story." The novel was inspired by his grandfather's accounts of the plight of the draught horses in Flanders during the Great War—for in the rural areas of Devon it was not only the men who disappeared to France in droves, but the horses, too.

Brian Carter's desire to be a writer dates back to a very early age. "As a child I was prone to illness, and some of the time my mother taught me at home," he told me, and he attributes his ear for language to those early lessons. "You see, my mother, being Welsh, has a wonderful sense of language. If I had gone to school in the normal way, perhaps I would never have been an author."

His knowledge of wildlife and nature, however, has grown through his own lifelong interest, stimulated by living in the West Country. He is a keen conservationist, writing a daily column for a South Devon newspaper, *The Herald Express*. To Carter's obvious pleasure the newspaper recently won a RSPB award for furthering conservation, and although modesty doesn't allow him to admit it, his contributions played a major part in winning the award. He has also worked for television: a year ago he wrote and presented a 4-part series called "Dartmoor—The Threatened Wilderness", and he is currently researching a follow-up programme about the Isle of Mull, which he also knows intimately. For the past twenty years or so he has gone there to walk, climb and simply look at the wildlife. "I go there whenever I can for its solitude, and for its wild beauty," he says.

Despite his involvement in television and journalism, his first love is writing fiction. At present he is working on his sixth novel which, he says, has an excitingly original subject—so original that he won't reveal it in case someone steals the idea!

C.C.

The
CHARM
SCHOOL

A CONDENSATION OF THE BOOK BY
NELSON DEMILLE

ILLUSTRATED BY LARRY SCHWINGER

What a holiday—driving through Russia in a powerful new sports saloon, courting an exquisite mix of discovery and adventure behind the Iron Curtain! Greg Fisher, a young American tourist straight out of college, is having the time of his life.

Until he takes a wrong turn and sees something he shouldn't see: Mrs. Ivanova's Charm School—the KGB's most explosive secret.

Suddenly, for Greg Fisher the holiday is over.

CHAPTER 1

"You are already staying in Smolensk two days, Mr. Fisher?" she asked.

Gregory Fisher was no longer confused or amused by the peculiar syntax of English as it was spoken in this part of the world. "Yes," he replied, "I've been in Smolensk two days."

"Why don't I see you when you arrive?"

"You were out. So I saw the police—the militia."

"Yes?" The Intourist representative leafed through the papers on her desk, a worried look on her face, then brightened. "Ah, yes. Good. You are staying here at Tsentralnaya Hotel." She examined his visa. "Occupation?"

Fisher had become impatient with these internal control measures. It was like making a major border crossing at each stop. He said, "Ex-college student, currently unemployed."

She nodded. "There is much unemployment in America. And homeless people."

The Russians, Fisher had learned, were obsessed with America's problems of unemployment, homeless people, crime and drugs. "I'm voluntarily unemployed."

The woman slapped a big red rubber stamp across the paperwork. "You must stay on the designated highways. Night driving in the countryside is forbidden for foreign tourists. You must be within the city of Moscow by nightfall."

"I know."

"When you reach Moscow, you must report directly to the Intourist

379

representative at the Rossiya Hotel, where you are staying." She glanced at his itinerary. "You are authorised one small detour to Borodino. But I would advise against that."

"Why?"

"It is late in the day, Mr. Fisher. You should be hurrying to Moscow."

"Thank you. But I'm sure I can make Moscow before dark."

She shrugged and pushed the papers towards him.

"*Spasibo*," Fisher said, using the Russian for "thank you" as he stuffed the documents into his shoulder satchel.

"Drive safely," she replied, adding, "Be cautious."

Fisher walked out into the cool air of Smolensk considering that last, cryptic remark. There was a crowd of people surrounding his car. He sidled through the throng. "Excuse me, folks." He unlocked the door of his metallic-blue Pontiac Trans Am, smiled, and slipped inside the car. He started the engine and drove slowly through the parting crowd. "Goodbye, Smolenskers. *Do svidaniya.*"

He proceeded slowly through Smolensk, referring to the map on the seat beside him. Within ten minutes he was on the Minsk–Moscow highway, heading east towards the Soviet capital. It was a windy October day, with grey clouds scudding past a weak sun.

Fisher saw that the further east he drove, the more advanced the autumn became. The wheat here had been harvested on both sides of the highway, and the occasional orchards were bare. A stone kilometre post informed him that he was two hundred and ninety kilometres from Moscow. He looked at the digital dashboard clock: 14:16.

Greg Fisher thought about things as the landscape rolled by. The restrictions and procedures were not only annoying but a little scary. Yet he rather liked the Soviet citizens he'd met. And he liked the way his car literally stopped the traffic. The Trans Am had Connecticut number plates, cast-aluminium wheels, a rear spoiler and custom pinstriping— the quintessential American macho car—and he thought that nothing like it had ever been seen on the road to Moscow.

From the back seat of the car came the aroma of fruit and vegetables given him by villagers and peasants wherever he'd stopped. He in turn had given out felt-tip pens, American calendars, disposable razors, tubes of lip gloss, and other small luxuries he'd been advised to bring. Greg Fisher felt like an ambassador of goodwill, and he was having a marvellous time.

His parents had given him the car and the vacation after he'd completed his graduate studies at Yale. He'd had the car shipped to Le Havre and spent the summer touring Western Europe. Heading into the Eastern bloc had been his own idea.

The landscape, Fisher noticed, deserved its reputation for being monotonous. And the sky seemed to be a reflection of the terrain: grey and rolling, an unbroken expanse of monotony for the last eight days.

The excitement of being a tourist in the Soviet Union, he decided, had little to do with the land (dull), the people (drab), or the climate (awful). The excitement derived from being in a country that didn't encourage tourism, a country where xenophobia was a deep-rooted condition of the national psyche, a nation that was a police state. The ultimate vacation: a dangerous place.

After an hour or so he turned off the highway onto a smaller, parallel route that had once been the principal western road out of Moscow. In a few minutes he found himself on the outskirts of Mozhaisk, a hundred and twenty-eight kilometres from Moscow. His Intourist guidebook informed him that this was a thirteenth-century town, but there weren't any signs of antiquity evident in the plain concrete and wooden buildings. He drove through Mozhaisk, affecting nonchalance behind the wheel as people turned to stare at the metallic-blue Trans Am.

With the town behind him he accelerated up the road and thought about the Rossiya Hotel in Moscow. That would be his first decent accommodation since Warsaw. He kept looking for a sign directing him back to the main highway. A stone kilometre post read 108km, and an arrow pointed to the highway via a one-lane road with crumbling black asphalt. An arrow to the left pointed towards a rising road in better condition. The sign was in the Cyrillic alphabet, but he could make out the word "Borodino". He looked at his dashboard clock: 16:38. Impulsively he swung onto the Borodino road, heading west into the setting sun. He wanted to see the place where Napoleon and Field Marshal Kutuzov had fought, where fifty years later Leo Tolstoy had stood and pondered his epic novel *War and Peace*.

The road rose gradually, flanked on either side by poplars. Fisher drove slowly through a pair of stone pillars with open iron gates. The road crested a small hill, and he saw spread before him Borodino Field, where Napoleon's *Grande Armée* had met the Russian regiments. The road led down to a small parking area, beyond which was the Borodino museum, a white limestone building with a red-tiled roof and a neoclassical portico. Two old muzzle-loading cannons flanked the entrance. Fisher got out of the car, mounted the steps of the museum and tried the doors, but they were locked. "Typical," he said softly. He turned and looked out at the grass-covered fields and hillocks where a quarter of a million French and Russian soldiers met on a September day in 1812, the French intent on taking Moscow, the Russians intent on defending it. For fifteen hours, according to his guidebook, the two sides fired at each other, and in the evening the Russians withdrew towards Moscow. A hundred thousand men lay dead and wounded.

Greg Fisher was suddenly overcome by a sense of history and tragedy. A cold east wind blew tiny birch leaves over the granite steps where he stood. "Russia," he said softly. "*Rodina*—the motherland. Bleeding Russia. But you made them all bleed too."

He walked back to his car. It was much colder now, and a chill passed through his body. He drove slowly down the lanes, past a black granite obelisk honouring Kutuzov, past other monuments and gravestones.

He had lost track of time, and it had become noticeably darker. He tried to retrace his route through the low hills and clusters of birch trees, but he realised he was lost. He found himself going uphill through a towering pine forest and reluctantly continued on the narrow, paved lane, looking for a wide place to turn. He put on his headlights, but they revealed only walls of dark green pines on each side.

Suddenly the headlights illuminated a large wooden sign attached to a tree, and Fisher stopped the car. The lettering was in Cyrillic, but he was able to make out the familiar word "Stop". The rest of the sign was incomprehensible. "Do I need this?" he muttered with a quaver in his voice.

He noticed what appeared to be a small opening in the trees on the right verge, beyond the sign. He didn't want to pass the sign with the car, so he took a torch from under his seat and got out. He walked the ten metres to the opening. It was a gravel turning place, obviously intended as a means of allowing the unwary motorist to obey the sign. "Russian efficiency," he said aloud. He turned back towards his car, and froze.

Over the hum of the engine he heard branches rustling. He remained motionless and breathed through his nose, noticing the resinous scent of the trees. He heard it again, the brushing of pine boughs, closer this time. Somewhere in the distance a dog barked—an unfriendly bark. He took a step towards his car.

"Russian efficiency," said a voice a few feet to his right.

Fisher felt his knees go weak.

CHAPTER 2

Lisa Rhodes noted it was 5.00 p.m., and poured a cup of coffee. She walked to the window of her office in the press attaché's section of the American embassy. A pale sun was just sinking beneath the flat horizon.

The internal phone rang. She turned from the window and answered it. "Rhodes."

"Hello," said a male voice she recognised as belonging to Seth Alevy. "Today is the first day of Sukkoth. The Jewish harvest festival. Sort of like Thanksgiving."

"Is that so?"

"I've been invited to a party in Sadovniki. Religious dissidents. You might enjoy it."

"I'm duty officer tonight."

"I'll get you switched."

"No . . . no, thanks, Seth. I have to finish a press release."

"Is it completely and finally over between us?"

"I'm afraid so."

"Well, at least think about it, Lisa."

She didn't know if Seth meant about them or the party. She replied, "Sure will."

She hung up, slipped off her shoes and put her feet on the desk. Holding the coffee on her lap, she lit a cigarette and contemplated the acoustic-tile ceiling. The new American embassy, she reflected, had been more than a decade in the building. The work had been done mostly by a West German firm under subcontract to an American concern in New York. If the Soviet government was insulted by this snub, they never expressed it verbally. Instead, they'd indulged themselves in petty harassments and bureaucratic delays of monumental proportions, which was one of the reasons the project had taken so long.

Lisa knew there was a good deal of residual bitterness among the American staff, and it influenced their decision-making. In fact, whatever goodwill there had been between the embassy people and their Soviet hosts was gone, replaced by almost open warfare. The State Department was now considering replacing the entire staff of two hundred or so with less angry diplomats. She hoped not. She wanted to continue her tour of duty here.

Lisa thought of Seth Alevy. As the CIA station chief, he could pull strings to keep her in Moscow even if State ordered her home. And she did love him. Or had once loved him. But somehow, being involved with him meant being involved with his world, and she didn't like that. It was too dangerous. Just being in Moscow was dangerous enough.

GREGORY FISHER got his bearings from the Kutuzov obelisk, shining in the moonlight. He found the white limestone museum, and within a minute he was on the poplar-lined exit road. Approaching the iron gates, he hit the accelerator, and the Trans Am roared through.

Fisher pressed harder on the accelerator as he negotiated a series of bends. Coming out of one of these, he saw the signpost he'd passed earlier. He made a hard right into the farm lane that led back to the main Minsk–Moscow highway. His chest pounded as the Pontiac bumped over the potholed paving. He could see lights from distant farm buildings across the flat, harvested fields. He had an acute sense of being where he wasn't supposed to be, when he wasn't supposed to be there.

The farm road seemed to go on for ever. Finally he reached the intersection of the main highway. He turned quickly onto it and headed east, towards Moscow. He saw no headlights coming at him and none in his rearview mirror, but there were towns and villages ahead, and if there were police in any of them, he would be stopped and questioned.

After a while he saw a strange, haunting shimmer of light sitting on the black horizon—Moscow.

The Trans Am rolled eastwards, and Greg Fisher kept his eyes on the distant lights. Ahead, the road dipped beneath a highway bridge, and he knew this was the outer ring road, the unofficial city limit. Eventually he passed the Triumphal Arch commemorating the Battle of Borodino, and suddenly there were streetlights and vehicles. He felt somewhat calmer now that he was mingling into the traffic of Moscow.

Soon he found himself on the Kalinin Bridge which spanned the Moskva River. On the far bank he could see a modern building of dark red brick, and he was fairly certain that it was the American embassy. "Thank God!"

Fisher came off the bridge into a confusing interchange. He was looking for a turning that would lead back to the embassy when a green-and-white police car pulled up beside him. The policeman in the passenger seat motioned him to pull over. Fisher took a deep breath and pulled over to the kerb. His knees were so weak he had trouble applying the brakes.

The police car stopped behind him, and two policemen got out. They were dressed in green overcoats and fur hats. One of them came to his window.

"Visa. Passport."

Gregory Fisher controlled his shaking hands as he produced the documents. While one policeman studied them the other man was walking round the car, touching it. He seemed intrigued.

No one said anything for a long time. Suddenly a man in civilian clothing appeared. He stared at Fisher through the windscreen, then came to the driver's side. He spoke in heavily accented but correct English. "The car documents, please. Also your licence and your itinerary."

"Right. *Da*." Fisher handed the man a large envelope.

The civilian studied the papers, then snapped his fingers, and one of the policemen quickly handed him Fisher's passport and visa. The civilian said to Fisher, "Turn off your ignition and step out of the car."

Fisher did as he was told. He noticed that the man was tall and slender for a Russian. In fact, he was fair and Nordic-looking.

The man studied Fisher's face, then his passport and visa photographs. He said, "You just arrived in Moscow from Smolensk?"

"Yes."

"You were driving in the country at night?"

"No."

"But you said you just arrived in Moscow. You were seen coming past the arch. You were driving in the country at night."

"Yes." Fisher looked closely at the man. He was about forty and wore a leather coat and a black fur hat. He seemed neither friendly nor hostile, just inquisitive. "I got lost."

"Where?"

"At Bor—at Mozhaisk." Fisher thought he might not have the right to remain silent, but he had enough brains not to incriminate himself further.

The man regarded him for an uncomfortably long time, then motioned Fisher to follow him. They went to the rear of the car, and the man unlocked the hatchback and opened it. The interior light revealed Fisher's cache of spare parts and lubricants.

"What does this mean?" asked the civilian. He pointed to the nameplate on the bumper. "Trans Am?"

"Trans—across. Am—America."

"Across America." The man smiled, and Fisher noticed it wasn't a pleasant smile. He turned away and joined the two policemen. They spoke for about five minutes; then he returned. "You have broken a law: driving in the country at night. It is very serious for a foreigner. I suggest you go now directly to the Rossiya and stay there for the evening. You may be asked to give a full account of yourself later." The man handed Fisher his papers. "Welcome to Moscow, Mr. Fisher."

The man walked away, and Fisher watched him descend into a metro station. The two policemen got into their car without a word. They remained parked, watching Fisher.

Greg Fisher closed the hatchback, then climbed behind the wheel and started the engine. He pulled out into the traffic. The police car followed. Greg was trembling so badly now that he wanted to pull over, but he continued down Kalinin Prospect. The police car stayed with him, so the embassy was out of the question for the time being.

Fisher recalled from the map what he was supposed to do, and turned onto Marx Prospect, went down to the embankment road, and cut left. On his right was the Moskva River, to his left the high, crenellated south wall of the Kremlin. The Moskva reflected the glow of the red stars on the Kremlin's towers. Ahead he saw an underpass beneath the ramp of a Moskva River bridge. Rising up beyond the ramp was the Rossiya Hotel. It was a massive modern building with a glass and aluminium façade. He drove under the ramp and saw in his rearview mirror the police car still behind him. Fisher pulled up in front of the hotel and switched off the engine.

A uniformed doorman stood inside the glass walls of the outer foyer. Fisher got out of the car with his shoulder bag and approached the man. He motioned towards his car. "*Bagazh*. OK?"

"OK."

He handed the doorman his car keys. "*Garazh*. OK?"

"OK."

Fisher entered the lobby, which seemed deserted and, like most public places, overheated. The Russians equated heat with luxury, he suspected. He looked around. There was no bar, no newsstand, no shops, no services in evidence. He walked over to a sort of ticket window that he assumed was the front desk. An uninterested young woman looked up. He gave her his Intourist reservation, his passport and his visa. She examined the passport a moment, then without a word disappeared through a door behind the desk.

Fisher said to himself, "Welcome to the Rossiya, Mr. Fisher. How long will you be staying with us? Oh, until the KGB comes for me. Very good, sir." He turned and looked outside. He noticed that someone had moved his car, but he didn't see his luggage being brought in, and that bothered him. He thought it was probably being searched by now. The police car was gone also.

He needed a drink. He looked at his watch: 8.30. Someone behind him said, "Gree-gory Feesher."

He turned back to the desk. A middle-aged woman with short red hair said, "I am from Intourist. I may see your papers?"

Fisher handed her the large envelope. She went through each paper carefully. "You are late. We were worried about you."

"Nothing to worry about now, is there? May I go to my room?"

"Of course. It's on the seventh floor." She handed him his papers minus his passport and visa, then gave him a green hotel card. "This is your *propusk*. Carry this always with you. Your passport and visa will be returned when you check out. You must produce the *propusk* when anyone in authority asks for it."

"Where is my luggage?" he asked.

"It will be along presently."

Fisher took the elevator to the seventh floor. The doors opened to reveal a small vestibule where a pretty young blonde sat at a desk. Fisher knew this woman was the floor's *dezhurnaya*—a guardian of public morals and, according to a Pole he'd met in Warsaw, also a KGB snoop.

Fisher gave her his *propusk*, and she handed him his room key. "Give me key when you leave. I give you *propusk*."

"Sounds fair."

She pointed down the hall, and at a turn in the corridor Fisher found his room, 745. He opened the door with his key and went in.

It was a medium-sized room, clean except for the window. He had not seen a single clean window in the whole of the Soviet Union. Fisher fell onto the bed and picked up the telephone. He dialled room service and ordered a bottle of vodka.

He had managed to suppress his fear so far, but his resolve was draining away fast in the quiet, empty room. He began to shake again, then bounded off the bed and paced the room. What if they come for me now? he thought. Maybe I should try to get to the embassy. But they're watching me. Can they know what happened at Borodino?

There was a loud rap on the door, and Fisher turned with a start. Another knock. He took a breath, went to the door, and threw it open. A matronly woman stood there with an ice bucket, from which protruded

386

a litre bottle of vodka. Fisher showed her in, gave her a tube of toothpaste, and showed her out.

His hand shook as he poured a half tumbler of the chilled vodka. He drank it down, and it made his eyes water. He refilled his glass and continued pacing. "The next knock will be my luggage or the KGB. The lousy K—" He stopped. He'd heard that every room was bugged. He put down his glass and took his shoulder bag. He slipped quietly out of his room into the hall and retraced his steps to the elevator lobby.

Fisher put his keys on the *dezhurnaya*'s desk. She looked up. " 'Ello, Mr. Fisher." She gave him his *propusk*, and he gave her a tube of frosted pink lip gloss from his bag.

She smiled as she examined it. "Thank you."

Fisher pushed the button for the elevator. When it came, he stepped in. Two Russian men who smelled of salami stood quietly behind him. Fisher felt perspiration under his arms.

He stepped out into the lobby and felt somewhat better in a public place. He found a foreign-exchange window, but it was closed. All he needed was a lousy two-kopeck piece. He noticed a well-dressed couple speaking French, and he approached them. "*Pardon, monsieur, madame. J'ai besoin de . . . deux kopecks. Pour le téléphone.*"

The woman smiled and searched through her bag. "*Voilà.*"

"*Merci, madame. Merci.*" Fisher moved off and located a single telephone booth in a dark corridor. He went inside and closed the door. He found the number of the American embassy in his guidebook, inserted the two-kopeck piece and dialled. The blood was pounding in his ears. He kept his eyes on the corridor as he listened to the short, distant ringing.

LISA RHODES had just crossed out a line on her press release when the phone rang. She picked up the receiver. "Rhodes here."

"This is Corporal Hines, ma'am. I have a call from a man who says he is a US national. Says he wants to speak to a defence attaché. Sounds young. Won't say where he's calling from."

Her eyebrows rose. "Put him through."

The phone clicked. A male voice said, "Hello?"

"This is Ms. Rhodes speaking. Can I help you?"

"I have to speak to a defence attaché. Air force, if possible. It's important. National security."

She checked the recording device to make sure it was activated. "Then perhaps it's not a good idea to speak on the phone."

"I know that. But I don't have any choice. I have to tell you now— before they come for me."

"Who is going to come for you?"

"You know who."

"All right." She thought a moment. There was a possibility that this was a prank, but her instinct said it was not. "What is your name, sir?"

He ignored the question. "Is your phone tapped?"

"You must assume it is."

"Oh, God! Can you send someone to get me? I need help."

"Listen to me," she said with authority. "Talk to me, and if I think it advisable, I will locate a defence attaché. All right?"

"Yes . . . Yes, OK."

She found the duty officer's procedure manual in a drawer and flipped through it as she spoke. "Are you an American citizen?"

"Yes, I—"

"What is your name?"

There was a pause; then the voice answered, "Gregory Fisher."

"Where are you now?"

"The Rossiya Hotel. Room number seven forty-five. But I'm not in my room. I'm in a phone booth in the lobby."

"What is your business in the Soviet Union?"

"No business. I'm a tourist."

"What tour group are you with?"

"Group? No group. I drove—"

"You *drove* to Moscow?"

"Yes. My own car. That was part of the problem. A Trans Am sticks out."

"Yes. All right. Tell me briefly why you need help and why you would like to speak to a defence attaché."

He sighed, then said softly, "In case you can't get here in time, I'll tell you all I can before they get me. I was in Borodino, about five p.m. tonight, visiting the battlefield. I got lost in the woods."

"Were you stopped by the police?"

"No. Yes, but in Moscow."

"Why?"

"For driving in the country at night."

She thought that this wasn't computing. A travel-itinerary violation was one thing. Asking to speak to a defence attaché—a person who was more or less an intelligence officer, a spy—was quite another. "Go on, Mr. Fisher."

"On the road, north of Borodino, I met a man. An American. He said he was an American air-force pilot."

"And he was on the road at night? Alone? In a car?"

"Alone. On foot. He was hurt. Listen, I don't know how much time I have. His name was Major Jack Dodson. He said he was registered as missing in action—a POW—shot down in Vietnam."

"What?" She sat up in her chair. "He told you that?"

"Yes. And he said he had been a prisoner here in Russia for almost twenty years. A place he called Mrs. Ivanova's Charm School. Near Borodino. He escaped. I gave him maps and money. He didn't want us to travel together in my car. He's heading for Moscow cross-country. To the embassy. There are other Americans held prisoner who—"

"Stop. Hold the line." She hit the "hold" button. In the duty book she found the number of the air attaché, Colonel Sam Hollis. She rang his office, two floors above. The phone was picked up on the first ring. "Hollis."

She said in a controlled voice, "Colonel Hollis, this is Lisa Rhodes on the duty desk. I have a US national on the line. He sounds very distraught. I'll play the tape for you."

Lisa transferred the playback to Hollis's line. When it was finished, Hollis said, "Put him through."

She put the phone on conference call and released the "Hold" button. "Mr. Fisher? Are you there?"

"Yes. There's someone standing—"

Lisa said, "Here is the gentleman you asked for."

Hollis's voice came on the line. "Mr. Fisher, you say you are calling from the lobby of the Rossiya. Is the lobby crowded?"

"No. Why?"

"Who is standing by the phone booth?"

"A man. Listen, should I try to get to the embassy?"

"No. Stay there. Do not go back to your room. There is a restaurant on the top floor. Go to the bar there and introduce yourself to some westerners—English-speaking if possible—and stay with them until I arrive. What are you wearing?"

"Blue jeans, black windbreaker."

"OK, son. Get to the bar quickly. If anyone tries to stop you, kick, scream, yell and fight. Understand?"

"Yes. I . . ." Fisher's voice sounded strained. "Oh, please hurry."

Hollis's tone was soothing. "Ten minutes, Greg. Get to the bar."

Lisa heard the phone click as Fisher hung up. Hollis said, "Ms. Rhodes, I need a car."

CHAPTER 3

Colonel Sam Hollis, American air attaché to the Soviet Union, went directly to the duty office on the ground floor.

Lisa Rhodes turned towards him. "Colonel Hollis, I almost didn't recognise you in civvies."

"Have we met?"

"A few times." She regarded him for a moment. He was wearing a leather bomber jacket, jeans and leather boots. He was in his late forties, tall and lanky, rather good-looking in a tough sort of way, with pale blue eyes and unmilitary-length sandy hair.

Hollis said, "I don't want you to breathe a word of this to anyone."

"I know that."

"Good. There is someone, however . . . Do you know Seth Alevy? Political-affairs officer. He's at a party in town."

"I've already asked his people to get him here." She hesitated. "I know he's involved with things like this."

"Are you involved with things like this?"

"Oh, no. I'm just a public-information officer. Seth and I are social friends."

They looked at each other a moment. Hollis guessed she was in her late twenties. She was lightly freckled, with reddish auburn hair. She was not the type of woman you would forget meeting, and in fact he had not forgotten the times they'd met in the embassy. He also knew that she and Alevy had recently been lovers. But by instinct and training he never offered information, only solicited it. "Hold the fort. See you later."

He left and walked quickly through the lobby, pushed through the glass doors into the damp, misty night. A blue Ford Fairlane sat in the forecourt and Hollis jumped into the passenger seat. "Hello, Bill."

The driver, a security staffman named Bill Brennan, drove quickly towards the gates. "Where we going, Colonel?"

"Rossiya."

The car moved past the marine guard post, the gates swung open, and they passed the two Soviet militiamen in their booth on the pavement. Brennan kept the speed down so as not to attract the attention of the KGB embassy watchers in the surrounding buildings, but Hollis said, "Step on it. They know where I'm going."

"Do I stop for police?" Brennan asked. He was in his mid-fifties, heavyset and balding, and his nose had once been broken.

"No, you run them. Don't take the direct route up Kalinin."

"Gotcha." The Ford picked up speed in the outside lane and sailed past the Kalinin Prospect intersection. Brennan knew the streets of Moscow better than a cabbie.

Hollis looked at the speedometer and saw they were doing seventy miles per hour. They crossed the Moskva at the Crimea Bridge, skirted Gorky Park to the right, and continued east along the wide six-lane road. Brennan's route might take them a few extra minutes, but it would avoid any KGB who were out to intercept them. Brennan suddenly cut left, with squealing tyres, and headed up Ordynka Street.

Hollis hitched up the left leg of his blue jeans, reached into his boot, and pulled out a grey air-force survival knife. He slipped the knife under his jacket and into his belt. He could see the Moskvoretsky Bridge about half a kilometre ahead, and beyond the bridge he saw the Rossiya. Hollis heard a horn honking behind them. He looked out of the rear window. "The fuzz. He's on our tail."

"Not for long."

Brennan took the narrow bridge at eighty miles per hour, bounced off

390

it, then tore across the embankment road. As they approached the Rossiya, Hollis said, "You keep going. Back to the embassy."

Brennan swung towards the entrance. "Ready?"

Hollis saw that the parking area did not have a Trans Am in it, and took this as a bad sign. "Ready. Nice job."

Brennan slowed the car in front of the hotel. Hollis jumped out as Brennan accelerated up the exit ramp.

Hollis pushed through the front doors of the Rossiya, and the doorman said, "*Propusk.*"

"*Komitet,*" Hollis replied as he brushed past him.

The man literally jumped back. Hollis went directly to the elevator and hit the button. *Komitet.* Committee. The Committee for State Security— the KGB. Magic words. Open sesame. The fact that he'd arrived in an American car, wearing American clothing, made no difference to the doorman. No one else would dare utter that word.

The elevator arrived and Hollis rode up to the top floor. The Rossiya was a confusing amalgam of four separate wings attached to form a square round a central court. The east wing was an Intourist hotel, the west wing was for Soviet and Eastern-bloc citizens only, while the north and south wings were residences for favoured Communists. At the top, however, East and West met.

When he entered, Hollis saw that the bar was full. Here, for Western currency, you could buy Western hard liquor and brand-name mixers. The clientele were mostly West Europeans, and nearly all were guests at the hotel. Somewhere in the crowd there was also a resident KGB snoop who could eavesdrop in ten languages. Hollis walked round the lounge, but didn't see anyone who could be Gregory Fisher.

He elbowed through the crowd at the bar and spoke to the bartender in fluent Russian. "I'm looking for a friend. An American. He is young and has on blue jeans and a short black jacket."

The bartender glanced at him quickly but continued to make drinks. "I didn't see anyone like that."

Hollis left the bar and walked quickly to the east-wing elevators. He rode down to the seventh floor and got off. The *dezhurnaya* looked at him curiously. "*Gost?*"

"No. Visitor." He leaned over her desk and looked her directly in the eye. "Fisher. Gregory Fisher. American."

She rolled a tube of lip gloss in her fingers, then shook her head. He walked past her, and she called after him, "You may not go there."

Hollis ignored her. He found room 745 and knocked.

A voice from behind the door said, "Who is it?"

"I'm from the embassy."

Hollis heard the lock turn, and the door opened. A paunchy middle-aged man wearing a bathrobe peered sleepily out of the room. "Is everything all right?"

Hollis looked past him into the room. "I'm looking for Mr. Fisher."

The man seemed relieved. "Oh, I thought something had happened at home. My wife. My name is Schiller."

Hollis stared at him. "Mr. Fisher told me he was in seven forty-five."

Schiller's manner went from worried to slightly annoyed. "So? He's not here, pal. I don't know the guy. Try four fifty-seven. Anything's possible in this screwed-up country." The man closed the door.

Hollis stood there a moment, then walked back to the elevators. The *dezhurnaya* was gone. Hollis took the elevator down to the lobby. He rang the bell at the front desk, and the clerk appeared. Hollis said in Russian, "What room is Gregory Fisher in?"

The clerk shook her head. "Not here." She turned and disappeared into the inner office. Hollis looked towards the foyer and saw there was a different doorman on duty. People are disappearing left and right, before my very eyes, he thought. Amazing country.

Several possibilities came to mind, including the possibility that this was all a KGB *provokatsiya*—a ruse to draw him into some sort of compromising situation. Or kill him. But if they wanted to trap him, there were less elaborate ways. He thought about Fisher's voice, the words, the very real fright in his tone. Fisher was real.

Hollis considered the evidence. Fisher's phone call to the embassy had tipped off the KGB, but they would have needed time to react. Therefore Fisher could have made it to the lounge. Hollis took the elevator back to the top floor and went to the bar. He ordered a Scotch and said to the bartender in Russian, "Have you seen my friend yet?"

"No. I'm sorry. Three dollars."

A well-dressed man next to Hollis thrust his glass towards the bartender and said with a British accent, "Gin and tonic. Slice of lemon this time."

Hollis said, "They've been out of lemons since the Revolution."

The Englishman laughed. "What a place this is, eh?"

The man's drink came without the lemon, and the bartender asked for three pounds. The Englishman said, "They make their own exchange rates as they go along. Three dollars, three pounds—all the same to them. Name's Wilson."

"Richardson," Hollis replied as they tipped their glasses to each other. "Listen, I'm looking for a friend—American, in his twenties, blue jeans and windbreaker. Have you seen him?"

"I think I did. Those two over there—French, I think—had a young chap with them. Could be your fellow. He'd had a few too many, and two people from the hotel helped him out."

"When was this?"

"About fifteen, twenty minutes ago."

"Thanks." Hollis moved through the cocktail tables and sat down opposite the man and woman. "May I?"

392

The man grunted in reply.

Hollis asked, "Do you speak English?"

The man shook his head. The woman said, "A little."

Hollis leaned across the table and spoke softly and distinctly. "I am looking for a friend, an American, a young man named Gregory Fisher. I understand he had a drink with you earlier."

The woman glanced at the man beside her before replying. "Yes. He was ill. He was aided to his room."

"Did he seem . . . agitated? Worried?"

The woman did not reply but nodded almost imperceptibly. The man rose and said to the woman, "*Allons.*"

She remained seated. "He said they may come for him. I think the drink was drugged." She stood up. "My husband wishes to go. There is no more I know. I am sorry."

Hollis stood also. "You understand, madame, this is a matter of some concern to the authorities here. You may be in danger."

The Frenchman walked away impatiently. The woman lingered and looked Hollis in the eye. "Are you the attaché?"

"Yes."

"He said you would come. He said to tell you . . ." The woman thought a moment, then recited, "Dodson told him it was once a Red air-force school. Now it is a KGB school. There are three hundred Americans."

"Three *hundred*?" Hollis found himself holding the woman's arm in a tight grip. "What else did Mr. Fisher say?"

"Nothing. He became ill. They came for him. A Russian spoke to us in English, asking what the young man said. My husband replied in French, saying we spoke no English and could not understand the Russian or the young man."

Hollis released her arm. "Then perhaps you will be all right. But you should contact your embassy. Then leave the country immediately."

She nodded. "The boy borrowed from me two kopecks. He seemed a nice sort." She walked away.

Hollis left the lounge and took the elevator down to the Zaryadye Cinema. He mixed with the crowd in the lobby and exited through the door that faced the Moskva River embankment. He followed a group into the tunnel under the road and came out onto the pavement of the Moskvoretsky Bridge. A fog rose off the Moskva below, and there was a fine rain falling. He turned up the fleece collar of his leather jacket. I tried, Fisher, I tried, he told himself. He headed for the metro.

SAM HOLLIS GOT OFF the metro at Smolenskaya station and walked into the Krasnaya Presnya district, where the new American embassy was located. The district had once been a squalid industrial suburb. During the revolution of 1905 the workers here had fought the tsar's army, and the whole area had been subject to intense artillery bombardment. It was largely rebuilt, but Hollis still sensed its tragedy. Russia was a very sad country.

Hollis looked up and saw the towering chancery building, its windows all alight. A few minutes later he saw the red-brick outer walls and the embassy residences that rose above them. The streets were deserted.

The main embassy entrance was a hundred metres away, and Hollis could see the Soviet militia booth. He heard a car draw up behind him. It kept pace with him, just to his rear. The driver flashed his lights. Hollis did not turn round.

The car drew abreast of him and stopped. Hollis saw it was a Chaika, a black four-door sedan, the type favoured by the KGB. The driver stayed behind the wheel and two men got out. They both wore leather car coats, black trousers, leather gloves and narrow-brimmed hats—what Hollis called KGB evening attire. One was short and squat, the other taller and better built.

Hollis continued towards the embassy, his hands in his pockets, his right hand through a slit in his jacket and round the handle of his knife. He heard the footsteps of the two men behind him, but kept walking. Suddenly he felt a powerful blow in the small of his back and lurched forward, sprawling across the pavement. He rolled to the side and barely avoided a kick, then splashed into the wet gutter.

Hollis wanted to take out the knife, but he knew that was what they wanted too. He remained where he was. The short one spat on Hollis; then the two men turned and walked back towards the Chaika.

Hollis stood and brushed the filth from his clothes. He felt a raw abrasion on his cheekbone and a dull pain in his back. The Chaika sped away.

Hollis approached the embassy, and a Soviet militiaman stepped out of the booth. "*Pasport.*"

"You know who I am," Hollis snapped. "Get out of my way."

The militiaman stiffened. "*Stoi!*"

A marine guard appeared at the gates and called out, "What's going on there?" He was armed and could not cross the threshold of the property. Hollis yelled, "Open the gates." Then he brushed past the militiaman and walked to the entrance of the compound.

The guard saluted. "Are you all right, Colonel?"

"Fine." Hollis strode across the courtyard, and in the distance he could hear the bells of the tower of Ivan the Great, in the Kremlin, chiming midnight. He entered the chancery and went directly to the duty office.

Lisa Rhodes stood up as he walked in. "Oh, Colonel Hollis. We were getting worried. We—"

"Did Bill Brennan make it back?"

"Yes. He's in the infirmary. There was some trouble, but I don't have the details. What happened to your face?"

"Tripped. Is Seth Alevy here yet?"

"He's waiting for you in the sixth-floor safe room." She paused. "May I come? Seth said I could if it was all right with you."

"Is that so? Come along, then."

They walked to the elevator in silence, rode up to the sixth floor and stepped across the corridor. Hollis pressed a buzzer.

The door opened, and Seth Alevy said, "Come in, please."

Lisa Rhodes looked round the dimly lit room. The chancery had several safe rooms, but this was the first time she had been in this one. It was an interior room, like the others. The floor was covered with a thick royal-blue carpet, and the walls and door were carpeted in a camel colour. The ceiling was black acoustic foam rubber. The room was impervious to listening devices, and was swept for bugs two or three times a day.

Hollis looked at Alevy. He was about forty, some years younger than Hollis. He wore a nicely tailored three-piece tweed suit with a green knitted tie. He was too tall and too lean and reminded Hollis of an unbearded Lincoln, though somehow better-looking.

Hollis recalled what he knew of Seth. The man was a Philadelphian, a Jew, and a Princeton graduate. He had once told Hollis in a rare candid moment that he hated the Soviets and had joined the CIA "to do maximum damage".

"They rough you up, Colonel?" Alevy asked.

"You know very well what happened, Seth."

"Well," Alevy replied, "if they had gotten out of hand, my people would have stepped in. You were covered."

"How is Brennan?"

"He didn't fare as well as you. The cops finally caught up with him. They kept him standing around in the rain for half an hour, then just gave him a ticket and left. But before he could get back to his car, a bunch of KGB hooligans appeared and beat him up. He got his nose broken again. Doc Logan says he'll be OK, but he has to go to the West for proper care."

Hollis nodded. Score another point for the KGB tonight.

Alevy said, "I assume you have a tale to tell. We're listening."

Hollis glanced at Lisa.

Alevy said, "It's all right. I had a top-secret clearance done on Ms. Rhodes some months ago."

"OK," Hollis said. He related the events of the evening.

No one spoke for a while; then Alevy said, "I'm interested in the man in room seven forty-five. Was he definitely an American?"

"Right down to the aftershave lotion."

"He could have been an American in the employ of the KGB," Alevy speculated. "Or maybe Fisher got his room number wrong."

Lisa remarked, "We all heard the tape. I think he got it right."

Seth Alevy paced round the room in thought. He said finally, "Well,

I'll handle it from here." He turned to Hollis. "I'll take a report from you and forward it to CIA headquarters. You'll want a copy sent to your section in the Pentagon."

Hollis stood up. "That's right."

Alevy added, "I don't see any military intelligence angle here, Sam. You might think this Major Dodson thing concerns you because Major Dodson, if he exists, was or is a POW and so on. But I'll let you know if I need you."

Hollis went to the door. "Thank you, Mr. Alevy," he said. He left and walked to the elevator. Lisa joined him, and they rode down to the ground floor. They walked out of the rear of the chancery into the cold October night.

Lisa said, "My apartment is to the left."

"Mine's to the right."

"Will you walk with me?"

They took the path to the left, which was bordered by newly planted birches. To the right was the quadrangle formed on three sides by terraced houses and the marine barracks, and on the fourth side by the chancery building.

Lisa came to a stop. "This is my place."

They stood in the cold mist. "Well, I suppose we'd better get out of the rain." He held out his hand.

She seemed not to notice and said, "You and Seth were short with each other. Are you enemies, or just rivals?"

"Neither. We enjoy each other. It's just our way of speaking."

She considered a moment. "Do you have antiseptic for those cuts? I have some witch hazel."

"I'm going to the infirmary to see Brennan. I'll get something there."

"Good." She picked a wet twig from his fleece collar and handed it to him. "I have tomorrow off. I wanted to go to the Marx and Engels museum. I haven't seen it yet. Have you?"

"It's not on my list."

"Anyway, I'm a little . . . concerned now. About going out alone, I mean. I guess they know who I am now. From the tape."

He examined the twig thoughtfully, then spoke in a soft voice. "I don't think you have anything to worry about. Besides, you can't let them dictate how you are going to live. They are not omnipotent, nor omnipresent. They just want you to think that. It makes their job easier."

"Yes, I know. But that is not what I had in mind, Colonel. I'm asking you if you would like to come with me tomorrow?"

Hollis cleared his throat. "Well, why don't we have lunch and save the Marx and Engels museum for a special occasion?"

She smiled. "Call for me here at noon." She turned and walked to her door. "Good night, Colonel Hollis."

"Good night, Ms. Rhodes."

CHAPTER 4

"Yes. I . . . Oh, please. Hurry."

"Ten minutes, Greg. Get to the bar."

Seth Alevy hit the "Stop" button on the tape player.

Charles Banks, special aide to the American ambassador, sat at the head of the long mahogany table in the ambassador's safe room. Sam Hollis sat on his right, opposite Alevy.

"A voice-stress analysis was done on the tape this morning. Our expert says that Gregory Fisher was probably telling the truth and was under actual stress," Alevy said to Charles Banks.

"Really?" replied Banks. "They can tell that? Amazing."

Hollis looked at Charles Banks, a man near sixty, with snow-white hair, a ruddy avuncular face and sparkling blue eyes. He was a career diplomat, with easy social graces. Yet behind the diplomat's polish Hollis recognised a kindred spirit; Hollis thought that Charles Banks was the third spy in this room.

Alevy continued. "And as I've indicated, Colonel Hollis believes he can establish that Mr. Fisher was at the Rossiya last night."

"So, despite the fact that the authorities say Mr. Fisher was never at the Rossiya," said Banks, "you two are convinced he was. Let me ask you this: Are you sure there is an American called Gregory Fisher in the Soviet Union?"

"Actually," Alevy answered, "we know where Gregory Fisher is now. He is in Mozhaisk. In the morgue."

Banks leaned forward across the table. "Dead? How terrible!"

Alevy replied drily, "Yes, sir. A Soviet official called about twenty minutes ago. Mr. Fisher had a car accident. According to the militia report, peasants found Mr. Fisher's car at daybreak this morning, eighteen kilometres west of Mozhaisk, in a ravine just off the Minsk–Moscow highway. The car apparently had been heading towards Moscow and went off the road, crashing into a tree. We are requested to take charge of the body for shipment out of the Soviet Union."

Banks seemed to be pondering all this, then said, "That would indicate that Mr. Fisher never got to Moscow."

Alevy replied, "Fisher's call came through without operator assistance, so it must have been made from metropolitan Moscow. In addition, we have the voice-stress test and the witnesses. Mr. Banks, what we are suggesting is that the Soviet authorities murdered Gregory Fisher."

"Oh." Banks nodded slowly. "Yes, I see." He glanced at his watch and stood up. "Well, I'll speak to the ambassador about this. I trust you'll both keep in mind the political considerations that may arise as a result of this incident."

Alevy stood. "Of course, sir."

"Splendid. Colonel Hollis?"

Hollis remained seated. "Once, I bombed only politically approved targets. We lost the war."

Banks responded in a soothing voice. "War is too important to be left to generals and colonels. Especially cold war. Good day, gentlemen." He went out of the door.

Alevy said to Hollis, "Why didn't you just say OK? That's all Banks wanted to hear."

Hollis stood. "An American citizen has been murdered, and I'm a little teed off."

"You feel partly responsible, I know. But you have to see the diplomatic point of view. They're trying to crank up détente again— that's the numero-uno consideration right now. If I found two KGB men in the basement planting a bomb, the ambassador would tell me to forget it. One can't become personally involved."

"Why was Fisher murdered?"

Alevy walked to the door. "You know. He saw something. Heard something. Something big."

"Right. And we're supposed to find out what it is. That's why they put us here. I'm going to go for the body."

Alevy looked annoyed. "Wrong. Someone in the consular section is going for the body. That's their job."

"I don't think you heard me. *I* am going. I'll need two passes from the Foreign Ministry. I'm taking company."

"Who?"

"Lisa Rhodes."

"Is that so? How do you know she wants to go?"

"Everyone here would like to get out of Moscow. Even picking up a corpse is a treat."

"The *Komitet* may not be able to resist the temptation to get you to the morgue on *their* terms. Keep in mind, I can't cover you out in Mozhaisk."

"You can't cover me fifty yards from the embassy. Two passes in my office before noon."

Alevy opened the door to leave, but Hollis closed it and asked, "Did you find out if a Major Jack Dodson is listed as missing in action in Vietnam?"

"I'm checking it, Sam. I'll keep you fully informed."

"I know you will, Seth. It's a joy working with the CIA."

Alevy patted Hollis's shoulder. "Try not to get killed on the Minsk—Moscow highway."

SAM HOLLIS PULLED ON his blue jeans, then his leather boots. He slipped his knife into the left boot and strapped an ankle holster above the right one. He checked his Tokarev 7.62-mm automatic. If he had to shoot

398

someone, it was better to leave a Soviet-made slug in the body. He screwed a silencer into the muzzle and stuck the automatic into the ankle holster. He put on a black turtleneck sweater and over that his leather jacket.

He left his apartment and walked across the wide quadrangle to Lisa Rhodes's door. He rang the bell. The terraced brick houses for single people were narrow, but they were three storeys high. The ground floor was a laundry and storage room. A hall with a staircase led up to the living room, dining area and kitchen. The second floor held one or two bedrooms, sometimes a study. Hollis heard footsteps on the stairs; then the door opened.

"Hello," she said. She was wearing ankle-high boots, black corduroy slacks, and a dark blue quilted jacket, which the Russians called a *vatnik*.

"Are you going to tell me why you requested I dress in casual clothes in dark colours?" she asked.

"I'll tell you later. Let's go."

They walked through the pedestrian gate at the rear of the compound.

"Where are we going for lunch?" Lisa asked Hollis.

"The Prague."

"Then we can walk up Arbat Street."

They walked along a wide boulevard, then turned up Arbat, the Soviet Union's first and only pedestrian shopping street. Hundreds of people were out on this promising Saturday, every one of them carrying a big bag. Benches, decorative streetlamps and flower boxes ran the length of the street.

Hollis said to Lisa, "Do you like this area?"

"Sort of. But it's a bit sanitised, if you know what I mean."

"Have you seen the unsanitised parts of the Arbat?"

"Oh, yes. I know every block of what's left of old Moscow."

"Are you a Russophile?"

She smiled. "Sort of. Yes. I like the people, the language, old Russia. Actually, I have Russian blood."

"Oh, do you?"

She took his arm as they walked. "My grandparents were named Putyatov. They owned a large estate on the Volga. I have an old picture of the house."

"Is it still there?"

"I don't know. This is not like Western Europe, where you can go back and trace your ancestry. There's been a complete break here—whole families wiped out, two world wars, revolution. Besides, what would I do if I found the house, or found a Putyatov?"

"You'd know what to do. You have a Russian soul."

She smiled and Hollis gave her a sidelong glance. Now that she'd mentioned it, there was something vaguely Russian about her. She was quite pretty, with high Slavic cheekbones and sharp features. Her complexion was light, and her eyes were big and blue. Her auburn hair was cut in a shaggy style.

She led him down a side street called Kalachny, or pastrycook. The streets in the Arbat recalled the names of the sixteenth-century court tradesmen who once lived and worked there: Plotnikov, carpenter; Serebryany, silversmith; and so on.

"Where are you taking me?" Hollis asked.

"To lunch. Do you mind if we skip the Prague?"

"All right, but there aren't any restaurants this way."

"There's one."

He followed her into an old stucco building and down a set of stairs to the basement. Lisa opened a door, and Hollis saw a large, dimly lit room with a low wooden ceiling. The floors and walls were covered with Oriental carpets, and a cloud of aromatic tobacco smoke hung in the air. An old woman approached, smiling widely. *"Salaam aleihum,"* she said.

Lisa returned the greeting and followed the proprietress to a low table laid with a dirty red cloth and mismatched tableware. Lisa and Hollis sat, and Lisa ordered a bottle of plum wine. The woman moved off.

Hollis looked round. "Is this place in the guidebooks?"

"No, but it ought to be. It's Azerbaijanian, sort of Middle Eastern. It's owned and operated by a produce cooperative. It's legal. And the food is better than in the best restaurants."

"How did you find it?"

"Long story."

Hollis thought it could be told in one word: Seth.

The plum wine came, and Lisa poured. Hollis touched glasses with her and toasted, "As the peasants say, 'To a short winter, ample meat and dry wood for the fire.'"

"You forgot the last line."

"Yes. 'And a warm woman for my bed.'"

They drank. Lisa looked at him over the rim of her glass. She asked, "Sam, where are you from, originally?"

"All over. I'm an air-force brat—older brother, younger sister. We moved all over the globe until I was eighteen. Then I spent four years at the Air Force Academy and went on to fighter school. I did a tour in Nam in 1968, then another in 1972. I was shot down over Haiphong. I bailed out and was picked up by air-sea rescue in the harbour. I was banged up a bit, and the flight surgeons said, no more flying. My father was a brigadier general by this time and got me a posting in the Pentagon. Somehow I wound up taking a language course in Bulgarian. I did three years in Sofia as an air attaché, then did stints in a couple of other Warsaw Pact countries, and before I knew it, I was involved with this embassy attaché business."

"And then about two years ago they sent you here. The big league. How about your family?"

"My father retired some years ago. He and my mother live in Japan. I'm not sure why."

Lisa hesitated. "I seem to remember a wife."

"Wife? Oh, yes. Katherine. She went to London to shop."

"I think she's been gone about half a year."

"Has it been that long?" He poured more wine. "We're in the process of a divorce."

The proprietress came to the table. Lisa ordered for both herself and Hollis, then she remarked, "Bulgarian? I thought your Russian was odd. I don't mean American-accented or anything, but not Russian-accented either."

Hollis smiled. "It's an article of faith with the Russians that only a Russian can speak *Russian* Russian. Yet Seth Alevy is nearly perfect. If he were trying to pass, a Muscovite would think he was probably a Leningrader, and vice versa."

"Perhaps on the telephone. But there's more to being a Russian than the language. The Russians *are* different, in unique ways. Neither you nor I nor Seth could pass for a Russian, any more than we could pass for an Oriental."

Hollis said, "I wonder. Given the right training, could an American pass for a Russian in a group of Russians? Could a Russian pass for an American at a back-yard barbecue?"

"Perhaps for a while, if no one was looking for a counterfeit. But under close examination something would betray the person."

"Would it? What if a Russian who already knew English went to a special school? A school with an American instructor? A total immersion in Americana for, let's say, a year or more. Would you get a perfect copy of the American instructor?"

"The instructors and the students would have to be very dedicated." She added, "We're talking about spies, aren't we?"

"You are. I'm not. You're very bright." Hollis changed the subject. "Your Russian is good. Where did you learn it?"

"My grandmother taught me. Her name was Evelina Vasilevna Putyatova. She was a wonderful woman." Lisa lit a cigarette and continued, "I was born and raised in Sea Cliff, on Long Island's north shore. It has a large Russian community that goes back to tsarist times. The Revolution brought a second wave of immigrants, among whom were my grandmother and grandfather. They were in their early twenties and recently married. My grandfather's father was a tsarist officer, and he was killed fighting the Germans. My grandmother's parents had already been arrested by the local Bolsheviks and shot. Sensing the party was over, my grandparents grabbed the jewels and the gold and got out. They wound up in Sea Cliff."

"And your grandmother told you all this?"

"Yes. When I was about sixteen, she told me about the Revolution, the civil war, the epidemics, the famine. It affected me very deeply. But she taught me love too—love of old Russia, the people, the language, the Orthodox Church. She had a deep and lasting influence on me. She died when I was away at college."

Neither of them spoke for some time; then Lisa said, "I went to the University of Virginia and got my degree in Soviet studies. I took the Foreign Service entrance exam and was vetted for a top-secret clearance. My first United States Information Service job was in India. Then off to East Berlin for two years, where I finally used my Russian. That was a good embassy—exciting, mysterious, spies all over the place. After Berlin I finally got what I wanted. Moscow. And here I am."

"And your parents?"

"They both still live in Sea Cliff. My father is a banker, my mother a teacher. They can see the harbour from their porch. It's lovely."

The food arrived, and Hollis enquired, "What is this?"

"That's *dovta*, a soup made of sour milk and rice. And the meatballs are called *golubtsy*."

Hollis helped himself. They ate in silence. More plates of spiced food arrived. They washed the meal down with weak Moscow beer.

Hollis glanced at his watch. "How would you like to take a ride in the country this afternoon?" he asked. "I have to go to Mozhaisk on official business. I have a pass with your name on it."

"Do you? I'd love to go. What sort of business?"

"Bad business, Lisa. Fisher is in the Mozhaisk morgue."

"Oh, Sam. That poor boy. Was he trying to escape?"

"No. They say he was heading *towards* Moscow. They say he had a car accident and never got to the Rossiya."

"They're lying."

"Be that as it may, I want you to understand now that if you come with me, I can't guarantee your safety. Still want to go?"

"Yes. So that's why I'm wearing dark casual clothes."

Hollis stood up and put six roubles on the table. "Well, the food wasn't so bad, and the place has atmosphere. Two and a half stars. Send a letter to the Michelin guide."

They left the restaurant, and Hollis found himself in an agreeable frame of mind for the first time in a long while.

CHAPTER 5

Sam Hollis and Lisa Rhodes came out of Arbat Street into the square of the same name. Hollis took Lisa's arm and led her towards the east side of the square, where a small black Zhiguli was parked at the kerb with its engine running. "Get in."

Hollis went to the driver's side. A man whom Lisa recognised from the embassy got out. Hollis slid behind the wheel and closed the door. The man said, "Full tank; transmission is a bit sticky; your briefcase is on the back seat. Luck."

"Thanks." Hollis threw the Zhiguli into gear and pulled out into Kalinin Prospect, then made a sudden U-turn and headed west. He accelerated up the broad avenue and within minutes he had left the inner city.

He reached under his seat and pulled out a black wool cap and a dark blue scarf. He put the cap on and handed Lisa the scarf. "A *babushka* for madam. Please try it on."

She draped the scarf over her head, tying it at her throat. "It's against the law for us to drive cars without diplomatic plates," she said. "Where is this car from?"

"The Intourist Hotel. Rented and paid for with an American Express card." He smiled. "Moscow is getting too big for the KGB. Too much Western influence. Rental cars, AMEX, a couple of Western banks. It's easier for us to operate now."

Hollis thought that bringing an amateur along might not be the brightest thing he'd done all week. But in some vague way he felt it would be good for her. And a woman with no intelligence connections was good cover.

They crossed the outer ring road, and Hollis handed her a piece of flimsy greyish paper. "Your pass."

She glanced at the red Cyrillic letters and the Foreign Ministry stamp. "It's good until midnight."

"We'll be there and back before then."

Lisa turned her attention to the countryside. A small village of about two dozen houses sat starkly in an open field. Rough fences sectioned off garden plots from poultry and swine, and mud paths connected dilapidated dwellings.

She said thoughtfully, "If Greg Fisher came in from Borodino, this is the road he took."

"Yes, it is."

They lapsed into silence for some time. The sky had become gloomy again, and drops of rain streaked across the windscreen. Lisa gazed at the Russian countryside. "This is it, Sam. Russia. Not Moscow or Leningrad. *Russia.* Look at those white birches. See the small leaves, all red, yellow and gold. Watch what happens when a breeze comes along. What could be more Russian—tiny coloured birch leaves blowing across a grey sky, across a lonely landscape? It's so desolate, it's beautiful."

Hollis glanced at her as she turned to him, and their eyes met. He returned his gaze to the road ahead, and for the first time he felt the presence of the land. They continued in companionable silence, travelling west into the setting sun, cut off from the embassy, the city, the world—alone.

403

The Zhiguli was one of the few private cars on the highway, but Hollis knew it would attract far less attention than an American Ford with diplomatic plates. He knew, too, that he and Lisa could pass for Ivan and Irina out for a weekend drive. He turned off the main road and continued at high speed, churning up gravel as the Zhiguli bounced along a narrow lane. Referring to a sheet of paper in his hand he took a sharp left onto another road. "A Brit charted back routes around a lot of major towns some years ago. This route bypasses Mozhaisk. No road names, just landmarks."

"We're going to Borodino, I suppose?"

"That's correct."

They crossed the tracks of the Byelorussian railway, and a short time later passed the town of Mozhaisk in the distance.

Within fifteen minutes they came to the poplar-lined road to Borodino Field and turned onto it. Ahead were the stone columns and towering gates that led to the battlefield. The gates were chained shut.

Lisa said, "Outdoor exhibits close early, this time of year."

"That's what I counted on." Hollis swung the Zhiguli round and cut back onto the road towards the museum.

The sun had gone, and the evening had become very still. The deep, dark quiet of the countryside surprised Lisa. "Spooky," she said.

"Romantic."

She smiled despite herself. The glow from their headlights revealed a dozen polished obelisks standing like shimmering sentries.

"Fisher would have come this way," Hollis said softly. "The trick is to retrace how he got lost. Reach into my briefcase and find the aerial survey map . . . good. Now unfold it. Under your seat there should be a red-filtered torch." He turned off the headlights.

She reached beneath her seat and brought out the light.

"He found himself on a road in the woods north of Borodino Field. Further north is the Moskva River, so he must have been between here and the river. The only wood on that aerial map is the *bor*—the pine forest. See it?"

"Yes." She looked up from the map. "Over there, in the hills."

"OK. Now I'm coming to a fork in the road."

She shone the red light on the map. "Yes. I see it here. If you take the left fork, it will loop back and begin to climb that hill."

Hollis nodded. The left fork appeared to head back towards the museum but did not. This was where Fisher must have made his fatal error. Hollis took the left fork. The land began to rise. Then the road entered the thick pine forest, and it became very dark. Lisa cleared her throat. "Can you see?"

"Just shine the red light out of the window once in a while."

She rolled down the window, letting in a cold blast of air. The red light picked out the narrow road, and Hollis followed the beam.

Ten minutes later they saw a sign, and Hollis stopped the car. Lisa shone the light on the sign, and they both read the Russian words. "Stop. You are entering a restricted area. Turn back."

"This," Hollis said, "must be the place."

He got out and looked around, discovering the small turning place on the right side of the road. He opened the boot and ripped out the wires for the taillights and the brake lights, then got into the car. He drove into the turning place; but instead of backing out he continued between the pine trees until the Zhiguli was some twenty yards into the forest. He turned the car so that it pointed back towards the road, then killed the engine.

Hollis whispered, "Be ready to make a quick getaway. If I'm not back within the hour, you go on to Mozhaisk and take care of the morgue business. Tell whoever asks that I didn't come along. See you later." He got out, softly closed the door, and began walking through the woods on a course parallel to the road.

Lisa came up beside him. "You're crazy," she said.

"Go back."

"No."

They walked side by side. The forest floor was springy, covered with a carpet of pine needles and cones. There was no wind, and the resinous pine scent was overpowering. The forest was very quiet and very dark.

Within a few minutes they saw signs nailed to the trees at intervals. Lisa turned the red-filtered torch on one and read "Stop. Go back. You are in a restricted area."

Hollis put his mouth to Lisa's ear. "There may be sound sensors. Step lightly, like a deer." He drew his Tokarev pistol from his ankle holster and slipped it into his pocket.

They continued through the forest. A half-moon was rising and cast a weak blue light into patches of clearing. Within five minutes they found themselves facing an eight-foot-tall fence of barbed wire, topped with coiled razor wire. A metal sign on the fence warned "High Voltage". On the other side of the wire the pine trees had been cut to a depth of about fifteen metres. Hollis could see an inner ring of more barbed wire at the far edge of the treeless zone. A watchtower rose up from the inner wire. He whispered, "Mrs. Ivanova's Charm School."

She nodded. "Not charming. Sam, let's go now."

He pulled her down onto the pine carpet. "Listen."

The stillness of the forest was broken by the sound of a diesel engine; then they saw headlights coming towards them. There was a vehicle moving slowly through the raked sand of the cleared zone between the barbed-wire fences. Hollis could see it was a half-track with six helmeted soldiers in an open troop compartment in the rear. Two were manning a swivel-mounted machine gun, two manned a searchlight, and two stood at port arms. Hollis hoped it was a random patrol, but the soldiers looked too tense and alert. As the vehicle drew within ten yards of them Holli whispered to Lisa, "Pull the scarf over your face and cover your hands."

Hollis pulled his wool cap down, and it became a ski mask. He put on black nylon gloves and waited. The half-track came to a halt opposite them. The searchlight snapped on, and a beam shot down the cleared area, then began sweeping the woods beyond the wire. The beam came towards Hollis and Lisa, passed over and continued. Hollis felt Lisa shaking beside him. He found her hand and squeezed it. They waited. After a minute the vehicle moved on. They remained motionless, barely breathing.

After five full minutes Hollis rose cautiously to one knee. He listened closely, then helped Lisa up. They turned away from the barbed wire and Hollis saw, not ten feet into the trees, two KGB border guards moving towards them, AK-47 rifles at the ready.

In an instant Hollis realised Lisa had not seen them, and they had not seen him or her. Lisa moved towards him to say something. The KGB men saw the motion. Hollis, in a single movement, pushed Lisa to the ground, dropped into a crouch, and drew his Tokarev automatic from his pocket. He fired the silenced pistol and saw the first man slap his hand to his chest. The second man brought his rifle into the firing position. Hollis put two rounds into his chest, then walked towards the two men lying on the ground. Lisa came up beside him. "Oh . . . oh, God, Sam!"

"Quiet." He took her arm, and they moved rapidly through the pine forest. Hollis was no longer concerned about the sensors, since there were patrols out now, making their own noise.

Hollis got his bearings and within ten minutes they found the Zhiguli among the trees. They jumped inside. Hollis started the engine, but instead of heading onto the road, he turned deeper into the woods. "Shine that red light ahead," he said.

As Lisa leaned out of the window with the light, Hollis weaved through the pine forest. Behind them they could hear a vehicle on the road they'd come up. She said, "These trees are getting closer. Watch out."

Hollis crushed both wings between two tree trunks, and the Zhiguli was stuck. He tried to throw it into reverse, but the transmission jammed.

He finally got it into reverse, pulled out and found another way. He knew that it was possible to get a vehicle through an evergreen forest. Whole columns of trucks and armour had passed through these Russian pine forests during the war. It was just a matter of finding the spaces.

The ground began to slope down, and the Zhiguli started to slide. Suddenly they broke out of the trees and plunged headlong into a ravine. "Hold on!" Hollis warned. The Zhiguli hit the trough of the ravine and splashed into a shallow stream, nearly overturning. Hollis cut the wheels hard right and pushed the battered car on downstream. The banks lattened, the stream became deeper. Hollis angled the car towards a low pot in the bank and floored the accelerator. The Zhiguli came out of the stream-bed. By the light of the blue half-moon they saw Borodino Field spread before them.

Lisa lit a cigarette with shaking hands. "This is not what I thought you meant by a drive in the country."

Hollis pulled the car into a copse of birches. He flung his pistol and ankle holster into the high grass. "Burn the map."

Lisa hung the map out of the window and touched it with her lighter. It lashed and disappeared in a puff of smoke. Hollis put the car in gear and moved out over the rolling fields, cutting across country. He knew that time and place were critical. If they could get to the morgue in Mozhaisk, they could bluff it out. But if they were caught in open country, the evidence would be strongly against them.

They came upon a small dirt road that marked the boundary of the historic battlefield. Hollis turned north, towards the Moskva River. At the river road he flipped on the headlights and threw his wool cap out of the window. Lisa threw her scarf out and brushed pine needles off their clothing.

Hollis made a fast run into Mozhaisk without encountering another vehicle. The town seemed eerily deserted for a Saturday evening. At length they arrived in front of a white stucco building near the railway tracks. They got out of the car and walked to the door. He pushed a button marked "Night Bell", and they waited.

The heavy wooden door opened, revealing a man wearing the uniform of a KGB colonel. The man said in English, "Come in."

CHAPTER 6

Hollis and Lisa followed the KGB colonel into a cold room of white ceramic tile, smelling of chemicals. The Russian strode over to a freezer chest. Without formalities he opened the lid, exposing the body of a naked man lying in white frost.

The corpse's arms and legs were askew, and the head lolled to one side. Gregory Fisher's eyelids had not been closed, and the staring eyes revealed frozen tears. The chest and face were deeply lacerated. Hollis wondered if they'd tortured him to make him tell them about Dodson.

The KGB colonel handed Lisa a passport. She looked at the photo, then at the corpse, and nodded. She slipped the passport into her bag.

The colonel slammed the freezer shut and motioned them into a small cubicle. He took a seat behind a battered desk and indicated two chairs for them. In English he said, "You are Colonel Hollis, of course, and this must be Lisa Rhodes."

407

"That's correct," Hollis answered. "And you are a colonel of the KGB. I didn't hear your name."

"Burov." He added, "With the death of a foreigner, Soviet law states that the KGB must process the paperwork and so forth. You should attach no further meaning to my presence."

"If you say so."

Hollis placed Burov in his mid-forties. He was a tall, Nordic-looking man with pouty, boyish lips. His skin was fair, his eyes were blue, and his hair was a flaxen yellow.

Burov said, "You are late. What caused your delay?"

"Your Foreign Ministry held up the passes." Hollis added sharply, "Why does everything in this country take twice as long as it does in the civilised world?"

Burov sat back in his chair and lit an oval-shaped Troika cigarette. The heat from the first two puffs caused the flimsy paper and loose tobacco to sag. Burov automatically straightened the cigarette with his fingers. He said calmly, "That was not very diplomatic of you, Colonel, to insult your host country."

"Diplomat to diplomat, that may be true. But you know who I am, and I know who you are. Now, do you have something for us to sign?"

Burov stared down at the cigarette in his hand, then crushed it out on the floor and said, "Many things to sign." He opened a green file folder on the desk and withdrew a stack of papers.

Lisa asked, "How do you propose we transport the body to the airport?"

Burov replied curtly, "The mortician will provide an aluminium air coffin, with dry ice. As in any *civilised* country." He eyed Lisa's jacket. "You both seem to have dressed as though you intended to be gravediggers as well as pallbearers. May I examine your passes and credentials?"

While Burov studied their papers, Hollis studied him. The man spoke unusually good English and was quick-witted. Hollis guessed he had had a lot of dealings with English-speaking people and perhaps was a graduate of the Institute of Canadian and American Studies in Moscow.

Burov made a few notes, then returned the passports but kept the travel passes. He handed Hollis a paper and said, "First, the dead man's automobile has been impounded, and it will be easier if you sign that document waiving any claim on it."

Hollis replied, "I want to see the car."

"The car has been shipped to Moscow. I will have your embassy informed of the location if you wish. Will you sign that?"

Hollis glanced at the waiver, written in Russian and English. Clearly there was no way the Trans Am would get back to the States to be examined by the FBI forensic unit. He signed the paper. "I must have a copy of this."

"Of course." Burov gave him a faint carbon copy of the document. "Second," he said, "an inventory of the personal items on the body and in the automobile. The items can be shipped to the deceased's home address at your embassy's expense." He handed Hollis the inventory.

Hollis leaned towards Lisa and they both read the list. It included—in addition to clothes and luggage—two watches, a school ring, camera, and even items that were meant to be small gifts, such as pens, razors and postcards. It didn't appear as if anyone had helped himself to anything. This meant either that the peasants, local militia and morgue employees had all the Western consumer goods they needed or, more likely, that this had been a KGB operation from start to finish.

Burov said, "I have six hundred and eighty dollars in traveller's cheques, seventy-two dollars in American currency, thirty-two roubles and seventy-eight kopecks, which I will give you now."

Hollis thought of Fisher's words on the tape: "I gave him maps and money." And the Frenchwoman's statement that Fisher had borrowed two kopecks from her. Hollis concluded that Burov had thrown the Russian money in the kitty so as not to raise any questions. "I don't see any maps listed on this inventory," he said. "Fisher surely had maps." He studied Burov's face. "Perhaps someone took them."

Burov waved his hand. "They would be of small value."

"I'll bet you'd like to know where those maps are now, Colonel."

Burov stared at Hollis.

Hollis was fairly convinced now that Dodson was not in KGB hands, dead or alive. He pressed on. "If the maps should somehow turn up at the American embassy, I'll let you know, so you don't worry yourself about them."

"I'll bet you we find those maps before you do," Burov said.

"I'll take that bet. What are the stakes?"

"Very high, Colonel Hollis."

The paperwork continued for another half-hour. Finally Burov leaned back and abruptly observed, "You have been walking in the woods."

Hollis looked up from a document. "Picking mushrooms."

"Really? You are real Russians now. May I see the mushrooms?"

"I'm afraid we weren't very lucky."

"I should think not, in a pine forest."

Hollis assumed that Burov had noticed a few pine needles or smelled the scent that clung to them, or perhaps he had more solid information. It was difficult to know what these people knew for sure and what they were guessing at. He stood. "Will you find us a truck and driver now? We'd like to set out for the airport."

Burov remained seated. "That's not possible at this hour. You'll have to spend the night. Unfortunately, there is no hotel in Mozhaisk. However, there is a *sovkhoz*—a state farm—not far from here. They will be pleased to give you accommodation."

409

Hollis glanced at Lisa. "I don't see that we have any choice."

Burov gathered the papers, then made a note on their travel passes. "This is valid now until noon tomorrow and will also give you entry to the state farm. See that you're within the Moscow city limits by noon."

Hollis said, "I want to call my embassy."

"I don't think there's a phone here. You'll find one on the state farm. Follow me, please." Burov led them through the dark morgue.

They stood outside on the front steps, and Burov gave them directions to the farm. "I'm sure you won't have trouble finding it. An old couple sleep in the administration building. Knock loudly." He walked to the Zhiguli and looked at the licence plate. "A rental car?"

"There were no embassy cars available." Hollis opened the driver's door. "Good evening, Colonel Burov."

Lisa opened her door and got into the car, but Burov put his hand on the door so that she couldn't close it. He said, "Don't get lost. And be careful on the highway. We don't have room for two more bodies in the freezer."

Hollis said, "Go to hell, Colonel."

"And you as well, Colonel."

Then, as they both understood the rules of the game, they saluted simultaneously and bade each other good evening.

AS HOLLIS DROVE SLOWLY through the dark, quiet streets of Mozhaisk, he saw a black Chaika in his rearview mirror.

Lisa said, "Did Burov know about our trip to Borodino or not?"

"He made the correct deduction. Our best defence now is to be unpredictable."

"Meaning we shouldn't go to the state farm."

"Precisely." Hollis glanced in his mirror again. "We have company."

They were in the centre of town, a collection of two-storey wood and stucco buildings round a traffic circle. There was street lighting but not much other evidence of habitation. The main street of Mozhaisk was the old Minsk—Moscow road, and Hollis headed west on it, towards the state farm. Soon they found themselves travelling along a very dark stretch of bad road, utterly defenceless on the vast Russian plain. Hollis was sorry he'd thrown away the pistol.

Three kilometres out of town Lisa spotted a sign bearing the name of the state farm. Hollis turned into a gravel road and proceeded towards it. They could make out a large group of wooden farm buildings and corrugated-iron sheds. Lisa looked back and saw the Chaika turning onto the road. Hollis spotted the brick administration building. He shut off his headlights, drove past the building, and carried on.

"What are we going to do now?" Lisa asked.

"Our little Zhiguli didn't have much chance on the main road, but back here we can give the Chaika a run."

410

There was not much light, but Hollis could pick out the gravel road. He speeded up, hitting the brake whenever he saw an intersecting lane, and turning onto it. Without brake lights or headlights the Zhiguli was virtually invisible, and after fifteen minutes Hollis announced, "We've lost the Chaika. Unfortunately, *we're* lost too. Let's pull into a tractor shed and wait until dawn."

Lisa groaned. "It's nearly freezing, and it's only nine o'clock. We have to find shelter, Sam. If we can find a *kolkhoz*—a collective-farm village—we can get a peasant to take us in for a few roubles, no questions asked."

"No questions asked? In Russia?"

"A collective is different from a state farm. In a collective village you'll see Russian peasant hospitality."

"You've never even been in the countryside. How do you know the peasants are friendly?"

"Instinct."

He shrugged. "All right. I'll trust you on this."

They drove on, and within fifteen minutes they saw the silhouettes of telegraph poles against the horizon. They followed the poles and came to the first *izba*, or peasant house, of a small hamlet. Hollis stopped the car on the dirt track that ran between two rows of unlit log cabins.

They got out. Like most of rural Russia, this village boasted electricity, but he saw no sign of telephone lines, nor was there a vehicle in sight. It was nicely isolated.

A light went on in the front window of an *izba*, then a few more lights. The door of a cabin opened, and a man stepped out onto the dirt path. Hollis said to Lisa, "You talk."

The man approached, and Lisa said in Russian, "Greetings. We are American tourists."

The man didn't reply. A few other doors opened, and more people came out, until a crowd was standing round them.

"We are having car trouble," Lisa said to the man who had come out first. "Can you put us up for the night?"

The peasants looked from one to another. "You wish lodgings?" said the man. "The state farm near here will have lodgings."

Hollis replied politely, "My wife and I would rather stay with the people." At the word *narod*—the common people—the man smiled.

Hollis looked closely at the peasants around him. They were coarse folk, with leathery skin the colour of the earth. The men were unshaven, and the women had that unusual Russian combination of fat bodies and drawn faces. Half their teeth were black or missing.

Hollis said, "You must let us pay you for our lodgings."

The man shook his head. "No, no. But I will sell you some butter, and you can make a nice profit on it in Moscow."

"Thank you." Hollis added, "I'll put the car where it won't block the road." He backed the Zhiguli down the track and parked it behind a

411

hayrick. When he walked back, he found Lisa involved in a ten-way conversation. She said to him in English, "Our host is named Pavel Fedorovich, and this is his wife, Ida Agaryovna. This place is called Yablonya—apple tree."

Pavel introduced each of the twenty or so families in the village, as well as his own son, Mikhail, a boy of about sixteen, and his daughter, Zina, who was a year or so older. Then he led Hollis and Lisa into his *izba*.

The front room was the kitchen. There was a wood stove for heating and cooking, round which were half a dozen pairs of felt boots. A pine table and chairs stood in the corner, and utensils hung on the log walls.

Pavel pulled out two chairs. "Sit. Sit." He barked at his wife, "Vodka. Cups."

The outside door opened, and a man and woman entered with a teenage girl and a younger boy. The woman set a bowl of cut cucumbers on the table and backed away with the children. The man sat very close to Hollis and smiled. Another family entered, and the scene was repeated. Soon the walls were lined with women. The children sat on the floor at the women's feet. The men sat round the table on chairs the children had carried in. Vodka began flowing, and the table was soon covered with *zakuski*, or snacks, mostly sliced vegetables, a bowl of boiled eggs, and salted fish.

As the party went on, the questions about America began, tentatively at first, then in a flood. At one point Hollis saw Lisa joking with a young man opposite her. Something about her acceptance of these people and her affinity with them appealed to him, and he knew that he liked her very much.

He eventually glanced at his watch and noticed it was near midnight. He stood up. "We've kept you all up long enough. Thank you for your hospitality, and especially for the vodka."

Everyone began filing out. Pavel and Ida led Lisa and Hollis through an opening in the kitchen wall, curtained off with a quilt. They passed into a bedroom, but Pavel motioned them on through a rough pine door to the end room in the three-room log cabin. Hollis guessed it was the master bedroom.

The room was lit, as the kitchen had been, by a single bulb hanging on a cord from an exposed log rafter. Heat came from a single-bar electric heater beside the bed. The only furniture was a double bed and two wooden trunks. Spikes driven into the log walls served as clothing hooks.

Lisa felt the bed. "A feather mattress and three quilts." She smiled at Pavel and Ida. "This is wonderful. Thank you for showing us the real Russia."

Pavel smiled in return. "I don't think you are tourists, but whoever you are, you are honest people and you can sleep well here."

Ida said good night. "*Spokoiny nochi.*"

After they had left, Hollis moved to the curtainless window and

412

examined it. It was a swing-out type, factory-made. He tried the latch handle and satisfied himself that the window would open if it became necessary to leave that way.

He glanced at Lisa. She pulled off her boots and socks and there was an awkward silence.

Lisa said, "It's very cold in here." Fully dressed, she lay on the bottom quilt and pulled the two top ones up to her chin.

Hollis took off his leather jacket and hung it on a nail, then stuck his knife into the log wall beside the bed, his heart beating faster than usual. "Would you be more comfortable if I slept on the floor?"

"No. Would you?"

Hollis hesitated a moment, then took off his turtleneck and jeans and threw them over a trunk. He pulled the light chain, then slid into bed beside Lisa, wearing his T-shirt and shorts.

She put her hand on his shoulder. "You shot two armed KGB men and never flinched, but now you're shaking."

"It's cold."

"I'm nervous too. But I want you." She added, "There may not be any tomorrow for us."

"Sounds like my fighter-pilot line. But if there is a tomorrow?"

"We'll take it one step at a time."

"Right. And Seth? How will he take it?"

She didn't reply.

Hollis felt her bare foot touch his, and he took her head in his hands and kissed her. They undressed beneath the quilts and wrapped themselves in each other's arms.

LISA WAS WOKEN by noises coming from the kitchen, and a rooster's crowing cut through the dawn.

Hollis lay on his stomach, and in the weak morning light she saw the scars that started at his neck and continued down his back. "I guess you did get banged up. The plane exploded?"

"Well, not by itself. A surface-to-air missile went up its tail."

Hollis rolled onto his back. "Ironically, it turned out to be the last American mission over North Vietnam. I was over Haiphong, released the bombs, and headed back south. Then my copilot, Ernie Simms, said, 'Missile coming up.' The next thing I knew, there was an explosion, and the aircraft was out of control. There was blood all over the place. I thought it was mine, but it was Ernie Simms's. I jettisoned the canopy, and Simms and I blew out of the cockpit. Our parachutes opened, and we came down into the water. I floated around awhile, watching enemy gunboats converging on me and contemplating life in a POW camp."

Hollis sat up and stared out through the window. He said, "I saw Simms in his flotation seat, about a hundred metres away. One of the gunboats was bearing down on him. I swam towards him, but he waved

413

me away. I saw the Viets pull him aboard. Then they came for me. But by that time the marine air-sea-rescue choppers had come. A chopper plucked me up and flew me to a hospital ship."

"Do you think Simms . . . I mean, does it bother you to talk about it?"

Hollis answered her unasked question. "I don't know what I could have done for him. But I keep going over it in my mind. He was my responsibility."

She put her hand on his shoulder. A few minutes passed in silence, then Hollis said, "So, to come full circle, Ernie Simms was never on any North Viet list of POWs, so he's still officially missing. Yet I saw them take him aboard alive. And now with this Dodson business I'm starting to wonder. All the guys whose chutes were seen opening and who were never heard of again . . . I'm wondering if Ernie Simms and a thousand other guys didn't wind up in Russia."

"In Russia?"

Hollis looked at her. "We should get moving." He swung his legs out of bed and retrieved his clothes and knife.

They dressed and went into the kitchen, where Ida greeted them and gave them a bowl of hot water. They washed at a side table. Pavel was sitting at the kitchen table with his children, Mikhail and Zina. Ida served them all a breakfast of boiled eggs, *kasha*, tea and brown bread.

Finally Hollis looked at his watch. It was just seven. "It's time for us to go." He stood up.

Pavel stood up too, and Hollis followed him outside. They chatted for a while; then Hollis said, "I'm afraid if someone here speaks of our visit, it will not be good for Yablonya."

"I know that. We will discuss it after you leave."

Hollis took Pavel's hand and pressed a ten-rouble note into it. "Thank you for your hospitality. *Do svidaniya.*" Hollis waved away Pavel's offer of butter and walked back to the house. Lisa was ready to go.

Hollis thanked Ida and said goodbye to the children. Then he took Lisa's arm and they walked down the lane.

They went behind the hayrick and got into the Zhiguli. Hollis started the engine and pulled out onto the dirt road.

"Where are we going?" she asked.

"Gagarin." Hollis honked his horn and waved to Pavel, Ida, Mikhail, Zina and the others, who were waving from their front gardens. When he had passed the last *izba*, he speeded up.

"Why Gagarin?"

"There are people between Mozhaisk and Moscow who are looking for Major Dodson, and maybe for us. So we're heading west. We'll ditch the car, then take the train to Moscow."

They came to an intersecting road of gravel, and Hollis cut north on it. After a while he saw the telegraph poles of the old Minsk–Moscow road ahead. He turned onto the paved road and headed west.

414

"About twenty minutes to Gagarin," Hollis said as he pressed on the accelerator.

Soon they saw squat *izbas* on either side of the road, then buildings with painted wood shingles. Hollis slowed down. "Gagarin."

"Named after the cosmonaut?"

"Yes. He was born in a village near here. From a squalid *izba* to a space capsule. You have to give credit where it's due."

Gagarin was a town of over ten thousand people, big enough, Hollis thought, for neither the Zhiguli nor its occupants to stand out. He drove until he found the railway station, then pulled up in a small, empty parking area beside the concrete platform and got out. They made their way through the crowd to the wooden ticket shed on the platform. A timetable on a notice board indicated that the next Moscow train would be along in twenty minutes. Hollis purchased two one-way tickets.

As he moved away from the ticket booth Lisa took his arm. They walked down the cold grey concrete platform, which was crowded with black-coated and black-scarved humanity. Old peasants, men and women, with teenage boys to help them, lugged crates, boxes and suitcases filled with dairy products and the last fresh produce of the year. They were all heading for Moscow.

Soon the Byelorussian Express came lumbering down the track, and everyone moved to the edge of the platform. The train stopped, the doors opened, and Hollis and Lisa found two empty seats. Within a few minutes every nook and cranny of the carriage was packed with bundles. The train pulled out.

The journey was without incident. By late morning they could see the tall spire of Moscow University, in the Lenin Hills. "Almost home," Lisa commented. "How are we going to get into the embassy if the watchers are waiting for us near the gate?"

"I'll show you a spy trick."

"You'd better."

The train pulled into Moscow's Byelorussian Station at ten minutes to noon. Hollis and Lisa left quickly and pushed through the throng. They came out of the station into a square that was dominated by a huge statue of the writer Maxim Gorky. The sky was the usual grey, and the air seemed filled with fumes, compared with the fresh air of the countryside.

Hollis led Lisa into the Minsk Hotel, where he entered a phone booth in the lobby. He dialled the embassy, spoke to the marine watch-stander, then the Sunday duty officer, who turned out to be his own aide, Captain O'Shea.

"Ed, it's me. Photoflash," Hollis said, using the word for a personal emergency. "Get a car to me at location Delta. Ten minutes."

"Yes, sir. Welcome back."

They left the Minsk Hotel and walked down Gorky Street. Lisa said, "That was neat. Where is location Delta?"

"It's Gastronom One. You know it?"

"Sure. Best gourmet store in Moscow. The only one, actually."

They walked through Pushkin Square and eventually came to the ornate façade of Gastronom One. Hollis said, "We change the locations every time we have to use one. So there should be no one here from the KGB to meet us. However, they will have a car close behind the embassy car. As soon as the embassy car slows down, you jump in the back, and I follow. OK?"

They waited. In a few minutes a black Ford came at a good pace up Gorky Street, and Hollis saw two security men in the front and a man who looked like Seth Alevy in the back. Behind the Ford was a black Chaika. The Ford swerved to the kerb and braked hard. The back door flew open, Lisa slipped in beside Alevy, and Hollis got in and slammed the door as the car accelerated. Alevy addressed Hollis directly. "You had better have a good explanation, Colonel."

The Chaika got up close behind them, and the security driver speeded up. The cars weaved dangerously through central Moscow. Within ten minutes the Ford reached the embassy, shot past the militia booth and entered the gates.

The Ford stopped at the entrance to the chancery, where Hollis, Lisa and Alevy piled out. Alevy said, "Please be in the ambassador's safe room in thirty minutes. Both of you."

HOLLIS SAT AT THE FAR END of the conference table in the ambassador's safe room. Charles Banks sat at the opposite end, and Lisa and Seth sat in the centre facing each other.

Seth Alevy said to Charles Banks, "Someone from the consular section is headed for Mozhaisk to take care of the business that Colonel Hollis did not complete."

"Good." Banks cleared his throat. He looked at Lisa, then at Hollis. "Neither of you returned to your quarters last night, and neither of you informed this embassy of your whereabouts. This is contrary to regulations as well as a dangerous breach of security."

Hollis replied, "We were unable to finish our business in Mozhaisk by nightfall, so we spent the night on a collective farm. There was no telephone there." He was careful not to mention their side trip to Borodino.

Banks addressed Lisa. "I would like you to write a personal note to Mr. Fisher's parents indicating that you were involved with the disposition of the personal effects and so forth."

"Of course." Lisa added, "I have phone messages on my desk from a number of news agencies. Apparently, someone issued a press release regarding Fisher, and the journalists smell a bigger story."

Banks leaned towards her. "There is no story beyond the fact that an American tourist died in an automobile accident."

417

Lisa frowned. "Why didn't the press release give all the facts? The call from the Rossiya—"

Alevy cut in. "We're as aware as you are that there is more to this. But we're trying to get the truth before we make any accusations. You appreciate the current diplomatic thaw. Trust us."

Lisa nodded reluctantly.

Hollis took a decoded radio message from his pocket. "I sent a query to Defence yesterday asking if a Major Jack or John Dodson was on the Vietnam missing-in-action list. They replied in the negative."

Charles Banks said, "So right there we have to wonder about Mr. Fisher's story."

"Do you?" Hollis continued. "In my business, rule number one is trust no one, including your own people. So I went to our library here yesterday and found a book written by a former navy flier who was a POW in Vietnam. An appendix listed some one thousand men who are still unaccounted for. Among them is Major Jack Dodson."

Alevy said, "Sam, leave it alone."

Charles Banks added, "Colonel, we are conducting an official investigation through diplomatic and other channels. In the meantime neither you nor Ms. Rhodes are to concern yourselves with the matter. This is beyond your respective duties."

Hollis stood. "Mr. Banks, until I receive orders from my superiors, I will pursue my own line of investigation." He turned and left.

CHAPTER 7

Sam Hollis walked through the Monday-evening rush hour crowds on Kalinin Prospect. He stopped in front of a shop window and examined his reflection. His brown wool overcoat was Moscow standard, as was his narrow-brimmed black hat and his oversized briefcase. He looked at the passing crowd reflected in the window, but couldn't spot his tail.

He crossed October Square, and walked through the gate set in the red-brick wall of the Kremlin. Two guards looked him over but said nothing. He entered the sixty-acre complex of magnificent cathedrals, monuments and public buildings—the heart of Soviet power and the soul of old Russia. Sam Hollis, who was not easily impressed, was still impressed by the Kremlin.

He walked into Red Square opposite St. Basil's Cathedral. Only official vehicles were allowed in Red Square, and pedestrian traffic was heaviest now at rush hour, which was why he liked to use this place and this hour to lose people. Hollis darted through the throng diagonally in front of the Lenin mausoleum. He walked quickly past the huge GUM department store, and glanced back, but didn't see anyone. He went down a set of steps leading to the metro. A train came within a minute, and he squeezed on with the commuters, riding north one stop to Dzerzhinsky station.

Hollis came up the stairs into a small park at the southern end of Dzerzhinsky Square. In the centre of the square was the bronze statue of Felix Dzerzhinsky, founder of the dreaded state security apparatus. The large building behind was the headquarters of the KGB, the infamous Lubyanka prison.

The streetlights came on. Hollis took a small Lenin pin from his pocket and stuck it in his lapel, then sat on a bench. From his briefcase he took a green apple, a hunk of goat's cheese and a small paring knife. He laid a cloth napkin on his lap and went to work on the apple and cheese with his knife.

Hollis saw him coming. The tailored overcoat belted at the waist marking him as a military man in mufti. General Valentin Surikov, of the Red air force, walked directly in front of Hollis, scattering the sparrows. Surikov noted the lapel pin signifying it was safe, and sat at the opposite end of the bench. The general lit a cigarette, and took a copy of *Pravda* from his attaché case. He said in English, "Why did you pick this place?"

"Why not?"

"This is no game, my friend. If they catch you, they kick you out, with your diplomatic immunity. If they catch me, they take me there"—he cocked his head towards the Lubyanka—"and shoot me."

Sam Hollis did not particularly like General Valentin Surikov, but he wasn't sure why. He put a piece of apple into his mouth.

General Surikov said, "Shall we get on with it? I'm meeting my granddaughter in one hour. Besides, your note said it was urgent."

They had worked out a simple expedient for arranging a rendezvous. Hollis would send a note by messenger to his counterpart, Colonel Andreyev, in the Soviet Defence Ministry and request an inconsequential bit of information. Andreyev would naturally pass the request up the line, and it would come across General Surikov's desk. Surikov would place Hollis's note over a small, detailed map of central Moscow. A pinprick in the note would pinpoint the meeting place. The time was always 5.30 of that day. The word "response" anywhere in the note meant urgent.

Hollis said, "I need information on a former Red air-force training facility north of Borodino. The *Komitet* uses it now for other purposes. You know the one I mean, don't you?"

Surikov cleared his throat. "I know something about it. It is so important, Colonel, so potentially dangerous for the future of Soviet-American relations, that it is better left alone." Surikov, usually cool as ice, was agitated.

Hollis said, "Well, something leaked, and before it gets into the wrong hands, I want to control it. But first, tell me what you know and how you know it."

419

Surikov replied, "I have to think this over."

"You've been doing that since the first day you contacted me."

"Yes? You know my mind and my soul?" Surikov hesitated, then said decisively, "All right. I have thought this through. I want to get out. I want to spend my last days in the West."

"Do you think they're on to you?" Hollis asked.

"No, but they will be if I give you what you want. I want to go to London. How long will it take you to get me there?"

"It's not easy. I'll take it up with my people," Hollis said.

Surikov looked over his newspaper at a group of six KGB men leaving through the front doors of the Lubyanka. He said quickly, "If you know anything about the facility at Borodino, you will know that getting me out of here is a cheap price for what I can tell you."

Hollis took a *Pravda* from his briefcase and rustled the pages. He had learned not to underestimate General Surikov. Whatever his motives for treason, they were not base. The man had never taken a rouble, a dollar or a banked Swiss franc. But his motives were not lofty either. He had had no ideological conversion, as far as Hollis knew. And he had not suffered any personal harm from the system. In fact, he belonged to the Communist aristocracy—the *nomenklatura*—who lived a life of gross hypocrisy and privilege. Then one day, for reasons known only to himself, Valentin Surikov had decided he didn't like it here any more. It wasn't a scam. The stuff he provided was top grade—Red air-force postings, unit designations, command assignments. Apparently, Surikov was a—or *the*—personnel officer for the entire Red air force.

From behind his newspaper Hollis watched as the six men in front of the Lubyanka split up. Four headed towards Hollis and Surikov.

General Surikov stood. "We have been here long enough. I will be at Gogol's grave next Sunday, at one."

As usual, Surikov had picked a place that would send Hollis leafing through his guidebook. "Alternative rendezvous?"

"None. Gogol's grave. Sunday. One p.m. You will tell me how you are getting me to the West, and I will give you half a secret. I'll give you the second half when I'm in London." Surikov tucked his *Pravda* under his arm and picked up his attaché case. He seemed anxious to leave, but stood motionless as the four KGB men approached. They looked at Hollis and Surikov with a keen eye of appraisal, then passed on. Surikov, quite pale, turned without a word and crossed the square.

Hollis waited for the KGB men to reappear and arrest him, but nothing happened. He sometimes wondered if this game was worth his life. But this time he thought of Greg Fisher's life, which was over, and of Major Jack Dodson's life, which was in the balance. And he thought of Ernie Simms and the thousand others whose families and whose nation had given them up for dead. He thought that maybe, if he did everything right, he might bring them home again.

SAM HOLLIS ENTERED the bowling alley in the basement of the eight-storey chancery building at the embassy. He bought a Heineken at the bar and then took a seat at an empty lane. He noticed four female FSPs—Foreign Service Personnel—on the adjoining lane, laughing and drinking. There was something oddly frenetic in their laughter, Hollis thought, as though their mainsprings were wound too tight.

Russia, Hollis thought, changed you. An American, whether a tourist, business person or embassy worker, was under constant scrutiny from the locals and from the state. One woke up with tension, lived with tension, and went to bed with tension. Some people, like his wife, Katherine, fled. Some cracked up, some became mildly idiosyncratic, and some, like Lisa, embraced the Russian bear and danced with it, which, Hollis reflected, might be the only way to get out with most of your marbles.

Seth Alevy walked over and sat on the bench beside Hollis. The ambient noise cover down here was good, Hollis knew, and any bugs planted during construction were ineffective, as were the KGB directional microphones in the surrounding buildings. Which was one reason that Alevy liked to meet here. The other reason was that Alevy suspected the safe rooms were bugged by State Department intelligence.

Alevy said, "Now that we're alone, why don't you tell me everything you did and saw on the way to Mozhaisk? I assume you made a stop at Borodino."

Hollis shook his head. "I'm really into interservice rivalry, Seth. It gives me a sense of worth and importance."

"I think you're being sarcastic." Alevy added, "Did Ace show today?"

"Yes."

"Can he help us with this?"

"I think so. There's been a new development. He wants to head west."

"Maybe he wants to find out how we get people out of here."

"Maybe. Maybe he just really wants to defect." Hollis cradled the beer bottle in his hands. Alevy had a weak spot in his professional make-up: he personally didn't like most Russians. Not liking the Soviet regime was a job qualification. But Alevy was unable to concede that anyone who had been shaped by the regime was capable of anything but treachery and vileness.

"What's he offering?" Alevy asked. "The scoop on Borodino?"

"Yes."

"Maybe you planted that in his head. Maybe he'll make something up just to get out of here. I want to talk to this joker myself."

Hollis said, "I don't think it's a good idea for the CIA station chief to run around Moscow trying to rendezvous with Russian informers. Do you?"

"Let me worry about my job description."

As station chief Alevy was not allowed to leave the embassy

compound without at least two security men and one cyanide pill. Hollis knew he sometimes left without the former but was sure he never left without the latter.

Alevy asked, "So where and when are you meeting Ace?"

Hollis knew he couldn't very well refuse to answer. "Gogol's grave. Next Sunday. Three p.m. Give or take a few hours."

"Where is Gogol's grave these days?"

"Beats me."

THE NEXT DAY Lisa Rhodes called Sam Hollis in his office. Hollis looked at the wall clock. It was 5.30, and he hadn't spoken to her since he'd left Alevy and Banks on Sunday afternoon. "Hello, Lisa. How are you?"

"I feel used. You're supposed to call or have flowers delivered or something."

"They don't deliver flowers. Look, I'm not good at this. I don't get around much. Can I buy you a drink?"

"No. I want dinner. Tonight. Out of the compound."

He smiled. "Meet you in the lobby in half an hour."

Hollis called his aide, Captain O'Shea, on the intercom. "Ed, get me a Moscow cab at the gate in forty-five minutes."

"How about a car and driver instead?"

"No. It's personal. A taxi will be fine." Hollis hung up and went to the window. His office faced east into the heart of the city, and the Kremlin towers offered a magnificent view at night, with lights like perfect jewels in an ordinary setting. Not old by European standards, Moscow had begun in the twelfth century as a trading post. A nothing-town on a nothing-river, it had become the centre of an imperial empire, then a Communist empire. Its one resource, Hollis decided, was its people: Muscovites. Tough, stubborn, conniving, cynical. And the city was a magnet for every like-minded citizen in the Soviet Union.

Hollis straightened his tie. Burov was no local Mozhaisk *gendarme*. He was a Muscovite by choice if not by birth. Furthermore, Burov was somehow involved with the Charm School. Hollis didn't know how he knew. But he knew.

He got his topcoat and walked unannounced into Alevy's office down the hall. He pulled the heavy curtains closed, put some music on the tape player, then pulled a chair up close to Alevy and said softly, "Burov."

Alevy nodded. "That's our only name and face, isn't it?"

"We want to draw him out, right? To get a fix on him? Call Lefortovo restaurant. Make a dinner reservation for two in my name." The restaurant was a KGB hangout near Lefortovo prison.

Alevy stayed silent for a while, then said, "Long shot."

"Not really. The embassy listeners are keyed for my name. Even if Burov is somewhere around Mozhaisk, he can get to Moscow quickly."

"Who are you taking to dinner?"

"Not you."

Alevy smiled wryly. "OK. But if Burov wants to do more than talk, I'd be hard-pressed to bail you out in Lefortovo. I think you're pushing your luck, Colonel. Not to mention our friend's luck."

Hollis stood up. "I'll put it to her straight, and she can decide."

He left Alevy's office and took the elevator down to the ground floor. The lobby was filled with embassy men and women leaving work. He spotted Lisa walking over to him. "Hello, Colonel."

"Hello, Ms. Rhodes," he said. "We have a cab waiting." As they went out he added, "I wanted to call you the last two days."

"Forget it, Sam. I was swamped with work anyway."

Hollis took her arm and turned her towards him. "I still think I owe you an explanation. Just listen. Before we went to Mozhaisk, I told you it could be dangerous, and you saw what I meant. Every day is a danger now, every time we leave these gates. This is not just dinner tonight. I guess what I'm asking is, do you want to get involved with me and with what I'm doing?"

"Taxi's waiting," she said.

Hollis took her hand, and they walked through the gates to a white taxi waiting at the kerb. He and Lisa got in. He said to the driver, "Lefortovo restaurant."

They headed east towards the Lefortovo suburb. After a short time they passed the grim prison compound, and the driver stopped in front of a modern glass building. Hollis gave him five roubles and told him to keep the change.

Hollis showed Lisa into the restaurant. They handed their coats in at the cloakroom. The dining area was unremarkable in its decor but interesting in its clientele. Most of the patrons were men, in one sort of uniform or another. It was darker than most Moscow restaurants, though the effect was not romantic.

"Sinister. I love it," Lisa said.

The woman at the reservation desk led them to a centre table. Lisa said, "Everyone is looking at us."

"You're so beautiful."

"They know we're Americans."

Hollis said, "By way of background, the gentlemen you see are mostly employees of Lefortovo—prison, not restaurant. They are a collection of KGB interrogators, torturers and executioners. They work up big appetites."

A waitress came with a bottle of mineral water and set it down, with two menus. Hollis ordered a bottle of Georgian wine and she left without a word. She returned with the wine, and they ordered dinner. A moment later a tall man in civilian clothes rose from a dark corner table and walked across the room. It was Colonel Burov.

He motioned to their table. "May I?" He pulled out a chair and sat down. He snapped his fingers and a waitress appeared. "More wine."

Hollis said to Burov, "Can I assume this isn't a chance meeting?"

"It's a fateful meeting, perhaps. Since our last unpleasant business at Mozhaisk, I've been thinking about you two. By the way, we found your rented car at Gagarin station, and I had it examined—mud, pine twigs, and so on. I concluded that you entered a restricted area. Specifically, an area two kilometres north of Borodino Field."

Hollis said, "Will you pass the butter, Colonel?"

Burov slid a butter dish across the table. "I know who you are, Colonel Hollis. I know you were shot down over Haiphong. I know your sister's name is Mary and your mother used to drink too much. Let's get down to business and forget diplomacy."

"All right," said Hollis, "no more diplomacy. You murdered an American citizen. You beat my driver, and perhaps you would have murdered me and Ms. Rhodes. Yet you sit here and talk to us as though you are a civilised human being. You are not."

Burov seemed not to take offence. "Very well. There's no use denying some of the details in this matter. But what you conclude from those details is erroneous. It's like this: the Major Jack Dodson, who the late Mr. Fisher referred to in his phone call to you, was a turncoat. While a prisoner of war in Vietnam, Major Dodson requested an interview with a military attaché at the Soviet embassy in Hanoi. During their discussion Major Dodson said he would welcome the opportunity to come to the Soviet Union and share his military knowledge. He felt bitter, and betrayed by his country. He stated that America's limited air war had endangered his life, wasted his talent, and caused the deaths of his friends. Dodson asked if we would get him out of the Vietnamese POW camp. We did."

"And why didn't the Soviet Union announce his defection for propaganda purposes?" demanded Hollis.

"Dodson didn't want that. That was part of the deal we struck with him."

Hollis said, "What was Dodson doing in the pine forest at night when Gregory Fisher came upon him? Picking mushrooms?"

"And," Lisa added, "why did Fisher leave the Rossiya and get himself killed in an auto accident? Come now, Colonel Burov."

Burov helped himself to some wine. "Mr. Fisher's accident is not relevant to the subject of Major Dodson. However, as I did listen to the tape of Mr. Fisher's conversation with you, I think we can all agree that he sounded agitated. The militia report says that he was also drunk. My theory is he panicked and got back in his car with the idea of . . . Well, who knows what a drunk man thinks? As for Major Dodson, he was hiking, as was his custom. He met Mr. Fisher quite by chance, and out of nostalgia, perhaps, told him something about himself. But he did not tell Mr. Fisher he was a prisoner, because he is not."

424

"I want to speak to Major Dodson and hear all this from him," said Hollis.

Burov nodded. "Yes, all right. If he's agreeable."

"I don't care if he's agreeable or not. You will make him speak to me. Tomorrow. Here in Moscow. At a neutral site. Lacking a prompt decision, I want to see a photo of Major Dodson holding tomorrow's *Pravda*."

"That's very clever."

Hollis leaned towards Burov. "If you can't produce the man or a picture of him, I'll conclude that he is not under your control. In fact, I believe he is on the run from you and may surface soon in his own way."

Burov looked at Lisa, then at Hollis. "Tomorrow I've got other things on my agenda, as you Americans say. I'm involved with the investigation of the murder of two guards in that restricted area I told you about." He added softly, "What fools you are to come here like—"

Hollis interrupted. "By the way, who was the man who answered the door of Mr. Fisher's room at the Rossiya?"

"How do I know?"

"That man," Hollis said, "looked and talked like an American. He was, in fact, a Russian—a KGB man. Better than your schools usually put out. At first I figured he was a real American working for you. Then I got to thinking about Mrs. Ivanova's Charm School and Major Jack Dodson and such. And I started coming to some mindblowing conclusions."

Burov cleared his throat. "I would like you both to accompany me to my office so that we can continue this talk in private."

Hollis said, "I think we'll finish our dinner. Good evening."

Burov said tauntingly, "Are you frightened? There are two ways to go to Lefortovo. One is voluntary."

Hollis glanced round the dining room and saw three men rise.

Burov stood up. "Come with me."

Hollis put his napkin on the table, stood up, and took Lisa's arm. They followed Burov to the door. The three KGB men fell in behind them. They retrieved their coats and stepped out into the cold. "I think we'll say goodbye here," Hollis said. He and Lisa turned away.

Burov motioned to the three men. One of them shoved Hollis, sending him slamming into a parked car.

Lisa shouted, "You creep!" She kicked the man in the groin.

One of the other KGB men slapped Lisa across the face and pulled her to the ground by her hair.

Hollis spun round and caught Burov's jaw with his fist, then went for the man who held Lisa. The man drew a pistol and barked, "*Stoi!*"

Hollis stopped. The other men drew their pistols.

Burov dabbed at his bleeding jaw with a handkerchief, and said calmly, "You are both under arrest. Start walking. You know where you're going."

Lisa and Hollis walked down the dark, quiet street towards Lefortovo prison. They were about a hundred metres away from it when a car turned into the street and put on its bright lights. Another car came from the opposite direction. They drew close and stopped. The doors opened and four men in black ski jackets and ski masks got out.

Seth Alevy, not wearing a ski mask, stepped onto the pavement and went directly to Burov. "Good evening, Colonel Burov."

Burov looked at the black-clad men deployed around him.

Alevy said, "They're all carrying silenced automatics. If you want to be reasonable, tell your men to put their guns away. Now."

Burov told them.

Alevy stared at Burov. "Do you know who I am?"

"Oh, yes. You're the Jew who is the CIA station chief here."

Hollis joined Alevy and said to Burov, "I still expect a call from you tomorrow, regarding Dodson." Hollis and Alevy ushered Lisa into the back seat of one of the cars. The other security men piled in, and they all headed back towards the centre of the city.

Alevy said to Hollis, "I don't think punching a KGB colonel in the face was a good idea."

"It seemed like a good idea at the time. By the way, Seth, your timing was a bit slow. I expected you sooner."

Lisa said, "This was all planned?" No one answered. "You two are crazy. Now I really feel used. Look, I'll help. But in future I want to be kept informed, or it's no deal."

Alevy and Hollis both agreed. Hollis said, "I'm convinced now that Burov is a main player. And he's desperate. I've never seen one of those guys take so many risks, like trying to kidnap Americans with diplomatic immunity."

Alevy nodded. "Things are going to get hot in old Moscow."

HOLLIS AND LISA stood in the lobby of the chancery.

"Come over for a drink," Lisa offered. "I need one."

They walked along the path to the housing units. She opened her door and put their coats in the hall closet, then showed him upstairs to the living room.

While Lisa made drinks Hollis looked around. The apartment was modern, with a living room-cum-dining room and a galley kitchen. The furniture was from Finland, the closest Western country from which to import quality goods.

Lisa gave him his drink, and toasted, "Another good date."

As she put some Rachmaninov on the tape deck, Hollis examined an icon on the wall. "Is that real?"

"Yes. My grandmother's. I'm going to have a tough time getting it back out of the country. Could you put it in the diplomatic pouch for me?"

"Sure. You planning on leaving?"

427

"No, but somehow I have the feeling my days here are numbered." They sat on the couch. She said, "It's not just Dodson, is it? There are hundreds of them, aren't there? That's what you were saying when we . . . in Pavel's bedroom."

Hollis glanced at her. "I might have said too much."

"I don't repeat what you tell me." She asked, "Don't you and Seth compare notes?"

"We trade notes. My outfit, Defence Intelligence, is sort of junior to the CIA. So I have to protect my patch."

She nodded. "You did say it would be dangerous, whatever it is that's going on. Do you really need me?"

"I know this violates the USIS rules, not to mention Pentagon rules. But yes, I need you."

She nodded. "OK. You got me."

Hollis smiled. "Say, I'll bet *you* know where Gogol's grave is."

"Sure." She laughed. "Doesn't everyone?"

"Well?"

"First things first." She kissed him. "I want to wake up beside you. Like in Yablonya."

"That would be nice."

They climbed the stairs to her bedroom.

CHAPTER 8

The next morning Seth Alevy abruptly summoned Hollis and Lisa to an 11.00 a.m. meeting with Charles Banks in the intelligence officers' safe room.

Charles Banks cleared his throat and began at once. "Colonel Hollis, Ms. Rhodes, it is my unpleasant duty to inform you that the Soviet government has formally declared each of you persona non grata. You have five days in which to get your affairs in order and leave the country. You will depart Monday a.m."

"That's not fair, Charles," Lisa said with emotion.

Banks ignored this. "As you both know, Soviet-American relations are on the mend. The Fisher matter, and indeed your expulsion, must not compromise that process." He turned to Hollis. "There will, however, be nothing derogatory in your file or that of Ms. Rhodes. After you report to Washington, you will both be given thirty days' home leave. You will also be given new assignments that will be beneficial to your respective careers."

Banks looked pointedly at his watch. "I must go upstairs. Mr. Alevy will now give you your departure briefing. Personally, I'm sorry to see you both go. Sam, Lisa, good luck to you." He left.

Alevy said, "I will now read you certain provisions of the National

Security Act and instruct you on your duty not to disclose anything you have seen, heard or read while posted here." He proceeded to do so, then asked them to sign standard statements of acknowledgment, which they did.

Alevy continued, "I'm advising both of you not to leave the embassy alone for the rest of your stay here. If it makes you feel any better, our government has booted the Soviet air attaché and press officer out of DC. The score is tied, two-two. As of now you're relieved of your duties. A West German moving company will pack you up."

Hollis asked, "Who's going to meet Ace on Sunday?"

"You have to do that. Tell him that someone else will be getting him out if he has what you asked for." Alevy turned to Lisa and asked with a forced lightness, "So, where will you spend your home leave?"

"I don't know. This is unexpected. New York, I guess."

Alevy looked at Hollis. "You?"

"Not real sure. London, I suppose, to take care of some business with Katherine." He stood up. "Well, are we finished?"

"No. I want you to tell me about your side trip to Borodino."

"There's not much to tell," Hollis replied. "However, I did kill two KGB border guards. It was unavoidable."

Alevy said, "So that's what got their blood boiling. Why didn't you tell me? You're lucky to be alive. Both of you. What else happened?"

"I'll give you a complete report before I leave," Hollis replied. "But as they say in diplomatic circles, we want a quid pro quo."

"Like justice for Gregory Fisher," Lisa said. "Murder is murder. And if you won't do anything about it, I will have to offer my resignation and go public."

"You will *not* go public, Lisa," Alevy retorted. "You just signed a statement to that effect. Remember? I might also remind you that you are one of the embassy's foremost cheerleaders for cosy Soviet-American relations. I don't subscribe to that, but I'll write off Fisher's death if my government determines that is the way to save the upcoming summit. So if that is your goal too, forget justice. There are more important issues."

Hollis interjected, "Maybe I'm willing to write off Fisher, Seth. But I have a personal interest in Major Jack Dodson and any other Americans who are being held here against their will. *That* we don't write off."

"Noted and agreed." Alevy looked at Lisa and said in a conciliatory tone, "Look, I can tell you're upset. This is all new to you. But justice is done differently here, and it's not a matter of public record. The only justice here is revenge."

Lisa gave Seth Alevy a long, sad look, and Hollis had the impression they'd been through this before.

Alevy stood up and moved towards the padded, airtight door. He opened it for them. "So let me take care of this. As for you two, the diplomats would say this matter is *ultra vires*—beyond your power or authority."

"I'll make that decision," Hollis said as he went through the door with Lisa. "Not you, or the diplomats."

"I know you will, Sam." Alevy added in a lighter tone, "Oh, your farewell party is Saturday at six thirty." They all shook hands.

Hollis and Lisa took the elevator up to the seventh floor and walked to Lisa's office door. She asked, "You're not unhappy about leaving, are you?"

"I don't like the circumstances. How about you?"

"I'm sad. But I'm glad it was both of us. We can get together on the outside, Sam." She smiled and walked into her office.

AT 6.00 P.M. THE TELEPHONE RANG in Hollis's office. It was Alevy. "Are you free? We have business."

Hollis surveyed the packing cases around him. "I'm out of business."

"Oh, don't believe everything you hear. My place in ten minutes."

"Right." Hollis hung up and buzzed his aide, Captain O'Shea. "Ed, if a Colonel Burov calls for me, I'll be in Mr. Alevy's apartment. Transfer the call to me there."

Hollis hung up. He took the elevator down to the lobby and walked across the quad. He rang Alevy's doorbell.

Alevy showed him in, and Hollis followed him up the stairs. Hollis had never been in Alevy's place, and he was surprised at its size and decor. The living room was furnished with opulent Russian antiques. There were oil paintings on the walls, Samarkand rugs on the floor, porcelain and lacquer pieces on every polished surface. Hollis commented, "Not bad, for a mid-level political-affairs officer."

Alevy hit a wall switch, and background music filled the room. He went to a carved mahogany sideboard. "Scotch, right?"

"Right." Hollis sat in a green velvet armchair. "The Pentagon doesn't understand perquisites like your company does."

Alevy handed him a drink, and settled into a facing chair of black lacquer. He raised his glass. "To your safe return home." As they drank, Hollis continued to look round the room.

Alevy said, "I can explain this stuff to you, because you're in the business."

"Interior decorating?"

"No, intelligence. This stuff is worth about a million. It's tied in to how we pay the Soviets who help us here. You've heard of the commission shops where Soviet citizens can bring family heirlooms. I can't go into details, but this gives us an opportunity to channel money here and there. OK?"

"You don't owe me an explanation."

"Nevertheless, you got one." Alevy stood up. "Anyway, we have to

430

accomplish a few things, you and I, before you leave. So let's get professional."

"Accomplish what?"

"Well, a report on Borodino. Follow me." He opened a door in the hallway and showed Hollis into a small, dark, windowless room with padded walls. The room was lit by the glow of a five-foot video screen. "This is my little safe room. A few electronic gadgets. Just enough to do homework."

They sat down. Alevy picked up a remote-control device and pressed a button. The video screen flashed a photo of a man wearing the uniform of an air-force officer. Alevy said, "Major Jack Dodson. Missing in action since November eleventh, nineteen seventy. Last seen by his wingman, ejecting from a damaged F-4 Phantom near Haiphong. He appeared to be unhurt. However, he never showed up on Hanoi's lists of POWs. Now we think we know where he disappeared to."

"My copilot, Ernie Simms, disappeared similarly."

"Yes, I know." The picture of Dodson disappeared, replaced by one of Ernie Simms. "I don't know if he's in Russia, Sam. We can't refight the war, but sometimes we get a chance to change the present a little to make the past better." He turned off the video screen. "There's more. But now it's your turn. Borodino."

Hollis related the story of their excursion, telling Alevy what he had seen and deduced about the place. Alevy listened intently, then asked, "More like a prison than a restricted area?"

"Definitely. A local *gulag*. With KGB border guards."

"No Red air-force people, signs, markings?"

"None."

"OK." Alevy nodded. "I've had some people poke around there. It was a Red air-force installation about fifteen years ago, according to local memory. But then the uniforms started to change to KGB and civilian attire. The personnel inside the installation have virtually no contact with Borodino village, Mozhaisk or the surrounding countryside. They helicopter back and forth, presumably to Moscow. Conclusion: top-secret stuff."

Alevy hit the remote switch again, and the screen brightened to show a slow-motion aerial view of farmland. He said, "The reconnaissance satellite is passing from northeast to southwest. Very nice sunny summer day. There's the Moskva River coming up."

The picture seemed to be taken at about two thousand feet, though the satellite could have been a hundred miles above the earth.

Alevy continued. "All right. You see the beginning of the pine forest. Now you see what you saw from the ground—a cleared ring about fifteen metres wide. There. See the watchtower? Now, look at the top of the screen. That clearing is a helipad. And there we see a log cabin, but you won't see much else, because of the evergreens. The Soviets like to use their pine forests as cover from our satellites." He turned off the video. "That's it."

Both men sat in the semidarkness for a while. Alevy said, "We did spectrum and infrared analysis on the pine forest. There are heat sources and such down there. Vehicles, people, lots of small structures and a few larger ones, mostly wood. Population anywhere from four to eight hundred hot bodies."

Hollis said, "There are three hundred American POWs there."

"Three hundred? How do you know that?"

"The Frenchwoman. Fisher told her; Dodson told him."

Alevy said, "Well, you can guess the rest, Sam. These are not defectors, of course, but POWs from Nam. They were given to the Soviets by the North Vietnamese, probably in payment for those surface-to-air missiles that knocked you guys down. A quid pro quo."

Hollis nodded. "And the Russians opened a Red air-force training school, with their potential enemy as instructors."

Alevy said, "OK. But aircraft and tactics change. Those Vietnam-era pilots were used to train MiG pilots fifteen, sixteen years ago. Now they're useless. What good are they *now*? That is the question."

The telephone rang. Hollis said, "That might be for me."

Alevy waved to the phone, and Hollis picked it up.

Captain O'Shea's voice came on the line. "Burov."

"Put him through." Hollis said to Alevy, "The phantom of the Mozhaisk morgue."

"Be nice," Alevy advised as he stuck a plug tap into his ear.

"Colonel Hollis," Burov said. "I meant to call earlier, but I'm still involved with that messy double murder. I spoke to Major Dodson, and he's very reluctant to meet anyone from your embassy. He sees no point in it."

"The point is to see if he's alive and well and wants to remain in the Soviet Union."

"That's affirmative on all counts," Burov replied.

Hollis was somewhat surprised at Burov's American military jargon. He said, "How about the photo with the *Pravda*?"

"That I can show you."

"Unretouched. I want the photograph and the negative."

"I can't do that. For your eyes only."

"Then keep it."

"I don't know what more I can say, Colonel Hollis. I'll talk to Major Dodson again."

"Will you? What if I told you that Major Dodson is here, in this embassy, and that he has told us a most incredible story?"

Burov skipped a beat, then replied, "That's not possible, Colonel. I just spoke to the man, twenty minutes ago."

"I don't think so."

432

Burov's tone was controlled but anxious. "I'll get back to you on the whole question of Major Dodson."

"Swell. Where can I contact *you*, Colonel Burov?"

"You may call Lefortovo and leave a message. Incidentally, a friend of mine from the Foreign Ministry called and told me the news of your departure. Who will I be dealing with after Monday?"

Alevy pointed to himself.

Hollis said into the phone, "Seth Alevy. You remember him?"

"Oh, yes. Send him my regards. And if I don't see you, Colonel, have a safe trip home."

"I plan to. Good evening, Colonel Burov." Hollis hung up.

Alevy said, "Well, you got him exercised about Dodson. He's wondering now if we know only a little about the Charm School or if we know everything."

Hollis said, "If we know that American POWs are being held at that place, why isn't our government doing something about it?"

"We didn't know until Friday night."

"You people knew something before then."

"What were we supposed to do about it? If the President made enquiries of the Soviet government, they would say, What are you talking about? Are you trying to wreck the summit? Look, Sam, I do what they tell me. They tell me not to embarrass the Soviet government with revelations that they might be holding American citizens as prisoners."

Hollis said, "I keep thinking about the one thousand missing soldiers in Nam and the three hundred we know are in the Charm School. I suppose there were more, but through attrition—natural causes, suicide, executions . . . three hundred. I think it's up to us, Seth, to save them."

Alevy regarded Hollis a moment. "You're willing to break the rules on this one, risk your career, world peace, your very life to get those fliers out? Cool Sam Hollis, Colonel Correct, is a wild jet jockey again, ready to bomb and strafe anything in his way." Alevy smiled. "Yet everyone still thinks you're a team player and I'm the rogue. They don't know what I know about you, Sam Hollis."

Hollis made no reply.

"Let's say we got those men out, through negotiations or otherwise. Do you know what kind of public outrage that would produce? It would mean the end of the summit, the arms talks, trade, travel—the works. We might have our honour intact, but I wouldn't give odds on the peace."

"Are you saying Washington doesn't want them home?"

"You figure it out." Alevy got up and poured some coffee and brandy. "I'm afraid those POWs are causing us damage, God forgive them. So our concern—my company's concern—has to do with urgent matters of national security." Alevy walked towards Hollis and said, "To put it bluntly, we think that prison camp is a training school for Soviet agents who talk, look, think and act like Americans."

Hollis nodded. "I know. A finishing school, graduate school, charm school . . . whatever."

"Right. If our theory is correct, a graduate of that place is indistinguishable from a man born and raised in the good old U S of A. When an agent leaves there, he has a South Boston accent, like Major Dodson, or maybe a South Carolina accent or a Whitefish, Montana, accent. He can tell you who played shortstop for the 1956 Dodgers. In fact, you've already met a graduate of the Charm School."

"The man in Fisher's room. Schiller." Hollis thought a moment. "So you think these . . . graduates of this school have entered American life, in America?"

"We believe so. They may not work for my company, but they could work for contractors we hire, and they could live next door to me in Bethesda or empty the trash in CIA headquarters. They could install my telephone and audit my taxes. They could go to computer schools or join the military."

"How many do you think have graduated from that place?"

"The Charm School has been in existence maybe twelve to fifteen years. The course would have to take at least a year. Probably a one-on-one situation. So the school may once have had the capacity to graduate several hundred agents a year. But we don't think the KGB schools here in Moscow or in Leningrad could supply that many qualified students. Some of the Russkies probably flunked out. And we can't be sure all of the graduates were infiltrated into the States. So to answer your question, I would guess maybe fifteen hundred to two thousand."

"You mean there may be as many as two thousand Russian agents in America, posing as Americans?"

"Posing is not the word," Alevy said. "They *are* Americans. The earlier graduates have been there nearly fifteen years. Long enough to have realised the American dream, long enough to have married and have had kids, long enough to be in a position to do real harm."

"And none of them has been caught?"

Alevy shook his head. "Not that I know of. They probably don't spy in the conventional sense. Their covers are perfect, and they never draw attention to themselves. They have got to hand over their reports to a control officer. So they go on foreign vacations, like other Americans. All agent contact is made overseas."

Hollis could imagine the fear and distrust that would run rampant in America if it became known that there might be two thousand KGB agents there.

Alevy said, "Actually, I think we have found two. Right here. In the embassy, Sam. Our nice handyman and housekeeper. The Kellums. When they were hired, they were given only low-level security

434

investigations commensurate with their jobs. Now it seems their backgrounds are not checking out." Alevy rubbed his eyes wearily and continued. "I'm having the whole American service staff rechecked."

Hollis thought about the Kellums, trying to recall his brief conversations with them.

Alevy seemed to be reading his thoughts. He asked, "Could you tell the Kellums weren't exactly like us?"

"No. But then we're not exactly like each other either. America is as diverse as the Soviet Union. The Kellums had me fooled."

"Me too. Now that we know, we can clean house a bit. However, a lot of damage has been done. And we have only two down and about two thousand to go. We have to come up with a way to find these people, who are scattered from one end of America to the other. Not to mention in overseas military bases and, as we are embarrassed to discover, our embassies."

Hollis seemed lost in thought, then said, "Where's the weakness in their operation, Seth?"

"I'm not sure. I have some thoughts. But I know what our problems are. We have two major ones. The first is to identify and roll up this network that isn't a network but is more like a toxic organism in American society. And then we have to stop this school from pumping out more of the disease. I didn't make up that analogy. That's from headquarters. They like analogies."

"You forgot the third thing. Getting the fliers out of there."

Alevy glanced at Hollis. "Yes. But that's part of closing down the school. We had several options until a few days ago. But now, with Dodson on the loose and with you snooping around out there, they know that we know, and our options are narrowing down fast. They'll shut that place and remove every scrap of evidence. Then they'll offer to take an American delegation through the suspected site. By the time we get there, it'll be a rest home for Moscow pensioners. So we have to act quickly."

"Why don't we arrest the Kellums and make them talk?"

"I'd like to, but we don't want to tip off the KGB any more than they're already tipped."

"Are you asking me to help you or not?"

"You can help by not becoming part of the problem," Alevy said. "I told you everything to convince you that we're not sleeping on this. We're working on getting those pilots home. I'm taking it on pure faith that you will be reasonable. Don't get your people in the Pentagon all worked up. OK?"

"OK." Hollis did not think for one second that Seth Alevy took anything on faith. Nor did he think that Alevy had spent an hour briefing him just to tell him to keep his mouth shut. With only a few days left in the country, Hollis knew he hadn't heard the last of the Charm School.

CHAPTER 9

On Saturday evening Hollis appeared at Lisa's door in his air-force uniform. "How do I look?"

"Very sexy," she said. "I'm going to lose you to some young secretary at the party tonight." She touched his row of ribbons. "Do you arrange them by colour, chronologically, or what?"

"By order of importance. Good conduct last." He kissed her on the neck, and they went upstairs. Lisa got Scotch and a bottle of soda. Hollis filled two glasses with ice.

She said, "These packing cases are getting on my nerves."

"Where's the icon?"

"Over there on the bookshelf. I'm going to send it to my boss at the USIS in DC. I wrote and asked him to keep it."

"I'll get it cleared for you on the diplomatic pouch." He took the icon from the bookshelf. It was about two foot square. The painting was of a male saint. "Who's this guy?"

She came up beside him. "That's the archangel Gabriel. See his trumpet? An art historian once told me the icon was sixteenth century. It's painted on larch. Worth maybe twenty-five thousand."

"No kidding." He put it carefully back on the shelf.

She said, "Icons have a very special importance in Russia. During the Tartar invasions, when churches were burned and priests massacred, icons were small enough to be hidden, and each household had one. The people came to see them as symbols of the survival of Russian culture and Christianity."

The doorbell rang. Lisa went down the stairs and came back with Charles Banks. He said, "Hello, Sam. Lisa assures me I'm not intruding. This will only take a few minutes." He looked round the room. "Well then, a bit of music would be nice."

Lisa went to a tape player on the shelf. She put a tape in and hit the "Play" button. A soft guitar, then a beautiful, clear Russian voice filled the room. Hollis said, "Go on, Charles."

Banks cleared his throat. "Yes. First thing—you both disappeared the other day for some time. There was some fear here that you'd met with foul play. Therefore, the ambassador requests that you stay inside the compound until you are driven to the airport, Monday morning."

Hollis replied, "No. Lisa and I intend to go to church in the city tomorrow. Surely you don't think the Soviet government would make an attempt on our lives just as our diplomats are discussing a new era of Soviet-American friendship?"

Banks replied coolly, "Not the Soviet government, perhaps, but I can't fathom what the KGB is up to, and neither can you. Now, more recent news. As you know, Gregory Fisher's body was flown home. His parents have had an autopsy performed. The medical examiner's report states that the injuries were not the immediate cause of death."

"What," Lisa asked, "was the cause of death?"

"Heart failure. Partly due to trauma. But mostly alcohol. Mr. Fisher had a deadly amount of alcohol in his blood and brain tissue."

"The KGB introduced the alcohol before death," Hollis said, "through a stomach tube. The perfect poison, because nearly everyone takes it now and then."

Lisa said, "So we have no evidence that could be used in a court of law or in a diplomatic note of protest?"

"That's correct," Banks replied.

Lisa asked, "Do you believe that Greg Fisher was murdered?"

Banks considered a moment. "The circumstantial evidence points in that direction. I'm no idiot, Lisa, and neither is the ambassador."

"That's reassuring." She added, "I appreciate your position."

Banks smiled tightly. "Do you? Let me tell you that I personally admire your sense of integrity and moral courage. However, I'm here to tell you in the strongest possible terms that if either of you so much as breathes a word of this incident back in the States, you will both be subject to legal action. Is that clear?"

Lisa put her drink down. "Charles, you've been in the Soviet Union too long. We don't make threats like that in my country."

Banks seemed somewhat abashed. "I apologise. I'm passing on information." There were a few moments of awkward silence; then he extended his hand. "I'll see you both at your farewell party."

Lisa took his hand. "You probably will." She smiled. "Don't worry. I still like you, Charlie." She kissed his cheek.

SAM HOLLIS GAVE HIS UNIFORM a quick once-over, then strode into the large diplomatic-reception hall. Protocol demanded that, as a married man whose wife was temporarily out of town, he arrive without a woman. Lisa had gone on ahead, and he saw her across the crowded room, talking to some people from her office.

The reception hall was an elegant modern wing off the chancery building, with tall windows, walls of Carrara marble and three large chandeliers hanging from the high ceiling. People were standing in groups, glasses in hand. There was a long buffet table against the far wall where a few people helped themselves. Hollis scanned the room, looking for the bar, and saw James Martindale, the protocol officer, making his way towards him.

"Hello, Sam. We have a nice turnout for you tonight."

"I see that. I'm very flattered."

Martindale took Hollis's arm and led him to the front of the reception hall, where there was a raised platform on which stood a lectern and microphone. A four-piece band was grouped around a big Steinway piano. Hollis stepped onto the platform, and Lisa joined him. They exchanged brief smiles.

Martindale tapped the microphone. "Ladies and gentlemen, thank you for coming. May I present our guests of honour, Colonel Sam Hollis and Ms. Lisa Rhodes."

There was a round of applause. Martindale reached behind the lectern and produced two lengths of blue satin, which he unfurled and held up. Everyone laughed. Hollis saw they were bogus ambassadorial sashes, on each of which was written in red glitter PERSONA NON GRATA.

Martindale ceremoniously draped the sashes across their chests, then said into the microphone, "For the nondiplomats here who don't know Latin, 'persona non grata' means someone who doesn't tip."

Lisa whispered to Hollis, "This is embarrassing."

There followed more serious presentations by Charles Banks, Captain Ed O'Shea from Hollis's office, and a colleague of Lisa's. At the end everyone clapped, and Hollis and Lisa stepped down from the platform. Martindale said, "Dance music, maestro, please. Have fun, everyone."

The combo played "In the Still of the Night", and Lisa took Hollis onto the dance floor. As they danced she said, "This is the first time we've done this. I love it."

Hollis smiled.

She held him closer, and they glided over the parquet floor.

Lisa said, "There's obviously some status attached to being kicked out of the Soviet Union. Still, I'm sad. I don't want to leave."

"Things could be worse. We could be dead."

She didn't reply.

"Listen," he said. "I'd like to spend part of my leave with you."

"I'll think about that."

He stepped away from her. "What is there to think about?"

"Well, my parents. You're a little older, and you're married."

"Did you just discover that?"

She smiled wanly. "Let me think about how to make it right."

"Do that."

"Are we having our first fight?"

"Quite possibly." Hollis turned and walked towards the bar. He was intercepted by Mike Salerno, a reporter for the Pacific News Service. Hollis had met Salerno on a few occasions and found him somewhat pushy but straightforward and down to earth.

Salerno took him aside. "You know that we've kicked out your counterpart in DC and also some Soviet Tass jerk in retaliation for Lisa. The Reds are probably having a similar party in Washington tonight." He laughed. "What's the actual reason behind you guys leaving?"

"Pretty much what the official version is, Mike. We took an unauthorised trip." To forestall any further questions, Hollis added, "Moscow gets claustrophobic."

"Hey, don't I know it?" Salerno took two glasses of champagne from a passing waiter and handed one to Hollis, saying, "To a safe journey home."

Salerno finished the wine, then said, "Look, I know there's more to this Greg Fisher story than anyone is saying. I called his parents in New Canaan, and they told me about the autopsy. So I'm thinking about this kid who's tearing along the Minsk–Moscow highway at night under the influence of alcohol, and I'm not buying it. Mr. and Mrs. Fisher tell me Greg was very careful. OK, parents say that about dead kids—but I'm starting to wonder, now."

Hollis said, "We're not supposed to talk business here."

"Just hear me out, Sam, OK? So the other day I go on my own unauthorised trip. First I poke around Mozhaisk, and for a few roubles a truck driver leads me to the accident site west of Mozhaisk. The car is gone by now, of course, but I see where it went off the road and ploughed into the tree. The truck driver says something about the kid's car causing a big stir in Mozhaisk. How did the kid get to Mozhaisk if he died west of town? And why is he on the Minsk–Moscow highway at that hour? Was he on some kind of assignment for the spooks here in the embassy?"

"There are no intelligence personnel in the American embassy," Hollis said. "If there were, they wouldn't send them out in Pontiac Trans Ams."

"True." Salerno added, "Look, I'm booked on that Pan Am flight to Frankfurt on Monday. Let's sit together, and I'll tell you a few other things I discovered about this business."

"Maybe." Hollis continued towards the bar. He saw Alevy standing there and had the impression that he had been waiting for him. Alevy said, "What did Salerno want?"

"He knows a few things, Seth. Any reporter in this room could come up with some inconsistencies in the Fisher story. Coupled with me and Lisa getting the boot, it smells a little."

"I suppose. By the way, do you know anything about the Mi-28 chopper?"

"Newest Soviet transport helicopter. Why?"

"I have to do a report. Can you bring me what you have? Midnight, my place." Alevy turned and walked off.

Hollis said to himself, I knew it.

He spent the next hour talking to the various air attachés from the NATO member nations, then made his farewells. He slipped out of the reception hall and went up to his office, where he intended to stay until his midnight meeting with Alevy.

His phone rang, and he answered it. Lisa was on the line. It did not take long for them to make up. As Hollis put down the phone it occurred to him that two of the great puzzles in life were women and espionage, and that he was up to his eyeballs in both.

CHAPTER 10

The blue Ford Fairlane sat in the embassy's underground garage. Betty Eschman, the wife of the naval attaché, was behind the wheel. "Ready, Sam?"

"Ready." Hollis sat on the floor in the rear of the car, his back to the door. Lisa was opposite him. In the rear seat were two young women from the consular section. In the front passenger seat was Jane Ellis, a commercial officer.

There were only two places in all of Moscow where Protestant services were being held this Sunday morning. One was a small Baptist church in a far suburb. The other was the chapel in the British embassy. The American embassy did the honours on alternate Sabbaths. It was fortunate that today was the turn of the British and that the four American women normally went over there together. There was nothing that would arouse the curiosity of the embassy watchers.

The plan went without a hitch. The Ford went through the embassy gates and proceeded up the street. No one followed. Betty Eschman cut onto the embankment road. It was not the most direct route to the British embassy, but it passed Novodevichy Convent. Within minutes she pulled up at a little park in front. Hollis and Lisa got out quickly, and the car sped away.

They began walking through the park towards the high, crenellated walls of limestone and brick that surrounded the twenty-acre convent grounds. Hollis looked up at the ornate battle towers in the walls and the gold onion domes rising above them. "So this is the site of Gogol's grave. Incredible place. Which way in?"

"Follow me."

They made their way round to the north wall, which held the Church of the Transfiguration. A stream of people, mostly elderly women, passed through the massive church portals. Hollis and Lisa joined them. They passed through the tunnel-like entrance of the gate-church and came out into the convent grounds. The people round them glanced curiously at Lisa's well-cut trench coat. Hollis wore his "spy outfit"—baggy brown overcoat, narrow-brimmed hat and Soviet shoes that squeaked.

They walked arm in arm, following a wet cobblestone lane covered with dead leaves. Lisa said, "Novodevichy used to be a nunnery—a retreat for highborn ladies. It was also a fort, as you can see, the strong point on the southern approaches to Moscow. Odd sort of combination, but common in old Russia. After the Revolution the Communists turned it into a museum. They've never really cared for it, but it's still lovely and peaceful. People come here to meditate. It's sort of the unofficial centre of the religious reawakening in Moscow."

"And probably crawling with KGB because of it."

"Yes. But after seventy years of persecution, their priests shot, churches torn down, Bibles burned, they still worship God. I'm telling you, these people are the hope of Russia."

They crossed a square, and Lisa steered him towards a small, single-domed church of white stucco. She said, "That's where we're going to Mass. The Church of the Assumption."

Hollis saw six men outside the doors stopping some of the younger people and the families, asking for identification. The men jotted information from the ID cards into notebooks.

"They don't stop anyone who looks Western," Lisa said.

"Well, I'll look Western. I'll smile."

"But your shoes squeak." She took his arm as they approached the church. A KGB man intercepted them and said to Hollis, "*Kartochka.*"

Hollis replied in English, "I don't understand a word you're saying."

The young man looked him over, waved his arm in dismissal.

The church was lit only by the weak sunlight coming through the stained-glass windows, but the raised altar was aglow with the fire of a hundred white tapers. The nave had no pews and was packed wall to wall with about a thousand people. Hollis became aware of a strong smell of incense. The place was in bad repair, but there was still a magnificence about it. The gold on the altar gleamed; the iconostasis—the tiered altar screen made of individual icons—was mesmerising. Lisa took his hand, and they made their way to the middle of the nave.

Long-bearded priests in gilded vestments swung censers and passed a jewelled Bible from one to the other. The litany began, repetitious and melancholy, then, from somewhere behind the iconostasis, a hidden choir began to chant. Hollis looked round at the people, and it struck him that these were the most serene faces he had seen in Moscow.

The chanting stopped, and the censers ceased swinging. A young, full-bearded priest moved to the edge of the raised altar. He delivered a brief sermon, speaking of conscience and good deeds.

Lisa whispered, "The KGB are recording every word. There are hidden messages in the sermon, words and concepts that the clergy and congregation understand but which the KGB cannot begin to comprehend. It's a start anyway, a spark."

Towards the end of the Mass a large number of people either prostrated themselves completely or knelt and bowed their heads. Lisa dropped to her knees, but Hollis remained standing. He was able to look across the church now, and he saw to his left, about twenty feet away, a stooped old man dressed in a shabby dark coat that almost reached his ankles. At first sight there was nothing remarkable about him, and Hollis thought that what had initially caught his eye was the young woman beside him. She was about seventeen or eighteen, Hollis reckoned, and she, too, was dressed in a shabby coat, but her manner and her bearing,

if not her uncommon beauty, marked her out as someone special.

People began to stand up, and in the second before Hollis lost sight of the strange couple he realised that the stooped old grandfather was actually General Valentin Surikov.

Hollis and Lisa moved with the crush of worshippers through the open doors of the church. These people, Hollis realised, did not seem to know one another, nor did they try to make acquaintances. They had come from all over Moscow, and now they scattered like lambs that smelled wolves.

Hollis watched the people coming down the steps, but he did not spot Surikov or the girl with him. He and Lisa walked away from the church. Lisa asked, "Did you like the service?"

"Very much. We take so much for granted in the West."

"I know. Thanks for coming, even if you came because you had to go to Gogol's grave. It's not dangerous, is it?"

"No. I just have to meet an old Russian friend to say goodbye." Hollis looked at his watch. "I won't be more than thirty minutes. I'll meet you at that bell tower over there. How do I get into the cemetery?"

"Just keep on this path. You'll see another gate-church set in the wall, like the one where we entered. Go through the gate, and you'll find the cemetery."

He kissed her on the cheek. "See you later."

Within a few minutes he saw the towering south wall of the convent grounds. He fell in behind three young couples and followed them down to the gate-church. He passed through the portals and a tunnel-like passage, and found himself in the quiet cemetery.

Hollis followed a brick path among the overgrown graves. There weren't many people in the cemetery, which was good for privacy, but there were enough so that he and Surikov wouldn't stand out.

The visitors were mostly students, apparently looking for the graves of the famous. Hollis saw the graves of Chekhov, Stanislavsky and the film-maker Sergei Eisenstein. He turned up an intersecting path and found himself in a patch of ground mist. Ahead he saw Surikov standing near a tall pine tree, smoking a cigarette, contemplating a decaying slab of lichen-covered limestone. Hollis walked over to him and looked at the stone.

Surikov said, "Do they read Gogol in the West? Do they read *Dead Souls*?"

"Not so much. Colleges, I guess."

"Dead souls," Surikov said. "Dead souls." He stared at the grave for a while, then turned and walked away. Hollis waited, then followed.

Surikov stood near the base of a corner battle tower where it joined the brick wall of the cemetery. He pulled a *Pravda*-wrapped parcel from the pocket of his baggy coat and offered it to Hollis. "Do you want to buy fresh carp?"

Hollis could actually smell the fish. "Perhaps."

Surikov tapped the package as if extolling the virtues of the fish. He said, "So, my friend, *Pravda* tells me you are leaving Russia. I was quite shocked to hear that. Who will replace you as air attaché?"

"I'm not certain."

Surikov said, "I think you're lying. I know the name of your replacement is Colonel Fields."

Hollis nodded. It could have been the embassy listeners, or it might have been the Kellums. Whatever the route, it was a little scary to hear it from General Surikov. Hollis said, "The KGB told you that."

"Yes. They wanted to know if I knew a Colonel Fields. The KGB is apparently having trouble building a dossier on him, so they came to me."

"How was this KGB enquiry directed to you? Memo? Phone call?"

"I was summoned to Lefortovo. The KGB can even summon generals. One never knows if one will leave there alive."

"To whom did you speak at Lefortovo?"

"A colonel named Pavlichenko."

"Tall, blond, pouty lips, blue eyes?"

Surikov's eyebrows rose. "Yes. You know the man?"

"By a different name."

Surikov said, "After Lefortovo, I am more resolved than ever to leave here. Can you get me out?"

Hollis nodded. "I can if you have the fare."

"Half now, half in the West. Will getting out be dangerous?"

"Of course."

"It's not for me that I'm worried."

Hollis already knew that. "Is she your granddaughter?"

Surikov drew on his cigarette. "You saw us?"

"Yes."

"Then you know why I want to leave." Surikov stared at the wrapped carp in his hands. "Sometimes I curse the day I found God," he murmured. Then he said, "Yes, my granddaughter. Natasha. My only daughter's only daughter. The light of my life, Hollis. Unfortunately, she wants to become a nun."

"Does she? Well, she'll do what she wants, General. That's what it's all about over there."

"Is it? And me?"

"We'll find something for you to do."

"Yes." Surikov wandered away, down the line of tombstones. A few drops of rain fell, splattering the graves and the damp leaves.

Hollis walked past Surikov, then stopped to look at the next tombstone. "Borodino, General."

Surikov spoke. "Some kilometres north of Borodino was once located a Red air-force ground school. Classroom instruction on American

444

fighter tactics, capabilities and weaponry." Surikov paused for effect, then said, "The instructors were Americans."

Hollis drew a long breath. The one prayer he'd allowed himself in church was that Surikov would confirm what he and Alevy had discussed. He said, "That's the secret? I know all about that. They train KGB men to be Americans. How do *you* know that?"

"I supply the students. They're not actually KGB. They don't trust their own recruiting methods. They get very odd personalities wanting to be KGB. They wanted honest Russian patriots. Men who had volunteered to be air-force pilots. Men who would have something in common with their American instructors."

Hollis nodded. "Like when it was a pilot-training school."

"That's my understanding. When it was a Red air-force facility, our pilots seemed more interested in asking the Americans about America than in learning fighter tactics. The political commissar was very angry and reported several pilots to the KGB. It was then that the KGB had their brilliant idea. They took over the school and made it a spy school."

"And how are you involved with this school, General?"

"Air-force personnel have to handle the paperwork on the candidates. So I—" Surikov stopped. "There's more. Much more. Is it worth it to you, Colonel, to get me out of here?"

"You know what I need. The names of Soviet agents already in America. The *names*. That is your ticket west, General."

"But how do I know you wouldn't abandon me and my granddaughter if I gave you the list of names now?"

"You simply have to trust me."

General Surikov's body seemed to sag. Beneath the erect military man was a tired old grandfather trying to do one last thing right. "All right," he said. "Here is what you're getting: a microfilm of the personnel records of every man who's gone to the American Citizenship School— that's what the KGB call it. On the microfilm you will find photographs of the men, their Russian names, their fingerprints, dates and places of birth, blood types, identifying scars, dental records, and so forth. You will not find their new American names or addresses, and I cannot tell you how many of them actually made it to America. Only the KGB has that information. Your people over there—the FBI—will have to do a great deal of work."

It was a start. "How many?" Hollis asked.

"A little over three thousand. These men, incidentally, are all officially dead. Killed in training accidents. The Red air force gave them military funerals. Closed coffins. We buried a lot of sand."

Hollis nodded. Three thousand military-training deaths in the States would cause something of a national scandal. Here, no such death ever got into the newspapers. The families of the supposed deceased knew only of their own loss.

445

Hollis said, "Tomorrow at nine a.m. you will go the antique store in the Arbat. A man will ask you where he can find tsarist coins. He speaks fluent Russian. Have the microfilm with you."

"And this man will tell me how I'm going to the west?"

"Yes."

"I have a better idea. You tell me now. Before I bring the microfilm."

Hollis thought General Surikov needed a victory. He remembered Alevy's words of caution: "Maybe he wants to find out how we get people out of here." But there was no time for caution. He said, "All right. It's basically simple. You go to Leningrad this Saturday with Natasha. At one of the Kirov Islands' recreational parks you rent a fishing boat. Take it to the mouth of the Neva River, but not so far as to attract the attention of patrol boats, and fish in the marked channel. Whenever you see a freighter flying the flag of a NATO country, give a signal that you will be advised of. One of these freighters will take you and Natasha aboard. When the authorities find your boat capsized, it will appear you've both drowned. If the rendezvous fails on Saturday, you'll do the same thing on Sunday."

"And if it fails on Sunday?"

"Then the next weekend. General, if you are being honest with us, you will not be abandoned. With luck, and God's help, by this time next week you will be in a Western port city."

"This thing will need all of God's help. Natasha thinks she is blessed by God. We'll see." He handed Hollis the carp. "You poach them in sour cream."

Hollis said, "I shake your hand."

"And I yours." Surikov added, "Safe journey west. I will see you in London." He turned and walked away.

Hollis slipped the carp into his pocket and headed for the bell tower to find Lisa. When they got back to the embassy, there would be much to tell Alevy. It looked as if they'd hit the jackpot.

CHAPTER 11

Hollis and Lisa stood beneath the portico of the chancery building and said their final farewells to the people who had come out to see them off. Lisa kissed her coworkers while Hollis shook hands with his former staff and exchanged salutes.

The ambassador had sent his car, a stretch Lincoln with the great seal on the sides. The driver opened the rear door, and Hollis and Lisa got in. Everyone waved as the Lincoln pulled away.

Lisa turned and looked back through the rear window as the iron gates of the American embassy closed. Following closely was a Ford with Seth Alevy in the front seat, accompanied by three security men. Behind the

Ford was the embassy van, loaded with their luggage and personal items. Ahead of them was another Ford with three more security men and Bert Mills, who was a CIA officer and Alevy's deputy station chief.

The Lincoln swung into Leningrad Prospect, and they headed north, out of Moscow. Hollis regarded the massive grey apartment blocks, the bare trees and the dark sky. He suspected that this was how he would remember Moscow.

THEY ENTERED THE MAIN TERMINAL area of Sheremetyevo Airport on their way to the diplomatic wing. Alevy's deputy, Bert Mills, said, "Please wait here a minute," and left them.

Hollis and Lisa stood on the concourse of the large new terminal. Grey-clad militiamen were all over the place, and Hollis spotted a few KGB border guards. He picked out his own embassy security people scattered strategically around the concourse. Hollis normally wouldn't expect any trouble in a crowded public place, but to the KGB the entire country was their private hunting preserve.

Alevy came up behind them. "OK. Everything's set. Let's go."

Hollis and Lisa picked up their flight bags and followed Alevy, accompanied by the six security men. They entered a long, narrow corridor off the concourse that took them to the diplomatic wing, where Bert Mills was waiting.

The wing consisted of a front desk and a comfortable modern lounge with small conference rooms at the side. It was not much different from a VIP lounge in any airport except for the presence of a KGB border guard with a submachine gun at the rear exit door that led to the tarmac.

Their luggage was now piled near the front desk. A passport-control officer arrived and stamped their passports with exit visas, then left.

Hollis, Lisa and Alevy sat in the lounge. The embassy security men took up positions round the room. Hollis remarked to Alevy, "Why all the firepower? One or two would have done."

"Show of force."

It occurred to Hollis, not for the first time, that Alevy relished the fact that his lifelong game against Moscow was being played *in* Moscow. Hollis wondered what would become of Alevy when he had to leave here.

There were drink lists printed in several languages on the coffee table, and Alevy ordered Bloody Marys for them.

A waitress came with three glasses of green fluid. Alevy said in English, "Everything in this damned country is red, but the tomato juice is green." He raised his glass to Hollis and Lisa. "Have a safe trip home."

Lisa said, "You're in a good mood today. Glad to see us go?"

"No, no. Just happy for you. Both of you."

There were a few seconds of awkward silence. Suddenly Hollis realised that Alevy and Lisa might like some time alone together. He excused himself and left the lounge.

Alevy and Lisa remained seated. Alevy said, "I'm not happy to see you go. I'm sad. I thought we could give it another try."

"I thought about it too. But other things have happened."

"I know. Well, maybe our paths will cross again, in some other godforsaken place. This is a strange life we've chosen."

"But you like being the premier spy in the capital of the evil empire."

"Oh, yes."

She put her hand on Alevy's arm. "Be careful, Seth. I worry about you."

"Do you? You be careful yourself. You're not home yet." He finished his drink. "Piece of advice, Lady Lisa. His age is not that important. Neither is his present marital status. But if he enters that macho world of jet jockeys again, you've got a problem."

"Leave that to me. What, by the way, were you two talking about until six a.m? You both look like hell."

"I just needed some Red air-force stats. Sorry if I intruded on your plans. Won't happen again." Alevy glanced at his watch and stood. "I'm going to find Sam and say goodbye. You'll be all right here."

She got up and kissed his cheek. "Goodbye, Seth. Thank you for everything." She wiped her eyes. "We'll meet again."

Alevy suddenly pulled her close. He whispered, "Listen to me. You don't have to leave on this flight. There are two more flights to Frankfurt today. Tell Sam you're not feeling well, and—"

"Why?"

"I thought we could . . . Look, what I'm trying to say is that Hollis is a target. I don't like the idea of you being near him."

"I know that. But I'm not a wilting flower, Seth. I was willing to share any danger with you, and I will give him the same loyalty."

A sad smile came across Alevy's face. He nodded. "That's why I love you." They kissed, and he walked away.

ALEVY FOUND HOLLIS in the narrow corridor that led back to the main concourse. Alevy pointed at the ceiling to indicate hidden microphones, and they walked back to the crowded terminal building, where they could speak.

Hollis said, "I assume your meeting with General Surikov went well. You got the microfilm?"

"I did. It was good stuff. I'd like to see us go public with the photos—TV and newspapers, cinemas, shopping malls. That would blow every one of those Russian agents. However, I think the government wants the FBI to try to round them up quietly."

"What I don't understand is how anyone is going to resolve the problem of the Charm School without all hell breaking loose."

"There are ways to resolve it quietly. As long as Dodson doesn't show up. If by some miracle he makes it to the embassy, I think Charlie Banks is under orders to have him killed. Our government is ready to write off three hundred American airmen for some abstraction they call détente."

"Seth, we have to find a way to bring those men home. What did you think of General Surikov?"

"I spoke to him in the Arbat antique shop for half an hour. I agree that he's a legitimate defector. Incidentally, I scanned that microfilm and found a picture of our handyman, Mr. Kellum, born Anatoli Vladimirovich Kulagin, in Kursk, USSR."

"So we bagged the first one. How about Mrs. Kellum?"

"Haven't come across her yet." Alevy smiled. "The microfilm was an incredible counterintelligence coup. Three thousand agents, Sam, that's the biggest single catch in history. And with those Russian Americans in our pocket, maybe there is a way we can tackle the Charm School itself."

"A trade?"

Alevy nodded. "Three thousand of theirs for three hundred of ours. It's a possibility. And we have you to thank for that. You did it, Sam. I think you got your people home."

"But I thought Washington didn't want them home."

"We'll work on that. You have some clout yourself now. When you get to DC you're going to be treated like a conquering hero. Don't be surprised if the President pins a general's star on you."

"Surikov just fell into my lap, Seth. You know that."

"Don't be modest. Well, a personal note on the subject of Lisa—all I can say is good luck. I wish you both happiness."

"Thank you." Hollis put out his hand, and Alevy took it.

"We'll meet again, in a better place than this," Alevy said.

Hollis turned and walked towards the diplomatic wing. He had the impression that Alevy did not think there was a better place. The truth was that Seth Alevy liked it here, or more accurately, needed to be here. He needed to breathe Moscow air and smell Moscow river fog. He needed the KGB, and in some perversely reciprocal arrangement they needed him, or they'd have had him expelled or killed long ago.

A MAN IN A HEAVY OVERCOAT opened the door to the diplomatic lounge and looked at Lisa and Hollis. "Pan Am. Frankfurt. Follow, please."

As they picked up their flight bags Bert Mills came over. The three of them walked past the border guard with the submachine gun and followed the Russian with the overcoat outside, down a set of steps to where a small airport bus waited on the tarmac. A fine, powdery snow sifted down from an overcast sky. They boarded the bus, on which they were the only passengers, and the driver headed out to a mammoth Pan Am 747. Four border guards stood round it with submachine guns.

The bus pulled up at the boarding stairs, and they got out. Mills said, "I'll hang around awhile. But I think you're home free." He shook their hands. "Safe trip."

Hollis and Lisa went up the steps and were met by a smiling woman who introduced herself as Jo, their flight attendant. "Ciipper Class is right up that little spiral staircase there," she said in a twangy voice. "Make yourselves at home. Soon as the other buses get here, I'll be up."

Hollis led the way up the spiral staircase into the dome of the 747. They hung their coats and stowed their bags in a closet, then took two seats near the front. The cabin seemed eerily quiet, and Hollis had the fleeting thought that the 747 was a sham and Jo was a graduate of the Charm School. He laughed.

"What's funny?" Lisa asked.

Hollis took her hand. "Nothing. I think this place finally got to me."

The other passengers started to board. Mike Salerno, the Pacific News Service reporter, was the first person up the spiral staircase, and he sat in a seat facing them.

"How did you get up here so fast?" Hollis asked.

"Pushed and shoved. I'm a reporter."

Lisa asked, "Are you going home for good?"

"No. I put in for two weeks' therapeutic leave."

Hollis noticed that only six more people came into the Clipper Class section, which could hold about fourteen passengers. There was a middle-aged British couple sitting near the staircase and four German businessmen across the aisle in the other facing seats.

Jo, the flight attendant, went to the front of the cabin and announced that they had been cleared for takeoff. As the 747 began to move, Hollis saw Bert Mills waving, and waved back. The aircraft turned onto the runway and raced down the concrete. No one spoke. The 747 nosed up, the wheels bumped into their wells and the plane began its climb.

Lisa looked out of the window at the snow-dusted landscape. She saw the Minsk–Moscow highway, the tiny villages that dotted the open fields, and the dark green pine forests that covered much of the countryside. She said, almost to herself, "*Do svidaniya*."

Salerno snorted. "Good riddance. Admit it, Lisa. That place"—he jerked his thumb towards the window—"is tense. Paranoia incorporated. Soon as you leave, you breathe normal."

Hollis yawned. Lisa picked up a magazine.

Salerno leaned forward. "I'll tell you something else I learned about that Fisher business. I found out from his parents that he was booked at the Rossiya, so I went there on the hunch that he'd actually gotten to Moscow. And guess what? I found an English tourist who remembered the car with Connecticut licence plates parked in front of the Rossiya."

Lisa lowered her magazine. Hollis asked, "What do you think that means, Mike?"

"I'm not sure," Salerno said. "But you know damned well that Fisher got to the Rossiya. Fact is, guys, he called the embassy from the hotel. Spoke to you, Lisa."

Lisa asked, "How do you know that?"

"You got a leak. So how is the embassy going to handle this?"

Hollis thought a moment. He couldn't conceive of how that call from Fisher to the embassy had been leaked. He said, "I'll discuss this with you after we're out of the USSR."

Salerno nodded. "OK. Listen, something else I heard: that you guys were holding an American in the embassy. I don't know if this guy is supposed to be a spy, or if he was somebody who got into trouble in Moscow and made it into the embassy, or both. It was a very strange story."

"Sounds strange," Hollis agreed.

"Yeah." Salerno took a packet of Marlboros from his pocket and lit one. "Come on, guys. Give me a break. You holding someone in the embassy? Someone, one of the service people, tipped me." He drew on his cigarette. "Says there's at least one American in an isolation cell. Maybe two."

Hollis studied Salerno a moment. He wondered if Salerno was fishing for the Kellums or for Dodson. He wondered, too, where this man got his information. Hollis noticed that the fingers in which Salerno was holding his cigarette kept moving in a habitual way to straighten the cigarette to keep it from sagging. But since it was an American cigarette, it did not sag. "You ever smoke the local brands?" he asked Salerno.

Salerno glanced at him quickly. "No. Why?"

"Just wondered."

Salerno stubbed out his cigarette and picked up a pulp detective novel.

Jo came over to them. "Ms. Rhodes, I was asked to give you this after we got airborne." She handed a brown parcel to Lisa.

Lisa asked, "Who gave it to you?"

"A Russian guy. An airport official." She added, "It's usually against regulations to take anything aboard like that, but it was from an airport official, and he said it was X-rayed and all."

Lisa sat looking at the package on the seat tray. She said to Hollis, "This is the icon, Sam, addressed to USIS in DC. I thought it was cleared for the diplomatic pouch."

"It was," Hollis replied. "I told them in the mailroom. What did they say when you brought it there?"

"I didn't. Mrs. Kellum saw it and said she was going to the mailroom, so she took it." Lisa looked at Hollis. "It's been opened. The tape is broken." She ripped the paper off, then let out a stifled sob. Deeply gouged into the painted wood, obscuring the face of the archangel, was a hammer and sickle. Lisa tried to say something, but no words came out. Tears formed in her eyes. Hollis took her hand.

Salerno looked up from his book. "What's the matter?"

The PA system crackled. "Ladies and gentlemen, this is Captain Johnson speaking. We're experiencing a minor electrical problem, and

451

we've been instructed to land in Minsk. Nothing to be concerned about. Please fasten your seat belts for our approach."

Salerno said, "It looks like our farewell to Russia was premature."

CHAPTER 12

The Pan Am 747 touched down at Minsk Airport. Hollis saw four mobile stairways coming out to meet them, which was not normal for a routine deplaning. Behind the stairways were four buses. Hollis also noted that the 747 was some distance from the terminal.

Hollis looked back at Lisa. She was still staring at the damaged icon. "It can be restored," he said.

Salerno turned the icon towards him. "Damned shame. Who would do something like that?"

Hollis replied, "I can think of one outfit right away."

"You mean the KGB?" Lisa asked. "Why, Sam? It's so senseless. So petty and vengeful."

"That's them."

Lisa took a deep breath. "I'm going to keep it just as it is," she said. "Just the way they gave it to me."

The 747 had come to a halt. Jo stood near the galley door. "Ladies and gentlemen, the electrical repair may take a while, so we're going to deplane. Please bring all your personal things."

Hollis, Lisa and the others from Clipper Class went down the spiral stairs to the door, then descended the mobile stairway to the tarmac. In the bus were about a dozen people from First Class. The door closed behind them, and the bus headed for the terminal, where they were shown into a small waiting room that was not large enough to accommodate the coach passengers. Hollis had the feeling that he and Lisa had been neatly cut from the main pack and that there would be further isolation when someone offered them diplomatic courtesies.

A short, squat man in a ludicrous mustard-coloured suit walked into the room, followed by an attractive woman. The man held up his hand, and the room became quiet. "I am Mr. Marchenko, the Intourist representative here. I must inform you that there is no electrical problem on the aircraft. Soviet authorities have received a bomb threat—"

There was a gasp from the group.

"Please, please. Nothing to fear. However, the aircraft and all luggage must be searched. This takes a long time. So Intourist will take you all to Sputnik Hotel to have lunch, and maybe you stay overnight."

The woman with him repeated the announcement in German, then in French. Hollis was impressed with this uncharacteristic Soviet efficiency at such short notice. Obviously, Intourist had had help from another, more efficient Soviet agency.

452

Lisa said, "I don't like this, Sam."

Hollis said, "I'll be right back."

"Where are you going?" Salerno asked.

"Men's room." Hollis walked out of the waiting room and into a corridor, but a border guard motioned him back. Hollis said in Russian, "I have to use the toilet."

The border guard pointed down the hallway.

Hollis went quickly to the main concourse of the terminal. He found a payphone in a recess. He put two kopecks in the slot, dialled the Minsk long-distance operator and gave her the embassy phone number.

A hand reached over Hollis's shoulder and pushed down the phone cradle. Hollis turned round and found himself looking down at the short, squat Mr. Marchenko, now wearing an overcoat and flanked by two border guards. Marchenko said, "Colonel Hollis, everything is all arranged. No need to call."

Hollis snapped, "Why the hell are you interrupting my call?" He turned back to the phone.

Marchenko said, "Come, sir. The Soviet Foreign Ministry has wired, instructing me to extend special courtesies to you and Ms. Rhodes."

"We require no special courtesies."

Marchenko shook his head. "No, Colonel. I have strict instructions. Ms. Rhodes is in the car awaiting you. Come now. We will be late."

"Late for what?"

"A helicopter, sir. To take you back to Sheremetyevo. There is a Lufthansa flight leaving there at three fifty-five for Frankfurt. Come. Ms. Rhodes is most anxious about you."

Suddenly Salerno appeared. "There you are. What's all this?"

Hollis said, "It seems Lisa and I are being offered a helicopter ride to Sheremetyevo to catch a Lufthansa flight to Frankfurt."

"Well, lucky you. In my next life I want to be a diplomat."

"What were you in your last life?"

"A Russian." Salerno laughed and motioned to the phones. "I'll call the embassy right now and tell them that Intourist has rolled out the red carpet—pardon the pun."

"Bull," Hollis said to Salerno. Then he added in Russian, "It was the cigarette, Michael. You kept straightening it with your fingers."

Salerno winked. "Don't tell anyone, and I'll owe you a favour. You'll need one shortly." He turned and walked away.

Marchenko led Hollis out through the glass doors, to the waiting Volga saloon. Lisa was in the rear seat. Hollis got in, and she threw her arms round him. Marchenko slid into the front seat, and the driver pulled away from the terminal.

Lisa whispered to Hollis, "Are we being kidnapped?"

Hollis glanced out of the rear window and saw another Volga, in which were three men in brown leather coats. "In this country it's hard to tell.

Sometimes you just have to ask." He leaned towards Marchenko. "*Komitet*?"

Marchenko looked back. "No, no. Please. Intourist." He smiled. "Like you are an air attaché."

They turned onto a road that paralleled the airport fence and halted by a concrete helipad. "Here we are," Marchenko said. "But no helicopter. We rushed for nothing." He looked at his watch, then peered through the windscreen at the sky. "Ah, there it is."

Hollis could hear the sound of helicopter blades beating the dank, heavy air. A black shape appeared over the bare trees, silhouetted against the grey sky. He recognised the shape as that of the Mi-28, a six-seat helicopter with turbojet engines. As it dropped in closer Hollis saw that it had the markings of the Red air force.

"Please step out of the car," Marchenko said.

Hollis and Lisa got out. The driver retrieved their flight bags and Lisa's icon from the boot and set everything on the concrete near their feet. The rest of their luggage was still on the 747.

One of the men from the other Volga stood behind Hollis. Marchenko shouted to Hollis over the noise of the approaching helicopter. "He is called Vadim. He will accompany us."

The Mi-28 set down, and Marchenko urged Hollis and Lisa forward. A crewman slid open a side door. Hollis got in first, then helped Lisa up. The crewman motioned them to the two rear seats. Vadim climbed in and sat in front of Lisa. Marchenko struggled aboard and fell heavily into the seat in front of Hollis. The crewman slid the door shut and settled into the copilot's seat. The helicopter rose and headed back in the direction of Moscow.

Hollis put his arm round Lisa's shoulders. "How you doing, kid?"

"Awful." She looked down at the icon, lying on her lap. "This is what real faith is all about, isn't it? The belief that someone up there is looking after you."

"Yes."

"This icon has probably been kissed ten thousand times over the last three centuries." She brought it up to her face and pressed her lips to it.

Hollis said in a light tone, "Do you want to say the words 'I quit'?"

She looked at him and whispered, "You and Seth promised I would be kept informed in exchange for my help."

"I'm keeping you informed. We've been kidnapped."

"Not funny, Sam. I think you both knew this might happen."

"We suspected."

"More than suspected, I think. Do you know that Seth didn't want me to get on that flight?"

"No, I didn't know that." But that was very interesting, Hollis thought. No one in this business seemed to be fully informed. He said, "But you came along anyway."

454

"I love you, stupid."

Marchenko piped up, "I hear whispers. No whispers."

"Go to hell," said Hollis.

"That's where we are going, my friend."

CHAPTER 13

Nearly three hours after they'd begun their flight, the helicopter began to descend. Hollis spotted the old Minsk road running along the Moskva River, and then, unexpectedly, he spotted Yablonya. It was now a stretch of black, charred log cabins along a dirt road. A bulldozer had already pushed half the burned village into a long ditch. To the list of scores to be settled, Hollis now added the village of Yablonya.

About three minutes later he saw the beginning of Borodino Field, the earthworks, monuments, then the museum. The pine forest came up, and the helicopter dropped more quickly. He saw the barbed-wire fences and the cleared area between them, then the helipad that Alevy had pointed out in the satellite picture.

Lisa leaned over and looked out of the window. "Where are we?"

"Mrs. Ivanova's Charm School," Hollis said.

The helicopter continued its descent towards the landing area, which Hollis noted was a natural clearing in the pine forest. On the south edge of the clearing was the log cabin he'd seen in the satellite picture. A narrow dirt track, barely visible among the pine trees, began at the cabin and ran a hundred yards south to the main camp road. It was two winding lanes of black tarmac that bisected the camp from east to west. This road passed through the main gate and was a continuation of the one they had taken from Borodino Field.

As they descended to about a hundred feet Hollis saw a grim-looking concrete building in the centre of the camp, probably the headquarters. Not far from that was a long wooden construction with a green roof, whose purpose he could not guess. Some distance south of these two buildings was another clearing, but this one was man-made. It was, in fact, a soccer field. As the helicopter flew lower Hollis could see stands that would accommodate close to five hundred people. Between the soccer field and the south perimeter of the camp he saw long barracklike buildings that would be the separate compound for the KGB border-guard detachment.

As they descended his eye caught something odd in the treetops. He realised that he was looking at a huge camouflage net supported by living pine trees whose tops poked through the net. An axiom of both combat flying and spying was that neither aerial photographs nor overflights could substitute for a man on the ground. He was about to be the man on the ground.

The helicopter settled onto the snow-dusted landing field. The copilot drew his pistol and slid open the door. Marchenko and Vadim climbed out first. The copilot motioned with his gun at Lisa, and she took her bag and icon and jumped to the ground. Hollis followed.

Marchenko opened the rear door of a waiting vehicle, a Zil-6, which was somewhat like an American jeep, but larger. Lisa got in, followed by Hollis and Vadim. Marchenko climbed into the front passenger seat and said to the driver, "Headquarters."

The Zil moved across the grass field and entered the narrow track in the dark pine forest. Hollis took Lisa's hand and said in her ear, "They're going to interrogate you. Be brave."

She drew a deep breath and nodded.

The Zil came to the end of the track and turned left onto the tarmac main road. The pines rose forty to fifty feet on either side of the road, and the canopy of boughs was so thick that little light reached the ground. Now and then Hollis saw lanes leading off the main road, and houses that he hadn't seen from the air. He was not surprised to catch sight of an American ranch house, then a white clapboard bungalow. They were probably residences for the Charm School students and their American instructors.

Lisa spotted one, and pointed. "This is bizarre."

The Zil continued slowly along the road, and coming up on the right was the long green-roofed building Hollis had seen from the air. It was a single-storey building of white clapboard with a homey-looking front porch with rocking chairs and a red-and-white Coke machine. Through a picture window Hollis glimpsed some men and women, and noticed a large American flag hanging on a wall. As the Zil passed by, he saw a sign over the double doors that read VFW POST 000.

The Zil moved on, and came to a halt in front of the headquarters building, a grey two-storey hulk of precast concrete slabs. A KGB border guard stood in a plywood booth, to the left of the headquarters' entrance. Standing in front, wearing the long green greatcoat with red shoulder boards of the KGB, was Colonel Burov.

Marchenko and Vadim got out, followed by Hollis and Lisa. Burov looked at them for a long time, then said, "Well, this is what you wanted to see, wasn't it, Hollis?"

Hollis didn't reply.

Noticing the large icon in Lisa's hand, Burov said to her, "If you were Catholic or Protestant, you'd have to carry only a small cross for comfort." He laughed, and Marchenko and Vadim laughed also.

Lisa said in Russian, "Go to hell."

Burov slapped her face, knocking her to the ground. Hollis bent down to help her up, and as he did, Burov swung at him, catching him on the jaw and sending him staggering back. "Well, that evens the score for Lefortovo," he said.

Hollis struggled to his feet as Vadim grabbed Lisa by her coat collar and pulled her up.

Marchenko and Vadim saluted and got back into the Zil.

Burov said to Hollis and Lisa, "Get inside."

The border guard opened the door, and Hollis and Lisa entered with Burov. A guard with an AK-47 met them in the lobby where the duty officer, a lieutenant, sat at a desk facing the door. The officer stood up when he saw Burov. Burov said to Hollis and Lisa, "Leave your bags and that religious thing with this man."

As Hollis set his bag down he noticed an open door to the left, through which he could see a telephone switchboard and a radio transmitter. At Burov's order he removed his trench coat and shoes while Lisa pulled off her boots and overcoat. The guard yanked off Hollis's tie and belt.

"This way," Burov snapped. He led them down a long corridor. The guard followed. He threw open a steel door and shoved Lisa inside. Burov said to her, "Take off your clothes and wait for the matron." He slammed the door shut.

Burov opened the next door and pushed Hollis into a small, windowless cell. "For your information," he said, "I am the camp commandant, and I've never had an escape in the ten years I've been here. Then Dodson escapes, and two of my men are murdered. I know you killed them, and I think you and your Jew friend Alevy know too much about this place. Don't you?"

Hollis said nothing.

"I'll tell you something else. From the moment I laid eyes on you and your girlfriend, I wanted you both here. My superiors in Moscow said impossible, but I showed them how we could kidnap two American diplomats. There was a helicopter crash not far from Minsk Airport today. Your death in that crash is now being reported to your embassy. No one knows you're here, Hollis. No one is looking for you. You're all mine now, and you're dead."

Hollis read between the lines that Burov was in trouble and was trying to redeem himself with his bosses. So far, he was doing fine.

Burov snapped, "Take off your clothes and give them to me."

Hollis did as he was told; then Burov and the guard left. The door slammed, and Hollis heard the bolt drive home.

He looked around. Four bare concrete walls enclosed a space about ten foot square. The only light came from a dim recessed bulb in the ceiling, covered by a steel grating. Somewhere up there was a fibre-optic device watching him.

There was no furniture in the cell, and as far as he could see, no heat source either. In the far left corner a water spigot protruded from the wall, about four feet off the floor. Beneath the spigot was a waste hole. Hollis turned on the spigot and rinsed the blood out of his mouth. He felt his jaw swelling, and one of his teeth was loose.

He went to the wall that separated his cell from Lisa's and struck it with his palm, but it was solid, and he heard no answering signal.

Hollis sat in a corner, pulled his legs up to his chest and wrapped his arms round his knees. He slept fitfully.

ON WHAT HE THOUGHT was the second day of his imprisonment, the door opened. Someone threw a bundle of clothes on the floor and shut the door. Hollis found a blue track suit and socks, but no footwear. He dressed and treated himself to some water. He felt weak. The light overhead went off, and the cell was in darkness. Hollis walked for a while, then curled up and slept in his new clothes.

ON WHAT HE RECKONED was the third day, the door opened again, and a sleeping-bag flew in, followed by a boiled potato that steamed in the cool air. As Hollis moved towards the potato the light went off, and he had to get down on all fours to find the food. He climbed into the sleeping-bag and ate the warm potato.

Some hours later the door opened again, and a guard shouted in Russian, "Get up! Come here."

Hollis got to his feet and followed the guard down the long corridor and into a small room. There, at a long table, were five KGB officers. Burov sat in the middle. On the wall behind the table was a large painted sword and shield, the emblem of the Committee for State Security.

Hollis faced the five men.

Colonel Burov spoke in Russian. "This special tribunal of the Committee for State Security has been convened for the purpose of trying Colonel Samuel Hollis for the murder of Private Nikolai Kulnev and Private Mikhail Kolotilov." Burov recited dates and circumstances, then asked, "Colonel Hollis, how do you plead?"

"I plead guilty," Hollis said.

If the KGB men were surprised, they didn't show it. Burov asked, "Do you want to say something in extenuation or mitigation?"

"No."

Burov cleared his throat. "Very well. If the accused raises no extenuating circumstances, then there is only one penalty for the murder of a KGB man, and that is death by firing squad."

Hollis stared straight ahead.

Burov said, "You are required to write a full confession of your crime. If that is satisfactory, you will be allowed to write an appeal of your death sentence to the chairman of the Committee for State Security. If the appeal is turned down, you will be executed. Take the prisoner to his cell. Bring in the next prisoner."

The guard moved Hollis to the door. It opened, and Lisa stepped into the room. She was wearing a grey prison dress and looked pale and disorientated. He said to her, "Plead guilty. Be brave. I love you."

458

She focused on him as if trying to place him; then their guards moved them past each other, and Hollis found himself in the corridor.

Back in his cell, he saw a writing pad on the floor, along with an American ball-point pen. He sat on his sleeping-bag and rested the pad on his knees. As an intelligence officer, his primary obligation was to escape, and to do that, he had to preserve his mind and body. His instructions were to confess to anything as long as it didn't endanger another prisoner or compromise national security. In short, he was to play their game.

Hollis began writing his confession. He knew that if they had the time, they'd make him rewrite it again and again. But he also suspected that Burov was on a tight schedule and had to get on with the important business of finding out what he and Alevy knew. Hollis reflected on the sequence of the criminal justice system here: trial, confession, interrogation. He supposed it didn't matter. The bullet still came at the end.

Hollis paused to collect his thoughts. In truth, there wasn't much to tell. He'd been spying on the Charm School, run into two border guards, and shot them. His chance sighting of Yablonya from the helicopter removed that moral problem and gave him an opportunity to betray people who were already liquidated. Hollis filled the writing pad, then read what he'd written. It was a good confession, a mixture of hard fact, which Burov already knew, and hard-to-prove fiction. Hollis signed it, then lay down in his sleeping-bag and fell into a restless sleep. He dreamed about Lisa.

ON THE FIFTH OR SIXTH DAY, his cell door opened, and the lieutenant who had been the duty officer when he arrived walked in. "Your confession is accepted," he said in Russian. "Now you will write an appeal of your death sentence. Come with me."

Hollis, half starved by now, stood unsteadily and followed the lieutenant out into the corridor. The man led him to the rear of the building and into a small, windowless room that had a table and chair in it. On the table were a sheet of paper and a pen.

"Sit down."

Hollis sat, and the lieutenant moved behind him. Hollis saw that the pine boards of the table were stained with blood. Against the wall in front of him were bales of straw, to keep a bullet from ricocheting.

"Address your appeal to the chairman of the Committee for State Security."

Hollis picked up the pen and began writing. The lieutenant remained behind him. Hollis heard a holster unsnapping, the pistol sliding over the leather, the click of the hammer being cocked.

He continued to write. His mouth had gone dry, and his palms were moist. He finished the last line and signed the appeal. Then he waited.

He heard the hammer click again, the pistol slide back into the holster.

The lieutenant chuckled softly and said, "Leave it there. Stand up."

Hollis stood, and the lieutenant took him back to his cell. The Russian said, "Your appeal will be decided within twenty-four hours." He closed and bolted the door.

The light was on, and Hollis knew Burov was taking some pleasure in watching him. He drank from the spigot, retched, then drank again. He took a deep breath, went to his sleeping-bag, and pulled it over his head. The light went off and he found himself slipping into sleep.

THE DOOR OPENED, and a guard said, "Come with me."

Hollis stood and followed the man into the corridor. They went up the stairs to the second floor, where Hollis was led into a spartan concrete office. Colonel Burov sat at the desk. There was a single window in the wall, and Hollis saw it was evening.

Burov said, "Sit down, Hollis."

Hollis sat on a chair facing the desk. The door closed behind him.

Burov held up Hollis's written confession. "Fascinating. I'm glad to see you were truthful about Yablonya. Your girlfriend, however, was not. In fact, her confession has fewer interesting details than yours does."

"She doesn't know much."

Burov studied him a moment. "Your appeal for clemency is also interesting. You say you are willing to work here if you are not shot. What do you think we do here?"

"Train KGB agents to pass as Americans."

"How do you know that?"

"We guessed."

"I see. And have you caught any graduates from this place?"

"Yes. The Kellums."

Burov leaned towards him. "And Dodson? Where is Dodson?"

"I don't know."

Burov stood up and went to the window. He stared out at the dark pine forest, and then he asked, "If you people know about this place, why aren't you doing anything about it?"

"My government is pursuing a policy of peace at the moment. So they want to keep it quiet." Hollis knew that what he said was being recorded and perhaps fed into a voice-stress analyser. Later he'd be asked the same questions when he was attached to a polygraph. Any inconsistencies would be resolved with electric-shock interrogation.

Burov said, "I can't imagine that your government would let our operation continue. Even in the interests of peace. There are thousands of our agents in America already, and we're graduating over two hundred a year. What does Washington intend to do about that?"

That, Hollis thought, was the crux of the matter. He replied, "It is my understanding that the State Department in Washington is looking for a negotiated settlement."

460

"Are they? And what does the CIA want to do? And your people—the Defence Intelligence Agency? Something like rescuing one or two of these men and presenting them to the world as evidence?"

"Not that I know of. From what I see here, that's not possible."

"No, it's not." Burov was silent for a while, then said, "I want the names of all Soviet citizens you employ as American agents."

"I don't have any actual names. Just code names. Besides, why should I tell you anything if I'm going to be shot?"

"Because being shot is not as bad as what I can do to you. Let me ask you something. What do you propose?"

"I realise I'm officially dead. I'd rather work here, among my peers, than go to Siberia or be shot. I want Lisa Rhodes with me."

"Yes, you are officially dead. I'll show you the American newspaper accounts. Moscow wants you actually dead after your debriefing. But perhaps I can convince them that you and your girlfriend will be an asset here."

Hollis didn't reply.

Burov paced round the room and said, "Well, Hollis, do you want to see your girlfriend?"

Hollis nodded.

Burov opened the door to his office, called the guard, then said to Hollis, "Get out."

The guard marched Hollis down the stairs. The man unlocked Lisa's cell and shoved Hollis in. The door closed behind him.

Lisa sat curled up in the corner. She looked at him but said nothing. Her cheeks were drawn and her eyes seemed sunken. Hollis sat down beside her, putting his arm round her shoulders. She didn't move. They sat in silence for a long time; then Lisa put her face in her hands and wept. "I was sentenced to death," she said in a barely audible voice.

Hollis didn't reply. He was sure the room was wired. He wanted to comfort her but thought it best to say nothing that Burov could use. In fact, he knew he should not have even told Burov he wanted to see her.

After a few minutes she reached out and took his hand. "I don't blame you for this. You warned me."

Hollis made no reply.

CHAPTER 14

There were footsteps, and the door opened. The guard said, "Stand up. Follow me. No talking."

"I love you, Sam," Lisa said, as she got to her feet.

"I love you."

"No talking!"

They walked down the long corridor, and another guard opened the door to the room where Hollis had written the appeal of his death sentence—the execution room. Lisa hesitated, but the guard shoved her inside. On the bloodstained table were hot tea, boiled eggs, bread and jam. The guard said, "Eat all you want."

Hollis and Lisa ate slowly. Then the guard led them into a locker room. There was a sink, a toilet, and in the corner an open shower. The guard motioned to the shower. "Go ahead. Use it."

They showered with hot water and soap. A matron brought in towels, a shaving kit, underwear and clean track suits. Hollis dried himself, shaved, then dressed. Lisa dressed quickly, avoiding the guard's eyes. The matron pointed to a box full of running shoes, and they each found a pair that fitted.

The guard led them upstairs to Burov's office. As they entered, Burov said, "Sit down." They sat in chairs facing him.

"You'll be pleased to hear that both your death sentences have been conditionally commuted to life imprisonment."

"What," Hollis asked, "is the condition?"

"Two conditions. One is that you pass a polygraph test. The other is that you work for us here. If you say no, you'll be executed for murder."

Lisa said, "You're asking us to become traitors. The answer is no."

Burov said, "Ms. Rhodes, your friend has already indicated he would work for us here in exchange for his life."

"I didn't say I would subject myself to a polygraph interrogation," Hollis said.

"No," Burov replied, "but you will be thoroughly debriefed nonetheless. There are several methods of interrogation. I prefer polygraph and sodium pentothal over electric shock and a truncheon. The results are more reliable. I'm sure you and Ms. Rhodes would prefer that too."

Hollis said, "Working here is one thing. But I cannot give you intelligence secrets that would endanger other agents."

Burov tapped his fingers on his desk. "You're not in a position to make deals. The question is this: Do you want to live and work here, or do you want to be shot? Answer."

"I . . . I want to be with Colonel Hollis," Lisa said quietly.

Burov grinned. "Such loyalty." He looked at Hollis. "What is your decision, Colonel?"

"I would like both of us to be let out of the cells, to live here a while before we decide if we want to become instructors."

"You're stalling."

"For what? I'm dead. We are both dead."

Burov stood and went to the window. He stared out into the trees for a while, then turned to Hollis. "All right. I think when you see how comfortable you can be here, you'll decide you don't want to die in front of a firing squad. You'll have one week. Then you must submit to an interrogation. The moment I think you are up to something, or lying to

me"—Burov pointed to Lisa—"she dies. I'll torture her to death right in front of you."

Burov walked towards Hollis. "You are intelligent enough to know that I let you bargain with me because I'd rather have you alive. I want you alive so that I can question you, not only now but any time something comes up in American intelligence matters that you can enlighten us on. You are both valuable commodities here. I also want you both under my thumb. For ever."

Burov stared at them for a long time, his face impassive; then he spoke in an almost friendly tone. "Well, now. Are you feeling up to a walk in the fresh air? I'm sure you're curious." Burov motioned them to the door and summoned the guard. He said, "I'll join you in a while."

The guard led them downstairs and indicated a bench near the front door. Then he left them.

Hollis looked round the lobby. A picture of Lenin hung over the front desk. The duty officer there was the lieutenant who had played games with his pistol when Hollis was writing his appeal. Through the open door of the communications room Hollis could see the manually operated switchboard and short-wave radio he'd noticed when he first entered this building.

The lieutenant said in Russian, "My name is Cheltsov. So, you will be instructors here?"

"We're considering the offer," Hollis replied. "Do you speak English?"

"No. None of the border guards speak English."

"And do the American instructors speak Russian?" Hollis asked.

"They are not supposed to know Russian, but they pick up a little. You see, here the Russian students and American instructors may communicate in English only. The border guards may not speak to students or instructors unless absolutely necessary."

The lieutenant went back to his paperwork, and they sat in silence. Then Lisa said in English, "Sam, I know we're in a bad situation here. But I'm not going to submit to them."

Hollis rubbed his thumb and forefinger together, the embassy signal to remind people of electronic eavesdropping.

She touched her chin in acknowledgment and whispered in his ear, "It was an act, wasn't it? I mean your . . ."

". . . submissiveness." He nodded. "We'll talk later."

They waited for nearly half an hour. Finally Burov appeared in his greatcoat, and Lieutenant Cheltsov jumped to attention. Burov said to the man, "Get them some parkas."

The lieutenant produced parkas for them both, and they put them on. Burov said, "Follow me."

They went with him out of the headquarters building into the chill air. There was some thin morning sunlight, and Hollis noticed how pale Lisa looked. He drew a breath of pine-scented air.

464

Burov seemed to be enjoying the morning. "We start with a clean slate here," he said. "Here there is no past. The instructors have no personal past, only a cultural past that they transmit to the students. The students have no personal or cultural past, only a political past that they cherish but never mention."

Hollis had the distinct impression that Burov was looking forward to showing them his school. They followed him round the headquarters building and he led them through the woods to the soccer field, where Hollis saw two teams of young men playing touch football. There were two middle-aged men on the opposite sidelines and two on the field.

Burov observed, "Those are the coaches and two referees. I wish the students could play with their instructors as they once did. But the instructors are getting on in years."

"The Americans, you mean."

"The instructors and students are all Americans, so we don't use that term to distinguish one from the other. Anyway, all exercise here is some sort of American or universal sport." Burov led them across the field, talking as he walked. "Now they are playing much soccer in America, so my students can excel at something over there if they have an athletic inclination. Incidentally, one of the best amateur soccer teams in northern New Jersey is coached by one of our graduates."

"Do you know what becomes of all your students?"

"Alas, no. They are turned over to Directorate S for infiltration into the States. But we get a few anecdotal stories back now and then. It's good for our morale."

They reached the edge of the field and entered the woods by way of another path. The path ended at a small concrete structure that resembled a bunker. Burov directed them inside, where he pressed a button on the wall. The steel-plate floor began sinking.

They rode down a shaft for a few seconds, then stopped. Two sliding doors parted, and Burov showed them out into a smartly appointed room with chrome furniture and suede-covered walls. A young man sat at a desk in the corner, wearing a T-shirt and reading a *New York Times*. Burov said to Hollis and Lisa, "Welcome to the Holiday Spa."

The young man behind the desk put down the paper and said in cheery English, "Hello, Colonel. Who you got there?"

"New members, Frank. Colonel Hollis and Ms. Rhodes."

"Great." The young man put out his hand. "Frank Chapman. I read your obit last week, Colonel."

Hollis hesitated, then shook hands with him and said, "If you're Frank Chapman, I'm Leo Tolstoy."

Chapman did not smile.

Burov said to Chapman, "I'll just show them round."

"Sure thing."

Burov led them through steamy glass doors into an anteroom. "Men's locker room there. Ladies' over there. We don't have many female students, because we only have six female instructors. Maybe seven now." He glanced at Lisa, then continued. "This place is our gem. It cost over a million roubles to build underground, and there's half a million dollars' worth of Western athletic equipment here." They followed him down a long corridor. "Finnish saunas here, steam baths there, sun-rooms, Jacuzzis. Here's the workout room. We know that many important contacts are made in athletic clubs and that most successful Americans are involved in some sort of athletic pastime."

They walked to the end of the corridor, which opened into a large gymnasium. At the far end of the gym six young men in shorts were shooting baskets. "Come," Burov said. They walked round the hardwood gym floor and approached the six students. Hollis was surprised at how they carried themselves: their smiles, facial expressions and hand movements closely approximated to American subtleties. They were like no Russians he had ever seen.

Burov said to them, "Gentlemen, this is Sam Hollis and Lisa Rhodes. They may be joining the faculty."

The six young men greeted them pleasantly, pumping their hands and saying things such as "Nice meeting you," "Glad you could come," and "Welcome aboard." Hollis was impressed. This, he knew, must have been a difficult cultural breakthrough for them and for Burov.

They toured the remainder of the underground sports complex, and Hollis realised this place was at least a partial reason for Burov's not wanting to break camp and move the whole operation. They left by way of the elevator, which took them back up into the concrete bunker. Burov led them out and pointed to the south. "That barbed wire is the compound of the KGB border guards. They man the watchtowers and patrol the perimeter. Like everyone here, they're assigned for life. Moscow does not encourage transfers out of this place. Many of the Russians who work here, including the entire medical staff, are political prisoners who have been assigned here from the *gulag*."

The three of them continued their walk through the woods, and to an outside observer it would have looked like a companionable scene.

"The real deficiency of this school," Burov pointed out, "is that all the male instructors are former pilots. Their job experience and adult lives are too similar for us to get a good cross-section of American society. Two people like you, with some variables in their backgrounds, would make excellent additions to the faculty."

They crossed the soccer field again and came back to the main road near the headquarters building. Burov turned left, west towards the main gate. About a hundred metres down the road they saw VFW POST 000, the long wooden building with the pleasant front porch. Burov showed them inside. To the right of the lobby was a large, brightly lit recreation room with twenty or so people in it. On the opposite wall was the American

466

flag that Hollis had seen through the window. Also on the walls were cardboard decorations for the current Halloween season: pumpkins, scarecrows, a black cat.

Hollis noticed a periodicals rack on the wall, in which were dozens of American magazines and newspapers. In a rear corner was a reading area with shelves stocked with hundreds of books. There were tables for cards and board games, a pool table, a television set, even a video game. Burov said, "The older men, of course, are your compatriots. They keep up to date with American life through periodicals and videotapes sent to us by our embassy and consulate staffs in Washington, New York and San Francisco."

A few of the middle-aged men glanced at Hollis and Lisa, but Hollis noticed that none of them even looked at Burov. Hollis looked at his brother fliers from long ago, and his heart went out to them. He took Lisa's arm and moved her out of the door. Burov hurried out behind them, and they stood on the porch in front of the building.

"Is something bothering you?" Burov asked Hollis. "Oh, yes, those men. How insensitive of me. They're all right, Colonel. They've adjusted. Come, we'll walk if you feel fit enough."

They followed Burov down the steps of the porch and along the road. The buildings in the camp were spread out, and there were times when it seemed to Hollis as if they were in uninhabited woods. But then a building appeared, or men could be seen walking. Hollis spotted three men in overcoats coming towards them now. Burov said, "Instructors."

They met on the path, and Burov made the introductions. "Commander Poole, Captain Schuyler, Lieutenant Colonel Mead, may I introduce Colonel Hollis, United States Air Force, former American embassy air attaché, and Lisa Rhodes, United States Information Service."

The five Americans looked at one another. Colonel Mead broke the silence. "How the hell did you get here?"

Hollis replied, "Kidnapped."

Burov smiled thinly. "If you followed the newspapers more closely, gentlemen, you would have read of the deaths of Colonel Hollis and Ms. Rhodes in a helicopter accident."

Commander Poole said, "Then you're both real? I was thinking you might be two of Colonel Burov's flying worms from a much earlier class."

"No," Hollis replied. "We're real."

Poole nodded gravely. "Well, sorry to see you here."

"We're sorry to be here," Hollis replied. He could sense that they had a lot of questions for him, especially about Dodson. "We'll talk soon." They crossed the main road again and took a path that ran behind the VFW hall and into the woods. Burov said, "We are trying something new. Graduates who have spent at least six years in America are returning as instructors. This programme must continue and expand. One day this school will put out two thousand Americans a year. By the end of the century you will have a fifth column in your country whose size and influence will be sufficient for the Soviet Union to consider itself a minority shareholder in America. One day we might be chairmen of the board."

Burov showed them to a small clapboard cottage built in a Cape Cod style, with green shutters and a cedar shingle roof.

"This was Major Dodson's quarters. You may use it for the week you need to make up your minds. Come in." Burov opened the door and invited them to take off their parkas, then turned on several portable electric and propane heaters. At Burov's urging, Hollis lit the wood in the fireplace. The room was rustic but comfortable.

Burov said to Lisa, "Through that door is a small kitchen. Would you be kind enough to make drinks?"

Lisa gave him a nasty look, then went into the kitchen.

Burov said to Hollis in a low voice, "A word of advice: try to keep her mouth shut. We're very lenient here, but a few instructors have gone too far."

"And you shot them."

"Only as a last resort. Have a seat. You don't look your old self. Sit."

Hollis sat on a couch facing the fire.

Lisa came back with three glasses and passed one to Hollis. "Brandy." She took a glass for herself and put the third on an end table. Burov took his glass and raised it. "To your new home." He drank alone. "So, do you find this preferable to torture, starvation and death?"

Lisa replied, "Not yet."

Burov stared at her for a while, then said, "Sex. You must both wonder about that. You saw some women students, and there are those six American female instructors whom you haven't met yet. Also there are many other women here. Russian women. It would be unrealistic to expect men to function well for all these years without women. Life here is what you make it. As in the West." Burov added, "I think in an ironic way you will be less homesick here than you were in the embassy."

Hollis found that he was sick to death of Burov. "We'd like to be alone," he said.

Burov stood. "Of course. You've both had a trying few weeks." He went to the door. "Speak to the quartermaster at headquarters if you need anything. There's a shopping plaza at the east end of the main road. Everyone here draws a salary. I'll get you your pay for the week in advance. You'll find your overnight bags in the bedroom through that door. Unfortunately, your luggage has been sent to your next of kin."

Hollis asked, "And the icon?"

"Oh, that's there too. Who cut that hammer and sickle into it?"

Hollis replied, "The Kellums, I presume."

"The Kellums?" Lisa said. "Dick and Ann?" She looked at Hollis. He nodded. "I don't believe this," she said.

468

Burov smiled in pure delight. "Fantastic, isn't it? We don't often send them over as a couple like that, but they had the idea of hiring themselves out as domestic servants to a powerful political family." Burov added, "We teach individual initiative here too, which is unfortunately not a Russian character trait."

"If desecrating a holy art object is an example of the initiative you teach, you're getting it wrong."

"That was rather cruel of them. Anything else? . . . No? Well, I've had a pleasant morning. I hope you did too." Burov left.

Lisa put her arms round Hollis. "I want you to know and to never forget that I love you," she said.

"I hope so. We may be here for the rest of our lives."

"No! We are going to go home, or we're going to die trying."

"Don't be a fool." Hollis rubbed his fingers together.

She nodded.

"We'll take a walk later. For now, get some rest." He covered her with a parka on the couch, then sat in an armchair. He stared at the fire and thought of the three American officers he'd met on the path. They'd looked like unhappy ghosts, lost souls, adrift in a void between the living and the dead. He tried to imagine nearly two decades in this place, but could not. He tried to think of a way out, but could not.

CHAPTER 15

Towards dusk Hollis and Lisa left their cottage. They walked past the soccer field and the concrete bunker that housed the spa elevator. After a while Hollis turned off the path and led her into a small ravine. They sat side by side on the sloping ground, and Hollis said softly, "They may have listening devices on the paths, and maybe directional microphones tracking us. But we can talk here if we keep it low."

"Are we here for the rest of our lives?"

"I hope not."

"Seth knows we're here?"

"I think he knows we didn't die in that helicopter crash."

"So, are we going to be rescued or exchanged or what?"

Hollis took her hand. "The less you know, the better. The less I know, the better. You understand about polygraphs and truth serums. Burov is by no means through with us."

"I told Burov just about everything, Sam. I couldn't help it. But I didn't betray the people in Yablonya." She looked at him.

"The village is gone. I saw it from the air. They burned it." Hollis put his arm round her. "It was brave of you to try to protect them."

"Oh, Sam, I'm so tired of this ongoing vendetta. All I want is to be out of here—and to get our people out of here."

"Good." He rose to his feet. "Then let's talk to some of our people here and see how we can help them."

Lisa rose also and put her hand on his arm. "Sam, do you think they'd give me a Bible?"

"I think they'll give you nearly anything you want. That's the whole idea. They're not trying to brainwash us here. On the contrary. They want you to be Lisa. And they want you to turn out other Lisas."

"I won't. I'd rather be shot."

Hollis glanced at her. "Lisa, just play for time. All right? One week. Promise me."

She nodded. "One week."

They got back on the path and continued their walk. After a while they came to a ranch-style house set snugly among the pine trees. It was red brick with white trim and a green asphalt roof. A gravel driveway led to a one-car garage, but there was no sign that a car had ever driven over the gravel. To the right of the garage a man of about fifty was stacking firewood. A child of about five swung in a tyre suspended by a rope from a tree.

Hollis walked up the drive. "Hello," he said. "I'm new in town."

The man looked up. "Sam Hollis! I heard you were here. And that must be Lisa Rhodes." The man wiped his palms on his corduroy slacks and shook hands with Hollis. He spoke with a Texas twang. "I'm Tim Landis. I think we know each other, Sam."

Hollis was momentarily taken aback. "Yes . . . by God, you were a flight commander in our fighter group."

Lisa shook hands with Landis. She asked, "Is this like dying and going to purgatory, or is it a living hell?"

Landis seemed to understand. "Well, that depends on what you dream about in the night." He rubbed his forehead. "You see, I've been nearly twenty years here, and I still don't feel like it's home, but I don't know what home is supposed to feel like any more." He added, "Except sometimes when I wake in the night and can remember all of it and feel it again."

No one spoke for a while; then Landis smiled at Hollis. "Hey, Sam, I'm glad you didn't get downed."

"Well, I did. Over Haiphong harbour. Last run of the war. But I got fished out of the drink." Hollis hesitated a moment. "My copilot was Ernie Simms. Is he here?"

"Not any more. He came here from Hanoi . . . let's see, back in 'seventy-four. In fact, now you mention it, he said you blew out too. That you and he hit the drink together. Artery got opened, but the Viets fixed him up. He was fine by the time he got here."

"What happened to him here?"

"Well"—Landis seemed suddenly uncomfortable—"he told them that he wouldn't play ball. So they shot him. They had all the pilots they

470

needed. Then the war ended, and the KGB started taking over here. Sorry about Simms. But hey, there are probably a few other guys here you know from our bunch."

Landis rattled off a dozen names, and Hollis recognised three or four of them. Landis said, "Say, let me introduce you to my little guy." He turned and called to the boy, who ran over to them. "Timmy, this is an old friend of·mine, Colonel Hollis. And this is Ms. Rhodes." The boy smiled bashfully as Landis added, "Timmy is almost six."

The boy nodded. He looked at Hollis. "Are you from America?"

"Yes."

"I'm going to America some day, to work for peace."

Hollis didn't reply.

"America is a good country."

"Yes, it is."

"But bad people run it."

Hollis glanced at Landis, who said to his son, "Go on and play." Landis watched the boy, then said, "At first they thought that sex was enough; then they understood that some of us actually had a paternal instinct. So they let us have children. They want to keep us contented here, busy with everyday things. But solutions lead to new problems. Like the kids. There are about sixty of them now."

"And what," Hollis asked, "is the problem?"

"Well, they didn't know how to bring up these kids. So they came up with this hybrid system where they teach a modified American curriculum in English but also Russian history and Soviet ideology. It's kind of screwed up. They think they can send them into America like they do the Russian students. But I don't know. I think all these kids are going to go bonkers as they get older and realise they're in prison." Landis looked at his son, swinging again on the tyre. "My poor little guy."

"Do you teach him the truth at home?" Lisa asked.

"Ms. Rhodes, they told me that if they discovered I was doing that, they would kill the boy. Not take him away, but kill him. And kill my wife too."

"I'm sorry."

Landis shrugged. "It's all velvet gloves over steel fists here." He looked at Hollis. "Say, Sam, did you ever happen to hear anything about my wife? I mean my American wife? Maggie?"

"No, I don't think so."

"I had two boys. Timothy—my other Timothy—and Josh. They'd be grown men now. I sure hope they did all right. Hope Maggie remarried too." Landis passed his hand over his face.

Hollis had a strangely empty feeling in his stomach. He said, "Look, Tim, I think my presence is a little upsetting, so we'll—"

Landis nodded. "Yeah, well, thanks for stopping by." He turned away, then came back. "Oh, I remembered something, Sam. Simms said that

471

after you both hit the drink, the Viets sent boats out, and you swam towards him, yelling to him to come to you. He said he kept waving you off because he figured he was a goner, but you kept coming. He said he was glad when he saw the chopper rescue you, glad for you and glad there was a witness that he'd been captured alive. He spoke highly of you, Sam."

Hollis nodded. "Thank you." He turned and walked away with Lisa.

They walked for a while in silence; then Lisa said, "We'll be free someday. I know we will."

He took her arm. "I feel free. Poor Tim Landis just gave me my freedom."

"I know."

LATER THAT EVENING Sam Hollis knelt by the fireplace in the living room of their cottage and lit the kindling under the logs.

Lisa said, "I used to love a fire on a cold winter night. That's one of the things I missed in Moscow."

"Well, you won't miss it here."

They sat on the couch holding hands and watching the fire. After a while there was a knock on the door. The clock showed 10.15.

Hollis went to the door and opened it. A man of about fifty, dressed in a ski parka, stood in the cold. "Sorry to bother you, Colonel. We met earlier, in the woods. I'm Lewis Poole."

"Come in."

Poole stepped in and greeted Lisa. He stood by the fire and warmed himself. "Can we play a little music?"

Lisa put one of Dodson's tapes into a portable player, and the voices of black gospel singers filled the room.

Poole said, "Mostly they've given up on house bugs because we find them and squash them, but this cottage is probably all wired for you. Also, we use writing and sign language. Every one of us here can communicate by sign."

Hollis commented, "I suppose there are a lot of things we have to learn, Commander."

"Call me Lew. I'm the aide-de-camp for General Austin. Do you know him?"

Hollis replied, "Of course. He was commander of the Eighth Tactical Fighter Wing at Cu Chi. The only American air-force general shot down. Missing, believed dead."

"He's very much alive. According to camp rules, there is no senior man among us, and no command structure. But we've set up a sub rosa POW camp organisation, as we were trained to do. The spirit of resistance is still alive here. To be perfectly frank, though, we have not accomplished much, aside from sabotaging the curriculum as often as possible. In real terms, Jack Dodson is only the second man we've gotten out of here."

472

Lisa asked, "What happened to the first man?"

"That was Gene Romero, an air-force captain. He was recaptured and shot on the soccer field along with five other men as an example. That was nine years ago."

"And Dodson?" Hollis asked. "How did he get out?"

"I'm not at liberty to say." Poole glanced at Hollis and Lisa. "Your presence here has sparked a lot of hope." His eyes searched Hollis's. "Right or wrong?"

Hollis replied, "I'm not prepared to comment at this time."

Poole seemed to take this as a positive statement. He said, "Well, I'm here to invite you to meet General Austin."

Hollis took the parkas from a wall hook. "Lead on, Commander."

The three of them walked out into the cold night, Poole shining a torch ahead of them.

"Isn't there a curfew here?" Hollis asked.

"No. There used to be a lot of rules. There are very few now." Poole added, "The Russians finally realised that totalitarianism doesn't suit their purposes here. This is the most free square mile in the Soviet Union." He laughed, without humour.

They came up to the main road near the VFW hall, and as they turned right towards the headquarters, headlights approached up the road. The vehicle drew close to them, then stopped, and Hollis saw that it was a Pontiac Trans Am. Colonel Burov was behind the wheel. Hollis saw that the Trans Am's windscreen was intact, and there didn't seem to be any body damage.

Burov said, "Yes. Mr. Fisher's car. I suppose he didn't get into an accident after all. Not in this car anyway." Burov patted the steering wheel. "Nice machine." He added, "I assume you are on your way to pay a courtesy call on General Austin. Or perhaps you are going to pick mushrooms?"

Hollis said, "General Austin. How about a lift?"

Burov laughed. "I'm afraid if I let you in this car, the temptation to try something stupid would be too great for you. So you will have to walk. Good evening." He let in the clutch and stepped on the accelerator. Hollis watched the taillights disappear towards the main gate.

They continued their walk. The road dropped as they rounded a bend, and Hollis realised it had become darker. They were under the camouflage net he'd spotted from the helicopter.

Lisa said, "Look, Sam."

Ahead were dim lights suspended from lampposts. As they got closer Hollis saw a paved car park and a row of about ten darkened storefronts, looking very much like a suburban shopping plaza. The main store was a large 7-Eleven. There was also a Laundromat, a Bank of America complete with logo, a place called Sweeney's Liquors, a barbershop called Mane Event, and a beauty parlour named Tresses. To the right of the 7-Eleven was Kruger's Hardware, a stationery-and-tobacco shop, Main Street Pharmacy, a bookstore that also carried audio- and videotapes, and at the end of the row a sort of luncheonette-coffee shop.

Lisa stared. "Incredible."

Hollis moved down the row of shops. "I was told there was another training environment here. Offices and so forth."

"Oh, that's right below our feet. A large subterranean arcade. It's mostly to familiarise the students with office etiquette and equipment. Word processors, photocopiers, electric staplers. The works. Also, there are two very modern home kitchens, an extensive reference library, a hotel and motel check-in desk, airport customs, and a motor vehicle bureau desk. They also do house closings down there, employment interviews and so on. It's a very wide-ranging curriculum."

Hollis nodded. As an intelligence officer, he knew a good programme when he saw one. Whereas the American intelligence establishment had shifted the emphasis from spies to satellites, the Soviets still believed in the human factor. Hollis himself had always thought that that was the correct approach, and so did Seth Alevy, which, Hollis suspected, was why he and Lisa were in the Charm School.

"It's a strange little world we have here," Poole went on. "The milieu is mostly suburban, as you can see. That's because most of us were suburban, I guess."

"But no cars or PTA," Hollis said.

"No. And no travel agency," Poole added drily. He seemed lost in thought for a moment, then continued. "The population of Anytown is a little over a thousand: there were two hundred and eighty-two former American pilots at the last count and about an equal number of Russian wives, plus our children. Then there are the six American women—they were kidnapped in Finland and Romania—and there are some Russian service people and medical staff. There are about three hundred students at any given time. And there are about fifty Russian proctors, as they're called. Control officers, actually, one for each six students. They're KGB intelligence officers who speak and understand English. Then there is the KGB border-guard battalion, about six hundred men, living mostly in their own compound and patrolling the perimeter. We don't really count them as part of the camp population."

Poole stayed silent for a while, then took a breath. "So that's it. One thousand souls living in this miserable square mile, spending each and every day pretending. Pretending until the pretence seems reality. I tell you, sometimes I think I'm a certifiable lunatic, and other times I think the Russians are."

"My problem with this place is that it works," Hollis murmured.

Commander Poole nodded. "That it does. We've hatched thousands of little monsters here, God forgive us."

They walked back to the main road and continued on. Hollis was glad

474

to discover that the men here still had a sense of themselves as American military men and that they still held the Russians in some contempt. He asked, "How many of you have been imprisoned here?"

Poole motioned them closer and replied in a low voice, "It's hard to say. Before the end of the war in Vietnam hundreds of men passed through here. Most of them are dead. We've put together a list of about four hundred and fifty fliers who we know were shot, died of neglect, or killed themselves. It was a very turbulent time, and we were not in a position to keep good records. But we do have several copies of that list hidden about the camp."

"May I have one?" Hollis asked. "And a roster of the men who are here now?"

"Certainly. Are you saying you can get this information out of here?"

"I'm not saying, but that is what I have in mind."

Poole nodded. "Something else you ought to know. After the Paris peace treaty and after all the POWs were supposed to have been freed, we were still receiving American fliers from North Vietnamese prisons. There were about fifty of them. They said there were still American POWs in North Vietnamese camps. We have a list of the POWs they say were left behind. It would be very good if we could get all of this evidence to Washington."

They continued their walk along the main road, then turned left onto a narrow log path that climbed a rise in the forest. At the end of the path was a run-down *izba*, with a weak light in its single window and smoke coming from its stone chimney. "One of the last of the original structures," Poole explained. "General Austin prefers it to the so-called American houses."

They approached the door, and Poole said, "The general has not taken a Russian wife, as he says he is still married to Mrs. Austin." He added, "He has more will-power than I do. Also, you should know that the general refuses to teach classes."

Hollis asked, "Why hasn't the KGB gotten rid of him?"

"We made it clear that we would strike if they did. We have value as a commodity here, like any slaves when the slave trade is cut off."

Poole knocked. The door opened, revealing a man of close to seventy, very fit-looking, with a grey crew cut and steel-grey eyes. His skin was pale. Hollis thought he looked like a man who had borne too much, too long, and had borne it alone.

General Austin showed them in, then went to a stereo system strewn out on a wobbly bench and placed a record on the turntable. Vivaldi's "The Four Seasons" filled the small, sparsely furnished room. Austin indicated three wooden chairs near the stone fireplace and lowered himself into a rocking chair. He spoke in a barely audible voice. "It was good of you to come, Colonel. And you, Ms. Rhodes." He leaned forward. "Do you have any news of Major Dodson?"

Hollis replied, "No, General."

Austin asked, "What do you think our government is prepared to do if Major Dodson makes contact with the embassy?"

"I can't engage in a discussion of that nature with a man I've just met. And, excuse me, a man who has been compromised."

"I understand your reservations," Austin said. "However, I expected, at the very least, some message from the outside."

"I am not the bearer of any message. I am an intelligence officer, and I've been instructed not to speak to anyone on matters that they have no need to know, rank notwithstanding. What I want you to tell me is how Dodson got out."

Austin replied, "Only a handful of men know that."

Poole added, "If they catch Jack Dodson, they will torture him and make him reveal the names of the men on the escape committee. They will then torture those men to determine if there are others. If you want to know how Dodson got out, be advised you might get caught up in the bloodbath to follow."

Hollis looked at Lisa, who nodded.

Austin spoke. "All right. A catapult." He explained, "We cut our own wood for our fires. We designed a catapult, cut the pieces and scattered them about in the forest. A few weeks ago we assembled the catapult, wrapped Major Dodson in blankets and sent him over the barbed wire. We intended to send three more men over in quick succession, but unluckily a motorised patrol came along and we abandoned the rest of the escape and made it back to our houses just as the alarm went up." Austin looked from Hollis to Lisa. "So you see, they already know how we got Dodson out. I was testing your courage."

"We don't need testing, General."

"I don't know that. I don't even know what brought you two here. But I'll tell you something, Colonel. Much as we want to go home, I think we'd all sacrifice our lives if we thought one man could get out of here and tell the world about this place. As for the catapult, it is now behind the headquarters building under guard. Do you know why? You, Ms. Rhodes?"

Neither replied, and Poole spoke. "If they catch Dodson, he will be the first—without the padding this time. If they don't find him and they don't learn who is on the escape committee, they will just pick ten names at random. So even if you find us contemptible as traitors, don't think we are the Russians' docile house pets. We did do something that we are prepared to die for."

Hollis said to Poole, "I am not judging you. I'm only reminding you that you've all violated the Code of Conduct for prisoners of war by collaborating with the enemy."

Poole's face reddened. "Colonel, I don't think you can say—"

"The colonel is right," Austin interrupted. "The Russians long ago

476

eliminated those of us who refused to collaborate. What you see left here, Colonel Hollis and Ms. Rhodes, are the traitors. That's why we're alive. And why Ernie Simms, among others, is dead."

Poole stood. "Colonel, let me quote you some rules that apply to POWs. First, 'Even as a POW, you continue to be of special concern to the United States; you will not be forgotten.' Second, 'Every available national means will be employed to establish contact with you, to support you, and to gain your release.' Look me in the eye, Colonel, and tell me that my government has lived up to its obligation to us."

Hollis looked Poole in the eye. "If they had known you were here, Commander, they would have done something to get you out." Hollis got to his feet. "You have my word that I will do everything in my power to get you all home. Good evening, gentlemen." Hollis took the torch and he and Lisa left.

"You were cruel," Lisa said, once they were on the main road. "How could you be so hard on men who have suffered so much?"

"I can't endorse what they've done."

Lisa looked at him and knew he was upset. She said, "You saw yourself in their place, didn't you? They were your people once. It's not anger and contempt you feel for them. It's pity."

He nodded. "Yes, that's it." He put his arm round her shoulders. "But I can't give them hope, Lisa. That would be crueller than anything else I could say to them. They understand that."

CHAPTER 16

Hallowe'en dawned cold and frosty. As Hollis and Lisa jogged along, other joggers, mostly men, passed them in both directions. Everyone waved.

They turned right onto the main road and walked a few hundred metres. Lisa asked, "Where are we going?"

"To call on Burov at home. He's asked us to stop by."

The main road ended in a wide turning space, on the far side of which was a guardhouse, a tall razor-wire fence, and a wire gate. Two KGB border guards watched them approach. One of them unslung his rifle and cradled it under his arm. "*Stoi!*"

Hollis and Lisa stopped. "We have an appointment with Colonel Burov," Hollis said in Russian. "I am Colonel Hollis."

The guard went back to the guardhouse, where he made a telephone call. He motioned to Hollis and Lisa, and they passed through the gate. Adjacent to the guardhouse was a kennel, where a pair of German Shepherds roamed inside a wire-mesh enclosure. The dogs immediately began to bark.

Burov's *dacha* was a two-storey clapboard structure set among towering pines. Parked in the carport beside the house was the Pontiac Trans Am.

Hollis knocked on the front door. He and Lisa were admitted by a KGB border guard, who showed them straight into a large, pleasant living room.

Burov stood in the centre of the room wearing his uniform trousers, boots and shirt, but no tunic. "Good morning."

Hollis ignored him and looked around. The furniture, he saw, was all Russian, but not the junk that the masses had to live with. Everything in the room was the solid, made-to-last lacquered furniture of the 1930s. Adorning the walls were oversized canvases of uncommonly handsome peasants, happy factory workers and Red army men prepared to do battle.

"Please sit." Burov motioned to the far side of the room, where there was an ancient Russian porcelain stove with a wood fire in it. Hollis and Lisa sat down in armchairs, and Burov sat on the sofa opposite them. "I called you here because I have some things to discuss with you."

An elderly Russian woman entered the room carrying a tea tray. She set it down on the stove, then left.

"Is that woman a prisoner?" Lisa asked.

Burov made a clucking sound with his tongue. "That was actually my dear mother." He stood and poured three cups of tea. "Yes, I have a mother. And a wife, and my little darling, Natalia." He handed Lisa a cup, then gave one to Hollis. "I was wondering if you would like to work here?" Burov said to Lisa. "In this house. To teach my Natalia English. She is ten now. Perhaps you could be a sort of governess?"

"Colonel Burov, you must be joking."

Burov shrugged. "We'll see. Time heals many hurts."

Hollis put his cup down. "Is that why you asked us here?"

"No. Unfortunately, something has come up. My superiors in Moscow did not agree with my decision to extend you a week to consider. So I must have your decision about working for us here."

Hollis stood up. "My answer is no."

Burov looked at him incredulously. "If you will not work for us here, you will be thoroughly interrogated, then shot."

"Then I would have nothing to lose if I killed you right now." Hollis took a step towards Burov.

The Russian seemed undecided if he should call for the guard or not. He said to Hollis, "Are you armed?"

Lisa rose to her feet. "Sam. Please." She said to Burov, "I'll work for you." She turned to Hollis. "Please, Sam. We discussed this. It's not worth our lives. Tell him yes." She turned back to Burov. "He'll do it. Just give me some time."

Burov said, "I will give you until six this evening. If you don't say yes by then, you'll be taken to the cells forthwith."

478

Lisa nodded. Hollis didn't reply.

Burov said, "I'm in a good mood today, and I'll tell you why. Major Dodson has been captured not two hundred metres from your embassy. So whose side is fate on?" He smiled. "You may go now. Report to me at my office at six p.m. with your answer."

The guard let them out, and they walked down the path to the guardhouse, where one of the KGB men opened the gate.

As they strolled along the main road Hollis said, "It's too bad about Dodson. But maybe that takes the pressure off Burov to break camp."

"If you're concerned that this place stay put, you obviously believe someone is coming for us."

"That's a good deduction. But don't press me on it."

Hollis thought that undoubtedly Alevy knew he and Lisa had been kidnapped and, in fact, had anticipated their kidnapping, which was why Alevy had tried to talk Lisa out of taking that flight. And in the early morning session Hollis had had with him, Alevy had hinted at some sort of rescue operation at the Charm School—perhaps an attempt to get at least two or three men out, as evidence. Hence his questioning about the Soviet Mi-28 helicopter, which was obviously how he planned to do it. But then Alevy, at Sheremetyevo, had indicated a swap, now that they could lay their hands on most of the Charm School graduates in the States. Alevy never actually lied to his peers: he just gave ten correct answers to the same question.

Lisa said quietly, "What will you do between now and six p.m.?"

"Explore." He put his arm round her, and they continued down the main road. As he approached the VFW hall Hollis said, "I'm to run into Poole here by accident this morning."

They climbed the porch steps and went into the building. There were about a dozen instructors in the recreation room and twice that many students. Four men played pool at one end of the room, and a group was in front of the television watching a movie.

They found Poole at a card table, playing poker with three students. Poole had a stack of chips in front of him. He looked up from his hand. "Oh, hello, Colonel. Ms. Rhodes. Do you want to sit in?"

"No, thanks," said Hollis. "Someone told me you were on the firewood committee."

"Sure. I'll be with you in a second. Let me finish the hand."

Hollis and Lisa sat at a nearby table as the men played the hand out. One of the students took the pot with aces and sixes.

Poole said to the students, "That's called dead man's hand. It was the hand that Wild Bill Hickock was holding when he was shot in the back. It's an unlucky hand even if you win with it. Aces over sixes." Poole got up. "I'll be back later. Don't swipe my money."

Poole led Hollis and Lisa outside and stood at the edge of the main road, some distance from the VFW hall.

Hollis remarked, "Dead man's hand is aces over eights."

"Really? How stupid of me." Poole grinned. "I have to pull a fast one on them once a day. It may not seem much to you, these little lies. But maybe one of those bozos in there will be playing cards someday with a CIA man, and pulling aces and sixes, and will make a stupid comment. You understand?"

"Perfectly."

"We try." Poole drew them closer. He took two aluminium cigar tubes from the pocket of his track-suit jacket. He handed them to Hollis, who slipped them into his pocket. Poole said, "All the names of the Americans past and present who've been in this place. Signatures where possible, and dates of death where appropriate. That's dynamite there, Colonel, if you can get it out of here and to the embassy. Though maybe they don't want dynamite in the embassy."

"They'll do what they have to do."

"Will they? Do you have any hope of—well, I won't ask you again. How was your morning?"

"I assume you know we went up to see Burov. Basically, he wanted to shoot us. But he'll settle for our working here. We have to give him an answer by six. We'll tell him yes, but I'm trying to buy time between then and a polygraph interrogation, when he's likely to get things from us that I'd rather he didn't know. By the way, Burov says they've captured Dodson."

"Jack—captured?" Poole seemed stunned, then pulled himself together. "Now comes the bloodbath."

"I'll speak to Burov. I'll see what I can do."

"You can't do anything."

"But I'll give it all I've got."

"All right. There's an idiotic Hallowe'en party tonight. Begins at seven. We all have to show up, with our women."

"I'll talk to you then," Hollis promised.

SAM HOLLIS AND LISA RHODES sat in Colonel Burov's office. Two KGB border guards stood directly behind them.

Burov said, "So you have decided to work here. And you will both submit to interrogations with truth drugs and polygraph machines. Correct?"

"Yes," said Hollis.

"And if you lie even once, you go to the electric-shock table. If you lie twice, you may go to the firing squad. Understood?"

"Yes."

"Now, let me ask you some questions, without drugs or polygraph. And your answers had better prove true when you get on the machine. First question: does American intelligence know of the general nature of this facility?"

Hollis replied, "Yes."

"They know there are American fliers held here?"

"Yes."

"Do they know how many?"

"No."

"What do they plan to do about the Americans held here?"

"I don't know."

"You don't? That answer had better not send the needle off the polygraph paper. Did you and Alevy know you might be kidnapped?"

"No."

Burov's eyes fixed on Hollis, and he stayed silent for a long time, then asked, "Is there an American intelligence operation of any sort planned against this facility?"

"I don't know of any."

"I hope for both our sakes that you are telling the truth." He looked at them both. "Tomorrow morning two interrogators will arrive here from Moscow. The first is a polygraph and drug expert. Your sessions with this man may last several weeks, and aside from some drug hangovers, you will not be uncomfortable. The second interrogator is a man they call the *elektromonter*—the electrician. He dwells in the basement of the Lubyanka, and he has seen things there that would make the three of us sick." He added, "Luckily for you, the choice is yours, not mine."

Lisa said, "We've chosen."

Burov looked into Lisa's eyes a long time. "What, I wonder, has happened to your spirit?" He shrugged. "Well, anyway, I congratulate you on your wise decision."

Hollis asked, "What's going to happen to Major Dodson?"

"Dodson, aside from committing a capital offence, has seen too much of the country between here and Moscow. I don't want him briefing the others. The man will be executed tomorrow morning."

"If you kill him, you may have trouble here," Hollis said.

Burov looked at him. "You've heard that? Well, you can tell your compatriots that I'm prepared to shoot as many of their wives and girlfriends as I have to if they even think of trouble."

Hollis drew a deep breath. "May we go?"

"In a moment. I want you to report to this headquarters immediately after the execution tomorrow. Yes, it will be a public execution. On the soccer field at eight a.m. Any man who does not attend will have his woman shot. Any woman who does not attend will be shot herself. Children are exempt. There will be two hundred guards there, heavily armed."

"Will anyone else be executed?"

"Yes. Ten others. Major Dodson is now being interrogated regarding his accomplices. If he doesn't divulge any names, I'll pick ten people at random. Don't feel sorry for them. They knew the rule. Good evening."

481

Hollis and Lisa stood up and quickly made their way out of the headquarters building and onto the dark road. The night was very cold, and through the pine-boughs Hollis could see stars, but no moonlight. They both walked in silence towards the VFW building. Hollis suddenly stopped and kicked savagely at a fallen branch. "Damn him!"

Lisa put her hand on his shoulder. "Will there be trouble tomorrow?"

"I don't know. I do know that six hundred unarmed men and women have no chance against two hundred armed border guards."

They continued slowly up the road to the VFW hall, which was all alight for the party. Lisa asked, "What are we going to do about the interrogation, Sam? We both lied back there."

"We seem to be running out of time and space, don't we?"

Hollis thought of the secrets he had to protect. He had to protect Surikov in the event that Surikov had not gotten out of the country yet. He had to protect the fact that the three thousand graduates of the Charm School were about to have their covers blown and would be swapped for Burov's three hundred Americans. He had to keep Burov thinking that Alevy had no plans to try to grab a few Americans out of here to show the world. But he could no longer stall Burov, and Burov would get what he needed through drugs or electric shock. Then the KGB would alert its three thousand agents in America. The Americans in this camp would be sent somewhere else and probably shot, and the last of those missing in action would be lost for ever.

Lisa stayed silent as they walked. Finally she said, "Sam, tomorrow we are going to watch eleven good men and women die in a horrible way. Then we are going to be interrogated for weeks. We may not ever leave that building back there. You know that. I've been thinking. If we went to bed tonight and just kept on sleeping . . . together . . . you and I . . . for ever. Wouldn't it be better? In each other's arms?" She added, "We could use the propane heater . . ."

He looked at her. He felt totally responsible for her fate. "There have been a lot of sunrises I haven't looked forward to," he said. "But we'll see this one. Together."

CHAPTER 17

Seth Alevy put on his trench coat, took his attaché case, and left his room on the twelfth floor of the hotel located within the complex of buildings called the International Trade Centre.

He rode the elevator down to the large marble lobby, and crossed to the shopping arcade, a thickly carpeted concourse flanked by six *Beriozkas*—speciality shops where Russian and Western goods could be bought with Western currency.

Alevy walked into the jewellery store and picked out a string of amber

482

beads. At the counter he presented a credit card issued under the name of Thornton Burns. The salesgirl placed the necklace in a satin-covered box and slid the box into a colourful paper bag.

He went out into the concourse, where he found the Intourist service desk. He placed his passport, visa and airline tickets on the desk and said in English, "I would like to confirm my helicopter connection to Sheremetyevo and my flight to Helsinki."

The woman behind the counter glanced at the papers and replied in excellent English, "Your helicopter is already here, Mr. Burns. There is no problem with your Finnair flight."

"Thank you." Alevy slipped his papers into his trench coat. He walked back to the lobby and spotted his luggage. He found a porter to carry the bags out to the Aeroflot minibus. Alevy followed him through the doors and boarded the minibus where he nodded to three other men who were seated there. The porter stowed his overnight bag and suitcase in the rear. Alevy held on to his attaché case. The driver started the bus.

The four men, all Americans, exchanged small talk about their stay in Moscow. It turned out that they were all taking the 10.45 p.m. Finnair flight to Helsinki.

The bus took them round the hotel to a floodlit helipad. A white Mi-28 helicopter sat there, its turbojet engines warming up. Alevy regarded the helicopter for a moment. Like most Soviet helicopters, it sat on wheels rather than landing skids. The Mi-28 saw service with Aeroflot as a transporter of VIPs, as well as with the military. It was fast and reliable. Or so he'd been told.

The bus stopped, and the four Americans carried their luggage off. As they climbed aboard the helicopter the pilot stowed the luggage in the narrow space behind the last two seats.

Alevy sat directly behind the pilot. He noted that the copilot's seat was empty, as was usual on short hops to the airport. The other three men settled into the remaining seats.

As the helicopter lifted vertically over the trade-centre complex, Alevy leaned forward and quickly examined the instrument panel, as he said to the pilot, "Do you speak English?"

The pilot glanced back as he swung the helicopter north towards Sheremetyevo. "*Chto?*"

"*Angliiski?*"

"*Nyet.*"

Alevy nodded and sat back in his seat. So far, so good, he thought. One pilot, full tanks. He and two of the other Americans with him—Hollis's aide, Captain Ed O'Shea, and Alevy's deputy station chief, Bert Mills—had flown out to Helsinki during the past week, then come back to Moscow individually, with new passports and forged visas, checking in to the hotel at the trade centre. The man behind Alevy, Bill Brennan, had come directly from his convalescent leave in London, thankful for having a chance to even the score against the KGB for his broken nose.

Alevy looked out of the window and saw Sheremetyevo coming up on the port front. "Well, gentlemen, are we ready?"

They all answered in the affirmative. Alevy took a foil envelope from his pocket, ripped it open and extracted a chloroform pad. Reaching around the pilot's face, he clamped the pad over the man's mouth. O'Shea jumped into the copilot's seat and grabbed the controls of the wobbling craft. The pilot thrashed around, kicking the pedals and yanking on the stick. The helicopter began tilting dangerously. O'Shea shouted, "Get him out of there."

Alevy ripped the pilot's headphones off, then with Brennan's help pulled him over the seat onto the cabin floor. The pilot groaned, then lay still as Brennan tied his wrists and ankles.

Alevy leaned forward. "OK, Captain. The seat is yours."

"Right." O'Shea moved across into the pilot's seat, grabbing at the controls as his feet found the antitorque pedals. The craft yawed and rolled, then steadied as he got control.

Alevy sat in the copilot's seat. "Well, is it as easy to fly as it looks?"

O'Shea smiled grimly. "I haven't flown rotary wing in ten years. Takes a while to get used to." He swung the helicopter west, away from Sheremetyevo.

Alevy put on the headphones and listened to the radio traffic from Sheremetyevo tower. Towards the east he saw the bright lights of Moscow on the horizon. The sky was unusually clear, very starry, but there was only a sliver of a white, waning moon tonight, he noted, which was fine. Below, farmland and forests were in almost complete darkness.

Bert Mills looked at his watch. "We're about five minutes overdue at Sheremetyevo."

"Right," Alevy said to O'Shea, "let's kill all the lights."

O'Shea scanned the instrument panel and referred to an Mi-28 cockpit diagram that he and Hollis had made up with English translations some weeks ago.

"This says 'navigation lights'," Alevy said. He hit the switch, and the outside lights went out. "You just fly, Captain." He took the diagram from O'Shea and found the interior-lights switch and flipped it, throwing the cabin and cockpit into darkness. The instrument panel cast a pale red glow over the two men.

Alevy held the diagram on his lap and scanned it. He depressed the radio transmit button and shouted in Russian into the mouth mike of his headset, "*Kontroler! Kontroler!*"

The control tower at Sheremetyevo replied, "*Kontroler.*"

Alevy said excitedly in Russian, "This is Aeroflot helicopter P-113. Lost engine power—" He stopped talking but continued depressing the button the way a pilot would do as he contemplated the ground rushing up at him. He screamed in Russian, "God!" then shut off the radio power

484

and removed his headphones."That should keep them busy searching for wreckage. OK, Captain O'Shea. Let's head west."

O'Shea swung the tail boom round, then opened up the throttle and changed the pitch angle of the rotor blades.

Alevy looked out over the dark landscape. "Let's get down there, Captain, and find a place to park it awhile."

O'Shea began his descent from twelve hundred metres. As the ground came up, Brennan said, "Forest there. Open farmland over there. Too open. There's something—what's that?"

They all looked out to starboard at a light-coloured area about five hundred metres away. O'Shea dropped in closer. He said, "It looks like an excavation. A quarry or gravel pit."

"That'll do," Alevy said.

O'Shea banked round towards the excavation. "OK," he said. "Let's see if this helicopter knows how to land."

They passed over the edge of the excavation at one hundred metres' altitude, and O'Shea realised the pit was deeper than he had thought. As he brought the craft down, the rotor's downwash raised huge billows of dust and gravel, obscuring his visibility and creating turbulence that was interfering with his ability to hold the craft steady.

"Hold on," O'Shea said. The nose dropped, and the helicopter fell the last few feet, the left landing wheels hitting first. "Damn it!" He shut off the engines as the aircraft rocked from side to side, the rotor blades barely clearing the ground.

Finally the craft settled onto the gravel, and the rotors wound down. They all sat silently as the dust settled, clearing their view. Alevy looked round the excavation. It was indeed some sort of open quarry. He saw a few wooden sheds to the right, and earth-moving equipment, but no sign of workers or watchmen.

Brennan opened the door, and he and Mills carried the unconscious Aeroflot pilot off the helicopter.

Alevy and O'Shea carried their luggage out and piled it some distance from the helicopter. Alevy opened the suitcases and removed three KGB border-guard uniforms, along with black boots, caps, four Soviet watches, pistols and three KGB greatcoats. Alevy, Mills and Brennan changed into the KGB uniforms while O'Shea put on the Aeroflot pilot's flight suit. They synchronised their watches, heaped their civilian clothes, passports, visas and wallets onto the stack of luggage, then threw their attaché cases on top of that. Alevy took the satin box of amber beads from his trench coat and transferred it into his KGB greatcoat.

Brennan reached into an open suitcase and retrieved two cylindrical phosphorus incendiary grenades with timers. He set the timers for three hours and shoved them into the pile of luggage.

They returned to the helicopter, and Brennan rummaged through Alevy's large leather overnight bag, which had been left aboard. He took out the broken-down pieces of a Dragunov sniper rifle, which he quickly assembled. He mounted a four-power night scope, pointed the rifle through the windscreen, and turned on the electronic scope.

Alevy said, "There are two aerial survey maps in the bag."

Brennan found the maps and handed them forward. Alevy gave one to O'Shea, who laid it out on his lap. Alevy handed him a red penlight, and O'Shea studied the map. Brennan was still rummaging through the bag. "Phosphorus grenades, extra ammunition, a little of this, and a little of that. Inventory complete." He said to Alevy, "Well, I've seen some scary costumes, but these are the scariest outfits ever. Happy Hallowe'en."

THE VFW HALL held close to a thousand people, but it was the quietest thousand people Hollis had ever been among. The building was surrounded by armed KGB border guards, and no one was permitted to leave until midnight. The main recreation room was darkened, lit only by candles and grinning jack-o'-lanterns. Men and women spoke in hushed, angry tones. Occasionally someone would weep. The masks, Hollis reflected, were off, literally and figuratively; no one was acting his part.

Hollis, who knew he would not be among the ten picked randomly for execution, felt somewhat guilty at being one of only two Americans in the hall who wasn't contemplating his imminent death. Lisa, he knew, felt the same.

General Austin sat in a small study, speaking briefly with groups of men and women, twenty or thirty at a time, until most of the two hundred and eighty-two Americans under his command, and their wives, had been addressed. Hollis made his way into the study and heard Austin say, "To attempt to escape is our only pure and uncompromised act here. So we shall try again and again and again. And if they want to shoot us ten at a time for each attempt, so be it."

Hollis listened awhile, then took Lisa to the bar for a beer. Commander Poole found them there. "The men and women are prepared to stick together," he said. "We can start a revolt, right here and now."

Hollis looked at him, and both knew it was suicide. Hollis said, "They have the guns, Commander."

Poole nodded. "So we take the eleven losses and let it go?"

"Yes. We have to live to try again. That's what General Austin is saying, and he's the boss. And you know, I don't think things will be the same around here after tonight."

"No." Poole thought a moment. "And you know what? That's for the better. We've all gotten too cosy with these people. It was hard for us to get angry and stay angry." He looked at Hollis and Lisa. "I think your presence here was the slap in the face that we needed to bring us out of it."

At midnight the Americans and their wives left the hall. Some of the Russians, Hollis noticed, stayed behind to drink.

486

"We'll pray tonight," Poole said. "I will wish you both good night and see you on the soccer field in the morning." He turned and left.

Hollis and Lisa went out into the cold, damp air and took the path back to their cottage. Neither of them spoke. As they walked, it occurred to Hollis, not for the first time, that after all was said and done, Alevy had simply abandoned them.

IT HAD BECOME COLD in the cabin of the Mi-28. Alevy, Mills, Brennan and O'Shea each took turns outside the helicopter, scanning the rim of the gravel pit with the night scope mounted on the Dragunov sniper rifle.

Finally, at 1.30 a.m., Bert Mills, who was standing sentry, jumped back into the helicopter, and O'Shea started the two turbine engines. He let them warm up for a few minutes; then he manoeuvred the controls. The helicopter rose out of the pit and into the north wind. Below, there was a flash of brilliant light. The phosphorus grenades had exploded and were now consuming the pile of baggage and clothing.

The Mi-28 began a diagonal climb on a northerly heading. At eight hundred metres O'Shea swung the nose west. "I've got this thing tamed now. Bill and Bert, you spot for aircraft. They can't see us without lights. Seth, find me the Minsk–Moscow highway or the Moskva River."

Alevy looked out through the windscreen. The night had remained clear, and the starlight gave some illumination to the ground, though the moon had nearly set. He finally picked out the Moskva River, a ribbon of tarnished pewter winding through dark fields and forests. He said to O'Shea, "Slip south of the river."

They found the highway, and O'Shea followed it on a due west heading, land-navigating between the river and the highway. Within a few minutes they picked out the lights of Mozhaisk.

O'Shea descended towards the Moskva. No one spoke for some minutes. Then Alevy said, "Reduce air speed." He looked at his watch, then at his aerial map, and said, "Gentlemen, we'll be landing very soon."

They were scared now, but excited too. Alevy could almost feel the energy, the anticipation of actually seeing if a blackboard strategy would work on the ground.

Alevy scanned the south bank of the river. "It's somewhere in that pine forest there." He said to O'Shea, "Lower and slower, Ed. Turn in over the forest."

"Right."

Alevy glanced into the rear and looked at Brennan and Mills sitting in the murky cabin, scanning the terrain from the side windows. He had never asked their motives for coming or given them any sort of recruiting pitch. He'd only outlined the plan and asked if they thought it was feasible and if they wanted to come along, and they'd said yes on both counts. And that was that.

They passed over Borodino Field and swung round. Mills saw the spot first. "There. Ten o'clock, one kilometre."

They all looked to port and saw a cleared swath of ground in the thick dark trees. Alevy caught a glimpse of a watchtower and noted that there were no floodlights on the perimeter of the camp. This was the age of electronic motion sensors, sound detectors and night-seeing devices. Prison walls had gone high-tech. Alevy said to Brennan, "Let's get the wind direction."

"Right." Brennan reached into Alevy's overnight bag and found a smoke marker. He slid a side window open, pulled the pin on the marker and dropped it out.

O'Shea put the helicopter into a hover at two hundred metres' altitude and watched the white smoke billowing through the trees below. O'Shea said, "Wind out of the north at about five knots. If we're going in, we have to be lit."

"Right," Alevy replied. He threw the switch for the navigation lights. "You know what you have to do."

"Right." O'Shea went from hover to forward flight again. Keeping the air speed slow, he banked round to starboard, approaching the northern edge of the camp perimeter on a parallel run from west to east. They could all see the watchtowers now, spaced about two hundred metres apart along the cleared zone.

Alevy took four unmarked metal canisters from his overnight bag, ripped a protective yellow plastic wrap off their top lids and turned a timer dial on each one. He slid open his vent window and dropped the first canister out, about five hundred metres outside the northern perimeter of the camp. He waited a few seconds, then dropped the second canister, followed by the third and the fourth. He was sure no one in the towers could see anything falling from the helicopter. "OK. Into the camp," he said.

O'Shea swung to starboard, and they passed low over the watchtowers and barbed wire.

"The helipad is at the western end of the camp," said Alevy. "Keep on this heading." He hit the landing-lights switch, and a bright beam projected from the underside of the fuselage. By now, he thought, the Russians were trying to contact them by radio, but he didn't have their frequency. Here in the heart of Russia, he hoped they would ask questions first and shoot later. He hoped, too, that if they had seen the smoke marker they took it for what it was supposed to look like, a landing aid to determine wind direction, and not for what it actually was—a means to determine where to drop the four gas canisters so that the gas, when it was released, would blow over the camp.

Suddenly a beam of light rose into the air about a hundred metres ahead of them. It passed slowly over the fuselage, illuminating the cabin and, Alevy hoped, the familiar Aeroflot logo.

O'Shea said, "That's probably the helipad light."

"OK." Alevy could see the clearing in the forest now. He worked the landing-lights switch and flashed the international codes for "radio malfunction, permission to land". He said to O'Shea, "OK, Ed. Let's take it in."

O'Shea began a descent towards the helipad. "This is it."

The searchlight moved away from them, and the beam dropped, sweeping back and forth over the grass clearing, showing them the way.

Brennan was scanning with the night scope on his rifle, and Bert Mills said, "Is there a welcoming committee waiting for us?"

Brennan replied, "There's nobody on the field. I see a log cabin at the edge of it. Guy there moving that spotlight, but I don't see much else."

Alevy felt his heart speeding up, and his mouth went dry. He said, "There will be no money in this for you, gentlemen. No medals, no glory, no official recognition. There will just be a hell of a bad time down there and maybe an unmarked grave in this Russian forest. So I thank you again for volunteering."

The helicopter settled onto the grass helipad of the Charm School. Alevy looked at his watch. It was 2.03 a.m. The people in the camp would be sleeping, unaware that their release from captivity was at hand.

CHAPTER 18

The helicopter sat in the centre of the field, its engines still turning. Brennan and Mills dropped down below the windscreen as the Russian searchlight played over the cockpit.

Alevy said to O'Shea, "Captain, you will lift off not later than three forty-five, with or without passengers. Understood?"

"Understood." O'Shea shut off the engines. "Good luck."

Alevy slid open the port-side door and jumped down. He put on his officer's cap and strode purposefully towards the searchlight and the cabin.

The man behind the light shut it off and walked towards Alevy. He was a young KGB border guard carrying an AK-47. "Halt," he said, his finger on the trigger. "Identify yourself."

"I am Major Voronin. I'm here to see your colonel. Has he sent a vehicle for me?" Alevy replied in brusque Russian.

"No, sir. And I have no instructions regarding your arrival."

"How unfortunate for you. What is your name, Private?"

"Frolev."

"Well, Frolev, call and get me a vehicle."

"Yes, sir." Frolev did an about-face and marched back to the cabin, a simple structure of hewn logs. He opened the door and moved aside to let Alevy enter. Inside were two other men. One lay sleeping on a bunk along the far wall. The other, a middle-aged sergeant, sat at a field desk studying a game of chess. As Frolev pulled the door shut he yelled, "Attention."

The sergeant jumped to his feet, and the sleeping man stumbled out of the bunk and stood to attention.

Alevy looked round. Along the right wall was a long table on which were a VHF radio, a short-wave radio and two field telephones.

Frolev said quickly, "Sergeant, this is Major Voronin to see Colonel Burov. He requires a vehicle."

The sergeant nodded and said to the man near the bunk, "Kanavsky, call Lieutenant Cheltsov."

Alevy took a short, discreet breath. Things were going well. As Kanavsky picked up a field phone, Alevy quietly drew his silenced automatic and put the first round through Frolev's chest. He put the second round into Kanavsky's side.

The sergeant reacted quickly, pulling his revolver from his holster. Alevy fired first, hitting the man in the midsection. The man staggered back and dropped to the floor.

Alevy hung up the telephone and stepped outside. Brennan and Mills were already there, Brennan with the Dragunov sniper rifle and Mills with the leather overnight bag. Alevy said in a low voice, "Bill, you tidy up in there and stay put."

Brennan asked, "Are you sure I can't come along?"

Alevy shook his head. "We don't know if these guys make scheduled situation reports to anyone. If somebody calls, answer the phone with '*Da*'—yes. Then just say, '*Nechevo*'—there is nothing. Sound bored and tired. Yawn."

Brennan yawned and said through his yawn, "*Da. Necheyo.*"

"Good. If anyone comes round to check this post, let them in, but don't let them out."

Brennan took the leather bag inside the cabin. Alevy and Mills moved quickly up the narrow gravel track that led away from the clearing, and soon they intersected the tarmac main road. To the right, Alevy knew, should be the main gate. To the left should be the centre of the camp. They turned left, moving quickly.

Within a few minutes they saw the lights of a long wooden building that had a porch at the front. They approached cautiously, and as Alevy got closer he heard music. He pointed to the sign above the entrance that read VFW POST 000. Mills nodded.

They stepped up onto the porch. Through the window they could see a large recreation room in which about twenty men and a few women were sitting talking. On the wall were Hallowe'en decorations.

"Party. Hallowe'en," said Mills.

Alevy nodded. "I can't even begin to imagine what sort of a surreal world has developed here." As they turned to leave, he reached into the pocket of his greatcoat and took out a small radio receiver. He turned it on and listened. "We have a signal. It's somewhere in this area."

They found the path that ran behind the VFW hall and followed it into a thickly treed hollow. As they walked on, Alevy spotted a shingled Cape Cod cottage, set back in the trees, with its lights off.

As they approached the front door, the signal grew stronger. The door had no lock, only a knob. Alevy turned it, whispering to Mills, "Stay here."

Alevy slipped inside. He turned on a red-filtered torch and played the beam on the walls and furniture. Through an open doorway in the right-hand wall he could see the glow of an electric heater. He went through and found himself in the bedroom. His light picked out the icon on the wall over the double bed. Alevy walked softly to the bed and looked down at Lisa Rhodes, bundled under a stack of quilts. Involuntarily he reached out to touch her cheek.

The crook of an arm locked round his throat, and he saw a long serrated bread knife poised in front of his heart. Alevy managed to turn his head slightly, and said softly, "Hello, Sam."

Hollis released his grip. "Hello, Seth." He motioned towards the door, and they went into the living room. He turned on a table lamp, and Alevy saw that he was wearing a track suit. Hollis rubbed his thumb and forefinger together, then put music in the tape player. He said softly, "It's actually good to see you, for a change." He put out his hand and Alevy took it. Hollis said, "I was beginning to wonder."

"I came as fast as I could, Sam. I spent five days in Washington selling this operation. Why don't you go wake Lisa?"

Hollis went into the bedroom and closed the door. He returned a few minutes later. "She's coming."

Alevy motioned around the room. "Not bad."

"Not good, Seth. I could spend a week telling you about this madhouse, but I suspect time is short. How did you get here?"

"I misappropriated an Aeroflot chopper."

"Right. The one I briefed you on. Who's with you?"

"Your aide, O'Shea. My man, Mills. He's outside. And Bill Brennan."

"Good team. Explain the plan to me."

"Well, I dropped four canisters of something called THX, a new sleeping gas, code name Sandman. Very potent. The canisters are on timers. We have about an hour and a quarter left."

"Who are you taking out of here?"

"You and Lisa and two others. That's all I can take on the chopper, and that's all the evidence I need to effect the release of everyone else."

"Are Surikov and his granddaughter out?"

"Yes. Last Saturday. Leningrad route."

Hollis said, "You have to negotiate for the wives here too, Seth. Russian women, mainly politicals. Plus some sixty children and six kidnapped American women. They go into the deal for the three thousand moles that we're going to swap."

Lisa came into the room wearing a blue track suit and running shoes, and Alevy guessed that this must be the camp uniform. She stood back a moment, taking in Alevy in his KGB uniform, then moved quickly to him and put her arms round him. "Seth. Oh, Seth."

Alevy disengaged himself. "We have to move quickly."

She took her parka from the hook. "I have to get my icon—"

Alevy held her arm. "It's not your icon."

"What do you mean?"

"It's a reproduction, Lisa. It's got a transmitter in it. That's how we found you."

Lisa stared at him, then at Hollis.

Alevy said, "It was a contingency plan. In case something like this happened. I hoped, with the hammer and sickle carved in the icon, they'd let you keep it. The real icon is safe." He drew two Tokarev automatics with silencers from his greatcoat and handed one to each of them. He drew a small leather box from his pocket and handed it to Hollis.

Hollis opened it and saw inside the silver star of a brigadier general. Alevy said, "There are orders signed by the President, but I couldn't bring those along. Congratulations, General."

Hollis closed the box, wondering briefly if this promotion could be considered posthumous, or perhaps preposthumous. "Thank you for delivering it," he said.

Lisa kissed him. "Congratulations, General Hollis." She turned off the tape player and the lamp, and they left the cottage quietly.

Bert Mills stood with his hands in the pockets of his green KGB greatcoat. "Hi, folks. Ready to go home? For real this time."

They moved quickly along the path, and came to the main road near the VFW hall. Hollis whispered, "Where do you want to go?"

Alevy replied, "Headquarters."

Hollis pointed to the right. They hurried at a jog along the road and within minutes saw the lit façade of a grey concrete structure. They stopped and knelt in the drainage ditch by the side of the road. Alevy said, "We have to knock out all their communications if this thing is going to work. Then we need two more passengers."

Hollis said, "That's a tough call, Seth."

"I'll make it a little easier for you. Is Burov in the camp?"

Hollis nodded. "I guess that's the professional thing to do." He added, "Jack Dodson is in one of the cells, and he's the second person I want with us. He's earned the right to leave."

They went quickly over the plan, then walked towards the building, Lisa and Hollis in front, their hands behind their backs. As they came into the light the guard stepped out of his booth holding his rifle.

492

"Two prisoners for the cells," Alevy said. "Open the door."

The guard hesitated, then obeyed. Alevy motioned him into the building. Mills brought up the rear and closed the door.

The duty officer inside was Lieutenant Cheltsov. He stood to attention, then glanced at Hollis and Lisa. "Again?" He looked quizzically at the border guard, who shrugged. Cheltsov addressed Alevy. "Yes, Major?"

Mills drew his silenced automatic and shot the border guard. Alevy shot Cheltsov who fell backwards.

Alevy said to Hollis and Mills, "Bolt the front door, wait five seconds, then bring those bodies into the communications room." Automatic in hand, he crossed the lobby and opened the door to the room. The man at the telephone switchboard never knew what hit him.

Hollis and Mills came in, dragging the bodies of Cheltsov and the guard, which they pushed under the radio table. Alevy found the switchboard connection marked "Helicopter". He pushed the button and held the headset to his ear. A voice, sounding bored and tired, said, "*Da. Nechevo.*"

"Bill, it's me. Anything to report there?"

"No. Quiet. *Nechevo.* But both radios are squawking away."

"Hold on." Alevy moved to the radios and turned the volume up. He listened a few seconds, then said to Brennan, "Normal traffic. Don't worry about it. Lisa will be at this switchboard until further notice. See you later."

Alevy said to Lisa, "Connect any calls going through this switchboard and listen in. Monitor the traffic on these two radios as well. We shouldn't be more than fifteen minutes. If you hear trouble, call Brennan, then get to the helipad. I'd like one witness to this place to make it out."

She glanced at Hollis. He nodded and squeezed her hand.

"OK," Alevy said. "Sam, let's go."

Hollis went to the door and opened it slowly. "Clear." Alevy and Mills followed him into the lobby and down a short corridor that ended in a closed door to the guardroom. The three men held their pistols at the ready, and Hollis knocked.

A voice called out, "Who is it?"

Hollis replied, "Colonel Burov."

Hollis moved to the blind side of the door as Alevy and Mills holstered their pistols. The door swung out, revealing a young man in his shirtsleeves. The man saw Alevy and Mills, jumped back quickly and saluted, his eyes scanning left and right for Burov.

Alevy and Mills strode inside. A moment later Hollis, outside the door, heard bodies hitting the floor. Then Mills and Alevy came out, closing the door behind them. "The cells," Alevy said.

Hollis led them to the rear of the building. They came to the cell doors and quickly checked them until they found one that was bolted shut. Hollis opened it. Inside, a battered man lay on the floor. His track suit was ripped and stained with blood. His unshaven face was badly bruised and he was unconscious. Alevy said, "That's Dodson."

Hollis knelt beside the man and checked his pulse. "Alive. He's been tortured and heavily drugged, but he'll make it."

"Take him to the communications room," Alevy said to Mills. "Call Brennan, then jam the radios and destroy the switchboard." He turned to Hollis. "Where can we get a vehicle?"

"Should be a Zil out back."

"OK," Alevy said. "You come with me, Sam. Let's move."

MILLS WALKED QUICKLY to the door of the communications room with Dodson over his shoulder, and said, "Lisa, coming in."

The door opened. Lisa, pistol in hand, stepped aside. Mills laid his burden on the floor. "Jack Dodson," he said. "He's in bad shape."

"Where's Sam?" Lisa asked.

"With Seth. They're getting a vehicle." He went to the switchboard and put the headset on, then pushed the button.

A voice came through the earpiece. "*Da. Nechevo.*"

"Bill, it's Bert Mills. Everything OK?"

"I don't know. One of the watchtowers turned its spotlight on our chopper for a few seconds. And I still have radio traffic."

"OK. I'm going to jam both radios, and you do the same. Then I'm going to destroy the switchboard. See you later."

Mills aimed his automatic at the switchboard and fired. Sparks flew, and the smell of burning insulation filled the room. He turned up the volume on the two radios and asked Lisa, "What're they saying?"

Lisa listened. "Tower One calling the helipad."

"That's what I was afraid of." He reached into his pocket, took out a roll of tape, and taped the transmit keys down on both handsets. He pointed to a metal nameplate. "What's that say?"

She read the plate. "'Auto search.'"

"Good." Mills turned the switch above the nameplate. "That's like a car-radio scanner. When the mike is constantly keyed, the radio becomes a broadband jamming device." He did the same to the short-wave radio. "This will play havoc with their radio traffic."

"But it might also alert them that something is wrong."

Mills had the uneasy feeling that the KGB border-guard detachment already suspected that.

HOLLIS AND ALEVY PARKED the Zil-6 in front of the headquarters building. Lisa and Mills were waiting by the door. They picked up Dodson and rushed down the steps. Hollis dropped the tailgate of the Zil and helped them place Dodson in the space behind the rear seats. Mills

494

got in beside Alevy, Hollis and Lisa jumped into the rear seats, and Alevy drove off towards Burov's *dacha*.

"Seth, we got some problems at the helipad," Mills said, as the Zil moved over the dark road. He explained about the spotlight and about the watchtower trying to raise the helipad radio.

"Let's not get jumpy," Alevy said. "We're very close to pulling off the snatch of the decade."

A few minutes later they spotted a small booth—the *dacha*'s guardhouse. Alevy drew to a halt beside it. One of the guards walked up to the driver's side of the Zil. "Yes, Major?"

Alevy put a single shot between the man's eyes as Mills opened his door and stood on the running board. The second guard was still in the booth, furiously cranking the field phone. Mills fired into the booth, and the man dropped to the floor.

Hollis got out of the Zil as Alevy moved to the gate. Hollis grabbed Alevy's shoulder. "Burov is mine."

"OK." Alevy looked at his watch. "We have thirty-four minutes to get to the helipad."

Lisa said to Hollis, "Let me go with you. I can help you get past the guard inside."

Hollis agreed. He opened the wire gate, then turned to Alevy. "On the left side of the house is Greg Fisher's Trans Am. Keys are probably in the ignition. We may need the speed."

Alevy watched as Hollis took Lisa by the arm and began running up the driveway towards the *dacha*. Two German Shepherds suddenly appeared out of the dark, tearing towards them from opposite directions. Hollis dived into a prone firing position, steadied his aim and fired twice. The dogs dropped.

Hollis and Lisa got to the front door. Lisa turned the knob and slipped inside. The guard was sitting at a desk in the foyer. Lisa partly closed the door behind her and put her finger to her lips. "I am Lisa Rhodes, the new American woman," she whispered in Russian. "The colonel wishes to see me."

The guard smirked. "I'll have to sneak upstairs and fetch him." He pulled off his boots. "Go into the living room. That's where he has to do it, with his old lady upstairs." He stood up.

Lisa pulled the door open and Hollis ran in and fired as the guard reached for his rifle, then rushed forward and grabbed him before he fell. He sat the man back in his chair. He took Lisa by the arm and propelled her towards the front door. "Go. No arguing," he whispered, then moved towards the staircase.

The stairs creaked, but Hollis went on up. A woman's voice said, "Natalia, is that you, darling?"

Hollis stopped. He heard footsteps; then Burov's voice came back. "It is the guard. Come back to bed."

Hollis heard footsteps again and the sound of a door closing. He climbed the remaining steps and came to a large upper hallway. To the left were two half-open doors that would be the bedrooms of Burov's daughter, Natalia, and probably his mother. To the right was the closed door that would be the master bedroom. Hollis went to the closed door and listened. Then he turned the knob, threw the door open, and aimed his pistol at the bed. "Don't move." The room was dark except for one small bulb, and as Hollis's eyes adjusted to the light he saw the bed was empty. He understood, but it was too late.

He heard the revolver's hammer click behind him, and Burov's voice said, "Drop the gun. Turn round, on your knees."

Hollis dropped the gun and turned slowly. Burov flipped on an overhead light, and Hollis saw him in the doorway, barefoot, wearing flannel pyjamas and pointing a revolver at him.

Burov said, "Some families practise fire drills. We have other sorts of drills. Take off your jacket and sweatshirt."

Hollis did so, and Burov said, "Lie down on your back, hands under you."

Burov went through the parka. He tossed a spare ammunition clip aside, then said, "What is this?" He threw the silver general's star onto Hollis's bare chest.

Hollis made no reply, and Burov kicked the top of his head. "And what is this in these aluminium cigar tubes, Hollis? Names . . . ah, a class roster, living and dead. Where are you taking this?"

"One copy to Washington, one to Moscow."

"Yes? I don't think so." Burov's foot shot out again towards Hollis's head, but Hollis sat up quickly, causing Burov to lose his balance. Hollis swung his legs round, knocking the Russian off his feet. Burov let out a gasp but did not loosen his grip on the pistol.

As they rolled on the floor Hollis grasped Burov's revolver, and smashed his forehead down on Burov's nose. He heard it crack. Neither man uttered a word or a sound of pain.

Hollis found himself under Burov's heavy weight. He released his grip on the gun, and with his freed hand he reached round Burov's head, grasped his chin and pulled. To keep his neck from breaking, Burov rolled over onto his back letting go of the pistol. Twisting out of Hollis's jaw hold he got to his feet.

Hollis stood also, but he could see Burov was finished. His breathing came in short gasps. Blood poured from his nose. Hollis moved closer. "For Dodson, Fisher, the airmen, their women, and the children," he said, then drove his fist into Burov's face.

Burov toppled backwards and lay still on the floor. Hollis sank to his knees beside him. A figure appeared in the doorway, and Hollis could make out a pair of jackboots coming towards him. He looked up into the face of Seth Alevy. Behind Alevy was Lisa. "Sam, are you all right?"

496

He nodded, then let her help him get on his sweatshirt and parka. He stood up unsteadily, stuffing the loose papers from the cigar tubes into his pocket. Lisa handed him his star.

Alevy knelt to pick up Burov, but Hollis pushed him aside and with some difficulty got Burov in a fireman's lift and took him to the door. They made their way downstairs.

The Trans Am was now outside the front door, its hatchback open. Mills and Hollis put Burov into the rear compartment with Dodson. Mills tied Burov's wrists.

"I'll drive," Hollis said. He slid into the driver's seat, Mills and Lisa climbed into the rear, and Alevy got in beside him. Hollis accelerated quickly up the driveway and through the gate.

"We have twenty-two minutes before Sandman," said Alevy.

Suddenly a piercing siren cut the air. Ahead they could see the lit headquarters building with several Zils in front of it, and about a dozen KGB border guards milling around. Hollis put the pedal to the floor, and the headquarters shot by in a blur. He glanced into his rearview mirror. "Two vehicles coming up."

Mills took a phosphorus grenade from a holder on his ankle and set the timer dial at seven seconds. "Open your door a crack," he said to Alevy. He pulled the timer dial out, counted to four, and pushed the grenade through the door. "Five, six."

The lead vehicle, a Zil-6, was about two hundred metres behind them, flashing its lights and sounding its horn.

"Seven."

The phosphorus exploded under the first Zil, which veered off the road and crashed into the trees, its fuel tank exploding. Balls of burning phosphorus lofted into the air and ignited the pine trees. The second Zil, a big troop carrier, kept coming.

Lisa called out, "Sam. There's the road to the helipad."

Hollis hit the brakes and twisted the wheel to the right, the Trans Am fishtailing but holding the road. Soon he saw the outline of the radio cabin ahead, a dim light in one of its windows. The searchlights in the watchtowers were probing into the woods.

Alevy looked out to the rear. "Stop here and block the road, or that damned troop carrier will follow us right to the helicopter."

Hollis hit the brakes, and the Trans Am skidded to a halt diagonally across the gravel path. Everyone scrambled out.

The Zil stopped about a hundred metres away, its headlights illuminating them. Alevy carried Dodson, Hollis took Burov. Alevy sent Lisa to warn Brennan that they were coming in.

At least ten men were leaving the troop carrier. Alevy said to Mills, "Hold them for a few minutes, Bert."

"Right." Mills drew his automatic, rolled under the Trans Am and waited for the men to draw closer.

498

As Hollis and Alevy began running towards the cabin, carrying Burov and Dodson on their backs, the air was cut with the noise of AK-47s on full automatic.

Hollis and Alevy ran hunched over, their burdens becoming heavier. Lisa, ahead of them, called out to the radio cabin, "Bill. Bill Brennan!"

A voice called back, "Lisa Rhodes? Come on. Run!"

She sprinted into Brennan's arms. Breathless, she motioned back down the path. "Seth and Sam . . . Bert . . . they're coming."

"OK. Get into the cabin and stay low. Be right back." Brennan ran down the path and met Alevy and Hollis. A burst of automatic fire ripped into the boughs above their heads, and they all dived for the ground.

"You take Dodson here and get back to the cabin," Alevy told Brennan.

Brennan got to one knee and took Dodson on his back. Hollis hefted Burov over his shoulder and followed Brennan in a low crouch. Suddenly there was an explosion, and a ball of orange fire erupted down the path. The Trans Am had blown up. Alevy called out for Mills but got no answer.

Hollis covered the last few feet to the cabin and laid the unconscious Burov beside Dodson, just inside the door. The cabin was dark now, but Hollis could pick out Lisa, crouched below a window, and three AK-47s stacked in a corner.

Brennan picked up his Dragunov sniper rifle, knocked the glass out of the window and focused the night scope on the nearby woods where he could see figures moving through the trees. He said, "Why don't you two get out there and tell O'Shea what's happening?"

Hollis took Lisa's hand and led her to the door. "Keep low." He pulled her away from the cabin and towards the clearing, where they knelt in the knee-high grass. About a hundred metres out, Hollis could see the white helicopter outlined against the black pine forest. Above the sound of the gunfire he could hear the turbines running. "Tell O'Shea we're coming."

She looked at him. "You're coming with me."

"Later." Hollis grabbed her shoulders and looked into her eyes. "I need you to go out there and tell him we're on our way, or he might take off. I have to go back for the others."

"I'll jump off, Sam. I swear I will. If you're not there, I'll come back for you." Tears filled her eyes, and her body began to shake.

Hollis turned her towards the helicopter. "Run. Low. Go on."

She glanced back at him, then began running towards the helicopter, turning her head back to him every few strides. Hollis turned and found himself face to face with Alevy.

"At least she listens to you," Alevy said. "She never listened to me."

Hollis and Alevy sprinted to the cabin and dived in through the open door. Brennan said, "There are a lot more guards out there now. They've fanned out into the woods and are moving from tree to tree."

"We have to slow them up a little." Alevy grabbed an AK-47 from the stack in the corner, poked the muzzle through the window, and fired long bursts into the nearby trees. The firing from the woods slackened for a few seconds as the border guards took cover. Alevy reloaded another magazine. "OK, Bill. You take Dodson and get to the chopper. I have to wait for Mills a bit longer. See you later."

Brennan put Dodson over his shoulder and moved towards the door. "OK. See you on board." He disappeared into the darkness.

Hollis dropped down on one knee beside Burov. Alevy said to him, "Well, Sam, it's your turn. Take your prize home."

"Why don't you come along, Seth? Mills must be dead."

"Doesn't matter. The sleeping gas will pop in a few minutes. I'll be all right. You'd better go."

They heard the sound of running footsteps outside. "I'm coming in." It was Mills. He dived headfirst through the open door. "They're close," he panted. "Less than a hundred metres."

Hollis noticed blood on Mills's hand and on his neck. "You hit?"

"I'm all right. I got away from the car before it blew. Well, are we waiting for anything?"

"Just you," Alevy replied. "Take Burov. We'll cover you."

Hollis lifted the still unconscious Burov onto Mills's shoulders as Alevy tore open his leather overnight bag and removed a canister. He pulled a pin and flung the canister out through the door. A black smoke screen billowed towards the advancing border guards. Alevy said, "OK, Bert. See you in a minute."

Mills ran from the cabin with Burov on his back. Hollis lay in the doorway with an AK-47 and fired a full thirty-round magazine in a sweeping motion into the woods, getting little fire in return. He rolled back into the cabin. As he reloaded, Alevy knelt by the window and fired long bursts into the black smoke.

Hollis said, "OK. Mills and Burov are on board by now. You want to go first? I'll cover."

Alevy glanced at his watch. "No. You go first. We have a couple of minutes."

Hollis moved towards the door. He could hear the sound of the helicopter turbines in the clearing. "He's going to leave. Come with me."

Alevy sat with his back to the wall beside the door. He looked at peace with himself for the first time since Hollis had known him.

"It wasn't sleeping gas that you dropped from the helicopter, was it?" Hollis asked.

Alevy replied, "No, it wasn't."

"Nerve gas?"

"Yes. I used sarin. It'll be quite painless. Sarin is quick."

500

"Why? Why, Seth? Nearly three hundred Americans—"

"They can't go home, Sam. They can never go home. They have no home. This is their home. You know that."

"So the State Department and the White House got their way. This place never existed. And you went along with it?"

Alevy glanced at his watch. "Go on, Sam. I'm not asking you to die here." He looked at Hollis. "It was my idea. The poison gas. It was a compromise. In exchange for the CIA and the Pentagon not wrecking the peace initiatives, we can keep the Charm School graduates that we round up in America. That was made possible by you, and General Surikov's files. That's what broke the deadlock. We're starting our own Charm School in America. We're turning their intelligence offensive against them. Get it?"

"I'm afraid so."

"But I'll tell you something that *wasn't* my idea. Neither you nor Lisa were supposed to leave here alive. Your own people in Defence Intelligence agreed to that."

"Then why—"

"Oh, Sam. I couldn't leave her here to die. As for you . . . well, I like you, so I'm giving you a chance to get out."

Hollis looked at Alevy in the dim light. "Do you understand how monstrous this is? Has everyone in Washington gone crazy?"

Alevy said, "Scared is what they are. Get off your high horse, General Hollis. This is bottom-line survival."

Bullets were slapping into the log walls. Hollis could hear men shouting orders and guessed they were getting up their nerve for the final assault. He thought of Tim Landis and his little boy. He recalled the quiet suffering of General Austin, the bravery of Lewis Poole, and the tragedy of all the Americans he'd met here. "Damn it!"

Alevy stood at the window and fired a continuous stream of bullets until the rifle overheated and jammed. He threw it down and stooped for another rifle as a burst of bullets tore at the window frame.

Hollis picked up the remaining AK-47 and moved to a window that faced away from the gunfire. He raised the butt of the rifle and smashed away the glass and wood. He lifted himself into the window. "Cover me. OK?"

Alevy looked at him. "Sure. I always have."

Hollis rolled out through the window and lay still on the ground. Suddenly the air was split by the sound of AK-47s on full automatic as the border guards began their final charge.

Hollis ran towards the clearing. He reached the grass and dived to the ground. Behind him he heard footsteps beating on the soft earth. He turned and saw Alevy coming towards him; then Alevy stumbled, disappearing in the tall grass. Suddenly the undulating grass became the swell in Haiphong harbour, and the figure trying to rise up out of it was not Alevy but Ernie Simms. A voice called out, "Sam, Sam." And Hollis could not tell it if was Alevy's voice or Simms's echoing down through the years. Hollis ran towards the spot.

He reached Alevy, dropped low beside him and tore open his greatcoat and tunic. A dark stain was spreading over his snow-white shirt. "Lie still, Seth. Shallow breathing."

But already Alevy's eyes seemed clouded, and his breathing was coming in gasps. "Go. They're waiting. Don't let them wait."

"Not this time," Hollis said. "We sink or swim together, buddy." He grabbed Alevy under the arms and began to pull him up, but felt Alevy's body stiffen, then go limp. Hollis drew a breath, then said softly, "I'm going to miss you, my friend."

He rose slowly to his feet and peered out into the dark clearing. The helicopter was gone. He looked up and saw it rising into the air. He looked at his watch and saw it was 3.48. They had waited, but not long enough.

He glanced towards the trees and could make out a line of men moving in his direction. The searchlights on the closest watchtowers were turned inward now, and one of them caught him in its beam. The spotlight remained fixed on him, and he fired along its beam until it went black. From the direction of the cabin a voice called out in Russian, "Surrender. You are surrounded."

Hollis fired off the remaining rounds from his rifle, then drew his pistol and waited for the fusillade of bullets to rip into him.

He waited and nothing happened. He heard some retching, then a moan, and he understood. The nerve gas had reached the first group of men.

He looked back at the guards who had come from the cabin, downwind of him, and saw that they were still moving through the grass. Hollis felt no particular fear of dying, knowing in his heart that but for a matter of minutes in Haiphong harbour he might have spent the last fifteen years of his life here. And he thought it fitting that he should be here with the men who would never go home.

Hollis closed his eyes and conjured up a picture of Lisa. If he had any regrets, it was that he should have loved her more.

The wind picked up, and he took a deep breath. The pines and the damp earth still smelled good, their essence, at least, untainted by the deadly gas. He felt a slight nausea and an odd tingling sensation on his skin. He heard a man cry out briefly in the distance, then another. He wondered why the gas was killing the Russians downwind before it killed him.

Somewhere in the back of his mind he heard a steady flapping sound, like the wings of dark angels. The wind picked up, and he opened his eyes. The sky was pitch-black above him, and he saw the darkness descending on him like some palpable thing. Then he understood that it was the helicopter, clearing the air around him, creating a small pocket of life in the dead zone.

The helicopter slipped to the side, and Hollis saw Brennan throw down a looped line. He drew the line under his arms and felt his body leave the ground. Then he felt nothing.

CHAPTER 19

Sam Hollis opened his eyes to the familiar sight of a cockpit instrument panel. He focused on a clock and saw it was nearly six. He looked at O'Shea, sitting in the pilot's seat beside him. O'Shea glanced at him. "Hello. Feeling all right?"

"I feel fine. Where are we going?"

"The Gulf of Finland. To rendezvous with a ship."

Lisa leaned between the seats and kissed him. "Hello, Sam."

Hollis felt her squeeze his hand and, remembering his one regret, squeezed hers in return. "Good to see you."

She said, "We waited for you, but . . ."

"You weren't supposed to wait, and you weren't supposed to come back and risk everything. But thanks."

Hollis moved his arms, then his legs, but didn't feel any lack of co-ordination. His vision and his other senses seemed all right. Presumably someone had administered an antidote to the nerve gas.

He turned and looked round the dark cabin. Lisa was kneeling on the floor between the seats, Mills was directly behind Hollis, and Brennan was sleeping peacefully in the seat behind O'Shea. In the two rear seats were Dodson and Burov, both held upright by shoulder harnesses.

Hollis turned back. "How far are we from the Gulf?"

O'Shea replied, "About a hundred and fifty kilometres. We're on a heading for Leningrad. When we see the lights of the city, we'll take a new heading."

Hollis looked at the instrument panel. The only problem he could see was the fuel: there didn't seem to be enough of it.

No one spoke for some time, and Hollis noted that his companions were anything but jubilant. He said to Mills, "If I understand this correctly, Burov and Major Dodson will disappear into the American Charm School."

Mills nodded tentatively.

"And Lisa and I will get a ticker-tape parade in New York."

Mills was silent for a moment, then said, "Did Seth speak to you?"

"Yes. I know that Lisa and I were not supposed to be on this helicopter. But now that we are . . ."

Lisa looked from one to the other. "I'm not completely following this, as usual."

Hollis looked at her. "It wasn't sleeping gas. It was nerve gas. Poison. Everyone back there, including Seth, is dead. You and I were supposed to be dead too."

"What?" She looked at Mills. "Seth, dead? No, he can't be. Bert said he would be taken prisoner and exchanged for Burov. Bert?"

Mills sighed. "It's very complicated to explain, Lisa."

Hollis said, "No, it's not, Bert. It's very simple." He turned to Lisa. "The State Deparment, White House, Defence Intelligence and the CIA cut a deal. Mrs. Ivanova's Charm School is closed for ever, and Mrs. Johnson's Charm School is about to open." He related to Lisa what Alevy had told him.

"And that was all Seth's idea?" she said.

Hollis nodded. "To his credit, he felt remorse over the consequences. And he couldn't bring himself to let you die." He said to Mills, "I consider that my life and Lisa's life are still in danger."

Mills seemed uncomfortable. "I think that all Seth wanted from you two is a promise never to reveal a word of this to anyone."

Hollis looked at Lisa and saw she had her hands over her face. Tears were streaming down her cheeks.

Hollis had to concentrate on the problem in hand. The fuel needle was in the red, but the warning light was not on yet. He said to O'Shea, "You've done an admirable job of burning fuel. Reduce air speed."

"I can't. Our rendezvous with the ship must occur before dawn. The ship won't identify itself after daylight. There may be Soviet vessels in the area." O'Shea added, "First light is 0722 hours. We're cutting it close, even at this speed."

Hollis nodded. He'd thought the only problem was fuel. Now it was the sunrise. He looked at the air speed indicator, then the more accurate ground-speed indicator. Air speed was a hundred and fifty kilometres per hour, but actual ground speed was only a hundred and thirty. They were obviously bucking a strong head wind.

Hollis took the controls on his side. "Take a break." He knew that helicopter flying, which needed continuous concentration, could fatigue a solo pilot within an hour. O'Shea had been behind the stick for two hours, alone with the falling fuel needle.

Hollis said, "Let's go upstairs." He increased the collective pitch for a slow rate of climb, increased the throttle and held the craft level. At three thousand metres he arrested the ascent, and the air speed climbed back to a hundred and fifty kilometres per hour. The ground-speed indicator read nearly the same. "That's better," he said, and turned to O'Shea. "How are we supposed to rendezvous with the ship in the Gulf?"

"First we look for Pulkova Airport, near Leningrad. About a kilometre due south of the control tower we take a three-hundred-and-ten-degree heading. We'll pass over the coast to the west and continue until we see a lighthouse on a long jetty. From there we take a three-hundred-and-forty degree heading over the gulf. Somewhere down in the main shipping lane we'll see three yellow fog lights that form a triangle. Those lights are on the fantail of a freighter heading out of Leningrad. We land in the centre of that triangle, deep-six the chopper, and the ship takes us to Liverpool."

Fifteen minutes later the fuel warning light flickered on. A few seconds after that a reedy recorded voice said in Russian, "Your fuel reserves are nearly gone. Make preparations to terminate your flight."

Hollis and O'Shea exchanged glances.

They continued north through the black night. Lisa leaned forward and put her hand on Hollis's shoulder. "How much fuel is left after that announcement?"

"It's more a matter of how much flight time you can get out of the available fuel. That depends on load, temperature, humidity, winds, altitude, speed, engine performance, and the good Lord."

"Should I pray?"

"Can't hurt."

The voice said again, "Your fuel reserves are nearly gone," then, "Make preparations to terminate your flight."

Hollis looked at the instrument-panel clock. It was 06:59. Sunrise was in twenty-three minutes. He said to O'Shea, "Our options are two: We can decrease speed, conserve fuel, and probably make it to our rendezvous, but it will be well after dawn. Or we can increase speed and our rate of fuel consumption, which is the only way we could possibly make our rendezvous before dawn. But, if we increase fuel consumption, we may not get that far."

"I'm betting that there's more fuel left than we think. That's just my gut feeling. I say full speed ahead."

"I agree." Hollis pushed forward on the stick. They continued north. The fuel warning light glowed a steady red, and the recorded voice continued its warnings in the same indifferent tone.

O'Shea called out, "Look!"

Slightly to starboard, on the black, distant horizon, they could see a faint glow. Hollis announced, "Leningrad." He looked at the clock. It was 07:04. Eighteen minutes to sunrise.

O'Shea said, "Pulkova Airport should be to port . . . There! Is that it?" He pointed out of the left side window.

Hollis saw the familiar blue-white aircraft lights. "Yes." He banked left as he increased the rate of descent and took a heading of three hundred and ten degrees. They were so low now that Hollis could make out passengers in a bus below.

O'Shea said, "I think I see the Gulf."

Hollis looked out and could see where the scattered shore lights ended and a great expanse of black began. The minutes passed in silence, and they were suddenly out to sea.

O'Shea pointed directly ahead. "Lighthouse."

"See it." Hollis swung the nose round to the new heading of three hundred and forty degrees. To the east he saw a small red rim poking above the flat horizon, casting a pink light over the city of Leningrad. It was 07:21. They weren't going to reach the freighter before dawn. Hollis saw boats and channel markers in the dark sea below, but no triangle of yellow lights.

Brennan said, "I guess they've shut off their landing lights. They won't risk a Soviet ship seeing an Aeroflot helicopter land on their deck. I can't say I blame them."

Lisa said, "But I don't see anything that even looks like a freighter. We've missed him."

O'Shea said, "Maybe he's still in Leningrad, trying to clear red tape. Maybe he's off course, or we're off course."

Hollis looked at his flight instruments. He said to O'Shea, "You were right about the fuel."

O'Shea smiled. "But I think by now that empty means empty."

Hollis looked down at the white, curling breakers below. Suddenly he banked right and headed back into the rising sun.

Mills asked, "What are you doing?"

Hollis began a steep descent. Ahead, he could make out the lights of Leningrad, about fifteen kilometres away. "I'm going on two assumptions. One is that the freighter did not reach the rendezvous point in time and is still steaming out of the harbour. Two, if that holds true, then the skipper of that boat feels some sense of failed duty, and if he sees us, he will come to our aid."

The helicopter continued inbound towards Leningrad, and no one spoke. The steady sound of the turbines filled the cabin, and they listened only to that, waiting for the sound to stop.

O'Shea cleared his throat and said in a controlled voice, "Twelve o'clock, one kilometre." Steaming towards them was a medium-sized freighter, and on its fantail were three yellow lights.

Hollis figured they needed about thirty seconds' flying time. He banked right, away from the oncoming ship, then swung north, approaching the freighter at right angles, flying into the strong wind for added lift. He estimated his glide angle would take him over the stern for a hovering descent.

"Ground speed, thirty; altitude, thirty," O'Shea said. A horn sounded. "Oil pressure dropping."

The recorded voice, which had become inexplicably silent about the fuel, said, "Imminent engine failure. Prepare for landing."

They were within ten metres of the ship's upper decks now, and Hollis picked up the nose of the helicopter, reducing ground speed to near zero. The aft deck of the ship was pitching and rolling, but never had a landing zone looked so good to him. Then, as he passed over the aft deck, the

506

helicopter picked up ground cushion and ballooned upwards. "Damn it!" The stern was gone now, and the helicopter fell towards the water.

Hollis quickly increased the throttle and the collective pitch of the blades, causing the helicopter to lift, seconds before its tail boom would have hit the churning wake. Hollis turned the nose back towards the ship, focusing on its stern light. He felt like a man trying to grab the goods-van rail of a moving train. He pushed forward on the stick, increased the throttle and literally dived in, clearing the rail by a few feet.

O'Shea shut the engines down as the rear wheels struck the deck and the Mi-28 bounced on the pitching and rolling deck, nearly capsizing the aircraft. Hollis yanked up on the brake handle, locking the wheels. Finally the helicopter settled. Hollis looked up at the ship's mainmast and saw that it was flying the Union Jack.

The sound of the turbines and rotor blades died slowly in their ears, replaced by the sound of lapping waves. A salty sea scent filled the cabin. There were no crew in sight, and Hollis assumed that all hands had been ordered below.

Lisa suddenly threw her arms round Hollis's neck. "I love you. You did it! Both of you." She grabbed O'Shea's shoulders and kissed him on the cheek. "I love you both."

Mills reached under his seat and pulled out a plastic bag filled with black ski masks. "Here—everyone put on one of these. No talking to the crew; no names."

Mills went to the back of the cabin and slid a mask over Dodson's face and then did the same to Burov.

Brennan opened the door and jumped down onto the rolling deck, followed by Lisa, O'Shea and Hollis. Mills got out last. "I'll have Dodson and Burov taken to the infirmary," he said.

The door of the quarterdeck opened, and six seamen appeared. They looked curiously at their passengers, all wearing black masks, three of them in Russian uniforms. Mills held up two fingers and pointed towards the helicopter. The six men removed Dodson and Burov, laying them on the deck.

Hollis jumped back into the cockpit and released the brakes, then joined O'Shea, Brennan and the six sailors in rolling the helicopter to the port side rail. One of the men swung open the gangplank section of the rail. They all pushed from the rear of the fuselage, sending the Mi-28 over the side, nose first, into the churning sea.

Hollis walked away from the rail. Four of the seamen had stretchers now and were carrying Dodson and Burov towards the quarterdeck. One of them said to Mills, "Infirmary."

One of the other two sailors motioned and they followed him to an upper deck, into a white-painted chart room behind the bridge. The seaman left wordlessly, and Hollis pulled off his ski mask. Lisa, O'Shea, Mills and Brennan did the same. They loooked at one another, not knowing what their mood was supposed to be. Finally Brennan yelled, "We did it!"

Mills broke into a grin and said, "Next stop, Liverpool."

There was some backslapping and handshaking, and Lisa got a kiss from Mills, Brennan and O'Shea.

An electric urn sat on the chart table. Mills drew five mugs of coffee, then poured brandy into each one and passed them round. He raised his mug and said, "To . . ."

"To Seth Alevy," Hollis said, "and all those we left behind."

A moment later the door to the chart room opened, and a tall, red-bearded man of about fifty strode in. "Welcome aboard the *Lucinda*," he said. "I am Captain Hughes. Your names, I am told, are no concern of mine."

"I want to thank you for leaving the lights on beyond the sunrise," said Hollis.

Captain Hughes shrugged. "We were a bit off schedule ourselves. The bloody Russians don't move very quickly with the paperwork, and our pilot boat was late."

"Any radar indications of ships approaching?" Hollis asked.

"No, but we're watching Kronshtadt naval base very closely. Once we sail past there, I'll breathe easier."

"So will we all."

Hughes said, "Before I left Leningrad this morning, a stevedore pressed a piece of paper into my hand."

He gave it to Hollis, who saw that it was a page from the embassy's cipher pad. It had that day's date on it and a frequency. A handwritten note said, "Situation report, attention C.B."

Hollis looked up. "I'll have a message for your radioman shortly."

"Right." Hughes nodded and left the chart room.

Hollis found a pencil and paper, and began writing to Charles Banks at the embassy: "Dear Charles, I am sending you this message not from the grave but from the *Lucinda*. With me are Lisa Rhodes, Bill Brennan, Bert Mills and Captain O'Shea. Also with us are Major Jack Dodson, USAF, and Colonel Burov, KGB, our prisoner. Seth Alevy is dead. Charm School is permanently closed. I must tell you, Charles, I think you and your crowd are far more treacherous and cold-blooded than any combat general or spy I've ever met. I demand you meet us personally in London four days from today. Come prepared for a long session. (Signed) Hollis."

Hollis handed the page from the cipher pad and his note to O'Shea. "Captain, have the radio operator encrypt this. Stay with the officer as he sends. Wait for a reply."

"Yes, sir." O'Shea took the message and left the chart room. Some minutes later he came back and handed Hollis a note.

"From Charles Banks," Hollis said. He read it aloud: "'Delighted to

508

hear from you. Congratulations on a fine job. Very sorry to hear about Seth. We'll miss him. Looking forward to seeing you all. Drinks on me.'"

The radio reply was so typically Charles Banks that everyone seemed on the verge of laughter.

An elderly steward entered with a jug of orange juice and a tray of biscuits. "Compliments of Captain Hughes," he said, as he set them down on the chart table. He added, "The first officer offers the lady the use of his quarters. For you gentlemen, bunks have been set up in the officers' wardroom." He left.

They all sat at the chart table, eating and talking quietly among themselves. Finally O'Shea stood up. "Why don't we go find the wardroom and catch some sleep?" he said to Mills and Brennan.

After the three men left, Lisa and Hollis looked at each other across the table. Lisa said finally, "You look sad."

Hollis didn't reply. He'd been thinking of Landis's little boy, Timmy, and of Landis saying about him, "My poor little guy." Maybe, Hollis thought, just maybe they were all at peace now.

Lisa said, "We're all sad, Sam. We're happy to be safe, but sad about the others. Will you try to put it behind you?"

Hollis nodded. "I'll try," he said.

Lisa removed a satin box from her pocket, opened it, then lifted out a string of amber beads. "Seth gave me these while we were waiting for you outside Burov's house. May I keep them?"

"Of course." He added, "Just don't wear them."

She looked at him and couldn't tell if he was serious. She dropped the beads back into the box and closed it.

Hollis took some crumpled sheets of paper from his pocket and spread them on the chart table. "These are the names of the men, all dead now, who were in the Charm School from the beginning. I want these men to be officially recognised as dead and their families notified. I want this list put to good use."

She nodded, then asked, "Is that list dangerous to have?"

"I think it would be dangerous for us not to have it. This is the only real evidence that you and I have that the Charm School did exist. It is our insurance policy."

She nodded in understanding.

"I'll send this along with a letter to my father in Japan. I'll have a seaman post it in Liverpool before we get off the ship. Then when we get to London, we'll talk with our friend Mr. Banks." He looked at her. "So what do *you* want from all this?"

She smiled. "I've got it. *You.*"

He smiled in return.

She added, "And we have Gregory Fisher's murderer, don't we? A little justice was done."

A seaman appeared at the door and said, "Captain Hughes wishes you to know that we've passed Kronshtadt. We are in undisputed international waters."

"Thank you."

Lisa looked at Hollis. "Another step home."

"We'll get there." Hollis stood up and went to the starboard porthole. He stared out to sea, then turned and found Lisa facing him.

She threw her arms round him and buried her face in his chest. "Sam, can I cry for Seth? Is that all right?"

"Of course. You're shaking. Let me take you to your room."

"No, hold me. Sam, can we pretend that after our lunch in the Arbat we flew to New York and nothing happened in between?"

"No, we can't do that. But we can try to make some sense of it. Try to understand this whole mess between us and them. Maybe I'll teach you about Soviet air power, and you'll explain Gogol to me. We'll both learn something that no one else cares about."

She laughed. "I'd like that." She hugged him tighter, and they stood silently for a long time, listening to the sounds of the ship and the sea, feeling the roll and forward momentum of the freighter as it moved westwards, away from Russia.

NELSON DEMILLE

"When you're writing a book," says Nelson DeMille, "it seems every third person you talk to has some useful information to offer." Even a chance acquaintance can provide surprising insights: when DeMille was flying to Russia to research *The Charm School*, the man beside him on the plane turned out to be a retired US military attaché—"a spy by definition," says DeMille. The man had once worked in the American embassy in Moscow, and spoke freely about embassy life. By the end of the journey DeMille had a wealth of information to flesh out the world of his hero, Sam Hollis. He did a lot of firsthand research as well. His trip to the Soviet Union was fruitful, if occasionally dispiriting. "The Russian people are very friendly to Americans, although Soviet officialdom can be paranoia-producing." For instance, the brochures claimed that a side trip to Borodino would be no problem, but when DeMille applied for permission to visit the site, he was turned down. "There seems to be an enormous gap there between what they say you can do and what they actually let you do." He ended up researching the battlefield at the Borodino museum in Moscow. But the rest of the vivid Russian landscape of *The Charm School* is the result of on-the-scene observation.

DeMille, like Lisa Rhodes, the heroine of his novel, grew up on Long Island, New York, where he still lives today. And, like Sam Hollis, he served in Vietnam. As an infantry officer he flew giant helicopters on some fifty airborne assault missions. Following stints as an insurance adjuster and a reporter, he took up writing full time in 1978, when his book *By the Rivers of Babylon* became a best seller.

Has his life changed with success? "In most ways," he says, "I'm just like everyone else. I've got a six-year-old car, I live in an old house, and I've got two good suits and a couple of bad ones. But now I get to travel more, even at a moment's notice. That's what I love about success."